The Saved of Hymiriam

Michael B. Randolph

DEDICATION

Hello my name is Michael B Randolph. I am the author of the tale you are about to read. I would like to dedicate this book to my mother, whom encouraged me to write and publish this story.

There's been a lot of speculation regarding the age-old subject of the return of Christ. This is a fictional story I felt compelled to tell. I am not an overly religious man but I am however a strong believer in God.

Those whom know me would say I have an over-active imagination as most story tellers do, without it we would have no entertainment. So, I decided to tell this tale of Mary, she who would be Christ, she who would continue her son's work for God's Great Purpose! Along with her conforming Arch nunnery which Embraces every religion in the world. I am a storyteller not a writer. This is my first manuscript and it may be a little rough around the edges. So please pardon its imperfections and Typos. I hope you enjoy this Book for its story rather than its historical or religious accuracy. It is however intended for mature readers. For it takes place in the not so distant future and unfortunately these things do happen in the world in which we live. It is of course a fictional tale and Hopefully it will be enjoyed for generations to come and considered one of the greatest stories in HERSTORY!

The Saved of Hymiriam

For All Those who have fallen to Covid 19 May their families
Be strong and God be with them we shall prevail. Now we rebuild
For God's Great Purpose!

Adam is created first from the 'Dust of the ground' and then God desires that Adam be given a 'Helper fit for him' so the Lord caused a deep sleep to fall upon the man, and while he slept took one of his ribs and closed up the place with flesh, and the rib which the Lord had taken from the man God made into Woman and brought to the man Adam. She was to be his wife and his equal in dignity.

And Adam called the name of his wife 'Eve' (Haw Wah meaning life Bearer)

Because she was the Mother of all living things.

Through Eve Life is Born Into the world something that Adam was not able to do on his own. Eve was not made out of his head to be ruled over by him, nor out of his feet to be trampled upon by him. But out of his side to be equal with, under his arm to be protected and near his heart to be beloved!

Man and woman were made for each other not that God left them half made and incomplete: God created them to be communion of persons in which each can be a helpmate to the other for they are equal as persons

(bone of my bones) and complementary as masculine and feminine!

It is believed that Adam lived for 930 years. Eve's death is not mentioned in the bible or anywhere else. SHE STILL LIVES!

The Devil's greatest trick was convincing man that he did not exist. Eve's greatest trick is convincing man he is in charge but having influence in his every thought. Eve created the word 'Goddess' so she can feel equal and loved in a time when man dominated the land and law. Man has always had a very deep dark fear of female sexuality and its power over him.

In religious times to keep his 'Vow of Celibacy'. It was man that said women Nuns will obey him, live in poverty, wear no makeup, cover themselves and show no signs of Independence. It was also man that decided women Nuns will not drink alcohol for it made women more desirable to him and easier to seduce. She was not to partake in any tobacco smoking for this caused her mouth to move in seductive ways he also found desirable. The Testament of Reuben: V 1,2 and 5 says women are evil my children: because they have no power or strength to stand up against man, they use wiles and try to enslave him by their charms: And man, whom woman cannot subdue by strength, she seduces by Guile! There are those who believe the end is near!

'BEHOLD THE BEGINNING IS HERE!'

For the Beginning

A lone woman stands amongst the clouds. Her heart is heavy. She stands Motionless before a bush that burns but is not consumed by the flames. She Kneels and bows her head. "Oh God I pray to you creator of all things. I ask that you allow me the opportunity to Save humanity from itself. Your first Female of this world Seeks to destroy it!"

The voice of God can be heard ever-so-slight in the distance. "Mary...Mary...Mary...Mary." Calls the voice of God. "Thou calls upon me to ask a great thing."
"Yes, Oh Lord." Mary responses. "I asked Oh Lord! that I may be granted this opportunity to assist Humanity one last time and bring your first Woman home to the 'Ever Lasting.' Before you make your final judgement upon them, Oh Lord. Her influence over them is Great!"
The Lord knows what lies within her heart and so the Lord listens. She asks the Lord to grant her the power to walk amongst Humanity and assist them in any way she can. She asks that she be given the power to attempt that, witch so many Angels and Arch Angels have failed to do in the past. And the Lord listened to Mary whom has never asked for anything, to She who has given birth to the son of God. To she whose request shall be granted. And God said unto Mary. Be cautious for Humanity has changed. Gone are the simple times when man searched long and far over vast distances when he sought to find Jesus.
 Humanity today with their technology can find anyone, anywhere in a matter of days or weeks. All those who would mean you harm, and there will be many, can find you and do so with minimum effort. For this Reason, you will be reborn unto the world. Through the Grace of god, the Lord created a history of her for Humanity to later find and see, a history that will prove her to be human.

The word Christ meaning Messiah, Savior or the Anointed is a title, not a given name. So, this time the Designation of Christ shall be Mary, Mother of Jesus.
She is an Arch Angel of high rank and she shall be called Christ. So, on this day.
This, that must be done, shall be done! And she shall have one to assist her.
She asked her best friend in heaven 'A Guardian Angel, Warrior class' if she would help her. She was honored to do so and chose the name of Mother Teresa for herself.
God allowed Mary Ten of her choosing to serve as her children and be the ultimate administers of God's laws! These Ten will walk with 10% of God's Grace and the Holy Spirit.
They will be the physical incarnation of God's Wrath! When needed. Yet they shall remain human. This type of human rarely walks the Earth and only for Extreme circumstances. The Ten are to be Saved and Blessed so they may be charged with this Most Paramount Endeavor.

There was an orphaned girl adopted by a Christian family. On her 16th birthday, still a virgin, the arch angel Gabriel appeared to her and told her she will bear a daughter, a daughter that would be Christ. She was slightly intoxicated so she agreed but believed this to be a hallucination and continued to party with her friends and became more intoxicated. She became so intoxicated that she passed out. When she woke up, she believed her boyfriend had taken advantage of her. She confronted him but he denied this. In the coming weeks she realized she was pregnant. Rather than bring shame upon the good Christian family that adopted her. She decided to flee, and flee she did. This was the will of God.

She Came Upon a home that helped people in need. This home was run by nuns living in poverty. She was taken in and cared for throughout the pregnancy.

With her heart and spirit filled with shame, she spoke only to one young nun. A twenty-year-old Nun by the name of Teresa. She never spoke of her past or where she came from nor did she tell the nuns or Teresa her last name. She was just Sarah.

Unknown to her Teresa is a Guardian Angel sent by the Lord to guide and protect her. And on November 24 1981 at 12:01 am. She gave birth to a beautiful healthy baby girl. Upon bearing this child God took Sarah, and into the arms of the Lord she went and the designation of Saint was bestowed upon her. There were no prophecies, there were no wise men, there was however a Shining star, but unfortunately very few noticed. Sister Teresa took the infant into the city. She reported the incident and was allowed to adopt the child as her own. The Nun hood that sister Teresa represented was allowed to register one name with no last name attached. This too was the work of Lord.

So on that day sister Teresa, knowing the name God has chosen for the child, registered the infant as her daughter and the name shall be 'HYMIRIAM'!!!

She kept the child close to her and as she grew, she excelled in academics. She is a prodigy as such the world has never seen. When the world powers at the time, discovered her genius they to embraced her. This allowed sister Teresa to go out into the world and do the Lord's work. God did not allow man to corrupt or guide Hymiriam. They are to watch and Simply allow her to be.
FOR GOD'S GREAT PURPOSE!!!!

On the morning of September 11th 2001 at 8:45 am. A young Muslim woman on the 110th floor of the world Trade Center watches in terror as a commercial jetliner heads straight towards her and with a great flash!!! It is over. Lying on her back she awakes slowly, dazed, confused and disoriented.
Unaware of her surrounding as her vision clears, she notices she is laying at the bottom of a very large flight of stairs. She slowly looks around and realizes she is alone.

It is not written in any book nor mentioned in any Testament. But there is a bridge, this bridge is very special it is where some Souls not all, go to be judged. It is a bridge to everywhere or a bridge to nowhere. This bridge is called 'Heaven's Bridge Walkway of the Angels'.
It is a place where high-ranking Arch Angels take people, they have dealt with on Earth for instructions they've been given.

With God's grace, sometimes the living are allowed on this bridge to say goodbye to their loved ones, this is often perceived to them as a dream. People receive last minute instructions pertaining to very important things that will happen in their life from family or friends who did not have time or was unable to tell them face-to-face or was in another part of the world when they died
and have not yet passed over, but we're on their way to the Everlasting. This is where time stands still. This is where Hymiriam conducts her interviews and chooses those for that which is to come!!!

She tries to stand but cannot. A woman with a bright light behind her stands over her, she was not there a moment ago. Her sight becomes completely clear as she notices the woman is dressed like a Nun.

"Awaken my child" she spoke softly holding out her hand to assist her." I am Hymiriam"

She was very attractive and of medium build. Anyone else would have asked where I am. But the young Muslim woman's first words were "Is this a Catholic School?" "No!" Hymiriam replied." why would you think that?"

"Well you're a nun and these are really nice stairs."

"Let me help you to your feet my child." Hymiriam replies laughing." you have such a

wonderful personality." The young woman tries to stand but cannot. "I feel like I do when I go to spring break." She says as she puts her head in her hands. Hymiriam helps her up and sits her on the stairs.

"Gather yourself my child for I have something wonderful to give unto you." The young woman stands slowly. "I'm sorry" she says in confusion. "I mean no disrespect, but you keep referring to me as your child. I was in and out of orphanages and raised by the system". Then she becomes excited and asks." Are you my biological mother?"

Becoming more excited she shouts. "I hope you are because you're very pretty and I'm incredibly pretty!!! I just want you to know that I hold no animosity toward you for abandoning me and giving me up as a baby I mean you were probably a drugged-out prostitute and it was probably the best thing for me so I wouldn't grow up to be a drugged-out prostitute too."

Hymiriam being a saint and Arch Angel looked at her in disbelief and amazement. It took all she could to keep from uttering the words. "WTF". But instead found her highly delightful and amusing." I am not your birth mother but if you allow it, I will be your mother. I would ask, are you always like this but I already know that you are."

Hymiriam says with joy in her eyes. "Now come I have much to discuss with you."

"Oh-Ok!!" She stutters." My name is Agnes Smith" The young Muslim woman said with a grin.

"Really! so that's your name Child? "

" No!" She hesitates. "It's Tauheedah, tauheedah Mujahideen" She goes on with a big smile. "I think I should tell the truth here."

"A wise decision." Hymiriam said as they walk up the stairs. "Sooooo I assume I'm dead? "

"No! Agnes" Hymiriam answers jokingly. "You are very much alive, you are on 'Haven's Bridge where time as you know it stands still."

They continue up the stairs as they slowly reach the top Tauheedah begins to worry.

"Well then I guess I'm here to look back on my life and be judged." She hangs her head in shame and continues. "This is not going to be good." She pauses "I've done some things I'm not very proud of." She concludes with a low voice.

"I understand Tauheedah, but you are not here to be judged." She pauses. "YET" "You are here for an interview, sort of."

"What!" Tauheedah becomes anxious. "Like for a job, I can work in haven? Can I be a toll collector on this bridge? You know I used to be a toll collector at the Lincoln Tunnel years ago, I would never be late if I get the job." Tauheedah rambles on because she is nervous, frightened and uncertain. So, she continuously jests with Hymiriam to lighten the mood. This is the way she has always dealt with things. She hides behind humor which is often mistaken for sarcasm. Because of her being a very attractive woman. But she proceeds from a false assumption. Hymiriam is already delighted and pleased with her. As they approach the top of the stairs Tauheedah can see that there is nothing on the bridge. It appears to be sitting in the middle of the clouds. It's very beautiful and the view is breathtaking. It's very long but seems to go on for only forty feet.

"Is this going to be a long walk?" Tauheedah asks nervously. "cause I'm wearing heels but I can take them off, with no problem." Tauheedah stops Hymiriam looks in the eyes and says. "It's like The Ten Commandments when Moses met God in the form of a burning bush and had to remove his sandals because the ground was holy." She leans towards Hymiriam and adds. "It was one of my favorite movies of all time." Looking Hymiriam in the eyes, hoping to impress her. At that moment Hymiriam remembers that this girl relates a lot of things to movies and she had indeed seen quite a few. One would go so far as to say that she has seen way too many movies!!! Tauheedah grew up watching many movies from many different genres and years. She had quite a vast knowledge of movies and television shows.

Hymiriam stares at her with delight, puts her hands on her shoulders and tells her that she never ceases to delight her. Also, to keep her shoes on. Hymiriam then begins to explain to her why she still lives. She tells her she was taken from a disaster at the point of which she would have died and she still has the choice to be returned to that point. Hymiriam only asks that she listens before making such an important decision. For this will undoubtedly be the most important decision of her life. Hymiriam goes on to tell her things unknown to humanity. Things if not told to her by an arch angel would not be believable by anyone.

"The destruction of the World Trade Center has set off a series of events that can destroy all of humanity. There is one name, one person behind all of this. This person is responsible for a great many things throughout the history of humanity this person is from the beginning. It is someone everyone is familiar with. A name everyone knows. This person will ultimately be responsible for what we are calling 'The Fall of All'. This person must be stopped."

"Let me guess "Tauheedah interrupts." is it-" She pauses."
SATAN?"
Hymiriam looks at her and with a smile
Replies. "No! Tauheedah it is not SATAN! "
"Then who Hymiriam?" Tauheedah asks with great concern.
"Who is so wicked, so powerful, So Evil, so cunning, So-- I
can go on forever just so you know."
"I know you can tauheedah, I know you can."
Hymiriam says laughing.

The look on Hymiriam's face becomes very serious for the name she is about to speak is known in every corner of the world. She looks at Tauheedah and stares directly into her eyes. Tauheedah's curiosity is so high she can hardly contain herself. She eagerly watches Hymiriam's mouth, paying attention. Then her mind wanders for a brief second and she thinks to herself. 'I wonder what lip shade that is she's wearing? or if she's wearing lip shade at all'. Her expression goes from eager to slightly dazed. Hymiriam picks up on this and decides to keep her in suspense no more.

She realizing that Tauheedah has the attention span of a third grader in church on Easter Sunday. So, she just tells her "The person responsible for all of this is EVE!"

Tauheedah with a blank expression on her face simply says." Wait! the one and only true EVE. Has in Adam and Eve?"

"Yes tauheedah, God's first female. She is the most powerful and most influential person on Earth!".

Although Hymiriam knows everything about tauheedah. Every experience and everything she has ever done. She still decides to ask her how much she knows about Adam and Eve?

"well I know they ran around naked in the Garden, Eating." She answers. "Oh!

And they had two sons Cain who was Able to kill a guy with a rock and I forget the other guy's name." Hymiriam just looks at her in disbelief. But now has her full attention. So, it would seem. Tauheedah goes on to say. "I mean, Eve would have had to have the body of a stripper or something to keep Adams attention all day. If she's been on earth since the beginning, she has got to be OLD AS FUUU-."

Tauheedah stops herself just in time before she says a bad word on Heaven's Bridge standing before an Arch Angel. Hymiriam gives her a stern look and tells her to pay attention to what she is about to say to her. "We Believe the

Lord has no set gender! We do however respect the beliefs of others. God being a woman, God being a Man and so on. One thing is most certain tauheedah. GOD IS ALL THINGS, AT ALL TIMES. But ever one knows Lucifer is a male fallen angel. Eve was deceived by him disguised as a serpent. Convincing her to eat the forbidden fruit and told her that she would live forever and have knowledge of good and evil. We all know how that worked out. Lucifer appears to many people in many forms but, the 'SERPENT can only present itself to Eve in the form of a snake. For that is what it first appeared to her as. Lucifer has tried countless times to communicate with Eve. This is the reason she despises snakes and collects their heads.

She promised the Lord she would not Endeavor to eradicate them from the world. However, she does control the snake population worldwide. For this reason, Lucifer avoids her at all cost! Because eve has been alive from the beginning of time. She has made many, many fortunes. Strategically finding priceless historical artifacts. Because she knows where almost all of them are. She owns several museums around the world and funds almost every archaeological dig of importance. She's responsible for the start of every law enforcement agency in the world. Ever since eve convinced Adam to eat the forbidden fruit her influence over men is unmatched and unstoppable but she cannot influence or control a truly evil person, Or any true servant of the lord God! So, she simply arranges for them to be killed if they refuse her. Her many sons and daughters have become quite proficient at it. I'll tell you more about them later. Eve has become a constant threat to the divinely ordered state of affairs defined by men. Every man wants to believe he achieved his greatness and power on his own. But eve is behind all of them!"

"Every last one of them?" Tauheedah asks.

"All but those chosen by God! Eve is the wealthiest person on earth. And has become very good at hiding it. She has become very good at being the absolute 'Queen of the in between' The genesis story portrays eve as a naïve and sexless fool. That was then, this is Now! She is a calculating, Wicked Seductress SHE IS THE FIRST WOMAN AND MOTHER OF ALL THINGS!"

Hymiriam momentarily lowers her head and whispers. "Wo-Unto-Man."

Tauheedah is so overwhelmed that she begins to feel a little faint but stays strong hoping to impress Hymiriam. After all she doesn't want her to think that she is weak and not up to the task.

"I am putting together a small team, a family you might say " Hymiriam goes on to tell her.

"This family's primary mission is to serve and assist Humanity and to bring Eve home."

"Can't God just snap his fingers and bring her home?" Tauheedah asks.

"That is not how the Lord works tauheedah. Eve must come home by her own free will. But she has chosen not to do this. So, we will attempt to convince her." Hymiriam knows Tauheedah is very excited.

"I think you will do well and be a wonderful woman." And before Hymiriam can finish her sentence tauheedah interrupts. "Oh-My-God I'm gonna be like Wonder Woman?"

"No! That's not what I said."

"Do I get an invisible jet and a rope that makes people tell the truth?"

"What?"

Hymiriam enjoys Tauheedah's enthusiasm but urges her to stay focused. "You and a few others were carefully handpicked by me, for this great task."

Tauheedah trembles with joy, No one has ever chosen her for anything special.

As they walk across the bridge a large pearl white Arch way with what looks like a golden gate in its center appears. Tauheedah reaches out like a child in a toy store to put both of her hands on the gate has if to grab it.

"Do not touch it tauheedah" Hymiriam says quickly. "You are still bound to the laws of the living if you touch the gate without the blessing of God you will cease to exist."

Tauheedah's eyes widen and she quickly steps back. Hymiriam Puts her hands on her shoulders. Tauheedah takes a deep breath as Hymiriam tells her.

"You must first take the vows of the Arch Nun and receive the blessing and the Grace of God."

"An Arch Nun?" Tauheedah curiously asks. "I don't think I ever heard of them."

"Of course not my child, you are one of the ten chosen to be the world's first 'Arch Nuns'." Tauheedah proudly stands before Hymiriam. Words cannot describe her excitement or willingness.

"Are you ready 'Tauheedah Mujahideen to be part of this great journey?" Hymiriam pauses waiting for Tauheedah to say something silly but she does not. She stands still, Strong and steady. So Hymiriam continues. "There is no going back to 'that which was' Once you comment to this new life. You will give 'All' that you are in service to the Lord. For God's Great Purpose."

Tauheedah looks deeply into Hymiriam's eyes and responds from the bottom of her heart. "Yes Hymiriam, I am ready to give 'All' that I am in service to the Lord, For God's Great Purpose!"

Hymiriam smiles, Hearing tauheedah speak those words with such conviction almost brings tears to her eyes. She tells her to Kneel before God and bow her head. Without hesitation tauheedah does this, Humbling herself before the Lord. Hymiriam stands over her, raises her hands above her

head then slowly brings them down to her chest to the
praying position bows her head and begins to pray.

"Oh Lord God I, Hymiriam your humble servant ask of you
to except this woman as an Arch Nun. I ask of you to give
her your Blessing, your Grace and the Holy Spirit. I ask of
you to give her strength to carry on in the darkest of hours.
For there will be many dark hours on this journey before
her. I ask Oh god that you give her sight so she may see
clearly. I ask that you give her Speed so she may always be
there when she is guided by you Oh Lord. I ask that you
give her knowledge of past and present. I ask that you give
her new life and finally Oh God I ask that you give her
wisdom to teach those who must learn and compassion for
those who are weak. In the Name of our son Jesus! I thank
thee Oh Lord Amen."

   At that moment Hymiriam disappears leaving tauheedah
alone to be blessed by the Lord. She stays in the humble
position for she knows not to move. The great illumination
of the bridge Dems so the light of the Lord may shine down
upon her. The garments she wears are changed into the
Uniform of The Arch Nun, her hair is changed and a Habit
appears on her head, her makeup and nail polish Vanish, As
do any ink markings, body piercings are healed. The high
heels she was so fond of are changed to the shoes of The
Arch Nun. All this was done by the power of God.
Hymiriam reappears standing over her. Tauheedah is
trembling she cannot open her eyes no matter how hard she
tries. Her legs are so weak she can barely feel them, her heart
beats as if it were going to explode and her arms feel like
they were made of stone.

She slowly rises from the Humbling position to the praying position. And with the finger of God, The Arch Nun vows are written one by one into her mind then spoken aloud for Hymiriam to hear.

1. I vow to honor those who take me into their hearts and keep them sacred.

2. I shall have no other gods before the one true God.

3. I shall keep my body pure never to indulge in pleasures of the flesh until it is the will of God.

4. I shall not take the name of the Lord thy God in Vain.

5. To Live and Die as an Arch Nun.

6. If I am to take a life, it is God's will. I pray the Lord their soul to take.

7. To live my life with love and to serve humanity.

8. To protect all children for they are the future for God's Great Purpose.

9. To honor my fellow Arch Nuns.

10. To honor and obey my Mother Superiors.

As she completes the last of her vows her body falls forward, she catches herself but feels worse than she did before. Tauheedah can no longer bear this extremely nauseating feeling, she is about to pass out when she hears Hymiriam's voice.

"I cannot help you my child. The power and blessing of God is What flows within you now. You must embrace it, control it, and rise to your feet on your own." Hymiriam pauses then with a strong, stern and encouraging voice she shouts. "If you cannot stand for The Power of God, you cannot Wield The Power of God and you Shall not receive The Power of God!"

Tauheedah hears this and gathers all her strength, raises her head, opens her eyes and with a focused piercing stare she looks at Hymiriam and says in a seductively soft and strong voice "NOW BEAR WITNESS TO THE POWER OF GOD!"

As she struggles, then Rises to her feet. As she stands a beautiful pattern of light begins to form in the center of the Arch Gate. Tauheedah feels the light becoming one with her. She looks up, softly closes her eyes and Embraces the Feeling as she consumes the light. When she hears Hymiriam's voice again.

"Tauheedah Mujahideen is no more! Step through the Arch Gate to begin your journey and except your new way of life."

She who was once Tauheedah begins to slowly walk through the gate as she takes her last step on the other side of the gate the great luminous light of the bridge once again dims. She stands perfectly still in the praying position. She is now ordained as an 'Arch Nun', this title is created by Hymiriam and it is the highest rank a Nun can have and this woman wears it well. Hymiriam looks upon her with great joy and proudly says.

"From this day forth. You shall be known as Arch Nun Sister Amira(A-mirr-ra).

So, shall it be written-So, shall this be done."

Amira opens her eyes as she looks upon Hymiriam with the Grace of God and the knowing of what and who she really is. She knows now that she is in the presence of Mary, The Mother of 'Jesus Christ.'

The Grace of God prevents her from being overwhelmed and controls her emotions allowing her to stay calm in the presence of such greatness. She knows she is considered a daughter of Hymiriam and a humble servant of the Lord. A great Divineness Shines from her now. The young woman whom was filled with joy and Infinite Jest still resides within her, but for now is suppressed. She stands still as Hymiriam looks upon her with the encouraging eyes of a mother.

Amira looks deeply into these eyes and knows she is part of something Grand.

"Come this way my child" Hymiriam says. "My reference to you as my child has a more profound meaning does it not?" Hymiriam now jests with Amira. But Amira just bows her head and replies.   "If I spoke for a thousand years Oh Great Mother Hymiriam my words could not express the pride and joy I feel being considered as one of your daughters."   Hymiriam is pleased to see how Amira is adjusting to The Grace of God. She is strong, she is focused and she is of Pure Power. Which can be felt in the way she now speaks. This is the Natural Rhetoric of The Arch Nuns. Every word with conviction in the tone of Royalty. This will undoubtedly be considered an arrogant tone in the eyes of humanity. But they will soon conform. For an Arch Nun Walks and Speaks with the power of God. This demeanor has not been seen since Moses walked the Earth with the power of the Lord God within him.

Hymiriam guides her across the bridge and down the first flight of stairs. There are no words spoken for these few moments as they descent down the second flight of stairs. Amira notices they are starting to walk upon the clouds as though they were a solid surface. But she fears not for she is in the presence of the Lord. Although Hymiriam can now communicate with Amira telepathically and spiritually she communicates verbally.

"So, tell me my child." Hymiriam asks. "how do you feel?"

" like I can walk on the clouds." Amira answers smiling. Hymiriam laughs because she knows Amira's lovable and delightful personality of old are intact so, she says lovingly to her new daughter.

"I fell right into that answer didn't I my child?"

They both laugh and continue to walk among the clouds. Amira asks her new mother if her name Hymiriam has a meaning or was it created just for her?

20

Hymiriam tells her God blessed her with this name and the 'Arch Nunhood'. But the meaning of the name Hymiriam will mean: 'The HyHeld of God' or 'HUMANITY HELD HIGHER' so they may continue.

"That is so beautiful mother Hymiriam." Amira says.

"I love the name you have given unto me. If I may ask why have you chosen the name Amira for me?" Hymiriam laughs softly cuts her eyes at her and answers in a jest.

"Because my child, A mirror evidently is something you spent a lot of your time in front of-- when you considered yourself to be Exxxxtremely pretty!"

They both laugh hysterically enjoying themselves bonding as mother and daughter.

"Mother why have you chosen for us to be Nuns?"

"Well Amira Nuns were once highly respected and loved. But as time went on, they became sex objects and something to be possessed by demons and made fun of in movies." Hymiriam continues with a heavy heart.

"They took vows that bound them in matrimony to my son Jesus, they vowed to live in poverty and be set aside and discarded as second-class Citizens. So, I not only chose Nuns but created the Arch Nunhood to be held the highest form of Nunhood the world has ever seen."

In the eyes of God Arch Nun truly means 'Divine Nun' but Mother Hymiriam tuned it down to Arch Nun. It may change to its true name later but for now Arch Nun will suffice. Amira is amazed.

"I am so happy mother, you choose me to be an Arch Nun."

"I know my child, I know."

Hymiriam then continues to tell her new Daughter more of what the Lord allows her to know of Eve. She tells her Eve keeps millions of daughters and sons All over the world. The sons are sometimes named Cain and Abel. For her own personal reasons. She has Every culture and nationality meticulously covered. She is involved in Far too many things for Hymiriam to explain at this time and It is not included in the knowledge of 'past and present' to the Arch Nuns through the grace of God. Amira has many questions pertaining to Eve and how they will convince her to come home.

Like mosses journeyed to Egypt to free the slaves. Hymiriam will also have a journey to Eve. God will not give Eve to Hymiriam on a silver platter, she and her Arch Nun's path will be hard and full with peril. Just has God loves Mary the Mother of Jesus, God loves Eve the first female. God does not allow Hymiriam the luxury of knowing everything about Eve. God gave her enough knowledge to set her upon the path. But God will allow several face-to-face meetings between Hymiriam and Eve to give Eve a chance to yield, comply and come home. Eve is not in the public eye very often nor is she the recluse you would assume her to be. She does travel and enjoy life she is however very careful as to who she lets into her life.

Eve can reset herself at will and any place of her choosing. She sometimes does this on Mount Sinai (God's mountain) at the age of 70 to 80 years old. With her having the influence she does in the world and over many important people and leaders she always has elaborate, air tight plans in place to cover every detail in the deception of her death and rebirth. Also, where this new person has been from childhood. Because she was NEVER a child! There is always a history in place. She is announced and presented as a relative inheriting everything.

Eve can only reset herself as far back as sixteen years of age that's when she was created because she had no childhood nor was, she ever a baby. Eve's Vitality is completely controlled by her, it is impervious to any outside force. To her current Sons and Daughters, the world over she is simply presented as one of their siblings. But they know it is their mother and they hold her in a very high esteem and are always very obedient to her. With so many of her blood on Earth in various stages of life. She has built a sustainable perpetual Network for her life. Time is the fire in which we burn. But Eve does not, she is Everlasting on Earth!

Any child born directly from Eve is blessed with extreme Beauty. Being the mother of all she can control their gender and what nationality or combination of nationalities they will be. She of course can change her nationality or combination of, when she resets herself. Which doesn't just make it hard to apprehend her, but impossible to apprehend her! At five to eight years of age these children begin to develop slightly enhanced speed and strength because of Eve's DNA within them which gives them 3% strength and speed only Over the strongest and fastest human. Which is more than enough to physically kill most human beings with very little effort. But they get no additional knowledge. They still must train physically to maintain this which is why the Arch Nuns are giving 10% of everything through the grace of God to combat them.

The sons and daughters of Eve with her permission reproduce heirs to inherit their companies and take over all of their affairs. Eve's DNA is passed on to them and with that DNA they can never turn on her they are as obedient as their parents before them.

Eve has pioneered artificial insemination and owns countless facilities all over the world every time she resets herself to sixteen years of age. She uses her eggs and the most powerful and influential males in the world to fertilize them. This bloodline is loyal to her for two generations before it deteriorates and they become independent. That is why the children of her children are loyal to her as well. They do not get additional speed or strength. After two Generations the obedience dissipates and has it does that bloodline dies off. Then Eve acquires their companies through other means. God does this so the whole world would not be related to Eve or share her DNA.

23

At an early age they are perfectly groomed to take their place in society that Eve and their parents have prepared for them.

Amira listens paying attention to every word. She begins to truly realize how powerful and great Eve is and has always been. If there ever was a queen of the known world it was and is Eve. Eve has everything covered. She also understands why there had to be an equal or greater entity such as the 'Arch Nunhood.' If not for the 'Grace of God' that flows within her, giving her strength and courage Amira would surely be afraid, very afraid.

"Mother I have a question if I may." Amira asks in confusion. "With Eve having so much power and control on Earth, with so much influence in every law enforcement agency, controlling many world leaders how were you able to convince them to allow us to be the absolute highest level of law enforcement on Earth with so many liberties?"

"Well my child." Hymiriam answers and tells her. Humanity is unaware they are slowly being enslaved by Eve. They fear somethings coming they always have and knew if they didn't create one super agency their worst fears may come true and they would fall. Another reason the world leaders signed off on this agency was if it was successful, they can take credit for the glory and the good that it does for the world. For Hymiriam and the Arch Nunhood seek no glory at all. The ten are the ultimate Ministers of law enforcement.

The world leaders are unaware that Mother Teresa is an Archangel and the Arch Nuns are really 'Time Displaced Superior Human Beings' blessed truly with 'The Grace of God' and the 'The Holy Spirit'

Amira is amazed at how much she knows and has learned, her mind is moving at the blink of an eye. She is very inquisitive and wants to ask many questions. Hymiriam knows this and tells her she may ask as many questions as she likes. Amira hesitates then asks.

"Mother Hymiriam, can I wear one of those T-shirts I see people wearing that reads 'BLESSED AND HIGHLY FAVORED'?"

"NO Amira!" Hymiriam says sharply and laughing. "you cannot. For God favors no one person over the other. GOD LOVES ALL EQUITY!

Please don't think that because God gave you special abilities above everyone else that you are favored above everyone else!"

Amira's eyes widen and she becomes very nervous.

"I know, I know Oh great Mother Hymiriam." Amira says quickly. "I meant no disrespect I know the Grace of God gives me the knowing of all these things I just----"

Hymiriam stops her and says jokingly "Got ya"

Amira sighs with relief.

"Yes you did, yes you did indeed mother!"

"Your still not wearing a shirt that says THAT!"

Hymiriam loves the conversation she is having with Amira. She loves laughing with her for laughing is essential to life. She loves talking with her for she is so full of life. She also feels a strong sense of Love that emanates from her. For she is the very embodiment of 'LIVE, LOVE, LAUGH'...

They continue walking, a large home style ranch complex appears in front of them.

"This will be your new home my child it is called the Divine Elysium." Hymiriam says. Amira looks upon her new home with excitement and ask the one question she's been dying to ask her new mother.

"What 'Magical superpowers' do the Arch Nuns have?"

Her eyes light up with excitement and joy in anticipation of all the wonderful super things Hymiriam is going to tell her

the Arch Nuns can do. But Hymiriam looks at her like a
mother looks at a child eagerly waiting to open Christmas
presents and says.

"Settle down Amira! First and most importantly they are
NOT, I repeat NOT and you will NEVER refer to THE
GRACE OF GOD and THE HOLY SPIRIT as magical
superpowers EVER!"

Hymiriam says in a stern but loving voice. "That which
flows through All Arch Nuns is The Grace of God and it is
NOT to be associated with SCIENCE, MAGIC OR SUPER
POWERS, UNDERSTAND?"

Hymiriam continues firmly. Again, Amira's eyes widen, her
mouth opens but she remains silent. She does not want
Hymiriam to consider her inquiry blasphemous.

"They are considered, and will be referred to as 'SPIRITUAL
GIFTS' from this day FORTH!!! And you wield them for
'God's Great purpose!" Hymiriam concludes with a smile.
Although Hymiriam is smiling Amira cannot help but feel as
though she was slightly verbally scolded. Amira welcomes
this from her new mother as they laugh together.

"As for the SPIRITUAL GIFTS." Hymiriam says putting her
arm around Amira and guiding her toward the ranch.

"You will have to wait my child; I'll tell you tomorrow."

"Yes mother." Amira replies with a nervous grin.

They enter the ranch to which half of it is under the clouds.
Hymiriam commands the clouds to dissipate revealing a
very large complex and a Lake.

Hymiriam tells Amira to stand before her, close her eyes and
bow her head. Hymiriam puts her hands-on Amira's Head
so she may pray with her. Just as Hymiriam begins to pray
Amira interrupts and starts the prayer.

"Oh god! I am your humble servant I thank thee Oh god for
my new mother, I thank thee Oh god for my new life. I
thank thee Oh god for the opportunity to serve Humanity
and I thank thee Oh God for the Grace you have bestowed
upon me for I will use it wisely in Jesus name I pray amen."

Hymiriam is impressed and pleased with her new daughter especially for taking the initiative, saying the prayer and thanking the Lord. Appearing at the top of the stairs another Nun stands looking down at them. She is older than Hymiriam with kind eyes and a warm smile. Through the Grace of God Amira is able to determine this is 'Mother Teresa'.

She is not an Arch Nun she is an Arch Angel and a very dear friend to Hymiriam.

Hymiriam tells Amira she will be leaving her here with Mother Teresa.

"This is where I leave you my child". Hymiriam says sadly. Like a mother leaving a child for the first day of school. "Behave yourself" She says looking her in the eyes. "Don't make me come back here!" She jestfuly tells her winking her eye and giving her a hug.

Amira is tickled and amused at how loving and jestful her relationship with Mother Hymiriam is. She has never felt such a sense of belonging. So, she gives praise to God as Mother Teresa comes down the stairs to hug and welcome her.

"Welcome my child, welcome" Mother Teresa says greeting Amira with a long warm embrace and tears in her eyes. Amira is curious as to why Mother Teresa is crying and so happy to see her, but does not ask her. Because she is meeting her for the first time and wants to appear strong and focused.

"Your brothers and sisters are on the patio waiting to meet you." Mother Teresa walks her to the large patio area but no one is there. Amira was beginning to worry that they were there, but she could not see them because Mother Teresa continues to make references to them as though they are standing there. Amira just keeps nodding her head in agreeance and smiling.

Then mother Teresa summons the rest of the Arch Nuns. Mother Teresa knows everything about she who was

27

Tauheedah Mujahideen and she who is Sister Amira. Hymiriam felt everything regarding her interview on the bridge to Mother Teresa through The Holy Spirit. Mother Teresa is well aware of Amira's Flare for theatrics and the cinema. So, to Indulge and entertain her new Grand Daughter as she summons the rest of the Arch Nuns, they appear in a flash of light that resembles something from a big budget Hollywood movie. Amira is amazed at how beautiful and spectacular they appeared before her. Standing in a semi half circle formation proud, strong and in the prayer position. They lovingly gaze upon their new sister silently, and they smile. Mother Teresa gives them this moment of joy.

"Behold Sister Amira and welcome to-- 'The Arch Nunhood of Mother Hymiriam'."

Mother Teresa says with the greatest of pride and joy.

What a beautiful sight Mother Teresa thought to herself to see them all together in full uniform for the first time. Amira thinks to herself 'The Arch Nunhood of Mother Hymiriam. COOLEST NAME EVER!'

"Now come Amira, I will introduce you to your new family then you shall take your place among them.

This is your sister Dajairia: The Dancer.(she is of African-American and Egyptian descent.) This is Anna: The Golden.(she is of European descent.) and this is your Brother Superior Joshua: The Musician.(he is of Asian Indian descent.) and here we have Donna: The Deceptionist.(she is of Italian-American descent.) This is Navaeh: The Weapon of Haven.(she is of French and African-American descent.) and this is Elizabeth: The Stunter.(she is of British descent.) and on this side we have Lyn Yeoh-Hao: The Alley Cat.(she is of Chinese and Japanese descent.) your brother Zachariah: The Sports fan.(he is of Native-American descent.) and finally your Sister Superior Maria: The Stylist.(she is of Spanish descent.) Everyone this is your sister Amira: The Movie Buff."

The rest of the Arch Nuns gather closely around Mother Teresa and Amira so they may lay a hand upon Amira so she may feel their love. This is the way of the Arch Nuns. Mother Teresa feels the connection they have established and is pleased with the Union they have instantly formed. She tells them she is going to leave them for now so they may fellowship and she will return on tomorrow. She assures them that she nor Hymiriam will monitor or invade their privacy here, for this is their home. She will speak with Hymiriam for a few more moments here then they will leave so the Arch Nuns may adjust and bond. Just to amuse Amira Mother Teresa disappears in the same flash of light. As she leaves the circle, in the blink of an eye all but Amira are now dressed in casual attire. But Amira is still in her Arch Nun uniform. The Arch Nuns stand looking at her quietly for a few seconds then Dajairia breaks the silence.

"You know you can change out of that uniform, now right?"

"Unless you're gonna sleep in it." josh adds jokingly.

"And you can change your hair, style, length and color Instantly!" Donna adds.

"I don't really know what to change in to." Amira says nervously.

"You can wear whatever you like and you can do so with a simple thought" Darejareha tells her.

"Yeah!" Zac adds. "Think it and it is done"

But Anna urges Amira to be careful what she chooses. "After all we are Nuns!" She says. Amira looks at her brothers and sisters to see what they are wearing. They are wearing a wide assortment of garments. Sister Donna is literally wearing a tourniquet she says it's from her favorite TV show war band. sister Anna is dressed like a secretary. Brother Zach is dressed in basketball attire.

"Mother Teresa said that she preferred us not to wear anything too scantily clad you know?" Sister lin advises. Amira thought for a moment to herself then remembered

Mother Teresa also said she nor Mother Hymiriam would ever invade their privacy this was our home. So, Amira before her new brothers and sisters changes in to the most revealing tight-fitting mini skirt and high heels she can think of.

"Well". Amira says with a sexy look on her face. "I'm ready." The Arch nuns are in Shock. "No! Sister Noooo!!!!" Sister Maria yells hysterically.

"Can I borrow that?" Sister Donna asks. Amira's brothers and sisters plead with her to try again now! Amira thinks for a moment and then changes into a one piece skin tight pants suit with a revealing neckline so low it reveals her navel and of course high heels with a short sassy hair style.

"Ok" Amira says smiling. "This looks good right? "

"O.M.G, O.M.G, O.M.G" Sister Anna chants to herself in fear. "Mother Hymiriam is going to come back here and smite us all." She says.

" ♫Oh! Little sister, what have you done♫." Brother Joshua sings from the song made famous by Billy Idol laughing.

"I would look good in that!" Sister Elizabeth says looking her up and down.

"Alright, Alright!" Sister Dajairia says seriously. "let's get it together before Mother Hymiriam really does come back here!"

So Amira still having fun with her new brothers and sisters changes in to a pair of very short-shorts and a half top tied in the front and buttoned almost all the way down and yet another sassy hair style. "Third time's the charm" Amira says while posing in her outfit. "You gotta agree with this?"

"If anybody's looking for me, I'll be dead face down in the lake." Sister Navaeh says sadly. The Arch Nuns urge their new sister to try again and this time get her mind out of the gutter as they all laugh.

Amira then Changes into a pair of sweatpants, sneakers and a hoodie jacket. The Arch Nuns put their hands in the air and rejoice yelling Hallelujah. Thanking God their new sister has finally come to her senses as they laugh and hug each other.

Hymiriam and Mother Teresa are standing on the lake just outside the nun's

View observing their new Children bonding and becoming family. They had forgotten Mother Teresa did say she would be here a few minutes more talking to Hymiriam.

"You were most wise to choose one with such a Great Spirit and sense of humor." Mother Teresa says. "The years they have spent and are about to spend with her have done and will do them all such good."

"Yes Teresa, I have such a wonderful feeling about them. Now I better get to Earth for there is much to do for God's Great purpose!"

Hymiriam and Mother Teresa fade away slowly as their children continue to make merry in the distance.

"Hey everybody" Sister Elizabeth yells. "We can't just stand here, ♫bouncing around, bouncing around, bouncing♫" she continues reciting and singing the lyrics from a popular Rap song.

"I agree, I'm with that" Sister Navaeh says.

"I think we all, are with that but what do we do" Sister Dajairia asks.

"Well let's not leave it to Anna cause she'll have us all in bible study or knitting sweaters. "Brother Joshua says laughing.

"Only for a little while" Sister Anna agrees looking at her brother seriously but sarcastically joking. "Then I'll have everyone make hot coco and cookies"

"No wait!" Brother Zach interrupts. "Let's hold hands and sing Kumbaya then play Monopoly"

"Oh! That's a great idea Zach" Sister Maria says as she stares at him.

"Oh my, Oh my!" Amira says sarcastically jesting. "Those all sound like wonderful "Nun like' things to do, But!" Everyone turns and looks at her.

"Wait! Just hear me out" She continues urging them to listen. "Now Mother Teresa said her nor Mother Hymiriam would monitor us or invade our privacy this was our home, right?" "Yeah And?" Maria says with her arms folded smiling giving Amira a look. Everyone is curious as to what Amira is going to say next.

"Well" With an innocent look on her face. Amira States the obvious. She has always been very observant and always used it to her advantage especially when getting out of trouble. "You're all dressed so conservatively and worried about acting so perfect because you assume, you're being watched and you want to be perfect little Nuns."

Everyone looks at each in agreeance. Then Anna raises her hand and says.

"I would like to be a 'perfect' little Nun!!!"

Everyone turns and just stares at Anna for a few seconds. So Amira having her brothers and sisters undivided attention asks them.

"Why, I ask you brothers and sisters didn't Mother Teresa or Hymiriam return When I dressed myself so scantily, why did they not return to reprimand or Smite us all--or just me?" No one answers everyone remains silent. They realize they are not being watched. So, Amira continues confidently.

"You told me Mother Teresa 'preferred' us not to but did not say 'definitely' not to. Let me remind you brothers and sisters Mother Teresa said that we were home I suggest we start acting like it! Did you dress and act like this in the privacy of your own home on Earth?" Amira turns to Donna who is wearing a tourniquet from mid evil times and adds. "Ok maybe Donna did!" Amira says to her sister jokingly. What exactly is that Sis?" Dajairia asks Donna.

"Ok everybody it's a tourniquet from a movie called 'Warband'." Donna tells them. "It's something my favorite girl character tiaka wears and yes, I wore stuff like this when I was home alone!"

"Well" Amira says. "This is our home we're not being watched and we can have fun with it." Everyone remains silent for a moment then Elizabeth in a lovingly and sisterly way asks Amira. "You used to shoplift and get caught alot didn't you?"

"Wait, What?" Amira says with a big grin.

"That, or she was an attorney for the entertainment industry." Brother Zach adds Laughing and padding Amira on the shoulder.

"I was good, pure and innocent" Amira says trying not to laugh. "But really I was a stupid little promiscuous slut!" She concludes with a serious face. Everyone gets so quiet you can hear a pin drop.

"REALLY Amira!" Donna asks in amazement.

"No! Donna NOT REALLY" Amira replies as everyone laughs hysterically.

Then Sister Maria speaks. "As much as I hate to admit it, she may be right." The others agree.

"Well then! Amira." Navaeh says cheerfully. "I think we should leave it up to you, the patio is yours."

Everyone agrees and anxiously waits as Amira takes a few seconds to think. Then before their very eyes the patio is transformed into an outdoor party environment complete with a bar, alcoholic beverages snacks and a complete DJ booth. Everyone's eyes widen and jaws drop. Amira was a little surprised herself at how accurate and quickly her thoughts manifested.

"O.M.G, O.M.G, O.M.G" Sister Anna chants nervously to herself again.

"Be still little sister" Brother Joshua says to her. "For you are home!"

So, the Arch Nuns rejoice and there was much revelry they share stories of their lives on Earth and their time on the bridge with Hymiriam. They partake in alcohol but not to excessively. They are unaware alcohol does not affect them here they are incapable of becoming intoxicated at home, on earth maybe. This particular order of Nunhood may indulge in a great many things for they are the first of their kind. The Arch Nuns realize their new sister was right. But they know not to push Mother Teresa or Hymiriam's patience or take advantage of their leniency.

And for 40 days and 40 nights Hymiriam prayed for Humanity spoke with God and to the world leaders. To whom she was considered a prodigy and a genius. Making all the preparations for that which will be and that which is to come. There was but one legal contract between Hymiriam and the world leaders. This was the contract that God set forth. This was the contract that favored Hymiriam and the Arch Nuns allowing them many liberties and loopholes. Hymiriam and Mother Teresa will be recognized as the absolute leaders of 'The Arch Nuns' and the U.N.A. but Mother Teresa will make ALL tactical and law enforcement decisions, Hymiriam will be doing God's work, separate and apart from ALL Law enforcement activities, for she walks a different path! part of the agreed contract was she will meet with the world leaders only when they or she needs to. She ONLY meets with the highest leader of the land. Her whereabouts are never to be known and the leader or leaders she meets with is strictly confidential.   This is for security and for her safety. Leaders are never to inquire anything regarding who she was with or the content of the meeting. Mother Teresa will be the spokesperson for the U.N.A and assist Hymiriam whenever or if ever needed. In the absence of Hymiriam she is the undisputed voice of Hymiriam communicating with the world leaders and for their instructions. Whenever a world leader needs to meet with Hymiriam before doing so They are advised to shut down all surveillance systems and prepare for her arrival. She sometimes arrives disguised and well-hidden as does her team until she meets with the leader she came to see.

She also departs hidden and disguised this is done to help keep her meetings confidential and Secret. Her team members are experts in misdirection and blending in they are never seen nor recognized for they are angels...

During the 40 days and nights the Lord God took over All forms of media. Every cell phone, tablet and computer. Every Magazine, Newspaper and Television broadcast was bombarded with information pertaining to the coming of this new law enforcement agency.

It was considered an emergency broadcast across all forms of media

Worldwide. Every hour for 10 minutes. It was appropriately named by the younger Generation 'The Media Storm'...

This will start 11/1/2027 and End on12/10/27.

The contents of this message starts with: Attention this is a worldwide emergency message.

A new law enforcement agency has been formed by the United Nations of the world. It will be called 'The U.N.A' United Nations Agency.

This agency will be the highest level of law enforcement in the world.

It will be composed of a highly trained religious order. Trained exclusively for this agency and Extreme Tactical and Combat situations. They will cover all forms of law enforcement worldwide. They are the world's first Arch Nuns there will be new laws worldwide. Here are some but not all of the new laws.

#1 No one shall mock or make fun of the Arch Nuns in any way, shape or form it will be considered a felony worldwide. They are a religious order but will not impose their religion upon you.

#2 They will be enforcing the old laws, the current laws and the new laws with a fair, firm and consistent hand.

#3 dressing like them will not be considered a form of flattery but a form of mockery, if you are not a nun of any religion, the wearing of a Habit for fashion is forbidden it will be considered impersonating a government agent and a felony with unlimited fines including incarceration.

#4 They have the highest form of diplomatic immunity worldwide.

#5 They answer only to the world leader of the country they are currently in. presidential status or equivalent only.

#6 Everyone must go to (www.UNA.org) for more information this is mandatory worldwide! Fail to do so at your own risk! Negligence of the new laws will not be an excuse for breaking the new laws.

#7 Never resist or interfere in any business of this new agency or you will be detained, heavily fined and may include incarceration.

#8 They need no warrant for apprehension, incarceration or to enter any premise. They do not require probable cause to search anything pertaining to their current or any case they are involved in.

#9 The Arch Nuns can take over or insert themselves in to any investigation they see fit at any level. From the smallest of crimes to the largest of crimes.

 #10 Only an Arch Nun can invoke the 'law of Goliath'? (very important)

This message will repeat every hour for the next 40 days. It also interrupted Netflix, Hulu and other similar services and could not be deleted or skipped over. It interrupted everything to the point of annoyance. When the people complained about this interruption and complained they did. The message continued relentlessly. The people remembered the United Nations talking about this for years but always had excuses as to why the agency was never started the people begin to remember and flooded the internet with inquiries. They searched for any information they could find about the U.N.A or the Arch Nuns. Aside from the information on the official world wide-approved website most of the information pertaining to the U.N.A or Arch Nuns was Black Ops Hush Hush high-level government stuff.

They were annoyed, resentful, curious and very interested. But at the end of the 40 days there was not a man woman or child that did not know about the 'United Nations Agency', 'The new Laws' or 'The Arch Nuns'.

The world leaders told the people this was necessary and a state of emergency also confirming that it would continue for 40 days. To the world leader's knowledge this was thought to be Hymiriam Collaborating with tech companies temporarily taking over the internet and all forms of communication with some new technology they hoped to get their hands on. But it was actually the Power of God preparing the path for the Arch Nuns. For there is no technology that can match the Power of the Lord...

So God put the laws and will into the hearts of the leaders and in their minds, God wrote these laws. This is what compelled the world leaders and allow them the courage and wisdom to allow this new agency to be formed.

God revealed the "Word" to their minds and the word was "God". For God is the light of Eternal mind and the light of God is in every man, woman and child!

The leaders of the world would never have come to such a

decision without Divine intervention. IN GOD WE TRUST!!!!!

Each world leader made sure their country and people were well aware of the coming of the Arch Nuns and ALL their legal and law enforcement liberties. They made sure that the people knew they were law enforcement only not leaders or politicians.

They made sure the world knew that the Arch Nuns worked for the world leaders and it is the world leaders that would make the new laws the Arch Nuns will be enforcing. They told the people the Arch Nuns answer to no General, no governor or vice president. The highest seat in the country ONLY! Presidential status or equivalent and that Authority could not be passed down to anyone under them for any reason.

   Back at the Divine Garden the Arch Nuns continue in their revelry, telling stories and enjoying each other's company. "What were you thinking when you first awakened on the bridge and saw Hymiriam for the first time?" Zac asked everyone.

"I thought she was a beautiful angel" Anna says. "I thought I was in heaven " Dajairia adds.

"I was so amazed" Donna says with a smile. Zac says with open arms. "I'm in haven!"

All the Arch Nuns raise their hands cheering and laughing. "Why are you so quiet Amira what did you think?" Lyn asks with caution.

"Well" Amira says smiling. "I thought to myself she sure is filling out that coat."

She pauses for a moment. "But in a good way."

Once again everyone becomes very quiet.

Then Dajairia yells laughing. "Wait! You were actually checking out her figure?"

Anna stands and shouts. "What the Apple, peaches, pumpkin pie were you doing looking at her figure?"

"Hold on!" Amira replies laughing. "I wasn't looking like 'Hey baby let's go out' or anything like that. She has a great figure so I thought she was my biological mother."

Zac who was sitting on top of the bar almost fell off he was laughing so hard. Lyn did fall to the floor with laughter.

"Why did you say Apple, peaches, pumpkin pie Anna? " Joshua asks barely containing in his laughter.

"Cause I can't say 'H'-'E' double hockey sticks!"

" What's H-E double hockey sticks Anna? "

"HELL! Joshua okay I can't say HELL!"

"But you just said HELL Anna." Donna yells Laughing. At that moment Amira releases a piercing high pitch annoying scream at the top of her lungs and says in a little girl's voice pointing at Anna.

"You're a Nun, and you said a bad word, I'm telling Grandma Teresa!" Anna couldn't help but laugh with her brothers and sisters. But in the back of her mind she thought this all seems Vaguely Familiar.

The Arch Nuns were having such a great time with each other, they continued well into the night. The morning arrives and Mother Teresa appears on the patio which is now completely empty. The Arch Nuns knew to reset the patio before Mother Teresa's return. They cared not to awaken to a scolding. But the Arch Nuns Awakened to a most glorious gift from God.

Through God's Grace, the Arch Nuns were given 30 years of life together in
one night. They were reset to infants so they may grow up together and Bond as true brothers and sisters. They started this life in 1998, (1996 for Josh and Maria) as new born orphaned babies and grow to adulthood together raised by The Arch Angels Mother Hymiriam, Grandmother Teresa

and Saint Michael. So, when they are on Earth in 2028 there will be some history that they were born, raised and stories of their training. (bits and pieces, fragments here and there.) These fragments of information can be found on the internet and in books and some magazine articles. But they are always short, very vague and hard to find. This is the current life on Earth protected by God's Grace. Their original lives up until 2001 will still exist but hidden from humanity and protected by God.

The lord took everyone who knew any of them, Pictures taken with old friends mysteriously disappeared. Sometimes when they slept in the year 2000 and 2001 the last two years of their original lives before they were taken, they would sometimes see the beginning of their second life has a dream, a very weird dream.

It's like when you hear someone say last night, I dreamt I was a baby! The dreams only lasted until the day the World Trade Center was attacked. This is what happened when they fell asleep the first night at the Divine Ranch and this completes the 10% Grace of God and The Holy Spirit. As for how the babies came to be in the hands of Hymiriam and Mother Teresa, God will guide you where you Need to be! They gave each other many nicknames as children that they carried well into their adulthood some are the nicknames Mother Teresa introduced them as when Amira arrived at the Divine Ranch. The Arch Nuns believed Mother Teresa gave them these nicknames for the first time while they were being introduced to Amira. But they were really the nicknames they gave each other during the 30 years they spent together. In one night. Amira now has a better understanding as to why Mother Teresa had tears in her eyes and was so happy to see her. Mother Teresa already knew her because she raised her in her Second Life, she raised all of them. Time is not linear for an Archangel they can move through it as God sees fit.

Anna now knows why Amira threatening to tell Mommy Teresa that she said a bad word seemed familiar to her because Amira was a little 'Tattle Tale' when she was a child and Josh and Donna were always making Anna say bad words. Like siblings do.

Everyone runs over to hug mother Teresa. The Arch Nuns gather around her hugging, crying and laughing with such love. For now, they had knowledge of an entire life together. The stories they spoke of this time were the stories they shared. So, Mother Teresa allows them this time to reminisce and enjoy it. They spoke of the times they helped each other during their training and lessons. They spoke of the times they fought as children over crayons and the television remote. They remembered many pranks they played upon each other and Mother Teresa. They recall attempting to be defiant as teenagers and paying the price with Mother Teresa. They remember Father Michael being a strong Father Figure in their lives. They look back at the periodic visits from mother Hymiriam to check on their progress and behavior. Which wasn't always good?

They remember their big brother Josh being the prankster putting their hands in warm water while they slept so they would urinate on themselves.

They were not perfect. But mother Teresa, Hymiriam and Father Saint Michael So loved them and wouldn't have it any other way. After all they are family.

The Arch Nuns also remember something else, something the female Nuns want to discuss with each other for a moment privately and immediately!!!

"Zac, Josh excuse us for a minute." Elizabeth says to her brothers. "GIRL HUDDLE!" She yells. "Hey! Does anyone else feel 'REALLY' funny in a certain area???"

"Yeah!" Maria answers." I wasn't going to say anything but now that you mentioned it. I feel strange just in one area"

"I don't feel anything" Donna says confused.

Amira adds. "I feel like I have never had sex and trust me

girls I REALLY, REALLY had sex."

"Indeed so have I" Anna says.

"I don't feel anything" Donna says again.

Amira looks at Dajairia and says. "That is absolutely amazing!!"

"What?" Navaeh asks.

Amira looks around at her sisters saying. "That Anna had sex and Donna didn't!!"

"That is astonishing!" lin states with wide eyes.

"I was getting around to it BUT excuse me I DIED!!" Donna says with frustration.

Amira looks at her with a smile saying. "I thought all of you computer geeks sat around watching porn, Japanese anime, eating Doritos, hot pockets and of course having sex, sometimes with yourself?"

"it was on my to do list" Donna answers looking down at the ground.

"Well our special areas are virgins again" Navaeh says Putting her hands on her belly.

"I'm glad I'm a virgin again" Lin says grinning. "My special area was starting to get a little large" All the girls' eyes widen as they look at Lin.

"Ok girls! "Maria interrupts.

"This is definitely a conversation for a night on the patio with frozen margaritas. When the boys are out. "

"I agree" Amira adds. "And on that night Lin and Anna will have the floor and our full attention!"

Hymiriam appears on the patio and everyone runs to embrace her with tears of joy and love. They remember, and it is the best of times.

"Ok everyone Gather yourselves and take a seat"

Hymiriam says wiping tears from her eyes. A table and chairs appear on the patio. Mother Teresa and Hymiriam sit across the table facing the Nuns.

Hymiriam continues to wipe tears from her eyes so she may speak.

"Ok, my children before we get started this will be your ONE and ONLY chance to change any physical part or parts of yourself you do not like or where never happy with whether it's your weight, height, moles, shape. ANYTHING at all. Speak now and it will be done or FOREVER hold your peace. The nuns take a moment to talk among themselves. Then all the Nuns stand and Donna answers for them. "Mother superiors we the Arch Nunhood of Mother Hymiriam Stand before you and our Lord God on this day and I speak for all of us when I say God made us into the shapes we are. Be it fat, skinny, short or tall.

You raised us to love ourselves and those who are different. Your lessons did not go unheard nor were your teachings in vain. We took a vow to live and love. For we love how God made us with all our imperfections and we shall change nothing!!!!!"

At that moment. Sister Maria yells proudly. "Amen Sister Amen!!"

Then Zac adds. "This is The Will of God!!!"

This time it is Mother Teresa's eyes that water. For it is moments like these that make Her very proud.

Hymiriam struggles to hold back her tears again but let's one or two go anyway. She also feels a great sense of pride and she decides to give her children a great gift, a gift they've been asking her about for 20 years. So, she motions for them to sit down and speaks the phrase she's been speaking to them for the past 30 years.

"Gather yourselves my children and settle down."

The nuns acknowledge their mother's request and comply.

"As you know we are an ever-evolving and constant changing religious order" she pauses for a moment looking over her children.

"You are the first Arch Nuns." She says with the greatest of pride. The pride of a mother.

"As times change, we will conform. I know some of you just couldn't wait to hear about some of the abilities." She pauses

43

for a moment to look at Amira.

Who is looking around attempting to avoid eye contact with her Then Amira looks at Maria and says chuckling "That sounds like something Maria would be concerned about."

"Are you kidding me right now?" Dajairia yells.

"Towards the end of the night that's all you could talk about!"

"Yeah Sis" Elizabeth adds. "You were hoping you could fly and see through walls and stuff."

"Nope." Amira responds with a serious face. "Sorry but you guys must have me confused with another sister Amira, Hymiriam bought to The Ranch yesterday and stayed up partying with you guys last night!!!"

All the Arch Nuns begin to laugh hysterically and carry on as they did when they were children.

"Excuse-me!!!" Hymiriam yells. "But what part of 'GATHER' yourselves did you 'NOT' understand?" All the Arch Nuns immediately become quiet as they did when they were children pointing and blaming each other for not being quiet.

"Now! As I was saying!" Hymiriam continues with a stern voice." I will tell you some of your abilities."

The Nuns are very quiet now. Hymiriam stands and continues with conviction.

"For in the beginning you will be subtle and discreet. But not so much gentle, you will be Stern and forceful. you will be fair, Relentless and fully committed to enforcing God's laws and the laws of humanity. An Arch Nun is held to a higher standard and shall be 'ALL' of these things a thousand-fold, For God's Great Purpose!" Mother Teresa stands and looks upon the Nuns and speaks the words.

"SO, SHALL IT BE WRITTEN!!!"

When an Arch Mother Superior speaks these words it summons the immediate attention of all Arch Nuns and at once they COLLECTIVELY respond.

"SO, SHALL IT BE DONE!!!!"

Mother Teresa and Hymiriam are so proud and impressed they can hardly contain their emotions. As Mother Teresa and Hymiriam Embrace this emotional moment. There is a brief silence. But because Hymiriam did not immediately go into detail regarding their abilities.
Amira asks. "Mother, not so much me, but 'MARIA' was wondering about those abilities???"
Maria gives Amira the big sister look. Amira ignores this and continues.
"Because 'MARIA', 'NOT me 'REALLY' wants to know!"
Mother Teresa looks at Amira and before she can say a word. Hymiriam grabs Mother Teresa's hand with tears of joy still in her eyes looks at the Nuns and says. "You children are so lucky mother loves you so much"
All the Nuns smile and begin to tell their Mother superiors how much they love them too.
Hymiriam goes on to tell the Arch Nuns about the new laws instead as to add to the anticipation, suspense and enthusiasm the Nuns are attempting to contain. She tells them she understands the world has changed a lot since the last time she was in it and how much she wants the Arch Nuns to be accepted. They will be dealing with many diverse cultures and age groups from around the world. So, she has made changes to the Nunhood that 'SHE' and only 'SHE' can do and undo at will...
She now explains the gift she is to give unto them before they interrupted her.
For makeup there shall be no Foundation to cover up imperfections in the facial skin. There shall be no blush to also Aid in disguising blemishes and other imperfections in the facial skin. Also, there is no need for lipstick. For those things were designed to disguise the face and arouse men. There may be eyeliner eye shadow and eyelashes to enhance the eyes for they are the windows to the soul. There may be nail polish and jewelry. There may be hair color and styles nothing too outrageous. Hymiriam allows her daughters to

45

have this and her son's May remove their shirts, when appropriate like men do. As for attire. She says looking at her daughters. "I will trust that you will not wear anything too, well you know."

Amira looks around again avoiding eye contact with her mother. The nuns are so excited they can dress as they please, when they are not in uniform and their uniforms can reflect their personal style a little more.

Hymiriam allowed this because this is a unique type of Nunhood. She wants them to be modern. They were raised to enjoy and embrace life and most importantly be themselves as well as an Arch Nun. There must be a perfect harmony between the two that is why during the 30 years of New Life. They were allowed to have some Talents. They can do better than their brothers and sisters that they could not do in their previous lives. Such as riding a motorcycle or skateboard for example.

They are allowed to have material possessions but nothing too extravagant and nothing they can't discard if needed to do so. The Nuns thank their Mother, or this is a big deal for them. Arch Nuns do not discuss one countries secrets with other when they are in one country they are bound to that country's laws and respect its discretion. They do not tell one country what weapons or technology another country has. Hymiriam being privately recognized as one of the world's most prominent prodigies in medicine over the last 30 years has gained the respect of the world leaders. And in 2020 Hymiriam could not bear seeing children that could not touch one another or play together. She could not bear the thought of a world where people could not hug one another, a world without hand holding, a world full of fear and paranoia. And on April 30th 2021 she cured Covid-19 the 'Coronavirus'.

The world leaders kept this private so they can take credit and of course make a lot of money from the vaccine. The world leaders were so happy they had no problem giving her what she wanted from time to time. She wanted her very own private craft for traveling and they gave it to her no strings attached. This to, was God's Will. The Lord made this journey for 'Christ' a little easier than the last. All the countries of the world collaborated and built the U.N.A technology over the years. Hymiriam did not assist in any way in the construction of these things. For they are after all, Weapons of Extreme Destruction!!
But these Technologies are Unfortunately Absolutely Necessary.
Hymiriam fears not for through the Grace of God the Arch Nuns will know how and when to use them. For the times and the people have indeed changed.
So God protects these things when they are used by the Arch Nuns.
Any ship Hymiriam travels in must be unarmed!!!!
There will also be a U.N.A Council to assist with the laws. For there will be many changes to existing laws as well as many new laws.
Arch nuns have a "license to kill" and the "right to die" Meaning if they choose to give their life for the service they can. An example of this would be running into a burning building to save children it's through the Grace of God they are guided to do so. This act would be preordained and they would be indestructible! only the Arch Nuns would know this. To the world it would appear that they risked their life to save the children. Whenever an Arch Nun is placed in harm's way. They walk with God. For they are God's chosen and will not be harmed!!!
Sometimes the Lord God allows the Nuns to use visual theatrics to emphasize these divine acts. This is not necessary, For the power of God-'IS THAT IT IS'!!!.
But sometimes people need to see something spectacular.

Sometimes people just need to see what a miracle looks like.
Thus, the saying 'Seeing is Believing'.

Hymiriam tells the Nuns they will each have a team of 7 of
the world's most highly trained black ops assault teams from
around the world. They were hand-picked by Mother
Teresa. For this will be their Road to Redemption for all they
have done and are remorseful for.

They will each have a private experimental aircraft that can
carry up to 60 people. They are called Battle Assault crafts
they use something called the 'Active Denial System' which
is a beam of heat that hits human beings causing them to feel
sick it is non-lethal.

These U.N.A drones are broken up into several classes
Pursuit drones Know as "Hyper Drones" surveillance drones
known as "UNA Eye" and the larger battle assault drones
known as "Something B.A.D"(all of these drones come in
various sizes) the larger ones use a combination of jet
propulsion and early experimental anti-gravity propulsion
for takeoff and landing enabling them to land on city streets
without Blowing a lot of air around or burning anything.
Although they can carry up to 60 people they are referred to
as drones because they can be flown remotely. The larger
ones shoot out the smaller ones and so on and so on down to
their smallest size to pursue anyone anywhere. They are a
world collaboration of corporate and military technology.
They represent one of the first steps toward a Unified
world.

The Arch Nunhood of mother Hymiriam does not accept
any type of payment from the world leaders for their service.
Only that they provide what is needed. So, the world leaders
came up with the idea of an unlimited credit card.

This agency is financed by every nation in the world its
finances are Unlimited making the United Nation Agency
the richest law enforcement agency to ever exist. Each Nun
will carry a credit card backed by the World Bank with no
limit. The card works with fingerprint recognition and will

only work in the hand of the Arch Nun it is assigned to. It is called the 'Electronic Banking Tracker'
E.B.T for short. As Hymiriam explains the credit card the Nuns look at each other in confusion and whisper to each other for a moment. Hymiriam pauses then tells the Nuns to pay attention.
She tells them in the event the card is lost due to extreme circumstances.
It will be canceled and tracked for retrieval. In this case an Arch Nun can write a voucher that will assure payment to the merchant from the World Bank with an added 2 to 10% for their inconvenience, Pending the amount charged. The voucher is a form of coupon with the stamp of the World Bank. Signed by the Arch Nun. Since this is controlled by the World Bank it is called the 'World in Control' voucher. W.i.C for short.
Again, the nuns look at each other giggling and whispering. Mother Teresa interrupts Hymiriam and asks the Nuns what they are laughing at as she pulls a ruler from her sleeve. Everyone knows what it means when a Nun or Mother Superior holds a ruler and is angry. Dajairia holding up her hand attempting to contain her laughter answers.
"No disrespect mother but---?"
"But what?" Hymiriam asks with concern.
Amira asks. "Sooooo we're the world richest law enforcement agency?"
"Yes' my child that is correct!"
"And we are going to earth." Elizabeth adds.
Amira cuts her off and yells.
"WITH WIC COUPONS AND E.B.T CARDS!!!!!"
"Yes my children"
"Ok mom" Zac interrupts. "Just making sure we understood that correctly that's all sorry to interrupt" he concludes laughing. The inside joke is W.I.C coupons and E.B.T cards are usually associated with people on government assistance and all of them were on government assistance during their

first life. Something their Mother Superiors would not have known. Because their financial status or lack of was irrelevant.

Mother Teresa slowly inserts her ruler back into her sleeve giving the Nuns a stern look and shaking her finger at them. The Arch Nuns are unaware of how slightly amused Hymiriam is when they get on Mother Teresa's nerves. They have been doing this for the last 25 years. Mother Teresa will NEVER let the Arch Nuns know, she is equally amused. Hymiriam continues on to tell the Nuns of the bag and which they will carry and what it will contain. She tells them the bag will be worn over the shoulder and will come in handy during tactical situations. It contains the 'Weapons of the Arch Nuns' they are: 5 plastic Frisbees, 5 plastic three prop boomerangs, two 12-inch rulers which will be worn under the sleeves made of titanium and can be combined to make a stick, One Universal Bible, One cross and One Gun. These are the things the world will know to be in the bag. But when an Arch Nun reaches into this bag it is God's Will and they shall pull from it. That, which is needed for any situation conceivable.

"We're getting GUNS!" Elizabeth screams in excitement standing and raising both arms in the air.

"Yes! Settle down my child" Hymiriam says.

"I'm so glad I don't have to throw a Frisbee at a bank robber mother" Joshua says.

"Or hit a perpetrator repeatedly in the palm of their hand with a ruler" Lin adds.

Mother Teresa slaps her hand on the table, Stands and pulls her ruler from her sleeve, lays it on the table looks at the Nuns and states with great conviction

"The 'RULER' is the most Recognized, Respected and Feared item carried by a NUN!!!!"

"Yeah!" Amira adds. "It's like a light saber to a Jedi"

Everyone just stares at Amira for a moment. Although Hymiriam knows exactly where she left off, she still asks.

"Ok! My children, where was I?" Immediately Anna raises her hand and answers.

"You were telling us that the bag contains anything we need. God will provide"

"Stop showing off Anna" Elizabeth yells.

"Don't talk to your sister like that" Hymiriam tells her. Mother Teresa slowly slides her ruler over to Hymiriam.

"No thanks Teresa, I have my own!!!" Hymiriam replies looking at the nuns. The nuns recall many a hand wrapping from their Mother superiors through the years and did not want another. Maria leans over and Whispers to Josh.

"I wonder if that hand wrapping would still hurt as adults as it did when we were younger?"

Hymiriam over hears this, pulls her ruler from her sleeve wraps it on the table and the entire Divine Elysium Ranch shakes violently! Amira looks over at Maria and says.

"Yep!!!, I believe it would!!!"

The Nuns decide to make a wise decision and interrupt Mother Hymiriam NO MORE, at least for a little while. Now that Hymiriam has their attention again she continues to explain.

The gun is multi caliber with interchangeable barrels and cylinders and can be combined with the cross by Electro magnets for perfect balance.

When an Arch Nun fires this gun the bullets are guided by God and Ricochet off many things to strike whatever they think of. The nun does not have to look in the direction they are firing.

They ARE ' GOD GUIDED BULLETS'!!!! If the bullet is to kill it is the will of God!!

They will also have a weapon which is a small bow and arrow no bigger than a coat hanger that fits in their bag. The arrows have adjustable feathers so they can fly in unorthodox ways. It too is Guided by God. It can fire two to three arrows at once with incredible accuracy. Like the gun it strikes whatever they are thinking of. It is God's will that it

51

shall strike what it is meant to strike. Or kill if it is God's Will.

It is referred to as the "Arc Bow" for its ability to curve arrows in flight.

The three prong boomerangs and Frisbees are controlled in the same

fashion. They cannot travel backward or forward it time. They can however move anywhere in the present with in the blink of an eye. This will be called Transitioning, but the Nuns will refer to it as 'Stepping to the rhythm of time' or 'Time stepping'. In the eyes of the world the Arch Nuns can read, write and speak twelve or so different languages five collectively and five different from each other to cover as much as possible(in the eyes of the agency) But with the 'Grace of God' they can read, write and speak All languages!!!

The nuns can communicate with each other through thoughts and feelings while having a verbal conversation with people at the same time. Mother Teresa fears they will enjoy this a little too much. The Nuns also through the Grace of God can throw small objects such as pennies very hard. The Nuns will later call this 'Pennies from Heaven'.

Another Spiritual Gift of the Arch Nuns through the Grace of God. They can speak to and read the conscience/soul of People. They can communicate both verbally and to their conscience simultaneously. But the person they are communicating with verbally always focuses on what they are saying to their soul or conscience.

As not to violate the privacy of the conscience/soul. It is not done often.

But when they do, Again Mother Teresa fears they will enjoy it WAY too much.

But she and Hymiriam know, it's just the playful human nature within them. The Arch Nuns can judge the person because they can and will arrest them for their crimes, but do not and CAN NOT judge the soul. God will be their final judge. The Arch Nuns can punish them for their crimes on Earth, but God can still forgive them on the bridge. The nuns are speechless staring at Hymiriam, now PAYING ATTENTION to every Noun, Verb and Syllable she speaks. Mother Teresa gives the nuns a look, a look they know all too well. A look she has been giving them for 30 years as she asks them.

"What's the matter? Where are your kooky little comments now?"

She then looks at Lin whom is very fond of cats and says. "CAT GOT YOUR TONGUE?????"

Lin is caught off-guard like only their Mother Superiors can do, but thinks to herself.

"Why does she have to pick me out?" But all of her brothers and sisters heard lin loud and clear in their minds. All the nuns look at each other and smile. Hymiriam sees this, puts her hand on Mother Teresa's shoulder saying.

"All will be well"

Mother Teresa hangs her head.

"You would have been better off giving them the ability to fly!!!" She says laughing with her best friend Mary.

Now that they are fully telepathic spiritually and mentally. Hymiriam looks at the nuns and asks. "What am I going to say now?"

All at once the nuns reply. "Gather Yourselves My Children"

Mother Teresa raises her head, looks at Mary and says.

"I don't think they used any telepathy to figure that out"

Hymiriam replies with a gentle smile. "Every mother has a phrase, that is mine."

She concludes for now telling them they have tactical responses more acute than any human on earth. The Nuns remain quiet looking at their Mother Superiors.

Mother Teresa gives them another one of her looks waves her hand at them and with a strain in her voice says. "Oh!! Go ahead let it out."

The nuns Rejoice so loud that Hymiriam holds her ears. This

went on for five minutes or so before Hymiriam says. You guessed it...

"Gather yourselves, gather yourselves and sit down."

The nuns run to their mother superiors to hug, kiss and thank them for all they have done and given to them.

Mother Teresa with a serious face of course taps her ruler on the table urging the nuns to take a seat.

As the nuns are sitting down josh pulls Amira's chair from under her in a playful fashion

almost causing her to fall. "Stop! josh" Amira shouts at him. "if I had fallen, I would have got up and knocked your teeth out."

"Sit down, both of you." Mother Teresa yells. "I can't believe you're 30 years old" she continues shaking her head. The Nuns take their seats as two Angels appear behind their Mother Superiors.

They are beautiful and glowing of light one male one female. With the most serious of expressions upon their faces. They did not smile nor did they appear to be happy to see the nuns.

Hymiriam introduces them to the nuns to break the silence. "This is Angelica and Peter my children, they too have gone through a life on Earth to lay down their history. They will be my personal pilots and escorts." The nuns just sit and stare in amazement.

Then Mother Teresa asks. "so, you are all Arch Nuns, raised by the mother of Jesus Christ, The Arch Angel Saint Michael and Mother Teresa but seeing Angels amazes you? Snap out of it and get yourselves together!!"

"Grandma did you just say 'gather yourselves' in a slightly different way?" Elizabeth asks.

"No, I didn't now pay attention!" Mother Teresa answers as she and Hymiriam laugh. The Angels Do Not Laugh for they do not have a sense of humor as such and do not care for the Arch nuns but are good friends of Hymiriam. They are only participating in this campaign for her. The Angels transition into U.N.A flight suits the world leaders have chosen to be the uniform of the pilots and escorts of Hymiriam.

Then they disappear, The Mother Superiors chairs rotate with their backs facing the nuns the table disappears, the Nuns chairs align two by two with Maria and Joshua seated in the rear. They are now sitting in Hymiriam's personal transport. It is unarmed and has a non-intimidating outside appearance.

The Angels reappear seated in the cockpit. Through the Grace of God, they are transported to Mount Sinai this is referred to as 'inserting' into the world. When this is done from the Divine Elysium Time stands still and compensates for their arrival so all is as it was.

This is only done with the permission of the mother superiors as they become accustom to this, they'll be able to do it at will. They are not to do this in the presence of their black ops team members for now. When it is the will of God then and only then will someone witness the insertion or transitioning of an Arch Nun! Hymiriam addresses the nuns once more.

"Okay my children I will not be traveling with you to the United Nations building in New York. You will be reinserted to your transport on Mount Everest. Mother Teresa will be traveling with you, she will explain your itinerary. See you there make mother proud"

Before the nuns can respond. They are reinserted into their transport. It unlike Hymiriam's transport is very intimidating in appearance and very heavily-armed. Each Arch Nun team will consist of One Arch Nun, Seven Black Ops soldiers and One pilot. When the pilot is not on board the craft, they will be piloting it remotely. One week before the 40-day media storm God put into the mind of the Pope to call for a meeting with Hymiriam, this meeting was to be private. So Hymiriam arrived at the Vatican and she met with the Pope who was confused and unsure as to why he called this meeting. But in his heart knew he was compelled to do so. He too felt this was the will of God. The pope sat in his chair has Hymiriam entered the room. They were alone she stood in front of the pope and kneeled before him. She took his hand into hers and looked up into his eyes. The pope being an elderly man suffered from many ailments and was beginning to feel a little weak. He closed his eyes for a moment, Then Hymiriam says in a soft voice, A voice only an Angel can possess.

"Open thy eyes and look upon me and know who I am"
As the pope opened his eyes and gazed upon Hymiriam. A ray of light shines through the window and down upon her, she stands before him and spreads her wings. For it is forbidden for an Archangel to reveal their wings kneeling before any human.

The Pope's heart begins to race as though it were going to burst from his chest.

"Be still thy heart and know of that which is to come and that which is expected of you." Hymiriam says softly. "All your ailments shall be healed and you shall live the rest of your days in pace." She concludes as her wings fold and disappear. This was truly the most beautiful sight the pope has ever seen. And God spoke directly to his mind and soul, now he is the only world leader and person on Earth to bear witness and have the knowledge that this is 'Mary Mother of Jesus' and this is truly the second coming of Christ!
From this day forth he is to do all he can to protect Hymiriam and the Arch Nunhood. This task is the will of God and shall be passed down to all future popes and kept sacred.

On top off of Mount Everest the nuns are receiving their final instructions from Mother Teresa.
"Can we go outside and look at the ship grandmother?" The Nuns ask. "Of course, my darlings, let's go outside and take a picture for the history books."

The craft is landed atop a small snow bank. In a freezing snow storm with strong harsh winds. The door opens as mother Teresa and the Nuns depart from the craft, the storm suddenly stops and the area is illuminated. Although the temperature is freezing, they feel no cold.

" ♫The cold never bothered me anyway♫" Amira sings a verse from the popular movie 'Frozen'.

"O.M.G!!!" josh says.

"This thing is awesome" Maria adds.

"It's so menacing" lin says covering her mouth.

Mother Teresa directs the Nuns to stand close together near the craft So the picture can be taken. She walks over and stands with the nuns. A camera appears from nowhere snaps the picture then disappears.

   January 1st 2028 7:15am Walking down a hallway in the white house president Ophelia Winfrey and her aids are preparing for this most important day.

"President Winfrey we just received word Hymiriam is at the U.N building" One of the aids informs the group.

"Ok everyone" president Ophelia replies. "Get the Chopper ready it's almost time, I haven't been this nervous since election day and make sure the Press understands we are not addressing anything regarding the forty-day media storm."

"Yes, Madam president." All the aids reply as they hurry about nervously.

"The Pope's E.T.A at the U.N is 7:45 Madam president." One of the generals tells her.

"Ok, that's fine" she responds as she looks at some papers she is holding.

Security at the U.N and the surrounding area has never been higher. Unknowing to most this is undoubtedly one of the most important days in human history. Hymiriam sits in the cafeteria in the United Nations building in N.Y with no escorts or important people surrounding her. She simply speaks with the staff and those who prepare the food and clean the tables. They do not know who she is only that she is kind, friendly and easy to talk to. She even assists them in cleaning the tables. She is not dressed in her Arch Nun Mother Superior attire. Nor is she wearing her habit. Through the Grace of God when an Arch Nun is not wearing their Habit they can choose not to be recognized. She gets to know the names of the staff and they simply know her as Mary, a very common name so they think nothing more of it. They confide in her, they laugh with her as they continue to clean the tables and empty the garbage.

Back on Mount Everest Mother Teresa tells the nuns to board the craft. As they start to board the ship Josh throws a snowball and hits Elizabeth in the back of the head. Then of course they had a snowball fight. Mother Teresa shakes her head in disbelief but allows this for a couple of minutes so they may enjoy themselves before they engage their 'Grace of God' and carry themselves as Arch Nuns... Mother Teresa takes the prayer position has the Archangel Gabriel, A very dear friend of hers appears behind her and blows his horn, then disappears.

It can be heard in the distance at base camp in the middle of Mount Everest and Echoes throughout the Himalayas. The Tourist, villagers and visitors of base camp hear this and look to the top of Mount Everest where a light seems to illuminate. This sound will become the Horn of all the Arch Nun's transports and it will not be commercialized for public use for any reason.

It will be associated with the Arch Nuns only! Man has always recognized The Four Horsemen of the Apocalypse to be males. He has also recognized the four Arch Angels to be males. This was man's version. Women Arch Angels serve with them and were equally favored by the Lord. She who is Mother Teresa is one such Angel she is a 'Guardian Angel, Warrior Class'

Heavenly rumor has it, The Archangel Gabriel is a very personal friend of she who is Mother Teresa that is why she has chosen Gabriel's horn to be associated with the Arch Nuns. At this time the 'live to love organization is holding their annual Workshop.

Mother Teresa calls the heads of the live to love organization to inform them that she will be stopping by for a brief moment and a prayer also to inform everyone not to be alarmed by the aggressive looking craft that will be approaching. Since this call was made directly to their private line, they knew it was not a hoax. For no one would dare impersonate Mother Teresa or any Arch Nun especially after the forty-day media storm. They were so excited because they knew Mother Teresa is supposed to be traveling with the Arch Nuns today.

So they immediately made the announcement on the loudspeakers for everyone to remain calm and not to be alarmed by the approaching craft and Mother Teresa will be making a short visit. Immediately the media that were there covering the live to love workshop call their home offices to tell them they may have a world exclusive. The workshops never attract the large news Studios they feel it's not important enough for them to cover. But today by order of Mother Teresa the smaller news studios shall have the biggest story. The first public appearance of 'The Arch Nunhood of mother Hymiriam'.

It will not be the rich, the powerful, the famous nor those who have paid to be spectators at the United Nations building. It will be the poor, the humble and the true believers that shall be the first to set Eyes Upon God's chosen on this day.

They quickly turn their cameras to the skies everyone anxiously awaits a first glimpse of this most wonderful site. Mother Teresa tells Peter and Angelica to approach the camp at 700 MPH then fire the braking Rockets. This is done intentionally to demonstrate the speed and breaking of the craft and for the Most Grandest of entrances. This is unimportant to mother Teresa but the world leaders want

the transports of the Arch Nuns to stand out and be distinctive. After all the technology is a world collaboration and cost a lot of money. So, when the time comes to commercialize the technology of these crafts, they stand to make trillions of dollars. Each country has their own version but are far from completion. After arguing over who gets what. The world leaders decided to work privately. President Winfrey decided to moved her production to Area 51. President Andrei to his countries private Base. The pilots accelerate to 700 miles per hour in 9 seconds. The crowd at Basecamp can see in the distance the craft arriving at a very high rate of speed. They watch in Wonder and amazement just before the craft arrives over Base camp, they fire the braking Rockets. These Rockets are located at the front of the craft. When fired for breaking they cause a large circular ring of smoke to appear in front of the craft. The craft flies through the ring and suddenly slows down. It is truly a sight to behold. As the craft slows down the crowd gets a clearer look at it and the entire camp begins to rejoice and cheer as loud as they can. The cheering is so loud the news reporters can barely be heard on their microphones. One of the reporters is repeatedly saying into the camera. "Are you getting this, are you getting this, please tell me you are getting all this?"
Many of the villagers and religious orders at the camp had tears of joy in their eyes. Some of the news reporters have tears in their eyes but for a different reason. They are hoping their cameras are working correctly.
Mother Teresa tells the pilots to hover and slowly rotate for a few moments before landing.
The leaders of the live to love organization give their staff instructions to play the song 'Believe' from The Prince of Egypt soundtrack. Through the loud speakers. The crowd continues to cheer and hold their hands in the air as they loudly sing along.

"Ok my Darlings, for this appearance wear the attire of Hymiriam." Mother Teresa tells the nuns.

"Josh and I too Grandma?" Zachariah asked. Mother Teresa looks at Zac, tills her head to the side and asks him. "Do you want to wear Hymiriam's outfit Zac?"

"Noooo" Zac answers quickly as they all laugh.

"You boys are fine." She tells them. Then the girls current outfit transforms into the outfit Hymiriam was wearing on the bridge.

"I was wondering if we were allowed to wear this." Amira says smiling.

The craft lands and the crowd's singing and cheering slowly begin to fade and the Music Stops. One would think that the media would seize this opportunity for a commentary but they are mesmerized. The door opens and Mother Teresa emerges from The Craft. The world has seen her several times through the years so they are accustomed to her appearance. But as a sign of love and respect they applaud her. One of the staff members quickly runs over to hand her a wireless microphone. She takes the microphone thanks the staff member then raises her hand for all to be silent.

 Base camp at Mount Everest is a fairly large outdoor environment and due to the festivals and workshops that are going on it is very crowded. There are only three small news crews covering the events. The crowd is so silent you can only hear the wind blow. Before Mother Teresa speaks one word. Hymiriam communes telepathically. 'STOP Teresa President Winfrey is very upset she just sent me a voice message she doesn't want the Arch Nuns introduced or identified to the crowd. She knew you were doing a flyby and didn't mind the demonstration of speed, but did not authorize a landing. She is saying it would be a breach of contract. They are to be identified and introduced to the world for the first time at the United Nations building ONLY!'

President Winfrey used her influence worldwide to limit
what footage can be uploaded or viewed from that location.
She stopped it from going viral but enough people saw it.
Mother Teresa smiles then tells the crowd she has brought
some friends and if they would indulge her, we would like
to join every one for a prayer.
Although they could not be identified or introduced. The
Humble, the poor and the True Believers were still the first
to set Eyes Upon them and in their hearts, they knew that
those who came to be among them and pray with them
we're God's True Chosen, The Arch Nunhood of Mother
Hymiriam. Mother Teresa quickly communicates with the
nuns telepathically.
'My children change into something else quickly and wear
No Habit. Before exiting the craft, and do not to wear the
same hairdo or outfit, also wear make-up. Maria help your
brothers and sisters and Maria, my sweet tone it down it's
not a fashion show.' Maria grins but her sisters know she is
quite the fashion plate and can't help but to look good in
anything she wears. President Ophelia is now arriving at the
United Nations building in New York. She immediately
starts asking for Hymiriam. Five minutes after the craft
arrived at Mount Everest's base camp and before it landed.
People were on their cell phones communicating with
people in New York. That is what infuriated the president.
Hymiriam is still in the cafeteria helping clean tables. She
knew the President was angry so she stopped cleaning and
begin to prepare herself for the premeeting of this most
blessed day.
 Whenever any of the world leaders find themselves a little
upset with Hymiriam it does not last very long.

The Russian president greets president Ophelia and asks if she has seen Hymiriam. "No not yet, I thought she was with you." They turn to their aides and demand they find her immediately. Although Hymiriam carries a state-of-the-art satellite cell phone. She is not obligated to answer if she is preoccupied. Nor does she have to explain why. This is in the contract. Also, she knows the phone can be tracked so she seldomly carries it but it was a necessity today. "I received confirmation she was here and I need to know her location now!" President Winfrey yells frantically. The generals that are with her give orders to their people to find her but be discreet.

Hymiriam says farewell to her new friends and she'll see them again soon. They all hug each other and she leaves the cafeteria. Like she knew the president was upset with Mother Teresa's detour she also knows she's eager to find her. She walks up the stairs from the cafeteria passing many people but does not wish to be recognized at this time as she enters the hallway, she now allows herself to be recognized. Several Secret Service agents quickly walk over to her. "Hymiriam" one of the agents says looking into her eyes. "Excuse me ma'am but we've been looking all over for you thank God we found you."

The agents are tall husky men that tower over her. She looks up at the agent with her billion-dollar smile and replies. "Thank God, indeed!" The agents inform their superiors and the world leaders that they have found her and are heading to the meeting room. The agent that looked into Hymiriam's eyes. Says to one of the other agents as they begin to walk "She has the kindest eyes I have ever looked into."

At base camp the nuns exit the craft in plain clothing. Mother Teresa tells Peter and Angelica to join them and wear plain clothing so there would be 12 of them. The world is expecting 10 Arch Nuns and this would make it difficult for the crowd to verify if they are who they think and hope they are. The crowd begins to applaud and cheer again. Mother Teresa Just Smiles as everyone exits the craft to stand with her. Then the crowd comes closer taking pictures and videos with their cell phones. Mother Teresa gives them a few minutes then raises her hand again for all to be silent. The news reporters know not to ask Mother Teresa any questions as this was covered during the forty-day media storm regarding questioning an Arch Nun. They want to ask Mother Teresa so badly is this the 'Arch Nunhood of mother Hymiriam'. They know if Mother Teresa did not offer an introduction do not ask for one. Those that are closest reach out to touch them. All others know not to rush or push. So, they hold their place. The Nuns are smiling, waving and greeting people. But Peter and Angelica are not so happy to be there. They are a little upset that Mother Teresa made them walk with the nuns and the crowd may think that they are one of the Arch Nuns.

At the U.N building in New York Hymiriam feels Angelica and Peter's slight animosity and finds it amusing. So, she reaches out telepathically to them. "Cheer up you too it'll get better." Angelica responds telepathically back to her. "I hope so being mistaken for one of these Arch Nuns wasn't on my to-do list today, or being considered one of your children but LOL we love you so, whatever!"

The nuns are unaware of this communication between them so they are just simply enjoying the crowd and awaiting Mother Teresa's prayer. The Sibling jesting is put on hold, for now.

"Thank you everyone, thank you for welcoming and accepting us." Mother Teresa says. "Now I ask that you bow your heads"

Almost immediately everyone, the nuns included bow their heads. Then Mother Teresa begins the prayer.

"Oh Lord thy God I ask that you bless us on this day' I ask that you bless this camp and all who reside here, I ask that you bless the youth of this camp for they have endured great hardship and have endured much I ask that you watch over them and protect them in their future endeavors, I ask you Oh god please guide us on our journey I thank thy Lord God Amen."

Mother Teresa keeps the prayer short so the crowd may enjoy their presents a bit longer. The news crews are too small time to have worldwide broadcast capabilities so it is only locally televised. But the internet and social media were a blaze with speculation and rumors. Who were these 12 people with Mother Teresa and which ones if any were Arch Nuns? Or was this merely a diversion. The craft in which they came in, has been seen on the cover of Popular Science and Aviation magazine covers. over the past 10 years. So, it was not a big deal for the world to finally see it.

   As Hymiriam and the Secret Service agents enter the meeting room. Russian president Andrei kuznetsov and president Winfrey along with several other world leaders are seated at a table and are very upset. One reason was Mother Teresa's detour and the fact that she almost introduced the Arch Nuns to the world. Something they believe she had every intention of doing. The other is Hymiriam not responding to her cell phone, when everyone was looking for her. But as she comes closer to the table All Is Forgiven and the world leaders are at ease. She has that effect on most people after all she is 'Hymiriam' Mother of Jesus. But not all the leaders in the room feel that way some do not trust and despise her but do not let it be seen and the Lord does not allow her to be aware of this. For this is one of the many trials of Christ. SHE SHALL NOT KNOW ALL! Some of the world leaders only signed the contract because other more powerful countries have done so and they didn't want to raise suspicion upon them, for some of the have a hidden agenda. They hope like all things 'This too shall pass'. Then the world will continue as they see fit and man shall reign supreme once again. Within the contract with the world leaders it states Hymiriam is the director of the

United Nation Agency. Mother Teresa is not the assistant director. She is the co-director and equal with Hymiriam in any and all business of the U.N.A and the Arch Nunhood. Many of the world leaders are under the impression they can take advantage of Hymiriam's kindness. Their opinion of Mother Teresa is that of a Stern Nun whom cannot be moved, swayed or intimidated. They know not how right they are. Hymiriam will not be meeting with world leaders as much as they assume. She like her son before her will be in the presence of the poor, the humble, those in despair, those in need and those whose Faith must be rekindled. This is how Christ walked in the past, this is how Christ shall walk NOW!

She shall not be involved with the violence the Arch Nuns must face.

She shall not be involved in the pain the Arch Nuns will inflict upon those who harm children, oppose the law or mean Humanity harm. For the Arch Nuns are 'The Hammer of God'.

As Hymiriam is the soft whispering 'Word and Voice of God'.

The Arch Nuns will protect the children and enforce the laws of God. So, all those who oppose t God's Laws and the new laws of humanity, shall fear them Greatly! This is necessary for without it too many attempts would be made upon Hymiriam's life. All those who wish her harm must fear the Arch Nuns, Not her! For she like her son would gladly give her earthly life if it is for the greater good. When Jesus walked the Earth there were no smart weapons or face recognition technology. He was not easily found by those that wished him harm and everyone knows what happened when they did find him. This is not the case today. This is why Hymiriam walks a separate path. Hers is the path of righteousness. The Arch Nuns is the path of Justice.

At base camp on Mount Everest the leaders of the live to

love organization are thanking Mother Teresa and her 'friends' for visiting with them. The crowd is so enthused they do not want them to leave. Mother Teresa tells Peter and Angelica telepathically not to enter the craft first to enter with the nuns as a group. Everyone enters the craft as the crowd continues to cheer wildly. Inside the craft the Nuns are overwhelmed by the reception they have received. Their happy, they rejoice and of course jest with each other.

"I feel like a rock star" Elizabeth yells.

"I feel like I'm, whoever the biggest A-Lister in Hollywood is, right now!" Amira adds.

"Maria you were killing that outfit, girl!" Donna tells her sister.

"Hey Zach did you and Josh get any phone numbers?" Lin asks.

"I'm not allowed to get phone numbers smarty" Josh answers the turns to Mother Teresa and says. "wait! can we get phone numbers Grandmother?"

"What do you think?" Mother Teresa replies with a serious face.

"I know Grandma I'm just kidding"

Peter and Angelica look at each other and shake their heads in disbelief. The nuns continue enjoying the moment and having fun with each other and with Mother Teresa. The pilots can wait no longer they quickly transition back into their flight suits.

Basecamp continues to play music as the ship lifts off slowly.

"Ok Angelica make it impressive!" Mother Teresa tells her. The craft rises 30 feet above the crowd and slowly turns 360°. Music is playing the crowd is cheering wildly. Angelica pushes the button to Sound the Arch Angel Gabriel's horn. The crowd gets louder than in a burst of light the ship takes off quickly straight up into the air at 500 MPH. The Crowd Goes Crazy. One female news reporter looks into her camera and says. "WOW! I really hope we got all this cause I'm

applying for a job at CNN World news tomorrow"
The crowd continues to cheer as they watch the craft
disappear into the clouds.

In the meeting room at the U.N building. Hymiriam tells
the world leaders Mother Teresa and the Arch Nuns are on
their way and will be here in twenty minutes. The world
leaders decide they would like to look at the news footage in
full from Mount Everest Base Camp before they get here.
Upon viewing the footage, the world leaders are pleased
that the nuns were not introduced or identified. But they feel
their entrance was a little too good. So, the U.S Secretary of
Defense and a few of the generals. Contact the pilots and
give them a new flight plan for approaching the building.
Peter receives the General's orders and informs Mother
Teresa of the new Flight Plan approved by the Secretary of
Defense. It must be Eye catching and Thrilling in order to
impress the world leaders, the crowd and the World....
This is a perfect opportunity for the world to see exactly how
maneuverable this craft the world will know as The Battle
Assault Drone of the U.N.A. can be. It uses a state-of-the-art
'Anti-Ion-Fusion' propulsion system with self-analyzing
sensors, these sensors allow it to fly very close to objects
without hitting them, these sensors cannot be disturbed by
reflective surfaces such as glass or water.
Angelica and Peter don't mind showing off for the crowd.
They accelerate to eighteen hundred miles an hour the
crowd can see the craft as it streaks across the sky in the
distance. The news crews covering the event at the UN are
among the world's most prestigious.
Unlike base camp at Mount Everest. For every one person
that believes and agrees with this agency there are at least
five people that disagree and reject this agency. The Arch
Nuns understand they may not be met with the same love
and respect as they received at Mount Everest. Mother
Teresa was aware of this. That is why she detoured to
Basecamp first. She believes her grandchildren, The Arch

Nuns deserved a warm welcome of love first, before they received a not so warm welcome in New York.
This crowd is literally tens of thousands the streets are blocked off in a fifteen-block radius it is an absolute traffic nightmare.

Every major television network in the world is covering the event there is literally nothing else on television. Even the Cartoon Networks are broadcasting the event.
It is being broadcast in every language around the world. Everyone in the vicinity of the United Nations building is being told not to panic' not to look up to the sky while driving and to pull over, safely if they wish to observe.

All the world leaders along with Hymiriam are now coming outside the front of the UN building where there is a podium with two movie theater size screens on both sides. As the president of the U.S Ophelia Winfrey approaches the podium the crowd becomes silent.
She is very nervous but anxious to start and get this event over with.
"Good morning ladies and gentlemen and happy New Year to you all." She says smiling into the cameras. "We're not going to make this a very long event we're going to try to keep it as short as possible so we may continue inside and get the streets cleared and the city back to normal."
The Secretary of Defense walks over and stands next to her. He politely interrupts and ask that everyone remain calm and not to be alarmed by the flight pattern of the oncoming craft. It will be flying low and it is approved to do so. He did not want the city to think it was under attack, again. There are many military and news helicopters in the area as well. The craft gets closer to the UN building and fires the braking Rockets. The spectators are amazed by this. The craft accelerates again circling around the UN building.

The craft is doing this at 200 miles per hour and very close to the building itself. Not disturbing the structure or the glass of the building.

 It stops in the front of the building, hovering over the flags of the United Nations. Then sounds the Horn of Gabriel. At the exact moment the craft stops the song 'God's plan' by Drake plays over the loud speakers. The Crowd Goes Absolutely Wild as the craft rotates slowly to the music. Now the crowd is cheering but it is more so for the craft and its maneuverability. President Wenfrey says into the microphone with great pride.

"ladies and gentlemen I present to you. The 'Battle Assault Drone' of the United Nations Agency."

Cameras are flashing, news crews are reporting, cell phones are recording and uploading to all their social media accounts it is absolutely hectic. This is undoubtedly the loudest cheering that has ever been heard in New York City ever, Mostly due to the amount of people in attendance. President Ophelia quickly asks. "Whose idea was it to play that song, I want to see them after the event they're getting a raise!" She says to her aides happily with her eyes wide.

"It was Hymiriam Madam president, it was her idea"

The Secretary of Defense answers. The world leaders were ecstatic as what seemed like the whole city singing along to 'God's Plan' by Drake. As the news crews filmed the spectators, the craft and the world leaders. President Ophelia, her staff and many of the leaders of the world where filmed singing along as well. Hymiriam held her head down and prayed silently. The cheering continued for more than five minutes and the leaders allowed it. For it was good....

"Ok my children" Hymiriam Felt to the nuns telepathically. "Do not be lured into a false sense of security by the cheers, they cheer more for the song and the maneuverability of The Craft at this moment."

The nuns remain silent and in the prayer position on board

the craft with Mother Teresa. Hymiriam continues to tell them again how proud she is of them. Mother Teresa adds. "Very appropriate song my daughter, very appropriate indeed."

Mother Teresa tells them now they may wear the outfit of mother Hymiriam.

The nuns remain seated in the prayer position as the Girls transition into the outfit of Hymiriam and Mother Teresa tells them the makeup May remain. So, the world can see they are a very different type of nunnery and for them to become accustomed to seeing the Arch Nuns wearing it. She also asked Josh and Zachariah if they would like to wear some 'Guyliner' as not to feel left out. Josh opens his eyes raises his head and responds smiling.

"Good one, Grandma!" Then lowers his head again.

Mother Teresa made this small jest with her children but Lord knows she does not want to get them started with their comradery. The music Fades the crowd quiets down as the ceremony continues.

She tells the Pilots to bring it to a close and land the craft on the roof of the U.N building where there are more news crews awaiting.

The craft accelerates so quickly to the roof the news cameras can barely follow it. The craft slows down as his approaches the top of the building so the camera Crews on the roof can get some good footage.

The world leaders invited several religious leaders to make short speeches before the nuns are introduced. During this time. Some of the leaders went to the roof to greet the nuns and take pictures. President Ophelia and Russian president Andrei kuznetsov stood with the religious leaders as they made their speeches. They will have many opportunities for photos with the Arch Nuns later. Since they will be spending the majority of their time in the United States and Russia for this first year. Other world leaders did not oppose this because they wanted to see if this would work. If it were to fail, let it fail in America and Russia. Then that may simply be the end of the Arch Nuns and the U.N.A.

They will be watching very closely from what they consider a safe distance.

The craft lands on the roof, the military and news helicopters are circling the area. There is an Eerie silence as everyone watches the craft. The newscasters are Whispering into their microphones as though they were in enemy territory. The door opens slowly Mother Teresa is the first to emerge from The Craft. This of course is being broadcasted to the crowd below staring at the screens in silence. If this was the loudest cheering city a moment ago it was surely the quietest now. The pilots emerge from the craft next wearing their flight suits and stand behind Mother Teresa. She looks to the world leaders, then to the news crews, greets them then simply says with the most serious of expressions.

"I present to you my Grandchildren, 'The Arch Nuns of Mother Hymiriam'.

The nuns emerge from the craft casually waving to everyone. The small crowd on the roof cheer and applaud them. One newscaster says. "They appear to be friendly rather than law enforcement."

Another reports. "They seem to be a bit young for such a big job at hand. But time will tell."

The crowd below watches in semi silence not yet sure of what to think of them yet. So, they applaud them as a courtesy but cannot wait for them to come down so they may be introduced individually. Mother Teresa leads the Arch Nuns down a small flight of stairs from The Landing platform and through the small crowd where there are more personal greetings and again some wish to lay their hand upon them. As a gesture of Goodwill, or good luck. Mother Teresa tells the crowd. Their names will be given downstairs. For all the world to know. The Black Ops soldiers that will soon be members of each Nuns team wait in a separate room watching on monitors. They are the world's current most lethal military men and women from around the world.

They are skeptical, and believe they'll be doing more babysitting than anything else. They feel they'll be doing all the work and the Arch Nuns will get all the glory. They look at the male nuns and find it amusing that there is such a thing as male Nuns.

You can imagine what else they thought of the male nuns! They think the female nuns are too pretty to serve any purpose other than eye candy. The Soldiers are simply not impressed by them at all. If the Arch Nuns we're supposed to have such Advanced tactical experience the soldiers were not seeing or believing it. From what they can determine they do not think these Arch Nuns are fit to lead them. Some of the soldiers are considering declining the job offer and returning to their combat units and letting someone else watch 'The children'.

Mother Teresa deliberately leads some of the staff and her Arch Nuns through the room in which the soldiers are waiting. So, they may look upon each other.

They watch as the nuns enter the room, looking them up and down and sizing them up. Then one of the soldiers named Mikolai, A midsize man of great physical strength and well known amongst the other soldiers for his many confirmed kills, looks at Zachariah and blocks his path with his big arms folded in front of him sarcastically saying. "Good morning Sisters"

Referring to Josh and Zachariah. Most of the soldiers laugh and point at Zach and Josh. 'Mama said there be days like this.' Josh feels to Zachariah. Everyone stops the staff are very intimidated by the soldiers so they remain quiet. Amira quickly steps toward them and shouts.

"Good morning privates!"

All the soldiers immediately stop laughing.

"Oh! I'm sorry you are privates, Am I right? we were expecting black ops super soldiers"

Maria joins her adding. "you guys are more like orange amateur soldiers"

Then Zachariah steps closer to Mikolai grinning and says. "But I guess Orange is the new black" All the Arch Nuns laugh lightly. The Soldiers nod their heads in agreeance smiling then laugh with them and a small bond is formed. One of the female soldiers named Antonia leans over and says to another.

"Well! I guess they talk, the talk and that tall Hispanic one can definitely walk, the walk on me any day." Referring to Maria. Military soldiers have always enjoyed playfully insulting each other. Mother Teresa knew by bringing the Arch Nuns face to face with these Elite soldiers this friendly verbal competition would ensue. She was also very pleased at how quickly the girls stepped in to defend their brothers. They exchanged a few more insults. The laughter grew louder and more friendly. There are even a few high fives between them. Mother Teresa is receiving text messages from the leaders to bring the nuns to the meeting room the time is approaching. "Okay everyone let's keep it moving now." She tells everyone. Some of the soldiers who are fond of Mother Teresa hug her and tell her and the Nuns they'll see them later. There are now friendly waves to the nuns as they leave the room. They're kind of cool the soldiers think. But still are unsure if they would follow their command. Mother Teresa tells the staff she and the Arch Nuns will take another elevator so she may speak to her grandchildren alone for a moment. She is far from naive to believe that the government does not have eyes and ears everywhere. She is well aware of the electronic audio and video surveillance in every elevator. So, she verbally tells the nuns to bow their heads so they may pray silently.

Then she communicates with them telepathically. "Okay my daughters, what are you wearing under these coats?"
"I'm not wearing anything grandma." Amira answers.
Mother Teresa had her suspicions and they were just confirmed.
Navaeh adds. "I don't think any of us are grandma it's kind of hot under here."
Quickly Zachariah feels to everyone. "This is too much information, grandma! I really don't need to know how naked my sisters are under their coats right now!"
Josh adds. "Please my brain can't take anymore."
This amuses Mother Teresa and she lets her grandchildren know this. So, it may lighten the mood. She knows how cruel a crowd in New York can be, she knows the cruelty of humanity all too well. She is weary of the reception her Grandchildren will receive here. The Arch Nuns are full of their usual comradery telepathically and are enjoying every moment. This pleases the Reverend mother. But like all mothers she still worries. To the security officers watching them on the cameras in the elevator. They remain in the prayer position while all of this is going on amongst them within their minds. She feels to her daughters to wear the traditional Arch Nun uniform under their coats. Because they'll be taking their coats off when they get to the meeting room. They will be introduced to the world wearing the traditional uniform of the Arch Nun. They arrive at their floor; the elevator door opens and of course there are more news crews and cameras. Although the media cannot ask any questions. There's still loud talk amongst them.
The nuns again casually smile and wave to everyone.
Several presidential aids and military personnel join them to escort them to the meeting room where president Ophelia and other world leaders are waiting.
 The Arch Nuns enter the meeting room, everyone becomes silent, Hymiriam is with them.
many of the leaders have met with Mother Teresa and

Hymiriam in the past few years but have never really met the Arch Nuns. Some of the leaders have seen them in the distance when they were training. But did not give them much thought. They assumed this agency would never be sanctioned. Ever! Now they stand before them ready for the world. President Andrei breaks the momentary silence. "I think I speak for everyone when I say I can really use a drink right now." The room is filled with light-hearted laughter everyone is at ease now. He goes on to explain some small changes with the itinerary for the event. Assuring the media understands there will be no questions directed to the Arch Nuns. All questions will be directed to him or President Ophelia. Other world superpowers such as China, United Kingdom, Germany, France, Japan, and Israel. Are present and their leaders are in the room. But they choose to remain silent for now. They're just here for the personal introduction to the Arch Nuns, photos and to represent their countries for this big event. Some of the leaders casually confront Mother Teresa regarding her decision to Land at Mount Everest base camp.

She accepts her slight reprimand and smiles. Hymiriam feels to her. 'Please do not be angered, but amused my friend Teresa it makes them feel Superior to give us direction from time to time'

'I am amused, my friend believe me' She replies. 'Very Amused'

One of the presidential aides knocks on the meeting room door to inform the leaders their ready for them on stage again. Everyone leaves the room heavily escorted by secret service and military personnel. President Ophelia and president Andrei go to the podium the crowd applauds them. Mother Teresa and the Arch Nuns remain backstage with the military personnel and some of the Secret Service agents.

President Andrei addresses the crowd. "My apologies everyone for the delay but this is kind of, how do you say? A big deal."

President Ophelia cut in. "A very big deal, to say the least!!!"
The crowd laughs with them a little. But are most eager for the introduction of the Arch Nuns. President Andrei continues as the crowd laughs lightly.

"I am told this is the biggest crowd in recent history. If we had known this perhaps, we should have sold tickets." The crowd continues to laugh with president Andrei. "I am glad we decided to have this party in America had this been Russia, I would have to make the big speech!"

The crowd is enjoying the lighthearted humor of the Russian president. It is not often the people get to see their leaders so relaxed and at ease.

"So at this time, I will turn things over to my good friend and president of the United States. Ophelia Winfrey. The crowd begins to applaud and cheer loudly. Some Spectators are yelling. "WE LOVE YOU OPHELIA!!!!". President Ophelia is very well known the world over long before she entered politics or became a world leader. She is the ultimate International Celebrity. She is the first female president of

the United States and the only world leader to be loved by
'BILLIONS!!!' worldwide.
She approaches the podium slowly she cries tears of joy? she
has never felt such appreciation especially under the
circumstances of imposing a new law enforcement agency
Upon the world. The Crowd Goes Wild, although she was
on stage earlier and has already addressed the crowd, they
know now she's about to make her speech and introduce the
Arch Nuns.

 She approaches the podium, takes a deep breath then
almost immediately starts to speak confidently. "Cheers to a
new year and another chance for us to hopefully get things
right."   The crowd applauds in agreeance. She pauses
looks out at the crowd and then continues.
"This agency was formed by the leaders of the world to save
us from ourselves.
We can't personally stop anyone from walking into a school
with an assault rifle nor can we single-handedly assure that
the rights that your parents and your grandparents fought
so hard for will be preserved for your children and the next
Generations to come.
Unfortunately there are people in this world that are capable
of unspeakable things. These same people are very rich,
powerful and seem to be immune to all forms of
apprehension, prosecution and accountability. No one wants
to acknowledge the existence of these people but they do
indeed exist. We have some leaders that are helpless, they
are bound by old laws written by the same people they are
trying to stop.
 We have some leaders turning a blind eye to this and even
making a profit from it.
Every organized crime syndicate and every street gang has
been raising and conditioning children to be their next
Generation. Some government agencies have even raised
children to be super soldiers and super agents even killers

by any means necessary. The truth exonerates, convicts and galvanizing. The truth has always been and will always be our Shield against corruption, our Shield against despair it has always been our Saving Grace. You are here today to see it, to Proclaim it and hopefully to accept it."

The people listen quietly as she continues.

"Where there is no struggle there is no strength and believe me, this generation will most definitely struggle with this. But we will gain strength from this."

She can hear talking amongst the crowd as many disagree. President Andrei walks over to stand by her side.

"For the first time. We the world leaders have come to an agreement. This concept has been on the table for a very long time. More than a few decades and I am proud to say, myself and many world powers agree this will assist in a brighter future for us all." The crowd applauds lightly.

"But I say with a heavy heart, I say and hope with every fiber of my being.!!"

She says squeezing her eyes shut and clenching her Fists. President Andrei puts his hand on her shoulder for comfort. She puts her hand on his, takes a deep breath and continues.

"Cause I know, and you all know, this generation will have the most difficult time adjusting to it."

The people applaud a little louder for a moment. President Ophelia is a very emotional and powerful speaker she always has been and today is no different but today is the most difficult. She must convince the world that the leaders are not imposing martial law upon them but building a better future for them. So, she Treads lightly as she continues.

"This agency is the first of its kind and these children are "Raised" to be exactly what they are the absolute ultimate Ministers of law enforcement. The worlds' first Arch Nuns. It's time that we take a stand together as one to make this world a better place for our children. If we are to have a better future!!"

She and Andrei hug each other as the crowd applauds.
Although Her speech was sincere the Arch Nuns are
something the crowd definitely holds in contempt. The
leaders feel this would be the best time to introduce the
Nuns and get it over with. The crowd's temperament was
not likely to become any better.

President Andrei takes the podium and tells the crowd He
agrees with Ophelia 100% and they are preparing for the
difficult times ahead. He then introduces Mother Teresa.
As she walks to the podium the crowd applauds a little
louder there are even a few cheers. The world is familiar
with her work through the decades as a humanitarian and
all the wonderful things she has achieved. As she takes the
podium, she thanks everyone then raises her hand for the
crowd to be silent. She tells them of Hymiriam and some of
the wonderful things she has done over the past 30 years.
Not once seeking the spotlight or even Financial
compensation. She spoke for more than 40 minutes and the
crowd did not mind. For she spoke of her daughter and her
many accomplishments. As she speaks the large monitors
display photos and video of some of her achievements.

The world has heard the name Hymiriam mentioned from
time to time in many magazines over the past 30 years but
thought nothing of it.

Now the crowd's temperament changes just a little for the
better. But they have not changed their perception of the
Arch Nuns. But they have a little better attitude towards
Hymiriam.

She then introduces her daughter to the world. There is an
equal Number of 'JEERS' and Cheers as Hymiriam
approaches the podium. There are several verbal altercations
in the crowd between supporters and non-supporters. But
they are quickly dealt with by security.

"Why is it just ten Arch Nuns?' A woman yells. "I will tell
you." Mother Teresa Answers. "Because Ten is God's
Number of government and order!" Upon hearing this the

crowd begins to settle down a little.

Many hold up signs of support but many more held signs of contempt. One sign reads

'THE ARCH NUNS WILL BRING THE END OF DAYS!!!' another reads.

'OUR LEADERS WANT 2 ENSLAVE THE WORLD!!!'

Watching on monitors in the cafeteria in the UN building. Those who she helped clean and take out the garbage watched in amazement and disbelief as their new friend she who assisted them in doing such dirty work is someone so important.

"OH MY GOD! That was Hymiriam cleaning with us "One of the older women named Shalonca says putting her hands on her head.

"I should have recorded that on my phone, nobody's gonna believe this." Another says.

The cafeteria workers Rejoice, cheer and applaud loudly. So loud in fact they are asked by their supervisors to quiet down. They feel blessed and proud of the friend they will always know as Mary.

President Ophelia and Andrei rush to the podium to take control of the situation. Hymiriam holds up her hand to stop them. She tells them it is ok, everything is fine, THIS TO SHALL PASS. Then she feels to Teresa and the nuns.

'Fortunately for me this is not the first time I have been verbally abused by a crowd. I'm so glad they weren't allowed to bring rocks with them!!'

Hymiriam, Mother Teresa and the Nuns make light of the situation in their minds with each other. Hymiriam stands at the podium before the crowd. Mother Teresa stands with the leaders. The Arch Nuns are backstage enjoying their Reverend mother's amusement.

The Secret Service agents standing with the Arch Nuns are getting a little nervous. There is a lot of radio chatter between the military and the Secret Service agents. Some of the leaders are concerned a riot may be imminent. Hymiriam asks Ophelia and Andrei to have faith. For there will be no Riot on this day she assures them. The military are ordering the helicopters to clear the area and bring the Battle Assault Drone online.

President Andrei disagrees and orders everyone to stand down immediately, Ophelia agrees with him. Hymiriam feels to the Nuns to reassure and comfort the agents and staff to ease the tension. General Coleman, a five-star general and several important military personnel walk over to the Secret Service agents standing with the Nuns and staff. He orders them to be ready and to protect the Nuns at all cost, he blatantly disregards the president's orders to stand down. He orders Elite Strike Teams into position and gives orders to power up the Battle Assault Drone. The Arch Nuns over hear this and Sister Amira confronts the general.

"Excuse me sir" she says respectfully. He turns to her and tells her to step out of the way. He knows what he's doing and this is for their own protection. Again, Sister Amira says. "Excuse me sir but--"

He puts his hand on her shoulder and moves her to the side. Sisters Lin and Elizabeth step in front of the general. He looks at them then to his staff and smirks. Amira in a not so respectful and very demanding voice shouts. "You will cease your present course of action and take heed to president Andrei command NOW!" The general is wondering how she knew about the order to stand down, but quickly dismisses it. He is appalled by the little Nun's request. With an angry look on his face he opens his mouth to speak again but is quickly cut off by Sister Amira. "Silence" She demands in full Arc Nun rhetoric. "As of 12:01am this morning the Arch Nuns and U.N.A are sanctioned and fully empowered, making us your superiors. Do not confuse my orders to stand down immediately as a request. Your compliance is not optional."

The general stands there for a moment. He is so angry he can almost spontaneously combust. But as she speaks to him, she simultaneously feels to his mind and conscience. The message she feels to him is. 'Or do you have a hidden agenda we should look into?'

General Coleman's facial expression immediately changes as he tells his Elite Riot teams to stand down.

'A wise decision' brother Joshua feels to the general. The general quickly turns to Joshua and asks him did he say something. Joshua responds. "No, I did not" he pauses for a second then adds. "Say Anything!" Then asks if the general is feeling okay. General Coleman is beginning to perspire but does not want everyone to think he is losing his mind or that something is wrong. So, he smiles and tells his staff to join him as they walk away. The presidential aides and Secret Service agents are speechless and in Shock. They have never heard anyone speak to General Coleman that way.

So the Arch Nuns speak to them with firm, confident voices. Sister lin walks over to address the agents and staff saying. "The people are restless; they are unsure this is to be expected."

Sister Dajairia joins her adding. "There will be no violence on this day. This is a blessed day given unto us by the Lord God. And it is the power of God that will see us through this day."

Sister Navaeh speaks loud for all to here. "There is no need for concern have faith in the Lord and all will be well."

Sister Maria slowly walks toward them. "I asked you to fear not and stand still." She says. 'So, you may witness the salvation of the Lord!"

They were silent as they listened to the Nuns and their Spirits were calmed. While Sisters Lin, Dajairia, Navaeh and Maria spoke to them. Sister Amira and brother Zachariah felt to their souls and Minds telepathically.

The message they sent was.' The Lord Is Our Shepherd, The Lord is our savior, Trust in the lord. All will be well!'

The agents and staff all felt this but will never speak of it.

For they now know in their minds and in their hearts. The Arch Nuns are TRULY SOMETHING SPECIAL!

Back at the podium. Hymiriam feels the calmness her children have brought to the agents and staff and she is pleased. Security gets the situation under control and the crowd quiets down. Then Hymiriam speaks.

"Good morning everyone, I understand, I understand Believe me I truly do." She pauses deliberately so some may still yell some obscenities. Many hold up signs of support. They are few, but they are most appreciated.

"Today will be a day such as the world had never seen! I know it's cold, So I will not take much more of your time. I know this is way too much to take in and way too much to accept right now. So, going forward Mother Teresa as Co-director of the U.N.A will be the voice of the Arch Nuns and agency. She will answer all questions and elaborate on many of your concerns."

Much of the crowd is silent others seize this opportunity to yell obscenities. President Ophelia is becoming agitated. Hymiriam concludes. "I feel and respect that many of you are not ready to hear from me on this day. Many of you may never want to hear from me. This will weigh heavily upon my heart but I will respect it. But I want you all to know that every day of my life I will be praying for you. In conclusion I only ask that you be kind to one another, I asked that you love one another."

Most of the crowd now cheer because that is one thing they can agree upon. Hymiriam speaks as the crowd continues to cheer. "Thank you, thank you everyone for hearing me." She concludes.

Mother Teresa walks over joining her at the podium to introduce 'The Arch Nuns'. She takes advantage of the loud cheering crowd to quickly bring the Nuns on stage. hoping they will continue to applaud. As the Arch Nuns enter the stage the crowd slowly becomes quiet. They are dressed in the Arch Nun uniform, Chosen and given to them by

Hymiriam when they stood upon the bridge.

There's a few seconds of Silence then those who support cheer and applaud as loud as they can. Those who do not are silent. Mother Teresa considers that to be acceptable at least now they are not yelling obscenities. She allows the supporting crowd to cheer a little longer. The Nuns gaze over what seems like an infinite sea of people. Mother Teresa stands at the podium she looks back at the Nuns, then back to the crowd.

"For those of you who do not support the decision of the world leaders to sanction this agency" She says. "That is understandable, but most unfortunate. Many of you the world over believe this to be worldwide Marshall law. It is not, it is Education, it is direction and Protection for the future. I can explain it, but it is something you must see for yourself. Because you know not the light of God's law, you are as children who have lost their faith if you're indulge me by the power of God, I will rekindle it." The people begin to applaud. "I would like to introduce the Ten that will Assess in the Construction of this hopeful future." The crowd quiets down as she continues.

"People of the world, I present to you 'The Arch Nunhood of Mother Hymiriam". 35% of the crowd are supporters. So, they cheer and applaud as loud as they can. As for the 65% of non-supporters. They curse, jeer and hold up signs of resentment.

President Ophelia has had enough of this disgraceful disrespect. She approaches the podium and asks the crowd to quiet down so Mother Theresa may continue. The crowd complies with Ophelia's request. Ophelia apologizes to Mother Teresa who responds simply by saying this was to be expected. Then she leans in and Whispers to Ophelia.

"Now you see why I detoured to Mount Everest Base Camp first." She says with a wink.

Ophelia responds laughing. "I ain't mad at ya girl, I ain't mad at ya!"

Mother Teresa then introduces the Arch Nuns individually to the world.

Starting with her daughter Maria the Sister Superior and ending with her son Joshua the Brother Superior. The supporters cheer and hold up many signs of love, Respect and Support. But they are overshadowed by the non-supporters' signs and their contempt. President Andrei addresses the crowd briefly regarding the cold weather. It is New Year's morning it's a cloudy day and the forecast calls for light snow flurries. Mother Teresa concludes with an Arch Nun pledge.

"We the Arch Nunhood of Mother Hymiriam vow:

TO honor and respect all of humanity.

TO protect ALL children, their protection is Paramount for they are the future.

TO never abused the power bestowed upon us by the leaders of the world or our Lord God.

This is how the Arch Nunhood will live and die!"

As she speaks the vows are displayed on the large monitors. 50% of the crowd begin to cheer and applaud. Then Hymiriam returns to the podium and stands beside her and adds with strength, pride, and conviction.

"SO SHALL IT BE WRITTEN"

Then all together. The Arch Nuns stomp their right foot to the ground, assume the prayer position and shout as loud as they can.

"SO SHALL IT BE DONE!!!"

This was so impressive it gained 70% of the crowd's approval with a very loud round of Applause and Cheers. There were not as many jeers and obscenities this time. Of those that did hold up signs of non-support there was one that caught the attention of Hymiriam.

The sign reads. 'Hymiriam! What leader sent you here to do this to us? What do you truly represent? And Who do you really serve?'

She points to the group holding the sign and asks the news cameras to focus on it. The cameras focus and display the sign on the large monitors for all the world to see. She reads the sign aloud for the crowd to verify. The cameras then focus on her and display her on the monitors.

She looks out at the infinite sea of people for a few seconds then gently closes her eyes,

Holds her hands to the sky, looks up into the clouds and slowly lowers her hands to the podium. A slight opening appears in the clouds allowing a small array of sunlight to shine down upon her. As the crowd witnesses this, there is much talk amongst them. Then they become still and very quiet. Hymiriam answers the question in a way the modern world will not soon forget. With a firm and confident voice, she replies.

"'I AM'!!!! SENT ME UNTO YOU AT THIS TIME! AND I REPRESENT THE KINGDOM OF THE MOST HIGH!!!!, AS FOR ME AND MY HOUSE, WE SHALL SERVE THE LORD!!!"

The group holding the sign drops it to the ground and fall to their knees many in the crowd feel faint, some begin to cry, Some who were non-supporters apologize to the supporters they were fighting with only moments ago. president Ophelia reaches out to hold president Andrei's hand and says softly. "My God! what did we just Witness?"

The crowd slowly begins to applaud. Hymiriam ends her statement saying.

"look upon these 10 Arch Nuns and behold this great sight that you may know the power of the Lord and you shall know that GOD IS GOD!!! " She quickly turns leaving the stage followed by her nuns then Mother Teresa. The Crowd Goes Wild! there are still many opposers and non-supporters but for now they cannot and will not be heard. As the Arch Nuns walk down the hallway backstage which is filled with Secret Service agents, Military personnel and aids to the world leaders from all over the world. They are applauded and cheered. Everyone quickly steps to either side of the hallway allowing Hymiriam and the Arch Nuns to walk down the center. Those amongst them who believe want to reach out and touch Hymiriam's coat but refrain from doing so to remain professional.

On a small privately owned island near Singapore. A woman in her late fifties' baths in her private Lagoon. On the beach there are several athletically fit female bodyguards and personal assistants. She watches the event in N.Y on a large television monitor on the beach. As she watches the clouds open, the sunlight shine down upon Hymiriam and the crowd's reaction to it. She is most concerned with what her eyes have beheld.

As she walks towards the beach and emerges from the water, she is naked her skin slightly aged, for a woman in her late fifties, she has the body of a Greek goddess, the beauty of her face is enchanting, she is absolute female perfection. As she steps on to the beach she stands still and holds her arms open wide.

Two of the personal assistants walk to her, bow their heads and wrap her in a very expensive robe. Although she is a Caucasian woman. She speaks softly in perfect ancient Egyptian to one of the personal assistants with a very sexy tone. Telling her to summon five of her top sons and daughters. The personal assistants and guards when standing close to her do not look upon her directly, they know never to look upon her directly unless she allows it! Some of the guards are recruited and taught how to conduct themselves in her presents. They are also paid handsomely to serve her. So they do not mind her Narcissistic superiority complex.

Most of them are ex-military, well educated, can speak many languages, but not this from of ancient Egyptian and are no strangers to killing.

The personal assistants are always Sons and Daughters of hers.The assistants escort her to a lone Cabana, Prepare a frozen margarita and kneel beside her as they serve it to her. To the average onlooker she would appear to be a rich old white lady with way too much money and treats people like slaves.

Her bodyguards like many the world over to whom serve her. know not who they serve.
They will never know. She is GOD'S first female 'EVE', The True Mother of All!!!

President Ophelia and Andrei give their closing speeches to a very shocked crowd. It will take hours to get the area cleared and the city back to normal. Radio stations, television stations and the internet are broadcasting replays and statements on the events of the day. Especially 'The light of God' as it is being referred to by the media. Religious leaders all over the world are taking to the internet and the streets. Many of the True Believers are exiting the area Celebrating and chanting.
'GOD IS GOD!!' There are still far more Skeptics, non-believers and non-supporters who are dismissing this as a mere coincidence. Stating 'Hymiriam was simply standing in the right place at the right time, NO BIG DEAL!!'
Hymiriam and the Arch Nuns are waiting in the main meeting room. They are kneeling before their Reverend mothers. The room is quiet they appear to be praying as military personnel and staffers enter the room. As a sign of respect everyone who enters the room speaks softly as not to interrupt what they perceive to be praying. But they are really communicating among themselves and their Reverend mothers.
' God sure Shined the Light on that subject. wouldn't you say mom?' Joshua feels to everyone.

'Mom, you should have flown straight up into the air.'
Navaeh adds jokingly.
'And then landed in a superhero stance.' Amira adds
quickly.
Anna tells everyone. 'You kind of scolded them a little mom,
like you used to do us'
'What do you mean used to, she still does!' Dajairia adds
Laughing.
The Reverend mothers and the nuns laugh are enjoying
these few moments together within their minds. Hymiriam
ends what appears to be praying
By saying "Amen" Aloud for all to hear. The Nuns reply
loudly "Amen". Then quickly and simultaneously jump to
their feet.
Everyone is so impressed by the respect and discipline the
Arch Nuns display in the presence of their Reverend
mothers. As the Nuns spring to their feet they are greeted by
cheers and applauds by everyone in the room and all who
enter. The sounds are so loud they can be heard outside the
room and halfway down the hallway.
   Everyone in the room begin to surround the Reverend
mothers and the Nuns still applauding, cheering and
reaching out to touch them. Hymiriam feels to the nuns. 'Go
forth my children and relish this moment, rejoice and be
merry.' Then she and Mother Teresa discreetly leave the
room as not to draw attention away from the Arch Nuns. As
mothers they wanted this to be another pleasant moment
their children can embrace. For the road they are about to
travel will be filled with many unpleasantries.
   So the Nuns mingled with the crowd. They laughed and
spoke with many people. Conducting themselves as Arch
Nuns. As president Ophelia and all the leaders of the world
entered the room, they were happy to see everyone getting
along and at piece.
"Ok, everyone may I have your attention please"
President Ophelia shouts several times to get everyone to

calm down and get their attention. But there was too much joy in the room. So, she decides to give them a little more time.

The president of Japan Kaito Tanaka, walks over to Ophelia and asks if he and several of the other world leaders may have a private word quickly with Hymiriam and Mother Teresa. Before they begin the broadcast. President Kaito, Queen Diana of England, and the president of Israel Donald Weizmann are taken to the small office. As they enter the room, they notice the Reverend mothers are kneeling and silently praying and Hymiriam's pilots are silently standing to the side. The leaders are respectful and quietly wait for them to finish. They complete their prayer and president Tanaka and president Weizmann rush to assist them to their feet. President Tanaka tells them he wishes to apologize for not having full confidence in this endeavor or agency but will do everything in his power to support it from now on. Queen Diana and president Weizmann share his enthusiasm and offer their full support as well. Although the support of the leaders is appreciated, the support of the people is essential. The leaders escort the Reverend mothers back to the main meeting room, the news crews are entering the room and setting up their equipment preparing for the mornings interviews that will take up most of the day. Hymiriam made previous arrangements with the world leaders for her not to attend the news conference. The news anchors are aware of this.

Mother Teresa will now represent and speak for her and the Arch Nuns. She hugs several of the world leaders then exits the room with Peter and Angelica. There was so much excitement in the room no one else noticed them leaving.

All the world leaders take their seats in the main meeting room. Mother Teresa sits between President Ophelia and president Andrei. The news reporters are very excited to finally have the opportunity to speak in depth with Mother Teresa and her Grandchildren who she is referring to as The

Ten Nuns of the Present. Of course, they would have preferred Mother Hymiriam but that is covered in the contract with the world leaders. Hymiriam will only be interviewed when and if she chooses. As they enter the crowded hallway. Hymiriam engages her Grace so they will not be recognized by anyone. They walk a few feet down the hallway unrecognized, Time slows to a standstill and then they are gone. Mother Teresa instructs the Nuns to sit behind her and the presidents Girls on the inside. She tells them to be cordial and act normal until the interview begins then they are to remain seated, bow their heads and take the prayer position. She tells them this to deter cameras from zooming in and staying focused on their faces.
Mother Teresa knows most of the cameras will be on her and the Nuns 90% of the time. President Ophelia reminds the media to ask the approved questions only. Also, to keep personal comments to a minimum.

  Now that the morning event has ended the entire world is focused on this broadcast, this will be the most anticipated interview in history. The room begins to quiet down as the media begins the countdown to start the broadcast. Two weeks ago, ten countries were selected to ask five questions each.
Since president Ophelia and president Andrei are hosting the event, they select who will be first to ask their questions. Israel is selected. The moment the broadcast Begins. The reporters dive right in with the introductions and then go straight to the questions. The Israeli news reporter steps up to the podium which is facing Mother Teresa and the world leaders. He greets the Reverend mother in his Israeli native tongue of Hebrew, Extending the salutation to the Arch Nuns as well. Mother Teresa smiles and raises her hand slightly off the table signaling the Arch Nuns.
Sister lin stands, opens her eyes and in perfect dialect speaks Hebrew. Returning the salutation.

(English translation) "Shalom! On behalf of The Arch
Nunhood of Mother Hymiriam. We would like to extend
greetings and warm wishes to you and your country as
well."
The entire room explodes in a very warm Applause.
For it is the first time the world hears the voice of an Arch
Nun. Also, it's not often you hear an Asian woman speak
perfect Hebrew. The Israelis are impressed as was everyone
in the room with the rhetoric of the Arch Nun.
Sister lin remains standing until the Applause slows down
and Mother Teresa signals for her to sit and resume the
prayer position. Joshua leans over for a moment and Pats his
sister on the back. She looks at him with gratitude and
smiles. This was caught on camera and displays compassion
by the Arch Nuns. There is no doubt they are very close
siblings. The Applause comes to an end. Then the first
question is asked.
"Mother Teresa, are these new laws and changes to existing
laws the doing of the world leaders or you and your
daughter Hymiriam?"
The reporter asked this in a very condescending tone
something everyone noticed. The room is silent eagerly
awaiting Mother Teresa's response. "They are a collaboration
of both parties." Mother Teresa says. "For the world leaders
they took the opportunity to change laws that were
outdated, Unfair, and abused. The Arch Nuns embrace,
enforce and Obey God's law for it is just and fair to all, it
cannot be manipulated and it will not be abused! The
things that go on in this world man inflicting his law unto
society. God did not mean for this to be so. I stand before
you on this day and I say to you. Woe unto thy humanity for
you have sinned a great sin in the site of the Lord. Please!
allow me to set your feet upon The Path of Knowledge and
love." She pauses briefly. "Do not fear the change of law or
new laws to come. For this is the only way we can move

forward, Always forward. Please forgive me if I become a little preachy! After all I am a Nun!" There is light laughter and applause in the room. The crowd settles down.
Then the next question is asked.
"Why is there a need for 'The Village raising child Act' included in these new laws?"   Mother Teresa immediately answers. "Children are NOT Respecting their parents or any other adult for that matter, they hit, Spit, Yell at, Curse and Abuse their parents, their school teachers or any adult that tries to prevent them from doing something wrong or corrects them when they do wrong things are met with disrespect, their parents seem to be subconsciously teaching them. The few times they are corrected by their parents, they throw temper tantrums and the parents conform to the child's will. This shall be NO MORE.
The 'Village raising child act' comes from the old proverb it takes a village to raise a child. Parents will accept the help and concern of others when they are overwhelmed and exhausted. This does not mean that strangers will discipline your child or tell you how to raise your child.
They will simply assist you in making sure your child is dressed properly for the weather and not being mischievous. This will assist you in knowing that more people are concerned and care about your child and their safety." She pauses as the crowd whispers amongst themselves.
"Parents who discipline their children are frowned upon and considered to be abusers or horrible parents. The Bible STATES 'Spare the rod and spoil the child' you can physically discipline a child without physically harming the child. There is a difference between Discipline and Abuse. Anyone who abuses a child physically, mentally or emotionally will be in violation of the law and will be harshly dealt with by the law! Anyone who does these things to a special needs child the accountability will be a hundred-fold! For those with special needs children I'm pretty sure they'd welcome and appreciate the help and

concern"

On this matter Mother Teresa spoke with such conviction it commanded the attention of the entire room.

"The 'Village Rising Child Act' is a policy created because parents are not rising their children to respect them as parents or an Adult Authority. Through this law, this and every law enforcement agency in the world will hold the parent accountable for any and all acts of their children. (under 18 years of age). This act includes Social Service intervention, involvement of all law enforcement agencies and also carries unlimited fines and unlimited jail time. Simply put 'The care of children is Paramount for God's Great purpose"

There is more Applause and a few cheers,

Mother Teresa continues.

"No more will there be children screaming at the top of their lungs crying in public places, while their parents ignore them because they are on their cell phones, Shopping or talking with their friends. Too much crying can produce so much cortisol that it can damage a baby's brain, If your child is screaming or crying stop time, move Heaven and Earth if needed but tend to your child immediately! Children have been known to damage their vocal cords doing this. I challenge any and all of you, scream as loud as you can for as long as you can and see what it does to your throat. Not to mention the disturbance to others around you."

Everyone applauds cheers and laughs.

"Generally, a baby's cry can be about 130 decibels," she says "That can be startling and painful especially if you are already hypersensitive to loud sounds due to an existing hearing loss."

People in the crowd agree with her.

"These disrespectful, Screaming, Tantrum throwing children of today are the ones that will be leading you in the future. Unfortunately, they will be the same adults challenging the

new laws and the Arch Nuns."
Mother Teresa leans forward motioning for the cameras to
zoom in on her face, she looks directly into the camera's lens,
squints her eyes and says in a spine-tingling voice.
"On that day 'THEY WILL SURELY LOSE!" An expression
the world will definitely remember. "So, I beg of you." She
concludes. "Please be better parents today for a better
tomorrow. I say to everyone on this day from the world
leaders and the richest families down to the poorest family
in the world. Tend to your children nurture and teach them.
The last thing you want is for your child to grow up
disrespect the law, this agency or become a criminal because
sooner or later they will encounter an Arch Nun! So, that Mr.
television reporter is why there is a VILLAGE RAISING
CHILD ACT!" Matthew 18:6 for protection of the children.
  Everyone in the room is shocked they don't know whether
to applaud or be frightened. They choose to applaud even
cheer a little then an Eerie silence comes over the room.
There is some whispering amongst them. But everyone now
has a better understanding of this law.
Mother Teresa being a Guardian Angel begins to sense fear
from some of the people in the room. So, she feels
telepathically to her Arch Nuns.
'Perhaps, I should tone it down a bit.'
'Ya think Grandma, you're scaring the holy crap out of some
of them' Zac answers laughing.
'I just wet myself, Grandma' Amira says like a little girl as all
the nuns laugh hysterically together with their Reverend
Grandmother.

Mother Teresa stands and addresses the crowd once more. "I
know this sounds harsh but I just want everyone to embrace
the passion I have for the well-being of children please
forgive me if I get a little carried away" the crowd seems
relieved as she continues." Please remember, I am a nun and
we tend to overreact. My apologies."

She concludes as everyone laughs with her feeling a little better. Everyone enjoys laughing for a few moments. The laughter and calmness are much needed before the news reporter asks the next question.

"Mother Teresa, 'The Sarum procedure' dubbed 'The Saruming' why is something like that included in the new laws will it not destroy the rights and privacy of the people?" Mother Teresa Smiles as she replies. "The time, resources and expenses of the average police investigation come at too high a coast to the people. Too much revenue is exhausted on building cases against mid-level and high-level criminals. They manipulate the system and make a mockery of Justice at the taxpayer's expense." The crowd agrees. "They arrange for others to take the blame and punishment. They bribe and threaten anyone and everyone they can, disregarding the safety of children and the elderly. They destroy entire families to elude apprehension and incarceration."

She pauses for a brief moment. "When incarcerated they still manage to maintain the status of their illegal endeavors. Again, at the taxpayer's expense!"

The room applauds. Mother Teresa elaborates more on the way criminals manipulate the Justice system around the world. The more she speaks to this the more the room agrees with her.

"Imagine a world if you will, where criminals are afraid to commit crimes, a world where the smallest of criminals committing crimes will be able to lead us to bigger criminals instantly, at no cost to the taxpayers! A world for the first time were criminals of all levels are truly afraid of being caught by the U.N.A. A world where the people are not concerned with telling on criminals, it will be the criminals telling on themselves." The room applauds more.

"There are criminals that enjoy incarceration because they have no fear of it, they consider it a vacation. TO THIS I SAY NO MORE!" The room begins to cheer.

"Jail will no longer be the pleasant experience for those

97

accustomed to the lifestyle."

The every one cheers louder.

"Incarceration will be the harsh punishment it was intended to be, it will not be three Square meals a day and regular exercise, free dental, free education and free health insurance! All at the taxpayer's expense. The people should not be forced to pay or take care of the criminals who mean them harm and have done them harm!!!!"

Everyone in the room is applauding loudly and cheering. Mother Teresa raises her hands for the crowd to settle down. As they settle down, she continues to speak.

"All the new incarceration facilities around the world will be built and financed at the criminal's expense, this agency will cease their homes, their cars, their businesses and liquidate it ALL!"

The every one begins to applaud again. "From now on when a criminal is incarcerated, they will be isolated, they will be ALONE, they will not be allowed to speak to any family member or friends. They will be fed tasteless food and water only. If they refuse to eat, they will be fed intravenously. Their interactions with their attorneys will be through correspondence and closely monitored." The room applauds.

"Their only intent was to harm Humanity. So, they shall be removed and separated from humanity!!! And it is the criminals who will finance this not the taxpayers."

Every one applauds in agreeance the Reverend mother continues.

"We have already made arrangements with the leaders of the world."

She pauses briefly so everyone can settle down. She waits patiently for the room to become quiet. Then she says loudly.

"All taxes will be decreased!!!!" The room applauds and cheers as loud as they can.

This is being broadcast all over the world in many languages, and all over the world people are watching their television and cheering. So, the Reverend mother continues to speak loudly into the microphone.

"This is just a small example of the power the 'Serum Procedure' and the new laws bring to humanity." The room's applause and cheers are so loud the news crews must turn down their microphones. The world leaders are pleased by the response. They are also aware of how fickle the people can be and how quickly things can change. All the world leaders in the room allow the cheering and applause to continue. Again, Mother Teresa raises her hands so she may continue to speak to the people.

"There will be no more multibillion-dollar companies manipulating the justice system whenever and however they see fit. Imagine people within these companies under investigation and being put under the serum, imagine what they will say and all of this will be transparent for the world to bear witness too" The room cheers and applauds as mother Teresa continues. "The serum procedure does not mean people will be given the serum for misdemeanor crimes. It will pertain to all felonies and felony investigations involving children, human trafficking and crimes ageist the elderly and It will not be abused!"

The news reporter interrupts briefly speaking loudly into the microphone. "With all due respect Mother Teresa, we all hope so. But someone is going to find a way to abused it"

The room quickly quiets down for a moment. The Reverend mother quickly responds.

"I assure you that will be impossible, Only an Arch Nun or myself can give the order for this and we or top-level agents of the U.N.A will be present when it is done."

The room is convinced for now so they applaud loudly.

The serum procedure was included in the contract to justify to the people how the Arch Nuns know exactly where to be and who to get. The Nuns can also obtain this information by looking into the conscience and soul of the people they are investigating. But they do not. Violating the privacy of the Soul is forbidden without the permission of Mother Teresa. The fact that the leaders are allowing the serum SHOULD! put the fear of God into the hearts and minds of criminals at all levels. Criminals will be uncomfortable in the presence of an Arch Nun. They will also fear carrying out their plans of treachery and deceit, they will fear returning to the leaders of their criminal organizations or gangs. Through this, many plans of Destruction, plans of killing, plans of hurting, plans of stealing or anything that opposes the laws or means to harm people SHOULD decrease tremendously. Simply because those who orchestrate and are involved in these activities will worry if any of them have encountered an Arch Nun, and If so, did they or did they not tell everything!

The world leaders have imposed a statute of limitations. So, it will not be used on most cold cases, depending on the circumstances. Also, any information obtained from the serum will remain confidential and assessed by the world leaders if it will bring about catastrophic events.

The sound of Applause subsides as Mother Teresa taps her finger on the table and all the Arch Nuns rise.

As the Arch Nuns stand behind their Reverend mother. The crowd slowly becomes deathly silent. Mother Teresa begins to speak again.

"For all the horrific things done un to humanity and children in the name of the church or in the name of God. The Arch Nunhood of Mother Hymiriam would like to apologize if we appear to be yet another mockery of religion. I can assure you we are not. All I can ask is that you look upon us and be patient. But we are living in times where people involved in the church or speak the word of God are thought to be deceitful. Unfortunately, far too many of them are guilty of this. Humanity asks the question why a religious order was created and chosen to enforce the new laws. Well, as a new more modern religious order we will attempt to rectify the perception of religion and God in the eyes of this new world.

It is most unfortunate that we are living in a time where children consider superheroes and supervillains in movies more powerful than God.

THIS CANNOT BE! That is why the arch Nunhood has requested 80% transparency. The world leaders explained to us why they cannot do that at this time and we understand. We want the children of this generation and all generations thereafter to look upon those involved in the church, those whom speak the word of God and to know they can trust them. On the U.N.A website we invite all to look upon some of the government-approved actions of the Arch Nuns. Yes, the world leaders will have final approval of the content you see. But take comfort in knowing that I will be actively involved to allow as much unfiltered content as they will allow. Most of the content will be quite graphic many will say inappropriate for young children, but it is for the young children to look upon and know, however harsh it may be. Children look up to the drug dealers The Pimps and the gangs. The children familiarize themselves with their violence and their way of life.

They grow up wanting the fast money, The respect and fear in the streets. I for one say let them look upon their false idols. Allow them to watch as those they consider to be Invincible are defeated by the law and humbled before God. When the children watch them fall, and fall they will!! The children will grow to honor thy mother and thy father, they will respect adults as they should. But most importantly they will have absolutely no reason to fear an encounter with an Arch Nun. For their relationship with them will be most Pleasant. Take heed and embrace the New Path God has prepared for you."

President Ophelia and president Andrei we're unprepared for the lengthy and thorough responses from Mother Teresa. Nor was the media or the world. But they were welcomed and most appreciated. However, they were very long and consuming too much time. So rather than have her shorten

her responses. Because Lord knows that would mean more questions the world leaders would have to answer. President Ophelia and president Andrei interrupt the Israeli news reporter for a moment. They did not ask to speak to mother Teresa privately. Instead they both stood while the cameras were still rolling and asked Mother Teresa publicly before the world. if she would mind answering these questions on a daily or weekly basis. The news media and world leaders are beside themselves with joy, but contain themselves. For they know this would give them unlimited opportunities to ask a great many more questions.
The Reverend mother Smiles keeping them in suspense. The world leaders are desperately hoping she agrees. Mother Teresa turns to the world leaders, nods her head in agreeance then turns to the cameras and responds.
"As long as the World wishes to hear from me, I will speak to them and answer their questions every day. But keep in mind I am an old woman, so it may be weekly occasionally... and of course I need my beauty sleep." She concludes laughing.
Everyone in the room stands applauding her. All the other news reporters are happy to know their questions and concerns will be addressed. The broadcast started at 10: a.m. it is now 3:p.m. President Ophelia addresses the room and the world.

  Everyone is talking loudly amongst themselves, as the room quiets down. President Ophelia apologizes for the inconvenience. She and President Kuznetsov had unreal expectations regarding finishing the broadcast today. But they are very relieved that Mother Teresa agreed to answer questions from the news reporters and the world on a weekly basis. Since the broadcast will be from the United Nations building in New York City the spoken language will be English but translated to every language in the world.

President Ophelia asks Mother Teresa on camera and before the world when she would like to begin.

Mother Teresa smiles and replies "In two weeks my friend, we shall begin in two weeks the Arch Nuns will be in the field operating under some of the new laws, and I am sure you will all have many questions."

Presidential Ophelia tells the news crews to start wrapping it up. In two weeks starts the beginning of what may be a brand-new television show. The news reporters make their closing statements urging everyone to Tune in, not Just in two weeks but from now on, until further notice. As the reporters address the world, President Ophelia speaks to mother Teresa. President Andrei joins them and motions for the Arch Nuns to come over. As the nuns stand everyone backs away as if in fear, clearing a path for them to join Mother Teresa and the presidents. The Nuns casually walk over to join their Reverend mother. The cameras are still rolling because many of the news reporters are still wrapping things up. But of course, many cameras are still focused on Mother Teresa and the Arch Nuns.

The Nuns laugh and casually speak with their Reverend mother and the presidents. The rest of the world leaders in the room slowly make their way through the crowd to join them and extend their best wishes. Mother Teresa is aware the cameras are focused on their every move. So, she communicates with her grandchildren telepathically while speaking to some of the leaders and their friends.

'You always wanted to be on television Maria.'

'That's right grandmother I'm ready for my close-up Mr. DeMille.'

'Buffy make sure the cameras gets your best side.'

'All my sides are the best grandma.'

'Donna don't be shy my child, Zachariah!! try not to pick your nose my son.'

'Come on grandma! I wouldn't do that, girls are watching' Zachariah replies as everyone laughs and enjoys the moment. The cameras are still fixed on Mother Teresa and the Arch Nuns watching their every movement.

Before the watchful eye of the world it would appear, they are casually conversing with the world leaders. But as usual they are in their own world making light of the situation and enjoying the moment. Remember they can carry on a verbal conversation with undivided attention, a serious facial expression and remembering every detail of the verbal conversation while communicating telepathically with their Reverend mothers or making fun of each other simultaneously. Through the Holy Spirit their brains can truly perform several tasks at once, something no human can do.

Another benefit of 'God's Grace' is the Arch Nuns can displace themselves in time. Turning seconds, minutes and hours into days at the Divine Elysium. An example of this is when they excuse themselves to be alone or using the restroom. For they must be alone in order to do this. Then through the grace of God they are removed from Earth and sent to the Divine Elysium. To everyone's knowledge they were only gone for a few seconds or minutes, that's all they need. That time is converted to days or hours depending on the need. This is used to rest or simply get away for a while. Also, every Sunday by order of Mother Hymiriam all the Arch Nuns she and Mother Teresa as well meet at the Divine Elysium (Home) to have Sunday dinner together as a family. President Andrei tells Mother Teresa she and the Nuns will be his guests and will be staying at the Waldorf Astoria Hotel here in town. A lot of the international camera Crews that are filming the Nuns make comments to one another. "The girl Nuns can arrest me anytime they want, the men Nuns, not so much" Says one Israeli cameraman. "They are a good-looking group. They look like they were hand-picked for a Hollywood movie or something." Says another.

An Italian cameraman sarcastically tells the others. "Men Nuns! What will they think of next? Maybe a female pope!"

"Don't give them any ideas." A French cameraman adds as
they all laugh. A Spanish news reporter was Brazen enough
to walk over to Mother Teresa and make a comment while
the cameras are still rolling.
"Mother Teresa, your daughters are absolutely beautiful and
your sons, magnificent!"
Mother Teresa raises her hand the Nuns move closer to her
and while the cameras are focused on her, Her laughter
Fades and she becomes very serious. Everyone notices this
immediately and stops what they are doing tapping the
person next to them to take notice. All attention is on Mother
Teresa. The Reverend mother looks at the reporter and yells.
"You dare to make inappropriate comments regarding this
Arch Nunnery?"
The reporters eyes widen; his mouth drops open but he can
speak no words. The look of Terror engulfs his face. This
gets the attention of the entire room; it becomes very quiet
and the cameras are still rolling. Mother Teresa continues to
yell at him.
"Since you have chosen to be the first to disrespect the Arch
Nuns. You shall be the first to be arrested under the new
laws"
The reporter immediately starts to beg, plead and apologize.
Mother Teresa raises her hand for him to be silent. Then
commands Zachariah to take him. As Zach walks towards
him, the reporter drops his microphone. Zachariah picks up
the microphone and hands it to him. All the Arch Nuns are
staring the poor reporter down.
The reporter is so frightened he cannot even extend his hand
to accept it. Then Mother Teresa and the Nuns start smiling
and laughing. Mother Teresa yells out to everyone as she
hugs the reporter. "Got ya! you see we do have a sense of
humor and love for everyone, sorry my friend we were just
joking."
The reporter was so relieved he almost fainted as Mother
Teresa and the Nuns hugged him in friendship. Everyone

was so relieved to see that Mother Teresa was jesting with the reporter. The world leaders suspected she was jesting. They knew the Reverend mother wouldn't abuse her power like that. They to found it amusing as did the world watching at home. It ended the day's events on a very pleasant note. But there is still a very, very long and hard road ahead. The news crews are told by their world leaders to leave their equipment in place this is where they'll be doing all the broadcasting for Mother Teresa. Most of the world leaders are staying in town for a few days. Those who aren't, say their goodbyes to Mother Teresa and the Arch Nuns. Russian and U.S. Secret Service agents are standing by to escort the Nuns to the hotel. Normally such high-level guess would stay at the United Nations Building under heavy guard. But president Andrei wanted to extend his Hospitality at the Waldorf. Only he and president Ophelia had knowledge that the Nuns will not be staying at the U.N building. The news reporters will be on the air at least another hour bringing today's events to a close and preparing the world for the continuation in a few weeks. Many of the news crews and staffers were concerned, wondering if there would be an attempt on the Arch Nuns lives today. President Winfrey on the other hand wasn't concerned at all, not with a Battle Assault Drone parked on the roof of the U.N building.

After observing a small demonstration of how that thing can move, if there was a terrorist cell considering an attempt today. They were wise to reconsider!

 However, there was a great concern for Hymiriam since she was publicly introduced and identified to the world today. Hopefully this can be an evening of peace for the Arch Nuns.

For in the coming weeks and months there will be many high-level criminal syndicates making numerous attempts on their lives, it is inevitable. The news crews make the Assumption on the air that the Arch Nuns will be staying

here at the United Nations Building and joking to New
Yorkers that any chance of seeing them in public up close
and personal tonight are zero to NUN. All pun intended.
The staff of the Waldorf are accustomed to world leaders
and people of great importance. Staying at the hotel and
they are well-versed in their conduct while they are their
guests. As the heavily escorted and guarded motorcade of
SUVs and limousines approach the private entrance of the
hotel reserved for guests of discretion. The security is
heavier than usual. Every world leader has some sort of Elite
security detail throughout the hotel and the surrounding city
blocks. Russian Security Forces open the door to one of the
SUVs and president Andrei exits the vehicle. He turns and
extends his hand to assist Mother Teresa from the vehicle.
The Trusted staff members of the Waldorf Astoria that are
accustom to handling guests of such importance were very
excited to see such a pristine guest at their hotel. They felt
honored to have her there.
They were also a little concerned that a guess of this stature
may provoke an assassination attempt or trouble for the
hotel. To spite the fact that the hotel is literally crawling with
Elite security from every country in the world and now they
understand why.
The hotel workers are a little frightened, not just for
themselves but for the Reverend Mother. Two limousines
pull behind the S.U.Vs The chauffeurs open the doors of the
limos; the workers are expecting more leaders to emerge.
That's what their paperwork tells them. So, they patiently
wait for more leaders to exit the car. But the Arch Nuns
emerge from the limos, Escorted by President Ophelia
Winfrey.
The staff of the hotel gasp in amazement. All the fear and
concern the workers were feeling was replaced with relief
and joy. All the hotel workers that are assigned to this
particular area of the hotel were handpicked by the world
leaders themselves, so they are very trusted.

For what their eyes now behold brings them great peace. Not to say they did not have confidence in all the world leader's elite security teams. But they're not God's True Chosen, 'The Arch Nunhood of Mother Hymiriam'!

 The workers are not allowed to have any cell phone or recording device of any kind on their person while they work this detail. But for the first time they truly wish they were allowed, so they may take pictures of this great site. One of the older gentlemen who has worked this detail for many years and is well respected amongst the entire staff of the Waldorf Astoria. Turns to a younger co-worker and says to him.

"I'll be retiring next year, my body has grown old, my strength has withered away. I may not live to see all the great things these Arch Nuns will bring. But I ask you, please respect and honor them. please, help them spread the word of God to the world."

The young man replies. "After seeing that light shine down on that woman today, I can truly say, Now I'm starting to believe."

President Ophelia and president Andrei lead the Nuns to a private elevator.

The Reverend mother stops them and asks. "If we are to be your guest at this hotel then let us go through the lobby so we may be among the people."

President Andrei looks at mother Teresa and says with a smile.

"Nice try mother Teresa, but you're already checked in so we are taking the private elevator it goes straight to your rooms so everyone can change for dinner"

The Nuns find it amusing that President Andrei superseded Mother Teresa's wishes. So, they smile and softly laugh amongst themselves as hotel workers greet them and Pat them on their shoulders. There are six large elevators that go to private Suites. President Andrei rides with mother Teresa, two Russian Secret Service agents and five of the Nuns. President Ophelia rides with the rest of the Nuns and four U.S. Secret Service agents. President Andrei reserved three presidential Suites. One for Mother Teresa, One for the female Nuns and one for the male Nuns. Everyone meets for a brief moment in Josh and Zac's Suite. Mother Teresa thanks president Andrei for his hospitality. President Ophelia reassures Mother Teresa and the Nuns they are safe, they have Apache helicopters on standby, the Reverend mother extends her appreciation.

"There are several fine restaurants in the area does anyone have a preference?" President Ophelia asks.

"We'll trust your decision. We are sure you will choose well." The Reverend mother answers.

"No offense Mother Teresa" President Ophelia says. "But they don't have to be so quiet, they can talk and be themselves around us!"

Everyone pleasantly laughs and Mother Teresa tells her. "Be careful what you wish for my friend!"

"Okay!" Zachariah says loudly. "Can everyone get out of here now please! Josh and I want to run around in our underwear playing video games while we figure out what to wear"

The look on the two president's faces was priceless. Mother Teresa turns to them saying.

"I told you. Be careful what you wish for, my friends."

"I apologize Madam president." Zac says Putting his arm around her. "I was just kidding, please! forgive me."

She smiles and shakes her finger at him. But is also relieved that they are starting to feel more comfortable.

"Boy! You had me going for a minute there."

President Andrei can hardly contain his laughter as he agrees with her. He then informs the Nuns their luggage is being bought to their rooms. The presidents excuse themselves and leave the room so they can make sure everything is in order for dinner. Mother Teresa tells her grandchildren to change and while they are with the world leaders, they will allow themselves to be recognized by all. Security will make sure pictures are at a minimum. This is after all a photo opportunity day for everyone. All the girls go to Mother Teresa's Suite to change for dinner.

Since they are on earth, they decide not to transition into whatever outfit they please but prefer to take the opportunity to enjoy dressing themselves and doing their own hair. Sister Superior Maria has taught her sisters to do this as they were growing up and relishes every opportunity to be a big sister to them. Mother Teresa on the other hand being a Guardian Angel simply transitions into another outfit. She tells her daughter's they may leave their habits off tonight. While the girls are having the time of their lives, helping each other with their hair and makeup in the mirror. They can hear the Sister Superior loudly humming 'I feel pretty' from the 1961 hit movie 'West Side Story' So of course they all join in singing loudly. Mocking their sister, having fun and singing off-key. Mother Teresa has always enjoyed watching her children have fun as all grandmothers do, and occasionally joining in, as all grandmothers should do.

So she walks over to the girls and begins to sing the song 'Tonight-Tonight' also from 'West Side Story' They all laugh and deliberately sing horribly off-key as they continue to get dressed. The garments within their luggage of course or anything their hearts desire they simply think it and it is there.

Now the Suite where the men Nuns are staying. Well let's just say they are doing exactly what Zac said they would be doing. Sitting on the couch in their underwear playing video games with their clothes scattered on the floor. The girls have finished dressing and knock on the door to their brother's Suite. In a millisecond the men transition into their clothes, their hair is neatly groomed and they are ready to go.

The Secret Service escort them to the main lobby where the presidents and of course more security are waiting. The guest and clientele of the Waldorf Astoria. Are known for containing their composure when in the presence of celebrities, world leaders and people of great importance. How ever seeing the Arch Nuns dressed in stunning evening wear is quite eye catching to say the least.

The Nuns are dressed so elegantly as is Mother Teresa but she is still wearing her habit. She being the Grand Mother Superior she is seldomly seen without it. The world leaders and the Nuns enjoyed a splendid evening dining. The Secret Service assured picture taking was at a minimum and he evening went smoothly without incident, and it for now is good.

A large private luxury jet sores across the sky approaching Singapore. Aboard the jet is a Caucasian woman in her mid-forties. She is surrounded by an Entourage of supermodels, fashion designers and image Consultants. She is sophisticated, elegant and very glamorous.
She is well-dressed and speaks with a slight English accent. She sits ever so elegantly in her seat sipping a glass of wine. While everyone around her is enjoying the flight and looking through fashion, ballet and Opera magazines.

She is the most influential person in the fashion industry today. All the top fashion designers in the world owe their success to her. There is no one in the fashion world more loved, Hated and respected then her.

She is Zsazsa La'more and she is a daughter of Eve.
Upon Landing everyone exits the jet, on the runway are two
SUVs for her Entourage and one limousine for her. The
SUVs take the group to a five-star hotel the limousine takes
Zsazsa to a private dock where there is a large luxury yacht
waiting. There is no one else at the dock other than the staff
of the yacht. The chauffeur opens the door and assists Miss
La'more as she exits the vehicle.

  As she boards the yacht the captain and two of his crew
mates are there to greet her. They escort her to the top deck.
There waiting is a very attractive and shapely fair
Skinned African American woman in her early thirties
sunbathing in a string bikini. This is her sister 'Ka'ren Margo
Eleganza' also known as 'Leggz- Dimond', for her thick
gorgeous legs and incredible figure. She is an Arms Dealer,
Human Trafficker, Drug Dealer' and an Assassin whom
absolutely loves to kill!!
She is extremely sexy with a very, very, very short temper
and has a zero tolerance for incompetence. All of Eve's
children are born with perfect mental and physical health.
So, there is absolutely nothing wrong with Ka'ren mentally,
she simply enjoys portraying psychotic.
In the urban streets the world over she is most Hated,
Envied, and definitely the most FEARED!

Most street gangs and High-level crime lords respect her but prefer to avoid her. She has a strong voice in the drug underworld including the cartels. She also has a very strong influence in the entertainment industry. She, like her sister Zsazsa are very high level undercover top-secret C.I.A agents. Their identities and affiliates are protected at the highest level by many governments. They were placed in this position like many of their siblings by high level government friends of their mother Eve.
They have licenses to kill and diplomatic immunity in every country they go. That is why they cannot be arrested only the Arch Nuns know this. Most law enforcement agencies in the world do not have this information. Zsazsa keeps an extremely low profile in the crime world it is almost nonexistent. To maintain her celebrity status this is a must. She knows everyone who is anyone and anyone who is of great importance wants to know her. This allows her to set anyone up for her siblings to kill, she is trusted by most. She only carries out assassinations for her mother. With her 3% speed and strength She always prefers to do this up close and personal. She is an accomplished ballet dancer known to the world. Secretly with her MI6 status and training she also excels in the martial arts calling herself 'Madame Butterfly' in the crime world for her graceful style of fighting and her use of the Shaolin Butterfly Swords.

Ka'ren Margo's field operations are designed to invoke fear. Her work unlike her sister's. Is very dirty and requires a lot of cleaning and covering up, she also enjoys it to the fullest. To say she acts like a crazy, unstable, narcissistic Loose Cannon. Would be in understatement! If all the world is a stage. She would definitely get an Academy Award. She even has the C.I.A convinced. As the yacht makes the short trip to the island their mother has summoned them to They relax and enjoy being themselves for a while and talking to each other as sisters. Without C.I.A Handlers or governments to deal with they are simply too very, very rich, Egotistical, Self-centered women enjoying a cruise. The trip is short taking only 45 minutes the yacht is quite fast. The ship's dock is within a mansion on the island. Zsazsa and Ka'ren exit the ship eager to greet their mother. They board an elevator that takes them to a large office. It has a breathtaking view of the island. The office has twenty monitors displaying news feeds from around the world. All of which are displaying recaps of today's events and the broadcast afterwards at the U.N building in New York. The two ladies watch in Amusement as one of the monitors is repeatedly showing and commenting on the light shining down upon Hymiriam.

"This chick, by coincidence was standing were the sun was shining and their treating her like she's a god or something! " Ka'ren says with an attitude.

"Don't get yourself worked up my dear" Zsazsa tells her. "I'm sure mother is a hundred steps ahead of this and the Arch Nuns will be over soon, very soon darling!"

During the media storm Eve gathers and increases her weapons and Technology in preparation for the arrival of The Arch Nuns and the U.N.A.

Including the "I.D.A.C. device (iris- disruption - audio - cancelation". It prevents camera irises from focusing and sends an ultrasonic sound unheard to the human ear that prevents microphones from picking up sound.

   A door opens and in walks another Daughter. Aston Vetta is her name and she too is a deep-cover N.I.A agent (National Intelligence Agency of Africa) with the same International status as her sisters. She is based in Africa and it is there where she carries out her mother's plans.

She is a tall, fair woman with beautiful dark skin. She is gorgeous, fashionable and quite the seductress. She maintains conflicts in Africa according to her mother's wishes. She is nocturnal by nature and prefers to carry out assassinations for her mother at night. Earning her the codename. 'Midnite Endeavor' amongst her brothers and sisters. Like her siblings she excels at hand-to-hand combat. But also has several small armies at her disposal. Whom follow her orders without question. "Greetings my sisters" she says with open arms as the three women hug each other. They barely have time to say hello when. A large set of double doors automatically opens on the other side of the room and in walks their mother. The three women immediately stop what they're doing and drop to one knee bowing their heads.

"Greetings Oh, Great Mother" They say.

"Rise my daughters and give your mother a kiss"

She says with a smile and opening her arms for a hug. The three women rush to hug and kiss their mother. Eve then turns their attention to the monitors. "How did this happen?" Ka'ren asks. "Did the leaders on our payroll forsaken us, do they hope to separate themselves from us?"

"That my sister" Aston interrupts. "Would be their darkest and last day on Earth!"

"For them and everything they hold dear!" Zsazsa adds with a laugh.

Eve has no problem giving orders to her children to kill entire families. It has become her way of being thorough and sending a message to all who oppose her. This is something she has learned from the Great Pharaohs and kings of the past and her children love when she gives such orders because they know she wants it to be bloody and almost impossible for forensic teams to explain.

The more foreign and harder to explain the murders appear, the more the governments will have to cover them up. So, they use their 3% speed and strength. Killing every family member and any military forces protecting them. Also destroying all evidence that they were ever there. In all the years her children have been doing this they have never been identified. If they leave a half dead Survivor it is Eve's instruction to do so and for her Amusement so, she may watch the government finish them off. Sometimes they blame other world leaders for the assassinations. So, they can wash their hands of the situation. This further corrupts them and keeps them under her power.

Eve calls one of the world leaders on her payroll and puts the call on speaker so her daughters may here. She uses many aliases with the world leaders she deals with. Being the owner of a few cell phone companies. Her calls are rerouted hundreds of times as not to locate the point of origin. Junlong, The President of Singapore answers the phone. He knows her only as Lady Vil'e.(VILE, she who is Wicked and most Unpleasant!)

He answers the phone in his native language, Mandarin. Eve is fluent in every language known to man. So, she speaks with him in his language. (English translation) "Hello My Dear" Eve speaks in a sexy tone, as if she has any other. "How are you?"

"I'm fine my lady and to what do I owe the pleasure of this call."

"I am delighted you find this call pleasurable. Do you have any more information regarding THIS THING that HAPPENED?"

She asks referring to the birth of the U.N.A agency/Arch Nuns.

  Eve does not concern herself with every little political detail. That is how Hymiriam was able to keep the Arch Nunhood under her radar. She remembers it being mentioned through the years. But to Eve it was just another one in a million inceptions that would never see the light of day. Eve Prides herself on being a perfectionist and she does not take well to being wrong or making errors. She is however quite proficient at CORRECTING THEM!

"It's as I told you before." President Junlong tells her. "This contract came out of nowhere they passed it around the U.N and I was pressured like many others to sign. Maybe if 'YOU' had gained control of the United States and Russia like you said the so-called organization you represent could do; THIS would not have HAPPENED!" He replies yelling angrily.

"Perhaps you are right my love"

"I know I'm right," He yells cutting her off. "And a few others feel the same way. You claim to have things under control but we could blame you and your people for this as WELL! And speaking of which many of us are starting to believe we may have to rethink our relationship with you. In light of this new agency YOU! Allowed to grow right under our noses."

Eve looks to her daughter's and with a sexy sinister smile replies.

"My apologies, forgive me if I appear to have lost my influence. Allow me to reassure you that is not the case, I will assess and rectify the situation. Please inform the others whom share your opinion of this. After all, The Arch Nuns and the United Nations agency with all their new rules and laws. Did take us all by surprise, and not a pleasant one I might add. But! know this, as sure as the sun rises in the morning. I will DEFINITELY CORRECT these ERRORS!!!!!, Good bye, My love."

"Glad to see you take the initiative, My SWEET!" He concludes sarcastically as he hangs up the phone. Eve's daughters laugh and give each other high-fives.

"That Mother fu#ker must have bumped his goddamn head!" Ka'ren yells.

"Be still my sisters, Mother will now speak!" Aston tells them holding both hands up for her sisters to be quiet. Eve looks at her daughters with her Sinister smile, a smile all too familiar to her children. As she stands her daughters immediately dropped to one knee and bowed their heads.

"For He Who DARES to speak to me in such a fashion!" She briefly pauses takes a deep breath and continues. "He and ALL that he loves, SHALL LIVE NO MORE! Wait a few weeks I want him to believe he is safe."

Her daughter's reply. "We Obey, Oh Great Mother!"

Her daughters were pleased. For They Knew by the tone of the conversation that their mother will now unleash them to wreak havoc upon president Junlong and all who follow him. He just condemned his entire family to death. Every man, woman and child in his known blood line. Shall be no more. As for those who endorse his opinion. They will live, but for the mere thought of disobedience, they will know death within their family to appease the Mother of ALL!

Mother Teresa and the Arch Nuns are returning to the hotel. After a wonderful and most intriguing evening of dining and conversation. They dined with as many as 27 world leaders, it was more of a meet and greet for leaders that were not acquainted with them. The conversation was casual, not much business or politics were discussed. All the world leaders were very concerned about Hymiriam's state. After the not so warm reception she received this morning from the crowd. The Reverend mother assured them. She was absolutely fine and she can take it on the chin with far more restraint than anyone in this room, they were relieved to know that. Fellowship, laughter and rejoicing were the order of the evening. Especially after a day such as this.

Mother Teresa asks for all the Nuns to meet in her suite for a final meeting and prayer before retiring for the evening. The Reverend mother being in Archangel knows there is no audio or video surveillance in any of their rooms. She speaks freely to her children regarding the events of the evening and the events that will take place on tomorrow.

"Did everyone have a nice time tonight my children?"

The Nuns all give pleasant responses, But the night is still young for them. So, Buffy asks.

"Can we go out and paint the town red Grandma? Like they used to say in the olden days."

"Oh yes! Granny can we, please" Dee adds with excitement in her eyes.

Then Maria joins in. "Just for a little while please grandmother?"

The Reverend mother just looks at her grandchildren with a serious expression upon her face. There is silence as she continues to look at them, and she looks. Then she breaks the silence ignoring their request.

"Anyway, like I was saying, my children get a good night sleep tonight, tomorrow is a big day. Josh! you and Zach better not stay up all night playing video games, I mean it!"

In the blink of an eye Hymiriam inserts herself into the room. All the Nuns hug and kiss her. To the point where everyone almost fell to the floor.

"I just wanted to personally say goodnight, and again tell you how proud I am of all of you."

Navaeh quickly asks Hymiriam.

"Hey Mom, can we go out for a little while?"

All the nuns join in pleading with Hymiriam.

"What did I just tell you?" Mother Teresa yells stomping her foot.

"It's okay with me if it's all right with your grandmother?"

They all turn and look at their grandmother.

"Come on grandmother Superior, you know we require very little to almost no sleep when we're here on Earth." Maria says putting an arm around her.

"It's impossible for us to be fatigued or anything like that, tomorrow or any other day" Elizabeth adds. Like all children no matter the age, have a way of playing the parents against the grandparents to get their way and the Arch Nuns are no different, when it comes to Mother Hymiriam and Grand Mother Teresa.

"We know you worry about us, grandma, you always have and you always will and we love you for it" Maria says. "If it will make you feel better. Josh will hold Buffie's hand when we cross streets."

Amira was smiling a moment ago now she's just staring at Maria with a straight face.

119

"We'll use our 'Grace' to make sure no one recognizes us."
Zachariah says.
Mother Teresa folds her arms looking at them.
"you guys are thirty plus years old and still pleading to go
outside and play?"
The Nuns look at each other and respond.
"Yep"
"same as it ever was"
"Yes we are"
Mother Teresa turns to their mother. Hymiriam shrugs her
shoulders and laughs. Then Mother Teresa does what all
grandmother's do, but not as often as most she lets them
have their way.
"Oh very well It's 9 p.m. transition to the destinations of
your choice." She tells them because the elevators go directly
to their privates Suites and security would know they were
in use.
"You are not to involve yourselves in anything. No matter
how severe the situation may seem or how violent the crime
unless you receive direct feeling from the lord."
The Nuns agree, Mother Teresa has physical currency in her
possession from the world leaders for whenever the Nuns
are on Leisure Time. This is done because the Arch Nun's
E.B.T card transactions can be tracked. She gives them
money and looks at them once more, shaking her head
saying. "I'll be Coming for You at seven a.m. sharp."
And so the Arch Nuns went out into the City of New York
and among the people. Maria and Anna went to a trendy
upscale fashion bar, Joshua went to a jazz club to sit in on a
few sessions with the musicians, Zachariah of course being
the Sportsman went to a sports bar, where he can yell and
argue with other fans, Donna and Nevaeh went to a cyber
cafe in a questionable neighborhood, Elizabeth went to a
country bar and rode a mechanical bull.
Dajairia, Lin and Amira went to a nightclub to dance, also in
a questionable part of town. All the places you would never

find traditional Nuns, EVER!!!!
They were loud, Rowdy dressed in a fashion accustomed to
the environments they were visiting, consumed alcoholic
beverages and they ran amok. But most importantly they
were themselves, they were in control and they had fun.
Their Reverend Mothers promised them privacy and respect
as adults which is good for the Nuns. For if their Reverend
Mothers looked upon them at this current moment.
'THE RULER WOULD NOT BE SPARED'!!! L.O.L.
 The next day as promised Mother Teresa came for her
grandchildren at 7 a.m. The Nuns returned to the hotel at 6
a.m. Wide Awake, their minds sharp and their bodies
purged of the evening's events. They were eager to meet
their teammates and begin God's work. The Reverend
mother conducts their morning prayer, then they transition
into the outfits they will be wearing this morning.
   The front desk had instructions to bring breakfast for
everyone in Mother Teresa's Suite. After breakfast the Nuns
were driven to the U.N building and taken to a private
section. Where Mother Teresa tells them to wait until she
calls for them. She is going to meet with the Tactical squads.
that will become their teammates and brief them on today's
events. The world leaders are on their way as well. Mother
Teresa enters a large gymnasium filled with the world's
most Elite Tactical squads. These are the same Squad
members the Nuns encountered yesterday upon their arrival
at the United Nations building. Every last one of them has
been handpicked by Mother Teresa. She chose from: China's
snow leopard Commando unit, Britain's special Boat Service,
Polish GROM, The special services group of Pakistan, Delta
Force, France's National Gendarmerie Group, The sayeret
matkal of Israel, Spain's special Naval Warfare Force,
Russian Spetsnaz and the U.S Navy SEALs and many more!
Since America and Russia are the countries the Arch Nuns
will be starting in. All the soldiers studied English and

Russian. They have also gone through extensive interviews over the past year with her. She has become quite fond of them and they have come to absolutely love and respect her. She is confident that they will do well with the Arch Nuns. It doesn't hurt that they will be receiving strong six-figure salaries as well. As she enters the room the soldiers are all sitting on the floor talking with one another. They all rise and stand at attention. "Good morning" She says.

"Good morning, ma'am" They all respond together, as soldiers do. She tells them all to relax. The soldiers knowing Mother Teresa for the past year or so are very comfortable around her. She allows them to be candid. But they to, like her children know not to go too far. Mikolai from Soviet Special Forces raises his hand to ask a question.

"Hey Mother Teresa, good morning again I was just wondering. If it's too early to ask for one of your granddaughter's hand in marriage?"

"Of course! my future son-in-law." Mother Teresa responses smiling. "let's see if you still have the same feeling after today's meeting with my grandchildren."

The soldiers enjoy a little lighthearted humor for a few moments. The world leaders have now arrived and are taking their seats which overlook the gymnasium where Mother Teresa and the soldiers are talking. There are one hundred soldiers in all. Seventy-seven will be chosen for A.N.T(Arch Nun Teams). Seven to each nun including Mother Teresa. With the remaining thirty-three on standby and backup to cover the severely wounded team members or fatalities. There's a saying in Texas about the Texas rangers; One Riot, One Ranger! The U.N.A will have a saying of their own; One War, One A.N.T!

All of the soldiers have undergone the sarum procedure. The confidentiality of their past missions has not been compromised they were asked specific questions regarding their reasons for joining this agency and if they have any animosity to this agency, Mother Teresa,

Hymiriam, the Arch Nuns or a hidden agenda for themselves or their world leader. This was done my Mother Teresa and the world leaders of their countries. The one-hundred chosen by Mother Teresa have all passed. The world leaders are talking amongst themselves as they look over the assortment of soldiers in the gymnasium. Each leader has the utmost confidence in their soldiers. These are their most Elite Tactical teams.

Mother Teresa summons her Arch Nuns, they enter the gymnasium single file in their prayer position girls first with the males in the rear. As they enter the room all the soldiers whistle at them and make sarcastic remarks. The soldiers are well aware that these are going to be their bosses so they don't say anything too harsh.

Mother Teresa raises her hands for everyone to be quiet and settle down,
she stands in front of the Tactical squads with her Arch Nuns behind her. She addresses the world leaders. Then she speaks to the soldiers.

"Just a few short years ago many of you were engaged in cold wars with the country and the brother or sister that stands next to you. Look to your right, then look to your left and behold what the Lord has brought together on this day. You will stand United for God's Great Purpose. I cannot thank you enough but know that Hymiriam loves you all." She pauses as the soldiers applauded in agreeance. "long ago there was an old proverb that states. 'you never truly know someone or respect someone into you are engaged in physical combat with them' before me stands the best warriors of the present age. Each of your countries have spent absurd amounts of money on your training. You have proven this to your leader's countless times. The fact that you are standing here. Not only proves that you have endured this, but you have survived this. You have proven to your leaders you are well worth every penny they have spent on your training. You have truly earned the opportunity that has been offered to you." She pauses for a moment looking at all the soldiers.

"Everyone in this room has signed contracts to be part of this agency and I am proud to know you and I am glad that you are here. You are the absolute best Warriors of the past present and future" All the soldiers cheer, whistling and applauded loudly. The world leaders are applauding also. The Arch Nuns are standing in the prayer position looking at the soldiers with serious expressions on their faces. Mother Teresa allows the soldiers to applaud themselves a little longer.

"Behind me stands fighters Trained in every form of traditional and modern hand to hand combat. Fighters who spent the majority of their adolescent life training at high altitudes in the Himalayas. Witch allows them better endurance for physical activities. But they are Fighters that have never fought for their lives, fighters whom are not proven. They have only competed in honorable sparring competitions. Where the rules were many and the environment safe. But today they stand before you"
She says as she steps to the side allowing the Nuns and the soldiers to face each other.

"Today there will be very few rules. Do not try to kill each other and try not to break any bones. This is a 'knockout' or 'tap out competition. The Arch Nuns have no egos to bruise they will accept their losses and be wise enough to tap out before bones are broken. I sincerely hope you are wise enough to do the same. Due to the Arch Nus high altitude training. The world leaders would like to observe their endurance."
The soldiers look confused Mother Teresa notices this and elaborates.

"like masters of yoga, they are able to control their heart rate and breathing.
While remaining in motion. Retina training with flashes of light to sharpen the peripheral vision."

"Rectum training?" Yells one Soldier causing the others to burst into laughter.

"I'll bet the two guy Nuns loved that!" Shouts another as the laughter gets louder.

"All right, all right, THATS ENOUGH NOW!" President Ophelia yells over the loudspeaker.

"Don't make me come down there, have some respect all of you. Do not forget this is a religious order of Nuns. There better not be another word from the US troops!" She was livid, but the Arch Nuns are good sports and they enjoyed a little laughter to. Josh and Zac took the joke like men and laughing with everyone.

"Okay everyone." Mother Teresa says urging everyone to settle down again. "Each Arch Nun will fight three opponents before resting. Whether they win or lose."

"Excuse me Mother Teresa" A soldier from Italian Special Forces interrupts.

"But if every one of them. Has to fight three of us back to back. We can't accurately keep count of how bad we're kicking the crap out of them because they'll be too tired."

"You have a valid point my son but it is also not fair to the Nuns to not truly know the pressure of fighting. What you'll be teaching them while you're, how did you put it? kicking the crap out of them. No one is going to have pity or Mercy on them in combat because they are a Nun.

All of you have been in Wars you know what it's like to push on when you know you can't, when you have nothing left, when you are ready to lay down and die. But still you push on.

My children have the mental capacity, the spirit, and of course the faith to push on. But their physical ability is unproven."

She has their full attention so she pauses for a moment then continues with a smile on her face.

"Especially while they're getting the crap kicked out of them." All the soldiers agree with Mother Teresa and laugh while making jokingly intimidating faces at the Nuns whom do not find this amusing. As the expression on Donna's face is not only of concern but that of intimidation, she is frightened. Several of the soldiers notice this and begin to point at her making crying jesters. Mother Teresa explains to everyone that no one will be allowed to touch the fighters once engaged in combat or their side will be disqualified. They have several medical teams standing by. Everyone is to wear lite protective gear for their feet and hands as to have full use of them during combat. Mother Teresa draws everyone's attention to the world leaders whom are watching them in a large booth. Every world leader tells their soldiers to defeat the Nuns to honor their training and bring glory to their country. They also remind them that this is still a friendly competition. But also know when to yield and not to kill anyone. But in the event, someone sustains severe injuries. Their position on the team will be held while they recover.

Upon hearing this Donna's eyes begin to water and her lips begin to quiver. The Soldiers noticed this also. At this point many of them consider her to be the weakest link. Mother Teresa tells everyone the entire gymnasium is their Arena.

As the fighters move around everyone is to get out of the way. She tells the soldiers to choose their Fighters. They are to choose 30 champions of hand-to-hand combat to participate.

She and the world leaders understand although every soldier in the room has been trained in hand-to-hand combat. Not all of them excel at this some are weapons experts, demolition experts, I.T experts, medics and so on. Mother Teresa asks for everyone to be silent. So, she may pray with her grandchildren. As she walks toward them, they bow their heads, then she feels to them telepathically. 'Ok everyone, I will tell you when you are to be victorious and when you are to lose. Some of you will appear to be damaged and a couple of you will be unharmed, maybe slightly bruised. Remember these are the people you will be working with and we have to make them look good. SO, SHALL THIS BE WRITTEN!'

The Nuns respond.

'SO, SHALL IT BE DONE!'

Mother Teresa now prays aloud for all to hear. As she speaks. Some of the soldiers bow their heads as well.

"Oh God, we ask that you watch over and protect these Warriors during this friendly but most serious competition. Oh God, please keep them calm, prevent them from becoming angry and most importantly Oh Lord! Protect them from sustaining serious injuries.

Hallowed be thy Lord God Amen."

She turns and looks at the soldiers one more time. Before joining the world leaders above the gymnasium.

They all stand at attention and salute her as a sign of respect. Once she is in the booth, she 'FEELS' one more time to her grandchildren to tell them. They may jest with the soldiers and enjoy themselves. But to keep it light. She speaks into the microphone and asks. If the soldiers have chosen their first champion?

"We have Mother superior." A couple of soldiers respond. Mikolai walks through the crowd of soldiers as they cheer, whistle and pat him on the back to encourage him. He is the number one master of M.M.A (mixed martial arts) in the Russian military. He is known by many of the soldiers if not personally, Then by his reputation. He has also assisted in training many of them. As he stands in front of the soldiers facing the Nuns. Zachariah eagerly walks out to face him. With the biggest smile in the world upon his face.   The Nuns applauded and cheer their brother. Mother Teresa quickly orders him to stand down and return to the line. The smile Fades from his face in disappointment. Mikolai laughs and points at him saying. "Don't worry nun boy! You shouldn't be so eager to get your face knocked in!" All the soldiers laughed loudly and pointed at Zac.

But he just throws his hands in the air and smiles then walks away. He knows his grandmother Superior knows best.

"The Arch Nunhood calls fourth Sister Dajairia."

Mother Teresa's voice came through the speakers in the gym loudly.

"She shall be first to represent the 'Arch Nunhood of Mother Hymiriam!"

The Nuns cheer for their sister as loud as they can. But the soldiers applaud, cheer and whistle much louder. Mikolai puts both hands over his heart and blows her a kiss saying.

"Your beautiful face, I am definitely NOT going to knock in, gorgeous one!"

"I know you're NOT" She responds smiling and batting her eyes at him in a playful and flirtatious way.

"Oooooooh!" Most of the soldiers' yell continuing to cheer.

"I don't mean this in a disrespectful way sister."

Mikolai says with a devilish grin. "But I can't wait to get my hands on you!"

Slamming her hand on the table president Ophelia yells.

"UNBELIEVABLE!!!!" As she looks at President Andrei who is sitting right next to her.

"I know, I know comrade I will have words with him afterwards." He tells her trying to contain his laughter. Ophelia gives him a look.

"ENOUGH!" Mother Teresa yells. "WARRIORS COMMERCE!"

Sister Dajairia assumes an aggressive Shaolin fighting stance. Mikolai walks to the left of her flexing his muscles and looking her up and down. As everyone in the room begins to whistle and applaud. Then he turns to the right continuing to look her up and down stopping directly in front of her. She is still, she does not move a muscle she is looking down at the floor. Mikolai asks her. "Do you not, want to see what's coming?"

He moves closer to her. But she still does not move. Mother Teresa knows Mikolai does not mean any harm. It's just his way, he has been a soldier most of his life. But the Reverend mother has grown weary of his jesting and mockery of her grandchildren. The other soldiers respect him so much they appear to follow his lead. So, Mother Teresa feels to her granddaughter. 'Dee you will be the victor of all your bouts, you will be Flawless, you will be graceful and you will demonstrate your superiority for all to see.

 This is for Mikolai only! The next two bouts give them a fighting chance and make them look good. This will give everyone the impression Mikolai's jesting cost him the fight and he will not be shamed before his leader and Country. Hopefully he will learn from this.

Now my granddaughter, humble him before the Lord.'
Dee raises her head slightly to look him in the eyes.
"Mikolai" She Whispers. "Yes" He whispers back over confidently.

"WITNESS THE POWER OF GOD!!!!" She says as she attacks him with a flurry of kicks he cannot counter. With the last kick Landing directly in the center of his nose breaking it and knocking a tooth out. All of the world leaders stand in amazement. But Mother Teresa remains seated. The soldiers are amazed they have never witnessed such speed and accuracy. Mikolai is down on one knee holding his nose. The soldiers are no longer cheering. The Nuns are laughing and cheering. Zach is rolling on the floor pointing and laughing at him. Mikolai of course is embarrassed and Furious. President Andrei is concerned that he is going to attempt to kill her now.

Dee stands in the prayer position looking at him. He looks up at her. Then slowly rises to his feet. Dee Like a ballerina raises her left leg straight in the air demonstrating a standing split with her left leg extended completely over her head, she flips over onto her left leg with her right leg now straight in the air, she slowly spins around on her left foot demonstrating extreme strength and control. She confidently folds her arms while holding this position and looks down at

Mikolai. This is her signature 'Prima Ballerina Maneuver!' She does this to show off and whenever she is in complete control of a fight.

He wipes the blood from his nose, spits out another bloody tooth, moves his hair back off of his face and tells her. "Now, I'm gonna knock head off shoulders!"

Dee's response is. "I don't use 'Head & Shoulders' shampoo!" She lowers her leg as he attacks. He continuously misses her throwing punch after punch. She taunts him as she out Maneuvers everything he throws at her. The two square off for a moment so Mikolai can catch his breath. Dee raises her leg in the air again and taunts him to come on. He moves towards her with Extreme Caution. She lowers her leg and walks slowly towards him. He stands strong awaiting her attack. She takes an attack posture, the two lock eyes. With blinding speed, she fakes him out as if to do a spinning kick but hits him hard with a spinning fist instead. Mikolai's fighting stamina is amazing. He takes the hit and rushes towards her to grab her. She spins around him and punches him in the back of the neck. He throws a back kick at her, she ducks under it as she sweeps his leg from under him, jumping in the air twirling her body as his body hits the ground. She comes down on top of him with her knee on his shoulder, dislocating it.

She stands over him with her foot on him, pointing down at him shouting. "BAD DOG, STAY!"

The soldiers cannot believe this. They don't know whether to cheer her or curse her. None of them wanted to anger their leader so they cheered for Mikolai to get up. Dee does a series of gymnastic flips and lands on the floor in a Russian split. Mikolai pops his arm back in the socket and stands up. Zachariah yells to him. "I think my sister's too much for you, Better stay, LITTLE DOG!"

Mikolai is furious but he keeps a straight face, turns to Zac, points to him and says.

"YOU WILL BE NEXT!"

Amira quickly yells. "Yeah! the next one to pull the other arm out the socket." The Nuns laugh pointing at him and the Soldiers. He turns back to Dee; she is still in the Russian split position arms folded in front of her. He wipes his face and again Spits more blood.

"Hey! gorgeous" He says winking at her. "Bring that big beautiful booty back over here."

"Ok! Baby" She responds crawling a little toward him like a stripper. Almost all the soldier's eyes widen and jaws drop, the Nuns are shocked as well.

"WHAT KIND OF NUNS ARE THESE?" one of the soldiers yells loudly from the back of the gym. Anna got so nervous by this; she starts to whisper to herself. "O.M.G, O.M.G, O.M.G!"

The gymnasium becomes quiet. Mikolai says. "Yeah! I'm your baby alright, sister."

Dee stands, fixes her hair and blows him another kiss. But what she is about to say to him will be remembered for a very long time.

"I call you baby!" She says in a very sexy tone as she slowly raises her leg straight in the air.

"Because I'm about to rock you to sleep!"

Of course, she is referring to Knocking him unconscious but all the soldiers go crazy whistling and cheering.

131

The nuns join in cheering and whistling as well. Anna decided to join her brothers and sisters. If one's going to get in trouble then they will all get in trouble together.

Antonia one of the female soldiers turns to another and says. "I know this is dead wrong of me and I'm gonna probably burn in hell for this. But I am totally turned on right now."

In his entire career Mikolai has never felt such pressure to win. Nor did he ever want to win as much as he does now! If it was his intention to get into Dee's head and psych her out, it is she who is in his head psyching him out. Mikolai has been in tougher situations and fights than this. But he underestimated the Sister Dajairia. His overconfidence in himself was his weakness.

His disrespect for the power of women is another. Now he is paying the price. He calms his temper, uses all of his military training and attempts to strategically attack her with punches and kicks. She easily out maneuvers him with jumps, flips and acrobatics striking him lightly with every move to demonstrate her superiority. These light strikes and slaps are beginning to anger him. But he does not give into this anger. The cheering is so loud you would think it is a professional sporting event. Then he has a revelation and accept his fate. Dajairia raises her leg straight in the air again ready to attack. He stands before her with his face bloody, his body sore, his eyes beginning to swell shut impairing his vision.

He knows if he continues in this condition. She will surely knock him out or tap him out. He didn't want to lose this way. Not like this, in front of all his comrades and leaders. So, like the Fearless soldier and great tactical Squad leader he is. He raises his hands for everyone to stop cheering. He turns to the booth where the world leaders are watching. The Russian world leader stands. Mikolai salutes him saying. "I have fought in many battles against many strong enemies I was the Victor in many of these resulting in my being here today, but I also stand before you now my comrades. I concede this fight today to this woman, This Arch Nun that I will respect for the rest of my life." He concludes saluting. Dajairia lowers her leg as president Andrei and his party return the salute. All the soldiers cheer and chant his name. That which he thought would be his most disgraceful moment, will be recognized as one of his finest. The Nuns salute Mikolai as the soldiers continue to cheer. He walks over to Dajairia and solutes her. She nods her head to him then gives him a big hug whispering in his ear. "You are by far the strongest man I have ever fought." Dajairia knew by telling him this his ego would not be bruised and his pride would be restored. Arch Nuns through the Grace of God always know the right things to say at the right time to be uplifting and encouraging when it is necessary. As president Andrei sits down, he looks over at Mother Teresa. She looks at him smiles and Winks her eye. Mikolai whom had very little respect for women, he who treated women so badly, he who thought their only purpose was to cook, clean and bare children has been humbled before the Lord on this day and from this day forth he shall hold all women deer and cherish them.

Immediately the next fighter is Antonia, representing Spanish Special Forces. She runs towards Dajairia performing an acrobatic Kick. Dajairia moves to the side to avoid being hit. The two women exchange a few punches and kicks before squaring off to size each other up and of course catch their breath. The soldiers cheer to encourage Antonia.

Dajairia attempts to raise her leg in the air, but Antonia attacks her quickly before she can do so. Antonia is fluent in many forms of hand-to-hand combat her specialty being ground grappling and submission holds. Dajairia makes Antonia look good before her leaders and the other soldiers before knocking her unconscious with a series of stylish kicks. The soldiers reluctantly applaud and the Nuns cheer. But before Dajairia can take a bow or even catch her breath.

Arsenio a large and very strong Brazilian fighter runs and kicks her to the ground. The soldiers cheer loudly as she hits the ground rolling and quickly gets up. With rage he throws very hard hits and kicks at her. There is no doubt in anyone's mind, he is definitely trying to hurt her, Bad! She out Maneuvers every attack. The harder he swings and misses the more fatigued he becomes. Dajairia punches him several times. Just enough to knock him off balance, but he is so strong and determined to harm her, he loses himself in his rage.

Dajairia finds this amusing and since her grandmother Superior gave her permission to win all three of her matches and demonstrate superiority she decides to take advantage of this again.

She lands a punch in the center of his body with just enough strength to knock him back a few feet. A blow which surely had taken his life if she so wished it. She takes this opportunity to raise her leg straight in the air. She is of course an accomplished ballerina; she has superb agility and this is just one of her favorite fighting postures. He moves in attempting to tackle her to the ground. She does two backflips then a no hand somersault kicking him under the chin. He can hardly contain his anger and in doing so he forgets himself and makes a critical error in his attack.

Dajairia seizes this opportunity to hit and kick him numerous times, knocking him to the floor.

He is exhausted and, on his hands, and knees attempting to stand. The soldiers root for him to get up. But before he can do so Dajairia executes a front somersault kicking him on top of his head as she lands. He falls flat to the floor unable to get up. His pride will not allow him to accept defeat especially from a female! As he struggles to stand, his arms tremble, his knees are weak and his vision distorted. The cheers of the soldier's echo in his head. He forces himself to one knee.

Dajairia sees his determination and slowly assumes an attack posture ready to strike. She can hear her brothers yelling. 'FINISH HIM'! Like the popular video game, they used to play. He manages to stand for a second before falling to the floor unconscious. Dajairia stands and raises her arms in the air as the victor.

The Nuns jump up and down cheering. The soldiers are in disbelief but they applaud her. Dajairia walks over to the soldiers holding one finger in the air. As she struts back and forth in front of them, stops, strikes a pose with attitude and flips her hair. The soldiers applaud, then they cheer and laugh but they give her respect for she has truly earned it. Some of the female soldiers come over to give her a hug. Many of the male soldiers Pat her on the shoulder and wink their eye at her. She runs over to her cheering brothers and sisters. Zach is holding his arms open she runs into his arms; He picks her up and Spins her around. President Andrei announces her as the winner over the loudspeakers. All the world leaders are standing and applauding. Mother Teresa remains seated and calm. President Ophelia attempts to contain her excitement but cannot help but to applaud and cheer. Josh rushes over to help the soldiers with their fallen comrade. Then rejoins the Nuns.

Mother Teresa stands and announces Elizabeth to be the next fighter. See struts away from her brothers and sisters like the sexy biker babe she is. The Reverend mother knows the soldiers will definitely rethink their fighting strategy. Mother Teresa will not allow any of the Arch Nuns to be knocked unconscious they are to tap out or concede only. So, she tells Elizabeth to win one, lose two of her matches and show no superiority but make them earn their victories. Elizabeth does exactly with her grandmother Superior asked of her. The next fighter Mother Teresa calls is Nevaeh. She tells her to win one, lose two matches and damage all her opponents but not too badly.

The soldiers are feeling very confident. She then calls her granddaughter the Sister Superior Maria. She tells her to win two show superiority, lose one.

Maria struts like a sexy supermodel walking the catwalk to meet her opponent. Most of the soldiers are captivated at how elegant she carries herself. Esmeralda another well-known female fighter representing French Special Forces. Slowly walks to Sister Maria. Like all the Nuns Maria has a personal fighting style as well. Her brothers and sisters jokingly call maria's

Martial arts 'Charisma-Fu'. Maria takes three sexy steps back and seductively stares her opponent down. Esmeralda is not intimidated by this at all she removes her jacket, she's wearing a tight-fitting tank top underneath and she is a very fit female fighting machine. She assumes her fighting posture and flexes her muscles. Maria assumes what looks like a flamingo dancing posture. Like almost everything she does it is magnificent to gaze upon. The soldiers admire her fighting stance so, they applauded and whistle for her. Esmeralda joins the Applause but as soon as she begins to clap her hands Maria viciously attacks her kicking and punching her with such finesse and style. It draws Applause from the world leaders as well. She dances around her occasionally stopping to strike a stylish flamingo dancing pose hitting her at will.

Esmeralda is overwhelmed Maria strategically avoids striking her in the face. But the blows she sustained to her body were very hard and precise. She thinks two of her ribs are cracked. The blows to her neck and back have her feeling weak in the knees. She is relieved the Nun whom stands before her in a flamingo fighting stance decided to stop hitting her. Maria stands still as a statue, Esmerelda begins to slowly bleed from the mouth before coughing up blood, falling to her knees and raising her hand to concede the match. While everyone is applauding and cheering the next male fighter, Adolf also from French Special Forces. Quickly runs out, jumps over Esmeralda and attempts to punch Maria.

She jumps in the air executing a spin kick with perfect form, knocking him unconscious before he hits the floor and sliding like a limp rag doll. As she lands and Spins in to another Flamingo fighting stance. Immediately ALL the Applause stops. Esmeralda looks at the fallen soldier shaking her head in disbelief and shame for he was her lover. The world leaders gasp in amazement.

"Oh my Lord" President Ophelia says covering her mouth. Maria is well aware of the rules. She is expecting the next fighter at any second and she is not disappointed.

The soldiers are beginning to strategically combat Nuns. Attacking them quickly between matches as not to let them catch their breath. Maria's third opponent 'pal yen chow' of China Special Forces. Runs at her then ducks just before her, causing her to throw a kick, missing him and throwing her off balance. He immediately grabs her and throws her to the ground. The two-wrestle exchanging submission holds until finally he gets to his feet as Maria attempts to stand, he grabs her one last time and throws her to the ground gaining a submission hold on her legs. She struggles to break free but deliberately does not. She finally Taps out; he is named the Victor and the soldiers go crazy. He helps Maria to her feet bows and salutes her.

President Ophelia turns to president Andrei saying. "I didn't think anyone would beat her"

Andrei nods his head in agreeance. Mother Teresa calls sister Anna to fight next. Telling her to win one lose two and to hurt one of her opponents. Anna decides to lose her first two matches and have a spectacular final win on the third. She then calls Joshua giving him the same instructions but to win his first match and show no superiority. He does what his grandmother asks making his opponents look like the Hand-to hand specialist they are. But the soldiers couldn't help making numerous female Nun jokes about him. Josh took the insults with a grin for God's Great purpose.

Both sides are tied for wins the soldiers are feeling very confident now. They also feel the time has come to gain some easy victories. They have been watching sister Donna throughout the competition. She appears to be frightened and reluctant to compete.
She also attempts hiding behind her brothers and sisters so the soldiers can't see her.
Mother Teresa then calls Donna. Her brothers and sisters Pat her on the back and shoulders for confidence. She slowly and nervously walks to meet her first opponent.
"You can do it Donna!"
Amira yells to her sister. All the Nuns yell words of encouragement to their sister. She stands in fear awaiting her opponent to walk through the crowd of soldiers. She appears nervous and frightened the soldiers talk amongst themselves for a brief moment. They decided this would be a good time for some of their lesser fighters to get a few victories under their belt.
"I'm just gonna go out there, put her in a gentle headlock, she'll immediately tap out and that'll be that. And don't rush out after her immediately like we do the other ones. Give her a chance to cry and get herself together in between matches" Anthony from Italian Special Forces says. All the soldiers agree.
He is not as large as some of the other Fighters. He's an information technology specialist but a warrior none the less.

He steps out and begins to quickly walk towards Donna. She steps back in fear. He puts his hands up in peace and explains to her that this will be quick and painless. As he Gets closer to her she punches him in the center of his chest with such Force his heart skips a few beats. He slowly backs away clenching his chest with his eyes wide open gasping for breath. Donna stands firm holding her fist extended, he falls to his knees choking and gasping for air.

Donna assumes a Shaolin Drunken kung fu fighting stance as he drops to the floor before her, slowly raising one hand to concede the match. The room is silent once again. The Nuns are falling all over themselves with laughter pointing at the soldiers whom cannot believe their eyes. Then Amira yells. "We call her, 'The Deceptionist'"
"Bet you wonder why we call her that" Zachariah adds.
"Because 'Decepticon' was already taken" Amira yells.
 The soldiers laugh with them shaking their fingers at the Nuns and quickly urge the next fighter to attack Donna. "Go, go, go" several soldiers scream. Two Soldiers quickly run out to fight Donna. The soldiers call one of them back. The other, Homayoun from Special Forces Afghanistan continues to run towards Donna then stops just in front of her hoping she would make a false move. But she does not, she just stands swaying back and forth in her Drunken fighting stance with a fierce look upon her face. He walks around her with caution looking her up and down. Still she does not move. He does not want to attack her from behind for that would be considered dishonorable amongst the soldiers. Everyone is cheering him and urging him to attack even the Nuns are telling him to attack her. As he slowly makes his way behind her. She does a front-flip kicking him under the chin very hard. He steps back holding his mouth which is bleeding profusely. He lets out a Fierce Battle Cry and runs to attack her. Donna being a stout woman defends herself using her two favorite fighting styles. Shaolin drunken style combined with light body skill techniques. As she flips, stumbles and somersaults around him out maneuvering and countering every blow he attempts to hit her with the angrier he becomes. He will not lose this match to this Woman's trickery. He believes once he gets his hands on her. He can then break a few of her bones. Something he will undoubtedly enjoy. He has become very tired and is now attempting to conserve his strength. He stops attacking her for a moment to catch his breath. Donna stumbles around

him in something she calls the 'Dance of the drunken Empress'. The soldiers who are very familiar with Shaolin drunken boxing. Watch in amazement as she executes these Maneuvers flawlessly, for a big girl!

They applaud and cheer her. The Nuns do the same for encouragement. Homayoun is beside himself with anger. He feels his comrades no longer have confidence in his ability to win the match. Donna stumbles and falls to the floor, rolls over then crosses her legs and begins to Fan herself with her hand, waiting for her opponent to attack. He approaches her with caution, anticipating an attack at any moment. Donna pretends to fall asleep. Homayoun is embarrassed.

"Stomp her!" One soldier yells.

"Get her in a submission hold, NOW!" Another screams. She rolls over and assumes the fetal position still pretending to be asleep embarrassing him further. He can bear this no longer so he attacks. He tries to kick her in the back while she is lying down. But she rolls over just in time and he barely misses her. He makes a second attempt she rolls backwards into a handstand awaiting another attack. He is hesitant and cautious of her now.

"She's upside down, get her, get her now!"

The soldiers scream. Donna flips herself over so she is now standing in front of him. She puts her arms behind her back, looking at him with a serious expression on her face. All the Arch Nuns can be very intimidating with Facial expressions, and Homayoun is beginning to feel this. With him being in Iraqi soldier, He would rather die than let this be known. Losing to a woman is one thing, losing to a woman this easily will surely be a blow to his pride. Donna is biding her time for she has not received instructions from her Reverend mother yet regarding winning or losing her matches. Since she has already defeated her first opponent with mischief and trickery, Mother Teresa tells her, she may win one more demonstrating superiority, but lose the last match and make it difficult. This will cause the soldiers to fight at their very best. Homayoun slowly assumes an attack posture, Donna dose the same. All the soldiers love Donna's fighting style for she does it so well.

He eases towards her. She executes two perfect backflips and a no hand somersault with perfect form. Everyone is very impressed with the Way She Moves. Donna can sense his fear. She takes one step towards him; he takes two steps back. She takes another step towards him hoping he would attack. She plans on allowing him to beat on her for a little while, for his self-esteem. She steps toward him a third time he punches her in the face with a right cross then a left hook and a kick to her chest knocking her to the floor. The soldiers cheer and scream instructions to him on what to do next. He immediately goes in to grab her. The two wrestle on the floor for a few moments before Donna gets him in an arm lock. He begins to feel the power of her legs as she squeezes his neck. He refuses to tap out so he continues to struggle. Donna will not let go of his arm he manages to get his other hand up to her chest area. Acting on Primal Instinct and being in great pain he instinctively grabs one of her breasts and squeezes very hard. Her eyes widen as she screams in pain looking down at him, his eyes do the same as he looks up and screams at her.

President Ophelia quickly jumps up and begins tapping and banging on the glass yelling at Homayoun. "Hey! what did I say!"

Most of the world leaders are lightly laughing to themselves. Donna breaks his wrist; due to extreme pain he taps out. Then she kicks him off of her. The two stand before each other exhausted and a little bloody. Homayoun quickly begins to apologize to Donna.

"A thousand pardons, I did not mean to- sister, please forgive me."

He then looks up to president Ophelia.

"I'm sorry madam president but with all due respect, you were not the one between those big pretty legs getting the

life squeezed from you. Again, my apologies."
Everyone in the room is now laughing, not at him, but with
him. Mother Teresa is shaking her head and lightly laughing
with the world leaders as they applaud. Donna is breathing
very heavily. She is giving the impression that she is
exhausted. She is bleeding from her nose and her eyes are
watered. She is also holding her side as though she were in
pain. The next fighter runs to attack her but approaches her
with caution. She takes a few steps away from her opponent,
still holding her side. Her opponent is an athletically fit
female by the name of Sophia from polish Special Forces,
GROM. She is reluctant to make the first move. She jumps as
if to throw a punch at Donna but kicks her in the face
instead. Sofia lands and immediately tackles Donna to the
ground. The soldiers go wild cheering Sophia on. Rather
than attempt a knockout. Sophia decides to beat Donna's
body instead, attempting to wear her down punching her
chest and ribs. The Nuns are cheering for their sister to get
up. Donna catches her arm and flips her over putting her in
an arm lock.

Sophia quickly gets out of it and jumps to her feet. But is
hesitant to immediately rush back in. After all the Nuns have
proven they can take it, as well as dish it out. Donna appears
to be exhausted and in pain. Sophia punches and kicks her
several more times backing her toward the wall. She stops
hitting her and immediately backs away in case Donna is
luring her in for the kill. Sophia is fighting very wise against
the Nun referred to by her siblings as 'The Deceptionist'.
However, she has been hitting and kicking Donna with all
her strength. She is certain the Nun is truly in pain and
cannot take much more. So, with Extreme Caution she
builds up her confidence and attacks the Nun once more.
She fakes Donna out with a kick and then grabs her
throwing her against the wall. The two-struggle attempting
to get a hold on each other. They lock against the wall
holding each other attempting to catch their breath. Sophia

breaks Donna's hold, giving her two quick punches to the face. Donna responds with a hard kick to Sophia's chest knocking her back. Before Sophia can raise her hands in defense Donna runs at her jumps and knees her in the nose breaking it. Sophia drops to her knees in pain. Donna lands and falls to her knees as well. The soldiers are cheering and screaming for Sophia to get up. The Nuns are doing the same. Both women manage to stand. Everyone can see Donna appears to be in great pain. So, she raises her hand to concede the match.

Sophia raises her fists in the air as the victor. She's in great pain and her nose is bleeding. But she is tough and like every Elite Tactical Squad Member. She has a high tolerance for pain. Donna has earned her respect as a warrior and she assists the Nuns as they tend to her. Although the soldiers are losing the competition so far, they applaud Donna as a sign of respect. After witnessing the determination and willpower of the Arch Nuns the soldiers realize they are very formidable opponents. The soldiers take a moment to talk amongst themselves regarding their strategy for the remaining matches. They decide to bring out only the strongest and best fighters for the remainder. The female soldiers inform the men that they will not be excluded from the selection.

Mother Teresa calls her grandson Zachariah. He removes his shirt and eagerly runs out to meet his opponent. Before the soldiers can make a choice. Keeva a female Soldier representing Irish Special Forces runs out to face Zac. Mother Teresa tells her grandson to win one match only but hurt his opponents and make them earn their victories. She runs to Zach but stops just in front of him. The soldiers have learned their lesson about being the first one, rushing in and attacking Arch Nuns. She holds out her fist, Zack taps her fists with his, she assumes a Japanese karate stance Zach responds with a Muay Thai kickboxing stance.

The two fighters slowly Circle each other. When one of the soldiers yells to her.

"Come on Keeva don't let the sister get the first hit, knock her on her ass."

Zach stops for a moment laughing and turns to the soldiers to tell them to cut it out and to remind them he's a guy Darn it! Keeva takes the opportunity to Tackle Zach from behind throwing him to the ground face first. His nose and mouth are bleeding and he sustained a knot on his forehead. The two-tussle on the floor attempting to gain submission holds, as the two fighters jump to their feet, she quickly grabs a handful of Zacks hair and pulls him to the floor again. Holding on to his hair, she punches and knees him repeatedly while they are on the floor.

Her determination to win by any means necessary is amusing to him. He decides to allow her the victory. But first he's going to return the bloody nose and mouth, with INTEREST! He does just that before allowing her to grab his hair again pulling and punching him. He allows her to put him in a headlock before tapping out and conceding the match.

The soldiers cheer loudly as she gets up spitting blood. One of the soldiers yells to the Nuns.

"You're not the only ones that can win with trickery mate" Referring to Keeva attacking him from behind while he was distracted.

Zach stands awaiting his next opponent. Keeva runs over to the Nuns and takes a bow in front of them everyone is laughing and enjoying themselves. The Nuns hug her and Pat her on the back as a sign of respect and love. She runs back to her soldiers many of them give her high fives. She is very excited and breathing heavily. She says loudly to her fellow soldiers.

"Mates! Grab em by the hair and treat em like a lassie!" (Meaning a little girl)

All the soldiers cheer and hold both Fists in the air. In all the excitement the soldiers didn't realize they are giving Zach a chance to catch his breath as if he needs to.

Amira steps forward waving her arms in the air to get the soldiers attention.

"Maybe, just maybe, You guys might not have wanted to say that hair pulling strategy out loud." Putting her hands on her hips.

"I'm just saying!" She concludes shaking her finger at them and walking away.

"Alright already! I'm well rested and reloaded" Zach interrupts touching his fists together.

"Let's get on wit it, Laddies!"(Meaning little boys) He concludes in an Irish accent urging them to send the next fighter.

Another female fighter attempts to run out but the soldiers grab her and whisper in her ear they're going to send a big strong fighter out and that she will definitely be next. She agrees, the soldier then send a strong fierce male fighter called Za'heem out to face him. He walks out slowly staring at Zach attempting to intimidate him the two touch fists and immediately attack each other. Zach makes short work of Za'heem with his Muay Thai kickboxing. As Zack is turning around slowly with his fists in the air claiming his victory. The soldiers quickly push the female, Lisa from American Special Forces who was anxiously awaiting her chance to fight. For the brief moment Zach's back was turned he allows her to kick him in the back of the neck, knocking him to the floor. Repeatedly punching and kicking him trying to grab his hair. He does not allow this and returns several punches and kicks of his own. She sustained massive bruises and a few missing teeth but Zach allows her to gain a leg lock on him. He Taps out and she is named the victor the soldiers are ecstatic. They have gained the lead once again. But are concerned, they yelled their strategy and the Nuns will not make hair grabbing easy.

"The little 'Arab chick' was right! We should've kept that hair pulling thing to ourselves!"
One of the soldiers says to another. Mother Teresa calls upon her granddaughter Amira. The soldiers all clap their hands whistle and point at her in anticipation of beating her to a bloody pulp. The soldiers truly want to put a hurting on poor little Amira. They do not Harbor animosity or contempt toward her. They just want to shut her loud mouth! In the name of fun! A task they will see is more easily said and thought of, than actually done. Mother Teresa gives her the same instructions as her brother Zach. But to show superiority on her victory.
Amira being a fan of theatrics and the cinema. Struts out holding both Fists in the air and
decides to give them quite a show for this first match.
 All the male soldiers are pointing at her, running their finger across their neck making the Cut Throat sign laughing. The Nuns are not surprised that after all these years their little sister can still get on people's nerves to the point that they just want to smack her. But it is one of her most lovable traits and they wouldn't trade that for anything.
Surprisingly to the male soldiers none of the female soldiers want to fight her. Not that they are afraid, but many of them have taken a liking to her, many of the male soldiers feel the same way. They greatly respect all the Arch Nuns now. But! She's got to go down. Amira stands ready with her arms crossed, pouting her lips and tapping her foot on the floor waiting.
"Alright, Alright, Alright, Alright" she says quoting the actor Matthew McConaughey.
"Come on now don't everybody rush out at once who's gonna come put Sister Amira to sleep?" She concludes as she assumes a Shaolin kung-fu fighting stance. Alfred a large British male fighter from British Special Forces walks out to face her.

"Don't take this personal Sister, but I may enjoy this just a little!" He says.

"I understand" she replies. "Be gentle with me it's my first time" she continues winking her eye and blowing him a kiss.

"What kind of Nuns are these?" A male soldier yells from the back of the crowd.

Alfred is a strong fighter specializing in grappling and very hard hits. He throws several hard punches. Witch she easily evades.

"Tag! Your it" she shouts as she executes a perfect sidekick hitting him in the forehead knocking him back and to the floor. She holds her leg in position then raises it higher holding it with her hand. He looks up at her, slowly stands, shakes his finger at her and smiles.

"You'll have to do better than that little one"

Amira quickly lowers her leg, stomps her foot, turns around and starts to walk back to the Nuns screaming. "That's it! I'm going home, I can't hurt him. He's too big, too strong, too Superior to little ol me. I'm just a Girl!"

The soldiers are confused. They're Whispering among themselves wondering if she's really walking away. The Nuns are also confused. She turns back towards Alfred walking very fast. With the signature intimidating expression of the Arch Nun upon her face. She yells at the top of her lungs. "I AM WOMAN! HEAR ME ROAR!!!"

She hits him with a Flying Phoenix kick demonstrating excellent form. Then attacks him with speed style, and such finesse the soldiers cannot help but cheer. The female soldiers are going crazy cheering for her to spite the dirty looks from their male comrades. As she attacks him, she recites phrases parents often use when chastising their children.

"DIDN'T-I-TELL-YOU-TO-CLEAN-THIS-ROOM-AND-TO-STOP-MAKING-FUN-OF-GIRLS?" The Nuns are laughing hysterically and rolling on the floor the soldiers are laughing as well. The female soldiers are jumping up and down with excitement as they cheer.

"LOOK-WHAT-YOU'MADE-ME-DO!" She continues reciting as she punches and kicks him to the floor. "THIS-HURTS-ME-MORE-THEN-IT-HURTS-YOU! Who's your mommy?"

She concludes stopping his head to the floor. He is beating, he is bloody and he is humbled but he is not angered. He is so strong, not even the beating she gave him can keep him down. For she did not hit him with all of her strength.

He stumbles to his feet Dazed and Confused but smiling. He raises his hand to concede the match. While everyone cheers Alfred hugs Amira and slowly turns her around with her back facing the soldiers. The moment he lets her go another soldier, Johnny from American Special Forces. Sucker punches her from behind hitting her hard in the ear. With her ear bleeding he continues to punch and kick her with all his strength. She allows him to hit her repeatedly, only preventing him from grabbing her hair.

"Grab her hair!" The male soldiers yell and scream to him. One of the female soldiers yells to the male soldiers. "You guys sound like a bunch of ghetto girls screaming instructions during a fight on 'World-star hip-hop'"

Amira fights her way to her feet, spins around evading what would have been a very hard punch. and smacks him across the face very hard. The smack was so hard and loud, it left her handprint on his face. His eyes begin to tear both from the impact of the hit and his anger.

"That's right!" Amira says holding her ribs bleeding from her mouth and ear.

"Squirt some tears, you little punk!"

The Nuns and the female soldiers burst into laughter.

"I can't believe she said that." President Ophelia says laughing with Mother Teresa.

Some of the world leaders join in the laughter. Mother
Teresa Smiles, rolls her eyes and says to them.
"All of you here, have one of 'THOSE' too much to handle
children as well."
The leaders laugh and agree with her. johnny circles her
slowly the print of her hand is clearly visible as he moves
around her. Everyone is still pointing and laughing then he
rushes in, grabs her and slams her to the floor. He attempts
punching her but she prevents him from doing so. She
deliberately reaches up grabbing him by the throat allowing
him to gain an arm lock on her.
It was his intention to dislocate her arm and he did. She
screams in pain and taps out, conceding the match.
   As soon as Johnny releases her and stands, she relocates her
arm as the third male fighter Alex from the U.S. Navy Seals
rushes and attacks her while she's still lying on the floor. He
does not attempt to punch or kick her. He simply puts her in
another arm lock and she of course Taps out immediately.
The male soldiers cheer him, the female soldiers shake their
heads and reluctantly applaud. He very gently releases her
and lifts her to her feet. "Can you stand Sister? "He asks.
"Barely, but I must" She replies as she stumbles to her feet.
The female soldiers push their way through the male
soldiers and run to her.
"Get your hands off her!" Antonia says pushing Alex away.
"That was uncalled for and fu#ked up what you guys did to
her!"
By this time all the soldiers are now standing around Amira,
one of them says.
"We just wanted to give back a little deception and trickery
of our own. We didn't mean to hurt anyone that BAD!"
Amira raises a hand for everyone to settle down.
"Why aren't your brothers and sisters coming over here to
see if you're all right?"
Lisa asks with attitude.
"The answer is right in front of you, do you not see it?"

Amira asks her.

"No! I don't"

"Because the Lord sent me you!" A calm look falls upon the female soldier's face. She being of Christian faith believes the Lord is a man so she responds.

"Yes, yes He did!" Putting her arm around Amira to assist her. The Nuns stood on their side of the room gazing upon that which their sister has brought together with the GRACE OF GOD.

And they know that it is GOOD! Most of the soldiers walk with Amira helping her as she returns to her brothers and sisters. President Ophelia turns to Mother Teresa and says.

"She is quite special" The Reverend mother replies with a smile. "Quite special indeed my friend, quite special indeed!"

The soldiers returned to their side of the room and prepare for the conclusion of the matches. There is but one Arch Nun left to compete. Sister lin with her hands on her hips she slowly walks out to face her first opponent. The tension is high among the soldiers for these final matches. Mother Teresa tells her to win the first match show superiority lose two. A female fighter named Metiko from Japanese Special Forces

walks out to face her the two women assume they're fighting stances. They stare at each other for a few seconds then engage in Fierce combat. Metiko desperately tries to punch and kick Lin. She Paces herself as not to make any false moves giving the Nun the advantage. Sister Lin's personal favorite fighting styles are Dragon, Eagles claw and various cat styles. This is the reason her siblings refer to her has the 'Alley Cat' cause she loves to use her very strong fingers as claws when fighting. Lin is simply evading her opponent for now hoping to ware her down. Metiko attempts a karate side kick against the Nun. Lin jumps back avoiding the kick and lands in a Shaolin Eagles claw fighting stance. Everyone cheers both women for their form is flawless although no one has actually landed a blow.

Lin like her siblings stands still as a statue in her fighting stance with perfect form. Metiko slowly moves closer to her. "Pretty birdie! come on don't be scared now!" She says to Lin smiling and winking her eye to let her know she's just having fun. Lin jumps high in the air at her, Metiko attempts to dive under her but is not quick enough. Lin does a front twisting somersault making the sound of the American bald eagle as she claws into both of Metiko's shoulders, tearing her shirt and into her skin. Lin did not claw her too deep she didn't want to damage her for life. But Metiko's shoulders are damaged and bleeding.

Lin decides not to use her eagle's claws against Metiko she does not wish to tear her to shreds. So, she hits her repeatedly with good old-fashioned punches and kicks knocking her to the floor. Metiko is having trouble attempting to stand. Lin gives her a few moments to catch her breath and get herself together. While Metiko is struggling with this Lin decides to turn around and walk towards the soldiers. As she approaches, they slowly back away, holding their hands up, laughing and shoving each other jestfuly. Lin walks right up to one of the biggest soldiers in the lot. A large red-headed man of Irish descent. They call 'HULK HOOLIGAN'.

She looks up into his face, points at him and says licking her lips. "YOU-ARE-NEXT!"

"Oooooooh" Most of the soldiers say Softly.

She backs away from him slowly never taking her eyes off of him. The soldiers can see Metiko in the background desperately attempting to stand. She is on her hands and knees trembling in pain. Lin with her eyes still gazed upon Hulk Hooligan performs five backflips and a no hand double somersault landing with one leg on Metiko's back slamming her to the floor.

"Daaaaaaaaaam" most of the soldiers scream.

Metiko is a medic and is certain her spine is broken; she cannot feel her legs. Lin does a half backflip into a

handstand holding the position. With all the grace of an accomplished gymnast. She slowly lowers herself near Metiko's face. Gazes down upon her and Whispers.
"I apologize my friend. It was not my intention to harm you in this way." Metiko made a critical mistake fighting today, unknowing to her comrades she hurt her back in the gym working out a few days ago and did not tell anyone of this. She was in no condition to fight today especially against such a superior opponent. The Lord helps those who deserve a second chance and Metiko has saved many lives on the battlefield some of which have go on to do the Lord's work. So, she shall receive a blessing on this day. Metiko looks up with tears in her eyes.
"you will now witness the power of the Lord, Stand!"
"I, I, I can't!" She responds bleeding from her mouth Sister Lin Definitely broke Metiko's back.
"Believe in the power of the Lord and you shall stand! Your wound has healed." Lin assures her. Lin flips herself upright and helps Metiko to her feet. Metiko made a poor decision fighting which could have cost her dearly!
Mother Teresa said no one will be permanently damaged and by the power of God, No Soldier shall sustain permanent injury on this day!
The soldiers are unaware of the severity of Metiko's injury they are still yelling for her to fight not just stand there exchanging cooking recipes. She stands in front of Lin with tears in her eyes but has not yet conceded the match. She is deliberately taking a few moments before legally doing so. She believes she is allowing Lin to catch her breath she looks at lin, bows her head and very gratefully says thank you.
Metiko has experienced firsthand the power of our lord God and from this day forth she shall TRULY know that 'GOD IS GOD'!
She is aware of Lin's challenge to Hulk Hooligan he is an absolute Terror in combat, and she believes Lin is going to

need every ounce of her strength. Metiko concedes the match. As she slowly walks away, she looks back at Lin several times, lin is pacing back and forth like a leopard in a cage staring at hooligan. The soldiers are oblivious to the Divine Act Which just transpired. They continue to applaud both Fighters. Some of the female soldiers can sense Metiko is a little different, In a good way.

Hulk Hooligan does not run out to attack Lin like the other Fighters would. He stands in the crowd with his large arms folded and asks Lin if she is ready. The soldiers are applauding and cheering their champion. The Nuns are jokingly chanting.

"LIN-YEOH-HAO, LIN-YOAH-HOI, LIN-YOAH-HOI"

Hooligan walks out and takes off his shirt off, he is extremely muscular and towers over Lin.

The two fighters assume their fighting stance Hooligan is in a traditional boxing pose. Lin is in a standard fighting pose. Then suddenly Lin screams like an alley cat and changes her fighting stance to Shao Lin tiger style, spreading her fingers like claws.

This does not phase nor intimidate him the room is completely quiet. Although Lin is considerably smaller than him and ASSUMED to be WEAKER. The soldiers are not taking any chances they've seen what her fingers can do. She slowly moves towards him he does not move. The soldiers are becoming concerned. Even the female soldiers are alarmed because Lin is getting closer to him. So, they scream and yell to him.

"Don't let her get close MATE!" Yells one.

"She'll scratch your eyes out! And you're a sniper" Screams Antonia.

"Give her a ball of yarn" Mikolai yells. The Nuns are laughing and pointing at the large man whom stands like a mountain. But is reluctant to throw the first blow.

"You're not afraid of my little sister are you, mountain man?" Josh yells. Hooligan cuts his eyes at Josh, smiles and Winks his eye at him with confidence. He is not about to make the same mistake Mikolai made underestimating an Arch Nun. However, he did underestimate her proximity. She quickly lunges towards him screaming like an alley cat.

Clawing both sides of his face and kicking him in the chest causing him to stumble backwards. As he stumbles Lin jumps into a forward roll clawing the front of his legs, from his belt to his knees tearing the skin just a little again screaming like an alley cat.

"Oooooooh NO!" Most of the soldiers scream putting their hands on their heads.

He reaches out to grab her, she evades him and scratchers him straight down his back tearing his shirt open, he arches his back in pain and quickly turns around in an attempt to grab her.

She ducks under him and scratches him across the abdomen and chest again now tearing the front of his shirt open. He is slightly out of breath and perspiring causing the scratches to sting. But he is a Tactical Squad Commander and this pain is nothing to him. Unknowing to Hooligan Lin is in full control and can easily kill him at any time if she wished. She is simply playing 'cat and Mouse' for now. He is a patient fighter with a high pain tolerance and Lin intends to test this to the fullest. Slowly he inches his way towards her with caution, Extreme Caution! Lin kicks him hard to the knee causing him to fall forward onto his hands and knees.

"Oh Noooooo" Navaeh yells.

Lin jumps on his back mounting him he quickly throws her off. But before he can stand, she grabs his buttocks, tearing his trousers as she scratches into his buttocks exposing them. The expression on his face was priceless as he stands holding his buttocks. The Nuns are falling over themselves with laughter. The soldiers are shaking their heads in disbelief, they fear this match is lost. You can clearly make out the claw marks on his buttocks through his torn pants. He is a good sport looking at Lin and shaking his finger at her

saying. "BAD KITTY!"
The mighty Hulk Hooligan Looks as though he were put
through a shredder. He himself finds this amusing as well.
During this match Lin has become quite fond of Mr.
Hooligan as she shall call him from this day forth. She
decides he has endured her shenanigans with the best of
spirits. She feels this to her siblings and they all agree. She's
now formulating an exit strategy that will allow him the
victory and honor him. She throws a few kicks, Punches and
scratches at him which he easily blocks and evades. Then she
lunges at him once more allowing him to catch her by the
throat. He spins her around a few times to gain momentum
before slamming her hard into the wall. She hits the wall
with such force it leaves an imprint of her body, she
Immediately goes limp for a few seconds as she slides to the
floor.
"Ooooooooooooooooh!" Everyone says almost collectively
the leaders included.
"Oh dear lord! I think she's dead." President Ophelia says
with great concern.
The soldiers are cheering and urging Hooligan not to go
near her. She is now sitting on the floor with her back
against the wall he steps back quickly, waiting for her to
attack. The Nuns are quietly watching but laughing amongst
themselves in their minds.
Lin struggles to stand using the wall to assist her.
"Be careful mate! Don't Go Near her." One soldier screams,
then everyone starts screaming and yelling. "Their tricky
ones, these Arch Nuns careful now"
"Don't fall for it Brother." Even the soldiers with missing
teeth, split tongues and broken jaws are attempting to shout
instructions to him. Hooligan's mother didn't raise him to be
a fool. So, he keeps his distance but expresses sincere
concern. "Are you all right sister?" He asks. "Please take a
moment to 'GATHER YOURSELF' sister I will not attack
you." With all the noise and shouting in the room. She can't

believe he actually said 'GATHER YOURSELF' to her. She quickly looks up at him and asks.

"What did you just say?"

"I said I won't attack you!"

Mother Teresa and the rest of the Arch Nuns simultaneously feel an amusing little message to Lin. 'GATHER YOURSELF LIN-YOAH-HOI'

Lin cannot help but be tickled by the joke so she laughs telepathically with her family.

She is pleased he has chosen not to attack her. She also knows to be careful conceding the match while she is still on the floor and against the wall. She looks up at hooligan then turns her head and looks at the soldiers whom are eager to send the next fighter, puts a wicked smile upon her face and quickly says she concedes the match. Then waves her hand to the soldiers to send the next fighter. The soldiers look into her eyes and assume she is attempting to trick them. Instead they take this time to cheer Hulk hooligan and make jokes and jest with the Nuns.

"They're are not falling for it, sorry sister" Sophia yells to her. Then the crowd of soldiers' parts as a very large Samoan Soldier from U.S Delta Force slowly walks toward her grinning from ear-to-ear. The room becomes quiet once again anticipating the start of the final match, Amira yells loudly. "REALLY! Someone tell that Samoan ta stop Growing!" The room erupts with laughter for a moment.

"Be careful Fetu!" As he is known amongst the soldiers.

"She's a dangerous wounded Tigress now"

He walks straight up to her, she attempts to attack him, he evades and grabs her. throwing her to the floor then quickly smothers her with his weight.

She allows him to make short work of her. She quickly Taps out and he helps her to her feet.

The soldiers go crazy hugging each other, jumping around, cheering and running around the gymnasium. The Nuns applaud them and go crazy right along with them. Although most of these Elite Tactical Squad members will never admit it. But this was indeed the best and toughest fight of their lives and they loved every moment of it. The world leaders hug each other shake hands and exchange opinions. They are all most pleased with today's event. If they had any doubts or concerns regarding the Arch Nuns physical abilities they are now dismissed. How they will be applied in the real world remains to be seen. They have a long and hard road before them and the leaders of course will closely monitor their progress. Mother Teresa asks for everyone's attention so she may conclude the event.

"On behalf of the Arch Nunhood of Mother Hymiriam. I would like to thank everyone for attending today's event." She says to the leaders then addresses the soldiers and Nuns. "To the soldiers of the world's most Elite Tactical Squads, you are truly great representations of your country's military might. You are superb Warriors. I applaud you and I welcome you with open arms to the world's most powerful and influential law enforcement agency to ever exist. Welcome! you are the first UNITED NATIONS AGENT'S".

Again, the soldiers cheer loudly hugging each other jumping and dancing around. Then she addresses the Arch Nuns.

"To my grandchildren, you are the world's first Arch Nuns. You have been trained and conditioned since birth. You've had countless physical competitions throughout your life. But you have never been called upon to defend yourselves as you were on this day. These soldiers put forth a great effort to do harm unto you. To physically hurt, damage and break you. If they we're successful, this agency would have been reconsidered today."

The room is silent she continues as a tear runs down her face.

"Not only did you honor and represent your teachers well, to whom many of which are no longer with us. You made me the proudest grandmother to ever live. I think I can speak for the leaders of the world and the soldiers as well, when I tell you my grandchildren. You fought with great inspiration and determination."

Most of the soldiers that can still stand raise one fist in the air cheering and slowly walking toward the Nuns. As they approach, they welcome them with open arms and those who's ribs are not too badly damaged exchange hugs. The leaders look upon this and they are pleased. All the leaders give a short speech before Mother Teresa gives final instructions.

"It is my great hope, that all of you." Referring to the Nuns and soldiers. "May consider yourselves comrades now."

"Yes ma'am" They all respond. She then gives them some news they were not expecting.

"Wonderful, I am so glad to hear that. Because all of you will be staying the night right here in this room." Everyone becomes very quiet.

"I know many of you are hurt some more so than others. Going 24 to 48 hours without professional medical attention is nothing new to any of you."

She pauses for a second.

"However! This will bring you all closer together and strengthen your bond. You will be given the same medical supplies that you receive when you are in the field. So, you may tend to each other's wounds, fellowship and nurture what I hope will be a growing friendship."

Many of the soldiers who did not compete in the physical competition are well-trained Medics the Arch Nuns are also well-versed in the medical field as well. Everyone is still quiet listening to the Reverend mother some of the wounded soldiers are shaking their heads in disbelief. They were looking forward to that professional medical attention and hospitalization.

"Also my children, tonight you shall feast. You will have whatever your heart's desire. For those of you who cannot open your mouths or chew my apologies." Everyone Applause and cheers. Mikolai stands and yells. "VODKA!

Mother Teresa VODKA PLEASE!" All the soldiers agree and applaud.

"Whiskey, Scotch?" Shouts one soldier.

"And some Brandy?" Says another.

Then the Nuns join in making Maria their spokesperson.

"Oh, Grandmother Superior may we have wine?"

Elizabeth adds. "Please! grandmother we need a drink after getting the crap kicked out of us by these elite soldiers"

"Yeah, we can't let them celebrate alone!" Dajairia shouts.

Zac whom is lying on his back in pain rises his hand and says. "It's Miller Time Grandma!"

Everyone is begging and pleading with her at this point. She looks to some of the leaders they shrug their shoulders and smile. She looks down upon them shaking her head, then waves her hand saying. "Very well, as you wish my children, you deserve it, I will allow it."

They were brought their medical field packs to address their wounds they were also brought much food and of course the alcohol they so desired. Mother Teresa tells them they will not be monitored. Their privacy will be honored and she will see them tomorrow afternoon. The soldiers and Nuns United assisting one another with their wounded. They ate, drank, shared stories and there was much unsupervised merrymaking to say the least!

1/3/2028 At the Mansion of the president Bae Wei of
Singapore. He and his family, his mother, wife, her sister,
and his three daughters ages five, seven and fifteen are
preparing for dinner. They are expecting a dinner guest. A
friend of his Dwayne a representative of Somalia who is also
reconsidering his relationship with the woman they know
only as 'Vil'e'. She has them convinced she is only a
messenger, a representative of a much larger more powerful
group. They are about to realize it is she that is All-powerful
and they shall know her true name given unto her by her
one and only husband.

Like all presidential leaders their homes are virtually
impenetrable. Eve has access to many blue prints of the
current world leader's homes. Many of her children were
and are currently world-renowned architects and were
involved in one way or another in their design and
construction. Bae Wei's home is guarded by private and
Military security teams. It is also equipped with the latest in
surveillance technology.

But it will not be enough. For 'Something Wicked' his Way
Comes. Approximately one mile above his home is a stealth
helicopter. It will serve as the command center for this
operation run by 'Midnite Endeavor' Her sisters Zsazsa and
Ka'ren are on the ground accompanied by four African and
Asian strike teams. 'Midnite Endeavor' with her military
influence has access and can Assemble strike teams in a
moment's notice.

She and her team bring the blueprints of the home up on
their monitors. They have a ten-minute window to kill
everyone on the grounds and in the house before outside
military forces are dispatched due to Communications
failure when she jams their radio transmissions.

'Midnite Endeavor' counts down. 5,4,3,2,1. She engages the
I.D.A.C device. Before the outside guards realized they were
unable to communicate with each other they were already
being killed by the strike teams. They were very silent,

precise and coordinated.

Everyone in the house is unaware as to what is going on. The teams cover all the entrances to the house. Midnite Endeavor who now has complete control of the house and all its electronic systems. Except the safe room which has a manual door that must be physically locked and unlocked. She strategically opens electronic doors for her teams to enter the premises. Once inside they systematically kill all the security guards and staff.

Only six remaining guards are in the dining area with Bae Wei, his family and guest. They dine and Converse in an enclosed dining room as they enjoy their meal. Bae Wei's 5-year-old daughter must use the restroom so a guard is asked to escort her. As soon as the guard opens the door. The room goes completely dark. ZsaZsa stabs the guard through the heart with her sword.

Aston turns the lights on, the guard falls to the floor, she steps over his body and slowly enters the room accompanied by a Strike Team. Pointing their guns at the guards. They order them to lower their weapons. The guards refuse to do so as they shout back and forth to the Strike Team each ordering the other to lower their weapons and surrender.

During this commotion Bae Wei guides his family and friend through a door that leads to a long corridor. They run as fast as they can to get to the safe room. They were so frightened they didn't notice that no one was pursuing them. A firefight erupts in the dining room. The Strike Team and guards take cover as they attempted to shoot each other. ZsaZsa utilizing her 3% speed and strength advantage. Takes this opportunity to very gracefully and stylishly kill many of the security guards with her swords her personal weapons of choice. But only she could and would bring knives to a gunfight!

Her accompanying Strike Team cannot believe what their eyes behold. A woman of her age that moves with such

speed, precision and strength. Many of her Strike team members were mesmerized at how gracefully she moves. To the point of nearly losing their lives due to the fact that they were unable to pay attention or focus on what they were doing. As the debris and smoke Fades from the room.
The strike teams stare as if they were dreaming.
ZsaZsa can be seen standing in a stylist fighting pose holding her two swords unscathed.
"Come Now!" She says with her perfect English accent. "You would think one had never seen someone killed before."
Bae Wei and company quickly turn a corner. As they approach the safe room door, they are met buy another Strike Team. Unarmed, exhausted and frightened they immediately surrender.
Bae Wei begins to plead with them not to kill him and his family. They are ordered to be silent by the Strike Team.
ZsaZsa followed by her team slowly walks up behind them. They turn in fear, Bae Wei moves his family behind him. ZsaZsa walks closer to him.
"I know you" Bae Wei shouts.
"Of course you do my dear! I am All the Rave" She responds fixing her hair.
"Please don't kill us, I'll give you whatever you want"
"I wouldn't dream of killing you. my dear, I do believe I've done my fair share of killing for the evening. Besides darling I already have everything!"
Bae Wei is relieved he believes his family will be spared and this being only a message, but sent by who. Of course, he begins to suspect his Simoleon friend standing beside him. Then a sexy soft laugh can be heard and the sound of high heels walking down the corridor.
"No one! And I mean No one speaks to our mother as did you, And LIVES!"
Ka'ren says holding a custom handgun in each hand. All her guns are custom-made and colorized to match her outfits.

The team members move to the side as she struts past them as though she were in a music video. Many of the strike team members are males and cannot keep their eyes off her. "Who are you, Are you behind this? TELL ME WHO YOU ARE!" The Simoleon leader demands. ZsaZsa orders the strike teams to leave the corridor. Then Bae Wei realizes who is behind this. "Your mother is 'Vil'e' the plunky for the Unseen, powerful world group we've heard so much about. Don't get me wrong that group has done some incredible things which is why we've considered doing this in the first place but your mother, we have absolutely no confidence in AT ALL"

"Well! aren't you the unappreciative disrespectful one." ZsaZsa interrupts.

"I have a good mind to kill you myself! But what kind of lady would I be? if I went back on my word."

Ka'ren grabs Bae Wei under his chin turning his face toward her saying.

"Our mother that you have no confidence in and spoke to so disrespectfully. Is the greatest of ALL women and you don't deserve to be in the same world as her!"

She pushes him away with such force he hits the wall behind him with a loud thump. looking him up and down with discuss she continues. "Our mother is The Mother of All, our mother is God's first female, EVE!"

Bae Wei looks at her holding his hands in front of him in an attempt to calm her down. Agreeing with every word she says to spite how absurd it sounds to him.

"Just ask your mother" Ka'ren says cutting her eyes at Bae Wei's mother.

"She's about to know everything"

"What do you mean?" He asks. Ka'ren quickly points her gun at his mother's head and pulls the trigger. The children scream in terror, his sister attempts to calm them and Bae Wei is in shock.

"When you die, you know everything!" She concludes laughing sadistically. She then goes on shooting every last one of them, Saving Bae Wei for last. He gazes upon his fallen family; He does not know if he is hallucinating but he can vaguely make out a vision of Hymiriam standing with open arms among his fallen family. A sense of calm falls upon him as he falls to his knees not to beg for his life, like so many before him have done. Only to have Ka'ren kill them anyway. But to ask the Lord to forgive him for bringing this tragedy upon his family and so he prays aloud. She allows him a few seconds to do this.

"Are you finished" She asks. He looks up at her weeping for his family, but with a stern look in his eyes tells her. "I regret that my family had to pay the price for my arrogance and mistakes.

For this I hope the Lord has Mercy on my soul. But I take comfort now, in knowing I made the right decision by signing the contract to invoke the Arch Nuns. Tell your mother to take heed, repent and reconsider her acts of world Destruction. For Hymiriam 'IS TRURLY THE VOICE OF GOD'!"

Ka'ren looks at ZsaZsa smiling, ZsaZsa looks back telling her.

"Get on with it my dear! we're pressed for time."

Ka'ren shot everyone else in the head for a quick death. But for Bae Wei she shoots him near his heart so he may die slowly. Then she and her sister turn and leave. As he lay dying, he now knows that Hymiriam is the mother of Jesus and she is 'THE SECOND COMING'. He also knows now the woman he knew as Vil'e. Is indeed God's first female Eve!

ZsaZsa, her sister and the strike teams leave the mansion. They meet at a designated undisclosed airstrip where there is a large privately owned helicopter. All the strike teams enter the helicopter.

Ka'ren and ZsaZsa await their sister Midnite Endeavor' to retrieve them.

Midnite gives orders for the helicopter to depart she is landing to pick up her sisters. The aircrafts depart and fly out toward the open ocean where a private yacht is waiting. As they approach the yacht. Midnite releases poison gas from canisters she had installed in the other helicopter. It kills everyone on board including the pilots. The craft goes down in the ocean. She waits until it is completely submerged before she detonates a bomb on board to assure there are no survivors. No one knew of their mission and of course they are expendable.

She does this to ovoid satellite tracking of heat signatures or boats in the distance that would have seen the flames.

Midnite is an excellent stealth assassin and tactical commander, she seldom fails.

They do not have to report back to Eve. Her instructions on this were simple and absolute!

"I charge you with this task go forth and FAIL ME NOT!"

It is very rare for any of her children to fail her when she gives instructions directly to them. The circumstances would have to be extreme. The helicopter lands Ka'ren and ZsaZsa exit then it departs. 'Midnite' will be returning to Africa until her mother requires her Services again.

ZsaZsa and Ka'ren go to the bar for drinks. ZsaZsa due to her world-renowned status in the fashion industry is seldom asked to go on any missions by her mother but relishes the opportunity when it arises. Ka'ren asks her sister if she would like to join her tomorrow at a meeting regarding a new shipment of girls. This excites her and she accepts the invitation. She loves to cover her face and be mysterious from time to time.

"I'd love to Darling" She responds eagerly with a devilish grin. "Perhaps something will go wrong and I can kill some of them" The two laugh and enjoy their drinks as though life is a party.

Back at the mansion of the recently deceased president Bae Wei. Military forces close the area. The vice president junlong and military leaders are on the scene. Their first priority is to contain the situation and fabricate a story for the media. There are many investigators on the scene. Being that many were killed by sword the investigators are not ruling out the 'Japanese Yakuza'. But vice-president junlong whom was also invited to dinner this evening at the mansion. But his wife had taken ill. knows it was something else, something a hundred times worse.

Because of the I.D.A.C device there is no video footage. He and Bae Wei were not only reconsidering their relationship with Vil'e and the organization they believed her to represent. But were also attempting to convince others under her influence to do the same.

Eve had emails sent out to everyone and anyone who is important in the entertainment industry, business world and all political leaders in Singapore. Including junlong and the deceased Bae Wei. They are sent by one of ZsaZsa's companies. Announcing a large extravagant Gala for tomorrow night.

This was done several hours before the incident at the mansion so junlong will have no choice but attend to keep up appearances. The investigators are shocked and intrigued at how such a strike could have been done with such precision. They suspect it was multiple Insiders that were deliberately killed during the attack. They are fearful that they may never know. If junlong knows what's best for him. He will do well to use his newly appointed presidential power to assure this remains a mystery for all time!

On the morning of 1/4/28 the yacht Pulls to Keppel Marina in Singapore. ZsaZsa and Ka'ren receive instructions from their mother regarding the Gala. At a moment's notice ZsaZsa can call upon many Hollywood A-listers and important people in the entertainment industry to come together or attend whatever function or purpose she needs

them for. Many of them are her siblings and children of Eve.
ZsaZsa is well known for throwing Galas like this with very
little notice and always having a massive turn out. She refers
to them as her 'Flash Pop Parties' and through social media
the word spreads instantly and flash mobs rush to them.

 The paparazzi hang out at the marina in hopes of getting
photos of celebrities. ZsaZsa is well aware of this. Although
she does not mind a good photoshoot. Her sister on the
other hand must be a lot more discreet. Ka'ren changes her
makeup, puts on a wig, sunglasses, Beach hat and long Sun
gown. Then blends in with her sister's staff as not to be
noticed. Staying as far away from ZsaZsa as possible
because all the attention and cameras are focused on her.
It's like her sister said back at the Bae Wei's Mansion 'She is
All the RAVE' and does indeed enjoy the spotlight. Of
course, there are some reporters from fashion and media
magazines.

"Miss La'more, what do you think of the new Arch Nuns?
"One reporter asks.

"I'd like to sign some of the female Nuns to a modeling
contract." She replies looking into the camera.

"The men on the other hand are an atrocious fashion mess,
but very handsome I might add."

She responds in a typical ZsaZsa La'more fashion, waving
her hands about as she speaks.

"What are your thoughts about the light that shined down
on Hymiriam? "
Asks another.

"Coincidence darling!, simply a coincidence, I do wish it
were me standing there."
Everyone laughs with her.

"Now! they'll be no more talk of Nuns, I'm sure they have
their hands full, as do we, preparing for tonight's Gala."
The reporters Focus their remaining questions on fashion
trends and of course the list of attendees for tonight's Gala.
Ka'ren slips away and discreetly Fades into the crowd

changing her appearance once more. Being a high-level
undercover CIA agent, she's a pro at blending in. ZsaZsa's
on the other hand her MI6 status requires her to be seen,
heard and noticed as much as possible. Ka'ren calls her sister
to give her the details regarding the meeting this afternoon.
ZsaZsa is very happy and looking forward to the meeting.
Like the assault on Bae Wei's mansion she adores wearing
flamboyant apparel that compliment her exotic fighting
styles and of course wearing a mask to hide her famous
world-renowned face.
This is how she earned the code-name of 'Madame Butterfly'
and it happens to be her favorite Opera. Ka'ren sometimes
jokingly calls her sister 'Batgirl' or 'Mothra' The beautiful
giant moth from the Godzilla films. If anyone other than
family attempted to refer to her as this, she would most
certainly kill them. She like many of Eve's children do not
take well to insults from Outsiders.

Vice-president junlong is stricken with grief and rage he
and Bae Wei have been very close friends for a long time. He
could almost understand if it had only been Bae Wei, but to
kill his entire family and household was Despicable.
Singapore and the world are unaware of Bae Wei's death
and for now the Singaporean government wants to keep it
that way. If this is the group Vil'e represents. junlong
decides he will not let any of them get away with this most
disgraceful Act.
He will lure them into a false sense of security with
Singapore, then expose them for the monsters that they are,
and in doing so gain the esteem respect from the world
governments. The Arch Nuns and United Nations agency
included. He still has a few world leaders on his side that
resent being under the influence of this unspoken, unnamed
group and its female representative they know as 'Vil'e'.
  He informs his advisers that he will be briefly attending
ZsaZsa's event. As to not raise suspicion. He or Bae Wei are

always honored guest of Miss La'more and the public would be concerned as to why neither was in attendance. The story they are giving the media for now is food poisoning. But of course, the internet is going viral with its own hypothetical interpretations regarding all the military, police and ambulances at the mansion.

The Singaporean government will do a good job at keeping the situation under control. Security detail for Junlong and his family have quadrupled. He cannot tell his family why but for now he knows they are safe. Before he enters his home, he must pull himself together as not to arouse concern from his wife.

Ka'ren arrives at her hotel The Mandarin Oriental there she is met by her Entourage. They are mostly mid-level female and male LGBTQ drug dealers from some of the bigger cities in the United States. That is her temp base of operation for now. They consider her to be their Queen and will do whatever she asks. She will be joined later at the party by some of Singapore's high-level crime Lords. This is the company she keeps around the world for the CIA. But work has very little to do with it. Arms dealing, human trafficking, drug dealing, assassinations, and the list goes on. if it's something illegal she has everything to do with it. This is what she does to serve her mother and she truly enjoys every second of it. There are always special daughters and sons held high in Eve's favor they will always have unlimited resources for their positions in the world and when Ka'ren, ZsaZsa and the lot Parish. Their very young successors are currently being groomed to take their place. They go to their penthouse suite which has a stunning View, a private pool, a master bedroom and several smaller bedrooms.

"Alright everybody I'm a little tense rite now and need ta release da tension. Y'all feel me?"

Ka'ren says with a hip-hop, street like tone. Because sometimes she has to communicate at their level and Style of speaking. Everyone's eyes light up with joy for they know they are about to partake in one of their favorite pastimes, A sex orgy. This is one of Ka'ren's vices and she indulges herself quite often.

ZsaZsa is staying at the Fullington Bay. As she and her staff enter the Lobby her body guards assure the picture talking has stopped. When ZsaZsa says that's enough she truly means that's enough!

She has several high-profile males she dates from all over the world. She's been seen and photographed jet-setting, dining and kissing some of them. There have been more than a few marriage proposals but she lets them down easy.

  It's 1:30 pm at the UN building in New York. Mother Teresa walks down a hallway accompanied by staff members of the many world leaders whom will be shadowing her often and a very large medical staff. They enter the gymnasium where the Nuns and soldiers spent the night. It appeared as though a tornado went through the room, there were empty liquor bottles, beer cans, unfinished food scattered about, clothing and bandages thrown everywhere and the stench of what can only be described as cheese and coconuts in the air. It was very reminiscent of the aftermath from a rock concert. Mother Teresa and the aides stand to one side so the medical staff can tend to the injured. Standing in the middle of all of this drinking coffee with Smiles on their faces are.

Dajairia, Josh, Maria, Anna, Navaeh and Elizabeth. The rest of the Arch Nuns are lying on cots with the rest of the wounded and will be treated for the wounds their grandmother Superior gave them instructions to sustain. The Reverend mother walks through the soldiers as she does many of them awakened and some walk with her. Many of them are either too hung over or too hurt to notice she is even there. She walks over to her granddaughter Lin. She is lying on her back wearing a neck brace, she looks up at her grandmother Hooligan runs over and Neels beside her taking her hand.

"Mother Teresa, please forgive me I didn't---"
She puts her hand upon his head and assures him
everything is alright.
Lin jokingly says to her grandmother in a crying little girl
voice and pointing at Hooligan.
"He tried to put me through a wall. Get em grandma!"
The soldiers laugh lightly unknowing to lin they deliberately
have her lying right under the imprint she made in the wall
where hooligan threw her.
Josh feels to Lin 'If I had a cell phone sis, this would be the
funniest picture'
Since no one can hear them but each other. Lin responds.
'And I would make you swallow that cell phone brother of
mine. It's a good thing no one can harm us cuz, Amira got
BEATDOWN.'
All the Nuns laugh amongst themselves Amira included.
Mother Teresa says to her, patting her on the shoulder.
"Settle down Lin, after all you did try to tear the skin from
his bones and Shred a friend of his."
More of the soldiers are beginning to awaken enjoying the
laughter and jesting. Lin lays there pouting then notices she
is lying under the imprint in the wall and yells for someone
to move her from this wall, NOW!
Mikolai approaches the Reverend mother. "Good morning
Mother Teresa, I was wondering if I could have word with
you?"
"Of course, Mikolai walk with me." He has spoken with the
Reverend mother many times over this past year. But this
time he is very nervous. "It's about the team selection if I
may, I know you told us it was going to be random"
"Am I to believe you do not wish to be placed with my
granddaughter Dajairia?"
"No, Mother Teresa on the contrary. I would very much like
to be placed with her!"
Mikolai of course is unaware he is speaking to a Guardian
Archangel and has been doing so for the past year and by

doing so she knows what's in his heart.

"I don't mean to ask for favoritism and I would not think of it to be such, but I am hoping you would consider this for me please." He concludes as he starts to fall to his knees before her.   She quickly stops him and tells him. "Do not Kneel to Me, Mikolai. You will take no knee except in prayer. Have you prayed for this Mikolai?"

"I am not a praying man, Mother Teresa but believe it if you will, I did Mother Teresa I did in my own way. I only hope that if there is a God like you speak of, He listened."

She looks him in the eye for a moment. He feels as though she is looking directly at his soul. She puts her hand upon his shoulder and says to him.

"I will consider it, Mikolai I will consider it."

"Thank you Mother Teresa thank you very much and please, you can keep between us yes?"

She looks at him for a few seconds before motioning with her hand for him to go away. He Grins and quickly walks away to rejoin his comrades. There are many sprains, cracked ribs, missing teeth, bruises and black eyes of both Arch Nuns and soldiers. The Arch Nuns do not feel any pain and can heal themselves immediately at any time. But Mother Teresa tells them to allow their wounds to go full term so the doctors may follow up over the coming weeks and months.

   The doctors and Medical Teams give Mother Teresa their assessment of those who require immediate medical attention and those that can be patched-up and go on with the day. With more than a few of the soldiers. Zach, Donna, Amira and Lin as per their grandmother's instructions will go to the medical wing of the building so the doctors can further evaluate their condition. Mother Teresa wants this done so there can be documentation of wounded Arch Nuns. The doctors will have x-rays and blood samples to run tests on and study. Aside from the DNA samples all the world leaders have on the Arch Nuns and every last member of their teams. This will further confirm and conclude that the Arch Nuns are human. This is one of the many strategies Mother Teresa uses to prevent controversy. As the Medical Teams prepare to move the wounded Amira feels to Lin. 'I bet I can act more hurt than you sis.'

'Are you kidding buff, I'm gonna make em think I'm dying'

'lin, I'm gonna give em the impression they have to do emergency surgery on me'

Everyone is talking, laughing, and enjoying breakfast which was bought in with the medical teams. Due to the amount of people in the room it is very noisy.

Mother Teresa raises her hands in the air for everyone to be quiet. This took a few moments for everyone to notice but the room slowly quiets down.

"Everyone I ask that you be silent. So, I may pray for those that require medical attention."

With the exception of the medical staff. All the soldiers no by signing the contract and joining an Arch Nun Team. It is mandatory to be silent and bow their head when an Arch Nun commands a prayer. Their individual religions are respected but they must realize they are part of something special and act accordingly. Failure to do so will void their contract. All the soldiers bow their heads. The presidential aides, doctors and medical staff do the same as a sign of respect.

"Oh Lord Our God! please watch over these injured ones, please aid those that tend to their wounds and please Oh mighty god. See them to a speedy recovery Oh God in Jesus name I pray Amen!"

Together everyone in the room says "Amen". The Reverend mother is pleased so she smiles and nods her head to everyone. A pair of orderlies begin to move Amira. She screams loudly and grabs one of them tearing his shirt. Everyone becomes immediately concerned and attempts to run to her but there are too many. The doctors rush in and urge everyone to move back. They make way for Mother

Teresa to go to her granddaughter. The soldiers assist her in kneeling at her side. She takes Amira's hand and presses it to her forehead as though to pray. Everyone becomes silent once again. Then she feels to granddaughter for all the Arch Nuns to hear in their heads. 'IF I HAVE TO STOP TIME AND TAKE YOU BACK TO THE DEVINE ELYSIUM YOUNG LADY --- You will regret it!"
'Grand Mother' Lin interrupts.
'You know Buffie Loves movies and she was just going for an Academy Award for her portrayal of a woman in great pain.' All the Nuns are laughing inside as everyone stands around concerned about Amira.
'I can't believe you're 30 years old' She feels to her grandchildren before releasing Amira's hand. The soldiers help the Reverend mother to her feet the doctors assure her they will do everything they can for her granddaughter.
The medical staff begins to move the injured out of the room. Mikolai walks over to Josh and Pats him on the shoulder.
"It's funny when your sister Lin does the little girl voice, no?" Josh looks at him laughing and replies. "Brother, you haven't heard anything yet my friend."
Mother Teresa continues to look at Amira and Lin as the orderlies take them away because they are attempting to compete with each other for the sympathy of the doctors. Mother Teresa shakes her head and smiles to herself. She then announces for everyone to go to the designated area for placement. There is much excitement in the air as the soldier's shower and prepare for team placement. The Reverend mother tells her grandchildren to clean up and meet her in the assembly area. Two hours later everyone gathers in the assembly area. As the soldiers enter the room Mother Teresa is standing with her remaining Arch Nuns at her side and Sixty-two Representatives of the world leaders. The soldiers are quiet and eager to learn which Arch Nun

Team they will be a member of. Two highly decorated five-star generals enter the room one Russian one American. All the soldiers immediately stand at attention and salute them. The generals congratulate them and inform them of how proud their leaders are of them. They also remind them of how the world will be watching them. All the soldiers were taught how to properly conduct themselves in the presence of Mother Hymiriam, Grandmother Teresa and their Arch Nun Commanders. From this day forward they no longer have to stand at attention before military generals, unless instructed to do so. Their immediate commanders are now the Arch Nuns. Many of the soldiers thought they would never amount to anything more than secret soldiers destined to die in the jungle fighting in private Wars. The Lord works in mysterious ways and it is the Lord that will watch over and guide them. This is yet another step on their road to redemption. For all the Unspeakable things they have done for their governments the Lord still and always will love them. They will know this and they will know peace. All they must do now is open their hearts and accept it. FOR GOD'S GREAT PURPOSE!

Behind the soldiers is a large monitor which now displays the names and team assignment. The generals salute the soldiers and give them the last order they will hear from them. "About face and check the monitor." They eagerly approach the monitor like high school students during S.A.Ts. Mikolai attempts to be calm. But his heart is racing, he too is anxious to find out which Arch Nun he will serve. Deep in his heart he hopes it is Sister Dajairia. Some of the soldiers are secretly hoping they are not chosen for Sister Maria's team. They've only spent the one night with the Arch Nuns. But some are under the impression she would be a bossy, self-centered 'A#s Hole'. Ever since the Arch Nuns were teenagers, they would tell their Sister Superior that she has a way of looking at people that indicates she's an 'A#s Hole'! Mother Teresa would tell her to pay no attention to her siblings. She's not an 'A#s Hole'! She's a 'NUN' and a Sister Superior as well. Over all everyone is pleased with the selection and placement and they rejoice. Mikolai is selected for Sister Dajairia's team. The Reverend mother thought it would be amusing to select some of the others that seem to have personal grudges against certain Arch Nuns to serve on their teams. Mikolai continues to play it cool amongst his comrades. He would like them to believe that he is somewhat disappointed. But deep inside he is jumping for joy and as giddy as a school boy. The generals and presidential aides mingle with the soldiers Whom Shall now be referred to as Arch Nun Teams. A.N.T for short followed by a number Between one to ten Representing the Arch Nun they serve. Mother Teresa motions for her grandchildren to join everyone and rejoice. Some of the soldiers notice Mikolai is watching Sister Dajairia attempting to be discreet as though he cannot keep his eyes off her. Many of them know him and hope he does not Harbor any hidden animosity toward her. She did indeed give him one embarrassing beating.

Mother Teresa raises her hands for all to be silent. She seems to do that a lot when people are having fun. As she would say.

"I am a Nun, I'm supposed to ruin fun. it goes with the territory". She informs them they have food and drink in the next room and they will be spending the remainder of the day and evening preparing for tomorrow, the day they are set out upon the world. Before everyone goes to lunch, She informs them someone would like to speak to them.

Hymiriam appears on the large monitor. "SALUTATIONS A.N.Ts" She yells with joy.

The A.N.Ts cheer, applaud and yell her name.

"I would like to say welcome and congratulate you on your recent career promotions. I know you're all famished and I won't take much of your time. So, know this." She pauses for a moment just to look at them and smile.

"By myself I am nothing. It is the Power of the Lord which uses me to work the will of God.

There is no freedom without the laws of God. The things that go on in this world, man inflicting his law on to society, God did not mean for this to be so. I hang my head in sorrow for the things I know you will Witness on your journey, the decisions you will make and the things you must do. But always remember. It is the Lord who executes judgement not I, nor you. Humanity shall be ruled by law not by the will of man." She raises her arms, looks toward the sky and continues.

"And so I ask, Oh God with a strong hand, I ask that you guide us on our paths."

She concludes bringing her hands down into the prayer position closing her eyes and bowing her head. The A.N.Ts paid close attention to every word she said. For they are great words of inspiration. They are accustomed to military motivational speeches. But they have heard nothing like this before, spoken directly to them. Each A.N.T member feels these words deeply in their heart as though she were speaking to them personally.

They do not know whether to applaud or cheer so they look to each other for a brief moment then do both, they are military that is how they respond. Her Image Fades on the monitor as the A.N.Ts continue to applaud, whistle and cheer. The Arch Nuns applaud with them. Mother Teresa the aides and generals smile and cover their ears. They enjoy a meal before being transported to Langley Air Base, given their uniforms, and joining their commanding Arch Nuns.

They will be moving all over the world at random. But for now, while some of them are still hospitalized. Mother Teresa gives them Specific Instructions.

Joshua, Dajairia and Nevaeh Will go to Russia for a few days. Maria, Anna and Elizabeth Will stay in the United States. Mother Teresa her Arch Nuns and the presidential aides stand at the door way of the cafeteria. She tells all the A.N.Ts to form a single line. So, she may hug each and every one of them as they exit the cafeteria. The presidential aides whom many are female become very excited for they get to put their arms around big strong military Heroes. Many of them look to each other with excited eyes grinning to themselves. The first A.N.T member steps to Mother Teresa she gives him a big warm hug then releases him. The A.N.Ts have not felt this loved or respected in a very long time and they most certainly welcome it. Immediately one of the female aides' steps toward him but is stopped by one of the generals. The excitement fades from their eyes as the Reverend mother continues to hug each member exiting the room.

 At the Sea Aquarium south west, One of Singapore's hottest party venues. Zsa Zsa's Gala is well underway. it is a who's who of Asia. With many of the country's most popular celebrities in attendance. Some of the world's top male and female DJs are performing.

Zsa Zsa's parties always host the most epic dance battles. Dancers come from all over to compete for her one and only $10,000 first prize.

The massive thrust from the bass in the music is so loud it can be heard outside and into the streets. Where there are hundreds of people still attempting to get in and just be seen in the area. The news media is all over the event covering every possible angle. But it is overshadowed by news from a few days ago. The start of the United Nations Agency. Since Zsa Zsa's parties draw diverse crowds of all ages, Eve

occasionally attends, this is one of those occasions. She
arrives by private helicopter. The party is in full swing.
Ka'ren and her Entourage are there enjoying the atmosphere,
drinking and dancing. Some of Asia's most notorious and
Powerful crime Lords are present as well, some of the young
extend salutations to her. The elder crime Lords gaze upon
her in disgust as she dances, feels and kisses women. But
they know to keep those feelings deeply suppressed.
Secretly appointed president junlong arrives at the party
with a very heavy Undercover security Force.
The venue contains a five-star restaurant which is being
used as a VIP area.
Junlong goes to this area to avoid the crowd he orders a
drink and his security detail discreetly blends in. He sends a
couple of security officers to find Zsazsa so he may be seen
with her, have some quick photos and leave. He is definitely
not in a festive mood. Nor does he wish to be disturbed or
engage in conversation with anyone, when a well-known
Asian action film star approaches him. He sits at the bar
beside him. Junlong not wanting to be rude looks at him
smiles and tells him he's a fan of his movies. The actor
thanks him then tells him.
"I'm not really into older chicks but that very attractive older
lady over there has been giving you the eye."
"I'm not interested I'm married" Junlong replies staring
down at the bar, not giving so much as a glance in her
Direction. The actor puts his hand on junlong's shoulder and
with a firm squeeze. looks him directly in the eye and says.
"I don't think she's asking you to come over, I think she's
telling you. if I were you, I'd do it."
He looks over and sees Vil'e sitting alone at a corner table.
With a cold, piercing stare. she looks right at him then
motions for him to come over to the table. He quickly
finishes his drink, smiles then walks over to the table. He
doesn't want to give the impression that something is wrong
and he is not yet sure if she or the organization she works

for had anything to do with Bae Wei's death. So, he is cordial and sits with her.

"Vil'e, a pleasure to see you here. Surely an attractive lady such as yourself is not here unescorted?"

She smiles and sips her drink.

"You flatter me sir? if you weren't married. Well I'll leave that to your imagination and your morning shower." She says with a wink. "I spoke to Bae Wei the other day and he told me the most interesting things." She continues looking down stirring her drink. "I apologize, where are my manners, would you like a drink my deer."

He accepts her offer and orders a drink. "You say you spoke to Bae Wei the other day what did you two discuss if I may ask?" She begins to answer but the waitress comes over to bring the drink. She pauses for a moment then tells him. "He had the audacity to accuse me of allowing the United Nations Agency."

"How absurd!" He says.

"That's what I thought, he then went on to tell me he represents a group that stands against the organization I represent."

"REALLY!"

"Indeed, he said they were reconsidering our business together and seriously considering separating themselves from us."

"I was not aware of such things."

"I'm glad to hear that junlong. Could you imagine what my associates would do." Then a serious expression falls upon her face and she looks directly at junlong and says in a soft sexy voice.

"Nothing human in their house would survive!"

At that moment he knew it was she and her organization that was responsible for his good friends' death. He remains calm. But like so many since the beginning of time. He really wants to jump over the table and strangle the life from her with his bare hands. She continues to stare at him without saying a word. He quickly finishes his drink to ease his nerves and orders another. She slowly leans forward and asks him. "Why don't you give our friend Bae Wei a call. So, he can reassure us of his loyalty?"

Junlong hesitates for a moment then replies.

"It's late and he wasn't feeling well. I'll be sure to give him your regards."

"Of course" she says with a soft smile. "Certainly, if you became the leader of this country, junlong you would do a far better job of serving my associates. I'm sure you've already seen what happens to those who don't!" And like the Great Pharaohs of Egypt her rhetoric is absolute and unchallenged.

Before junlong can respond. She stands and walks away like the TRUE QUEEN she is. As she leaves the restaurant, he notices half the people follow her.

No doubt they were her protectors he thinks to himself and there were quite a few of them.
Singaporean Security Forces know not to approach their leader unless they are called. He sits at the table alone for a moment as the hostess brings him another drink.
ZsaZsa and her friends enter the restaurant she approaches him apologizing for her tardiness and explaining of course how everyone wants to speak to, and take pictures with her.
"Are you feeling okay darling? you look as though you've seen a ghost." She says with concern sitting down beside him.
"No, no! " he replies giving her a hug. "Just a little too much to drink. you always throw one hell of a party and have the best bartenders."
"I do understand, darling. they're from some of the hottest clubs in Singapore half the drinks they make aren't on the menu." The two engage in small conversation so photographers can snap pictures for tomorrow's newspapers. Then junlong says his farewells and tells her he's calling it a night. he has a big day tomorrow.
"Undoubtably!" She says giving him a hug and kiss on the cheek.

Hymiriam is working in Cambodia with the Peace Corps. For now, she is among the many who are assisting in poor Villages throughout the country but that is about to change. She is assisting the doctors and nurses with the children whom many are very sick. This particular Village has been stricken with famine and many diseases for a long time. The medicine deliveries are few and far between and when they are delivered sometimes the soldiers confiscate them. Leaving very little medicine for the surrounding villages. On a cot in the corner lie a native woman and her 8-year-old son, she has named Paul. After his father whom was American and died from illnesses earlier this year.
Both are very ill and dying the doctors and nurses are

tending to as many as they can. But they are overwhelmed. Soldiers have confiscated much of the medicine and food from the last delivery for their troops. When they feel they need or want more they come to the Villages and take it by force. This is the way it has always been. This is just one of the many perils' charity organizations face. But do not speak of. The villagers and staff of course know Hymiriam as Mary, a very common name. As Mary walks by the cot Paul and his mother are laying on Paul reaches out and grabs Mary's hand, clenching it tightly. His mother who is called 'Chamroeun' which means prosperity. Attempts to restrain her son but is too weak. She apologizes to marry but she can only speak softly.

"I'm sorry I don't know what has gotten into him." She says Breathing heavily holding her son who lies in her arms and on her chest. She holds him as tight as she can urging him to release Mary's hand but the child will not. Mary kneels beside their cot; she moves the hair from Chamroeun's face and wipes her forehead with a cool rag.

"It's okay" Mary says to her Softly. "He may hold my hand as long as he wishes"

The child will not remove his eyes from Mary's face. He is becoming very weak and can barely move or speak. Mary moves closer to him. He releases her hand and puts it upon her face. Looking directly into her eyes he speaks with absolute clarity. "I know my mother will take very good care of you."

He says pointing to Mary. "For she shall serve you well!" Chamroeun looks down at her son, he looks up at her. She Whispers. "I love you my son"

His hand slowly slides down Mary's face, she catches it, kisses it softly and with a smile he passes away. As Chamroeun weeps the room slowly grows dark. She believes now she is to take her last breath. She slowly turns to Mary. She sees the light of God illuminate from her; at that moment she knows. She sees her son standing under her spread wings.

Her breath quickens, the paleness of her skin Fades, her slowly Beating Heart becomes regular and stable as her body becomes strong. The brittleness of her hair softens, the lesions around her face and upon her body are No More. She holds her son's body close to her as she sits up and turns toward Mary. Mary stands back so she may put her feet upon the floor to stand. As she stands, she falls to her knees, not from weakness but from sorrow. Mary joins her on the floor the two embrace with the child's body between them. Then Chamroeun looks into Mary's eyes and with the deepest sincerity says to her.

"Oh, Great Hymiriam, mother of Jesus. I know my son has gone home and is in the arms of the Lord. it would be a great honor to serve as your apostle. Will you accept me, I recognize and accept you as Hymiriam Christ!" The lord has just sent Mary her first Disciple.

There is much despair and commotion in the room. No one has taken notice of the two women kneeling. This is something that is all too common in villages such as this, the sickness, the deaths, the hopelessness and the constant praying. The Lord has now answered their prayers and they shall know the Lord's blessing from this day forth.

Dr. Andrew Stephens an older gentleman in his mid-forties and once-prominent and renown surgeon from London. Whom gave up a prosperous career and millions of dollars to do humanitarian work. He liquidated all of his material possessions and wealth and gave all of it to numerous Charity organizations around the world. He is a good man and travels to many villages to help in any way he can. He notices the two women kneeling and runs to them. He is familiar with Chamroeun and her son's condition. He knew Paul did not have much longer to live and he insisted Paul be allowed to stay with his mother till the end. He helps Chamroeun and Mary to their feet. Chamroeun is still holding her son's body. The three slowly walk through the

chaos as others are tending to the sick. As they exit the medical tent three military vehicles enter the village. It is Commander Bona
and his soldiers. They are rude to the villagers and demand more medicine for their troops. Dr. Stephens approaches them with his hands above his head in a non-threatening manner. He asks that they leave the village and explains they have no more medicine to give, there are people dying here. "This young boy" he attempts to explain pointing to Paul.
"Has died only moments ago please I beg of you. Leave me what little medicine I have to help these people and let this woman mourn her son"
The villagers are frightened and know not to look at the faces of the soldiers.
Chamroeun holds her son's body tight against her chest. Mary has her arms around Chamroeun comforting her. Commander Bona punches the doctor in the stomach then in the face knocking him to the ground. His soldiers Point their guns at the villagers so they will not interfere. The villagers as always are petrified and too scared to move. Shots are fired in the air as a warning. All the villagers immediately drop to their knees pleading with the soldiers. Dr. Stevens is being kick repeatedly by Bona while he is lying on the ground. Through all of this Mary and Chamroeun remain standing. Bona stops kicking the doctor and looks at the two women and tells the villagers.
"If you don't give me what I want this woman will join her son"
He draws his gun and points it at Chamroeun's head walking toward her.
The doctor tries to stand but is pushed back to the ground by the soldiers. As he gets close to Chamroeun, Mary steps in his path, he strikes her across the face and points his gun at her. As she turns her face back towards him, she allows herself to be recognized by all.

She looks the Commander in the eyes and says to him. "It is your choice, But I will ask you to leave this Village and let these people live in peace!"

Bona is the first to recognize her. He immediately drops his gun and falls at her feet. His soldiers witness this and slowly lower their weapons. The doctor is hurt badly but he stands, wipes the dirt from his face, clears his eyes and looks upon her and his heart nearly stops. Although he is in a foreign country. He still has a satellite phone and internet access and is well aware of who she is and the events of the last few days. The villagers on the other hand have no internet access and can barely read or write. They saw no television broadcast and are oblivious to the events of the past few days. To them she is simply Mary, one of the many who came to help care for the sick.

They know nothing of the United Nations Agency or the Arch Nuns and at the moment are very confused. They have never seen Commander Bona fall to his knees and weep. The villagers begin to whisper among themselves, the soldiers are now joining their commander on their knees. Bona remains in the humble position weeping with his head touching the ground. He is praying harder than he has ever prayed in his life. Mary looks to the doctor and holds out her hand for him to join her. The doctor's heart is filled with rage there is only so much a good man can take and he had seen this consistent behavior in soldiers in villages many times. He is a little reluctant to take Mary's hand he believes she is going to pray for the soldiers and he does not believe at the moment he can pray for those partially responsible for so much death. He does not wish to be disrespectful so he takes her hand. A couple of the elder women in the village go to Chamroeun to take Paul's body from her arms. Mary holds Chamroeun's hand. Then the three of them kneel over Bona whom has not stopped weeping nor lifted his head from the ground.

"Oh God I thank thee for guiding these three souls in to my

path. I shall do all I can with the power bestowed upon me. I will teach them, Oh God! so they may teach others, I will love them, Oh God! so they may love others. I thank thee Oh God! for allowing me their companionship we shall go forth and Proclaim Liberty so all may know your Greatness"

As Mary concludes Bona slowly looks up into her eyes. She steps back and slowly opens her arms. His eyes now behold the luminance of God's light that seems to radiate from her body. The doctor looks upon her and sees the same and knows he too has been chosen.

He and Chamroeun assist Bona to his feet and escort him to Mary's embrace. She, who could have easily summoned just one of her Arch Nuns to destroy Bona and every military force in Cambodia.

Demonstrates to thy Lord God that she is truly worthy of the Divine Grace bestowed upon her.

God will test Mary many times on her journey and she is confident the Lord will be pleased. The villagers are not shown the Divine Light of Hymiriam. But they are beginning to feel in their hearts who she truly is. And through this knowledge they understand why Mary is so kind to Bona. As they walk to attend a short service to honor Paul. Bona hangs his head in shame Mary puts her arm around him to walk with him they walk behind dr. Stevens and Chamroeun. "I will follow you and give my life in service to Christ" Bona tells Mary. "But my heart hangs heavy I have done so many terrible things." He looks at Mary and with the saddest of eyes he asks.

"Why did you choose me? I have lived nothing but a life of sin - and I hurt people."

"That, Bona is why I have chosen you, We Are All God's Children and God loves us so much none of us are perfect we all make mistakes and all are welcomed in the arms of the lord."

"I would like for God to have mercy on me but I think I'm nothing but a stranger to God!" Bona says.

"There are no strangers among those who seek God's mercy"
Bona looks at Mary and a pleasant look falls upon his face.
He whose heart was filled with hate, rage, destruction and
contempt. Shall now walk with Hymiriam and spread the
gospel of the Lord throughout the lands. FOR GOD'S
GREAT PURPOSE!

During the service for Paul, Mary is asked to speak. She
speaks not of Paul. For he was one in God's plan she now
speaks for the many. She tells them this Village shall no
famine, sickness and despair no more. The men who were
once Bona's soldiers now stand amongst the villagers. She
asks that everyone close their eyes, bow their heads, join
hands and prepare to receive a great blessing. And with the
power of God she cures the entire Village of sickness. As
everyone begins to open their eyes and look around. They
see no more sickness amongst their friends and family. They
see vegetables that were planted just this morning in full
bloom. The villagers are amazed they hug one another and
cry tears of joy. The laughter of healthy children can be
heard. The doctor and Chamroeun walk amongst the
villagers hugging and laughing with them. This is a Joyful
Noise that everyone takes comfort in. Bona approaches the
soldiers that carried out his treachery and inflicted pain
upon others.
"Bona you look so different." One of them says to him.
"You look as though you know peace" Says another.
"I have seen the error of my ways and will spend the rest of
my life atoning for it. I have not only done great wrong to
these people, but I have done wrong to many others. I have
also led you astray my brothers. But if you believe in and
give the Lord a chance you too, my brothers will know joy."
The soldiers gather around him and listen as they always
did.
"We will do anything for you Commander, anything!"
"Do not seek fulfillment for me, my brothers. Seek it to be
better men and to serve God."

The Soldiers throw down their weapons and Swear to protect these people in service to the Lord. Mary enters the medical tent with the doctor, Chamroeun and several of the villagers. Those that were too sick to move or attend the service now know the power of the Lord. Mary and her three new apostles are escorted to one of the military vehicles. The entire Village comes to see her. To gaze upon the new Messiah and most importantly give thanks to the Lord. As the vehicles depart, the villagers fall to their knees and pray. For the world will be a better place.

In an underground parking lot in Bangkok four SUVs are parked. Standing outside the vehicles are Malik Haze, an African American, mid-level and well-known pimp in Bangkok. He is waiting with fifteen of his gangster crew members. They are awaiting the arrival of Ka'ren whom they know as Leggz Diamond. It is 10 a.m. and she is already a half hour late. But since she is making a five-million-dollar purchase of young girls her tardiness is accepted by Malik. His younger brother Ha'zeem however is a bit agitated.

"Yo! Malik, man I'm Fu#king Sick of Dis Bit#h. Being Fu#king late all da time we need ta handle Dat"

Ha'zeem says out loud smoking a cigarette.

"Dis ain't Nutting Nu ta you Dis bit#h always late, whoever she works for pay good though"

Malik answers in a low voice. Then the group spends the next 20 minutes discussing all the sexually perverted things they would like to do to her. How they would drug her, make her an addict and turn her out on to the street to make money for them.

Two motorcycles followed by an armor SUV pull into the garage. A few seconds later the Roar of a classic exotic car can be heard entering the garage, it is followed by another armored SUV. The second SUV stops on the off ramp blocking the exit. The motorcycles go to the far side of the garage away from everyone. The other SUV and exotic car pull right up to Malik's vehicles.

Leggz exits the Car, leaving the door open and the motor running.

She's wearing very expensive one of a kind red bottom high heels and her diamonds of course.

She walks toward Malik with her signature sultry Style wearing a long form-fitting skirt with splits on both sides to show off her gorgeous legs.

Ka'ren dresses herself in the apparel and style of the people she is doing business with. Since she is doing business with Ghetto Gangster Pimps. She dresses accordingly and it gives her a laugh, to dress like a prostitute and give males such as them, orders they had better OBEY!

To spite their opinion of her Malik's crew loves the way she looks and Carries herself. like a QUEEN Ghetto, BOSS, Stripper with authority. One of her security guards shuts off the motor and closes her car door. (WARNING EXPLETIVE CONTENT!)

"Bout Fu#king time you got here" Ha'zeem says sarcastically looking her up and down.

"Shut da fu#k up, for I shoot you're Dum a$s!" She replies as she walks by him and puts the palm of her hand in his face.

"Who da fu#k you think you talkin to BIT#H!" Ha'zeem yells walking behind her. Two of Malik's crew quickly grab him and hold him. Ka'ren stops, cutting her eyes at him as she turns around.

Before she can say anything Malik rushes over to talk to her. She lets NO man call her the B- word in anger. Especially ones she considers to be low life's. Malik steps between Ka'ren and Ha'zeem his main concern is getting the five million dollars. He knows his brother is a bit of a hothead and has never gotten along with Leggz. She gave Malik instructions to never bring him again after the last meeting, advice he should have taken. The driver steps out of the armored SUV and opens the rear door. He steps back as Zsazsa emerges from the vehicle. She is flamboyant in her attire which resembles the colors of a butterfly. Malik's crew stands ready in case of gunplay. She is careful, as not to display the characteristics of the renowned Zsazsa La'more. Like her sister Ka'ren she hides herself very well. She is wearing a spray-on suntan to darken her skin and a mask in the shape of a butterfly to conceal her face. A headdress is worn over a wig to conceal her hair. There is no evidence to confirm her identity. She stands beside her sister and speaks to her in Italian a language unknown to Malik and his crew.

"Who da fu#k is dis?" Malik asks.

"I don't think your crew would have heard of her but perhaps you have?"

Leggz answers looking at her sister, in that seductive way she does oh so well.

"This is 'Madame Butterfly'" Malik and his crew look to one another shrugging their shoulders.

"Dis who you work for?" Malik asks pointing his finger at Zsazsa making a funny face.

"No! she's my sister" Leggz answers. ZsaZsa says to her sister in Italian.

"This is why mother should allow me to come out more, my name is fading!"

Leggz giggles to herself then pats her sister on the shoulder and replies in Italian.

"Then by all means, my sister. Reclaim Madame butterfly's Fame!" She tells her, now cutting those sexy eyes at Ha'zeem. He notices the way she looks at him as she spoke and realizes she said something about him. He gets a cocky attitude; Smiles then leans over and says something to one of his crew members and laughs with him. Malik attempts to resume the business conversation but is interrupted by Ha'zeem making a smart comment toward Zsazsa.

"Dis clown Bit#h suppose ta scare us or some 'em?" He says laughing with his crew.

"I have a proposition Malik I think you'll love" Leggz interrupts. "I Got five mil here today, your brother Ha'zeem against my sister one on one, fair fight. If he wins keep the five mil straight up and I'll get another five million to buy the girls that's ten million dollars for you, right here, right now!"

Ha'zeem has been in and out of jail most of his adult life. Primarily for beating and raping women. His brother Malik was a well-organized pimp in New York City before moving his operation to Bangkok. His little brother has always enjoyed beating and abusing the women when they do not make enough money. He is feared by most of the prostitutes on the street circuit, for he is a murderer and rapist of women.

Ha'zeem begins to take off his shirt he is well built and strong. His body is chiseled like that of a professional bodybuilder or a convict. Malik is quiet rubbing his chin, considering her challenge.

"Leggz how long it take you ta get the other five mil?" He asks smiling.

"I can have it here within the hour"

"REALLY" He says rubbing his hands together. Malik has been doing business with Leggz for seven years now and knows she has plenty of money. So does the organization he thinks she works for. But he is still a little hesitant. "I'll sweeten the deal" Leggz says putting her hands on her hips. "Not only do you get the money, also if he wins all Y'all could pull a train on me, right now and video it!"

She concludes moving her hands down her thighs. She knows how to deal with small-minded men.

Malik's eyes light up he's been wanting to do that to her ever since he set eyes on her years ago and he knows she's not kidding; she has no sense of humor with him or his crew.

Ha'zeem and the crew begin to cheer. "Hell yeah! Do that Sh#t get ready ta make that call!" Malik yells.

Ha'zeem runs over to Leggz telling her. "Imma be da first ta fu#k you after I knock your crazy lookin sister Da fu#k out!" Leggz looks him up and down in a sexy way and replies. "Of course you are, I can hardly wait- Daddy"

Malik puts his arm around Ha'zeem and Whispers in his ear. "Yo little brother don't play with this bit#h just get in there, get it done, ex that bit#h, cuz Leggz still gotta call for that money ta get here."

"For sure, I got dis my Nig--er, plus it's gonna take at least 2 hours for all of us to hit that!"

Referring to all of them having sex with 'Leggz' Ha'zeem assures him the fight will be quick shaking his brother's hand. Everyone is now standing in a circle with Zsazsa in the center. She stands poised with her hands behind her back. Ha'zeem enters the circle and his crew starts to cheer him on. He circles Zsazsa laughing, joking and doing a little dancing then stops in front of her.

And like the low-life coward he truly is. He attempts to sucker punch her.

As he swings his fist at her, she quickly spins doing a kick and hitting him in the lower jaw with such force it nearly tears his jaw off his face, then in a millisecond she spins again as his body turns, she punches him directly in the back of the head. Sending his head through the window of his brothers' vehicle. With half his body inside the vehicle up to his waist. leaving his legs dangling. Everyone almost collectively yells. "Oooooooh" Then begin to laugh, but the laughter quickly Fades as they see Ha'zeem's legs begin to tremble.

Madame Butterfly still stands poised. Malik and his crew run to his brother; they slowly pull his body from the vehicle. When they turn him over to see his face they are horrified. His face looks like he was hit by a speeding truck. As they lay him on the ground his eyes roll to the back of his head.

His body begins to shake violently. And he who has brought nothing but trouble, heartache and physical pain to every woman he has ever encountered. Now lies dead his life had no meaning and he shall be missed only by his brother. There is a brief moment of silence as Malik and crew look down at Ha'zeem.

Leggz walks over to her sister, kisses her on the cheek then turns to Malik and his crew with her hand on her crotch and politely says.

"Well, I guess this pu$$y's gonna have ta fu#k itself! Cause you guys definitely ain't doing it!"

This infuriates Malik he quickly jumps up yelling at Leggz, but his crew holds him back. But not before he yells some very fatal words.

"Bit#h!" He yells with an insane anger in his eyes.

"I don't give a fu#k about you or who you work for, Y'all both dead! my word is bond! Y'all dead!"

Leggz and her sister stand laughing and pointing at him, then they stop laughing. Malik's crew know not to draw their guns. For they are outgunned many times over. Leggz slowly walks toward them with a sadistic look in her eye. "In all the years I have known you, you have never made the error of raising your voice to me or have been stupid enough to threaten me or my family"

More of her security teams emerge from the SUVs as she speaks.

"For this I will punish you in front of your entire crew"

"You think you got it like that bit#h? Fu#k you and your guns I don't give a fu#k how many guns you got right now. You think I'm gonna just stand here and let you hit me bit#h you got another thing coming."

Madame Butterfly walks over and Whispers in her sister's ear.

"I've lost count of how many times he referred to you as a bit#h my dear"

Malik's crew continue to hold him back in fear of her team shooting all of them.

"No I don't want you to just stand there." She says tuning away from him. "You may TRY to fight me."

She removes her very expensive high heels and urges him to get up and come toward her.

"I just want you to know if they let me go I'm gonna kill you wit my bare hands bit#h!"

"Based on you, and your crew's track record of disappointments today I highly doubt it!"

His crew is a little reluctant to release him but do so anyway. He immediately runs at her swinging his fists and kicking at her wildly in anger and with no form. She effortlessly out Maneuvers him.

He throws another wild punch and misses in doing so she grabs him in a headlock from behind and with her Superior strength she holds on to him for a moment. He struggles but cannot break free.

Then she starts to yell at him as if he were a child for everyone to hear.

"First you would lead me to believe I'm going to lose 10 million dollars. THAT didn't happen, Then I had my heart set on being GANG RAPED by a bunch of ignorant Gang bangers, THAT didn't happen.

AND now! you promised to kill me and I'm pretty sure THAT'S NOT gonna happen either!"

She concludes sarcastically, pushing him away from her, he turns to strike her. But she executes a perfect sidekick hitting him in the nose, breaking it, his face explodes with blood as he stumbles back. He struggles to remain standing but he was struck too hard. Before he can fall, she catches him by the neck holding him in place. "like all MEN you are filled with broken promises. Here I stand, awaiting my death, but of course--THAT DIDN'T HAPPEN!" She screams, shaking him like a rag doll.

He looks at her with his blurred vision, too weak to break free or hit her in his weakened state he says to her what any real gangster pimp in his position would say at this moment. "S*CK MY D#*K! — BIT#H!"

She looks to his crew as if daring them to laugh, they do not! They wonder how she is able to do this? She doesn't appear to be that physically strong. Yet she handles him like a toy.

Ka'ren extends her hand, the door of the SUV opens and a very attractive secretary type woman exits, carrying a briefcase. She walks over to Ka'ren, opens the briefcase and hands her a custom-made handgun. She lowers him to his knees still holding him by the throat as if he were nothing. He struggles for a brief moment. She puts the gun down by her crotch area and puts the barrel into his mouth. "S*CK MINE FIRST!" She yells before pulling the trigger, his crew remains silent. She looks at them and Squints her eyes as she asks. "Does anyone else want to say that to me or refer to me as a female dog?" They all remain silent. She looks at one of the crew members whom she recalls having a few Pleasant conversations with over the past few years. Although he is petrified, he looks at her and recalls the same. "I remember you, what's your name again?" She says pointing to one of them.

"Benjamin" He answers trying to be cool and keep his swagger. She slowly walks toward the crew, still holding the gun in her hand. "You will be rich, you will be powerful, you will be feared and you will be Envied. Do you know why you will be all of these things BENJAMIN?"

Still trying to be cool and also not knowing how to answer he just replies. "I don't know"

"Because I will allow it, all of this is now yours, I'll call your bosses, I have influence with them your in control of the Bangkok operation now-- BENJAMIN." He starts to smile. "You wouldn't ever think of speaking to me as they did. would you Benjamin?"

The smile quickly Fades from his face.

"No, no never Dat. you get mad respect from me, I'll Killa mother fu#ker before I let ANYBODY Dis you. That's my word!"

Madame Butterfly walks up and stands beside her sister. After what they have just witnessed, they are absolutely terrified of them. But like so many men will never admit it and attempt to hide it.

Leggz Taps her foot on the ground softly the secretary comes
over, kneels down and puts her shoes upon her feet, stands
and opens the briefcase. Leggz puts the gun inside.
"Your Bangkok boss will make all the arrangements and put
everything into your name Benjamin.
I'll call you in a few days so we can reschedule this deal at
half price of course"
"Ok, OK yes ma'am" He responds fiddling about nervously
unable to contain himself. Madame Butterfly steps over to
him and reaches out to touch his shoulder. He immediately
jumps and becomes tense, she does this to assure his fear of
her. She looks at him and speaks to him in English so he may
understand but not in her true voice.
"Service us well Benjamin! and I will be pleased!"
"I will" He responds staring into her eyes. She turns and
walks back to the vehicles with her sister. They drive away
leaving the two dead bodies for Ben and his newly-acquired
crew to clean up. They are relieved and happy with the way
things turned out. But none of them will ever forget the
name 'Madame Butterfly'!

  A motorcade of military SUVs arrives at an undisclosed
military airfield not too far from the UN building, they are
transporting the A.N.T agents. At the airfield Mother
Superior Hymiriam's air craft awaits. She herself is not there,
but Peter and Angelica are. They will be flying the A.N.T
agents to Area 51 in Nevada. The Battle Assault Drone
which transported the Arch Nuns to the United Nations
building will remain there until the wounded are released
from the Doctors Care.
The A.N.T agents being the super tough soldiers they are.
Can hardly contain their enthusiasm, they never thought
they would be at this level of the military or going to Area 51
of all places.
"Have ya ever been ta this place before, brother Joshua?"
Keeva asks with her thick Irish accent she deliberately dose

from time to time.

"Yeah, we came a couple of times with mom. when she was doing research here, but they kept us in a children's area. Are you afraid Kee? I can call you Kee right."

"Of course you can, I'll admit I'm a little nervous- okay a lot nervous. IT'S AREA 51!!!"

She replies hugging his neck and kissing him on the cheek, he looks at her in shock. "Oh my God, I'm so sorry Josh." She says rubbing his arm. "But I'm not on your team or anything. Unless ya want me UNDER you! So, what's up baby?" she concludes looking at him in a very sexy way.

He begins to perspire not knowing what to do. "Take it easy Joshua it's not like I'm gonna grab ya by the hair and treat ya like a lassie! Unless you really want me ta, Baby" She says with a wink patting him on the back. He hopes she was kidding but can't help feeling flattered. Everyone on the ship is too engaged in their own conversations, laughter and jokes to notice this go on between them. But it is all in fun.

'Hey Zach' Joshua feels to his younger brother, still at the U.N medical wing in New York.

'That girl Keeva who dragged you around by the hair just came on to me jokingly, I hope. it was kind of funny but it made me feel a little weird, you know WEIRD!'

'Don't let her grab your hair she won't let go and I can't believe Grandma put her on Buffie's team for now, UNBELIEVABLE!'

The craft lands at Area 51. There they are met by General John Randolph of the United States Air Force.

He's accompanied by twenty scientists that are very excited to meet them. He is also the first to test pilot a Battle Assault Drone.

"Welcome to Area 51 Ladies and Gentlemen or as we like to say 'NOWHERE'."

The general of course keeps his composure but he too shares their enthusiasm.

The A.N.T agents are like school children on a field trip for the first time. Their eyes are like sponges absorbing everything they see. They're escorted to dressing areas to change into their battle attire. Each Arch Nun is standing outside the entrance of their assigned Craft to welcome their team members. Battle Assault Drone 1 for A.N.T 1 and so on. Mother Teresa speaks to all of them through a very small earpiece in their ears.

"Okay everyone, let's get out there. You can go on a sightseeing tour next time, maybe. Now we have the Lord's work to do!"

There is loud cheering from the A.N.T agents as they greet their commanding Nun and enter their crafts.

Each craft has a pilot that was involved in the development of the craft and each A.N.T has an Apache helicopter pilot in training to be the primary pilot for their team. Eventually everyone on the team, the Arch Nuns included will have to have a basic knowledge of piloting the craft. Since the crafts can operate collectively the pilots merge the operational systems to B.A.D-1, Sister Maria's craft. Her pilot now has control of all six ships.

General Randolph clears them for liftoff. All six ships slowly and simultaneously begin to rise. They are in perfect formation and perfectly spaced as if they were one ship. They have several smaller drones flying around them recording for the world leaders.

General Randolph speaks to the pilot of B.A.D -1. "Looking Good Pilot, damn good!"

Many of the staff have come to the hanger to see them off. They cheer' applaud and whistle.

They have seen the ships operate collectively many times during testing but this time was special. For they now carry the Arch Nuns and their teams. And in the words of the Great Jean-Luc Picard of the Starship Enterprise. General Randolph says over the loudspeaker. "ENGAGE!"

The hangar is filled with sci-fi Geeks and they are all familiar with 'Star Trek the Next Generation'. So, they cheer as loud as they can and of course one of them plays the theme music through the loudspeakers. The general laughs and throws his hands in the air.

The ships slowly exit the hangar once cleared of the hanger, they stop and like one large ship tilts toward the sky, awaiting the general's order to depart.

"Permission to depart sir?" Sister Maria's pilot says which can be heard over the loudspeakers in the hanger. The general salutes, then Quotes Jean-Luc Picard again saying loudly. "Make it so, number one!"

The six ships jet into the sky as one disappearing into the clouds.

The General joins the applause for a moment then tells everyone to return to their duties.

Peter and Angelica approach the General and explain to him. They too must depart to retrieve The Mother Superior Hymiriam.

The ships go to their temporary areas of operation. The General informs B.A.D-4 Sister Elizabeth's team that they will be going to Los Angeles by order of Mother Teresa.

She and her team are to land and work with FBI agents for now. There are private air fields being built all over the world to accommodate the Battle Assault Drones. These are heavily guarded areas of 2 to 5-mile radiuses. But the craft can land anywhere the A.N.T agents need to including any rooftop or city street. The Landing fields will have a landing pad with numerous vehicles, weapons and equipment for the A.N.T agents.

These areas will be referred to as 'ANT FARMS' B.A.D-4 lands in a military airfield, the rear door opens and two heavily armored SUVs with several small drones atop the roofs, drive off the craft. A.N.T-4 is now headed into the city of Los Angeles.

"Hey boss! Should we check in with the FBI headquarters here?" Tommy one of her A.N.T agents asks.

"As a courtesy we will do this, but going forward it will not be necessary!"

"Ok boss"

"Oh and Thomas?"

"Yeah boss."

"Whenever we are in any City, WE are the commanding law enforcement agency!"

She says in a condescending tone. The Arch Nuns have engaged their 'Grace of God' their method of speaking. Will now be referred to as the Arch Nun Rhetoric.

There is no doubt they will be misunderstood and considered arrogant by many. Their team members will quickly become accustomed to it. As it was covered by Mother Teresa during the past year with them on how to conduct themselves in the presence of an Arch Nun.

She calls the office but director Hector Lopez is unavailable so she speaks to the deputy director William Vesuvio whom was already informed of her possible visit.

"Hello deputy director this is sis--" and before she can finish, he disrespectfully cuts her off

"Yeah, yeah I know who you are. listen there's no need for

you to stop by. you could just Patrol the streets or something for a little while we're kind of in the middle of something here. Maybe we'll have lunch or something in a few days. okay?" Then he hangs up the phone on her.

"F.B.I- Full-Blown idiots and self-centered pricks always." Thomas says shaking his head. Sister Elizabeth looks at him. "Continue on to the FBI building please sir."

"yes ma'am"

  They arrive at the FBI headquarters they enter the building and almost all activity in the lobby comes to a halt. Everyone admires their appearance; they look like the 'Bad Asses' they are. This is the first time they are seen in public on Official Duty. Two of the team members walk ahead of the rest. They approach the front desk and before the receptionist can say anything, they stand to one side. Sister Elizabeth silently walks by the desk and through the metal detectors without so much as a glance. The rest of the team follow her. Security teams run over to them. The last member of the A.N.T turns and holds her hand up stopping them. As the metal detectors are going off the elevator doors open.

A small group of FBI agents quickly run out to tell everyone that everything is okay, yelling for the security teams to stand down. Sister Elizabeth and her team walk through the agents and onto the elevator without saying a word. The elevator door closes and they leave the agents in the lobby. "She could have at least said hello!" One of the agents says. Then quickly gets on the radio to inform everybody that an Arch Nun is in the building. The elevator doors open, out steps Sister Elizabeth followed by her team. Everyone in the hallway immediately steps to one side. Some of them look upon the Sister in anger. They cannot believe the nerve she has. They enter the deputy director's office; He is having a meeting with several agents. Sister Elizabeth approaches him and the agents aggressively stand. The A.N.T do not react they stand calmly.

"Whoa, whoa, whoa" The deputy says looking at the A.N.T.

"Excuse me, YOU don't just barge in here, Sister!" Elizabeth looks the deputy in the eye then takes the paperwork he was holding.

Then commands he and his agents to sit down.

"Hold on Sis" he says with a sarcastic tone.

"That's Arch Nun Sister Elizabeth to you, and I will not tell you again deputy director, or should I end your career now?"

He is silent, but he and his agents sit down. She deliberately left the door to the office open so everyone in the hall can bear Witness to the authority of an Arch Nun. Mother Teresa told all of her grandchildren if they are met with animosity, contempt or resistance by any military or law enforcement agency, they are to quickly establish their Superior Authority. Elizabeth reads the paperwork; they are in the middle of formulating a plan for a current hostage situation at a local bank.

The robbers have hostages' women, children and infants. This changes the situation inserting the A.N.T into their plans.

Sister Elizabeth gives the agents the opportunity to quickly finish the plan. She does not interfere she stands quietly as they work things out. The deputy director is embarrassed and angry so he sits at the table silently, pouting like the child he was behaving as.

"Quickly everyone, time is of the essence, need I remind you children are involved!" She says to them.

"Understood ma'am two SWAT teams are currently on the scene, bomb squad is standing by." One agent responds.

"Yeah they used some pretty sophisticated electronic equipment to take out the surveillance system and they're keeping it pretty dark in there moving people around constantly."

Then the deputy director adds. "Plus, they're using all the males and Bank staff as a human wall in front of the windows. Snipers can't get a clear shot, not to mention all

203

the C4 they've got throughout the building."
Another agent tells her.
"The leader has a Deadman switch in his hand if he releases his grip, 'BOOM! It changes frequencies constantly so we can't Jam the signal. They're calling themselves, and I kid you not, 'The Statement!'"
What in the blue perfect hell kinda name is that?" Says yet another agent.
Sister Elizabeth interjects telling them.
"Statement is not so much a name as it is something they are determined to make. The bank robbery is just a diversion, they have every intent of detonating and killing everyone in the bank."
The agents agree with her and inform all law enforcement agencies on the scene.
"Come everyone, we need to be at the scene, and I mean everyone!"
She concludes looking at the deputy director.
"I seldom do fieldwork" The deputy director says with an attitude.
"You do today, come now" The Sister replies.
"Will we be taking your spaceship?" The deputy director asks sarcastically.
Elizabeth looks at him for a moment, turns and leaves the room with her team following her and the Agents not far behind. As they arrived on the scene one of the negotiators is talking to the male spokesperson for the terrorist bank robbers. He is outside the bank yelling into a bullhorn communicating with the negotiator. The terrorists are communicating this way to get as much media attention as possible and to keep the negotiations transparent to the world. It is already going viral on the internet. Sister Elizabeth suspects when they reach the desired number of viewers, they will detonate the bombs. She hopes to God that she is wrong. But it is not likely, everyone is coming to the same conclusion. Sister Elizabeth tells the negotiators to

not mention U.N.A presence at this time. For they have not shown themselves yet. She tells her team they shall stand Idle No More. "Infiltrate that building and await my signal."
"You got it boss!"
Tommy answers with a grin. "Alright, team let's get ready ta rumble"
The A.N.T were hoping they would be allowed to take over the situation. This will be the first time their Arch Nun Commander will see their military and tactical superiority and they are looking forward to making an impression. The FBI agents inform Sister Elizabeth that the media has been contained and the terrorists will be oblivious to their presence. But there is still the matter of the public with their cell phones and social media. So, she has them shut down the surrounding cell phone towers to create a temporary Communication blackout. She also has local law enforcement instructing the crowd of Spectators to be silent anyone making any noise of any kind will be arrested. She does this in the rare event they cheer at the site of the Arch Nun or her team. Her last orders are for all other tactical teams to standby, Her A.N.T agents will take point. Her team exits their vehicles first and turn on their body cams. The crowd sees them but thinks they are part of the S.W.A.T team. They are able to move unnoticed as they infiltrate the building and take their positions. They are very good at what they do and it does not take them long. They all report to Sister Elizabeth that they have infiltrated the building and are in position awaiting her orders. Sister Elizabeth exits the vehicle, activates her body cam, puts her carry bag over her shoulder and joins the other team commanders who are studying the floor plans of the building. They watch as she approaches assuming she is going to relieve them of their commands. Deputy director Vesuvio is standing with them. He has given them the impression she is here to evaluate their performance. She greets them and tells them to resume their duties asking if she may take a look at the floor plans.

She focuses her attention on the front door, and metal beams surrounding it and the lobby where the leader of the terrorists is holding most of the hostages.

Deputy director Vesuvio notices her doing this and Whispers derogatory remarks to the other commanders whom are friends of his. They are reluctant to agree with him because some of them respect the U.N.A.

"Attention team make sure your body cams are active and online." Sister Elizabeth tells her team. They confirm and continue to stand by. The news media has not yet noticed there is an Arch Nun among the commanders of the various tactical teams. They know not to point their cameras at any Command centers, if they wish to keep their video footage. The spokesman for the terrorist emerges from the bank Furious and yelling into the bullhorn regarding the cellular blackout. The FBI negotiators assure him they are working on rectifying the problem. While he is standing in front of the bank doors shouting. Sister Elizabeth steps forward, he immediately stops and looks at her with no fear.

The recording drones atop of the A.N.T vehicles. Liftoff to record every vantage point possible for the world leaders to View and evaluate later.

The Spectators to spite the L.A.P.D's request for silence couldn't help but to cheer at the sight of her.

The news media quickly Focus their cameras on Sister Elizabeth. The spectators watch in amazement eager to see what she is going to do. She stares at him in deep concentration.

He informs his leader that one of those Arch Nuns is out here and requests further instructions. "Come back inside now! and let's get this party started then!" The leader tells him.

Sister Elizabeth slowly reaches into her bag, he turns to enter the bank, the electric doors slide open, he walks through the doors as they begin to slide shut.

She quickly draws the custom made White and Gold

revolver, pointing it slightly above him, On the side of her firearm it reads 'THOU SHALL NOT KILL!' Time begins to slow down.

The split second before the doors close, she fires her weapon. The bullet passes between the small opening just before they close completely. The bullet ricochets off one of the steel beams in the ceiling, ricocheting off a concrete column in the lobby, then finally ricocheting off the concrete floor lodging perfectly in the center of the spine of the terrorist leader holding the Detonator switch, severely damaging his nervous system causing his fist to clench tightly, preventing the release of the switch.

Time resumes to normal, at that exact moment Sister Elizabeth commands her team to move in. A firefight ensues as the Arch Nun walks toward the bank.

L.A.P.D instructs the spectators and news media to get down and take cover. The sounds of gunfire can be heard within the bank. Deputy director Vesuvio tells the other tactical teams to hold their position. He wants the U.N.A to be solely responsible for what he perceives to be a massacre and epic mistake by the Arch Nun. Because it appears to him, she tried to shoot the terrorist negotiator in the back but missed.

"well, I guess we're watching the end of the United Nations Agency gentlemen" he says laughing to himself. He calls the director whom was avoiding Sister Elizabeth to happily give him an update on the situation. F.B.I Director Lopez is not a supporter or fan of the U.N.A. he would like to have as a little interaction with them as possible. He tells the deputy director he wants a CSI team in there immediately, the Nun fired first he wants that documented and to make sure the news media is aware of the Arch Nun initiating the gunfight, risking the lives of everyone especially the hostages. Gunfire can still be heard within the bank as Sister Elizabeth approaches the doors.

The doors slide open; she enters they close behind her and the gunfire slowly comes to a halt. The Deputy director informs the director that the gunfire has stopped. "With a little luck maybe she and her team got killed." He tells the director jokingly "Call me back ASAP!" Assuming but not hoping they're dead. "Now go take charge Vesuvio" He puts his phone in his pocket, Combs his beard and begins to walk toward the other commanders with purpose. "Everyone hold your positions, maintain radio silence and standby" he says over the radio.

Inside the bank and unknown to the deputy director the A.N.T have the situation in control.

"CLEAR" they all confirm over their private Radio Network. Sister Elizabeth enters the lobby. The surviving terrorists have been contained and the hostages are being attended to. Tommy is holding the fist of the terrorist leader; he is barely conscious his nervous system has been shattered. He struggles to open his hand but he physically cannot. He will be paralyzed from the neck down for the rest of his life. Another team member comes over to assist Tommy in securing his hand. The terrorist organization kept the explosive devices simple because they had every intention of detonating them. This allows the A.N.T to quickly disarm and disable the devices rendering them harmless. The hostages are free of their explosive devices but are instructed to stay where they are. The body cam footage is being live streamed directly to Mother Teresa, the world leaders and high-ranking commanders of the U.N.A.

The children are still frightened and crying as they cling to any adult they can. The adults cannot express enough gratitude to the Arch Nun and her team. Almost all of them kept their heads down and eyes closed praying during the entire gun fight. But they were very relieved to see an Arch Nun when they opened their eyes. "Behold, The Power of thy Lord God!" She said as she stood before them. An image they shall remember for a long time.

The A.N.T ask that everyone be quiet for the Arch Nun Sister Elizabeth. She kneels, bowels her head and prays. "Oh God, you are my savior and my strength I thank thee for the safety of these people taken hostage against their will, I thank thee for watching over my team, I ask of Thee Oh Lord to have mercy on those Souls delivered unto you on this day and I thank thee O Lord for allowing me the wisdom, strength and courage to carry out your Will. in thy name I pray and give all to I AM, amen."

The hostages look upon her, many silently join her prayer others gaze upon her and believe for the first time in their lives that GOD IS GOD!

None of the hostages were physically harmed, the Arch Nun killed NO ONE! The terrorists whom were killed by the A.N.T agents and chosen by the Lord to pass through the Pearly Gates on this day, have done so. And he who was the architect of this endeavor, he who has been struck with a bullet guided by the hand of God! Shall remain a quadriplegic for the remainder of his days until his final judgment by the Lord. THIS IS THE WILL AND POWER OF GOD!

Four black U.N.A investigation vans drive through the police lines and right up to the front of the bank. This is the United Nation's personal Crime Scene Investigation Unit they were dispatched by Mother Teresa the moment the U.N.A arrived at the bank. The investigation teams rush from vehicles and await further instructions from Sister Elizabeth. Deputy director Vesuvio makes his way to the news media, to inform them the FBI was not in charge here and to insinuate the Arch Nun made an attempt to shoot the terrorist in the back, starting the gun fight and risking the lives of everyone here. Some of the news media attempt to report this over the air but are quickly shut down by their bosses whom are currently on the phone with Mother Teresa.

The deputy director attempts to take charge but is ordered to Stand Down by Sister Elizabeth.

The bank doors slide open, the A.N.T agents exit the bank followed by their Arch Nun Commander. The U.N.A investigator in charge 'Horatio Bain' approaches Elizabeth, while his teams enter the bank, they Converse. Deputy director Vesuvio and the other team Commanders rush toward them but they are stopped by the A.N.T agents. The other Tactical Team commanders are respectful to the Arch Nun. But deputy director Vesuvio insists upon being included in the conversation. He desperately tries to use his authority to gain access to the bank with his own CSI investigators, who are now joining him. Although Mother Teresa can call the deputy director directly on his satellite phone, she chooses to allow her granddaughter to continue handling the situation.

"Sir with all due respect. The situation will be turned over to you as soon as our investigation concludes"

Horatio tells him. The Spectators are indecisive they are still in the dark as to what is going on and they have not yet seen any hostages exit the building. The news crews receive instructions from their bosses regarding how to proceed and what to report.

"This is Sally Struthers reporting for the LA News and I am pleased to report we have confirmation. ALL, I repeat ALL of the hostages are safe and unharmed Due to the actions of the U.N.A."

Sister Elizabeth and her team begin to walk to their vehicles. The crowd of spectators applaud and cheer them. All the Tactical teams and commanders join in as well, patting them on the back and shoulders
and shaking their hands as they walk by them.

"Any openings on your team Sister?" The SWAT Commander asks her as he applauds. The recording drones land, reattaching themselves to the roofs of the A.N.T vehicles.

"Ladies and gentlemen and people of the world. This is Jake wedemeyer of Fox news and you have just witnessed the first official Act of the U.N.A."

As the hostages are escorted from the bank, the cheering and Applause becomes louder. Deputy director Vesuvio could not bring himself to applaud the Arch Nun, but he does applaud for the well-being of the hostages. Then his satellite cell phone rings, it is director Lopez.

"What the fu#k is going on there why aren't you in charge" He yelled over the phone.

"Because the goddamn Arch Nun turned everything over to a U.N investigation team, why don't YOU call somebody and get me in there, before it's too late"

There is silence on the line before the director hangs up the phone.

"That's what I thought" Deputy director Vesuvio says to himself he makes another attempt to gain access to the bank but his efforts are in vain. The news crews continue to broadcast the good news to the world as the A.N.T Vehicles depart the scene.

Sister Elizabeth sits quietly in the vehicle with her head bowed and her eyes closed as if she were meditating. But she is communicating and celebrating with her family.

'Superb! my granddaughter, Superb!' Mother Teresa feels to her granddaughter. All her siblings join in with High Praise.

'I'm so proud of you my Sister, we honor you!' Amira feels to her.

'Honor you indeed! little Sister.' Maria adds.

'You have bragging rights for a few weeks kid Sister, we love you. Well Done!' Joshua feels to his little Sister.

'I love you all, so very much and thank the Lord you are in my life'

Elizabeth very emotionally feels to them all.

Her Mother Hymiriam will not communicate congratulations or praise for the acts of violence her children must do and be involved in. Her 'WALK OF CHRIST'

prohibits this. But she prays for their strength and well-being and takes comfort in knowing the Lord guides them on their path. For on this day Arch Nun Elizabeth made someone quadriplegic and her team took the lives of eight terrorist. The A.N.T agents being assembled from tactical assault teams from around the world usually celebrate after a campaign such as this. The Arch Nuns are aware of this, and as they are allowed by the Lord to be themselves. They must allow their teams members to be themselves as well. The vehicles return to the A.N.T farm but before boarding the Battle Assault Drone, Sister Elizabeth speaks to her team. "Everyone I am well aware of the celebratory procedures Tactical Teams such as yourselves indulge
in. I do not wish to deprive you of that. So, by all means enjoy your victory, you have performed beyond my expectations on this day."
Her team thanks her for her praise. But for the moment are hesitant to rejoice. Then Tommy asks.
"If you don't mind me asking. Was this the first time you shot someone Sister?"
"Yes" She answers softly.
"All of us had a first time as well, if you will let us, I think I speak for everyone when I say we would like to help you through it"
The Grace of God prevents the Arch Nuns from feeling remorse when they do the Lord's work the team is unaware of this. But Elizabeth allows them to do this to strengthen their bond. They go to the cafeteria section of the A.N.T farm so they may talk to her. She opens her mind so her siblings and grandmother may hear each of them open their hearts and share with her.
They all share tales with the Sister of the first time they shot someone, how it made them feel and how they overcame it. Mother Teresa is very pleased with the selection she has made for the A.N.T agents.
The Arch Nuns are moved by this sharing and hope to build

an equally strong bond with their teams. Mother Teresa has no doubt that they will.

The U.N investigation is swift in confirming the actions of the Arch Nun and her team were just. This took a few weeks while the world was unsure, some organizations seized the opportunity to slander the Arch Nun and her agents. During this time Mother Teresa gave instructions to all the A.N.T's to be as visible as possible assisting all law enforcement agencies internationally. This will also give the Arch Nuns still in the hospital a little more time to be cleared for Duty along with the remaining agents. Dr. Barbara Randolph is the wife of General John C Randolph of Area 51 and also the Chief of the medical staff in charge of the Arch Nuns and their agents without her medical clearance no A.N.T agent is leaving the U.N medical wing. She is a woman of very little patience to which Sisters Amira and Lynn are trying to the fullest.

"Doctor with the current medications you have me on. May I have salt on my food now?"

Dr. Randolph being fully aware of Sister Amira's knowledge of Medicine being a prodigy and genius is well aware of what she can and cannot have with certain medications.

"Why did you ask me that?" The doctor responds in a stern tone.

"Oh! I didn't want to know, it's my Sister Lin, she was wondering, not me of course but Lin, it was Lin"

Amira says smiling as she looks away. The doctor hesitates for a minute. then responds with frustration.

"If you OR your Sister would like to have salt, you may do so in moderation"

Amira begins to feel she is getting on the doctor's nerves so she changes the subject. Noticing the doctor is wearing three very beautiful diamond rings. Amira compliments her on her taste in jewelry and the two begin to converse. Sister Amira has a way of finding a common bond with people and she just discovered Dr. Barbara Randolph's love for fine jewelry. The doctor sits at the edge of Amira's bed and makes a delightful discovery that Amira is quite the movie buff with a love for classic MGM movies. The two spoke of the great Classics Such as 'West Side Story', 'The Wizard of Oz', The Thief of Bagdad and many, many others. Dr Randolph gave the rest of her rounds to her staff as to spend more time talking with Amira. Who reminds her so much of her deceased granddaughter Adrienne Marie Randolph. Outside Zachariah's room four nurses are standing in the hall. The door is partially open, they peek through the opening making comments as to how handsome he is. Three nurses are already in the room tending to him. They are gigging like school girls as they give him their full attention. The head Registered Nurse Dorothy White enters the room and she too is taken by his appearance but attempts to hide it. Zach lies in his bed watching sporting events on television enjoying the attention. Dr Randolph clears the remaining Arch Nuns and A.N.T agents for active duty.

Mother Teresa wanted this time, for things to settle down regarding Sister Elizabeth. The Deputy Director Vesuvio was fired by President Winfrey.

During this time the Arch Nuns were seen throughout the United States observing and working with various law enforcement agencies.

The crime percentage rose 30% worldwide, taunting the United Nations Agency. But Mother Teresa did not allow the A.N.T agents to respond, yet.

Hymiriam has also been seen around the world with her three apostles. Where there is famine, there is Hymiriam, where there is suffering, there is Hymiriam, where there is hopelessness, there is Hymiriam. She could not be everywhere but she was where the Lord willed her to be and the sick were cured, those in parve Saw Green Pastures, where there was famine and barren fields there is now fruit and vegetables. These things were reported by the news media and shown to the people of the world.

For all of this was the work of the Lord. But Eve in her bitterness and to be spiteful, used her influence, power and wickedness to assure these things were dismissed as hoaxes trickery and government deceit. The people were uncertain, unsure and conflicted. And Eve instructed a few hundred of her children to wreak havoc upon the world at their leisure. And wreak havoc they did, they rallied the religions and churches that are skeptical of Hymiriam and the Arch Nuns. They made assassination attempts against some of the world leaders managing to succeed in a few. The Singaporean government used this to their advantage announcing the death of their president Bae Wei and empowering junlong as their new president. Mother Teresa knew this was an attempt at drawing the Arch Nuns all over the world chasing them. So, she allowed the C.I.A, F.B.I, D.E.A, Interpol and all the law enforcement agencies of the world to handle it after all the U.N.A are not here to do THEIR jobs! Mother Teresa walks down the hall of the medical wing accompanying her are eight assistants, they are pulling luggage containing the uniforms of the Arch Nuns. The Reverend mother informs the doctor of the urgency

regarding the release of the A.N.T agents. The doctor
concurs and the Arch Nuns change into their uniforms.
'Hey Grandma' Sister Donna feels to her grandmother. 'Can
you please come to my room, Now!'
'Yes my granddaughter, allow me to finish talking to the
doctor and I'll be there momentarily' she responds, as she
simultaneously concludes talking to the doctor.
The assistants deliver the uniforms and wait in the hall for
Mother Teresa.
Sister Donna is in the bathroom changing as her
grandmother enters the room. They continue
communicating telepathically as not to be recorded.
'I don't have to come back and see Dr Randolph again do I?'
'Why my child'
'She had the nerve to talk to me about type 2 diabetes
prevention' Mother Teresa laughs hysterically.
'It's not funny grandma'
'It is my granddaughter, it so very much is'
To the video surveillance security team that monitor
everything in the UN building. It simply appears to be
Mother Teresa sitting on the bed silently awaiting her
granddaughter to exit the bathroom with no words spoken.
'Type 2 diabetes of all things. I know she was insinuating I
was overweight. Why didn't she just offer me insulin and get
it over with'
Mother Teresa continues to laugh hysterically. She is so
amused at her granddaughter.
'Come on Grandma stop laughing'
'Okay my child, settle down soon Dr Randolph and the
world will see that you are faster than the wings of a
hummingbird and lighter than air itself!'
'Thank you Grandma, please don't let my stupid brothers
and Sisters get a hold of this'
'I will not my child, it will be our little secret. Now let us join
the others, and be off'
Mother Teresa gives Donna a hug then leaves the room to

see Zachariah. They too communicate telepathically. He is still lying in bed watching sports on television.

'Well! don't you look snug and comfortable'

'I am Grandma, everybody here is so nice. Doctor Randolph said I remind her of her great grandson.'

'Did she now I'm sure she took good care of you!'

She communicates as she hugs him. Exiting his room to see Lin. Upon entering the room Lin hugs her grandmother as she continues to get dressed. Mother Teresa continues to stare at her then asks aloud. "What did you do"

"I have done nothing grandmother it was Zach all Zach"

Lin failed to tell her grandmother that three days ago during the night while Zach slept, she very discreetly as not to be seen on camera, submerged his hand in warm water causing him to urinate on himself. Upon discovering this he used his Grace of God to correct the wetness of himself and the bed as not to be embarrassed. Knowing at a later date and all in good fun, he will have his retribution as they have done since they were children. Mother Teresa knew she did something but was not angered by their playful acts. They were very discreet.

But now it is time to tend to humanity and the world. She shakes her finger at Lin with a smile then leaves the room to see Amira. As she approaches Amira's room, she can hear laughter from within. Dr Randolph is in the room talking with her.

She enters and hugs her granddaughter before Amira goes to the restroom to finish dressing.

"You have a wonderful granddaughter Mother Teresa."

Doctor Randolph says leaning in for a hug.

"Well thank you" The Reverend mother replies with a confused look on her face as she Embraces the doctor in a hug. She goes on to say many wonderful things about Sister Amira. Mother Teresa listens with delight and amazement. Then the bathroom door opens, Amira steps out in her full Arch Nun uniform, makeup and habit. The doctor looks at her with great admiration, before telling her she looks absolutely stunning. Amira is now conducting herself as an Arch Nun. She silently bows her head to the doctor in gratitude then exits the room to join her brother and Sisters who are waiting in the hallway.

"Sister Amira" The doctor calls to her she stops and turns to face the doctor.

"knock 'em dead girl" The doctor tells her putting a hand on her shoulder and looking in to her eyes.

Amira Winks her eye with a slight smile then turns and leaves the room.

"Wow, she seems so different now, so focused!" The doctor says to Mother Teresa.

"Indeed, for she walks with the GRACE OF GOD! Now!" Mother Teresa hugs the doctor again.

"Thank you so much for taking care of my grandchildren doctor. See you soon, good day to you."

"Good day to you Grandmother Superior."

Dr Randolph follows behind as they exit the room but stopping in the doorway to watch as they walk down the hall. Zach, Donna and Lin along with the assistants are waiting in the hallway. As Mother Teresa and Amira approach, they step to one side allowing the Reverend mother to lead followed by her grandchildren than the assistants. Doctor Randolph remains in the doorway watching as they continue down the hallway and on to the elevator. She continues watching until the elevator doors close completely.

   Ka'ren Margo's private jet lands at JFK airport in New York she is finalizing arrangements for another shipment of young girls into New York's Port Harbor.

This will be a rather large shipment to compensate for the mishap in Singapore. They will be using a Cargo Carrier. Owned of course by one of her countless brothers, he will take care of all the paperwork assuring everything is in order for his Sister Ka'ren.

Ka'ren is keeping Zsazsa in the loop. But she must be careful, mother never said for Zsazsa to sit on the side, she also never condoned her direct involvement. If anyone were to remotely associate Zsazsa with, Madame Butterfly'. They of course would have to be killed and killed quickly even at the peril of others. Meaning taking an entire building down or destroying a shopping mall would not be out of the question. The things 'Midnight Endeavor' enjoys so much. Eve has many favorites amongst her sons and daughters and Zsazsa does indeed enjoy being considered one of them. She adores her mother's respect and relishes her attention. So, she must be careful, very careful being around her younger Sister Ka'ren!

Mother Teresa sends her remaining four grandchildren to Area 51 along with their teammates to get their Battle Assault Drones and join the other A.N.T agents in the cities of the world. For days the A.N.T agents were seen among various law enforcement agencies. The news media did everything they could to ease the transition of laws. But this was hard and too many of the people were rebellious and fearful of the local street gangs and drug dealers. So, Mother Teresa communicates with her grandchildren telepathically. 'Arch Nuns, hear me my grandchildren separate yourselves from your teams for a moment. The Divine Elysium is where I shall meet with you.'

Each of the Arch Nuns make excuses to be alone for a few moments. Ranging from restroom breaks to momentary prayers. But they all found a private place immediately. Once they were alone, they confirmed to their grandmother. Mother Teresa whom was already alone in her Chambers at the UN building tells her grandchildren to use their Grace of God and transition to the Divine Elysium.

Time slows down then stops. She is first to arrive on the patio of the Elysium, immediately followed by her ten Arch Nuns. They stand before their grandmother in the prayer position. They are still wearing their uniforms. Since it was

Mother Teresa that called this meeting and summoned them. They know there shall be no comradery amongst them. For this is the business of humanity.

"Welcome my grandchildren. The world looks upon you and is reluctant to see you as anything--but Liaisons of the United Nations. Your mother is doing a great many things that are slowly gaining recognition. Very slowly to say the least. Elizabeth's campaign saving the hostages is already old news. Eve is doing everything in her power to discredit your mother, this Nunnery and the U.N.A."

She pauses for a moment to let these words sink in.

The Arch Nuns are focused on her every word. They were not summoned here for their opinion they know to remain silent.

"When you return to Earth. I will allow you to invoke The Challenge of Goliath' to select individuals. The Lord will guide you to them and it is the Lord that will decide their fate. When You Face these individuals in physical combat you will show them the superiority of the Arch Nuns and the Power of thy Lord God! if they are to be judged by God on that day it is you that shall send them forth. This decision has been made on this day." She then Stomps her right foot to the ground shouting.

"SO SHALL IT BE WRITTEN"

Collectively the Arch Nuns respond as they stomp their right foot to the ground.

"SO SHALL IT BE DONE!"

She smiles. A table appears from nowhere; she sits at the end asking her grandchildren to sit. As they begin to sit their uniforms transform into their personal attire. For the Mother Superior Hymiriam appears at the opposite end of the table. The Nuns are delighted to see their mother but before they can say a word, she raises her hand to silence them, so she may speak.

For she speaks to them now not as the woman who raised them but as the Mother Superior of The Arch Nuns.

"Salutations, my children" she says lowering her hand.
"It is so wonderful to see you all, but be still and take heed to the words I speak. I will not hear of your violent endeavors they shall never be spoken to me by any of you. I am forbidden, nor do I wish to indulge in such conversations. We walk different paths, For God's Great Purpose. Your grandmother being a Guardian Archangel is the only one allowed to speak to me of these things and only when permitted by the lord to do so! With that being said. I miss you my children and from this Sunday forth we shall have dinner as a family and speak of pleasant things and happier times. So, shall this be written"
The Nuns respond appropriately. "So, shall it be Done"
Hymiriam sheds tears of happiness as her children run to hug and kiss her. And for the next four hours they enjoyed Sunday dinner. The Mother Superior gives her children a fond farewell.
"Okay my children, I'll see you next Sunday, I would say be good and mind your grandmother."
She smiles and rolls her eyes.
"But I know with the Ten of you, everything goes in one ear and out the other." She says lovingly.
"I won't say any names."
She pauses for a moment then says with a grin. "Amira!"
"Why does it always have to be me? Mom Elizabeth is the name you should be saying."
"Throw me under the bus, why don't you? Ya bloody bus driver! For your birthday I'm gonna get you a cap that says 'BUS DRIVER' on it!"
Anna adds laughing with her siblings.
"Make sure it has a picture of a Greyhound on it as well."

The Nuns are playfully arguing amongst themselves, until Hymiriam has to tell them to. "Gather yourselves"
The Nuns applaud and cheer hugging their mother almost pulling her to the ground with excitement.
"Am I going to have to say that every time I see you?"
"Pretty much, Mom"
Nevaeh says.
"That never gets old mom"
Joshua adds putting his arm around his mother and kissing her on the cheek.
Grandmother Teresa looks at everyone shaking her head trying so hard not to smile. "I can't believe you're thirty years old." She says.
" thirty-two for Josh and I grandmother, thirty-two"
Maria interrupts correcting her grandmother with a smile.
Hymiriam Fades away as does the merrymaking as they transform back into their uniforms. This was the first of many Sunday dinners they will enjoy together. For they shall always remember and honor their family bond.
"Okay everybody get back on a clock and back to your teams" Mother Teresa tells them. The Nuns hug and kiss their grandmother smothering her with love. Something they cannot do in the presence of others on Earth. For it would be considered unprofessional. So, the Nuns returned to their teams. The four hours they spend with their family having dinner at the Divine Elysium. Went by quickly to them but only four minutes has passed on Earth. They returned unmissed and unnoticed, as the Lord allowed time to resume and compensate for their absence. Mother Teresa returns to her Chambers at the UN building telling the command center to send landing coordinates to a remote part of the Sahara Desert to all ten Battle Assault Drone Pilots. So, Zach, Lyn, Donna and Amira may sort out their team agents. All Ten teams will be properly placed to their assigned Arch Nun.
Keeva so desperately wants to run to Zachariah and jest with

him about their fight but knows not to. Now that all ten
Battle Assault Drones and teams are assembled in one place.
General Randolph instructs the pilots to conduct a test of the
collective maneuverability of all ten ships together.
Since many of the general's team of scientists are sci-fi fans,
they decided to refer to the A.N.T agents in the following
manner.
Team: 1 of Maria.
Team: 2 of Navaeh.
Team: 3 of Donna.
Team: 4 of Elizabeth
Team: 5 of Lin.
Team: 6 of Amira.
Team: 7 of Dajairia.
Team: 8 of Anna
Team: 9 of Zach.
Team: 10 of Josh.
The U.N.A and A.N.T agents are unaware of this. But the
scientists hope they will not mind.
"B.A.D five You have the Com, all craft Lift-Off and conduct
sequence." The general tells them.
 B.A.D five launches several recording drones so the general
May observe.
All ten crafts Lift-Off simultaneously and begin to conduct
sequenced Maneuvers that look like a symphony of ships
dancing In the Wind. The general and his team are satisfied
with the test but are concerned of B.A.D Seven's anti-gravity
engines cooling system.
The crafts break formation and head on their separate
courses. B.A.D Seven's destination is New York the general
informs the pilot to disengage the anti-gravity engines and
accelerate to 2000 MPH. He wants the craft in New York as
soon as possible. Once there he will have a team check it out.
In the City of Cairo, the largest city in Egypt. Eve sits at a
desk watching the footage of the ten Battle Assault Drones.
She is joined by two of her children her daughter Aston vetta

and her son Cain. Eve through her many children has access to many things' technology and video feeds of Area 51 included.

Whenever recorder drones are used, she can usually access the footage, for now.

"We're going to need crafts that can match their maneuverability if we are to remove them from the sky" Aston says to her brother.

"Easier said than done my Sister. We cannot display technology such as this, without exposing ourselves. I'll look into the legality of it. So, we may reveal our technology without risk of exposure."

Eve looks upon her children with proud eyes. "Splendid my darlings, splendid. There is no need for my personal involvement from here on. I know you'll take care of everything and make me proud as you always have." She stands. "Farewell for now, my children mother loves you." She says walking away from them for she knows through their vast network they will work it out.

   Mother Teresa tells Zac and Josh to return to the U.N building for their assignments and additional team agents. A.N.T seven arrives in New York and lands at the farm. Mother Teresa informs them they will be working with the F.B.I. because they deal with and cover many categories of law enforcement so they will be the main hub to which the Arch Nuns and U.N.A will coordinate with for the time being.

She wants the girls to work in the United States for the special tasks she has charged them with.

Joshua and Zechariah will be with her for a few days before moving on to Russia. The rest of the Arch Nuns go to their assigned cities. Josh and Zach meet with their grandmother at the UN building they walk down the hallway accompanied by several aides and assistants. There are many people in the hallway going about their daily duties. Many of them smile at the Reverend mother and her grandsons. They meet with a small group approaching. They hug her and stand to one side. So, Others May pass. She is going to introduce her boys to a few very special people they'll be working with. One is

Supervisory special agent Valentina Correll. She is a tall very beautiful woman of Argentinian and Caribbean descent, in her mid-thirties with the physique of a high-end supermodel, with big beautiful sexy eyes to die for. Men are usually taken by her appearance. Zach is under the impression being a holy man and an Arch Nun that he would be immune to this. But that which has stricken his brother Joshua now hits him like a ton of bricks. His body temperature begins to rise and he finds himself slightly attracted to her and cannot understand why.

Tall attractive women were his weakness in his first life. So, while his grandmother is introducing him and talking, he feels to his brother, some very confused thoughts.

'Hey Josh, why do I feel funny in that special man way I thought mother said this wouldn't happen! What's going on, Big Brother?'

'keep it together. But that's what I was feeling on the ship with Keeva, just a little, but I wasn't sure. That's why I didn't want to say anything about it.'

While they are communicating with each other on the inside. They simultaneously talk and

smile at everyone on the outside. Josh notices someone walking toward them, he has a slight expression of Terror on his face and like his brother his body temperature begins to rise. She is alone, who is this goddess of a woman who approaches them? She is supervisory special agent Betty Miller she is of African American and Brazilian descent, medium height, extremely curvy, very well endowed in the buttocks, hips and legs. With beautiful dark skin that appears to be a gift from God.

Curvy women were Joshua's weakness in his first life. He begins to perspire and fumble about. He sincerely hopes that this woman is to simply walk by and continue walking way, someone's secretary perhaps or maybe even an intern. They are after all standing in a crowded hallway. But Noooooo! She walks right up to Mother Teresa and gives her a big hug. 'Of course!' He feels to his younger brother.

'You okay man? it's happening to you isn't it?'

'You have no idea, I think I'm going to be sick'

The two brothers attempt to jest with each other telepathically, to ease their minds. Then Mother Teresa introduces her to Josh. Whose weakness in his first life were women with beautiful skin, hourglass curves and of course a big butt. When Mother Teresa introduces her grandchildren, she seldom refers to them as such. She addresses them as Arch Nun and their name.

"And this is Arch Nun Brother Superior Joshua." She says putting her hand on his shoulder then suggests they all have lunch at a local restaurant, rather than a stuffy office or boardroom.

'Josh the Lord truly does have a sense of humor.'

'I don't think the Lord had anything to do with this selection little brother.'

Mother Teresa looks at her grandsons with a big smile on her face and laughter in her eyes. While she is still talking to the group verbally, she simultaneously communicates with her grandsons. 'What's wrong my darling boys?' She asks with sarcastic concern.

'Soooooooo grandma were there no aging, bald, hairy men available and qualified for this job' Josh asks and Zach agrees.

'Of course there were my boys, there were many men as qualified. But I took a liking to these two.' Although she is having a different verbal conversation with the group she slowly turns and smiles at her boys. At that moment the boys remember their grandmother also has a sense of humor, from time to time putting these great Temptations before them.

'We'll talk later my darlings, now! let's all have lunch. I'll make sure Valentina and Betty sit next to you two.'

At the FBI headquarters in New York. Sister Dajairia, her team and several agents are discussing mid-level drug dealers. With Arc Nun Rhetoric She tells them to give her several names on their list she has a proposition for one of them. The agents know not to question the U.N.A so they grant her request. But are intrigued at the proposition she is going to offer.

They give her all files pertaining to Diego Lugo, the meanest drug-dealing pimp in Manhattan. He is a former heavyweight boxer and likes to turn out girls at a very young age through drug addiction and intimidation. He is ruthless and well connected to the cartels Sister Dajairia selects him. The FBI agents tell her he's hosting a basketball tournament this morning in Central Park. Sister Dajairia tells the agents that is where she will see him. The agents are very confused this is happening very fast, maybe a little too fast. But she brings forth the new law and the power of the U.N.A. "if you don't mind me asking Sister what proposition?" The special agent in charge William Moseley asks.

"You'll see and it will indeed, be a sight to behold!" She responds.

"I only ask Sister, because a lot of us put a lot of hard work and man hours into these cases."

"You needn't worry about your MAN HOURS agent Mosley I'm not here to take your case or glory. What I offer is sanctioned by the world leaders and is THE WILL OF GOD!"

"May we accompany you Sister?" Another agent asks.

"Of course agents, by all means, all who wish to witness the power of the Lord are welcome"

The agents chuckle to themselves a little, because she didn't refer to the power of the U.N.A.

they mean no disrespect but are a little amused by her rhetoric.

But are very relieved that she is not here to dismiss or take their case from them.

"She did have to throw God in there." One of the agents Whispers to agent Williams.

"She's a holy woman and a Nun, what did ya expect. let's go!" He responds as they wrap up and head out to Central Park.

She communicates this information to Mother Teresa who is delighted. She tells all the major FBI headquarters in the United States to be expecting the Arch Nuns and to provide them with similar information. She assures them they will reap the rewards of their hard work.

They will be exempt and not held accountable for the events that are about to take place. They are glad to hear this but very concerned as to how this will be done.

A.N.T 2 Lands in Detroit and goes to the FBI headquarters. In a large office talking with FBI agents Sister Nevaeh and her team requests files on the same types of individuals. They give her the files of Samuel Jenkins. He is the Absolute King of the city. He specializes in moving many types of drugs including fentanyl a very addictive and Dangerous Drug made popular during the big opioid crisis. He forces young girls into prostitution and stripping at a very young age. Some as young as thirteen many of which die or are killed. To him they are nothing but merchandise. He also controls many of the street gangs their violence is merciless. Mr. Jenkins rules with zero tolerance for Disobedience.

"Where can we find him?" Sister Nevaeh asks taking a seat at the meeting table. Two of her team stand behind her.

"Are you kidding me, right now? He owns the largest strip joint, I'm sorry Gentlemen's Club downtown." One of the agents shouts.

"We can't just barge in there; you know how many warrants we'll need? He pretty much runs everything from there." Another agent adds wiping his forehead nervously.

"Hold on a second everyone." Bob Newheart, the special

agent in charge says.

"From what I understand the U.N.A is going to take this guy down and we're going to receive all the credit. Is that right Sister?"

"Yes, it is by order of Mother Teresa and the U.N.A."

"Then gentleman what are we waiting for. I for one would like to see this sh#t! We've been working on this case for the past three years. I'd like to see him go down and see who takes his place." Special agent Newheart concludes siting down taking a sip of his water.

"Hopefully no one will be too eager to take that position after this day." Sister Nevaeh tells them.

"We of course can accompany you, right Sister?"

"Of course agents, every step of the way. This is your case. I am merely going to demonstrate the power of thy Lord and ALL will bear witness to this."

Special agent Newhart and his team are glad to hear this and find her rhetoric interesting. "Alright ladies and gentlemen we're going to a strip club." He says to everyone. "Are you actually going to go inside Sister, or do you want us to go in and clean it up. They have both male and female strippers there ya know?"

He continues telling Sister Nevaeh with a smile on his face. Then everyone in the room turns and looks at Sister Nevaeh.

"Ok everyone I have seen naked bodies before!" She says putting her hands on her hips then begins to fumble around in her bag as though she is searching for something. Special agent Newhart asks her if everything is all right and she replies.

"Does anybody have change of a twenty, I'm going to need some one-dollar bills?" She concludes smiling back at everyone to lighten the mood. They enjoy a light laugh and the agents are pleased to know with her harsh condescending rhetoric she has a sense of humor.

A.N.T eight goes to St. Louis. To meet with the FBI, there Sister Anna is given all information pertaining to Valencia

Tobler. She's the current crime Queen of the city. She specializes in various narcotics and male prostitution taking in young boys as young as five years old. Valencia is a middle-aged, well-educated, Black woman who clawed her way up the crime ladder by killing and manipulating numerous boyfriends and husbands. She has no love for men other than exploiting them. She surrounds herself only with the strongest fighters and killers. The agents working the case do not mind U.N.A assistance, especially since they'll be receiving all the credit. They welcome the A.N.T with open arms.

As they sit in the boardroom discussing the particulars of the case. Sister Anna is seated at the head of the table drinking coffee.

"So tell us Sister, if you don't mind how are you gonna bring this case to a close today." Head agent Randy Graves asks.

"Yeah Sister! no offense but that's a pretty tall order." Adds special agent Erica Cooper.

"But considering what happened with deputy director Vesuvio we're not going to ask too many questions. I'm sure everything is in order, so we're just gonna hold on and go along for the ride."

Sister Anna sips her coffee and slowly lowers her cup to the table and softly says.

"And quite the ride it will be agents, quite the ride indeed! Am I to understand you have an undercover agent close to her?"

"Yes we do Sister" Special agent Graves replies handing her a file with the undercover agent's picture and information. She passes the photo around to her team so they know not to harm him. Special agent Graves informs her that they are currently on an airplane returning from a trip to the Bahamas and will be landing within the hour. Miss Tobler always travels with six large male bodyguards to protect her.

They must be top champion Fighters and ruthless Killers to be by her side.

Sister Anna informs the agents that she wishes to confront her in public at the airport. The agents are not sure if this would be a wise move but this is imperative to the proposition, she is to offer her. The agents assume Sister Anna is attempting to avoid a firefight to keep everyone safe. It wouldn't be the first-time law enforcement chose a public place for a meeting it does have its advantages and keeps everyone calm. Sister Anna stands and asks for everyone to Bow their heads and join her in a prayer. Special agent Graves and several of his agents respectfully decline stating they are not religious or the praying type. She respects their wish but the A.N.T agents know to bow their heads. Even if they do not pray or believe. They do this to respect and honor their Commander.

"Oh God I am thy humble servant and I ask that you watch over these agents and my fellow team. Oh God I ask that you keep Miss Tobler of sound mind and body and finally Oh Lord I ask that you keep her companions calm cool and collected in our presence, for the light of YOUR Laws, her way comes. Thank you, God Amen."

The agents look at each other shaking their heads in disbelief. They do not wish to hear her praying or any other religious mumbo-jumbo while they are doing their jobs.

"Okay everybody we should get going now if we're going to intercept them at the airport" Special agent Graves tells the group.

"Again Sister, no disrespect it's just that there isn't a lot of room for praying in our line of work"

"It's okay special agent Graves, I only ask that you join me in a prayer. I would never demand that you do. Oh, and Special agent."

"Yes Sister"

"There is always room and time for prayer!"

"Of course, Sister of course"

At Sakura a popular Japanese restaurant near the UN building. Mother Teresa and her party arrive. Although she does not condone, she does not mind from time to time being treated like a celebrity. The staff too which many are religious respect her highly. Everyone in her party is laughing and being festive with the staff as they are being seated. All but Zachariah and Joshua. For they are struggling with their masculine emotions. They appear amongst the group as two spoiled boys who did not get what they wanted at the toy store. They are sulking and attempting to hide it. But their grandmother knows them all too well and is relishing this moment and she made sure Valentina and Betty we're seated beside her grandsons.

The party is engaged in small conversations amongst themselves when Betty puts her hand on Josh's shoulder and asks with concern.

"Are you okay, Brother Superior Joshua?"

"Yes! Thank you, I do not mean to be distant but I am a man of God." He answers calmly then turns to Mother Teresa and shouts.

"BUT MY thoughts are on the lord! ALWAYS on the Lord and the many ways I can serve."

"AS ARE MINE, YEP, YES INDEED ON THE LORD!" Zachariah shouts also looking at Mother Teresa who is seated at the far end of the table currently engaged in a conversation with the waitress and ordering drinks. Shouts to her boys with a big smile on her face.

"As they should be!"

A.N.T-7 and the FBI agents arrive at Central Park. It is a beautiful afternoon. The basketball tournament has not yet started, but it is very crowded. They received confirmation that Diego is already here. Several SUVs pull directly up to the main entrance to where the tournament is being held. Everyone pulls out their cell phones to videotape this. The FBI exit their Vehicles first. They are wearing their blue uniform jackets with the large yellow F.B.I letters on the back. Diego's staff at the door immediately inform him that the FBI is here. He sits calmly with his friends telling them confidently. "They must be here for somebody else but keep an eye on em I wanna know their every move."

The agents assure everyone that everything is okay and to remain calm.

The A.N.T agents exit their S.U.Vs. they are wearing their black uniforms with the letters A.N.T largely displayed in bold White across the front and back. "Who the fu#k are these guys?" Someone shouts.

Mikolai walks to one of the SUVs, he is wearing a small PS 92 assault rifle under his arm, he opens the back door and out steps Arch Nun Sister Dajairia. Immediately a crowd attempts to gather but the FBI agents quickly take control of the situation ordering local law enforcement to call for backup and crowd control. She stands proudly before the crowd representing the Arch Nunhood. Every cell phone camera is fixed on her.

"OH SH#T!" Is the only thing many in the crowd can shout, without hesitation Diego's staff call him back.

"What you calling me for, just tell me where they at. They ain't gonna do nothing. Don't bother-----"

Before he can finish that sentence he is interrupted.

"Yo man! there's a fU#KING Arch Nun, OUT DIS MOTHER FU#KER."

Diego's jaw drops and he immediately stands up. He begins to notice the crowd around him talking and whispering about the Arch Nun at the entrance. Diego always travels with his bodyguards and a member of his lawyer's legal team. Like the old Teflon Don of New York 'John Gotti' No law enforcement agency has ever made a case stick to him. He is very well connected. He gets himself together and regains his composure.

"Alright y'all! don't trip, I got this. They just trying ta shake us. EVERYBODY be cool and enjoy the game."

He tells his group. His lawyer agrees reassuring everyone to remain calm.

Since the sanction of the U.N.A, he like so many crime bosses have been very careful as not to be directly involved in anything illegal. Diego takes comfort in this. He wants to show the U.N.A that he is not shaken nor moved by them. Two police officers walk ahead of Mikolai followed by Sister Dajairia and the rest of the A.N.T. As they walked down the corridor heading toward the stadium everyone is taking pictures and video. Some shout sarcastic remarks as typical New Yorkers would. But many show them respect and wonder what brings an Arch Nun to Central Park. They enter the stadium bleachers and there are many gasps from the crowd. The Arch Nun and her team are truly a magnificent sight to behold. She walks with such confidence as she makes her way down the bleachers to the main Court. Mikolai her second-in-command stays close to her. "Send Em' up" Mikolai tells Francesco the team's I.T specialist who controls the small recording drones atop the A.N.T vehicles. The team activated their body cams as soon as they exited their vehicles. This is standard operating procedure of course. The drones quickly acquire their optimum vantage points.

The crowd is definitely not accustomed to U.N.A drones flying around. Many hide marijuana and other contraband. They also try not to look directly at them in fear of facial recognition.

But everyone knows not to try and leave for that would bring unwanted attention to them.

As they have learned from the 40-day media storm. When an Arch Nun is present and on official duty. These things record EVERYTHING!

Sister Dajairia makes her way down to the basketball court. There are many jeers and obscenities shouted from the crowd, not directly toward her but pertaining to the delay of the game. The crowd simply wants them to finish their business and leave. The recording drones can also serve as audio speakers for the A.N.T agents using the small microphones in their headsets.

"May I please have everyone's attention for a moment please." Sister Dajairia asks the crowd politely. But they continue to talk amongst themselves. She increases the volume on the recorder drones and asks again. Only this time with the rhetoric of an Arch Nun.

"ALL BE SILENT!" Is heard loud and clear through the recorder drone's speakers.

This gets the attention of everyone instantly.

"Well, she did ask politely the first time." One FBI agent Whispers to another laughing.

"I BRING YOU THE WORD OF GOD! FOR I HAVE COME TO DO THE LORD'S WORK. your compliance is not optional."

Sister Dajairia says slowly walking in the center of the basketball court accompanied by Mikolai. The crowd finds her rhetoric a little funny. For they have never heard someone speak like this.

"We are also here on official business of the U.N.A, you have 45 minutes until the start of the game and it will start on time. I promise you."

To that everyone applauds.

"This event is sponsored by Diego Lugo."

She pauses while everyone applauds and whistles, he holds a hand up in appreciation for the crowd's response when hearing his name. She motions for them to settle down.

"DIEGO" someone shouts from the bleachers.

"THE KING OF NEW YORK"

Shouts another again the crowd applauds stomping their feet loudly on the bleachers creating a very loud rumble.

Sister Dajairia begins to talk over the crowd.

"Diego Lugo is accused of a great many crimes to which many he is guilty of. Many of you have lost loved ones to his influence and violence and many of you are afraid to stand up to him in fear of the repercussions it will most definitely bring upon you. So, you praise him, honor him and respect him."

She deliberately pauses for crowd response.

"That's right! we do!" shouts a woman from the crowd.

"More then we can say about Your ass!" Shouts a teenage boy. Then a young Puerto Rican woman stands up holding her baby on her hip. She makes her way across the bleaches and down to the center of the basketball court. She walks directly up to Sister Dajairia whose headset microphone can pick up her voice as well. She looks the Arch Nun directly in the eyes as she speaks.

"If all these things you say are true. The police, the mayor and politicians ain't done nothing about it. I don't care if you don't like what I have ta say, sister! and I don't care if Diego doesn't like what I have ta say. But if you can't do anything about it once and for all. Then get the fu#k outta here now! and leave us alone. We have to live here, you don't." The crowd agrees cheering and applauding.

"May I know your name?" Sister Dajairia asks.

"What you wanna know my name for?"

"So I may simply know who I am addressing, that's all."

"Don't worry bout my name Alright!" She says putting her hand up to Dajairia's face and walks back to her seat. The crowd is still cheering so Dajairia motions for them once again to settle down.

"It's true many have promised you everything and given you nothing." The Arch Nun says.

"But what I offer you on this day is my life!" She definitely has every one's attention now. For she offers the law of Goliath! A Warrior's challenge similar to The Challenge the Philistine champion Goliath made to King Saul. If Goliath wins all will belong to the Philistines if the Israelites when all will be theirs. As King Saul said the warrior that defeats Goliath shall be a rich man.

That is why the crime Lords are allowed to choose a champion if they wish and make them Rich if they are the victor, it was a fight to the death. There is NO due process Simply put WINNER TAKE ALL!

"I challenge you Diego Lugo or a person of his choosing to a fight to the end, for everything! This is approved by the President of the United States and the U.N.A. they will waive all charges and dismiss any pending cases against you. He will leave here with a clean slate and can truly call himself the 'King of New York' if he defeats me on this day right here, right now. Or I will arrest him right now and he will answer for all crimes against him as he will undergo the serum and be convicted thereafter."

There is much talking amongst the crowd as they struggle to understand this.

Upon hearing he will be placed under the serum. Diego turns to his legal aid and asks can this be done?

She regretfully tells him it can! under the new law. He knows the F.B.I doesn't know all his illegal businesses, but the new U.N.A might! With no time to call his friends in the C.I.A he tries to play it cool.

Sister Dajairia signals to Mikolai who tells awaiting FBI and SWAT teams standing by at all of Diego's businesses and residents to commence operation 'CHOKE-HOLD'. Within minutes they storm all of his properties and businesses securing everyone inside but make no arrests. All Squad leaders check in confirming to Mikolai they have complete control and are awaiting further instructions.

"Stand by for further orders." Mikolai tells them.

All the managers of Diego's Empire are told what is going on and allowed by the S.W.A.T teams to call Diego's primary attorney Jacob Weinstein, who understands the new laws and immediately calls Diego.

"Diego, Diego listen to me! Just listen, everything that Arch Nun is telling you is correct if she's stupid enough to challenge you to a fight and the President is willing to wipe your slate clean and close all existing investigations. Then Oh my God! I am telling you to take it, knock her on her ass in front of every one, and even though you can't and won't be charged for murder knock her out ONLY, show Mercy but DON'T, I repeat DON'T kill her just because you can get away with it! The world is most likely watching and People need ta like you, right now and who knows maybe after this you can run for mayor. The new Goliath law states if you don't wanna fight you can choose someone else ta take your place and pay them. But if you delay the fight, they will hold EVERYTHING of yours for three day before it is considered a forfeiture and they CAN and WILL take you and your ENTIRE EMPIRE! All you have ta do is win or choose somebody that can and your home free, my friend, HOME FREE!"

Diego's mind is now put at ease, he smiles. But would very much like to kill her, in front of everybody. He is however going to break as many of her bones as he can. He's still angry but knows he absolutely cannot be put under the serum or taken into custody the cartels would be furious and his life would be worth NOTHNG!

"You won't just have the respect of other bosses in the city. You'll have respect from all the bosses in the world!" Jacob tells him. Diego's thoughts are no longer on his businesses all he has to do is win a simple fight. He knows everything, will be just fine now. Because he's going to go down there and put that Arch Nun through the pavement.

"OK Dogg, you just made my day!"

"Remember, DON'T KILL HER! We're gonna make a lot of

money after this."

Diego is now feeling confident and full of himself; he stands. "What are you doing?" His legal representative asks taking hold of his hand.

"It's okay" he tells her gently removing her hand. "I can't pass up dis opportunity ta kick these motherfu#kers outta here." He takes his shirt off displaying a finely chiseled body of a heavyweight boxing champion. He throws both fists up in the air, the DJ of the event plays the rap song 'HOOLIGAN'

The crowd cheers wildly as Diego walks down to meet the Arch Nun. The news media have been called but they have not yet arrived, no one was expecting this. The FBI agents are very concerned that Sister Dajairia is going to get physically hurt, very bad and they'll be back to square one as Diego goes free.

"I can't believe we came down here for this" One of the FBI agent says to special agent Newhart.

"Well, Vesuvio was a friend of mine, so maybe this is Poetic Justice."

Diego enters the basketball court doing a little Shuffle dance. "Go Diego, Go Diego, Go Diego." The crowd chants. He is given a wireless microphone by the DJ so he can speak to the crowd.

They cheer for him, but not from love, respect or appreciation but from Fear. For them there has always been and will always be a Crime Boss to control their lives. To them the U.N.A is just another empty promise of Hope to keep politicians in office and adding religion to it will not make it more acceptable.

"Yo, Yo, Yo New York what's crackin" Diego shouts into the microphone waving to everyone. "First off, I wanna apologize for this little inconvenience. But Y'all gonna get a show and a basketball game. I wanna let Y'all know something right now. They want to challenge me to a fist fight and if I win, they'll leave me alone. They told me by the

new law only the Arch Nuns can do the fight. Oh well!"
He says shrugging his shoulders.
"It's ten of these Nuns, it's gonna be nine when I'm done." He
looks at Sister Dajairia and drops the mic, blows her a kiss
and waves bye-bye to her. The crowd goes wild.
"Shut these motherfu#kers down Diego.!" Shouts a man
from the crowd.
"Knock that bit#h the fu#k out!" Shouts another.
How disrespectful they are to Sister Dajairia but she knew
this was to be expected.
Diego is feeling great like the old days when he was boxing
in the heavyweight circuit. So, he picks the microphone up
from the ground telling everyone that there will be a large
block party tonight to honor his victory and the liquor and
food is on him. The crowd cheers even louder he continues
to extend the invitation to the FBI and the U.N.A.
  At this point no one seems to be concerned about the
basketball tournament. The crowd outside the basketball
court is getting thick the police are doing an excellent job of
crowd control but unfortunately the news media cannot get
through. So, they begin to report what they can. A New York
crowd is hard to keep silent when they are excited and they
are very excited. Mikolai has a few of the basketball refs
inspect the fighters to assure there are no hidden weapons or
body armor.
Also so the people will know there is no trickery this is very
much for real.
Mikolai assists Sister Dajairia in removing her coat.
She is wearing a black bodysuit with a long white cover
dress with four slits around it so she can move freely. Many
of the males make lewd suggestions and comments
regarding her figure. One woman says to another. "She may
be a holy woman, but she most definitely has a body made
for sin!" Behind them sits a man who overhears this and
adds. "Amen ta Dat, DAM!"

Diego flexes his muscles and the women in the crowd go wild. He turns and asks. "Are you sure you wanna go through with dis? if you forfeit, I win and you can spare yourself a lot of pain. Cuz I ain't holding back, AT ALL!" She stares at him as though she were looking through him and speaks into her headset for all to hear.

"Then I sacrifice my life today in an attempt to free these people of you!"

When the crowd hears this. they begin to quiet down. Can this be true, is she really willing to die so violently here today? This Arch Nun must be crazy. They think she's just saying and doing this for attention. Sister Dajairia urges all those with children that do not wish to look upon this, to take this opportunity and leave. No one leaves, their children have seen far worse, they are New Yorkers. The referees of the basketball game had no idea they would be referees to a fight as well, but are happy to do so. The Arch Nun and Diego stand facing each other. Sister Dajairia turns off her headset and removes her habit for it is sacred to her, she assures her dress strands are free to move as she does, she turns away falling to her knees, she assumes the prayer position and prays aloud for those close enough to hear. "Oh lord I pray to thee, you are my Strength as I fight to free these people, you are my guiding light, So Oh Great and Merciful God I ask that you guild me and for haven to take hold of me. I give all to I-AM Amen." She quickly jumps to her feet with her eyes closed, she turns to face him. She slowly opens her eyes and with a focused piercing stare, she says loud for all to hear.

"NOW WITNESS THE POWER OF GOD!"

The refs eyes widen as they hear this, they look at Diego then shout the word everyone has been so anxious to hear. "FIGHT!" The Crowd Goes Wild Diego immediately attacks her with all his strength and skill. The Arch Nun easily and gracefully out maneuvers his attacks. Kicking him numerous times to the body and legs just enough to weaken and anger him. He throws two very strong hits missing her, the two square off for a moment.

Diego is in a traditional boxing stance breathing heavily, the Arch Nun is in a kung fu fighting stance. She hits him with three perfect spinning kicks to the left side of his face with the heel of her left foot, time slow down. She spins to the right hitting him with a reverse fist with her right hand followed by four more spinning kicks with her right foot knocking him back several feet and to the floor, time resumes. The crowd cannot believe what they have just seen, nor can Diego. She then raises her leg above her head to perform her signature 'Prima Ballerina' stance demonstrating the great strength of her magnificent legs. "Damn! she got mad skillz" Says a young woman to one of the FBI agents standing near her.

Dance Style kung fu was always something for exhibition only this is the first time anyone has seen it applied affectively. Sister Dajairia is a master of this and does it so well.

Diego is exhausted and out of breath but does not want anyone to realize this. He knows now he has to hit her with all his might if she dies, she dies! He thinks to himself, but is determined to hit her as hard as he possibly can. He throws a wild Haymaker punch and misses. Dajairia executes a spin kick with lightning speed, the heel of her foot hits Diego in the jaw, breaking it! "Ooooooooh" The crowd yells. Many stand concerned for Diego. He absorbs the impact of the kick turning his body attempting to strike her with a backfist. She ducks and performs the same kick again with pinpoint accuracy. This time striking the back of his neck causing severe damage. He falls forward his body is limp, as he hits the hard ground. Upon doing so he breaks his nose and all of his front teeth.

"Oooooooh shit!" Many in the crowd yell in disbelief. They assume he, being the strong Champion fighter, he is that he'll be getting up immediately but this is not the case.

He lies in his own blood shaking and trembling; he is in shock and having convulsions. Dajairia stands over him with her leg straight in the air with perfect form. The crowd now realizes he will not be getting up, EVER AGAIN! This all happened so fast no one could hardly believe it Sister Dajairia slowly lowers her leg. The paramedics who were on the scene in case of injuries in the game, immediately rushed to Diego.

Sister Dajairia Falls to her knees and silently prays for the Lord to take care of Diego.

The noise from the crowd can be heard well outside the stadium. As she stands Mikolai assists her with her coat, habit and headset. So, she may address the crowd.

"It was not my skill, my speed nor My Strength to which I owe this Victory. It Is thy Lord God."

"Now you gonna preach ta us." A teenager shouts from the crowd. But before Sister Dajairia can respond many in the crowd Shout at the teenager.

"Shut up, before I come up there and throw your ass off the bleachers, Punk!"

Shouts a large man standing in the bleachers.

Many in the crowd agree and Shout things to the teenager who they are now starting to shove.

The FBI agents have been standing with their jaws dropped in astonishment since Diego hit the ground. But prevent the crowd from harming the boy.

"Please everyone settle down please" Sister Dajairia asks and they immediately comply.

"This was the man whom you were so afraid, he who has ruined many of your lives and harmed so many of your loved ones, he who has taken your sons, daughters, and wives addicting them to drugs and forcing them into prostitution. He who would see your children die! for profit. Many of you served him and treated him as though he were a king. He who children looked up to and admired, he who was your champion. Now look upon him and know. By the power of God! He shall harm you NO MORE! " she says with conviction as she points down at him.

There is loud chattering in the crowd as they speak to each other and point at Diego.

The paramedics stabilize him and are very careful as they ease him onto the stretcher. They begin to roll him away when Sister Dajairia grabs hold of the stretcher stopping them. The crowd gasped loudly they cannot believe she did that.

"I know many of you think there will be another one to take his place. That this is only temporary." She says holding tightly to the stretcher.

"Sister we have to get this man to the hospital immediately!" Pleads one of the paramedics.

"He can endure his pain a bit longer as many were forced to endure him."

She replies shoving the stretcher toward the paramedic. Mikolai grabs the paramedic by the arm.

"The Arch Nun said to wait!" The paramedic looks Mikolai in the eye and knows he had better listen. The crowd can hear all of this from her headset, so they begin to quiet down.

"Diego's lieutenants are sitting in the stands amongst you. let them come before me now. Let them and all others who dare to take his throne come before me now! And I shall lay them down beside him!" She says pointing to Diego again. She informs the crowd that Diego's money will be used to serve the community. Everything he owns has been seized and will be liquidated. His organization is now bankrupt! "The U.N.A will occupy Diego's properties and from there they will serve the people.

From this day forth you are free of his kind." There are loud cheers and happy tears as The Crowd Goes Crazy. Many politicians and law enforcement agencies have promised this, none have delivered. But on this day with the Power of God an Arch Nun has done what no one else could.

She motions for Mikolai to allow the paramedics to take Diego away. His lieutenants and all those who would have jumped at the opportunity to take his place, sit silently and lower their heads in shame. With no money to continue Diego's businesses they are helpless. They can only hope that upper management sends someone to replace Diego soon.

Sister Dajairia asks for the microphone from which Diego spoke. From her headset she asks for everyone's attention one last time. They gladly settle down and listen to her.

"The basketball game will be held and the prize money Diego promised will be awarded. The party he spoke of will commence. For you now have much to celebrate so rejoice and NEVER FORGET."

She holds the microphone high in the air for the crowd to see. "All praise be to thy Lord God!" She yells at the top of her lungs and DROPS THE MIC! Everyone FBI agents included throw their hands in the air and cheer as loud as they can. Because many of the spectators were live streaming on their cell phones. Almost everyone in the park was watching. This goes viral through the internet again nearly causing a shutdown and like the Breath of God it swept swiftly through Central Park.

Mother Teresa and her assistants were watching from the U.N building. The assistants celebrate and hug each other, they were worried about Sister Dajairia. They didn't what to see her beaten to death. This was the first time they, and the world bared witness to the fighting skills, strength and maneuverability of an Arch Nun and they are very, very impressed!

Mother Teresa telepathically communicates to her granddaughter. 'Magnificent! my granddaughter magnificent' While simultaneously speaking to her A.N.T agents through their headsets.

"Great job A.N.T -7 the crowd and traffic are extremely heavy so I grant you permission to remotely bring in your

B.A.D to retrieve you."

The FBI agents are hugging and shaking each other's hands because all their hard work was not in vain. Diego Lugo has been removed from the streets and they all get big raises, promotions and full credit for it, Mother Teresa will see to this. Many in the crowd approach the Arch Nun very slowly and with caution they simply want to thank her. Mikolai slowly puts his hand on his weapon. The recorder drones which are also armed, form a defensive perimeter around her. As they continue to approach, they open their arms as a sign of non-aggression. So, she allows them to get closer. But they still maintain a little distance between them and her. When the young Puerto Rican woman whom spoke so rudely to her earlier pushes her way through the crowd, she continues to rush toward Sister Dajairia. She is determined to reach the Arch Nun. The crowd closest to Sister Dajairia begin to back away in fear. She tells Mikolai not to draw his weapon.

The young woman attempts to kneel before Sister Dajairia who quickly catches her preventing her from doing so. The rest of the crowd is loud and celebrating those closest to this incident are silent. As sister Dajairia lifts the woman to her feet, she looks into her eyes and says to her.

"Do not kneel to me, my child but humble thyself before the Lord God. You will take no knee except in prayer, I am merely a servant of the Lord."

The young woman looks up at her crying hysterically.

"My name is Rosa Diaz and I'm so sorry sister. please, please, please forgive me."

"You have done nothing wrong for me to forgive my child and I shall remember your name as long as I breathe." The crowd of people who were closest, hear this and take comfort as they start to believe and slowly begin to approach the Arch Nun. The FBI agents come and stand with Sister Dajairia so they may be seen with her. They witness people they know worked for Diego showing gratitude and appreciation. The people have never experienced law enforcement such as this, and harsh as it may be. They know that it is GOOD!

On this day Diego Lugo the once King of New York challenged the Power of God and on this day, he lost everything! Mikolai informs Sister Dajairia the B.A.D is on its way. The announcer of the basketball tournament asks for everyone to clear the court and take their seats. The crowd attending the tournament is beginning to settle down however the mass crowd forming outside and within the park is getting larger. The traffic in the area has come to a standstill as people attempt to enter the park and take a look at an Arch Nun up close. Mikolai begins to escort Sister Dajairia through the crowd followed by the F.B.I. A teenage African-American boy stands in the way. Those nearby take notice and become concerned. The FBI agents escorting Sister Dajairia notice this as well, they slowly reach for their weapons. The teenager is a popular drug Runner for Diego and known by many. Four more teenage boys now stand behind him. The drones are still recording. The Arch Nun has not yet ordered them into a defense position. Mikolai immediately stands in front of Sister Dajairia and as he reaches for his weapon. She puts her hand on his shoulder and orders him to stand down. She steps around him, the boys keep their hands visible, stretching their arms wide. Then one of them speaks to the Arch Nun. "Sister my name is Walter Lynch they call me Wild Ass Junie on the streets and I don't wanna do this shit no more" He says with tears in his eyes tossing all of his drugs and his gun at her feet. More people in the crowd noticed this. They are familiar with him and know he and his friends are new to the drug game. The others in his group surrender as well. The FBI agents cannot believe what their eyes behold.
"I wanna do something better with my life" He concludes and the others join him. Sister Dajairia motions for the FBI agents to retrieve the drugs and guns.

"It is a brave thing you do on this day and for this you shall not be arrested, but you will accompany the FBI agents. They will process your weapons and contraband then a representative of the U.N.A will meet with you to discuss your now bright future."

The boys are relieved that they are not going to be arrested. As they walk the crowd Parts allowing them to pass. Almost everyone thanks the Arch Nun as she walks by, but are reluctant to put their hands upon her. Mikolai gives the order to bring in the drones and wrap it up.

The A.N.T and FBI agents enter their vehicles; the recorder drones reattach themselves to the tops of the A.N.T vehicles. Normally they would not drive the vehicles on the grass in Central Park but due to the massive crowd and traffic they must, after all Diego's money will pay for the repairs.

The news media did not make the event in time but Mother Teresa is going to allow them copies of footage from some of the recorder drones.

The police clear a hundred foot radius in the middle of Central Park so the B.A.D can land. The craft quickly enters the area and slows to a stop, hovering over the crowd then blows the signature Horn of Gabriel to identify itself. The horn Echoes through the park. The crowd is so large and cheering so loud it is almost unbearable.

The craft slowly descendants the second it touches the ground its rear door opens and the A.N.T Vehicles Drive on board. The door quickly closes and the craft immediately takes off. The crowd is impressed at how quickly the vehicles drove on board and the craft took off, it was almost instantly.

It took only one hour for this news to spread worldwide. All the FBI agents now have a full understanding of how their offices and the U.N.A are directing this business with operation 'Chokehold' and the 'Challenge of Goliath law' Crime bosses at all levels were receiving phone calls from their lawyers, assuring their comprehension of these new laws being implemented. Many of them are eager to receive this offer, this opportunity to fight for a full pardon of their crimes and continue their criminal activities with more respect than they had ever hoped for. At the higher spectrum of organized crime, they are already choosing their champions. But Mother Teresa has given instructions to her granddaughters to be spectacular and invincible, to show the superiority and 'POWER OF GOD'! And this they shall do!

At St Louis Airport Valencia Tobler walks through the terminal with her bodyguards and staff. She is on the phone with her attorney who is explaining to her what happened in New York. She didn't know Diego but her staff are watching the videos from the spectator's cell phones on YouTube. "DAM! she fu#ked him up." Says one of her bodyguards. "They saying this nigg#r was a heavyweight boxer?" Says another.
"She beat his ass like he stole something from her!"
They show Valencia one of the videos while she's on the phone. She watches for a few seconds then continues the conversation with her attorney.
"look I'm 42 years old. I'm not about to be out here fighting with any of these bit#hes. But whoever I pick fights for me and can kill the Nun if I want and get away with it?"
"That's right V, win or lose you don't get the serum but if you refuse, YOU GET THE SERUM! So, choose very carefully!" He urges her. She like Diego is confident her Champion will win and she will profit from this. "Oh I keepz my boyz on point. They are always strong and ready to fight."
She says patting one of her large male bodyguards on the back. She uses many of them in underground fighting competitions to the death.

"I wish one of those damn Arch Nun Bit#hes would approach me with this bullsh#t. That'll be the last goddamn thing she do, thanks Hal"

She continues talking to her attorney and assistant as they continue through the terminal. They notice a Ruckus and camera flashes as a crowd is slowly approaching them.

"Oh get the fu#k outta here!" She says coming face-to-face with Arch Nun Sister Anna. She tells her attorney who gives her instructions.

"Be careful what you wish for V" Her attorney is heard on the cell phone speaker.

"I'll stay on the line with you handle this carefully, very, very carefully 'V' and remember you can't ask for the challenge, it must be offered" He tells her.

"Miss Valencia Tobler" Sister Anna says politely with a European accent.

"WHAT" Valencia answers with an attitude staring Sister Anna in the face attempting to intimidate her.

"It appears you have several very serious outstanding charges against you with the Federal Bureau of Investigation!"

One of the F.B.I agents leans over and Whispers to an A.N.T agent.

"Couldn't she just say F.B.I?"

"Couldn't you just shut the fu#k up!" Is the response.

Valencia takes a step toward Sister Anna and pointing in her face very angrily tells her.

"My attorney is handling all of that! and---"

"Your attorney's time has come to pass, as does yours!" Sister Anna says loudly with authority and Arch Nun Rhetoric. The crowd is silent but recording with their cell phones they want to hear everything that is said and they're impressed at the way the Arch Nun speaks and conducts herself. But when she said that directly to Valencia, they couldn't help but to applaud. The attorney attempts to shout instructions to her through the phone. When Sister Anna snatches the phone from her and ends the call.

Valencia would never let anyone do that to her especially in public in front of people without a very vicious beating from her bodyguards.

"You should keep your line free you'll be receiving some very important phone calls in a moment" Sister Anna tells her retuning the phone to her. Valencia begins to receive several very important calls informing her that law enforcement has invaded all of her businesses and properties.

"Chokehold applied boss", her second in command Bernardo informs her.

Valencia is angry she can hardly contain herself. The small crowd of Spectators begin to Snicker fueling her anger. She forgets herself and walks right up to The Arch Nun's face shouting.

"Let's Do This SH#T, THEN BIT#H!"

She is so close Sister Anna can smell the alcohol on her breath. "A warning" The Arch Nun says purposely pouring on the European accent. "Watch your proximity, Step back, NOW!" She continues assuming the prayer position.

Valencia disregards this warning and continues to argue walking closer and closer showing off in front of the crowd.

"You have three seconds to comply" Sister Anna says. Valencia continues to hold her ground yelling at the Arch Nun.

"Three, two, one" Sister Anna counts down before striking Valencia hard to the chest pushing her back. Time slows, as she grabs the phone from her hand, slaps her across the face and hits her again in the exact same spot on her chest before returning to the prayer position, time resumes. She falls backward in to the arms of her Body Guards. The Spectators gasp in amazement capturing all of this on their cell phones. Valencia felt the AMAZING strength of the Arch Nun as she is struck. Her bodyguards grab hold of her in case she wants to fight back, but there was no need, she does not wish to be

hit again by the Sister Anna. Her eyes are tearing but she doesn't want to cry in front of everyone, although the blows were very painful. "It's okay Y'all don't do nothing"
She tells her bodyguards, as if they were going to do something. They too were amazed at Sister anna's speed and accuracy. The terminal is becoming congested. Airport security is urging people to move along. Many in the crowd wish to view this incident but they don't want to miss their flights. They also do not believe there is going to be a physical altercation in the middle of the airport terminal, and they are right.
"I have brought everything that you are to a standstill" The Arch Nun tells her, this time without the European accent. "I offer you the Goliath challenge to release the U.N.A's hold upon you, you are familiar with this, no?"
"Oh yeah! I'm very familiar with this, in fact I was praying for this." Valencia responds angrily, quickly wiping tears from her eyes.
"Wunderbar" Sister Anna says which in German. (meaning 'wonderful') "Be very careful what you pray for!" She concludes.
"So where we gonna do this at, so you can get outta my business once and for all?" Valencia anxiously asks.
"The Park is 20 minutes from here" Says one of her bodyguards.
"We can end this there in front of everybody, since you itching for an a$s whooping so bad!"
Valencia says loudly.
"We will leave the Airport." Sister Anna says with a cold look and orders the FBI to collect all their cell phones and escort them to the government vehicles.
"Why can't Valencia ride with us?" Valencia's secretary asks.
"Because my dear, Valencia is legally under arrest pending the outcome of today's event"
Sister Anna answers smiling.
"Ok then" Valencia interrupts.

"It's all good. Cuz I got somebody that's gonna knock that smile Right Da fu#k off your face, PERMANENTLY!" Chattering can be heard amongst the crowd some are disappointed they will not fight here, others are relieved. "We shall see" The Arch Nun responds calmly.
"Al vita Zein" she concludes in German which means "Until we meet again". She instructs her team and the FBI agents to gather Valencia's staff and take them to the park. Although the crowd did not see a fight, they were very entertained. For they know in thirty minutes they can watch the video of it on YouTube. They applauded as they disperse. Some attempt to follow but are stopped by airport security and the police. "This is reminiscent of an after-school fight of junior high school kids." Special agent Bryson says to Sister Anna.
"I'm afraid I must agree with you. But if they insist upon bullying people as though they were in the 8th grade. There would be no need for us to bully the bullies so to speak. They refuse to comprehend your language of law so, I shall speak to them in theirs, A fist for a fist!"
"I hear ya Sister Amen. The Bible says in eye for an eye."
"Unfortunately special agent in this case we'll be taking a head for an eye."
The FBI agents are both shocked and glad to hear this. They are also glad they will not be held accountable for any of this if it should go wrong.
They leave the airport and head to the park. Along the way Sister Anna notices a large vacant parking lot. "Pull into this lot" she says pointing. "This will do nicely."
The motorcade enters the parking lot and forms a circle as they park. Everyone exits their vehicles; Bernardo gives the order to send out the recording drones. As Valencia is escorted from an FBI vehicle, she asks. "I thought we were going to the park, why ain't we at the park? we agreed on the park!"
Sister Anna who is standing close to her turns and shouts. "Silence! we agreed upon nothing of the sort. The mutual

agreement was to leave the airport. Now, choose your champion!"

Valencia cannot stand the way the Arch Nun speaks to her and can't wait to see her Beat to Death!

Sister Anna is well aware of Valencia's staff informing more of her people to come to the park.

This would have put her at a strategic Advantage for an ambush. So, she changed the destination and ordered FBI vehicles to block the entrances to the parking lot and allow no one to enter. Valencia is well known for ambushing her enemies. She is about to win or lose everything and that makes her desperate and very dangerous.

Valencia chooses her champion his name is Abrafo which means 'Warrior/ Executioner' He is African ex-military and of course a very large and strong fighter. He is feared on the streets of St Louis by many. Sister Anna gives Valencia a few moments to talk to her fighter and her attorneys.

"Listen very closely Abrafo You won a lot of fights for me." Valencia tells him putting both hands on his face. "Since you can get away with killing her in front of the FBI and everybody, Do Dat Sh#t and I'll give you a million dollars, TODAY!"

Abrafo knows he can beat the Arch Nun to death as he has done to countless women in the past and gotten away with it. This time he can do it and get rich. He likes the sound of that so without hesitation he agrees. "Don't toy with her, don't play with her, just kill that bit#h. QUICK, FAST and in a GOD DAM HURRY!" Valencia tells him as she turns and gives the Arch Nun a hard stare.

Abrafo removes his coat. The A.N.T assist the Arch Nun as she removes her coat and Habit. Both Fighters are checked for weapons or body armor before they begin.

"I would ask if you're sure about this Sister but my gut tells me you got this."

Special agent Bryson says smiling at her.

"Thanks for the vote of confidence special agent, but if I

should die please tell my brothers and Sisters to be sure and water my plants"

The smile slowly Fades from the agent's face as he says. "Wait What?"

The Arch Nun slowly walks toward the strong African warrior. "Are you ready to kill me now?" She asks him. "I woke up this morning, ready to kill you!"

Valencia and her people cheer and applaud loudly as they hear this.

Sister Anna turns to special agent Bryson saying. "My plants, please don't forget my plants!"

Special agent Bryson with a concerned look on his face simply nods his head. The A.N.T agents silently Snicker to themselves.

One FBI agent says to another. "What the fu#k, are we just gonna stand here and let her be beaten to death?"

"law or no law I'm Catholic as soon as she hits the ground, I'm arresting everybody here I don't give a fu#k about my career!" Says another. A crowd of people have formed outside the parking lot with their cell phones out recording anything they could. As soon as the A.N.T entered the airport the news media was called. But they arrived at the airport too late.

"You gotta be fu#king kidding me" A news reporter shouts as airport security tells him they just missed them, they're on their way to the park.

Sister Anna begins to walk toward Abrafo, He tightly clenches his fists and starts toward her flexing his chest muscles. As they come closer together, they begin to Circle each other sizing one another up.

Abrafo takes a karate stance. Sister Anna decides to use her Iron Fist technique, she assumes a Shaolin crane fighting stance. Loud cheering can be heard from the still Gathering crowd outside the parking lot. As Valencia watches the two fighters, she rubs her chest discreetly. She is still in pain from the blows she received from the Arch Nun.

Abrafo throws numerous hard punches at Sister Anna, she evades. All he can think about is killing her and becoming a rich man in the process. He cannot stop grinning for he so enjoys beating up on women and he knows one of his punches will soon find her face then the fight will be his. He plants his feet firmly to the ground playtime is over he thinks to himself. He throws three left Jabs at Sister Anna attempting to set her up for his killer right-hand punch. As he throws the third Jab, then his mighty right hand cross. Times slows, Sister Anna with blinding speed evades and punches him behind his arm just above the elbow as it fully extends, snapping it like a twig. He immediately turns throwing a wild left hand punch, she Ducks as his body twists, she is now positioned slightly behind him. Using her Iron Fist technique, she strikes him in the lower spine, his eyes widen as his back breaks. He falls towards the ground but just before impact Sister Anna jumps in the air twirling her body placing her knee in the center of his back slamming him against the hard-concrete time resumes. He feels nothing from the neck down he is still conscious but quiet and motionless.

"Oooooooh sh#t" The rest of Valencia's body guards' yell. Everyone including the crowd outside the parking lot are going crazy cheering and applauding, the F.B.I agents are speechless. Valencia is silent as she looks despairingly at Abrafo, her once great champion, whom has now cost her EVERYTHING!

Sister Anna with her knee still placed upon his back slowly raises her head, she and Valencia's eyes meet, she slowly stands never taking her eyes off Valencia. She slowly closes her eyes, bows her head, assumes the prayer position and begins to pray for Abrafo for he shall be paralyzed from the neck down for the rest of his life!

'Well done! my granddaughter, well done' Mother Teresa feels to Anna.

The FBI had paramedics standing by who are now entering the parking lot. Valencia's legs weaken and she loses balance. Her staff and bodyguards catch her preventing her from falling. Sister Anna concludes her prayer the A.N.T assist her with her coat and Habit. She then approaches Valencia and her staff.

"You need not assist her." The Arch Nun says to them. "She has no currency nor means to compensate you for your trouble, she has nothing now and anyone attempting to take her place shall know the same! All those who were forced to work for her are now free. But you will still answer for the crimes you have committed under her rule. Fortunately for you it will not be the U.N.A apprehending you."

Sister Anna steps closer to Valencia one of the recorder drones follows her. She then proceeds to recite the U.N.A Miranda Rights and Conviction used only by the Arch Nuns this is spoken when an Arch Nun is removing someone from society and incarcerating them.

"It is with great regret and deep sorrow Valencia Tobler; you are no longer allowed to function in Society. You are condemned to spend the rest of your life in multiple incarceration facilities around the world. You will never see your family or friends nor will you speak to them ever again. They may communicate to you. But you will never be allowed to respond. You have proven yourself a menace to the world and it is the voice of the world that removes you from it. With the power invested in me by the U.N.A. I, Arch Nun Sister Anna. So says this on this day. Has it is written, so shall it be done!"

This is the first time this has been spoken for the world to hear. If Diego logo survives his wounds, he shall hear this and he shall know the same fate.

She motions for her second-in-command to take Valencia into custody.   "Wait, wait LET ME TALK TA MY LAWER, LET ME TALK TA SOMEBODY, WE CAN WORK THIS OUT. PLEASE,

PLEASE WAIT, YOU CAN'T JUST DO THIS TA ME! I GOTTA HAVE A TRIAL!" Valencia screams hysterically she can't believe this is the end of her and everything she had is gone. The Arch Nun approaches her but she will not be quiet. Sister Anna uses her head set to speak through the drone's loud speakers for all to hear. "YOU CAN NOT NEGOTIATE THE TERMS OF GOD'S LAW; IT IS ABSOLUTE AND JUST!" The Arch Nun turns off her head set and walks away. For Miss Valencia Tobler is now property of the United Nations Agency.

As Sister Anna walks by, the FBI agents pat her on the back and congratulating her. She stops, turns and says to the special agent in charge.

"I'll tend to my own plants special agent, thank you."

"Yes ma'am" he replies with a big grin.

The FBI will be given full credit for the apprehension and fall of Valencia Tobler. She is handcuffed and placed in one of the U.N.A vehicles. As they shut the door those who worked for her simply stare as though they are lost. But unknowing to them, on this day they were found and saved by Sister Anna. What they do with the rest of their lives is completely up to them.

"Bring em in" Arsenio tells the I.T specialist. The recorder drones reattach themselves to the roofs of the A.N.T vehicles.

The FBI offer rides back to the airport terminal to Valencia's ex-employees. They reluctantly accept because there is no one else they can call. There is no faster medium on Earth than the internet and it is the internet that gives the world a voice and this voice spreads the acts of the Arch Nuns to every corner of the world. Almost instantly! Unfortunately, this gives criminals a heads up to prepare for operation 'choke hold'.

The FBI and A.N.T-2 arrive at 'Pole Position' the largest ladies and gentlemen's exotic club in Detroit. It is owned by Samuel Jenkins it is his home away from home. The news media in every major city in the United States are on high alert. This has been an interesting day so far two Arch Nuns have been engaged in physical combat and apprehended two major crime bosses. Without any major news coverage, they do not intend to miss anymore. They are using every resource at their disposal to obtain information regarding the whereabouts of crime bosses. Just in case they are approached by an A.N.T.

The 'pole position' club is located on a very busy street near the center of downtown Detroit. Local police begin to block off the Street. News reporters staking out the area notice this and immediately flock to the building. A few of them pay admission to enter the club so they'll have someone on the inside. They are familiar with Mr. Jenkins and believe the U.N.A are here for him.

Mr. Jenkins is no fool and has not been in the crime world as long as he has without being a bit paranoid. He is already receiving information regarding the Distinctive U.N.A vehicles parked outside Although they are unmarked not many Sport Utility Vehicles have small Drones on their roofs. He is too old and smart to fight an Arch Nun.

He always has his number one Enforcer and head of security Steven McQueen an Ex-navy SEAL standing by his side. Mr. McQueen is so BAD ASS if he were not employed by Samuel Jenkins, he would have been on Mother Teresa's list for an A.N.T. Mr. Jenkins gives him emergency instructions for everyone in the club to carry out if things should go wrong. He also gives all of his legal and illegal businesses instructions on what to do if law enforcement enters the premises.

Sister Nevaeh tells everyone to remain in their vehicles for a few moments so her team can make a tactical assessment of the area.

"Ok everyone, listen up Mother Teresa's tactics so far have proved fruitful. But let's not get complacent and make assumptions on how we will be received. Let's pray for the best but prepare for the worst!"

She tells them as Keeva, her second-in-command coordinates operation 'Chokehold'.

The public notices the U.N.A vehicles which have been parked outside the pole position club and seen on the internet all morning and now the people know an Arch Nun is here.

"Well, the element of surprise is gone thanks to the internet" An FBI agent says over the radio.

"That element ladies and gentlemen was gone the moment my Sister defeated Diego Lugo"

Sister Nevaeh responds then exits her vehicle followed by her team.

Body cams are active along with several very small recorder drones worn on the shoulders of some of the A.N.T agents. The FBI order local law enforcement to block the intersections and redirect traffic. The A.N.T give additional instructions to evacuate nearby businesses for safety. The FBI enter the club first followed by the Arch Nun and her team, the staff at the door have orders to let them in. Mr. Jenkins has after all been aware of their presence since they've arrived. As the agents walk through the club customers begin to take notice of them. There are half naked men and women dancing on poles and tables. Some of the women are completely topless. Lewd acts are being performed in the open and in private rooms. The music is loud, some of the dancers stop dancing and attempt to cover themselves as a sign of respect to the Arch Nun, but are threatened to continue by the staff. They do so out of fear but bare the look of shame upon their faces. Mr. Jenkins does not want to show weakness or disrespect to the U.N.A as mentioned he is a very smart man. He's just waiting for the Arch Nun to make the first move. He stays in his office with his security team watching the agents on monitors. Sister Nevaeh tells one of the FBI agents to go to the DJ booth and stop the music. There are loud jeers and complaints from the patrons when the music stops. A couple of the small recorder drones are deployed.

"All be silent!" Sister Nevaeh shouts in the distinctive rhetoric of the Arch Nuns. Then orders Keeva to engage operation 'Choke Hold' The A.N.T agents draw their weapons, disarm the bouncers and staff, then take control of the club. This is done very quickly; they are quite proficient at it.

The Arch Nun now has full control of the club and all his businesses.

"I am Arch Nun Sister Nevaeh of the United Nations Agency. I am here to remove Mr. Samuel Jenkins from your lives. He will answer for the many crimes he has committed within this city and unto its people, for he has committed great sins in the eyes of the Lord!" The patrons of the club are silent they don't want Mr. Jenkins to see their excitement. Based on the many videos circulating on the internet pertaining to this morning's events with the Arch Nuns. They know the end is near for Mr. Jenkins and his reign over the city. The Arch Nun has the attention of the entire club.

"Agents of the FBI bring him before me!"

She concludes slowly pacing in a circle with her hands behind her back.

Mr. Jenkins is infuriated. "who does this bit#h think she is?" He shouts to as he and his bodyguards rush from the office and down the stairs to meet her, keeping their hands in plain sight as not to be shot. The closer they gets to her, the slower they walk.

Approaching an Arch Nun in anger should be done with Extreme Caution!

Many of the patrons shout his name but he motions for them to stop.

Sister Nevaeh deliberately stands with her back to him but her team is focused on him and his bodyguards who are standing very close to him opening their jackets to prove they are unarmed but they are still searched.

"What the fu#k you doing Coming in here like this?, Is there something I can do for you Sister?"

He asks angrily looking at one of the female FBI agents.

The Arch Nun slowly turns toward him looking him up and down.

"Shall We speak of the many charges pending against you or just the human trafficking of under age children for prostitution, perhaps?" She asks.

He doesn't want to lose his temper or have any of his staff do anything stupid. He believes the Arch Nun is aware of this that's why she is making such a scene using psychology, attempting to shake him up and provoke him. Not many know of his underage prostitution rings and he did not appreciate her accusing him of that out loud! But he hopes she came to offer him ' The Challenge of Goliath'. Because now he wants her DEAD!

  All day Mr. Jenkins and his security team have been watching videos of the Arch Nun fighting. In the event one came knocking on his door, and knocking on his door one most certainly came.

"Sister, I think we all know why you're here." Mr. Jenkins says with a devious laugh. "And I have every intention of cooperating and obliging you. I've already spoken with my attorneys, I know all there is to know and if your dumb enough ta take it there, Sister I've already picked my champion, you fake ass wanna be holy bi#ch!" He concludes placing his hand on Steven's shoulder. The customers and staff burst into laughter. Steven folds his arms and stares at the Arch Nun knowing this doesn't intimidate her at all.

He merely wants to express to her how serious he is when it comes to fighting.

"Well Mr. Jenkins it seems you have done your homework and in so little time" Sister Nevaeh says continuing to look at Steven. "But I caution you sir, be very careful what you hope for!"

"No,no,no Sister" Mr. Jenkins shouts to her. "it's you that should be careful what the fu#k your about ta offer, cause my fighter isn't a washed up, drunk ass Ex-heavyweight boxer with mediocre skills!"

Everyone continues laughing as he speaks. The Arch Nun receives conformation of the 'Choke Hold' Mr. Jenkins acknowledges the seizure of his businesses and properties. Then she raises her hand for all to be silent then speaks the words Mr. Jenkins has been waiting for. "Mr. Samuel L. Jenkins for ALL the pending charges against you. I Arch Nun Sister Nevaeh of the United Nations Agency, offer you the Challenge of Goliath!"

"I except Bi#ch let's get on with it!" Mr. Jenkins Screams. "Oh, and Sister Vader." He continues mocking her name. "Now I got something ta say out loud." He turns to Steven and says. "Steve, my man you can legally kill this Bi#th and NOT be charged with murder. So, do it and I will pay you Five Million Dollars, YOU ARE DONE SISTER!" He concludes pointing at Sister Nevaeh. "I can't begin to tell you how many times I've heard that." The Arch Nun says calmly. Steven unfolds his arms and tells her. "Well taday was the last time you heard it, cause you ain't gettin any older!"

The Arch Nun nodes her head. "Very well Then, let it begin." Everyone in the club goes wild Mr. Jenkins tells his staff to move the tables and chairs to make room.

Sister Nevaeh explains to the crowd that she fights for the people's freedom of Mr. Jenkins. If she should lose or be killed here today, he will be absolved of all pending charges against him and will go free with a clean slate. Everyone is aware of this from the previous videos on the internet but each Arch Nun must speak this aloud for the world leaders. This is a legal verbal agreement and is one of the many reasons everything is recorded.

"If you're finished with your little speech Sister, I'd like ta get on with my day please" Mr. Jenkins says confidently.

"Of course, Mr. Jenkins as am I" The A.N.T agents assist Sister Navaeh with her coat and Habit. Steven removes his jacket but not his shirt and tie. Both Fighters are checked for weapons and body armor. Now he is playing a psychological game leaving his tie on for the Sister to grab hold of and doing what the other two fighters could not do get his hands on her and break her neck. Sister Nevaeh stands in the prayer position silently praying. Steven knows this fight has no rules nor does it require a referee. So, he seizes this opportunity to attack her throwing several punches and kicks. Her eyes remain closed as she out Maneuvers him using the Shaolin clasp hand technique the spectators go Wild. The FBI and A.N.T agents are impressed at how effortlessly she evades him with her eyes closed and her hands clasped together as though she were still playing. This was indeed a very different Sister Nevaeh than the one they fought against weeks ago. Steven threw so many hard punches and kicks at her, he exhausted himself quite a bit. The Arch Nun stands on one leg poised ready to kick with her hands still clap together held over her head, her eyes still closed.

Steven breathing very heavily slowly steps back.

The Spectators cheering and applause slowly settles down. Steven is using every second to his advantage to regain his breath.

"Steven Alexander McQueen" she addresses him using his full name not known to many especially Mr. Jenkins or the staff.

"For he who has dared to attack a servant of thy Lord God in Prayer. Shall drink bitter waters, Now witness the POWER

OF GOD!" She concludes slowly opening her eyes and assuming a very impressive martial art stance. The Spectators who are recording every second of this with cell phones cheer and applaud so loud the FBI have to take control to quiet them down.

Steven has now fully regained his breath and is ready to continue the fight. Now he will take his time and allow her to come to him. Both Fighters stand still and focused. The room is somewhat quiet some of the spectators are whispering to each other in excitement. Mr. Jenkins is calm he feels his fighter is doing well thus far.

Then Steven breaks the silence. "Well girl, what you waiting fo---" Before he can complete the sentence Sister Nevaeh lunges forward punching him in the mouth. "Ooooooh" The Spectators Shout. Stevens head jerks back, before he can focus Sister, time slows Nevaeh quickly strikes him in the throat then again to his forehead then once more to the center of his chest quickly grabbing his tie as his body falls back, time resumes. The spectators and FBI cannot believe the speed, accuracy and power of her blows. Holding onto his tie she Maneuvers herself behind him quickly forcing him to the ground. He plants both Palms on the floor in the position of a push-up attempting to break his fall.

She releases his tie and Stomps on the back of both his arms breaking them has his face crashes to the floor. She then jumps in the air performing a front somersault Landing on his body one foot on his head the other on his upper back. She quickly reaches down grabbing his tie. With his arms broken his face smashed she pulls on the tie breaking his neck as well.

"Oooooooh SH#T WHAT THE FU#K" Many of the spectator's shout in disbelief. As the Spectators observe the fight the A.N.T agents are trained to observe everyone and everything else. They notice Agent Tanya Flemming of the F.B.I move closer to Mr. Jenkins. Her firearm is holstered but visible to him.

He quickly draws her firearm from the holster.
"GUN!!!" One of the A.N.T agents yells loudly. The
Spectators scream and drop to the floor, the Arch Nun
gently Shields Steven's body with her own as not to cause
any further damage to him. Mr. Jenkins is able to fire one
shot before he is shot dead by the A.N.T. agents.
That one shot grazes the Arch Nun's arm. The small assault
drones target the remainder of Mr. Jenkins bodyguards with
green lasers, who immediately surrender. The FBI secure
everyone else the A.N.T agents inform the staff and patrons
to remain on the floor with hands visible all cell phones will
be confiscated and they will submit to a full search before
exiting the building.
Sister Nevaeh carefully stands her medic fuquan runs to her
side.
"Boss, boss, boss, please take it easy. You've been hit."
"I know fuquan, I am fine, thank you. Please tend to him."
She responds pointing at Steven.
"Boss with all due respect, fu#k him! you're my top priority.
He knew what he was getting into when he fought you" he
turns and looks down at Steven for a moment.
"He is in Allah's hands now!" He concludes tending to Sister
Nevaeh's wound. Before she can order fuquan to tend to
Steven the F.B.I takes care of him, keeping him alive and
stable. FBI agent Flemmings is apologizing to the special
agent in charge for the incident.
"My apologies sir, he grabbed my gun before I knew what
was happening"
"It's okay agent Flemming these things happen as long as
everyone is okay that's all that matters."
Sister Nevaeh approaches the two as they continue to talk
with Fuquan Attentively by her side.
"Excuse me agents, may I have a word with the two of you
in private?"
"Of course Sister but how's your arm" He and agent
Flemming respond.

"I don't want to go to one of these rooms where God knows what went on in, how about we just go to the bar Sister?"
"That will suffice special agent" The three go to the bar the agents sit. Sister Nevaeh stands facing them. Sister Nevaeh begins to speak to the special agent regarding the incident. But at the same time communicating telepathically to agent Flemming regarding something else.

"It is most unfortunate that Mr. Jenkins chose to forfeited his life today special agent."

While the Special Agent is responding agent Flemming can feel the Arch Nun communicating to her very soul. 'Agent Tonya Fleming you have been on Mr. Jenkins payroll for some time now. You deliberately positioned yourself near him so he may draw your firearm.'

Agent Fleming screams holding her head and jumps to her feet.

"What the fu#k?" She screams Breathing heavily holding her head with both hands, staring at Sister Nevaeh.

"Flemming, you scared the sh#t outta me" Special agent Newhart shouts.

"What the fu#k is wrong with you? You've been through tougher things then this! I'm sorry Sister. I apologize for my agents Behavior. You were saying Sister."

But agent Flemming continues to stand for a moment before sitting breathing heavily and staring at the Arch Nun whom is staring back at her.

"Yes special agent as I was saying" Sister Nevaeh says slowly turning away from agent Flemming continuing to talk to special agent Newhart, while continuing to communicate with agent Flemming's soul. 'Agent Flemming, you currently have two million dollars buried under the back porch of your home. If you confess and surrender now the U.N.A and I will help you, but make no mistake agent Flemming. You will be held accountable and pay for your crimes. The question is will you do this with or without my help?'

While Sister Nevaeh is talking to the Special Agent, Agent Flemming interrupts.

"Excuse me, but may I speak to Sister Nevaeh alone, sir?"

"What the fu#k Flemming we're wrapping things up here." The special agent responds in frustration.

"Please just a moment" Agent Flemming says to him with tears in her eyes.

"Yeah! of course Fleming go ahead."

The special agent begins to walk away when Sister Nevaeh instructs him to wait at the end of the bar. Special agent Newhart has been with the FBI for a long time and he is now having suspicions and concerns. Sister Nevaeh motions for her second-in-command and I.T specialist to join them with one of the recorder drones. Agent Flemming confesses many things to the Arch Nun. One of which explaining how Mr. Jenkins controls some of the most powerful and violent street gangs in Chicago as well. That is where his Lieutenant operates from. The U.N.A now knows Mr. Samuel Jenkins secretly controlled Chicago as well. Agent Flemming dries her eyes and looks to the Arch Nun and asks.

"How Sister are you able to know these things about me and where I have money buried and exactly how much? It's been buried there untouched for fifteen years" Sister Nevaeh puts a hand upon her shoulder and says.

"You refer to the yellow and blue box with the bent handle that contains the money, your father's Purple Heart he received for his courage and a picture of your high school boyfriend James whom you kissed under the bleachers during the homecoming game. Even though his breath reeked of alcohol"

Agent Flemming's eyes and mouth open as wide as they could as the Arch Nun continues.

"The Lord sees and knows all things and no one, my child can hide things from the eyes of the Lord! You have made many mistakes and the Lord knows what's in your heart. Your world will be purged, for your crimes as for your cooperation. The U.N.A will have mercy with your conviction."

Agent Flemming slowly lowers her head and begins to weep. Sister Nevaeh hugs and Embraces her for a moment. Special agent Newhart is confused but fears the worst as the Arch Nun calls him over.

"Is everything all right over here, what's going on?" He asks looking at agent Flemming.

She just looks at him and sadly says. "I'm sorry"

Special agent Newhart drops his head.

"I'll tell you everything in a moment special agent." Sister Nevaeh says then orders her second-in-command to take her into custody.

"Wait! she was one of us shouldn't we take her?" Special Agent Newhart asks.

"No, she is in U.N.A custody and will be convicted as such, under the new laws her situation is not separate from Mr. Jenkins"

Through the recorder drones Mother Teresa has witnessed this live and she diverts A.N.T-6 to Chicago. She wants this loose end tied up immediately! She also wants to make a spectacle of it and she knows just the Arch Nun to send. She doing this to draw attention away from the events at the pole position and the demise of Mr. Jenkins. This will no doubt be important news for the world to hear and she wants to assure they receive it correctly. The Reverend mother alerts local and worldwide news media to inform them of Mr. Jenkins and what is to happen next and she will be keeping them in the loop as to where this will take place. With the confiscation of the cell phones at the pole position club there will be much speculation has to what happened inside. The undercover news reporters and patrons are still on the floor face down. They will be there for a few hours. The Arch Nun and her team exit the building with agent Flemming. They do not handcuff her until they enter their vehicles. The FBI is getting full credit for the apprehension and fall of Mr. Jenkins so they remain on site to assure everything goes according to Mother Teresa's instructions. The Arch Nun and her team head to the United Nation Building in New York to process agent Flemming. There she will be placed in a holding cell. Mother Teresa and president Ophelia wish to speak to her in person.

  A.N.T- 6 arrived at their Farm in Chicago. The Arch Nun instructs her team on how they will conduct this campaign. The Reverend mother already has Chicago News along with CNN, NBC and Fox on standby. She is watching the 'Cabrini Blue' housing projects. This is the home of 'The Lords of Bushton'
They are the head of a network of gangs that are referred to as the 'Thrones of Chicago'
They are the most violent and ruthless gang in Chicago. Many children and teenagers admire them. They are seemingly Unstoppable by law enforcement and are responsible for the deaths of countless men, women, children, babies, and pets.
There is no time to coordinate the chokehold. This will be a 'Hyper sweep' operation.

  The 'Hyper-Sweep' is a procedure reserved for extreme circumstances. It can involve multiple Arch Nuns, countless law enforcement agencies and branches of the military. Law enforcement agencies devote long hours and hard work to their cases. Unfortunately, they sometimes must rely on informants for critical information they can't get from undercover agents. Too often this important information is lost at the last-minute setting cases back days, weeks, months or years. This gave birth to the U.N.A operation 'Hyper-Sweep' which is similar to Chokehold but not as accurate and can be very messy, this operation must now be performed to conclude Mr. Samuel Jenkins entire Empire. Thanks to Ex F.B.I agent Tanya Flemming telling Sister

Nevaeh and the Mother Teresa everything she knows while being transported. She is definitely not looking forward to meeting with the president and Reverend Mother face to face.

One of the staff members at the pole position secretly sent texts of Mr. Jenkins death to his Lieutenant 'Giovanni Luciano'.
A man recently revealed to them by agent Fleming. The FBI were aware of Mr. Luciano but had no idea he was linked to Samuel Jenkins in such a way. They were under the impression he ran Chicago's crime syndicate independently and was under the influence of the Italian mafia. So, this is an extension of the Samuel Jenkins case.
Mother Teresa whom is still enjoying lunch is receiving all of this information on her tablet and making all the preparations for its conclusion. Special agents Betty and Valentina along with the rest of the staff are watching the videos that are bringing the internet to a crawl. Everyone at the table is impressed at how well the Arch Nuns fight. They have so many questions but dare not ask the Reverend Mother. Almost everyone in the restaurant are glued to their cell phone screens watching the YouTube videos of today's events.
The servers have brought the food several minutes ago but no one has taken their eyes off their cell phone screens. They are all mesmerized by the graceful maneuvers of the Arch Nuns.

"My goodness, you are worse than teenagers. "Mother Teresa facetiously says with a smile. "Down with your screens and prepare for your meal." They all enjoy a giggle as they Place their phones on the table. Some immediately begin to eat when the Reverend Mother slams her fist to the table with a loud thump. "BOW YOUR HEADS!" She shouts, those who have begun to eat have stopped chewing and immediately do as the Reverend Mother asks. "Let us thank the Lord for the meal we are about to consume." Mother Teresa blesses the meal and everyone slowly begins to eat when she interrupts them once more. "And don't think for one second I didn't notice you attempting to watch your screens during my blessing. But I will allow it in light of today's most exciting events." She concludes laughing. Betty leans over and Whispers to one of the assistants sitting near her. "I'm glad she was just joking, I was nervous as sh#t" "I know, I haven't felt like that since my Mother caught me smoking weed in the basement." The assistant responds as they giggle. Mother Teresa is enjoying the meal with her staff but at the same time coordinating the conclusion of today's events on her tablet. She is quite the multi-tasker. Today's events are being described by the world as better than any movie or television show EVER!

So far everything is going according to Mother Teresa's plans for 'God's Great Purpose'. They eat, drink and watch more videos of the Arch Nuns as they Converse and share their opinions. Interpol and the FBI inform Mother Teresa they are unable to locate Mr. Luciano. For the moment he has gone underground to avoid apprehension. He like all crime bosses have many in his employment and he has several in the news media whom have kept him informed of Mother Teresa's challenge to the 'Lords of Bushton' and 'Thrones of Chicago'. She did that to draw him out. So, he arranges a Fall Guy to take the blame and suffer the consequences until he can get things under control.

All this is happening too fast for these High-level crime
bosses and they are TRURLY overwhelmed. They know not,
what to do against the new U.N.A. And for that! Mother
Teresa is pleased. Mr. Luciano arranges for Joseph Dumas
known on the street as 'Joey Get-Down', a well-known
young African American street gang leader in the 'Cabrini
Blue' housing projects. He is of average height and very thin
build. But surrounds himself with very large bodybuilding
hardcore ex-convicts. His status in the street game was not
earned, but given to him directly by Mr. Jenkins himself for
reasons unknown. He is unattractive, arrogant and has a
short temper. He threatens to kill woman's children if they
don't perform sex acts on him. He mercilessly kills drug
addicts for amusement and will do absolutely anything to
maintain his status in the 'Lords of Bushton'.

Mr. Luciano informs the Lords that Joey Get-Down is the
big boss and will be making the decisions for all the gangs
until further notice. He has given him special instructions
and the authority to do what he sees fit. It only took 30
minutes for the entire city to know joey is the man in charge.

The 'Thrones' do not mind sitting back and allowing such
an idiot to take the driver's seat for the events that are about
to take place. The Thrones of Chicago intend to Prevail at all
cost. This sudden status boost increases Joey's arrogance. He
not thinking carelessly chooses one of his bodybuilding ex-
cons to be his champion just in case an Arch Nun comes
knocking at his door. He wastes no time telling everyone to
spread the word throughout the projects that he is in charge
of everything. Mr. Luciano informs his news media contacts
of Joey's status in the hood. Like the rest of the world Joey
Get-Down and his gang continuously watch the videos of
Arch Nuns Sisters Dee and Anna.

Sister Nevaeh's event videos have not yet been released due to the fatality involved. The early evening news will be the first to play those and report the death of Samuel Jenkins. The cell phones are being returned to those who were there the fatality footage has been removed and they will no doubt immediately upload their footage to YouTube and all forms of social media telling everyone how Mr. Jenkins was killed. This will work to Mother Teresa's advantage proving the A.N.T agents are a most lethal force and starting THE LEDGED OF THE ARCH NUNS.

The world now awaits the outcome of what is being called 'The Chicago Fire!' Mother Teresa wants these challenges done quickly. Removing eight High-level crime bosses in the United States will definitely be remembered as the Birth Cry of the Arch Nuns!

Chicago local news has its top reporters at the housing project with a large crowd of Spectators to which many are residents, anxiously awaiting the arrival of an Arch Nun. Mother Teresa herself has informed the news crews that this would be the next location for attempted purging. Local law enforcement is on hand with several SWAT teams for crowd control and of course the Chicago FBI branch. This is the Lords of Bushton's main turf. They too are in strong presence along with many members of the 'Thrones'. They stand quietly amongst the crowd, proudly displaying their different gang colors and logos. For that reason, many residents prefer to stay in their homes. Most of their lives the people have been bullied by these gangs. Their loved ones killed, if not by their stray bullets, by their drugs and violence. But for the first time in their lives they believe, they trust and they have hope.

Alone in her apartment sits an old woman her name is Miss Cicely Tyson. She has buried three sons, two daughters and a husband, all victims of gang violence. She is too old, frail and frightened to be among the crowds in the street even with the strong police presence.

So, she sits on her couch watching the event on television where she spends the majority of her time. Above the television is a shelf filled with pictures of her family. It is difficult and painful but she kneels, she cries and then begins to speak and pray to the Lord.

"Oh, merciful god please! I beg of you, hear me on this day. Please God whoever you send to fight these Thugs and gangsters. Please let them be victorious, let them be strong and let them be true! Oh God please! I've lost my entire family to the violence of this city, I know they are in your care Oh Lord, and I asked Oh Heavenly Father please allow me to live just a little while longer, Oh Lord so I may see the people of this city free, free from the wickedness that has corrupted it for so long. Please sweet Jesus I ask this of you. Oh Lord I'm ready, I'm ready to come home. All I ask, if you will Oh Heavenly Father please allow me to look into the face of the one that will deliver this city from the bondage of corruption and on to FREEDOM! Amen."

She concludes as she slowly lowers her head. In the distance sky, high above the city. The crowd notices a white streak appear across the sky. Something is coming toward them very fast. The news reporters instruct their camera crews to focus on this object. They know it is a Battle Assault Drone. As it gets closer it engages its Halo braking system, it flies through the Ring of smoke and slowly comes to a stop. Hovering over the housing project slowly rotating. Then the Horn of Gabriel is sounded echoing through all the housing projects signifying the arrival of an Arch Nun.

The craft softly lands in the Large Courtyard of the Housing projects. All cameras are fixed on it, the cargo door opens and four A.N.T agents exit. The crowd really wants to applaud but are fearful of retaliation from the gangs.

Many in the crowd can be heard talking. The A.N.T agents stand outside the craft as though they are waiting for something. Joey Get-Down shouts loudly. "LORDS OF" Then collectively all the gang members respond. "BUSHTON" Those who support the gangs and their lifestyle applaud. Unfortunately, those intimidated by The Gangs applaud as well. But in their hearts, they hope this is the last time they applaud any of the gangs in the network of the Thrones of Chicago. Many religious organizations and their leaders are in the crowd but are too afraid to speak against any of the gangs.

A motorcade of FBI SUVs and police cars are driving toward the housing project. Among them is one A.N.T vehicle. Sister Amira rides with two of her team in silence. It appears she is praying and mentally preparing herself for the task at hand. But she is really going over a playlist of songs she wants to remix. There are many people in the streets leading up to the housing project and the police presence is very heavy throughout.

Sister Amira instructs her team to pull over and let her out so she may walk the rest of the way amongst the people.

"You sure boss? These Fu#king people might Stone you to death or something."

The Arch Nun laughs. "This is 2028 I don't think they Stone people anymore."

"Well years ago During the riots in Los Angeles a truck driver was struck in the head with a large stone, you think that would count as a stoning boss?" The laughter Fades as Sister Amira responds.

"The person that strikes me with a rock, will be the easiest person for law enforcement to catch!"

"How's that boss?"

"Because that person will be walking around with that same rock lodged in the center of their throat!"

She concludes jokingly giving her team member a high five. Sister Amira hopes no one would attempt to harm her and she would never personally retaliate against anyone.

That is not the way of the Arch Nuns. She is merely having fun with her team member.

It is only a few blocks, but walking among the people is something she would very much like to do. For she, like all Arch Nuns walks with faith and goes with God!

The motorcade continues to slowly drive away. A small crowd begins to gather around the Arch Nun with their cell phones taking pictures and videos. Of course, they keep a safe distance.

She holds her hands high to the sky as her Mother Hymiriam did in New York, she bows her head, closes her eyes then slowly assumes the Prayer position. Most of the crowd respects the position and lower their voices. Then Sister Amira begins to pray aloud.

"Oh God I pray to thee give me the compassion to have mercy on those forced into their roles in this world by circumstance. Guide Me, Oh God on this most dangerous road I must traverse. I am driven forward, always forward for a God unseen but knows what's in my heart. If my time has come to die on this day I will not weep and ask for a little more time. I will celebrate the gift life you have given unto me and return home in peace.

I give all to 'I AM' amen." To her surprise the crowd shouts. "Amen!" She quickly opens her eyes to behold this great sight. Children do not fear the Arch Nuns they run to hug her. And the people witness this and know that it is GOOD!

The crowd at the housing project are eager and becoming restless everyone is talking amongst themselves. The news reporters are reluctant to interview people in the crowd. Any attempts are met with intimidation by the gangs.

Joey Get-Down is standing with his chosen champion, Raymone Iglesias an ex-convict bodybuilder known on the streets as 'The Rap-Tor' for his rapping skills he also has no shame with biting opponents during fights. He stands staring at the ground, deep in thought. He is reminiscing of a very serious Heart to Heart conversation he and his girlfriend had a couple of hours ago.

"Baby I just don't trust Joey get-down." She told him.

"You took a charge and did five years in prison for dem. They told you they were gonna take care of your family. Well you know what the Lords of Bushton did for your family. I never told ya dis baby cuz I ain't wanna start Nutting, but while you were in jail, they bought groceries for us twice. Then forgot all about us. They would see me in the rain at the bus stop and wouldn't even offer me a ride. They ain't do Sh#t for us, like they ain't gonna do Sh#t for you now!"

She concludes picking their three-year-old daughter up and sitting at the kitchen table.

"They told me I get a million dollars from Mr. Luciano."

"Did Mr. Luciano tell you that or did Joey Get-Down tell you that Sh#t?"

She shouts cutting him off.

"If, you win da fight all you gonna be known as is da Nig#r that won da fight."

She says shaking her head and starting to cry.

"You use ta go ta church and sing in da choir when you were younger before da gangs changed your life.

The choice you make today baby, is gonna ruin your life and ours." She says hugging her daughter tight. Please, Baby, please don't fight this Arch Nun for THEM."

Raymone is always fighting with his girlfriend who lost her Mother two years ago to cancer. But in the back of his mind he can strongly hear the words.

'PLEASE-DON'T-FIGHT- WITH-MY-DAUGHTER'

He knows not from where these words came, for he did not get along with his girlfriend's Mother in fact she couldn't stand him.

These words echo in his head. He knows deep down inside the words she spoke to him earlier are true. He did not hear this from Mr. Luciano and Joey has a reputation for taking advantage of anyone he can. If it weren't for Mr. Jenkins, they would have killed Joey long ago.

Joey's cell phone rings, it is Giovanni Luciano. Before Joey can say anything, he tells him to give the phone to Raymone. Mr. Luciano confirms the one million dollars promised to him and to publicly kill the Arch Nun. Now Raymone knows for sure he is getting a million dollars for this, if he WINS! He gives the phone back to Joey who is high on cocaine. Joey looks at him and says.

"What I tell you Nig#er, we got you, you know the rules of the challenge. Make sure you KILL dis Bit#h! in front of everybody, like Mr. 'G' said."

Raymone's girlfriend is standing by her man holding their daughter, she heard all of this and looks at him with tears in her eyes and slowly backs away. He does not look at her he stares forward in deep thought.

Suddenly everyone's attention is drawn to a new crowd of people slowly walking toward them. All the news reporters are receiving messages over their headsets.

Karen Wimbleton, Chicago News is one of them.

"Miss Wimbleton you're not gonna believe this. Check out what's coming your way."

Her news helicopter pilot tells her. Traffic slows to a standstill; people are coming out of stores and restaurants to join this new crowd as they walk toward blasting the song 'Jesus walks with them' by Kanye West.

"Oh my God! make sure we are getting ALL of this."

Miss Wimbleton tells her camera crew. As the cameras
Focus, they can see Arch Nun Sister Amira holding one child
by the hand and carrying another. Leading a very large
crowd of people.
The news cameras focus on Sister Amira's face.
"That is one very pretty Nun"
 One cameraman says to his reporter.
"It sure is, definitely not the face to be in a fight"
The reporter responds shaking his head. The crowd is still
uncomfortably quiet.
Minister Lolita Brown visiting from Savannah Georgia. Can
hold her tongue no more, the spirit takes hold of her and she
absolutely feels the need to speak. Knowing she can be killed
by a gang member at a later date for doing so. She has been
given a warning once before by the Thrones for speaking out
against them.
But it is God's will that she be heard, and be heard she shall!
She is a short middle-aged African-American woman well
known and respected in the religious Circles of Chicago and
Georgia.
   Not many can hear her as she screams as loud as she can
but she doesn't care as long as the Lord can hear her, she is
content. People around her stop talking and begin to listen.
Some of the news reporters notice this giving her a
microphone and are glad they finally found
someone brave enough to speak. So, she catches her breath,
closes her eyes and begins anew.
"People I just wanna say that it warms my heart and I thank
JESUS, that I lived to see this day. The day Jesus sent
somebody here to stop this madness and to put these gangs
to rest once and for all! thank you Jesus, thank you oh Jesus
thank you" she says stomping her feet hard to the ground.
To spite retaliation or their fear of the gangs everyone now
begins to applaud and cheer as the Arch Nun and the two
crowds slowly merge. Now Raymone must prepare himself,
for now he stands before an Arch Nun.

As the two face each other the crowd becomes quiet. It is an eerie silence for such a large crowd. The Arch Nun still holds the children. She looks Raymone in the face, puts the children down they attempt to cling to her but the parents pull them back. A few of her agents are now by her side. Joey stands next to Raymone smiling. Raymone is staring pass the Arch Nun and into the distance. The people begin to speak amongst themselves. The recorder drones were launched minutes before the Arch Nuns arrival. Minister Brown stands with the religious leaders of Chicago as they join hands and pray.

"Yo Bit#h, you scared?" Joey shouts to the Arch Nun with a loud disrespectful tone. Some find this amusing, many do not!

"All be silent!" Is heard through the recorder drone's loud speakers. With this command the crowd settles down.

"I Fu#king love when they say that" A detective says to one of the FBI agents.

"So, do I buddy, so do I! Times, They-Are A-Changing and it's about Fu#king time!" The two shake hands and Pat each other on the back.

Sister Amira keeps them in suspense a few moments longer, then speaks with the signature rhetoric of the Arch Nunhood.

"Raymone Evander Iglesias, you have been acknowledged by the U.N.A as the fighter for the Thrones of Chicago. You represent all they stand for. You have the opportunity to win everything for them or lose everything for them. My mind, body and spirit shall be God's vessel. The outcome will be determined by thy Lord God. I fight for the future of the children. On this day they shall bear witness to the fall of that which WAS you! Consider this your warning!" She says pointing at Raymone.

In the presence of the Arch Nun the people do not fear the notorious 'Thrones of Chicago' and with that they release a most thunderous Applause!

"You sir stand against the power of God, now you shall experience the wrath of God" Sister Amira says to him but the crowds cheering is so loud it could barely be heard but Raymone did, and the news reporters got it on camera for the world to hear.

Raymone is staring at the ground; he looks at the Arch Nun and remains silent. This is how he prepares himself before a fight. He slowly unzips his jacket and removes it. Joey takes his jacket and holds it up for the crowd to see proudly displaying the 'Lords of Bushton' logo on the back. This time only gang members and their affiliates applaud and cheer. Some of the gang members stare hard at Minister Brown attempting to intimidate her. But she fears not for she has the joy and love of the Lord in her heart. It is the middle of March and the weather is still a little cold. Sister Amira is wearing a custom coat designed by her Sister Maria and the crowd loves it.

Mother Teresa said she wanted this to be a spectacle and that is exactly what it is shaping up to be. It looks as though they are having an outdoor sporting event. The only thing missing are cheerleaders and a marching band. Sister Amira's second in command Lisa addresses the crowd through the loud speakers of the recording drones.

"Good afternoon everybody I just like to take a moment to explain briefly what's going on here. But I suspect you already know. A few Arch Nuns have already issued this challenge, you know the results and you know the stakes." There is a tremendous Round of Applause from the crowd.

"So, I won't waste your time with a long speech. This Arch Nun fights for your freedom!

This Arch Nun is willing to die here today for your freedom! She represents the United Nations Agency, the new laws and the Arch Nunhood! I am proud to stand with 'Arch-Nun-Sister-Amira!"

To say the crowd went wild would be an understatement the noise level was almost deafening the Applause and cheers could be heard clearly in the aircraft Hovering above.
Amira jokingly feels a message to Mother Teresa. 'Is this spectacle enough Grandmother?'
'indeed, it is my granddaughter, indeed it is my little show-off'
She assumes the prayer position then opens her arms for Lisa to remove her coat and habit. Law enforcement starts to move the crowd back so they may have room.
The moment Lisa removes Sister Amira's habit and while the crowd is still close. Raymone looks at the Arch Nun, he does not see a crowd of people, he does not see television cameras and news reporters. He only sees her, A daughter of Hymiriam, a daughter he is about to fight!

And the Lord sent Raymone clarity. And with this Clarity he made the wisest decision of his life. He opens his arms wide and yells as loud as he can. "I won't do this, I forfeit!" The crowd quiets down in disbelief.
"You can have all dis. let everybody be free of us. If my boys kill me, so be it then it'll be me dying for the people." He turns and looks to his girlfriend and daughter. "And I'll gladly do so"
He concludes holding his head high. The people are skeptical but slowly applaud for a moment then become quiet.

Joey Get-Down's eyes almost popped out of his head. The news is quickly spreading through the crowd. Lisa returns Sister Amira's Habit to her head. The people are unsure of what happens now, so they remain relatively silent. But talking can still be heard amongst them. As much as they would like it to be. They know it cannot be over that easily.
The Arch Nun must except and announce the conclusion of the event.
"Yo Nige#r you better fight dis bit#h if you know what's good for your azz"

Joey screams at Raymone, poking him in the face. The police searched everyone for weapons before allowing them into this area so he has no gun or he would have surely shot Raymone,
 Minister Brown and the Arch Nun. Since he is recognized as the leader of the Lords of Bushton he is allowed to approach Raymone so he may speak to him. One of the children Sister Amira carried earlier breaks away from her parents and runs to her.
The parents immediately attempt to stop her but Sister Amira tells them it is ok. She picks the child up and hugs her tightly. Again, there is a thunderous Applause. Raymone feels weak in his legs and falls to his knees and lowers his head. Joey repeatedly and viciously threatens Raymone to get up and fight! He makes threats against his girlfriend and daughter. Telling Raymone he will repeatedly rape them before killing them very slowly. This would enrage any man to tear Joey limb from limb. Raymone cannot understand why he is so calm but feels a hand upon his shoulder. Then he hears a voice in his head that assures him everything is going to be okay. He slowly raises his head and cannot believe what his eyes behold. Before he can speak, he hears.
"THANK-YOU-FOR-NOT-FIGHING-MY-DAUGHTER!"
There before him with her wings spread wide, for his eyes only. He sees a very faint image of
Mother Hymiriam then it is gone. It was her that spoke to his mind earlier.
The difference between Raymone and the other Fighters is simple. Unlike the other fighters, they loved harming others, they loved their lifestyle and were willing to die to preserve it. Killing an Arch Nun would have meant nothing to them. Raymone is conflicted and never wanted to fight or harm an Arch Nun. But he has harmed others in the past.
So, the lord gave him ONE chance, to change everything as the Lord does, for us all!
As sister Amira's prayer States.

'Oh Lord have Mercy on those born into their Lifestyle by circumstance.'

The Applause slowly comes to a stop so Sister Amira may speak. Joey realizes the crowd favors the Arch Nun. So, he walks over to her to shake her hand, he extends his hand as does she. Then Joey sucker punches her hard to the face. She could have easily evaded his attack but her primary concern was protecting the child she is still holding. It was Mother Teresa's plan for Raymone to strike her but Joey will suffice.

The crowd is shocked, Sister Amira turns quickly handing the child to Lisa whom knows not to interfere as Joey continues to punch her. The A.N.T inform everyone to stay back the situation is under control. Everyone in the crowd is shouting obscenities to Joey and all the gang members for this despicable Behavior. Joey reaches into his pocket pulls out a small screwdriver he was hiding and begins to stab the Arch Nun. The people are outraged and becoming frantic as Joey quickly stabs her body again and again. The gang members of course cheer him on. The crowd is now under the impression that this may be the actual fight. The people are confused and concerned very, very concerned. They fear they may have celebrated too soon. Joey in his rage did not take into account that the Arch Nun is wearing her bullet-resistant habit or coat. His stabbing dose not penetrate her clothing nor do her harm.

She is slumped forward with Joey standing to the side of her stabbing at her torso. She reaches down and grabs hold of both his ankles and with a quick yank pulls straight up causing his body to fall backwards. Slamming his body and the back of his head to the hard concrete.

He lies there motionless, his fists still clenching the screwdriver. The crowd becomes silent for a brief moment. Sister Amira raises her arms high in the air. The crowds cheering continues. Paramedics start to run to Joey but are stopped by the A.N.T agents.

"Just hold on a second" Pal yen chow tells them. "She'll let you know when you can tend to him!"

The paramedics know not to insist so they stand in wait. Joey lies on the ground with the back of his head bleeding, his neck broken. All he can do is stare up at the clouds as tears roll down the sides of his face. These are not tears of remorse nor are they for forgiveness for Joey these are tears of hate! Hate for the people that are glad to see this happen to him, hate for the Arch Nun for doing this to him and hate to God for sending her.

Sister Amira stands over Joey looking down at him. She can see the hatred in his eyes. She kneels beside him and asks. "Will you go before God with such hatred in your heart?" The crowd is making so much noise and his hearing is damaged so he can only hear this in his mind for she speaks directly to his soul. He cannot move or speak but she hears his thoughts.

'There ain't no god, Bit#h! If there was, he wouldn't let Sh#t like Dis go on and not do nothing about it. So, don't try ta preach ta me now bit#h you jus better pray I don't get up.'

'I do pray Joey; I pray regularly as should you! As for getting up, THAT is something you shall never do again. Make your peace with God Joey it is imperative that you do so.'

'You better be glad I'm gonna die bit#h!'

'But Joey you're not going to die the Lord is not finished with you yet. You will spend the rest of your life paralyzed from the neck down with neurological damage preventing you from speaking correctly. You will also be incarcerated for the rest of your days under the new laws. I know this may be impossible for you to conceive but the lord loves you so.'

With that conclusion she discontinues Communications with him.

For those who chose to watch this it appeared as though she were praying for him. But no one cared or expressed any concern for him. He has spent his entire life committing great sins in the eyes of the Lord and must reap what he has sown. He will be alone physically and mentally to reflect on his life. He is, as he always was and always will be. IN THE HANDS OF THE LORD!

The Arch Nun rises to her feet. She motions for the paramedics to tend to him. As they Rush pass, some of the news reporters approach her, not for an interview but to express their genuine concern for her well-being. "Oh my god! sister are you all right" One of the reporters asks. "That was a hell of a punch sister. "Says another.
"I'm fine thank you." She responds but momentarily loses herself as she so often does. Telling the reporters. "He couldn't hurt me, not with those little chicken wing arms of his, he had no strength at all. Besides my armor protected me."
It was such a natural response to the situation that Mother Teresa allowed it. But felt a message to her Granddaughter to be mindful of her words.
The reporters are a little tickled by her response. In all the fuss they forgot to turn off their microphones and cameras as they approached her. So, the world heard the Arch Nuns response and Mother Teresa was not angered for this makes the Arch Nuns more acceptable.
   The crowd rejoices disregarding Joey as though he never existed.
Now it is time for the Arch Nun to announce the conclusion of the event.
"Everyone settle down now."
Is heard loud through the housing project.
 "May I have your attention please. For her they immediately quiet down.

Many in the crowd could not help but to shout praise to her. The remaining gang members in the area are furious.

"People today you have reason to Rejoice, you have reason to celebrate. For today you are free of the gang's hold on this city."

Before the people can applaud one of the gang leaders quickly shouts.

"Y'ALL CAN BELIEVE DAT SH#T IF YOU WANT TOO, WE RUN DIS CITY AND ALWAYS WILL! WE GONNA GET ALL YOU MOTHERFU#KERS FOR DIS. BELIEVE DAT!"

The news crew's camera drones focus on him so everyone can see him. There is loud talk among the people but before sister Amira will allow them to be intimidated by them. With a firm hand she takes charge and speaks in the Arch Nun rhetoric.

"ALL BE SILENT! PEOPLE OF CHICAGO. FEAR NOT BEHOLD THE POWER OF THE NEW LAW! "

With that she snaps her finger and points at him.

The A.N.T recorder drones Red lasers Target him, immediately those around him step away so he is exposed and isolated. He shows no fear standing with his arms folded smiling.

"Take him, bring him before me!" The Arch Nun commands. Her Agents comply bringing him to her. She addresses him by his full name which no one ever told her.

"Ronald Hensley McCarthy" You dare to threaten the people of this city in plain sight of the Lord. You have blatantly defied the laws and threatened the people of this city for the last time. You are now charged with terroristic threats against the people of this city!"

"Yeah bit#h now what?" He says disrespectfully.

A.N.T agent Alfred grabs him from behind and covers his mouth forcing him to listen.

She takes one step toward him and looking into his eyes she recites the U.N.A conviction.

"With great regret and deep sorrow. You are no longer allowed to function in Society. You are condemned to spend the rest of your life in multiple incarceration facilities around the world. You will never see your family nor will you speak to them ever again. They may communicate to you. But you will never be allowed to respond. You have proven yourself a menace to the world and it is the voice of the world that removes you from it. HAS IT IS WRITTEN SO SHALL IT BE DONE!

The crowd recognizes this Special Miranda Right used only by the Arch Nuns
from the 40-day media storm and gasp in amazement. Can this be? Did she just arrest and convict him instantly, just like that? Loud chatter can be heard from the crowd.

Then the Arch Nun announces.

"BEHOLD, THE LORDS OF BUSHTON ARE NO MORE!"

The crowd is in disbelief, there is a momentary silence before the loudest applauds of the day is heard. He struggles and attempts to resist almost in tears.

The FBI and A.N.T handcuff and move him to one of their vehicles. The gang members watch in silence as the applause and cheers continue. Some of them attempt to leave.

When the voice of the Arch Nun is heard once more.

"Officers, do not allow any of the gang leaders or their Affiliates to leave. Someone has a special message for them."

The gang leaders are relieved for a moment they thought they were going to be arrested and convicted before they had a chance to plan their retaliation. So, they stay as if they had a choice!

The crowd is so excited they dismiss their Fear and begin to shout obscenities to the gang members. The Arch Nun asks that they settle down so she may continue to speak.

"People of Chicago although there is cause for celebration. My heart is saddened. A young man led astray so early in life as so many are. This young man Joseph James Dumas will spend the rest of his days unable to move or feel the touch of a loved one. This is the work of the Lord and it is For God's Great Purpose. May I ask something of you that would mean a lot to me."

The crowd agrees as they continue to shout praise to her.

"Anything for you Sister Amira!" Someone shouts.

"We love you Sister Amira" Is shouted countless times from many in the crowd.

Mother Teresa Witnesses this and she is most pleased. Sister Amira continues to speak.

"I will ask something of you that many will find difficult. But I would be grateful if you indulged me. I ask that you join me in a prayer for the one you knew as Joey get-down."

The crowd sies and shouts more obscenities toward the gang members. They not only hated Joey they despised him.

"I know dis bit#h don't want us ta pray for Dat Mother fu#ker! "

One woman says to another in the crowd.

"Hold on now! we not gonna refer ta her as bit#h!"
The woman replies.

"Damn girl, you right my bad. But Joey raped me more den once. I don't think I can pray for him." The woman says starting to cry.

"Girl! He raped me too and when my brother went down ta talk ta him about it, he shot him in the leg." She tells her as she puts her arm around her.

"But if this Arch Nun Dat did what she did for us today wants me ta pray, I won't do it for Joey, but I'll do it for her. Will you join me?"

"Yes, yes I will because SHE wants me to"

Some of the people standing near them put their hands on the women's shoulders. A man standing near them whom did not hear the content of the conversation only the end of it adds his comment.

"I'll do whatever that pretty woman wants."

Sister Amira assumes the prayer position, bows her head and begins to pray.

"Oh God, please watch over Joey. His path has been hard and his choices bad. His poor misguided soul has been under the influence of the street for a very long time. I pray Oh God for his remaining days. He comes to know and embrace your love. I pray that he acknowledges the error of his ways and when the day comes Oh God, on that day I hope you have mercy upon his soul. For he too is worthy of Your Love. Amen!"

The response is very weak and from very few as they say Amen.

"I thank you for allowing me this moment to pray for Joey. Before I depart and leave you to your rejoicing. There will be a brief word from Mother Teresa"

A word from the Reverend Mother this must be a special occasion indeed. The people think and speak amongst themselves for a few moments. Before the voice of Mother Teresa is heard through the loudspeakers.

"People of Chicago I would like to extend a salutation and take a moment of your time. I assure you; I will be brief!"

Hearing the voice of Mother Teresa herself brought forth an immediate Silence from the crowd.

What could the Reverend Mother of the Arch Nuns have to say to them. The Curiosity of the people was matched only by their suspense. "Now that I have your attention. Giovanni Luciano is the Man Behind the Thrones of Chicago. The Lords of Bushton were empowered by Mr. Luciano to represent him and all that he has. On this day the Lords of Bushton lost all that Mr. Luciano controlled. Effective immediately all gangs under the Thrones of Chicago will surrender themselves to law enforcement. You have two days to comply. Those who wish to surrender now may do so. The city will be blocked off preventing you from fleeing. Any who give Refuge to gang members will be charged accordingly.

This is by order of the United Nations Agency! It is the Lord who executes judgement! The Lord is our God, the Lord is one. Resistance to the Power of God is FUTILE! The city of Chicago shall be free of street gangs. Rejoice in thy deliverance and know that GOD-IS-GOD!"

The crowd could not have applauded or cheered any louder, they jumped, danced and waved their hands in Praise.

The people of Chicago have heard many promises such as this. But they know in their hearts and in their souls. If Mother Teresa said it. It shall TRURLY be DONE!

Seven gang leaders and members immediately surrender to the FBI. Among them three were undercover FBI agents seizing this opportunity to come in and debrief their fellow agents with valuable Intel that will be vital to the conclusion of this event.

Sister Amira's attention is drawn to a window in the distance. It is too far for anyone else to see but her agents notice her gaze.

"What cha looking at boss"

Pal yen chow asks as the paramedics roll the stretcher carrying Joey pass her.

Still staring at the window in the distance she replies.

"Three of you and few F.B.I agents accompany me. Tell the rest of our team to stay here amongst the people and assist however they can."

As they walk through the crowd, two recorder drones follow. The people step aside so many of them want to touch or hug her but they know to Admire from afar. They are content with taking selfies and any type of picture they can as she walks by. She is Guided by the Lord as she leads those with her to an apartment.

The Arch Nun knocks on the door. There is no answer she knocks again but there is still no response. "This is the FBI open the door please." One of the agents shouts, again no response. The Arch Nun gives instructions to force it open. Upon doing so they notice an elderly woman lying on the floor, she is dying. The officers immediately attempt to run to her but the Arch Nun commands them to stop.

Sister Amira slowly walks toward her and kneels beside her. She lifts her head onto her lap and slowly caress her face. The old woman with her last ounce of strength clutches Sister Amira's arm holding it tightly, she looks up into her face and with her last breath she says.

"Thank you for delivering the people of this city. They free from the gangs now. I know there will be a much better future for the children now."

And with that said she looks into the Arch Nun's face once more, reaches up and touches the face of the deliverer, before dying peacefully in the arms of an Arch Nun. The Lord allowed miss Cicely Tyson to look into the face the one that would bring peace to the streets of the city she loved so much. Two FBI agents are asked to stay and tend to the situation.

As the Arch Nun and her team leave the apartment building. The crowd outside appears to have gotten larger as word spreads that the Thrones of Chicago will be removed from the city. The Arch Nun walks through the crowd, but this time slowly with her arms extended and her team behind her. This time she is not walking through the people, she is walking to the people and now she shall walk with the people.

They know an Arch Nun will never stop to take personal pictures with them and to never ask an Arch Nun to do so. They are content just being in her presence and feeling the blessings of the Lord. Now that they are allowed to leave the area all the gang leaders and their affiliates do so. As they walk through the crowd people move but shout obscenities to them. They go quietly for now but if it were not for the strong presence of law enforcement. They would have surely taken their anger out on the people.

The Arch Nun and her agents are escorted to their vehicle by the Chicago PD, they slowly drive their vehicle through the crowd as the police clear a path. They drive to the courtyard where their Battle Assault Drone has landed. The small A.N.T recorder drones reattach themselves to the craft. Sister Amira exits the vehicle for a moment to blow a kiss and make the hand gestures- I-LOVE-YOU! To the crowd. The vehicle drives on board the craft with The Arch Nun walking behind it. The cargo door closes and the craft immediately takes off hovering a few hundred feet above the crowd slowly rotating as the crowd cheers as loud as they possibly can. Then it shoots straight up into the air at 600 MPH and disappears into the clouds.

"I wish the FBI had one of those."

An FBI agent Jokingly says to another.

"The country wouldn't be able to pay us if we had one of those, I heard through the grapevine they cost over a billion dollars! and the monthly maintenance is through the roof. They'd come out a lot cheaper buying every agent Lamborghinis, My friend"
The two laugh as they join the crowd in their rejoicing.

Evening arrives every Network in the world is broadcasting news of today's events. News networks and talk shows are bringing in fight experts to analyze the Arch Nun's combat maneuvers. This is part of Mother Teresa's plan. They speak of how Diego Lugo was a washed-up boxer far from his Prime and could have easily been defeated buy a highly trained military fighter such as an Arch Nun. They speak of Arch Nuns being the equivalent of highly-skilled neurosurgeons, tactical geniuses with extreme military hand to hand combat skills.

Sister Neveah's video footage of her event will be delayed a little longer, due to the fatality and her being shot. Sister Amira's combat footage is simplistic and requires no explanation. She displayed exemplary conduct and formed a very strong bond with the people, perhaps the strongest to date. It will be shown to the world and hopefully considered an example of how beautiful the future can be.

Sister Dajairia's footage is perhaps the most popular and most viewed. Not for being the first event of the day, but for the way the 'Dancer' moves. Sister Anna's footage requires an explanation for the speed, precision and strength she displayed. A lot of the fight experts work for the U.N.A and quickly validate the Arch Nuns combat skills! This continued on every Network well into the late evening. Then the late-night talk show hosts continued with more of the same. The parties and celebrations carried over into the next morning, With strong police presence of course.

And as the sun rose to start the dawn of a new day. Mother Teresa sent forth Sister Elizabeth to Miami Florida. There she challenged High-level Crime Boss Frank mosca of the Russian mafia. He has the largest child pornography ring in the city. He chose his sister Sapphire mosca whom is head of his security and a well-known MMA fighter. Sister Elizabeth was Victorious, Frank mosca lost everything and Sapphire, now a quadriplegic shall never be the same again.

Mother Teresa sent forth Sister Donna to Dallas Texas where she challenged High-level crime boss Garcia Hernandez known in the city as 'Tex Mex' he is connected to a well-known Mexican cartel and uses children to smuggle drugs. His son, known on the streets as 'Tex Flex' for his large muscular physique that he enjoys showing off to the ladies is also known to be the fiercest fighter in the city. He volunteers to fight on his father's behalf as any good son would. After seeing Sister Donna Mr. Hernandez didn't mind his son fighting for him. He thought himself fortunate that it wasn't one of the Arch Nuns he seen on YouTube yesterday. Mr. Hernandez thinks Sister Donna is so cute, almost friendly and looks forward to the victory.

As Tex Flex faced Sister Donna he was amused. This Arch Nun seemed to be a little afraid he thought and it would be a quick victory, very quick. This challenge took place at the very large home of Mr. Hernandez He unlike the others didn't want a large crowd. But the U.N.A recorder drones recorded everything. Tex Flex fought as best he could but was easily defeated by Sister Donna. She performed Maneuvers so beautiful and graceful to behold for a woman of her size, she amazed Mr. Hernandez, his family and staff. And as he gazed upon, she who Moved like a feather dancing in the Wind. His heart was quickly broken as was his son's neck! He will NEVER move again. And from this day forth the world shall know Sister Donna as the 'Deceptionist'. She who floats like a butterfly with the aggression of a HORNET!

Since this fight was on private property the FBI called a
helicopter to airlift his son to the hospital. Mr. Garcia
Hernandez will spend the rest of his life in jail and all that he
ruled and controlled was lost and now property of the
U.N.A.

The Reverend Mother sent forth Sister Lin to Atlanta
Georgia. There she challenged a Crime Boss of a slightly
higher caliber. One who controls several other cities in
Georgia. A man by the name of Kenneth Williams also
known as 'THE EMPEROR OF ATLANTA!' He is the biggest
human trafficker of children and Drug Boss in Georgia. Like
the other bosses he had not the time to properly select a
champion. With so much at stake a man of his stature would
have searched the globe for such a man. Mr. Williams does
not have the confidence in a woman's fighting ability to
defeat an Arch Nun. So, he chose the craziest and most
insane fighter in Atlanta and offered three million dollars for
the victory.
A man in his employment by the name of Paul Nesta. A
strong dreadlock wearing Rastafarian herbalist who mixes
his own performance enhancing drugs. He is not an overly
large man. But he is one of Atlanta's most lethal Fighters due
to his high tolerance of pain. Which he is surely going to
need fighting against Sister Lin!

When Mr. Williams received news of S.W.A.T and Military
Strike Teams seizing the other bosses under him and all of
his properties and businesses, he immediately doubles that
amount to six million. In desperation he attempts to reach
out to all of his political affiliates to call in favors. But no one
can help him in such short notice against the U.N.A. He too
did not want public humiliation and disgrace. So, the fight
was held at his private Villa on his tennis court. He only
allowed his family, closest friends and staff to be in
attendance during the fight. Sister Lin decides to allow her
opponent Paul Nestor to land one punch.

Upon doing so she grabs his dreadlocks, pulls him to the ground, landing on his face, she pulls him across the concrete shredding the skin from his face. All the while making her signature cat screaming sounds. Still holding on to his hair she flips over and plants both feet on his back. She pulls upward as she performs a backwards somersault pulling his hair and a piece of his scalp from his skull. Before he can react, she immediately performs a front somersault planting both feet in his back breaking it, still holding his hair and scalp she turns to Mr. Williams and says. "It's Over!"

The 'Emperor of Atlanta' Has Fallen, before a private crowd and the world shall now refer to Sister Lin as 'The Alley Cat'. The people of the world are paying very close attention to these events. They know there are still three Arch Nuns left. The two males and the Arch Nun Sister Superior Maria.

She was sent to Las Vegas Nevada. The city is no stranger to lights in the sky or on the ground. But when a Battle Assault Drone appeared through the clouds of the early evening sky and flew slowly over the hotels of the Las Vegas Strip from the Stratosphere Hotel to the Las Vegas Airport before landing. The city almost Stood Still. There was no sounding of Gabriel's horn, the Sister Superior wanted to make a Grand Entrance! There were far too many mid-to-high level crime bosses for the FBI to choose from in 'Sin City' But one stood out among the others Akihiko Watanabe. He is believed to be connected to the 'Yakuza' and pretty well-connected here in the United States. He controls teenage prostitution, drugs and a lot of the street gangs in California and Nevada. He unlike the other bosses always has a champion at the ready. His chosen champion 'Arakan' which means 'Worthy one, the hero' is considered to be a super assassin in the crime world and revered by many. He never leaves Mr. Watanabe's side.

The FBI locate Mr. Watanabe and his staff at the Bellagio Hotel. Where he is engaged in a high-stakes poker game. Every crime boss in Nevada knows an Arch Nun is here, for whom remains to be seen. Until the F.B.I agents enter the private playing room. A few other crime bosses from around the world are playing in the game as well. They became very nervous but Mr. Watanabe remains calm. No One knew who they were here for yet. The FBI are enjoying their suspense and watching them sweat. They disarm everyone and take their cell phones telling them to remain calm. "To what do we owe this intrusion agents?" Mr. Watanabe asks. The agents keep them in suspense a few moments more before announcing the arrival of an Arch Nun in the hotel.

A couple of the crime bosses slammed they're playing cards to the table shouting profanities, one became sick and still Mr. Watanabe remained calm. The agents Snicker among themselves like schoolchildren telling a secret.

"No one's allowed to leave the room so just sit tight for a few minutes you'll know who we're here for soon enough" An FBI agent tells them grinning from ear-to-ear. The A.N.T motorcade took Backroads and entered the hotel from the rear. But the Sister Superior sticks out like a sore thumb. Everyone that caught a glimpse of her and her team begin to post on social media. The word spreads quickly and people began to gather. The elevator doors open, the Arch Nun exits with her agents proudly walking with her. Hotel management and top security accompany them with several small recorder drones hovering above the group. The Sister Superior struts down the hall with her signature Super Model walk, as though she were on the catwalk at a fashion show in Paris. Her uniform designed by her of course is stunning, like something you would see in a fashion magazine.

She unlike her sisters is seldom seen wearing her Nun bag. She prefers to carry a mid-size pocketbook witch always coordinates and complements her outfit. As she enters the room one of the crime bosses begins to pray and do the Catholic sign of the cross as he finishes. The Las Vegas FBI agents in the room have not seen the Arch Nun and gaze upon her in amazement. This is their first time being this close to an Arch Nun and they are indeed very impressed. "Akihiko Yoshimura Watanabe" She calls, the other crime bosses let out a sigh of relief.

"I am The Sister Superior Maria, of the Arch Nuns." She says in the Arch Nun rhetoric.   Mr. Watanabe raises his hand to stop her from speaking.

"I know why you are here, Arch Nun!" He says calmly with a thick Japanese accent.

"Spare me your speech I care not to hear it; I know why you have come. You know of my alleged activities and all that I have. You hold it hostage hoping I will surrender everything and myself to you. So, you can use it against my associates." He concludes as he stands proudly.

"Alleged activities my ass!" An FBI agent says sarcastically. Mr. Watanabe gives him a cold stare and replies.

"That insolent tone, will be the end of you agent!"

"You must not be keeping up with current events, as$hole, this is the end of you!" The agent tells him.

The Arch Nun walks to the center of the room and turns to Mr. Watanabe.

"Enough of this bickering, evidently you fully understand the concept and consequences. We will delay no further, so let us begin!"

The Sister Superior says sternly. He receives conformation of his property and business seizures, the Arch Nun offers the Goliath Challenge, to which he gladly accepts.

Francis her second in command removes her coat and habit. The hotel staff and crime bosses admire her clothing. Francis then explains to the hotel staff whom will be the spectators and Witnesses. What is about to take place and if any of them are squeamish they will be permitted to go to another room until the event has completed, none do so.

Arakan slowly walks to the center of the room removing his suit jacket, leaving his vest and shirt on. Both are inspected for hidden weapons or body armor. "Do you mind if I keep my skirt on 'Bubala' my legs, they get so cold?"

The Sister Superior asks Arakan with a sexy Argentinian accent. The skirt has been inspected by him and he knows it is just regular material and he believes it would hinder her movement so he agrees. Not wasting anymore time the Sister Superior takes three steps back, twirls and assumes one of her elegant Flamingo fighting stances. Her skirt follows every movement so elegantly.

Her teammates begin to whistle, applaud, cheer and chant her name. This encourages the hotel staff to do the same. The Sister Superior immediately stops and turns to her teammates shouting.

"STOP IT! You, Stupid Good Looking's" Something she would say to her siblings when they were misbehaving which earned her the first nickname, they ever called her 'Madame Yes' from the cartoon series 'The Flintstones'. She turns and resumes her stance.

Arakan looks at the Sister Superior's fighting stance and he must admit, he too is impressed.

"Shall we dance, Sister?" He says.

She answers in Spanish.

"Deja que la Musica juegue" (English translation. Let the music play)

Then she viciously attacks him with Maneuvers he has never seen, Maneuvers very hard to counter or evade.

In the security room of the hotel, more security guards watch on the monitors and they too cheer and act as children at a school yard fight. This cannot be helped these challenges have been going on for the past two days and the world has never seen anything like it.

Sister Maria continues to show superiority as Arakan desperately tries to strike her. He realizes he is exhausting himself, so he deliberately works up a sweat. The two fighters step back to catch their breath. Arakan is perspiring heavily. He asks if the Sister Superior would return the favor and allow him to remove his shirt and vest, she allows him to do so. Mr. Watanabe grabs his Cane and slowly stands, closes his eyes and lowers his head as if he is in shame. Arakan approaches him, to hand him his shirt and vest. The Sister Superior stands in the center of the room allowing her opponent this courtesy.

Arakan quickly grabs the cane from his bosses' hand, draws a sword from it and with a swift strike he decapitates Mr. Watanabe.

He then swings the sword twice at the Arch Nun, causing her to move back. He was so fast and fluid with this maneuver her team barely had time to aim their weapons before

Arakan backs away and plunges the sword into his stomach and slicing left and right disemboweling himself to assure death.

"Holy Sh#t, WHAT THE FU#K" The crime bosses Shout hysterically. The small spectator group of Hotel staff are traumatized. The FBI agents are a little shocked but not much, the A.N.T are laughing and find it highly amusing and entertaining and the Sister Superior is overwhelmed with grief but she contains it well as she runs to him and falls to her knees. She lowers her head and assumes the prayer position. Francis takes his defensive position behind her ordering his team and the FBI to take care of the situation calm everyone down and secure the scene.

Arakan lies on the floor bleeding his life slowly leaving his body. He reaches out to the Arch Nun; she gently takes his hand. She can hear his final thoughts as he says to her in Japanese.

"I can see Kami's (God) light with in you, it was an honor to fight against you. I will go before Kami and accept my judgment. I have one regret and hope Kami will forgive me. knowing I have faced one of the True Warriors sent by him to save us all. I proudly accept my defeat; I have been humbled by it and pray the Kami has Mercy on my soul."

The Sister Superior communicates and prays for him in his native Japanese Tongue. To the hotel staff silently watching it appears as though she is just silently praying beside him. Mr. Watanabe and Arakan have died an honorable death for their Clan and the Yakuza.

The Sister Superior stands, Francis helps her with her coat and habit. He drapes his arm around her as they slowly walk away from the bodies. The Sister Superior tells two of her agents to drive the vehicles back to the airport the rest will accompany her to the roof for extraction. This was a very shocking conclusion and there is blood everywhere and the Sister Superior doesn't want to walk through the hotel with blood on her clothing.

One of the female hotel managers still in a State of Shock asks with a stutter to no one in particular. "Should I-ca- call-for maintenance?" She is not attempting humor. She is traumatized and on the verge of passing out. Others are in a state of Hysteria. No doubt the hotel will be offering this small group very large Severance packages after this experience.

Francis apologizes and explains to everyone that they will be detained for a while due to the circumstances.

As for the other crime bosses and their staffs they will be isolated and detained by the FBI before they are free to go. Horatio Bain and his U.N-C.S.I team have been very busy these past few days and are now on their way to Las Vegas.

The Arch Nun and her agents go to the roof of the hotel. The Battle Assault Drone is summoned remotely. If the people along the Las Vegas Strip were uncertain of an Arch Nun's Presence at the Bellagio Hotel. It was definitely confirmed when the Battle Assault Drone approached the hotel. It was unable to land on the roof due to its size, so the pilot remotely bought it in as close as he could. A small ramp drops down to the roof as they enter the craft news helicopters are recording them and traffic is at a standstill on the Las Vegas Strip.

That morning the events are televised minus Sister Maria's. President Ophelia's approval rating is skyrocketing. But she is very worried it can all fall apart in the blink of an eye. She has been asked by Mother Teresa to not address the nation just yet.

She would like to wait until the conclusion of the Thrones of Chicago. Which will be very soon.

At an abandoned building in Chicago. Gang leaders that make up the Thrones of Chicago Discuss their plans for retaliation and to take back that which they believe is theirs. The building is well fortified with one concrete, steel reinforced Panic Room with two months food supply and they are very well armed. This is also one of their main drug dens. They keep the place filled with drug addicts, prostitutes with their babies and children to be used as human Shields if needed. This place was protected by Giovanni Luciano and his political affiliates. It houses a small army of different gang members within its walls. All information pertaining to this building was acquired by the undercover FBI agents that surrendered at the housing project and given to their superiors and Mother Teresa.

The gang leaders are gathered in one of the rooms discussing their plans.

"We need ta getta bomb and blow Dat whole Mother Fu#king neighborhood up!" One of the leader's shouts.

"Hell yeah! Wit all them Motherfu#kers in it too." Another agrees.

One of the gang leaders they know as 'Fistacuff' asks for everyone's attention.

"Them Motherfu#kers gonna pay, you can believe Dat. But we gotta get this heat off us first. Mr. G still out there, he let us know he still got our back. We jus gotta hold it down for a minute."

They all agree so he continues to speak.

"in a few days this Sh#t gonna die down then it's on like popcorn."

"What about Mother Teresa and da U.N.A?" One of the female gang leaders asks.

"Fu#k a Mother Teresa!" Fisticuffs shouts standing and throwing his beer against the wall.

"This street-level crime that bit#h got Bond villains ta worry about. She only making those fake a$s promises ta make herself look good. In a week that bit#h won't give a fu#k bout Chicago, trust me" He says as he sits down.

"We got everything from AR 15's ta RPGs (Rocket Propelled Grenades.) If we need a tank all we gotta do is call 'Leggz' that chick can get anything for da rite price and that Sh#t is done.

If the U.N.A want us or this city they gonna have ta come fight for it. And you can best believe they ain't gonna do Dat Sh#t on these city streets for a bunch of poor Motherfu#kers." He is successful at boosting the confidence of his fellow gang leaders. And as they take comfort in their false sense of security. They drink, get high and party. But as the Clock Struck Midnight at the end of the two days Mother Teresa granted them. Three A.N.T s were on the ground and in position awaiting the command to strike. High above the building hidden in the clouds are three Battle Assault Drones standing by awaiting Mother Teresa's command. Surely three Battle Assault Drones were not needed but the president wanted a show of force.

Michael B. Randolph

They are being remotely piloted by the team members on the
ground.
The Arch Nuns assigned to this campaign are.
Sister Donna, Sister Amira and Their Sister Superior Maria.
President Ophelia and president Andrei are watching from
the White House with their vice presidents and secretaries of
defense. General John C Randolph and General William
Coleman are with them. They are all very, very nervous!
"This should have been a military operation!" General
Coleman protests.
"Shut up general!" Presidential Ophelia tells him.
Sisters Donna and Amira, we're told to stay on board their
crafts by the Reverend Mother. Sister Maria is on the ground
with the teams. Mother Teresa ordered SWAT teams to
surround a three-block radius but not to interfere until they
are called upon. This is to be a U.N.A operation only. Local
law enforcement is ordered to redirect traffic away from the
area. Mother Teresa feels to her oldest granddaughter.
'Maria my sweet most of the people in that building are high
on one thing or another. I charge you to go forth and be
spectacular. The people in that building desperately need to
see visual effects accompanying the Lord's work. So, my
granddaughter let them witness miracles! You will not need
your sisters. The choice is yours my sweet.'
'I understand my Grandmother' Maria responds. All A.N.Ts
check in and are ordered to hold their positions and standby.
The Sister Superior tells them she has the utmost confidence
in their ability to do that which they do best and to maintain
the safety of the civilians with in. She then feels a message to
Amira and Donna.

'Hey, Buffie, Donn listen to me. Grandmother has given permission for me to use Spectacular visual effects to accompany the Miracles of the Lord I will be performing. The surveillance system will be down. Our body cams will be fluctuating as not to capture this. It is not as important to me my sisters. But I know how you two like your 'SUPERHERO' stuff and you BETTER not let Mom find out I used that 'S' word, LOL. So, join me you two and Let us make Hollywood Magic.'

Amira is ecstatic she can hardly contain herself. She can't wait to go in there and

Do the stuff she sees in movies. Mother Teresa is pleased that the Maria shared this with her younger sisters. So, she FEELS to the three of them.

'Okay my darlings protect everyone you can, Commence Procedure!'

Sister Maria tells the A.N.Ts to Commence.

One hundred small recorder drones move into position as she walks toward the front entrance of the building. There are as many remote Pilots standing by at Area 51 in case the small drones lose contact with the main craft. President Ophelia wants every Vantage Point possible inside and out. As she approaches, she is immediately picked up by the surveillance system.

There are several gang members guarding the entrance with twenty-five more surrounding the building's exterior. From afar the gang members think she's just another prostitute drug fiend coming for a fix. But as she gets closer to their surprise, they realize it is an Arch Nun.

"Yo Nig#r! it's one of them Arch bit#hes." One of the gang members yells loudly as the others pull out their cell phones to alert the leaders. They raise and point their guns at Sister Maria. But before they can shoot. A.N.T snipers take them out with tranquilizers.

The Sister Superior wanted them to alert the leaders before they were taken out and alert them, they did.

Sister Maria enters the building. It has a rather large Lobby with two staircases on either side
and a large glass dome in the center of the roof, the only light is from the moon. The apartments are on the outside of the square with a view from top to bottom.
It was a ten-story luxury apartment complex owned by Giovanni Luciano before it was condemned. There are many drug addicts sprawled across the floor high on their drugs. The Thrones wanted to assure they had plenty of hostages in case of a standoff with law enforcement. So, they offered free drugs to get as many inside as they possibly could. There are ten gang members in the lobby heavily armed and watching over them. Sister Maria Walks in Plain Sight but the Lord does not allow them to see her, yet. She walks to the center of the lobby with gang member standing as close as 10 feet from her. But their eyes are still not allowed to see.
 "Ah man I thought you said an Arch Nun was coming in side?"
"She did, she came right up ta the front door."
"Ni#er the door never opened that bi#ch still outside."
A fluctuating circular light appears in the center of the room where she stands. Then Sister Maria speaks softly in a sexy voice for them to hear.
"You have been given the opportunity to surrender, yet you have chosen to resist. You have been ordered to cease your illegal activities and still you resist. You refuse to live by the law, so you will be punished by the law."
As she concludes the light dissipates and she stands before them.
"Oh Sh#t where that bit#h come from?" They shout in amazement.
They immediately draw their weapons and shoot at her. The bullets slow down as they approach her then stop in mid-air.
"Ooooh Sh#t!" A few of the gang members say in disbelief.

The bullets hang in the air as the Sister Superior speaks to them once more. "I beg of you, please do not fire your weapons at me again."

Then the bullet drops to the floor, of the ten gang members surrounding her. All but two fire their weapons at her again. As the Second Barrage of bullets approach her. She quickly Twirls around and the bullets follow her as she spins. Time slows down and each bullet returns to its point of origin striking only the gang members whom shot at her.

They fall to the ground hurt badly but they will live. If any of them could gather the strength to stand and rejoin the fight they would do so, but not after what they have just experienced and witnessed. As for the two whom did not fire their weapons she orders them to their knees and to put their hands behind their heads. Without hesitation they obey.

"Now witness the Power of God!" She tells them.

Most of the addicts are starting to take notice what is going on around them and even under the influence of Narcotics they cannot believe what their eyes behold. Hearing the gunfire in the lobby more gang members run down both flights of stairs. In the blink of an eye sister Maria disappears from where she was standing and reappears with a flash of light at the foot of the left stairwell to intercept the gang members running down the stairs. She makes quick work of them.

At that exact second sister Amira appears in a flash of light at the foot of the right stairwell, striking one of the gang members to the center of his body with such force, he flies up the stairs into three more gang members knocking all of them to the wall behind them. They are all hurt very badly and can barely move. The addicts are beginning to wonder if they are hallucinating. No one her size can hit with such strength, not to mention The Arch Nuns are appearing from flashes of light.

'Well, little sister you seem to be having fun.' Maria feels to Amira.

'Oh yes' Big Sis I can't thank you enough for this opportunity to do all my favorite movie stunts and effects'

'Don't mention it little sis, but I doubt if you'll have time to do all your favorite things LOL. I'll cover the lobby for now, party on Buffie.'

'Watch this Maria, I'm going to do my crunching Tiger, Hidden Dragon maneuver in the center of this stairwell.' Sister Amira walks to the center of the stairwell. She slowly assumes the take-off position made famous by Keanu Reeves in 'The Matrix 2' The floor beneath her feet begins to Ripple like a pebble being thrown into a still lake, then she jumps in the air twirling as she Rises. As she passes each floor, she releases a Halo of bright light. The Prostitutes and their children standing in the hallways that Overlook the stairwells are captivated by this beautiful sight. The prostitutes see a green burst of light, the children see an assortment of colored lights the gang members see a blinding sun-like light. This light of God instructed the women and children to go to the lobby there they will be safe. It commanded the gang members to Humble themselves before the Lord. And still they did not take heed. Amira reaches the top floor; she hovers a moment before disappearing. The gang members guarding the top floor are protecting their leaders. Many of them are ex-military. They cannot believe what they have just seen.

"Yo man, did that bit#h just fly up here and disappear?" One of the gang members yells in disbelief, after firing several shots at what he believed to be Sister Amira.

"Hey, dumb Asses! that's gotta be a Motherfu#king projection, bit#h! Don't waste your bullets on that Sh#t!" Fisticuffs yells then tells the rest of the gang leaders we should all go to the safe room now. An electrical field forms in front of The Gangs who are backing away in fear.

The field is producing winds blowing papers and garbage around. The electrical Distortion forms the silhouette of a woman. Then Sister Amira appears before them with her arms at her side slightly opened with electricity pulsating around her body.

The leaders were running down the hall to the safe room when they noticed this. The site stops them dead in their tracks. The winds and lightning appear to have disappeared into Sister Amira's body. She immediately starts to walk toward them.

"That's a projection Y'all don't shoot at that bit#h!" Fisticuffs shouts pointing his finger at her. But they fire their weapons at her anyway. She stops quickly assuming the prayer position, the Bullets stop in mid-air as they did for the Sister Superior. Sister Amira slowly walks to the bullets and swipes right as they fall to the ground.

"THAT AIN'T NO MOTHER-FU#KING PROTECTION, THAT'S HER, FA-REAL!"

Realizing this, four of the seven gang leaders attempt to run to the safe room. The gang fire their weapons at her again. This time the bullets stop halfway. She is on one side of the large Square opening the gangs are on the other. The bullets are sustained in the center of the square held by the hand of God. Sister Amira swipes her hand left and the gang members disappear and reappear in front of the bullets with their guns floating above them. The four gang leaders whom were attempting to flee slowdown and are unable to move. The three remaining leaders one female and two males are petrified. To them it appears as though a movie slowed down and then paused. Yet they and The Arch Nun can still move. How can this be they thought?

The female gang leader known as 'La-Rocker' has a revelation and Falls to her knees.

"Oh, Heavenly Father, Oh God please, please forgive me. Jesus, I beg you please don't let me die like this. Please give me another chance to turn my life around." She yells repeatedly asking God for forgiveness. As for the males they too are frightened but know not what to do. So, they stand beside her each with a hand upon her shoulder attempting to calm her.

Amira walks through the solid railing and continues toward them Walking on Air. As she gets closer the male gang leaders fall to their knees as well! Now they find themselves humbled before the power of God and kneeling before an Arch Nun. "Rise, do not Kneel to Me."

Sister Amira says softly.

"I wasn't kneeling ta YOU, I was kneeling before God and asking forgiveness."

La-Rocker responds sobbing like a baby.

"I said RISE! " Sister Amira commands. The three slowly stand keeping their heads down as not to make eye contact with Sister Amira. "Look upon me and know the Power of the Lord"

The three raise their heads trembling in fear. Sister Amira points to the gangs still hovering in the center of the square with bullets inches from their bodies.

The three of them look, the four leaders whom are suspended in time can only move their eyes but they too look at their associate's peril.

"Those who shall not live by the law, shall be punished by the law!"

Sister Amira says with conviction, swiping her hand to the left, time resumes, the bullets strike their marks and the four leaders continue running to the Panic Room.

The gang members scream in pain as the bullets penetrate their bodies, they fall ten stories to the floor below. The three gang leaders quickly run to the rail watching in Terror as the bodies drop. The bodies appear to have hit the floor yet they did not die! They levitate inches above it. With a smile and a wink Sister Amira says to them. "Perhaps they will Die Another Day."

"What do you want from us Sister? " La-Rocker screams hysterically.

"Go downstairs, surrender to my sister and be Swift, or I will assist you!"

They waste no time running down the stairs almost tripping one another. The other gang leaders Witnesses this continuing to the Panic Room which is on the same floor and not far away. Running as hard and fast as they can, reaching the entrance and inputting the code to unlock the door. They turn to look at Sister Amira. She is not pursuing them just watching as they enter the room with five gang members. When the leaders heard of an Arch Nun was approaching the building.

They ordered several women and children to wait in the Panic Room so they may use them as hostages or for bargaining. As the electronic door slowly closes fisticuff maintains eye contact with Sister Amira until it is fully closed and locked. Then she disappears in a large flash of light. The room is large and dark the leaders can hear the women and children crying.

"Somebody turn on da Motherfu#king lights."
Fisticuff says Breathing heavily.

"I got it" An unfamiliar voice answers, then Sister Donna turns on the lights. She is sitting on a couch with the women and children. The members of the gang raise their weapons and with complete disregard for the women or children they began to fire at her.

Sister Donna sits calmly as the bullets approach her; she stops them in mid-air.

Then claps her hands once and the children quickly fall asleep.

The women Express concern for the children but Sister Donna assures them they are fine.

"What the FU#K, Bi#ch how the FU#K you get in here?" They all ask.

"God let me in." Sister Donna answers crossing her legs. With the bullets still Suspended in time She holds up her index finger and twirls it around. The bullets turn and strike the gang members in the center of their bodies. They fall to the floor motionless

but they will live. The leaders do not wish to let each other know how frightened they really are. But they are definitely having a hard time keeping their cool.

Fisticuff in an Act of desperation, picks up a two-year-old girl and holds his gun to her sleeping body. The other two leaders decide this is too much to handle and quickly raise their hands and step away from him. They want no part in what he is now doing.

"Yo Fist what the fu#k you doing?" They ask.

"Shut the fu#k up, I got dis, these kids and Arch Nun are our hostages now!"

"Do you really want to do this?" Sister Donna asks calmly.

"Shut the fu#k up bit#h and stay your fat ass on that couch!"

"Do you really think after what you have just witnessed, the bullet will penetrate the child's body and not yours?" Sister Donna asks softly. Fisticuff is shaking and he is very unsure of himself at this moment. The other leaders have noticed that he is definitely not the calm cool and Fierce leader he was just hours ago. None of them are. The women whom they use as prostitutes and personal sex slaves. Look upon him and shake their heads in disgust. He who stands holding a gun to a child, he who has terrorized so many for so long, he who has witness with thine own eyes the Power of the Lord. And still refuses to respect it. He who shall know before the sun rises the true Power of thy Lord God!

One of the women Whispers to Sister Donna. "When you get the chance Sister, PLEASE break his Motherfu#king NECK!" "Be still my child and know that the Lord is with you all." Sister Donna responses taking her hand. Fisticuff pushes a button on the wall which signals all the remaining gang members to attack with everything they've got. Over a hundred heavily-armed gang members emerge from vacant apartments.

"It's on now bit#h!" He says with a devilish grin, then turns on the monitors so he can watch what's happening. From the perspective of the occupants of the building Thirty minutes have passed. Which has seemed like an Eternity. But in reality, only Ten seconds has passed since Sister Maria entered the building.

"A.N.Ts I have many hostiles and civilians surrendering in the lobby. Some of these dummies (referring to the gang members) are so high on drugs they 'SEEM' to have shot themselves and each other."

Sister Maria tells them over the comlink. This is not an Arch Nun telling a lie, she told them

'IT SEEMS' Not 'THEY HAVE' shot themselves and each other!

"The lobby is secure, repeat the lobby is secure. many more hostiles approaching from top floors. ALL TEAMS MOVE IN NOW!"

The four mid-sized B.A.Ds Circle the outside of the building covering the first floor traveling clockwise periodically firing fifty caliber bullets through the building to establish an impassable perimeter, the primary B.A.D circles the building counterclockwise covering all other floors using x-ray scanning systemically taking out gang members.

Realizing they are unable to cross the perimeter of the first floor. They use grenade launchers attached to their Firearms to disperse nerve gas into the lobby below. It was their intention to kill everyone in the lobby.

"Behold the power of thy God!" Sister Maria shouts holding her head high with her arms wide. And through the Grace of God holds the gas at Bay preventing it from passing the stairwell. Then orders the primary B.A.D to blow a hole in the top of the building.

The craft stops in place, rotating 180 degrees, rises to the top of the building and performs what can only be described as a backflip over the building momentarily stopping midway with its nose pointing straight down at the top of the building, firing a single missile blowing a very large hole in the building's roof continuing it's flipping motion. It then releases a fifth mid-size drone this particular drone also has propellers. It flies straight down the hole until it reaches the lobby. Using its propellers, it sucks the gas upward as it flies up through the hole. The gang members wearing gas masks attempt to shoot it down. It sustained some damage but was able to complete its flight.

"This is definitely blowing my high' but in a good way!" One of the addicts says to another. Barely conscious another asks. "Is this a movie if so I wanna watch it from the beginning."

Fisticuff orders some of the gang to the roof with Rocket launchers to take out the main Drone.

Three make their way to the roof. As they open the rooftop door, they can see the large drone hovering approximately fifty feet in the distance. All three aim and lock on to the craft. The large drone hovers as though it was taunting them. Three missiles are fired at the Drone.

"Yeah Motherfu#kers that's how you do it!"

Fisticuff yells watching on his monitors. The missiles are rapidly approaching the Drone. They are ten feet away from Impact when suddenly. The craft quickly darts upward in doing so it releases a titanium fine mesh net attached to a steel wire. Which closes instantaneously on impact containing the rockets and 80% of the explosion. Then they are dropped the to the surface for retrieval.

"Oh my God, now that is money well spent!" President
Ophelia says giving General Randolph a high five referring
to the cost of a Battle Assault Drone. The gang members on
the roof are exposed to return fire from the Drone. Three-
fifty caliber bullets are fired striking each member
simultaneously killing them instantly. The Drone proceeds
to take out the doorway to the roof with a small missile.
Several gang members were on their way to the roof but are
stopped by the blast and wounded by flying debris.
"You're right! that is how you do it." Sister Donna says with
a sexy smile.
The women join her in a giggle, this infuriates Fistacuff
fueling his rage. He points his gun at Sister Donna. "FU#K
YOU FAT BIT#H!" He says angrily.
Sister Donna asks the women. "How many times is he going
to refer to me as a FAT FEMALE DOG?"
"A lot" They respond.
"Y'ALL bit#hes shut the fu#k up! " He shouts. "As for you, I
had enough of your Sh#t die fat bit#h!" He screams at her
pulling the trigger. He was so angry he forgot what Sister
Donna warned him of. As the bullets approach her, they
pass through her and she is gone. In her place now sits Arch
Nun Sister Amira. "I'm not fat" She says as the women
quickly move away from her in amazement but meaning no
disrespect.
"Oh, HELL NO!" The other leaders say in disbelief. Fisticuff
still pointing the gun and holding the sleeping child, is
amazed, shocked and petrified with fear.
Sister Amira stands and slowly walks toward him asking.
"Now then, where were we?"
He throws the gun to the floor and puts his hand around the
child's neck telling her.
"I'll break dis Lil Motherfu#kers neck. Come at me BIT#H!"
The other two leaders remain sill with their hands up, they
are too afraid to speak.
Sister Amira stops and with a hash stare and says.

317

"I truly believe you would do it. Henry Bartholomew Barkly." Addressing him by his full name to which no one in the room ever knew.

Some of the women seize this opportunity to tease him.

"Nigg#r! Yo name is Bartholomew. I'd change that Sh#t too!" One woman says.

"Change it ta punk ass bit#h!" Says another.

The women are becoming more confident in the presence of the Arch Nun.

"Settle down ladies." She tells them. "I'm sure with a name like fisticuff he most certainly knows how to fight!" She goes on looking him up and down.

"Do you want to fight me---Mr. Cuff, or do you want to stand there with your hands around a sleeping child's neck?" He most definitely does not appreciate her sarcasm. Nor does he wish to fight her. But she is embarrassing him doing what 'Buffie' does best. The women all laugh at him. Tears of anger form in his eyes. If he had not thrown the gun to the floor, he would surely have fired upon all of them. His hands tighten around the child's neck.

"Keep laughing bit#hes!" He screams with a crazed look in his eyes. The women quickly stop laughing as they once again grasp the sincerity of the situation. Realizing their fellow gang leader may actually snap the child's neck. They attempt to intervene. "Yo fist it's over man!"

"Yeah man com' on our troops are losing out there." They plead. "These Arch Nuns bit#hes are flying around, walking on air, stopping bullets, bullets are changing direction and not hitting these Motherfu#kers. They Disappearing and reappearing. Sh#t gotta STOP!" They continue hoping he'll understand and come to his senses. Fisticuff picks up the gun holds it at his side for a moment, then points it at his fellow gang leaders and shoots them both in the face.

"Them bullets didn't change direction, now did they?" He shouts at their still bodies.

The women scream hysterically. Sister Amira stands calmly a few feet away from him. He holds the child by the throat close to his chest.

"No, no, no Where's all da laughing and jokes now?" He asks waving the gun at them. Since shooting his friends in the face he is now confident the bullets will not change direction. So, he points the gun at the women but before he can pull the trigger. Sister Amira tells him to stop! if he knows what's good for him. Not trusting the bullet's direction, he does not shoot. Truly knowing his options are limited. He comes to the realization that he would rather die then go to jail. He knows he cannot kill the Arch Nun for the bullets do not penetrate her. So, he decides to squeeze the life from the child then shoot himself in the head.

Sister Amira notices his hand beginning to constrict. With the look of a Madman upon his face he quickly raises the gun to his head. Sister Amira in a flash moves toward him, appearing to strike the child. A small but very visible Ripple passes through the child striking fisticuff.

On impact he releases the child and flies backwards in slow motion.

"Oooooooh Sh#t" The women collectively Shout. For they and the Arch Nun move freely, only fisticuff is flying backwards very, very slowly. The child still sleeping from Sister Donna's command is suspended in mid-air undisturbed as is the gun in which he was holding.

Sister Amira gently embraces the child removing her from the time slip and gives her to her Mother.

"Thank you, sister, Oh God thank you!" The Mother says hugging Sister Amira with the child in between them. All the women in the room join in for a group hug.

Fisticuff feels himself moving slowly but is unable to do anything about it. With all he has recently seen and experienced he still denies the power of The Lord. And with hatred in his heart looks upon the women in disgust still wanting to kill every last one of them.

The women who believed not, in the Lord but in the old Mighty Dollar, they who believed they were Unworthy of God's love, they who believed they were put upon this Earth to serve man and to fulfill his sexual desires, to bear his children and be his slave, to abandon their ambitions and live the life that he sees fit. They know now that the lord loves them and they were meant for so much more.

Sister Amira turns assumes the prayer position and Stomps her right foot to the floor. Upon doing so time resumes for fisticuff. He continues to fly backwards only to be stopped by the large heavy steel door behind him. For a moment he is stuck to the door then the Arch Nun allows him to fall. As he hits the floor, he hears moaning it is the gang leaders he shot moments ago, they still live. This too was the Power of God!

The five gang members that were shot earlier are still lying on the floor, suffering from their wounds unable to move or speak, they have witnessed all of this. Fisticuff is also in pain from hitting the heavy door. He struggles to stand but finds it very difficult to do so. The A.N.Ts are outside making quick work of the inexperienced gang members. They are no match for the world's most Elite tactical squads.

"They'll never get through that door."

Fisticuff says finally standing. The women shout obscenities to him and attempted to rush over to beat him but are stopped by Sister Amira.

"Can we finish him off sister, PLEASE?" The women plead.

"No ladies, you may not!"

The A.N.Ts are enjoying themselves taking out the gang members, perhaps a little too much. Those who are not killed, quickly surrender and are ordered to the lobby to see the Sister Superior. The firefight is coming to an end. The A.N.Ts secure the building. The bodies of the gang members litter the floor and stairwells.

The safe room was built on the tenth floor. Now the A.N.Ts have the slight dilemma of opening the door. The primary B.A.D is remotely maneuvered into position. It fires a single low-impact missile destroying a wall, blowing a hole in the side of the building. It now has a clear line of sight to the Panic Room's door. It fires a highly classified experimental fusion plasma laser. This weapon is reserved for the most extreme circumstances but there are children locked in there so Mother Teresa authorizes its use and General Randolph concurs.

With the Precision of a surgeon it cuts through the steel reinforced concrete like a hot knife through butter. It took six seconds and only used 40% of its power. The heavy door crashes to the floor. "What were you saying about that door?"

Sister Amira asks fisticuff before he has the chance to answer she is gone in the blink of an eye.

The B.A.D Shines a light into the room it is accompanied by many red laser sights targeting everyone inside.

"Everybody, down on the Fu#king ground NOW!" An A.N.T commands.

"Keep your Fu#king hands where we can see them. deviate from my instructions and you will be shot!" The A.N.Ts quickly move in to gather everyone and tend to the wounded. The room is filled with a heavy dust. One of the women lying on her belly with her foot near Fisticuff's face gives him a hard kick to the head. The A.N.Ts saw this and laugh.

"Bit#h you better hope I don't ever see your ass again!" He says grinding his teeth with a bump slowly growing on his forehead from her kick.

"Your mother's a bit#h! Bartholomew and don't worry you won't nig#er!" She responds attempting to kick him again.

"Shut the fu#k up both of you, NOW!"

A.N.Ts shout to them shining lights on both their faces. As the A.N.Ts get everyone on their feet the children awaken and the women ask where is the Arch Nun?

"She's down stairs in the lobby, you'll see her soon enough." An A.N.T tells them.

"Yeah, be careful what you ask for. An Arch Nun is the last person you wanna see right now." Says another as they start to handcuff everyone. The women wonder how did she get to the lobby so fast none of them saw her leave.

"Enough talking!" Shouts the commanding officer. "Shut the fu#k up, all of you I don't wanna hear another word from any of you dumb motherfu#kers." He concludes grabbing fisticuff by the shirt.

"Get da fu#k off me!" He says attempting to pull away. He still wishes to die and believes this would be the best way to do it by resisting the A.N.Ts.

Sister Maria senses a feeling from the Lord and intervenes. "All A.N.Ts listen up" She says over the comlink.

"Your orders are now capture only, repeat capture only!" Before they can bind his hands he begins to attack one of the A.N.Ts hoping to be killed. But instead he is lifted in the air then thrown hard, to the floor then secured and bound.

He kicks and screams like a child throwing a tantrum. "Kill me, kill me, kill me" He shouts repeatedly.

The women laugh uncontrollably pointing at him some of the A.N.Ts join in.

"That's enough I said!" The commander interrupts. "Get everyone downstairs now!"

Everyone immediately stops laughing and complies. They gag fisticuff and carry him down to the lobby. They don't want him shouting nonsense to the Sister Superior.

The president and her party are very impressed with the outcome of the event and the unbelievable performance of the Battle Assault Drones.

In the increasingly crowding Lobby. The women can see the Sister Superior.

"Where are the other Arch Nuns?" They asked.

"This is the only Arch Nun here." They are told by the A.N.T. After everything they have witnessed, they still find it just a little hard to process. They whisper among themselves for a quick moment and decide not to say anything further regarding the other two Arch Nuns. They do not want to be thought of as crazy, nor do they want to agree with fisticuff when he is telling the story. They consider themselves blessed to have witnessed the work of the Lord! As did the Hebrews and Egyptians when Moses wielded his mighty staff in the name of the Lord.

These women will not return to their previous lifestyle, they will form a strong bond and remain friends for the rest of their lives raising their children to love the Lord.

Sister Maria orders all three B.A.Ds to land outside the building so they may begin transporting the prisoners. The medical teams and coroners standing by are ordered in to tend to the wounded and dead. A.N.T agent Alfred walks over to Sister Maria carrying fisticuff as though he were a piece of luggage.

"We have ta keep an eye on this one boss, he's suicidal, very suicidal!"

"Very well, keep him separated from the rest sedate him if you must."

There is a lot of commotion as they get everyone outside and separated to board the B.A.Ds.

The addicts along with the women and children will be on one ship, the gang members will be on another. Everyone is considered a prisoner of the U.N.A at this moment by order of Mother Teresa. Sisters Donna and Amira walk over to join their Sister Superior. Fisticuff's women see them and their faces glow with excitement. They remain silent and cannot take their eyes off the Arch Nuns as they are escorted onto the ship by the A.N.T agents. "Oh Sh#t! there they go right there." The surviving gang members scream referring to Sisters Donna and Amira.

"THEM ARCH BIT#HES AIN'T HUMAN, THEM BIT#HES CAN FLY, THEY INDESTRUCTIBLE!"

Many of the gang members scream frantically, only to be laughed at by the medics and other law enforcement agencies now on site.

They continued relentlessly hoping someone will believe them.

"So let me get this straight, all of you guys were shooting at the Arch Nun?"

A.N.T agent Sophia asks. All the remaining gang members admit to firing weapons at them.

"Thank you very much for that gentleman, that's going to make things a lot easier now."

A.N.T agent Francis says with a big smile. For the gangs forgot the small recorder drones flying around are recording everything!

The addicts, women and children are divided among two crafts, the children and babies are allowed to stay with their parents. All the gang members will be on one ship heavily guarded. Sister Donna is overseeing preparations on board her ship as is Sister Amira. The women who were in the safe room are divided amongst the two ships and continue to watch the Arch Nuns.

"Stop staring at that Nun, we might get in more trouble." One of the addicts says.

"We're in the presence of God's love, trust me we are not in

trouble." She responds smiling.
Mother Teresa and president Ophelia are concerned as to
where and from whom a street gang received nerve toxin
from.
This particular toxin was very special, it only stays lethal for
20 minutes before dissipating. The news media are not
allowed on site yet, but they were filming the entire thing
live from a distance capturing a lot of the action firsthand
with zoom lenses and broadcasting live to the world.
There were 157 addicts including their children,62
prostitutes concluding their children and 225 gang members
representing the Thrones of Chicago.
The Arch Nuns saved all the addicts, all the prostitutes and
all the children. As for the gang members none were killed
by the Arch Nuns, twenty-seven were saved by them. The
rest were killed during the firefight by the A.N.Ts.
CNN, NBC, FOX and World News Tonight are the first news
crews allowed on site as the B.A.Ds are taking off.
Mother Teresa addresses the world from the U.N building in
New York.
It is heard through the speakers of the B.A.Ds hovering
overhead.
She is very brief and direct to the point.
"Attention! people of Chicago"
The cameras focus on the B.A.Ds.
"The 'Thrones of Chicago' are NO MORE! Woe unto ANY
attempting to take their place. Bask in this glory, for you
have witnessed the Power of thy Lord God, Hallowed be thy
NAME!"
Then the B.A.Ds disappear into the night sky. Loud cheers
can be heard throughout the streets as the people danced
and gave praise to the Lord, president Ophelia and The
U.N.A.
The city rejoiced well into the morning and at the dawn of
this new day, Eve
Once again used her influence to incite contempt from many

of the churches around the world. They rallied their congregations to take to the streets insinuating the Arch Nuns are nothing more than the government's murderers and hit squads. But this did not go over well with most of the people worldwide. They defended the Arch Nuns, bringing these absurd accusations to a swift close.

Mother Teresa was relieved this endeavor did not succeed in slandering the U.N.A or their intentions. The president's approval rating continues to rise it is now higher than any other president in the history of the United States.

President Andrei is also receiving recognition by Russia for his involvement as his country prepares to welcome the U.N.A.

Hymiriam is aware of all her children's Endeavors but this one in particular hangs heavy on her heart. It is not her intention to anger God's first female nor to give her the impression she is being challenged and she certainly does not want 'The Mother of All' to declare war upon her Arch Nuns. So, she asks the Lord if she may meet with Eve to discuss alternative peaceful Solutions. And the Lord heard Hymiriam. Now she shall meet with 'The First Created Female!'

While the city of Chicago and the world continue to celebrate. Eve watches from one of her many private Villas. This one is built into the side of a small mountain in France with its own private Winery. As always it is heavily guarded and protected with very heavy artillery.

Hymiriam's craft cannot approach this area at all. So, through the Grace of God She must transition there. Everyone at the Villa is very busy tending to their daily duties. Time slows down as Hymiriam transitions into the villa. She is dressed appropriately and all who look upon her will not recognize her. To them she was always there and they do not communicate with her, time resumes.

Eve sits on the balcony watching the afternoon News. The U.N.A and Arch Nuns are highly celebrated. There are a few

people tending to her bringing her wine and such. One
brings a pedicure station. Hymiriam politely takes over and
begins to wash Eve's feet. One of her personal assistants'
approaches.
"Pardon the intrusion My Lady, but there is a call from your
son 'Cane'
Hymiriam's worries are confirmed. If Eve is summoning her
current 'Cane' or 'Abel' things are going to heat up a
hundred-fold.
"I will speak to him later" She responds with her soft sexy
voice continuing to watch the news.
"Why, Oh Great One must you torture yourself, watching
these buffoons idolizing this manufactured military
nunnery? They are nothing more than a facade!"
The assistant asks with concern kneeling beside her.
"Perhaps you are right, NOW everyone but my pedicurist
leave me."
She commands closing her eyes and leaning back in the chair
to enjoy her pedicure. Hymiriam is a little nervous, opening
a dialogue with God's first female is an honor indeed.
But how will I begin she wonders. Then she realizes the
honor should be Eve's as well. She takes comfort in knowing
no one can recognize her unless she wants them to and so
she gathers herself. But just as Hymiriam's lips part to speak.
She hears something most disturbing.
"Welcome Mary, Mother of Jesus."
Hymiriam almost fell over. How is she able to recognize me?
She thinks to herself.
"Your son washed feet as well, a most humble act."
Eve says looking down at her. Hymiriam slowly stands
never breaking eye contact.
"Now that you are before me, I will ask you, why are you
here?"
"I am here to reacquaint Humanity with God, to assist in
establishing a stable future and hopefully convince the 'First
of Us' to come home to the 'Everlasting'"

"How Noble of you" Eve says as she stands. The two women slowly walk the large balcony. To Eve's children whom were tending to her begin to wonder. Who is this pedicurist their mother allows to walk with her. For through the Grace of God they cannot see her true identity.

"How are you able to see and recognize me, may I ask?"
Eve smiles ever so wickedly.

"Mine are the eyes that were among the first to look upon this world. Although I cannot see everything, I can see a great deal and I remember everything since the beginning of this world."

Hymiriam smiles and understands. But she is baffled as to why Eve has not mentioned what her Arch Nuns truly are.

"This military nunnery you have formed knows not the true power of my children; I hold high in my favor. Blood of My Blood is ABSOLUTE POWER!"

Then the Mother of Jesus realizes Eve does not know they are Time-Displaced, walk with 10% of God's grace and are Blood of her Blood. The Blood of Hymiriam.

She and Mother Teresa did an excellent job rebuilding the Arch Nuns history.

She truly believes her High Held children can physically defeat an Arch Nun. So, she allows her to continue believing this.

"Eve, if I may ask can you not refer to them as a Military Nunnery please."

"As you wish, my dear."
The conversation is quite cordial so far.

"You mentioned me accompanying you to the Everlasting?"
Eve asks.

"Yes! if you come home to the Everlasting. I will abort this endeavor, dissolve my Nunnery and the U.N.A"
Eve found that statement highly amusing.

"Oh no my dear, I have a better suggestion. You, your Nunnery and the U.N.A Will assist me in destroying ALL of Humanity and this wretched planet man has so desecrated!

Then you and I will enter the EverLasting hand in hand. 'The Mother of Jesus and the Mother of All' Sounds like a NetFlix Television series, Does it Not?" Eve says wickedly laughing.

Hymiriam was not surprised by Eve's temperament. She has lived so long and has seen man at his best and at his worst. She stops laughing and looks away from Hymiriam for a moment in remembrance of that which was.

"I assisted in the start of Humanity. Countless times I begged the Lord to help or save mankind but my prayers were in vain. And that is when I stopped praying."

"The Lord heard your prayers, Eve."

"I KNOW, THE LORD HEARD MY PRAYERS! MARY, MOTHER OF JESUS!"

Eve shouts as the two stopped walking for a moment.

"THE LORD HEARS ALL MY PRAYERS!"

She continues looking Hymiriam up and down almost in anger. Although she speaks loudly her servants and children are too far away to hear.

"Unlike YOU, the lord does not speak to me through Arch Angels, I have a more direct communication. I believe it was the Archangel Gabriel whom delivered a message from the Lord. Let's see how did it go? Oh yes, you will bare the son of God!"

It would appear she is trying to insult her with sarcasm or disrespecting the Immaculate Conception. But she is not this is how she speaks to everyone and the mother of Jesus is no exception. Eve tells Hymiriam how God spoke to her telling her of great things to come. It is believed that God spoke to Noah first regarding the destruction of the world by water. But the Lord told Eve years earlier. This allowed her to assure her marriage to one of Noah's sons securing her passage on the ark.

She tells her she has been many women throughout history and through the Grace of God she is always in the right place at the right time.

Eve motions for Hymiriam to continue walking with her and guides her to a table. The two sit so they may continue their discussion. On the table is a bottle of Red wine and four glasses. The servants quickly rush over to pour the wine. Hymiriam does not want to be rude so she allows them to pour her a glass. But she has no intention of drinking it, Eve takes notice of this and says.

"Let me guess, born unto humanity as a human but still a Celestial being, As was your son!"

Hymiriam smiles nodding her head.

"Your son's first miracle was turning water to wine at a wedding in Cana. I'm sure he must have tasted a little."

"I hope not, I would have taken his cell phone and grounded him for a week."

Hymiriam jestingly responds smiling attempting to lighten the mood. But humor is a difficult concept for God's first female as of late.

"How Quaint!" Eve says with a cold stare.

Her children and servants watching from a distance still wondering who is this woman, this pedicurist their mother speaks to.

Hymiriam notices them watching.

"Oh don't mind them."

Eve says starting to smile.

"They're just a bit concerned as to why I speak so long to a mere pedicurist and if anything were wrong you would be removed and Beaten! Sorry, old habits"

If anyone else had made this statement it would surely be a jest, but Eve is definitely not joking. She still has her servants beaten. This helps Hymiriam understand and how to better locate her children. It is this very distinctive arrogant trait that will assist in exposing some of them. If you ever have or are currently working for someone displaying this trait. Beware! You may be working for a child of Eve!

"I propose a toast my dear." Eve says.

"To the two of us, what a pair we make!"

Hymiriam toasts to be respectful but does not drink.

"So it is your quest to assist Man in bettering himself? Well, good luck with that! MAN, with the exception of a few is the worst thing this world will ever know!"

Hymiriam disagrees but Eve persists in convincing her otherwise.

"You look upon man and see the good in him. For he has indeed done a great many good things. But let us not forget it was MAN; who hunted and crucified YOUR SON!"

This definitely struck a nerve in Hymiriam. She bows her head and clenches her Fist.

'Heaven take hold of me' She prays silently asking for the strength to endure this encounter. As Eve continues to provoke her.

"It was MAN; who made him carry a cross while they beat and spat upon him, while many of the People, THE SAME PEOPLE you are attempting to save did nothing, NOTHING! THEY LAUGHED." She shouts slamming her hand to the table.

"YOU were there feeling EVER lash of the whip, EVER hammer of the nails, AS WAS I!" Hymiriam quickly raises her head looking at Eve almost in Disbelief. They stare deeply into each other's eyes for a moment, Mary remains silent as Eve continues to speak.

 "There were some who felt true remorse, but they were few, oh so few compared to the masses that wanted him DEAD! And when MAN nailed him to the cross, I FELT EVER POUND OF THE HAMMER! Man, did all this to your son and STILL you believe there is hope for Him, still you believe there is good in him"

331

The eyes of Eve have not teared in Centuries but she speaks from the heart with such passion that Mary begins to truly realize EVE WAS THERE! She knew and loved her son Jesus. And from the emotions she displays. She knew him rather well.

But who was she at that time? Could this woman who speaks to her now, have been MARY MAGDALENE at that time?

Eve continues to describe in great detail the pain Jesus went through.

The two women shed tears and mourn. One weeps for the pain and sacrifice of her son, the other weeps in anger. Just when Mary believes she can take no more. The Lord comforts her, gives her strength and allows her to speak the 'WORD OF GOD'!

Hymiriam stands, Gathers herself and in Full Arch Nun Rhetoric, She says unto Eve.

"Prepare thyself, Oh Great Mother of ALL, FOR CHRIST WALKS THE EARTH AGAIN!"

Upon speaking these words she dips her index finger in the glass of wine before her and with the Power of God it is transformed into water.

Eve's wine is transformed as well, As is ALL the wine on the property!

Then as silent as she appeared. Hymiriam is gone. Anyone else would have been amazed and fell to their knees before such Power. But Eve is accustomed to the miracles of the Lord. For she has witnessed them many times in the past. She remains seated smiling to herself in remembrance of such might, but it does not change her mind.

One of Eve's children approaches her with an itinerary for the day's events.

"Has your guest gone mother or will she be staying for the afternoon festivities?"

Eve staring off into the distance slowly turns and replies.
"Do not concern yourself with her my child, carry on with
your duties."
Eve who has from the beginning of time received messages
from God pertaining to Monumental events. She who has
seen the rise and fall of Mighty Empires, she who has
survived the GREAT FLOOD and she who has witnessed the
Power of God through Moses.
Received no warning regarding the coming of Mary Mother
of Jesus with the designation of CHRIST!
Several of the servants quickly approach her with news of
the winery. They inform her that the entire stock of wine has
somehow been switched and replaced with water.
"How can this be?" They ask.
"Who could do such a thing so quickly and undetected?"
They are baffled, Eve must act the same as not to reveal the
true identity of her visitor. That is something she never
wants the world to know. It is too late to cancel the lunch,
nor does she want to. Her guests will be here shortly so she
instructs everyone to remain calm, definitely do not speak of
this and have security look into it. Also, to fly in more wine
immediately! A few of the guests have arrived early. Some
of their private chefs were assisting Eve's staff.
When they received word of all the wine mysteriously being
replaced with water. They thought it to be absurd, A farce
and amusing.
But they immediately post the news to social media anyway.
This infuriates Eve, not that Mary turned the wine into
water. It was the news going public on the internet.
She takes hold of her expensive garment and tears it ever-so-
slightly.
The tearing of clothes was an ancient custom when one was
very angry or sad.
Her guests do not know her true identity. To them she is one
of the many high-level corporate representatives hosting a
luncheon event.

She excuses herself so she may be alone in her Chambers for a moment.

Two of her security officers also, children of hers escort her. As they walk down the hall Eve begins to feel a little faint.

"MOTHER!" The they cry.

"I'm fine my sons"

She enters a large luxurious bedroom and walks over to the television monitor. It is a hundred-foot screen with three smaller monitors to both sides. She places her hand to one of the smaller monitors for identification. The monitors separate revealing the most beautiful of altars, in its Center is a large crucifix. It does not bear Jesus Christ upon it just a simple crown of thorns draped over the top. At the foot of the altar lies, Gold for the King of Kings, Frankincense for the priest of all priests and the gift of myrrh to honor thy sacrifice.

Eve removes her shoes from her feet and kneels at Her private Sacred altar. This altar is to Praise and honor Jesus. But Eve does not speak to the son in the Everlasting, she speaks directly to God!

She clasped her hands together and slowly bows her head. Something she has not done in a very long, long time. Then she prays in a rhetoric like no other.

"Oh great, Powerful and Almighty God. I, who have turned away and refused you for so long, kneel before you now. You, who know all things and that which is truly in my heart know of my undying love for you. But MAN; is a true pestilence to this Utopia you have created. He is most undeserving of it.

Time after time HE denies you, he has explained you away with science and has

Enslaved himself with his stupidity and arrogance. For so long I have conformed to his traits for this I truly apologize. Now, preferably with your blessing I will use this against him a thousandfold. I will send them ALL to the Everlasting and there they will praise you for the rest of their days. I ask

almighty God for your understanding and forgiveness. For
this is something I am compelled to do. I thank you for your
anticipated cooperation.

Oh Great and Mighty Lord God!"

Then she stands with a Sinister grin. The altar disappears
behind the monitors and wall from which it came. She feels
in her heart the Lord will grant her this request. Or at the
very least keep Mary out of her way.

She tells her children to disassociate her from this event. This
includes wiping all video footage. Allowing her to dismiss
the wine incident without explanation.

"Mother we need the video footage, if we are to find out
what happened to the wine." One of her sons States.

"Disregard that for now and do as I wish!"

"I Obey"

Her Sons are well aware that Mother Knows Best and this
works to her Advantage for she can simply dismiss Mary
turning the Wine to Water without explanation to anyone
her children included. They are currently discrediting the
wine incident on social media as a private in-house hoax.

Since talking to God, Eve is beginning to feel better
spiritually and emotionally.

"Well! my sons it appears we will not be having lunch here
today."

She says as she puts both arms around her boys.

"Locate a nice place and I will take you to lunch, you must
be famished"

The men are beside themselves with joy. It is not every day
they are invited to lunch with their mother. Besides her good
moods are few these days and they relish her attention.

Her children do an excellent job of disassociating her from
the luncheon as though she was never there. Hymiriam's
distinct craft is spotted buy the residents of the city and
tourist flying near the Villa before it disappears into the
clouds. Eve's staff is aware of this and assumes it is merely
passing by on unrelated business.

At the United Nations building the U.N.A are wrapping up their case against the Thrones of Chicago. The surviving gang members are being separated and sent to prisons around the world.

President Ophelia has been in the news constantly. She is fast becoming the most loved and popular president of all time. There is talk of extending her presidency beyond two terms. The doctors at the U.N are thoroughly examining the addicts, women and children. Almost all of the addicts are in very bad shape due to years of drug abuse. Many of them are infested with AIDS, syphilis and tuberculosis. Unfortunately, so are some of the women and children. The doctors are discussing containment options. Since this is a U.N.A case it has a certain level of transparency for the public. By order of Mother Teresa.

So, the news media is allowed to cover this very closely. Keeping the world informed of how sick these poor people really are and everything they recently went through at the hands of the gangs.

The media is referring to them as the 'Prisoners of the Thrones'. But for now, they are prisoners of the U.N.A they are separated in to several groups and are being treated as guests.

The world loves the transparency of the U.N.A and it is aiding in the growing popularity of the Arch Nuns. But many still regard them as the United Nation's hit squad. The prisoners

A few days later new instructions are given regarding the prisoners by the Mother Superior Hymiriam. All of the prisoners will be immediately transported to Syria once there they will be taken to the River Jordan. All of these decisions are done before the eyes of the world.

Rumors circulate among them that they are being transported to a private facility for the rest of their lives. They become worried and begin to panic. But two of the women who were in the safe room with fisticuff and the Arch Nuns convince them to remain calm and keep their faith.

"They gonna take us ta a private place and kill us cuz of what we saw" Shouts one addict.

"I hope so I got nothing ta live for anyway." Say another.

When a woman by the name of Jasmine whom was also in the safe room with fisticuff and

It was her child he held and threatened to kill. She listens to the speculations, then raises her hands for everybody to listen to her for a minute.

"Hold on now Y'all. They didn't save us, to take us someplace else, just to kill us. That don't make no motherfu#king sense, do it?"

No one answers.

"Now imma keep it real wit Y'all. I'm sick, I'm really fu#king SICK! alright. But they told me my child only got T.B. Hell They can cure That."

She stops for a moment to wipe tears from her eyes.

"I know I'm dead already, I ain't gonna see my child grow up, and I'm cool wit that. But after what these Arch Nuns did for all of us and what I seen them do. I ain't no religious bit#h, or Nutting like that but I'm glad God sent this different type of Nun ta handle Sh#t."

Another woman from the safe room joins her adding.

"I ain't no religious type bit#h either, but amen sister amen!"

Many of the prisoners join in shouting. "Amen!" For she speaks the truth.

"I wanna say one more thing ta Y'all then I'll shut up." Jasmine says.

"I ain't never thought I would say no Sh#t like this. but I think God he sent the Arch Nuns ta save us!"

Those condemned to die and those who have lived a life of sin agree, welcoming their fate, whatever it may be with open arms.

Mother Teresa and president Ophelia are watching this in the Oval Office. The Reverend mother will assure the news media receives all of this footage.

The international Manhunt for Giovanni Luciano is still underway.

The media has dubbed Him 'Lucky Luciano'.

Mother Teresa is allowing him to stay at large for the time being. So, he may lead the U.N.A to higher-level bosses. Now that he has nothing, she's hoping he may become desperate.

From Johannesburg Africa 'Midnite Endeavor' speaks to her sister 'Leggz Diamond' who is currently in Brazil wrapping up a twenty million-dollar drug deal.

"Yo Midnite, what's up?" She is in a very sexy form-fitting dress that compliments her figure and shows off her legs, of course.

"Find Giovanni Luciano sister of mine and keep him safe, for now!"

"I'll find him, he doesn't know Mr. Jenkins dealt with me on a regular basis. From what I understand this Giovanni motherfu#ker has a problem with female authority figures. If he says something stupid to me, he's going to be missing a lot of teeth and maybe his tongue!"

The two women laugh as they enjoy a bit of small talk.

Two Battle Assault Drones enter Syria, they land at a military base. Four large buses are standing by to transport the sick to Mother Hymiriam who awaits them at the Jordan river. The Syrian military are in full Hazmat uniforms has not to come in contact with them. The Syrian government protested but granted Hymiriam's wish.

The news media has not taken their cameras off these people since they were removed from the building after the short battle.

Their skin is dry and infested with lesions, their hair thin
and falling out many have lost the will to even walk but are
helped by others. The women that were kept as sex slaves,
appear to be healthy. But they are not they too are infested
with AIDS and other terminal diseases. The gangs kept
them looking their best so they may be used for prostitution.
Escorting the sick aboard the buses are four FBI agents and
one A.N.T agent. The FBI wear hazmat suits for their
protection the A.N.T agent is in full air tight battle gear. As
they ride the sick look past the FBI at the A.N.T agent which
is a most menacing sight.
"See, I told you they gonna Fu#king kill us!"
A very thin male addict says to one of the prostitutes.
"Shut the fu#k up!" She sharply responds.
"If you ain't got Nutting good ta say then don't say Sh#t at
all. Wit your skeleton looking ass. After all the Arch Nuns
did for us, Nig#er! you still thinking like that?"
She angrily concludes pointing her finger in his face. Deep
down inside he knows she speaks the truth but he like so
many others have been through too much and has already
given up on life. Too many agree with her but remain silent.
For tensions are high among them. The Syrian Military
remain for backup if needed. The news media use drones to
film the prisoners and the Beautiful Jordan River and
Countryside. Many religious leaders are present as they
always are at this most holy and Renown place. The FBI and
A.N.Ts are ordered to remove their Hazmat suits as a
gesture of Goodwill and faith. Also, to show the world the
prisoners are not contagious.
The Syrian military refuse to remove their suits so they are
ordered by Mother Teresa to vacate the area and return to
their base immediately!
With the Syrian military gone and no one wearing hazmat
suits. The area no longer resembles a Zombie Apocalypse
movie. The prisoners are engaged in their own conversations
and enjoying the scenery.

"You still think they gonna kill us?"
The Prostitute asks the Thin Man whom she spoke to earlier.
"YES!"
He replies sarcastically, Crossing his thin arms and turning away from her.
She laughs and puts her arm around him.
"Then I guess we gonna die together, Ya Fu#king skeleton."
"Will you grant this dying man one final wish?"
"LIKE WHAT?"
She asks giving him a fierce look.
"No, no, no it's Nutting like that!"
He says holding his hands up.
"I couldn't get it up, let alone do da deed. I just wanna know if I could feel that Ass one time before I die?"
She takes him by the hand and pulls him close. Seductively looking into his eyes. She is a fair-skinned black woman, in her early twenties and very attractive. She is wearing government-issued clothing but her figure is still very noticeable.
She has slight lesions on her face but she conceals them with makeup. From her appearance it would be hard to assess that she has AIDS. But to him she is the most attractive woman he has seen in a very long time. He also has not been sober or off drugs in a very long time. If he can physically touch her in this way. He thinks to himself he can die a happy man. As she slowly pulls him closer gazing deeper into his cloudy bloodshot eyes.
She grabs him by the face.
"NOPE! NOT TODAY!" She says gently pushing him away.

"Dam! Girl, Really. It's like that? Can I get your name at least beautiful?"

"Of course, skeleton I'm Danielle but they call me 'Dannie-Daaaam! Or Dee-Dee for short. What's your name?"

"Hold up, why they call you Danny Daaaam?"

"Cuz when nig#er walk by me, they turn around look at my ASS and all they can say is DAAAAM! Now tell me your name?"

The man laughs so hard he almost falls.

"Nah, you gonna laugh."

"No! I'm not, okay fu#k it, I probably am but you wanna real laugh you herd of fisticuff leader of the thrones?"

"Yeah, everybody know him."

She can hardly contain herself as she reveals to him his real name is Bartholomew.

"That's fu#ked up, I'd change my name to something tough to. But for real my name is 'Samson'"

Danielle finds this very funny because the man is not only anorexic thin, but has pale white scaly skin riddled with Legions and almost bald and he can barely stand. Surely, he would have broken his own hands had she allowed him to grab a handful of her ASS! Still she is flattered.

The two smile at each other not noticing a silence overtaking the crowd. The silence is replaced with gasping, whispering and pointing. The two were so caught up in their moment of amusement, they didn't notice the crowd parting.

Now they can see the image of a woman walking toward them. She is wearing a simple robe and sandals. She has a small earpiece with a microphone so she may be heard through the speakers of the Apache helicopters broadcasting from above.

"Oh my God! It's, it's Hymiriam!"

A woman screams then many begin chanting her name and applauding.

The news media's drones maneuver to get the best vantage points zooming in on her face. She wears no habit, her hair blowing naturally in the soft Wind.

She and her disciples walk among them. She slightly extends her arms so they may touch her and know that she is not afraid of Contracting their diseases. She breathes the air they breathe and allows those who are the sickest to touch and hold her hands as she walks by to let them know, God has not forsaken them. They are LOVED!

As the media broadcasts this to the world. They are amazed at the reception she is receiving from people that are in U.N.A. Custody.

The world also shares in this growing admiration for her. As the Applause grows louder. many are being baptized by their religions in the river, they too join in the Applause.

She stops in the center of the sick. They stand close but do not want to crowd her, forming a Circle around her.

They continue to applaud and chant her name. She slowly turns so all may see her face. This is not for the media or the world. it is for the sick to look upon her and take comfort in knowing the love of the Lord. Many are atheist and do not believe but they respect her and are grateful for all that she has done for them.

"Thank you, thank you so much" She says over the Applause.

Many of the sick respond. "No! Hymiriam, WE THANK YOU!"

She puts both hands over her heart, smiles and bows her head in gratitude. The crowd settles down almost becoming completely quiet, those in the river continue their business. Not wanting to get involved as long as they keep their distance.

"For those of you whom do not know who I am, allow me to make your acquaintance. I am the Mother Superior of the Arch Nuns, I am Hymiriam."

The sick applaud with all their strength. They applaud and cheer until they are almost out of breath.

"Damn! my heart is beating fast!"
One of the sick says to another.
"I feel like I'm about ta Fu#king die!"
"Me too, but I don't care, I'll die applauding for her."
The two men can barely stand but they assist each other for
they refuse to fall. Hymiriam knows they are exhausted and
weak many of them are on the verge of collapsing from all
the excitement. She knows she must be brief.
"I know all of you have been through so much"
She says motioning for them to settle down.
"Are we gonna be taking ta a new place ta live, Hymiriam?"
Shouts a woman.
"The doctors say a lot of us are too far gone and can't be
cured."
Shouts another.
"let me ask you this?" Hymiriam interrupts. "How many of
you believe in God?"
A few raise their hands but most remain still.
"What God, Jehovah, Buddha, Allah?"
Some Shout.
"There are many names, but there is only one true God!"
She assures them.
"yeah da one God that addicted me ta drugs!"
A man yells from the crowd.
"The one God that had me turning tricks on da streets for a
living!"
Screams a prostitute from the crowd.
Many of the sick agree with them.
"These were choices of yours, not the Lord's"
Hymiriam tells them.
"You have seen people born in poverty, yet rise above it. You
have seen people go down dark roads and turn around. You
have seen people make life-changing decisions. But you
have chosen to do nothing. When the going got tough you
simply gave up. You let life beat you down and you chose to
stay down! Then you dared to blame the Lord for your

misfortune. But I am here today to give you the love of the Lord!"

The sick are silent they look to each other in confusion.

"You brought us here ta preach ta us?"

A woman asks but not wanting to seem disrespectful.

"No, my child." Hymiriam respond laughing. "I apologize, I am after all raised by my Mother Teresa, We are Nuns and we are passionate about the Lord."

Everyone enjoys a light laugh for a moment before the Mother Superior continues.

"However, I would like you all to pray with me."

Before she can continue a man shouts.

"I don't believe in God but I'll do it for you, Hymiriam."

They are so appreciative for what the Arch Nuns did for them that everyone reluctantly agrees.

"Thank you all, I just have one more little thing to ask of you, and it would mean so much to me."

One of the prostitutes cutting her off, throws both her hands in the air and yells.

"Hymiriam I don't care how many things you ask me ta do, I will do them all!"

Everyone laughs and applauds in agreeance. They are becoming more comfortable with her.

"You want us ta stand out here all day okay I'll do it"

Yells one of the addicts.

"You want us ta stop doing drugs we'll do it"

Then I weak male voice is heard from the back of the crowd.

"I don't know about that last one, um I'll have ta think on that I really, REALLY like DRUGS!"

Everyone the news media included burst into laughter, the Mother Superior as well.

"Well maybe the Lord can be your drug from now on!"

Hymiriam says hopefully.

The laughter dies down and the Mother Superior continues with her request.

"I would like all of you to join me in the Jordan River so I may baptize you."

This takes everyone by surprise.

"But I'm not a Christian!" A prostitute screams.

"I can't swim!" Another adds.

"I was baptized as a kid, and look at me now! can't we just go to McDonald's?"

Shouts one more. Again, they laugh but they gave Hymiriam their word so that cooperate.

"You don't have to be a Christian, I represent GOD! and God is in ALL religions!"

She tells them. As they walk down to the river. Those being baptized by their religions become concerned. Her disciples remain with the A.N.T agents.

"Is she seriously going to bring THEM! into this River as sick as they are?"

One of the ministers says to his congregation. They and many others discreetly leave the river as Hymiriam and the sick enter the water. To her surprise many choose to stay. For they too are sick, some with cancer, some with tumors, some are blind, some crippled by advance stages of diseases and many are terminal.

They are of various ages and religions. They also believe no worse can happen to them.   But if so, it be the will of God. Nor did they wish to be rude or disrespectful to those who have been through so much. So, they remained in the water and welcomed all who entered. Danny holds on to Samson whom is worried of falling. Hymiriam encourages everyone to keep walking until the water is at waist level. The news crews' interview some of those who have left the water. They express their contempt for this intrusion and what appears to be Hymiriam's blatant disregard for the health of the people that were already here.

"She should have taken them someplace else."

One of the ministers says during an interview.
"This is an Outrage!" Adds another.
But they do recognize and respect her as a holy woman. So,
they try to be mindful of what they say. "This is pretty
boring, definitely didn't need this much news coverage for a
baptism."
A news reporter says to his crew.
Hymiriam takes the hands of the two nearest her and asks
for everyone in her group to join hands. They slowly comply
until everyone has joined hands.
All the news cameras focus on her and the sick.
She bows her head, then begins to pray aloud.
"Oh Heavenly Spirit thy Lord God! Those who stand before
you on this day are in despair. They are victims of humanity
at its worst. I speak to you for them. For this very moment I
shall be their voice. Many of them are non-believers, Oh
Lord and have dismissed your existence like so many before
them. I do not feel this is the mind, body and soul of those
whom hands I hold. For theirs is a faith that can be
rekindled. They claim to indulge me but in their heart of
hearts they truly stand before you asking for your love and
forgiveness. They come to you, Oh God! to repent and turn
from their sins."
Samson looks to her and says.
"I don't believe we gonna be forgiven"
Then hangs his head in shame.
"Oh he of little faith, be still and behold the salvation of the
Lord."
She replies looking up at the sky.
"I now baptize all of you in the name of the MOST HIGH for
the Forgiveness of your sins. Behold this gift from the Holy
Spirit."
She guides everyone to completely submerge themselves in
the water exactly seven times for a brief moment. Without
hesitation they do so. Her words were so powerful that the
other religions and everyone within the sound of her voice

considered this to be their baptism as well and quickly submerged themselves seven times.

As everyone lifts their heads from the water, after the seventh dip they stand with the water at their waist. They look at each other and cannot believe what their eyes behold. Miraculously their bodies have regained muscle mass, Those who were losing their sight or were completely blind can now see, the lesions that covered their skin were gone, their hair has fully regrown, those who were weak have regained their strength, tumors and cancer were no more, those with AIDS were now free of it. They submerged themselves as the dying and emerged as the LIVING!

And all those who submerged themselves at Hymiriam's request where cured of all ailments. The Spectators and news crews could not believe their eyes. Those who left the water in disgust and contempt for the sick quickly run back submerging themselves repeatedly in hopes of receiving this blessing, but they are too late.

"Surely this must be some kind of trick."

" How could she have done this?"

" They must have been treated at the UN building and bought here for some type of show."

These are the opinions many have expressed.

But they are quickly discredited. For not everyone in the river was at the UN building. The tourist, Spectators and Ministries that remained in the water were cured as well. This could not be dismissed as trickery or a hoax. It is recognized before the eyes of the world, for that which it TRURLY is, A MIRACLE!

Danny turns to Samson who now stands before her as the man he was prior to his extreme drug addiction. She can no longer refer to him as skeleton. For he who stands before her now has the physique of a true man. As his body mass returned, he can no longer fit the shirt he was wearing so he removes it. Danny looks upon his finely chiseled body with lust in her eyes.

"Dammmm!" Is the only word she can utter. There was so much commotion going on with everyone in the water hugging, rejoicing, talking, crying and showing great appreciation and love for Hymiriam.

They are grateful and most importantly they are now firm Believers in the Power of God!

The Press is recording and broadcasting every moment of this, most joyous event to the entire world. Nothing like this has been seen since the days of Jesus Christ.

Most of the alleged Miracles done by Hymiriam in the world from January until now where on a smaller scale and have not received the attention this one is about to receive.

"Thank you for your forgiveness oh merciful Lord. THANK YOU, THANK YOU, THANK YOU!" The people Shout repeatedly.

And for the first time in their careers, some of the news reporters lose their professionalism as they too fall to their knees in prayer. HALLELUJAH! ALL PRAISE BE TO GOD! Hymiriam Walks from the water with everyone following her, they are immediately given large towels to dry themselves.

People all over the world who have witnessed this on television are being humbled before the Power of God. Atheists the world over are at a loss for words at what they have just seen. Those who dismiss faith as science are silent as well. Standing at the edge of the River Bank Hymiriam exchanges hugs with many. The A.N.Ts are a little uncomfortable with this. For they have seen many leaders killed in this fashion by those they trusted and loved. They close their battle visors and begin communicating with each other formulating a defense strategy. A few of them consider Mother Teresa and Hymiriam their parents as well and if anything should happen to either one of them, they may become most uncontrollable!

In time through Mother Teresa's teaching they will learn to control this rage, Hopefully! But for now, it is a work in progress. Samson and Daniel work their way through the crowd attempting to get to Hymiriam. Who is surrounded by people wanting to touch her robe.

The internet is so overcrowded; it once again comes to a halt. The world has witnessed a great miracle on this day and from this day forth they will refer to her as 'HYMIRIAM CHRIST'!

She believes this to be the Lord Paving the way for her to be widely received and appreciated by the world. The people chant the new name they have given her. Only Mother Teresa and her children know this designation was given to her by God. Still many believe referring to her as 'Christ' is Blasphemous, these are the people Eve will influence the most.

President Ophelia Watchers the broadcast from the White House and unfortunately, she shares their sentiment. But the majority have spoken.

"I have the highest respect for that woman, but I will not refer to her as Christ."

President Ophelia says to her aides. She feels Hymiriam may have breached terms of the contract by curing those people. She and president Andrei have concerns as to whether or not she used cures they own the patents to. So, she calls an emergency meeting with president Andrei and Mother Teresa. She wants Hymiriam in transit to the white house immediately!

She is not angry; she is concerned and requires reassurance. President Andrei feels the same.

At the Jordan River the rejoicing continues. Samson and Daniel have finally gotten close enough to Hymiriam to speak to her. Like everyone before them they are so excited, they forget to introduce themselves.

As they attempt to kneel, she stops them informing them that she is merely a humble servant of the Lord and request they stand with her, not kneel before her. She puts an arm around each of them and pulls them closer for a hug. Daniel feels what she considers to be the Holy Spirit take hold of her as her body momentarily goes limp. Hymiriam attempts to hold her up but cannot. Samson takes hold of both women and guides them slowly to their knees.

The A.N.Ts notice this and immediately rush to Hymiriam fearing the worst.

"Be still my great protectors and know that all is as it should be."

Hymiriam Whispers softly over the comlink.

The A.N.Ts are trained men of science but even they cannot deny what they have just seen. Everyone begins to notice Hymiriam kneeling with Samson and Daniel. The A.N.Ts gently move the crowd back. This provides an opportunity for the Press to take some very beautiful still photographs and videos while playing the song 'Live you say/ I Believe. By Lauren Daigle.

Around the world believers put a hand to their television screens wishing they were there.

Daniel's strength returns as she looks into Hymiriam's eyes thanking her and swearing to live her life for God and to raise her children to do the same.

Samson whom was an extreme atheist since he was a small boy, takes Hymiriam's hand and looking deep into her eyes telling her.

"I ain't never believed in god until ta day and I swear ta you I will NEVER use drugs again."

He says squeezing his eyes shut and holding her hand to his forehead struggling to continue speaking.

"I got two kids out there somewhere, I pushed them out of my life when I lost my battle ta drugs. But I promise you I'm gonna find them and do right by them and spread God's word along da way."

He concludes dropping his head and weeping.

Hymiriam is silent listening to his heart felt words. She puts her hand under his chin raising his head and says to him.

"I believe you, my child. I believe you."

Samson helps the women to their feet. Hymiriam gives them a final hug before they walk away.

As they walk Daniel holds Samson's hand.

"I didn't wanna say this in front of Hymiriam cause I ain't wanna put you on da spot or make you feel pressured or anything."

She says grinning at him no longer afraid to show her perfect new white teeth.

"But if you'll have me I would very much like ta join you and be by your side as you look for your children. But I'll understand if you don't, I was kinda mean and dissing you before."

He takes her by the hand and pulls her close.

"I'm glad you ain't say this in front of her, cause I don't want you ta think I'm puttin
up a front wit my answer."

Still holding her hand he puts his arm around her and they continue to walk slowly.

"Imma keep it real wit you girl. I dropped outta school in the 7th grade and I don't got much of an education. I got hooked on drugs at a early age and you know the rest from there. I'm scared of what's out there. But with you by my side. I promise you; I will be strong and true til the day I die!" And with that said he pulls her close and the two embrace.

The traffic around the Jordan River is becoming hectic and congested as far back to the city of Jericho. There are many minor traffic accidents as people break traffic laws attempting to get to the river. "Hymiriam Christ" The people chant repeatedly.

President Ophelia asks Hymiriam to return to the UN building in New York immediately with all of the people once referred to as the sick/ prisoners. The news reporters respectfully ask if Hymiriam will grace them with a parting statement, she agrees.

The A.N.Ts begin guiding everyone on board the buses then all cameras focus on Hymiriam.

One reporter is chosen to ask a universal question.

"Hymiriam, this is impossible please, please tell us what happened here today?"

She stands before the cameras, her robe still a little wet, wrapped in a large towel she closes her eyes and very calmly says.

"The Lord spoke on this day and made it so, for nothing said by God can be or will be impossible. Behold their salvation"

She slowly opens her eyes and with an almost seductive look asks as the cameras focus on her face. "How is your faith, now?"

The people applaud, cheer and continue to chant the name 'Hymiriam Christ!'

The news reporter puts down his microphone and joins them.

Her aircraft 'God Speed' Slowly descends behind her, touching down for a brief moment lowering a ramp so she and her disciples may enter. The people are mesmerized by the sight of this.

The craft slowly Rises a hundred feet, then accelerates straight up into the sky.

Mother Teresa tells the news networks to keep some cameras on Hymiriam's aircraft until it is gone. So, the people in the surrounding cities will be assured she is no longer at the Jordan River and cease their Reckless attempts to get there.

Once the craft is gone, she has them focus on the river and the people entering the water hoping to be cured, but their efforts are in vain. Mother Teresa wants the world to see the water at the River Jordan is normal!

The people in their rejoicing sing praise to God as they dance jump and Shout! The FBI keep a sharp eye on the crowd as the A.N.Ts escort and secure Hymiriam's newly 'CURED' and the accompanying news crews back to the buses. Strangers who remained in the river and were cured attempt to join them. They assumed they were to accompany everyone back to the UN building.

But Mother Teresa informs the A.N.T to simply tell them to enjoy the rest of their lives. So, they remain behind and are interviewed by the Press. Those once referred to as the prisoners were given security bracelets, so all may be accounted for.

In the past few days, they have been given many titles. They were the 'SICK', they were the 'PRISONERS' now they will be referred to as the 'CURED'!

In the city of Beijing Eve watches the event at the Jordan River with several of her children, who are some of the most powerful and influential people in Asia. With the current president of Japan Kaito Tanaka anxiously awaiting the arrival of the Arch Nuns.

Eve is forced to make some unexpected decisions. She summons one of
her many sons, she has named 'Kane' to be by her side during these most uncertain times.

Her children are using every resource at their disposal to discredit Hymiriam as a charlatan and her alleged Miracles as Elaborate hoaxes.

Eve would never physically harm or allow any physical harm to befall Mary. There are countless people the world over whom would gladly kill her and love to see her dead! If any one person or organization in the world not under her influence, ever did Hymiriam harm and eve knew who they were she would have them and everything they love Wiped from the face of the Earth. For she loves the mother of Jesus as she did Jesus himself.

This of course like so many things about Eve is unknown to Hymiriam. She is under the assumption Eve Dislikes her. As for her new children, The Arch Nuns when Eve is done with them, The U.N.A will be dissolved! and she who is the deliverer, she who is Hymiriam Christ will walk alone!

The A.N.T watch over the Cured as they laugh, sing, cry, rejoice and give praise
to God.! Those among them whom were atheist join in the revelry, they finally Believe, Embrace and Acknowledge there TRURLY is a God! For they are atheist NO MORE!
One of the cured, a middle-aged Asian man turns to a young Hispanic male sitting near him who is crying.
"I know, I know brother I feel like crying happy tears myself."
The Asian man says to him patting him on the shoulder.
The man, wiping his face replies.
"It ain't that man, it's jes that I don't think I'm strong enough ta not go back ta drugs. My mom got me hooked when I was ten. then pimped me out ta turn tricks in the streets.
this is all I know man! I got little schooling. I appreciate what Hymiriam did for me and all, I feel great! But for me it ain't gonna last. I was born a failure, getting a second chance I'm sure I'm gonna fail again!"
He holds his head in shame continuing to cry. Almost all the cured feel this way. But they don't want that to dampen their Spirit or ruin their mood for this most joyous day. The man feeling for his newly found cured friend. Makes him a sincere promise. Gently putting his hand on his back and holding his hand. He says to him.
"Fifteen years ago I was a college professor. I had a beautiful wife, but we were unable to have children. I was unfaithful to her with a lot of my students, hell I was unfaithful to her with any woman. I was weak, so weak that I begin to hate myself then I turned to drugs and it cost me everything! and ruined my life as you can see. I know what it's like to be weak my friend and I know what it's like to fail. But I promise you, I'm going to stay by your side, educate you and make sure you succeed, I will not let you fail. The power of God cured us today. I look forward to reacquainting myself with the Lord! What's your name?"

"Orlando, my name Orlando but day call me skidz on the streets"

"Why did they call you skidz, my friend?"

"Cause I always had skid marks in my underwear"

The older Asian man cannot help laughing.

"Well, ORLANDO I'm pleased to meet you, I'm Frank"

There are many friendships forged among the cured by today's event.

This too is the work of the Lord. They will now return to the U.N building in New York for a thorough examination and the media is invited to stay by their side.

But Mother Teresa prevents them from turning this into the world's best reality television show.

She does however want the media's cameras on the cured at all times until further notice.

In Brazil Giovanni Luciano is escorted down a hallway buy four heavily-armed gentlemen. They take him to a large rooftop luxury swimming pool area.

It is a beautiful day and the sun is shining brightly.

Behind the bar mixing a drink is a middle-aged dark-skinned Brazilian man Carlos Moreno whom Mr. Luciano is affiliated with. He is one of Brazil's most notorious high-level crime bosses. He and Samuel Jenkins have done a little business in the past.

"Well, well, well if it isn't the man. The U.N.A is calling 'Lucky Luciano'! Come in my friend, come in."

Mr. Luciano whom is appalled by being referred to as lucky. A nickname he knows was given to him by Mother Teresa herself.

He asks Carlos for a shot of whiskey and responds with a little hostility in his voice.

"There's nothing lucky about me I'm alluding them because the U.N.A and every other law enforcement agency are Fu#king stupid, OK!"

Mr. Giovanni turns to the four men telling them to leave,

they do not. He notices a woman lounging in a beach style chair wearing a very revealing bathing suit and dark sun glasses.

"And take this piece of a$s with you." He says pointing to her. She doesn't look at him or jump at his command she ignores him and looks away.

"Does this bit#h understand English Carlos?" He yelled walking over and kicking her chair.

"Come on bit#h get the fu#k outta here, move that pretty ass!"

He says again kicking the chair one last time then turning away and walking back to the bar for another shot of whiskey.

Carlos finishes mixing the drink, puts it on a silver tray and walks around the bar past Mr. Giovanni who gives him a puzzled look. He walks over to the woman and kneels handing her the drink then stands at her side while she takes a sip.

Mr. Giovanni walks toward them and sarcastically asks.

"Is this your wife? over here, or is this some kinda sick S&M thing. If so, you can play 'fifty Fu#king Shades of Grey' later! Right now, we got problems capiche?"

The woman holds out her hand for Carlos to assist her standing. She is texting on her cell phone as Carlos helps her putting on a robe.

Mr. Giovanni looks her at her face asking.

"What the fu#k, you got something to say to--?"

She holds up her index finger, cutting him off signaling for him to wait a moment, she sends a final text before placing her phone on the silver tray Carlos is still holding and removing her sunglasses.

Mr. Giovanni doesn't think too highly of women other then something to sleep with and he barely remembers their faces.

Samuel Jenkins was well aware of how disrespectful Giovanni can be to women.

So Mr. Jenkins made sure he dealt directly with the woman who stands in front of Mr. Giovanni now. The woman they know to be 'Ka'ren Margo' also known as 'Leggz Diamond' Whom just sent a text to her sister 'Midnight Endeavor' that reads.

'Giovanni Luciano will be delivered as planned minus his TONGUE!' Message SENT'.

Carlos introduces her. "This is Leggz Diamond"

"Oooh yeah! this is the Arms Dealer Sammy dealt with. I thought Leggz Diamond was an Italian guy who could dance well, go figure! So, you're sleeping with the Arms Dealer and think I'm supposed to do whatever the fu#k this bit#h says?" And with a thick classic Italian mafia accent he concludes with the traditional.

"GET OUTTA HERE!"

She just stands for moment looking at him. Mr. Giovanni looks back at Carlos shrugging his shoulders.

"No man calls me a bit#h without receiving a severe beating, Unless I allow him to in a jest and that is after dinner or during sex. Which I have not received from you, not that I want these things from you. I doubt you'll be able to do either when I'm done beating the Sh#t out of you!"

She says softly removing her robe handing it to Carlos.

To be a middle-aged businessman Mr. Giovanni has kept his body in Peak physical condition.

He knows this woman has some sort of combat training but if she thinks he won't knock her unconscious and toss her pretty ass in the pool, she has another thing coming.

"Oh! You don't say, and what do you think I'm gonna be doing while you're TRYING ta beat the Sh#t out of me?" He says with a sarcastic smirk.

Ka'ren looks at Carlos then back to Giovanni and politely tells him.

"I'll start easy at first to demonstrate my physical superiority over you, you will attempt to fight back and I will find this entertaining, then I'll progressively hit you harder and harder until you fall to your knees before me. As all MEN eventually do."

Mr. Giovanni stands shaking his head with his hands on his hips.

"How long is this speech of yours gonna be BIT#H! cause I'd like ta put you ta sleep and throw you in the pool now!"

There is an awkward silence for a moment before Mr. Giovanni attempts to speak again.

"Ya know what? Carlos, I don't have the time for this sh#t get this BIT----"

With blinding speed she strikes him in the throat with her right hand, the chest with her left hand then stomach with her right hand again. He stumbles a few feet back before falling but immediately gets up, choking and struggling to breathe, he clinches his chest tightly. But he'll have no time to catch his breath for she is now walking quickly toward him, seductively licking her lips like an animal about to feast. Still out of breath but filled with rage he lunges toward her. She takes one quick step toward him, punching him in the center of his body, stopping him in his tracks. Again, he stumbles backwards falling to the floor this time unable to get up so quickly.

He lies on the floor rolling back and forth clutching his chest tightly. He feels as though he were hit by a moving truck. Combat training is one thing. But where did she get that strength he wonders. She doesn't have the muscle mass nor is she a bodybuilder. She simply doesn't look like she can hit this hard. There must have been something in my drink he convinces himself.

Rather than accept the fact a beautiful woman is beating the crap out of him.

He catches his breath and she allows him to stand.

Still in pain and a little slumped over. He cuts his eyes at Carlos.

"Carlos, you son of a bit#h you put something in my drink, Paisano?" He asks Breathing heavily.

"Nah, Amigo this is all you."

She slowly approaches him. Refusing to give up or admit defeat he clenches his fists tightly, anticipating from which side she will attack. As she gets closer to him their eyes lock, then suddenly she lunges forward and quickly punches him in the forehead. His head snaps back and again he hits the floor. He stands immediately but struggles keeping his balance before falling once more. For all the women he forced to have sex with him and smacked around, this is Poetic Justice at its best.

He grabs hold to the back of a chair to help him stand and to use as a crutch.

Ka'ren does a roundhouse kick striking him to the left side of his face, he stumbles sideways landing on a nearby table.

"You definitely drugged me! There is no FU#KING WAY this is happening!"

He yells pushing himself off the table but still holding on to it.

"Did this bit#h put you up to this?"

He asks his good friend Carlos throwing a glass at him.

Ka'ren catches the glass and throws it back hitting Mr. Giovanni in the head.

"That's the last time your calling me a bit#h. Now I'm gonna cut out your Fu#king tongue, kapeesh gumba?"

Her cell phone goes off with a distinctive ring tone.

It's an urgent call she's been expecting from her sister Aston vetta.

"Hey! 'Rocky Balboa' I gotta take this call. Then I'll be right back to take your tongue!"

She turns to answer the phone Carlos looks at him shaking his head from side to side and shrugging his shoulders in disbelief. How could his good friend Giovanni have gotten in so much trouble so quickly. He thinks to himself.

"Hey sis, give me a minute I'm about to cut out Giovanni's tongue."

She says to her sister as she's fixing her hair.

"Hold on Ka'ren, don't do any permanent damage to him Kane wants him in one piece. You may have your fun, but don't cut anything off or out of him"
"I sort of promised him I would cut out his tongue."
Ka'ren says giggling.
"I know, Ka'ren and one day soon you will keep your promise and cut whatever you want from him, but not today! See you soon little sister." (WARNING EXPLICIT CONTENT AHEAD)
Placing her phone on the table, Ka'ren is a little disappointed. She did so have her heart set on cutting his tongue out and placing it in his anus. But that will be for another day.
She begins to walk toward him. He had a little time to rest and catch his breath during her short phone call.
He's bleeding from the head a little where the glass struck him but he feels strong and believes he can defend himself better against her now. He also thinks he should keep his mouth shut. She stands in front of him but he is reluctant to throw any blows this time.
"Carlos, come here for a moment please." She asks.
"This man who stands before us is TRURLY the luckiest man in the world. He is definitely 'Lucky Luciano'"
"How's That"
Carlos asks putting his arm around her.
"He gets to keep his tongue, for now!"
Mr. Giovanni feeling relieved and full of himself again, Smiles and says to her.
"It Ain't luck baby, I got connections, Big connec---"
Before he can finish his sentence she quickly punches him in the nose the blood splatter ruins her bikini.
"MOTHER FU#KER" He screams holding his nose. Carlos checks his clothes and is glad none of the blood got on him. Ka'ren points her finger in Mr. Giovanni's face touching his forehead.
"There's another connection for your collection, did you feel

that? I connected with you!
Now wait here."
She concludes pushing his face away with her finger.
Looking at her ruined bikini shaking her head, she steps
back keeping her eyes on him. Then removes her bikini
dropping it to the floor in front of him. Eve's children are no
strangers to being naked.
She turns and walks to the pool standing at the edge she
looks back once more at Giovanni before diving in and like a
mermaid, she swims the length of the large pool in a matter
of seconds emerging on the far side. She exits the pool very
seductively, the water dripping from her naked voluptuous
body. Slowly she walks running her hands through her hair
pulling it back from her gorgeous face.
Even though this woman just beat him and broke his nose,
he is still strangely aroused by her. He looks at Carlos whom
he knows loves women more than anyone, but he nor the
four-armed guards are paying her any attention.
Do they not see this naked woman strutting around in front
of them? He asks himself. Or is he hallucinating. The bikini
on the floor and his bloody nose assures him he is not.
But still he wonders why they're not looking at her.
Samuel Jenkins and Giovanni Luciano to spite all they have
built and accomplished in the crime world. Are NOT
Children of Eve's.
Carlos Moreno and the four guards are CHILDREN OF EVE!
And they dare not look upon their sister with lustful eyes.
In his opinion they are giving this Arms Dealer Woman way
too much respect. She walks up to him and smacks him hard
to the right side of his face causing him to stumble sideways
and with a laugh tells her. "I love you too sweet heart!"
Carlos helps her with her robe then she tells Giovanni.
"Never and I mean NEVER forget you owe me your tongue.
And I will COLLECT!"
Carlos directs everyone's attention to the television monitors
above the bar which were on mute.

Every station in the world is broadcasting the event at the Jordan River.

They all watch and listen.

"It's all smoke and mirrors."

Mr. Luciano says slowly sitting at the bar to accommodate his sore back.

"She puts on the 'Hocus Pocus' miracle act while her Arch Nuns break every law there is. But everybody's too busy calling her Christ now ta notice."

Ka'ren cuts her eyes at him.

"That's probably the smartest thing you said, in the short time I've known you. But you're a little late everyone already thinks that! Now shut the fu#k up, or I'll make another connection with you."

Carlos and the guards laugh. His sister is having fun belittling him. But this is Giovanni Luciano a man who does not take disrespect lightly. He has no choice but to play their game for now. But he promises himself the first chance he gets he's going to kill Ka'ren with his bare hands, very slowly. As they watch the news coverage of the Jordan River Event, breaking news interrupts.

'This is Joanne cappadonia with Breaking News: Two days ago, we have received video and confirmation of a large private Winery in Paris where the entire stock of wine was allegedly turned to water. Sources say they think Hymiriam may have been on the property, her craft was seen flying nearby.

The entire stock of wine on the property and in the delivery, trucks was allegedly turned into water. No video was obtained as of yet from inside the winery but Hymiriam's craft was videoed by tourist flying nearby shortly after. We will continue to investigate this keeping you updated. I'm Joanne cappadonia Now back to the event at the Jordan River.'

Ka'ren and Carlos stand silent staring at the screen. This must be why their mother summoned Kane and if

Hymiriam met with Mother, why? They pondered. But knew not to inquire. For No one questions Eve.

Flying above the clouds two Battle Assault Drones transporting the cured back to the United States are cruising at 500 miles per hour trailed by Hymiriam's Craft 'God Speed' approximately two-hundred feet behind. There is still much rejoicing on board the crafts and everyone is in a good mood the Pilot's especially. The A.N.T agents piloting the Battle Assault Drones challenge Hymiriam's craft to keep up. "B.A.D-6 to Godspeed come in Godspeed you having a little trouble keeping up?"

Peter and Angelica who seldom display a sense of humor are amused at the challenge, turn to Hymiriam who is reluctant to go faster because they are transporting passengers is communicating with Mother Teresa.

The Reverend mother feels to Hymiriam advising her to allow this. With the media accompanying the sick and recording everything. Mother Teresa feels a little lighthearted fun would do everyone well.

Hymiriam gives Peter and Angelica the playful node to indulge themselves.

The A.N.Ts left the intercoms on so everyone May here the playful conversation, it fits the joyous mood. As the cured take heed to the conversation they begin to settle down for a moment.

"Godspeed to B.A.Ds-3 and 6 if it's a race you're looking for we accept the challenge"

Angelica says calmly.

"Hey everybody, we gonna race." One of the cured yells.

The pilots display a 360-degree view on monitors in the crafts for all to see. There's loud cheering as everyone braces themselves for harsh acceleration.

The news crews cannot believe their luck not only are they traveling on board Battle Assault Drones and Hymiriam's craft, but they are about to experience an up-close-and-personal demonstration from within.

Those who are frightened say nothing they don't want to ruin the fun for everyone else. Besides if Hymiriam said its okay, then by all that is HOLY it is OK and they will fear not, they know it's safe for they are with Hymiriam Christ! The Battle Assault Drone's engines Roar as they accelerate to 1,100 miles per hour breaking the sound barrier. With Hymiriam's craft now trailing far behind. They continue to accelerate.

Everyone is amazed at how smoothly the crafts accelerates with zero turbulence. The Battle Assault Drones continue to accelerate to 1,600 miles per hour still with no turbulence and Hymiriam's craft now trailing very far behind them. Everyone is jumping up and down and cheering for No One in particular to win, they are just having fun. Sisters Amira and Donna are smiling and watching everyone enjoying themselves but must remain cool and calm, on the outside to keep up their image. But on the inside, they are having just as much fun as everyone else, May more!

"B.A.D-6 to Godspeed I thought that thing was supposed to be the fastest aircraft ever built!"

Godspeed accelerates to 3,500 miles per hour, quickly pulling up to the rear of the Battle Assault Drones matching their speed for a moment. Everyone is amazed at how fast Hymiriam's craft REALLY is. It slowly rises above the other two crafts, moves to the lead position, again matching their speed. The Assault Drone Pilots can see the craft as they attempt to pass. Pushing their engines as hard as they'll go. Peter and Angelica toy with them for a few seconds giving them hope, remaining in front of them then slowly start to pull ahead.

"WE NEED MORE SPEED!"

Page, the pilot of B.A.D-3 shouts.

"I'm giving her all she's got Captain, I can't get any more!" Co-pilot Connor replies with a thick Irish accent, imitating Scotty from the TV show 'Star Trek' everyone is cheering those familiar with the television show burst into laughter.

Then Godspeed accelerates to 4,000 miles per hour and is gone from view.

"Whoaaaaaaaaa" Everyone says almost collectively.

"Well, they named that craft appropriately!"

One of the A.N.T pilots says.

Now the media has a first-hand look at how Hymiriam gets around so quickly.

This is part of Mother Teresa's Public Relations strategy.

Thirty minutes later the Battle Assault Drones transporting the cured approach the landing strip at Langley. President Ophelia had them redirected there for the time being. They are met by staff and more news crews. There is still much revelry among them it's very hard to regain their composure after such events.

"This is Philip Trebek with CNN news we're here at Langley Air strip where the cured have just touched down.

The mood here is very festive it's similar to a New Year's Eve celebration."

Another member from the NBC news team who traveled on board Hymiriam's craft stands beside Mr. Trebek and shouts.

"Dear diary today I traveled at twice the speed of sound! Oh Yeah!"

President Winfrey has arranged for them to stay in a private facility temporarily constructed for them at Langley, the news crews are invited to stay as well. Mother Teresa wants the cured visible to the world at all times, for now.

Hymiriam is ordered to the White House for a private meeting with President Ophelia and president Andrei. She is told to leave Godspeed, her pilots and disciples at Langley she'll be helicoptered in.

At the white house president Ophelia and president Andrei anxiously await the arrival of Hymiriam. Mother Teresa is attempting to convince them that what they witnessed was truly a miracle and there has been no breach of contract.

"You both had samples taken of the water. I'm sure both your countries scientist will come to the same conclusion." Mother Teresa explains.

"And what conclusion might that be, Mother Teresa?"

"The water is pure, untampered with and the same as any other River."

President Andrei walks over to Mother Teresa who is Seated on the couch he puts his hand on her shoulder.

"I want very much to believe this, but we'll have the results soon."

President Ophelia sits next to the Reverend mother and explains.

"This may give the world the impression we are holding out on cures for terminal diseases and we can't allow that!"

"Are you open to suggestion?" Mother Teresa asks calmly.

"Of course we're open to suggestion. We wouldn't be having this meeting if we weren't."

Mother Teresa thinks for a moment then tells them.

"Be transparent with your investigation and allow the world to accept it as a miracle."

"My dear Mother Teresa miracles do not exist in this day and age."

President Andrei says taking a seat next to Mother Teresa on the couch. The Reverend mother gives him a look as though he were one of her grandchildren.

"Presidents might I suggest we simply allow this to play out. This generation has a short attention span and things, tend to end quickly. In a few weeks they'll be more concerned with celebrities and things of that nature"

The presidents know she is right. The Reverend mother

convinces them that all will be well once they have the results from the water at the Jordan River. Now convinced there has been no breach of contract the presidents are a little more at ease.

"Well, we'll give it a few more weeks Mother Teresa, I sincerely hope this blows over!"

"I'm sure it will."

The Reverend mother feels to Hymiriam informing her of the two presidents moods. Which are now, thanks to her a lot better and to listen and act accordingly.

"let's arrange for the media to start playing it down. Thank you for your time Mother Teresa, that will be all."

President Andrei agrees.

She dismisses the Reverend mother; president Andrei accompanies her president Winfrey then calls for a staff meeting before Hymiriam arrives.

"Madam President we cannot dismiss the fact that those that were born blind can now see."

One of her advisors tells her.

"Nor were they part of the original group transported there. The facts are too great Madam president people infected with AIDS knocking at death's door left the river as though they, well to be blunt as though they just left the gym!"

The president knows she has to control the story. So, she and Andrei inform their Adds to create the assumption that an experimental chemical might have been secretly used to which they will neither confirm or deny. The government controls conspiracy theory websites for just such occasions. For it is stated in the contract no world leader can discredit Hymiriam's acts EVER!

If they are considered acts of God by the people. So, shall it be!

The helicopter transporting Hymiriam lands on the White House lawn. The personnel exit the chopper first, then Hymiriam followed by the pilots. Immediately after confirmation of Hymiriam's presents.

The Press and paparazzi descend upon the White House causing a large media circus outside the gates. Military Apache helicopters are called in to circle the premises. To deter any hostile intentions. But that is the furthest thing from anyone's mind the people simply want a glimpse at HER!

President Ophelia wanted the media to know Hymiriam was called to the White House. So, the people may know, she is still in charge. She had no idea it would get this hectic so quickly.

"That's the last time I have her publicly flown in."

Ophelia says to Andrei as the two look out the window at the growing crowd of spectators.

"I agree my friend, I must prepare Russia for this."

As President Ophelia watches Hymiriam being escorted by the military, she tells her staff to stop for a moment and let Hymiriam wave to the crowd for a few minutes. She doesn't want the world to get the impression she is forcing her to come here.

The white house P.R staff rush into the oval office very excited. They suggest this presents the perfect opportunity for she and Andrei to take photos on the steps of the White House with Hymiriam.

President Ophelia thinks this is a wonderful idea. She can tell Hymiriam this is the reason she called for her and send her back to Langley to be with the cured.

The presidents join Hymiriam on the steps of the White House they are accompanied by private photographers. Hymiriam stands in between the presidents as their pictures are being taken.

"They'll take pictures of us all day, if we let them. Perhaps we should go to your office for the meeting?"

"Oh your MOTHER took care of that for you"

President Ophelia responds before realizing she spoke to Hymiriam as if she were a child.

"Oh, I apologize Mary, I didn't mean to insinuate your

mother fights your battles. It's just--"
Hymiriam puts her hand on Ophelia's shoulder and the two laugh.
"Alright let's get you inside girl, you are causing too much commotion and I'm starting to get a little jealous"
President Ophelia says Jestingly then guides everyone inside. As they enter the oval office Hymiriam like her mother attempts to convince Ophelia to believe in miracles.
"I do"
Ophelia says.
"I just prefer my Miracles a little more subtle or discrete Mary."
Hymiriam sits on a couch in front of the president's desk, with Andrei beside her.
"I can't tell you how much I wish these were simpler times Madam president."
"As do I, Mary as do I. But tell me, how do you feel about so many people referring to you as Christ?"
Hymiriam finds it hard to hide her enthusiasm, so she does not.
"Well Madam president, it does State clearly in the contract I may choose to be what the people deem me to be. I am pleased they chose this instead of something else."
The three of them laugh out loud.
"Well that's wonderful Mary the world leaders can take comfort knowing Christ works for them." They continue laughing as Hymiriam responds.
" You mean they may take comfort knowing Christ is in their lives."
"Amen to that, sister Amen to that!" Ophelia adds.
Andrei is laughing noticeably louder than the women so president Ophelia says to him.
"keep laughing mister remember when she gets to Russia, they'll be calling her Christ there as well." They continued laughing and enjoying the moment.
"Mary do me a favor? please." Ophelia asks.

"Of course what is it Madam president."

"Please, please, please don't walk on water until you get to Russia!"

Andrei begins to choke.

"Don't worry Andrei, my son Jesus already walked on water"

Hymiriam seriously tells him as she repeatedly pats him on the back as he's coughing.

"Well enough of this fun."

President Ophelia interrupts.

"I'll let you handle the whole Christ thing, with the media Mary, For now return to Langley and be with the cured a few days, then return to your duties. I'll see you accordingly. Always a pleasure and thank you for your time."

Hymiriam turns to Andrei and asks him if he is all right.

"Yes, yes I'm fine my dear"

She hugs them both and heads straight to the cafeteria to say hello to everyone. The business of the cafeteria is greatly interrupted as Hymiriam enters. Everyone wants to touch her and be near her.

President Ophelia is forced to put her foot down and demand she return to Langley immediately!

Hymiriam understands and complies.

A team of scientists and presidential aids along with the Secretary of Defense enter the oval office, they have to test results from the Jordan River.

"Madam president the water tested negative. There are no impurities."

One of the scientists tells the presidents.

"What about other parts of the river?" President Andrei asks.

"The same sir." The Russian scientist confirm the same results.

"Thank you everyone that will be all"

Presidential Ophelia says asking the Secretary of Defense to stay.

"Madam president are we really going to allow the world to

call her Christ?"

"That's not up to us Mister secretary the world may refer to her as they like. If these are elaborate tricks she'll slip up soon enough and everyone assisting her will be exposed."

"I really hope she doesn't walk on water in Russia."
President Andrei says wiping his forehead with a handkerchief.

"Speaking of water, let's announce the results of the water to the world and get it over with"
President Ophelia says laughing at Andrei.

At the Divine Garden it is Sunday and like every Sunday all the Arch Nuns gather for their weekly meeting and Sunday Dinner. Hymiriam has not yet arrived so Mother Teresa conducts the meeting. The Arch Nuns are as impressed with their mother as is the world. But the Reverend mother tells them not to be complacent; For the memory and love of humanity are brief.

"Ok my children. President Ophelia would like us to tone down our Hammer of God philosophy for a short while. It seems we are disrupting years of undercover work which could cause catastrophic events. So, they say, we'll give them a little time before the next wave."

"So wait, we can't offer the Goliath challenge anymore?"
Navaeh asks.

"She not going to take away our guns is she grandma?"
Elizabeth adds with great concern.

"I can still kick people in the face though right grandma?"
Dee says leaning forward in her chair.

"Can Buffie still get punched in the face grandma?"
Zach shouts.

"I can still punch you in your face, ZACH!"
Buffie replies quickly standing up jesting with her brother.

"Wait! Or like Keeva said I can grab you by the hair and treat you like a lassie!"

Everyone bursts into laughter, even Mother Teresa cracks a

smile. The Nuns are enjoying each other's company as they always do and of course Mother Teresa will never admit it, but it is music to her ears.

"Alright everyone" She yells. "Every GOSH-DERN Sunday! I can't believe you're thirty years old. Now settle down"

The nuns exchange a few more insults before settling down than the Reverend mother continues.

"Going forward you will still offer the challenge, but the stakes will not be as high for now.

We'll be using the same formula as your fight against the soldiers whom are now your teammates. It will be a 'knockout' or 'tap out' situation and you will show your superiority on every fight which should last no more than ninety seconds or so.

You may offer this when people refuse searches of property or to acquire information. Upon losing if they refuse to honor the terms, they will be taken into custody with a 90% chance of being sarumed. That will assure their compliance. Now that the world leaders have seen how effective the Goliath Challenge is, they just want to be kept in the loop a little more and that's fair, for now. I can still change it as I see fit, if I suspect foul play. But don't worry my darlings we are dealing with world leaders and unfortunately there will always be FOUL PLAY!"

"So what about the seizure of property grandma?" Anna asks.

"Immediate property only my darlings. You are to seize the property that would have been searched.

The car they are driving, the boat they are on, the private plane they are in

or their house. We won't be taking all that they are, for now.

When you offer the challenge, they will sign legal documentation pertaining to these temporary new rules and be recorded doing so."

"Will the Press be involved grandma?" Donna asks.

"No! this will be quick, private and on the spot. But if they

are in the area, they can cover it
Again if they lose and refuse to comply. Seize their property
and take them into custody it's as simple as that."
"What about Spectators grandma?" Lin asks.
"Only those that accompany them and those lucky enough to
be in the vicinity at the time. I'm sure they'll be recording it
with their cell phones and immediately uploading the
video."
"That makes sense they'll be a lot less internet traffic and it
won't shut down as much."
Maria says as she stands. "But may I make a suggestion
grandmother?"
"Of course Maria"
"Rather than show our superiority, ending the fight quickly.
Perhaps we should allow ourselves to be struck periodically.
Before ending the fight victoriously. We will endure the pain
for the moment and where the bruises. It will give the fighter
hope and a chance to remorse, if they are to do so. If they
perceive this as a sign of weakness and attempt to kill us.
Then let them know the difference between an Arch Nun
fighting for a simple end, and an Arch Nun fighting for their
life or the freedom of the people.
Jesus endured far worse and I believe we can endure a little
physical pain to honor thy sacrifice! This is the least we can
do!"
Mother Teresa is so very proud of her granddaughter at this
very moment for speaking with such wisdom. Her siblings
all stand in agreeance applauding her.
"You are all well aware, I say this often. But with thy Lord
God as my witness I am so very proud of you all. SO,
SHALL THIS BE WRITTEN"
And collectively the Arch Nuns loudly respond.
"SO SHALL IT BE DONE!"
Like every Sunday the Nuns conduct their meeting in full
uniform and habits. They conclude the meeting with the
usual prayer for those who have fallen before them. Then

they transform into casual attire to greet their mother, business is now over.

It is now time to make Merry, enjoy a fine Sunday meal and be one as a family. For this is a day the Lord has made.

A stretch limo rides along a private Road in Brazil heading toward the marina. Inside the limo are six-armed female and male guards along with Giovanni Luciano. These guards are to deliver him to Kane.

Mr. Luciano who is always seen in a fine tailor-made suit is wearing a multi-colored shirt, shorts and flip flops. This is the only clothing Ka'ren deliberately gave him to wear. She cannot physically harm him but she intends to humiliate him. She also ordered the guards to tease him the entire way. This is shaping up to be the worst experience in Mr. Luciano's life and when the time comes, he's going to make Ka'ren pays for every minute of it. In his mind her death will be slow and agonizing.

They arrived at the marina where Ka'ren is waiting. Mr. Luciano looks out the window at her with contempt and doesn't take his eyes off her. She is wearing a blue bikini, with a long blue sheer skirt and matching hat. You can clearly see every curve of her voluptuous body through the sheer material. Her high heels compliment her gorgeous legs. If it weren't for his hatred for her, he could have easily fallen in love with her. All of Eve's children held high in her favor are stunning as they are arrogant and absolutely breathtaking to behold.

As they exit the limo Mr. Luciano quickly walking toward Ka'ren, he's angry. But the closer he gets the slower he walks. He begins to point his finger in her face but quickly realizes she would gladly break it. So, he puts his hands in his pockets.

"Enjoy the ride, lucky?"

She asks sarcastically, looking him up and down with disgust. Rather than tell her what's REALLY on his mind he simply responds.

"Loved it, really enjoyed the company."

Mr. Luciano being the boss of bosses in Chicago, has owned his share of yachts. Finds himself impressed by Ka'ren's extremely large luxury yacht complete with helicopter landing deck on its roof. Her yacht is named the 'SEA LEGGZ'.

The dictionary describes the term 'Sea Legs' as the ability to adjust one's balance to motion of a ship, especially in rough seas. So, her yacht is appropriately named.

Onboard are many friends and associates of Ka'ren's. Some are aware of her CIA status. Others know her as one of the most dangerous arms dealers in the world!

Her parties are always a who's who of the crime world! and Everyone on board always signs a non-disclosure agreement. Cell phones are absolutely prohibited. These are the rules when anyone enters her private domain and no one would dare break them. As they enter the yacht Mr. Luciano is applauded for eluding the U.N.A. He is a bit of a celebrity to them currently being at the top of Mother Teresa's most wanted list so Leggz doesn't mind being seen with him for now. she uses everything to her advantage.

Unknowing to Leggz a few of her prestigious guests are deep undercover MI6 and Interpol agents. Whom must now find a way to get this information to Mother Teresa, something they will find difficult to do even with their 'James Bond' like gadgets.

By providing her with this intel she would be grateful and owe them a favor No Doubt?

Back in the United States at the Port of Miami Sister Lin
and her team are investigating the most heinous of Acts. The
air holes poorly cut in to a container trafficking women and
small children was blocked and everyone inside died from
suffocation.
Due to the many adolescents found dead the local police
alerted the FBI. This drew the attention of the U.N.A who
joined the FBI in the investigation.
It is also being covered by CNN and world news.
The bodies had been festering in the container for weeks. As
Port workers moved surrounding containers, they realized
the holes were not deliberately blocked. The surrounding
containers reduced the amount of air to the container with
the women and children inside.
The FBI no longer consider the U.N.A or Arch Nuns to be an
intrusion on their investigations, but an Alliance welcomed
with open arms.
"The containers point of origin is Thailand. Interpol may
have Intel on what gangs are involved in this, Sister Lin. I'm
sorry you had to see this."
Special agent Levites explains shaking the hands of her
team.
"Indeed special agent, but unfortunately it is the way of the
world."
She covers her mouth with a handkerchief and enters the
container followed by some of her team. Of course, their
body cams are active and transmitting directly to Mother
Teresa,
whom immediately assigns Brother Zachariah and Agent
Betty to the case and charges them with the task of bringing
her all information pertaining to the Thailand gangs
involved to her within the hour. They partner with Sister
Donna and her team they are the closest A.N.T to Thailand
and set a course immediately to the city of Bangkok. High
above the city residents point to a white streak across the
sky. B.A.D-3 quickly descends Upon the City engaging the

Halo braking system and sounding the Horn of Gabriel for they are on official business of the U.N.A.

Every crime syndicate and street gang in the city are aware of the dead women and children found in the container in Miami and the involvement of the U.N.A due to all the news coverage.

B.A.D-3 hovers above the city high enough for everyone to see. Mother Teresa is speaking with the government of Thailand, who are reluctant to grant A.N.T-3 access to the country or city.

"This Uninvited intrusion is considered an insult. Our country and law enforcement agencies will handle this matter. You will leave our country immediately or you will be met with deadly force."

The president of Thailand tells her as they lock missiles and launch several aircraft.

he is both embarrassed and angry that his country is possibly being blamed for this crime. But as angry as he may be, he most certainly did not intend to threaten The U.N.A and must now find a way to deescalate this situation without making himself seem weak.

Upon hearing this response Mother Teresa orders B.A.D-3 into Extreme Defense Mode.

Instantly the four attack drones detach from the main unit, they hover close as they detach one hundred smaller attack units that surround the crafts like a swarm of bees.

The citizens of the city watch and record presuming it is a friendly display unaware of the true nature of the situation. Then with a Stern voice the Reverend mother demands his compliance.

"By order of the United Nations. you will stand down. We are investigating a single crime not invading your country. Our contract with you, States these terms clearly. You have sixty seconds to comply!"

Mother Teresa did not intend for a showdown before the world. But sometimes the arrogance of man must be put in its place. The Taiwanese government realize they acted in haste. The A.N.T are protected by the contract signed by the president of Thailand.

He is too proud to apologize to the Reverend mother so he simply orders his troops to stand down and allow them entrance. B.A.D-3 does the same then enters the city.

Yu-Chen a deep undercover officer in the Taiwanese police. Risks his life contacting Mother Teresa to inform her of a location where women and children are held for trafficking. He is fifth in command of the largest street gang in Bangkok, the 'Thai-Tings' their specialty is human trafficking of women and children. The container in Miami was shipped by them.

This is not the first time they have been investigated for the death of children. They sell children into the sex trade as young as seven years old. He isolates himself in a restroom where he and several gang members are having lunch and makes an emergency call to a private number set up by the U.N.A reserved for undercover police officers worldwide. He speaks to his superiors demanding to be connected directly to the U.N.A. his superiors procrastinate knowing time is of the essence. He is connected to a U.N.A representative in New York.

He quickly identifies himself; his identity and status is confirmed then he is immediately connected with U.N.A Betty. He gives her the location of the gang's primary holding facility.

Yu-Chen has been Undercover for the past three years and has done some things he is not too proud of to climb up the ranks up the 'Thai-Tings'.

After witnessing the power of Hymiriam. He wants to do all he can to help make things right. He has been giving Intel to his government for years but they seem to do nothing. He knows if the gang discovered his true identity his life would be over. He considers this a small price to pay to assist Hymiriam in making the world a better place. He is not

fluent in English but he hears the words of Hymiriam
resonating in his head 'FOR GOD'S GREAT PURPOSE!'
He flushes the toilet, washes his hands and exits the
restroom.
He is shot 22 times by his fellow gang members who were
waiting outside.
Yu-Chen's superiors wasted no time exposing his identity.
As he suspected for a long time they are on the gang's
payroll. They deliberately refrained from shooting him in
the head, they wanted him to lie there and die slowly. They
say your entire life flashes before you when you die. Yu-
Chen proudly goes into the Embrace of the Lord with one
image on his mind.
An image that inspired him to make his decision. It is the
image of Hymiriam standing in the Jordan River curing the
sick.
   Betty passes the information on to B.A.D-3. They set course
for the holding facility. Which is a large abandoned
warehouse. With plenty of room for B.A.D-3 to land.
The gang often leave the facility with just a few Young male
gang members to guard the women and children. These are
often new inexperienced members who are unaware of what
they are guarding or what to do in case of an emergency.
They are more thieves and vandals then they are killers.
There are only four of them. Two seventeen-year-olds, one
sixteen-year-old and one fourteen-year-old and of course
they are on their cell phones playing video games. When
'Paithoon' the sixteen-year-old, receives a call from one of
the gang leaders ordering them to kill the women and
children NOW! And set fire to the building. He tells the
teenager they are in the basement in a large locked room. He
tells them there's a red lever above the door pull it and it will
fill the room with poison gas. He ends the call and slowly
turns to the others.
"WHAT THE FU#K? There's women and children here and
they want us to Kill Them All?"

He says to the group.

"I thought we were guarding guns and drugs."

Anurak the fourteen-year-old replies.

The boys know what would happen to them if they didn't carry out the boss's instructions. They also know that carrying out these instructions would get them respect and they can quickly move up the ranks and make a lot of money. (WARNING EXPLICIT CONTENT AHEAD)

"I'm doing it, and buying me a Mercedes with the money they pay me."

One of the seventeen-year old boys says.

"Fu#k Yeah! I'm getting an Oculus VR system and two bit#ches to su*k my di#k."

Paithoon adds starting to smile urging the others to join him as he heads down stairs to the basement.

With pistols drawn the boys run and jump down the flights of stairs, eager to get to the basement.

Once there they approach the door. Paithoon sees the small red lever above the door, he reaches to pull it.

When suddenly and without hesitation Anurak Shoots him three times then exchanges gunfire with the other two teenagers at near point-blank range. Paithoon was hit in the buttocks, upper thigh and Center torso.

Anurak and the other two teenagers lie dead on the floor. Paithoon trembling with pain still tries to stand so he can pull the lever.

He still wants to carry out their boss's instructions but loses consciousness.

Anurak's spirit stands over what was once his body.

He looks down and remembers his older brother who was killed in front of him by a rival gang.

The last thing he said to Anurak was "When the time comes little brother do the right thing, it will make a very big difference and I will be so proud of you, be better than me."

That is exactly what Anurak did. His mother named him Anurak, after the Male Angel in Thai mythology. Because of his noble sacrifice this fourteen-year-old boy is responsible for saving 62 Women and children.

And with this a calmness comes over his spirit, he smiles, feels the warm embrace of the Lord and is welcomed into the Everlasting.

Five minutes later the A.N.T storm and secure the building. Local law enforcement joins them at the scene with the news media not far behind.

"The building's clear and secure boss."

Sister Donna's second-in-command Sophia tells her over the comlink. She enters the building with Bangkok's military police and Joins her team members who are waiting for her in the basement. They inform her of a survivor, it is Paithoon he is still unconscious.

Mother Teresa and Betty watch from the UN building in New York. She orders them to stabilize the boy and bring him there.

The door to the room where the women and children are is steel-reinforced concrete and sound proof.

They bang hard on the door to let everyone know inside that help is here.

This room was used as a bomb shelter for the employees when the factory was open for business. The A.N.T disarm the gas system, disconnect the gang's security cameras and begin cutting through the door. Upon entering the room, they are surprised at how maintained everything is. it appears to be a large live in cafeteria with several bathrooms.

Cots were supplied for sleeping these women and children were well kept but cut off from the outside world. They had no cell phones; television was DVD only.

The gang hadn't addicted them to drugs yet. Also, they were from mixed nationalities but predominantly Taiwanese.

They are frightened and unaware of how close they came to
death, if not for the sacrifice of a fourteen-year old boy. They
are told to form a single-file line so they may be searched
upon leaving the room by the A.N.T. As they leave the
building they are greeted with cheers from the police and
news media. Mother Teresa wants B.A.D-3 to process them
and turn them over to the Taiwanese government. This will
take approximately three hours. In the meantime, Sister
Donna takes one of the A.N.T vehicles and two of her team
to follow up on the locations of the 'Thai-Tings' bosses. The
police officers on the scene are very nervous because they
can be connected to the Gang's prostitution businesses many
of Bangkok's City officials are involved as well. They get
word to the Thai-Ting bosses ordering them to disappear for
a while. But the Thai-Tings are not known for their smart
decisions. Like the very small holes in the container that
killed everyone in Miami, or the four young teenager boys
left to guard such an important part of their trafficking
business.

The Thai-Tings may not have known who the 'Thrones of
Chicago' where but every gang in the world Knows what an
Arch Nun and the U.N.A did to them.

On her way to a well-known Thai-Ting hang out a
restaurant called 'Chewz'
Sister Donna is joined by several Bangkok police vehicles.
Inside the gang leaders discuss their options and there is
heavy gang security inside and out.
'A-wut' whose name means weapon is very angry.
He is the big boss over the others in the gang and must
answer to higher bosses and their political partners for this
catastrophe.
(speaking Taiwanese).
"Who put those stupid motherfu#kers in charge of watching
the facility?"
He shouts at the other two bosses.
'Noom' a twenty-two year-old Leader of the gang in charge
of drug operations
and Chai, A twenty-four year old in charge of prostitution.
"Yo-yo is not happy she went to Miami to close the deal and
that idiot man Giovanni lost his entire operation. And now
no one knows where the fu#k he is!"
A-wut continues, pointing his finger frantically at the others.
"He didn't have a back-up plan in place yo-yos been in
Miami for a while!"
Noom asks while texting to other gang members.
"He had several back up plans in place."
A-wut assures him.
"But when you lose everything like he did. We'll let's just say
that's not going to happen to us!
Chai, you've been awfully quiet, you have nothing to say?"
Chai is a man of few words, quick to anger and can be very
unpredictable. But he knows the bosses are going to blame
him for this. Especially for leaving four teenagers in charge
of the building. He knows something must be done and he
intends to do it, something that will make the bosses take
notice and make the Thai-Tings the most feared gang in
Bangkok instead of a laughingstock for the city.
The A.N.T and police vehicles pull into the parking lot of the

restaurant. The police officers were attempting to lead the A.N.T on a wild goose chase away from the bosses. But Betty had already received information from undercover agents as to their exact location. The moment the vehicles were seen the gang members alerted their bosses.

"How did they know we were here, what are we paying the police for" A-wut shouts in Rage.

"Keep calm" Noom tells him. "They don't know who you are, move away from us and go sit at the bar." He continues.

The Bangkok police enter the restaurant first followed by the A.N.T then Sister Donna with two more police officers behind her. Looking at the A.N.T and Sister Donna Noom is now petrified. Chai notices this and pats him on the back and with a big grin says to him.

"Watch and learn, my friend watch and learn."

He stands, flips his shirt collar up, moves the hair from his face, looks down at Noom who is still seated. He folds his arms and stands in wait.

Sister Donna recognizes him and Noom from the pictures Betty sent her. She and her teammates approach the table. A-wut unfolds his arms holding two pistols. He fires several shots at Sister Donna. Time slows down as the bullets approach her face. She turns 180 degrees her habit fluidly following her motion. The bullets strike her in the back of her head, but do not penetrate the armor of her habit. Time resumes and Chaos ensues inside the restaurant as the patrons attempt to flee. The A.N.T are quick on the draw but unable to return fire. There are too many innocent people in the way. Sister Donna is now facing the two officers whom were standing behind her. They too quickly draw their weapons. But instead of firing at the gang, they began firing at Sister Donna. The first few bullets destroy her body cam. But not before it captured them shooting her. Again, she slows time, she allows for the officers to remain in her time frame so they may realize what they have done and behold the wrath of God for doing so.

Since they were recorded shooting her, she would be well within her right defending herself and killing them. But this is not the way of the Lord or the Arch Nun. They witness the bullets striking the bare skin of her face but do not penetrate.
"What in Buddha's name"
One of the officers' yells.
As Sister Donna pulls out their eyes so they may see no more. Before they can scream she strikes them in the throat damaging their vocal cords so they may speak no more. Then she extends her hand and with telekinesis gently Guides them to the ground and knocking them unconscious. She resumes time and as she turns to join the fight.
She locks eyes with Noom who has witnessed what she did, but to him it was at lightning speed. He has been in many gun fights with rival gangs, but this one was different.
This is a gun fight against highly trained tactical military soldiers, and an Arch Nun. The A.N.T are killing his gang members with ease. They are no match for A.N.T Firepower nor can they penetrate their body armor.
The only thing he and Chai can do now is run!
Sister Donna tells one of her agents to secure the police officers and the crowd. The other to go after Chai she will pursue Noom.
"You want me ta hold yer bag, Boss?" Connor yells to her.
"No! I got it"
She answers running through the restaurant after Noom who has gotten a little bit of a head start on the Arch Nun, but she is in hot Pursuit. Noom is an expert parkour champion. He has been doing it since the age of twelve. He bolts through the rear door of the restaurant and down the alley. He begins to climb up a fire escape. If he can make it to the roof, he can run along the rooftops he knows so well executing his advanced parkour maneuvers.
He makes it to the roof with Sister Donna not far behind. He ducks, jumps and maneuvers over rooftops and obstacles with ease. He stops for a moment to catch his breath,

laughing to himself he turns around to see if the Arch Nun has given up.

To his amazement she is still in Pursuit and executing some of the most graceful Parkour maneuvers he has ever seen. "WHAT THE FU#K" He says to himself; how can this Fat woman keep up with him? He has seen her fight videos on YouTube. But parkour is a totally different sport. He turns and runs picking up as much speed as he can preparing for a big jump. Surely this Fat woman would abort her Chase once he makes it to the other side. As he gets to the ledge he jumps, lands and rolls. Stopping once more to see if she'll jump cause she's far too heavy and will plunge to her death, then he has a realization. He stands waving his arms frantically for her to stop. He does not want to be charged with her death.

"STOP! PLEASE STOP" He yells at the top of his lungs hoping she will hear. Sister Donna jumps the ledge and does a perfect flying eagle pose as she Glides through the air.

"I CAN SEE MY HOUSE FROM HERE!" She yells with her uniform, bag and habit flowing in the Wind.

Noom can't believe his eyes, not only did she jump, but she's doing it with better form than him. She absorbs the landing performing a front roll, then a dive roll followed by a front two hand flip springing to her feet and slowly walking toward him straightening her habit and adjusting her bag. If he thought he was amazed by her jumping form, he was even more so by her Landing. He now understands why they call her 'The Deceptionist'

"Will you continue to run, little boy?" She asks as she gets closer. Noom backs up slowly he's still breathing heavily but she is barely out of breath. He realizes he can't outrun her this isn't his first time running from the law. So, he decides to lure her down into the city streets where he can maneuver through people and throw obstacles in her path. He looks around for a door, spotting one on the other side of a large air conditioner. He smiles at Donna and runs around the air conditioner. She does not pursue instead she reaches into her bag and pulls out the small plastic 3-prong boomerang. She throws it, it curves around the air conditioner striking Noom in the side of his face while he is running this startles and distracts him throwing him off balance just enough to stumble forward and run headfirst into the heavy rooftop door. With a loud thump he falls backward to the ground with a large knot growing on his forehead he is too dizzy to stand. Sister Donna slowly walks around the air conditioner. From the corner of his eye he sees her approaching. She stops, leans over and puts her hands on her knees as though she were addressing a child and says. "Oh! Did em fall down?"

Noom to spite what he does for a living is a member of the 5% of Christianity followers in Thailand and has a sense of humor. He looks up at Donna, Smiles, shakes his head and gives her the thumbs up sign. He then struggles to his feet turns and pulls the door open. Still stumbling with Sister Donna a few feet behind him. He struggles with the door so sister Donna holds it open for him. She opens her bag and the boomerang returns to it. As she continues to assist Noom grabbing on to the handrail of the staircase, he attempts to maintain his balance, slowly negotiating his way down the staircase with Sister Donna walking right behind him. He makes it down the flight of first stairs but as he turns to go down the next he stumbles and falls landing on his back looking up the staircase at Sister Donna.

Laughing and pointing at her he says.

"Ha, I'm getting away and you can't catch me."

This is amusing to her so she smiles just a little as he rolls over and falls down the next flight of stairs. He knows she didn't lay a hand on him but he still yells.

"Stop pushing me!"

Rolling over onto his back he can no longer see the Arch Nun. She knows her body cam is inoperative. So, she decides to show him something spectacular!

"Hey! My friend where'd you go?" He yells to her. For a brief moment he believes he did get away or that she allowed him to. But then to his amazement she passes through the solid floor and floats down and lands in front of him. He like so many who behold the Power of 'God' find it hard to believe. Sister Donna looks down at him, extends her hand and tells him.

"Take but one step toward the lord and the Lord will take ten steps toward you!"

"What are you?" He asks.

"I AM OF HYMIRIAM! AND WE ARE OF GOD!"

He hangs his head in shame for all that he has done and reaches up to take her hand. She effortlessly pulls him to his feet. He notices the absolute strength and power of her body. Still dizzy and his balance unsteady. He takes comfort in her presence and decides to confide in her.

"My cousin Chai sent that container to Miami." He tells her.

"The original order was for young girls eighteen and over, Sister."

"Who was to receive the order, Noom?"

"Miami was just the drop point. one of our Representative was going to meet someone there then take the girls to Chicago, that was the final destination."

"Whom did you deal with in Chicago?"

"A guy named fisticuff. But he said at the last minute his boss put someone else in charge and the new guy wanted to add the Young kids so they can be raised in the game, you know, to be turned out on the street at an early age."

"Did he say who this new guy in charge was?"

"Yes! A guy called something 'Get Down' those black guys have funny Street names."

"Why have you decided to tell me this?"

"Well I had no intention of telling you anything. But when I saw you fly through the air and land like you did. I'm starting to think all this talk about you guys being angels and Sent from Heaven is true."

Sister Donna smiles and replies.

"We're Not Angels, I can assure you. But we are sent unto you by God."

Noom knows he has been caught by an Arch Nun.

Under the new law he is now in U.N.A custody, he has no rights at ALL!

He won't be bailed out and the U.N.A cannot be negotiated with or threatened by his bosses. All he can do now is cooperate and repent!

"Chai and me were raised in the streets by the Gang. This is all we know. I seen a lot of my friends die or get killed in the street and nobody gave a fu#k. I know I should be loyal to the gang, but I never been as tough as Chai. Because you caught me, Sister they'll never let me back in I know they gonna kill me now. If I'm gonna die! I want it to mean something. But know this! I don't owe you, The U.N.A or that Fu#ked up Mother Teresa Sh#t! But I do think I owe God and that is a debt I intend to pay!"

Sister Donna puts her hand on his shoulder, and quietly thinks to herself. 'Did he just say my grandmother was F-ed up? If I weren't a Nun, I'd thrown him down these stairs.

She and her siblings maybe Arch Nuns, but they are still human, and they have very REAL human thoughts and opinions REGULARLY!

This is allowed by the Lord and their parents find it amusing.

She puts her arm around his waist and helps him down the stairs.

A.N.T agent Page is in pursuit of Chai he is approximately ten feet behind him. He feels he should not have to bring this piece of sh#t in alive who shot at his Arch Nun.

He stops, drops to one knee and takes aim at Chai. His green laser targets the back of his head.

Tightly holding the handle and gently squeezing the trigger he has a revelation.

He is finally part of something good. He no longer has to

tarnish his soul carrying out dark orders from his
government. He thinks of all the innocent lives he has taken
because of government disagreements. He remembers his
interview with Mother Teresa when she selected him from
so many others, His conversations with Hymiriam who
assured him of God's love and is now performing what the
world is describing as miracles.

He fires two shots deliberately missing him but striking a
wall very close to him to stop the bullets. "On the ground
NOW" He commands, in Taiwanese.

"Or I WILL separate your head from your Fu#king body."
Chai knows his bullets cannot penetrate the A.N.T agent's
armor he also cannot surrender. The gang will not only
abandon him but, they will send many to kill him. At least if
he dies in battle with the A.N.T the gang will have no choice
but to honor his death and give him the street respect he
deserves. What better way to die then at the hands of such a
great warrior, a military super soldier and a Stone-Cold
heartless killer, just like him!

He puts his headphones on playing Taiwanese rap music,
turns and stares at the agent Page intensely. A door opens in
the alley it's a waiter coming out to empty the garbage. He
sees the two men pointing guns at each other but is too
frightened to move. Chai motions for the waiter to come
over to him. "Don't do it, kid!" Agent Page shouts.

Chai continues to motion for the waiter to come over
pointing his gun at him. Agent Page fires hitting Chai's hand
holding the gun clean off. Chai screams, grabs his wrist and
falls to his knees.

Agent page walks over and smacks the headphones off his
head. (WARNING EXPLICIT CONTENT AHEAD)

"I know I promised you head, but I decided to give you a
hand job instead"

Agent Page says sarcastically.

Paramedics are called to tend to him. He will not be going to the hospital. He'll be kept stable, transported to the B.A.D landing site and taken to the United States.

Sister Donna and Noom exit the building. A large crowd of Spectators begins to form. Noom who is well known in the city is embarrassed. Not so much for being caught, but for the large lump on his forehead. The Arch Nun is holding him by the arm and he dare not pull away or attempt to run again. With everyone watching she puts him in handcuffs. As soon as he is secured he begins to pull away a little and act tough for the crowd.
Sister Donna Yanks him close to her and Whispers in his ear. "You better stop acting like a tough gangster, or I'll take out my ruler and spank your Butt in front of everyone."
He gives her a dirty look again performing for the crowd. He has cooperated and given important information to her. So, she gives him a little grin and a wink then allows him to continue with his show. As not to lose face with the gang and with her consent a show is what he puts on
Yelling obscenities and trying to pull away from her. The police are now on the scene offering to transport the Prisoner. But Sister Donna refuses and with good reason the local police cannot be trusted for the time being. They attempt to insist but Sister Donna dictates U.N.A policy demanding their names and badge numbers and they immediately Stand Down. She calls for a U.N.A vehicle for transportation directly to the B.A.D landing site.
Back at the restaurant Chai is being stabilized for transportation to the B.A.D. Standard operating procedure and U.N.A policy is to stabilize and sedate wounded prisoners. But Sister Donna is not there nor is her second-in-command. Just agent Page and agent Conner.

They decide not to sedate but to keep him conscious while
he is being treated so he can feel EVERYTHING!
Agent Page walks over to the stretcher leans over looking
into Chai's face. Repeatedly asking the paramedics.
"Can I offer a 'HAND'?
Do you guys need a 'HAND'? Can I 'HAND' you some more
bandages?"
Agent Conner adds.
"I got to 'HAND' it to you, kid. This is some pretty 'HANDY'
work huh?"
This goes on the entire time he is being treated they tease
and torment him. But in comparison to what they could
have done Chai is very, very FORTUNATE!
Mother Teresa has made it clear to the Taiwan government.
Chai and Noom have committed crimes against children
resulting in multiple fatalities and made an attempt on an
Arch Nun's life.
They are in U.N.A custody and will be Quickly and Publicly
Convicted under the new laws. The police officers whom
attempted to murder an Arch Nun will be turned over to the
U.N.A
Immediately! President Ophelia and Andrei stand behind
her. The Taiwan government has no choice but to comply.
Sister Donna sends Mother Teresa the information Noom
has provided along with all of the information in his cell
phone. In his photos there is a picture of a Young very pretty
Thai Girl with a heart emoji beside it with the caption: 'I
WANNA GO UP&DOWN ON- U!'
Agent Valentina's team has identified her as 'Boonsri' whose
name means 'beautiful' but is nicknamed 'yo-yo' for her
violent mood swings and bipolar Behavior.
She is A-wut's niece and the Thai-Tings representative sent
to Miami to conclude the business of the women and
children in the container. But has lost contact with Giovanni
Luciano. Only to find out that everyone in the container is
dead. Her bosses knew the Thrones had been purged but

Mr. Luciano always has backup plans and with him eluding law enforcement they assumed their business deal was still intact.

They would not have sent her to Miami if they thought anything was wrong. They tell her everything that has happened in Thailand and to return immediately. To their knowledge the U.N.A have no idea what she looks like or her real name. If the Thrones of Chicago had not been purged by the Arch Nuns. The Thai-Tings would surely be at war with them over this $500,000 trafficking deal! This was one of many illegal business deals Mr. Luciano was working on at the time he lost everything.

Back at Langley there is still much joy and celebration. The cured are still being examined and interviewed. Hymiriam followed the president's instructions to stay with them for a little while. This is something she had every intention of doing anyway.

In a short interview with CNN and Fox news. She was asked the question how does she feel about the world referring to her as Christ? She took into consideration the world leader's position on religion nor did she wish to upset any religions. But she did want to sustain the hope of the people and continue to spread the gospel. So. her response was enlightening.

"I am honored to be associated with such a divine title and if it helps bring people together, helps people to love each other and brings hope to this new generation of children. This is the will of God! And I embraced the title bestowed upon me by God! So, shall this be written on this day so shall this be done!"

This is a worldwide broadcast and all over the world people are falling to their knees, weeping and praising the Lord. Everyone there looks around at each other in wonder. Did she just accept herself as CHRIST? They whisper. loud chattering can be heard amongst the crowd.

Her acceptance of this title was most unexpected. Hymiriam

asks for everyone to settle down so she may continue.

"I am here for God's Great purpose and it is God's plan for Humanity to prosper. I am not sent here by the Lord to answer your questions. Nor am I here to perform tricks at your command. The power of God is Not for your entertainment. I only ask that you trust in the Lord and know that you are loved. From this day forth I shall answer your questions no more! The Lord said unto you 'I am' that 'I am'!'"

She says with conviction in closing.

"Hallowed be thy name"

She assumes the prayer position and closes her eyes.

The people repeat her closing remark.

"Hallowed be thy name!"

And praise her with Applause and cheers.

Those around the world watching on their televisions do the same.

Kathy Pritchard a reporter for CNN has one of her cameras focus on her for her closing commentary. "I probably won't have a job in the morning after saying this. But I guess that's the holy equivalent to the 'Mic Drop.' As for this reporter, I believe! This is Kathy Pridgen signing off."

President Ophelia cannot be any happier. Hymiriam exercised her right as an Arch Nun excluding herself from any media questions and will only give statements at her leisure.

The president hopes this will expedite the closing of the peoples 'Christ' Designation of her and she can go back to being Mary.

The president arranged for luxury accommodations for her but she refused. Instead Choosing to stay with the cured. She and her disciples ate and slept amongst them teaching and spreading the gospel of the Lord.

But now it is time for her to resume her mission for 'God's Great Purpose'

She will make no departing speeches, there will be no special

photo opportunities for the media. She will quietly and
humbly be escorted to her craft unnoticed in the night.
Godspeed slowly lifts off. Those outside enjoying the night
sky, watch in Wonder at the beauty of the craft.
"Look! Hymiriam's leaving."
Some Shout alerting the others. All those she has cured run
outside to wave farewell.
Outside the area and throughout Island County Washington.
Many groups large and small have camped out and are
coming together, making friends, praising the power of the
Lord and bonding with one another.
The people knew Hymiriam was at Langley Air Force Base
and we're hoping for a live Glimpse at her. But the president
was concerned and requested she stay on base for the
duration of her stay. There has been too much commotion in
Washington since the recent Jordan River Event.
General William Coleman and the Secretary of Defense are
called to the Oval Office for a private meeting with president
Ophelia. She is seated at her desk with her chair turned,
looking out the window. They enter the office and make
themselves comfortable.
"Is it done General?" She asks.
"Yes, Madam president. It wasn't easy, but my team installed
several tracking devices. You should be able to track her
craft now."
Several such devices were installed since the crafts
completion. But none have ever worked. The Secretary of
Defense explains that the new devices have been installed
within the computer system and are state-of-the-art GPS
tracking. Unlike their predecessors they should be
impossible to detect.
He opens a briefcase inside are three seven-inch tablets.
"These tablets can track her craft anywhere in the world,
Madam president."
"What about when it's outside the atmosphere Mister
secretary"

General Coleman interrupts.

"like the Battle Assault Drones, Godspeed can only stay above the atmosphere for three to five minutes at a time. According to spec."

President Ophelia slams the tablet on her desk in anger.

"This is why we're here gentlemen. The craft is no longer to spec, she's modified it into something else!"

"With all due respect Madam president." General Coleman interrupts.

"That's exactly my point and what I've been saying all along. We should not have signed off on giving her a single unarmed custom craft of her own under a special law declaring it her home!

What in the blue perfect hell, were we thinking?"

"I'm afraid you're right General." The President says taking a seat at her desk. "We should not have, but I can tell you what we were thinking, gentleman. With the countless diseases she has given us the cures to not to mention pioneering the anti-gravity engine technology and turning its patents over to us. We were thinking hundreds of trillions that's trillions with a 'T'."

She takes a deep breath and exhales. "It was our greed gentlemen but fortunately for us she is not a threat and most likely never will be."

Shaking his head disagreeing the general mumbles.

"She's more of a nuisance and I don't believe this Christ crap for a second!"

"Nevertheless gentlemen we can track her now, and I thank you for your excellent work. That will be all."

Mother Teresa has always been aware of the president's attempts to plant tracking devices on her daughters craft and takes great pleasure in foiling their efforts.

A.N.T-3 is wrapping things up in Thailand. They are awaiting the Thai governments release of the police officers. Sister Lin is following up on a possible lead to Giovanni Luciano. So, Mother Teresa asks Sister Elizabeth to assist in

Miami. A.N.T-4 is in California; they are putting the fear of God into one of the largest human trafficking organizations in the city. CNN's current coverage of the Thailand incident makes Sister Elizabeth's California job way too easy. Some of the largest human trafficking organizations in California are closing up shop or moving further underground to avoid the U.N.A.

Mother Teresa is pleased, for the world is beginning to notice and take heed that the presence of an Arch Nun is not only the presence of the new laws but the presence of God's law!

Yo-yo and several gang members carry on with their daily activities of shopping and site seeing as though they were tourist, still under the assumption law enforcement doesn't know why they're here or who they are. It's a Saturday afternoon and they are attending a motorcycle race at the Homestead-Miami Speedway.

Yo-yo loves motorcycles and is a notorious Street racer and Street stunter on the streets of Bangkok, where she participates in many illegal road races.

B.A.D-4 approaches Miami International Airport and sets down. People are still amazed by these crafts and cannot help but to take pictures and video of them whenever they get the opportunity. They do the same when they see an Arch Nun but with a lot more discretion and caution!

Sister Elizabeth and her team have all the information they need to apprehend Yo-yo and her accompanying gang members. Three A.N.T vehicles exit the craft heading to the Homestead- Speedway. Yo-yo stands out in the crowd because she is wearing yellow, pink and blue hair with K-pop style clothing. She is also surrounded by young Asian males, oddly dressed as well. The race is underway and The Spectators are paying close attention.

A.N.T-4 enter the stadium through a private gate reserved for the racers, bypassing the crowd.

They make their way up the stairs to the Spectator seats.

They are noticed by one of the gang members. He immediately calls yo-yo telling her and the others to get up and try to discreetly leave. But the moment she and the others stood.

A child assuming they were Korean celebrities points and yells.

"look Mommy K-Pop Stars can I go get their autograph?"

One of the male gang members turns to the mother and shouts in broken English.

"REALLY! you Fu#king gotta be kidding me?"

The child's mother is attempting to apologize. But it's too late it has already caused a scene.

Sister Elizabeth and her team make their way toward the commotion. An A.N.T agent motions for the gang to come over to him.

Yo-yo and her gang know they are boxed in by the spectators she nods her head for her gang to comply. As they work their way through the seated spectators. She's speaking softly to them in Taiwanese.

"When we are clear, start a fight and get me out of here! I don't care how you do it, BUT DO IT!"

Sister Elizabeth tells Thomas not to handcuff them yet, wait and bring them to the lobby. As they enter the lobby people start recording on their cell phones. At that moment three more gang members exit the restroom; they lock eyes with yo-yo.

"GO NOW!"

She screams loudly in Taiwanese.

The gang attack the A.N.T even though they are physically inferior. Sister Elizabeth assists her team fighting the Gang, knocking a few unconscious.

Yo-yo runs off accompanied by two of her gang. The Arch Nun and one of her agents pursue them while the others secure the Gang in the lobby.

Weaving in and out of the crowd, running as fast as they possibly can. Yo-yo shouts for the two running with her to

snatch a hat from someone, so she can cover her brightly
colored hair. He snatches I hat off a woman's head and
tosses it to her, they turn a corner, stop running and merge
with the crowd.
Sister Elizabeth turns the corner but can no longer see her
assailants.
(speaking Taiwanese)
"They're gonna have all the exits blocked. We're gonna need
some guns."
Yo-yo tells them.
"We're gonna have ta jump one of these guards, quickly take
the gun and fire in the air before some Good Samaritans
interfere."
Approximately 50 feet in the distance Sister Elizabeth notices
a commotion. Then suddenly shots are fired. The gang were
successful in acquiring a gun.
The panicked crowd scatters in multiple directions. Four
more guards quickly run to assist before they can assess the
situation, they are ambushed by the Gang they assumed
were innocent bystanders. The guards are shot fatally
numerous times and their guns taken. The gang runs
through the thick crowd, firing periodically in the air forcing
everyone to take cover and get out of their way.
Sister Elizabeth runs to the guards with agent beside her.
"Go! Boss I got Em"
The Arch Nun continues her Pursuit following the gunshots
she hears in the distance.
"We have ta split up"
One of the gang members says Breathing heavily.
"Don't you two Fu#king leave me!"
Yo-yo yells to them in a panic. Then she notices the crowd
parting, making way for the Arch Nun who is motioning for
everyone to get out of the way.
"Mother Fu#ker! You go, but shoot her first!"
Yo-yo screams hysterically throwing her hat to the floor. She
shoots the lock off a door, hearing the gunshot the crowd

begins to run. She kicks open the door it leads to a long stairwell. As she frantically runs down the stairs she's constantly looking up, hoping the Arch Nun isn't following her. The two gang members point their guns at Sister Elizabeth.

"EVERYONE GET DOWN, NOW!" She screams loudly. Those still in the area immediately dropped to the ground. As the gang members pull the triggers, Time slows down as the bullets slowly exit the barrels of their guns. The Arch Nun puts her left hand behind her back, extending her right hand in front of her face, telekinetically her gun flies from the bag at her side, spinning through the air Landing perfectly in her hand. She fires four shots two of her bullets collide with the gang members bullets dead center flattening them on impact. The other two rounds, strike each of them in the shoulder of the hand holding the gun, time resumes. One drops his gun and falls to his knees screaming in pain. The other runs through the door following Yo-yo down the stairwell leaving a trail of blood.

Sister Elizabeth takes a brief moment to ask if everyone is all right. Then continues through the door. The gang member has made it to the bottom of the stairs. As he opens the door to exit the stairwell, time slows down. Barely aiming Sister Elizabeth fires one round. God guides the bullet as It ricochets off the walls around the stairwell heading down until it striking the gang member in the back of his upper thigh, time resumes.

The gang member screams falling to the ground dropping his gun, it slides across the floor well out of his reach. He lies in the doorway with his body holding the door open crying out in pain.

Sister Elizabeth jumps down the center of the stairwell Landing perfectly before him. He cannot believe his eyes. How was she able to shoot him or jump from such a high place without sustaining injury!

"Behold the power of God!" She says looking down at him.

"Who the fu#k are you?" He asks in Taiwanese.

"I am Arch Nun Sister Elizabeth; I am a servant of the Lord!" She replies in Taiwanese before rendering him unconscious. She can see Yo-yo still running approximately fifty feet down the corridor.

"I have one down, I'm tagging his position for retrieval." She tells her agents who are running down the stairwell. She tells one to stay with the gang member. The other to join her in the foot pursuit of yo-yo.

Running down the corridor checking for open doors as she goes Yo-yo is becoming desperate. Finally, she comes across an unlocked door. She opens it, enters and slams it behind her. She notices the door has a sliding lock; she quickly slides the latch locking the door. Turning around and leaning on the door she sighs in relief catching her breath.

"Hey! little girl you can't be in here!" A male voice shouts. She's startled for a moment, still breathing heavily she stands up straight. Then suddenly there is a loud thump on the door she nearly jumps out of her skin.

"What's going on over there, you have to leave now!" The man says. Knowing the Arch Nun cannot get through the heavy metal door. Yo-yo begins to walk toward the man. He is a large Stout Caucasian man. The closer she gets to him he notices she is carrying a handgun.

Putting his hands up in a non-aggression manner, he slowly backs up, as she comes closer. She enters the room further, there are four racing motorcycles and two more male mechanics, one Caucasian the other a native of Thailand. She screams profanity at them in Taiwanese pointing the gun at them. With their hands in plain sight they hope to calm her down. Three hard thumps are heard on the door.

"All of you, over there now!" She demands pointing to the wall the men slowly back up until their backs touch the wall.

She begins strategically shooting three of the motorcycles puncturing the tires and damaging the engine. The two Caucasian men lunch at her attempting to stop her. She fires on both of them striking one in the abdomen the other in the chest. She then points the gun at the Taiwanese man.

"Please don't shoot, I'm from Thailand, I'm from Thailand please!"

He begs speaking their native tongue.

"How fortunate for you brother, if you know what's good for you. You better not say anything!"

Hearing the gunshots on the other side of the door Sister Elizabeth tells her agent to go find another way into the room.

Yo-yo mounts the undamaged motorcycle and speeds off. The moment Sister Elizabeth's agent is out of her sight. She uses the Power of God to pass through the solid door. She unlocks it and calls for her team member to return.

She approaches the men who are hurt badly but will live.

"She went that way Sister, she probably already crashed. She can't handle that bike, it's too powerful!"

The Taiwanese man says to her tending to his friends. Sister Elizabeth tells her agent to stabilize the wounded men.

The Arch Nun runs to one of the damaged motorcycles. As she mounts the bike the Taiwanese man shouts.

"Sister she shot up the engine and tires the bike won't work."

She sits on the motorcycle and with the Power of God.

The tires which were shot full of holes self-inflate, the engine repairs itself and starts. The A.N.T agent didn't notice this but the mechanic did. He knows those three motorcycles were severely damaged and inoperative. Yet one worked for The Arch Nun.

"Did you see that?"

The mechanic asks in disbelief tapping the agent on the shoulder rapidly.

"See What, God dam it!"

The agent screams in frustration pushing the mechanic back.

"Stop Bull Shi#ting and help me with these men, if you want them to live!"

The mechanic can't help but to watch and listen as the motorcycle roars down the Corridor leading to the outside with Sister Elizabeth working the gears like a pro.

"She really knows how to ride, Huh?"

The Agent looks at him.

"From what I understand, she was born on a motorcycle!"

Yo-yo was travelling so fast she had already cleared the parking lot, before the police could block it off. Several police motorcycles and cars are in Hot Pursuit. As Sister Elizabeth cleared the pit garage entering the parking lot. Two police vehicles accidentally block her path.

She applies the front brakes executing a stunt known in the motorcycle world as the 'Stoppie'.

The rear wheel of the motorcycle rises off the ground as the front wheel continues to roll, Sister Elizabeth balances the bike on the front wheel as it slows to a stop. The handlebars gently tap the fender of the police car. Balancing for a brief moment. Sister Elizabeth performs what looks like a Break-Dancing Freeze pose, for a quick second before the rear wheel lands on the ground and the bike slowly rolls backwards a few feet.

The police cannot believe the riding skill of the Arch Nun.

"HOLY SH#T! DID YOU SEE THAT!"

One of the officers shouts putting both hands on his head in astonishment.

"Back it up boys, I have to go! And tell everyone do not, I repeat do not shoot her"

She commands waving her arms for them to back their Vehicles up. She revs the motor building up the RPMs to launch the bike as soon as they are clear and with a mighty roar, she releases the throttle and the bike catapults forward. The police officers notified the others of the Arch Nun joining the pursuit on a racing motorcycle and to watch out for her.

News helicopters are tracking the Pursuit. Yo-yo notices the helicopters and slows down so the police motorcycles can catch up to her. She draws her gun and tells them to call off the helicopters and back off or she'll start shooting innocent people. Before the cops can respond she speeds off. The police motorcycles are no match for the speed and power of the racing motorcycle. All they can do is keep her in sight and call off the helicopters. The chase continues through the city streets with Sister Elizabeth not far behind. As she pulls behind the police vehicles, they part-way allowing her to ride between them. The police motorcycles notice her in their rear-view mirrors coming up behind them very fast. They too Part-way so she may pass. She zooms through the police motorcycles riding a wheelie with her right foot on the seat and her left leg trailing behind. She orders the officers to control the traffic so no one gets hurt and for all police officers attempting to join the pursuit to disengage and do the same.

Yo-yo notices the Arch Nun speeding behind her, quickly closing the gap between them. She knows now she must dismiss her fear of the high-powered bike and treat it as if it were her own. She accelerates weaving in and out of traffic at 170 MPH. Disregarding the safety of others and herself. Sister Elizabeth knows this cannot continue. All it would take is for one person to open their car door or swerve into her path and there could be multiple fatalities. She radios ahead for the police to start blocking the intersections guiding her away from traffic and the city. The racing motorcycles tires are composed of a special compound allowing them to stick to the track Like Glue during tight turns.

The police instruct a truck driver to use his eighteen-wheeler to block an intersection. They assist with the blockade leaving only a left turn exposed. Unknowingly Yo-yo rides over a manhole cover in the street. The hot sticky tires propel the two-foot circular sewer cover a few feet in the air, landing on the concrete and sliding behind her very fast. She leans into the left turn like a professional racer barely slowing down.

Sister Elizabeth accelerates to catch the sliding manhole cover before it hurts someone.

She lays the left side of the motorcycle on top of the manhole cover, moving her left leg out of the way, then lays the left side of her body over the motorcycle. Using the Grace of God to slide under the trailer of the eighteen-wheeler, time slows down as she fixes her habit as she slides under bringing the manhole cover to a stop time resumes. She Performs a few 360-degree donuts to bring the bike up off its side. The police and spectators applauded and cheer her on. She pops a wheelie riding off going down one block and taking the next left turn

continuing the pursuit of yo-yo, quickly catching up to her. The police strategically block her path guiding her toward a closed construction site where a damaged bridge is being repaired. Unfamiliar with the streets of Miami Yo-yo assumes she's getting away with only the Arch Nun chasing her.

 With no more vehicles in her way she can ride at her full skill level. The Arch Nun can as well. Accelerating to speeds well over 200 miles per hour.

Yo-yo is becoming more comfortable with the super powerful racing motorcycle. She sees a bridge ahead but is unaware of it being under construction. The closer she gets to the bridge she can see it is not complete. The entire middle section of the bridge is unfinished.

The opening in the middle is one hundred and twenty feet, too far for a successful jump. Yo-yo's eyes widen at the site of the hopeless road ahead.

Sister Elizabeth slows down giving Yo-yo a chance to realize there is nowhere else to go. Yo-yo stops at the foot of the bridge, drops the motorcycle and draws her gun. With only three bullets left she is desperate.

The Arch Nun stops the bike, puts the kickstand down and remains Seated on the bike with her arms folded. Yo-yo notices some concrete cinder blocks and Long flat wooden planks.

I know this chick is not going to make a ramp. Sister Elizabeth thinks to herself. But sure, enough she does. Sister Elizabeth throws her hands in the air in disbelief, continuing to watch with her hands on her hips as Yo-yo quickly constructs a ramp. She knows in her heart; she can never surrender now. Mounting the bike, she prepares for the jump.

The Arch Nun gives her a few more moments to think it over. A police helicopter has been trailing the two since they left the city streets, hovering not far away.

"I have a clear shot awaiting confirmation"

The police sniper says over the radio to his superiors.

"Negative!"

Sister Elizabeth interrupts.

"Do not take the shot, repeat DO NOT take the shot!"

For all the innocent people Yo-yo has shot and endangered during this Pursuit. The Miami Police Department would be more than happy to shoot her dead. But are contempt watching her kill herself.

The Arch Nun knows she must prevent this woman from risking her life. Yo-yo revs the engine several times. She has done similar jumps many times back home. But never on a bike this powerful or a distance this great. Spinning the rear tire, she releases the throttle. Working through the gears quickly to get as much speed as possible.

The Arch Nun takes off after her. Yo-yo looks up at the helicopter then behind her at the pursuing Arch Nun. Sister Elizabeth doesn't want to get too close to her, allowing her enough room for the jump.

With the Wind hitting her face and blowing through her hair. She decides this is the best way to go out in a blaze of glory. Hitting the ramp at 148 miles per hour, she Flies through the air. Holding tightly on the handlebars, she concentrates on her Landing.

Watching from the police helicopter. The officers can see she's not going to make it and cannot wait to see her Crash and Burn!

Sister Elizabeth closes her eyes and prays for a favor from the Lord.

'HEAVEN TAKE HOLD OF HER'

She successfully makes the jump. But the racing motorcycle was not designed to do such things.

Upon impact the suspension instantly breaks, severely damaging her knees and ankles.

The pain is excruciating, she struggles to hold the bike steady but due to her injuries she is unable to apply the rear brake. So, she uses wooden blockades and traffic cones to slow the bike down.

The police officers are laughing hoping for the bike to explode. She finally comes to a stop, falling over and rolling onto her back. Trembling from adrenaline and pain she can see the Arch Nun clearing the ramp.

Coming off the ramp Sister Elizabeth lays the bike into a tabletop position. But the racing motorcycle is too heavy for such a maneuver causing it to over rotate. Sister Elizabeth uses her Grace of God to bring the bike under control. As the bike continues to rotate, she yells.

"Air X-L-lon-tay baby!" (a word she made up to describe her motor cycle jumping skills.)

Before landing on the other side of the bridge.

The police officer's cheer. They've never seen someone So Graceful on a motorcycle and no one has ever seen such a stunt performed, 'EVER'!

Yo-yo watches as the bike lands hard, breaking the suspension but the Arch Nun controls the bike to a stop near her, uninjured she looks down at Yo-yo and winks her eye.

Sister Elizabeth couldn't help but say to her. "RIDE OR DIE"

Yo-yo slowly claps her hands sarcastically as the Arch Nun

Dismounts the bike. Believing she is dying she says to her.
"Good ride bit#h! I'll see you in hell."
She draws her gun and empties it into the Arch Nun. The
bullets pass through her striking a nearby tree. The Arch
Nun winks at her again.
Yo-yo can't believe what she has just seen. She knows she
didn't miss, not at such a close range.
Speaking with a British accent Sister Elizabeth responds.
"My dear, I am an Arch Nun, we don't do HELL! But I will
see you in jail."
At that moment the police and paramedics arrive.
Yo-yo begins screaming at them in English with her heavy
Taiwanese accent
"I shot-ta, she should be DEAD, SHE SOULD BE DEAD!"
The paramedics attempt to calm and tend to her but she
continues on.
"Oh my god, sister that was the most amazing jump I've ever
seen, are you okay, are you hurt?"
One of the police officers asks.
"I think I might have sprained my ankle."
Sister Elizabeth answers starting to limp a little.
"There's nuttin wrong wit her, she lying, SHE LYING!" Yo-
yo screams continuously until the paramedics sedate her.
Yo-yo has shot innocent people and endangered the lives of
many and for the crime of Shooting at an Arch Nun, she will
spend the rest of her life in jail under the new laws.

In the Mediterranean Sea Leggz and her guests watch the
chase in Miami. Undercover Interpol and FBI agents are
desperately trying to get word to their superiors and the
U.N.A. to inform them of Giovanni Luciano's presents on the
yacht. But the Sea Leggz is no ordinary vessel. It's equipped
with various types of Hi-End experimental technology, she
recently Included the I.D.A.C. To assure what happens there
can never be recorded.
This is Ka'ren's primary yacht and her home away from

home. Some of the vilest acts imaginable have been
committed here. This is one of the places she hosts fights to
the death to which she is a regular participant. Here she has
mercilessly killed, maimed and tortured countless men and
women. This is her world and a wicked one indeed it is.
The undercover agents know it may be impossible to get a
discrete signal through with all the ship's monitoring
technology. They'll have to transmit from the bridge using
the ship's radio, definitely a suicide mission.
Isabella, a young undercover D.E.A agent whom has been
working with Ka'ren for the last two years, and is not aware
of her CIA status. She has also been sleeping with Ka'ren for
the past year and is very much in love with her. In that short
period of time she's seen Ka'ren do some horrible things and
dismissed it. But Isabella is looking for a quick promotion to
the U.N.A and what better way is there then to give the
U.N.A this most wanted criminal. Isabella being a native of
Brazil is an exotic beauty with sun kissed skin and long
shiny black hair she seldom has a problem seducing or
getting men to do what she wants.
It's not suspicious for her to be seen in various parts of the
ship the bridge included. She picks up a bottle of champagne
and works her way to the bridge convincing people along
the way she is intoxicated.

   Once inside the bridge she asks to be alone with the
Captain whom has had a crush on her since the day he set
eyes on her. She's wearing a very revealing string bikini with
tropical patterns.
(Speaking Portuguese)
"You know I get it on with Ka'ren, Poppy but I swing both
ways baby and right now I want a man!"
She tells him, rubbing his arm. The captain has known
Ka'ren for a long time and knows she doesn't mind sharing
from time to time.

By offering him sex she knows he will turn off the security cameras on the bridge for privacy.

The captain known to his men as 'SirManly' is an older gentleman and needs to excuse himself for a moment to go to the restroom, so he may take a Viagra pill. He seals the doors to the bridge. The private restroom on the bridge is not far away and Isabella will have to be Swift. Isabella majored in Communications at Annapolis, graduating at the top of her class and is familiar with the yacht's complex radio system. She must send the message quickly and encrypted, buying her at least an hour before the transmission is detected. A piece of cake for her, with her telecommunication skills.

Working as fast as she can she decides to bypass the DEA and send directly to the U.N.A. after witnessing the technology of the Battle Assault Drones she knows their satellite technology would be far superior.

She successfully sends the message then knocks on the restroom door to see if the captain is all right. "You alright Poppy? She asks knocking on the door. (WARNING EXPLICIT CONTENT)

"If you don't wanna fu#k me baby, it's all right I'll get somebody else!"

"No, no, no! please I'll be right out."

The captain replies trying to buy himself as much time as possible for his pill to work. But doesn't want to miss this rare opportunity. He exits the restroom, walks toward her and takes her in his arms. With kissing and foreplay, he still needs a little more time. Isabella realizes he has a intermit problem and uses it to her advantage.

"Dam Poppy! You not hard I'm not turning you on?"
She says pushing him away.

"No! It's not that I just have a lot on my mind."

"Okay I'm going to let this go this time, Poppy cause I think Leggz wants me on deck, but you owe me! unless you want me to tell everybody about this?"

"Thank you, thank you, Beautiful. Please don't tell anyone. I have a lot on my mind we have a special guest and it's just kind of tense right now."

She kisses him on the cheek, he Pats her on the butt then she leaves the bridge. She can't believe how smoothly everything worked out and to her advantage. The encrypted message shouldn't show up on the ship's logs for another hour or so and with the Bridge surveillance cameras off, it would be almost impossible to prove who sent what or where it went. Returning to the party proud of her accomplishment. She mingles among the guests dancing and drinking. Ten minutes later Leggz and Giovanni Luciano join the party.

"Okay Lucky A#shole go tell everybody your tall tale of how you eluded the U.N.A." she says to him.

"Yeah, yeah anything you say. You want me to bring you a drink? Wit those gorgeous legs over here." He responds "Maybe I'll let you touch them before I kill you!"

"After I touch those, I can die a happy man, Baby!"

Giovanni says with a wink as he walks away.

Isabella brings Leggz a drink and puts her arm around her waist.

"All this trouble over that Motherfu#ker! you should just kill him and throw his a$s overboard, Baby."

Leggz sips her drink watching Giovanni walk away.

"Him, I'm going to kill very slowly! But when I find out who sent an encrypted message to a U.N.A satellite a little while ago. THATS the motherfu#ker I'm REALLY gonna kill slowly!"

She says with a cold stare into Isabella's eyes. Isabella encrypted the timestamps and bounced it off other radio systems in the ship so the time and location would be hard to find. But Leggz has her team on it and it won't be long before she knows the exact time and location it was sent. Isabella continues to mingle with the guests, trying very hard to hide her emotions. She is very, very frightened of what Leggz will do to her when she finds out. She excuses

herself and goes to the restroom for a moment to be alone.
She takes a long hard look in the mirror, then Falls to her
knees in prayer.

"Oh heavenly father, please forward me for the sins I have
committed while on this mission. Please forgive me for the
sexual acts, the drug use and the many unspeakable things I
have done to maintain my cover. Perhaps I was too
ambitious and career-driven. I don't know, and
I make no excuses for my actions Oh Heavenly Father. I only
ask for your forgiveness. If I should die at the hands of a
woman I am in love with, I only hope my message finds the
U.N.A. Please God! I beg of you, let Mother Teresa find this
man who is responsible for the deaths of so many women
and children and bring him to Justice. As for me, I gladly die
as your humble servant and hope you're welcome me into
your arms. Thank you Oh Heavenly Father, Amen!"

Cruising Above the Clouds in the vicinity B.A.D-6 receives the faint encrypted message.

"Boss I got a direct message from a deep cover operative, not far from here."

Sister Amira's Communications specialist tells her.

"Authenticate and put it on screen please."

The message reads. 'Emergency authentication code I-M-N-DEA-MIX. I have eyes on Giovanni Luciano. We are currently on a yacht designated 'The Sea Leggz.' Ship identification number and destination Unknown.'

Her Communications specialist tracks the message to its point of origin, they identify the yacht and its registered owner, a woman named Ka'ren Margo Eleganza.

The A.N.Ts are unfamiliar with that name or who she is. That information is above their pay grade and on a need-to-know basis. The registration does not show as CIA. They inform Mother Teresa then set course to intercept. There are three smaller yachts in the area not affiliated with Ka'ren but enjoying the Open Sea.

The guest aboard the Sea Leggz are indulging in many adult activities. When suddenly several of them notice a white streak high in the sky. They quickly alert everyone else, Leggz included. They slowly Stop Dancing pointing to the sky. Everyone knows it is the coming of a Battle Assault Drone.

Ka'ren tells everyone to be calm. Captain SirManly knows he'll be taking point and doing all the talking. He'll be wearing an earpiece and getting his instructions from Ka'ren.

She tells everyone to quickly go inside. She needs to hide Mr. Luciano in plain sight. Several of her guests are Arabic. So, she pulls him into a private room and disguises him with a beard, dark sunglasses and a turban.

"Are you Fu#king kidding me?" Giovanni protests.

With his tanned skin he Blends in nicely. The undercover agents are pleased to see someone got a message through.

Isabella is relieved at the site of the Battle Assault Drone and has made up her mind to give up her Mission and return with them, but how if Leggz thinks she betrayed her she will definitely put a hit out on her, or worse come for her, HERSELF!

Mother Teresa feels to Amira informing her of Ka'ren's location witch C.I.A intel confirms she is in Dallas Texas at this time.

So she should have no trouble gaining control of the ship and searching every inch of it.

B.A.D-6 approaches the Sea Leggz stopping just ten feet away, then sounding its signature horn to alert everyone on board an Arch Nun has arrived for official U.N.A business. Captain SirManly exits the bridge with his first mate.

Everyone else, the passengers included have instructions to remain inside. The undercover agents are having a hard time identifying Mr. Luciano. Ka'ren disguised him in private and merged him with the rest of the guest. The captain attempts to identify himself but is immediately cut off by a loud voice from the B.A.D's speaker system.

"We know who you are." Lisa says. "All passengers and crew are ordered on deck NOW! prepare to be boarded."

"You have no right to--"

Again he is cut off but this time by the launching of four midsize B.A.Ds.

"Everyone on Deck now!" Lisa repeats.

As the crew and guests comply. They are most uneasy, many would rather the U.N.A not know who they are or of the Contraband onboard. They look to Ka'ren to do something, anything! As her crew and guests slowly pour onto the main deck. Ka'ren stays cool like the boss she is, walking among them.

"Okay, that's everybody." The captain says looking up at the Battle Assault Drone.

"Hey boss, our cameras are having a problem focusing. We won't be able to scan the Yacht." Esmeralda tells Sister

Amira.

"If the cameras cannot focus our microphones are affected as well." The Arch Nun says.

"It would be a good idea ta not let them know that, boss."

"I agree, it is a good thing Mother Teresa made sure we have pre-recorded audio loops of all our essential commands."

"Shall I broadcast again boss to give the impression we are unaffected."

"By all means, do so."

Ka'ren stands with her guests smiling, confident the I.D.A.C is doing its job when suddenly she hears.

"Prepare to be boarded!" The smile is quickly wiped from her face. If the battle assault drone can still broadcast perhaps its facial recognition cameras are functioning as well. Unable to leave the main deck she has no way of confirming the I.D.A.C's status. She cannot have these guests checked by the U.N.A.

The Battle Assault Drone lowers its rear ramp and gently touches the main deck. Three A.N.T agents exit assault rifles at the ready, red lasers on.

"Spread out and Keep your Fu#king hands where we can see them, no sudden moves!"

One of the A.N.T agents yells. Ka'ren notices they didn't broadcast that through their craft's speaker system, like they did in Chicago. Maybe they are affected by the I.D.A.C.

This is not a chance she is willing to take she must do something and do it soon.

She tells the captain to continue protesting their search and to have the crew display a light level of resistance with a little show of force. Just enough to create a standoff. The captain calls the ship's security to be by his side and orders them to draw their weapons but do not aim.

"ARE YOU OUTTA YOUR FUC#KING MIND?"

The A.N.T agent yells pointing his assault rifle at the captain, as the red laser turns green.

"I WILL DROP YOU, LIKE A BAD HABIT! TELL THEM TO

STAND DOWN NOW!"
The captain does not flinch nor show Fear. He looks at the agent and tells him.
"I'm afraid I have orders not to do that"
The captain and agents exchanged a few more words and threats. But neither are backing down.
Now the guests are becoming restless and frightened.
They don't want to get caught in the middle of a shootout against A.N.T agents. This gave Ka'ren a little time to think.
Then she notices Sister Amira walking down the ramp accompanied by two more A.N.T agents.
This is what Ka'ren was waiting for. As the Arch Nun gets closer the captain is taken by her beauty and formally introduces himself.
Sister Amira stands firm with her hands behind her back looking out over the guests as he speaks and in full Arch Nun rhetoric interrupts him.
"You speak as though this is a social visit or request. This is official business of the U.N.A, We will search this yacht and look upon all its guests and crew."
The captain isn't easily shaken but finds himself more than a little nervous engaged in a confrontational conversation with an Arch Nun and resisting the U.N.A.
"like I stated before, I can't allow that."
"Is that so?"
Sister Amira says turning to face him and with a cold stare deep into his eyes she gives him a warning. "Resistance to the U.N.A is futile!"
Ka'ren tells the captain to remind her of the changes to the Goliath's challenge, Mother Teresa made available to the public and allow him to choose a champion and to speak loudly for everyone to hear.
The captain has a feeling in the pit of his stomach, a feeling he has never known before. He is feeling fear for the first time in his life!
This makes him very uncomfortable. For he is afraid, very

417

afraid of this woman, this Arch Nun that stands before him. He removes his hat and runs his hand through his hair, taking a deep breath he returns his hat to his head. His short-lived feeling of fear is gone.

"Sister, with all disrespect! you are not searching this ship!" He says with confidence ordering his men to stand steady.

"I believe there's been some changes to your Goliath's challenge law. We all know it; we prefer to remain current on such things here. Besides many of the guests are still protected by diplomatic immunity and--"

"SILENCE!"

Sister Amira interrupts.

"U.N.A business supersedes diplomatic immunity. How dare you sir, attempting to dictate the law when you are so ignorant of it. The addition to the law acknowledges the respect of one's personal property or place of residency and their right to protect it. Therefore, allowing this agency to offer a non-lethal fight. If this agency is the victor one's property may be searched, confiscated or seized. If this agency loses, one's property cannot be searched or confiscated for three days."

"Well Sister, the only way you're gonna search this yacht is if you go through me or my chosen champion. So, if you don't want your a#s royally kicked in front of your agents, I'd turn around and get out of here, now!"

Sister Amira turns away and begins walking toward her agents. The guest and crew begin to applaud the captain. She turns to face the captain once more with her agents behind her. She makes a hand gesture to her team and one of them steps forward.

The agent raises his hands for everyone to settle down. Then looks at the captain and shouts.

"CHOOSE YOUR CHAMPION!"

Without hesitation Captain SirManly responds.

"I'm responsible for this ship and it will be me that fights for it, the crew and passengers. Allow me to apologize in

advance for messing up that pretty face of yours, Sister."
The Captain hands his hat to his first mate and begins
unbuttoning his shirt.
The guests are ecstatic and angry. Ecstatic to witness an
Arch Nun fight Live, angry for not being allowed to have
their cell phones to record it. But to their knowledge the
ship's cameras are functioning recording everything and
Leggz will definitely sell them copies, at an astronomical
price.
"MANLY, MANLY, MANLY!" The crew member's chant.
A very loud round of applause and cheers from the guests
begins to drown out the chanting of the crew. The guest
divide allowing someone to approach the Arch Nun and to
Sister Amira's surprise walking toward her with a Fierce and
determined look upon her face, is the one and only, Leggz
Diamond. Sister Amira feels to her grandmother a most
unexpected message.
'Um grandma I have a little problem here. It seems as
though the CIA's information regarding Ka'ren was wrong,
very, very, very WRONG!'
'Why do you think that, my child?'
'Because she's walking toward me right NOW! and she is
pissed!'
'This is a surprise indeed. She will most likely be very
confrontational and offer to be the chosen Champion to
combat you.'
'What shall I do grandma?'
'Match her skill, showing periodic superiority. BUT do NOT
defeat her or allow her to defeat you. She must believe she is
physically Superior. I will create a diversion so the battle
will be Undeclared resulting in a stalemate so you and your
team can get out of there.'
'Ok grandma.'
Ka'ren now stands beside the captain, his shirt is open before
he can remove it. She places her hand on his arm for him to
stop. He stands still staring at the Arch Nun. The guests are

now certain Ka'ren is going to fight the Arch Nun. "I'm the owner of this yacht and if anyone is gonna defend it, it will be me!"

She tells the Arch Nun Looking her up and down with hatred in her eyes so deep it is unmeasurable!

Again the guests applaud. They have seen Ka'ren fight countless times to the death barely breaking a sweat, her opponents seldom striking her and often wearing a bikini or evening gown and heels. But Ka'ren is no fool after watching the Arch Nuns fight on social media. She anticipates her being a formidable opponent so she'll be dressing appropriately and wearing proper Footwear to face an Arch Nun in combat.

She tells Isabella to bring her some proper clothing. She puts it on over her bikini as Sister Amira steps back with her arms wide so her teammates may remove her bullet-resistant coat and Habit.

The captain inspects the Arch Nun for hidden weapons. One of the A.N.T agents does the same to Ka'ren. All of the guests remain quiet during this procedure. Many are secretly making high-stakes wages, not all in favor of Ka'ren. As with the original Goliath's challenge there are no separate rounds just a fight to the end. in this case until someone gives up or is knocked unconscious!

The A.N.T agents, Captain and crew step back to give the fighters room.

Ka'ren assumes a Muay Thai fighting stance. With legs such as hers, she loves to kick box.

Usually she just walks to her opponent punching and kicking them with her superior speed and strength, toying and dominating them the entire fight. In her adult life she has never known defeat.

 She has also never seen anything move like an Arch Nun! This will be a grand victory, she tells herself. Sister Amira has not yet taking a fighting stance, she eases closer to Ka'ren, closes her eyes for a brief moment, inhales then exhales opening her eyes.

"Now witness the Power of God!"

She says loud for all to hear. Ka'ren's guests dare not applaud or cheer.

Sister Amira whistles her signature Little tune. The guests are still silent eagerly awaiting Ka'ren to throw the first punch and she does not disappoint.

Attacking Sister Amira with punches and kicks.

She Dodges and out Maneuvers them, then with lightning speed strikes Ka'ren several times to the body making the hissing sounds of a snake and finally punching her with a solid fist to the face knocking her back causing her nose to bleed a little. Then she assumes a Shaolin Snake Fist fighting stance. The guest and crew cannot believe it. This Arch Nun holding her own against Leggz Diamond. Sister Amira stands still without motion in her fighting stance as Arch Nuns do during a fight.

The guest cheer and applaud. Giovanni is torn, on the one hand he wants the Arch Nun to kill Ka'ren and shut her BIG mouth. But then he would be in U.N.A custody. On the other hand, that would deny him killing Ka'ren himself. Something he looks forward to doing.

Isabella doesn't want the Arch Nun to kill the woman she loves, but is fearful for her life. One way or another she's getting off this yacht.

Ka'ren wipes the small amount of blood from her nose. Her guest and crew notice the look on her face. They've seen this look many times before just before she kills her opponent. She takes a few steps toward the Arch Nun. The Applause comes to a halt.

Then Ka'ren assumes a Shaolin Dragon fighting stance. Her guests know, play time is OVER! If the Arch Nun can defeat Leggz Diamond, she had better do it and do it quickly. The two fighters make eye contact. There is a Stillness among the guests and crew. Then with a sudden burst Ka'ren attacks the Arch Nun furiously with half her

Superior speed and strength. Repeatedly throwing various kicks with excellent form. Sister Amira continues to dodge and block them. But Ka'ren is determined to strike her. The Arch Nun knows Ka'ren is moving just a bit too fast and the guests are becoming silent in amazement. So, she allows herself to be hit a few times. Ka'ren executes a spin kick, her heel strikes Sister Amira's jaw breaking it, she's telepathically connected to her siblings so they may experience the fight and jest with each other.

'She just broke my jaw! Oh, wait I fixed it.' She communes to her siblings.

Ka'ren punches her hard in the chest, then the eye finishing with a kick to the rids Breaking them. Sister Amira moves with the punches and kicks as not to raise Ka'ren's suspicion. But feels every bit of the pain for a brief moment.

'This Bitty just crushed my eye socket and broke my ribs! Ok, Wait I'm fine'

The two women begin to grapple exchanging holds attempting to break arms or legs. The A.N.T agents are very concerned. No one has ever gotten their hands on an Arch Nun during a fight, except them and to their knowledge they didn't seem to do too well when they did, they recall Sister Amira needing medical care afterwards.

Leggz gets Sister Amira on the floor and punches her a few times in the face. The Arch Nun's face bruises but does not bleed. She tightly warps her legs around the middle of Ka'ren's body, holding her head close to her chest to prevent her from hitting her. Ka'ren lifts the Arch Nun off the floor with her legs still wrapped around her body, holding her head tightly and slams her to the hardwood deck. The cheering is so loud. No one heard or noticed the small exchange of words between the fighters.

"Why won't you BLEED, BIT#H?"

Leggz asks Breathing heavily. Sister Amira now holding Ka'ren's neck tightly, pulls her close to her mouth and calmly responds.

"Jesus bleed for the sins of humanity. I will not bleed for YOU!"

"We'll see about that!"

Leggz tells her breaking her hold, stomping HARD on her chest and performing three backflips to put a little distance between them.

Sister Amira rolls backwards and jumps to her feet. The two women slowly Circle each other as the crowd cheers and whistles.

'Heeeey, wait a minute, did this BITTY just stomp on my boobies?'

Sister Amira communes to her siblings.

'I think that would hurt me a lot more if she had stomped on my little boobies.' Dee communes.

'Anna would have gotten up, crying holding her boobies then told Grandma what Leggz did.'

Lin adds.

'Stop talking about boobies, All of you!'

Maria tells them.

'Shut up, Maria if she stomped on your tata's you would've shoved your fan down her throat.'

Amira communes as they all laugh.

'Enough!'

Brother Joshua communes loudly commanding their attention.

'Grandmother would be furious, if she knew of this blatant disregard for where you are and what you are doing little sister. FOCUS on the task at hand. Everyone dis-commune now. So, Buffie may continue the Lord's work.'

Joshua seldomly takes such a serious tone with his siblings, but when the brother or sister Superior speaks or communes with such a tone it is the WORD of the Mother and Grandmother Superior!

Their camaraderie comes to an immediate halt as ALL but the Sister Superior collectively reply.

'Yes, Brother Superior. IT SHALL BE DONE!'

Now that Buffie is not communing with her siblings. Sister Amira can get back to business.

She performs a 360 turn and assumes her snake fist fighting stance again hissing like a snake.

Leggz rushes toward her grabbing both her wrists, slamming and holding her against the wall behind them. Her teammates are concerned once more. They were hoping Ka'ren didn't get her hand's on Amira again. Ka'ren holds the Arch Nun's wrists firmly at waist level against the wall. Amira moves her hand back and forth quickly like the head of a snake going up the wall making the sound of a rattlesnake's tale. Ka'ren struggles desperately to hold her wrist but the sound is distracting. With her arm now extended high above her head, still holding the Arch Nun's wrist Ka'ren is off balance and with the speed of a King Cobra Sister Amira strikes Ka'ren five times with pinpoint accuracy to her rids. She cries out in pain clutching her body and quickly moving away from the Arch Nun.

The Applause and cheers stop. The guests and crew can't believe this. Leggz Diamond has not only been hit multiple times, but cries out in pain? They quietly joke amongst themselves, surely it must be the end of the world. So many of them Giovanni included are glad to finally see her meet her match and if they know what's good for them, they best keep it to themselves.

Leggz has now made the decision to kill Arch Nun Sister Amira. Enduring the pain, she slowly assumes her fighting stance; The Arch Nun does the same.

The cheering resumes. Isabella and the captain are standing ten feet behind the Arch Nun.

This is my chance, Isabella thinks to herself.

She runs behind the Arch Nun and jumps at her attempting to punch her, but Sister Amira is too fast, turning and kicking Isabella in the forehead knocking her unconscious. Ka'ren is very upset with Isabella as are the guest and crew. Now she must be arrested under the new laws for

interfering with the U.N.A and attacking an Arch Nun.
"Take her"
Sister Amira tells her agents. Then suddenly there is a loud
explosion on one of the nearby yachts. The engine has blown
with such force it punctured the hull causing the ship to
slowly sink. The fight is over.
Not far in the distance is a cloud of black smoke. The ship's
distress alarm has been sounded. Mother Teresa transitioned
to the Yachts engine room and blew the engine. This action
is allowed by the Lord, for she is a Guardian Archangel and
she would never consider abusing her status but the fight
was taking too much time.
No one aboard the Yacht will be harmed and insurance will
compensate its owner. Isabella is revived, placed in
handcuffs and taken to the B.A.D.
'There's my diversion, Buffie, bring that situation to a close
and tend to those in need.'
The Reverend mother communes to her granddaughter.
"No winner no search. How fortunate for you."
The Arch Nun tells Leggz Diamond.
The guest and crew go wild cheering and whistling. Did
Leggz just fight off an Arch Nun and now they're free to go,
they asked amongst themselves.
Because there was no Victor both parties must go their
separate ways for three days. Sister Amira and Ka'ren stare
each other down one last time. The Arch Nun's face is a little
bruised, her cheeks red, her chest and ribs sore.
Ka'ren suffered a bloody nose, a slightly bruised eye, a
sprained wrist' snake fist strike marks to her legs, back and
torso resulting in slightly bruised ribs. Both women look as
though they were in a hair-pulling street fight. Sister Amira
held back a lot for God's Great purpose. Ka'ren's only
purpose was to destroy her opponent and she cannot wait
for another chance.
The fight worked out just the way Mother Teresa wanted it
to. So, Eve's children can still believe they are physically

superior to an Arch Nun. There is no time to put her battle armor back on. For they must now answer the distress call of the neighboring yacht. As Sister Amira and her team enter their craft, Ka'ren continues to stare at them as the guest continues to cheer.

The midsized drones reattach themselves to the main craft as it slowly departs from the Sea Leggz flying the short distance to the distressed yacht. Ka'ren's guests and crew surround her cheering patting her on the back and hugging her.

She doesn't want anyone to know how much pain she's truly in, she uses her three percent strength of course to manage her very high pain threshold. So, she can endure their hugs, smiling, talking and exchanges high-fives.

"Leggz, please sell me a copy of this fight. Money is no object."

One of her guests asks.

"I'll think about it, Baby I'll think about it. Right now, I gotta go get cleaned up, fix my makeup and hair. And most definitely get out of these clothes!"

They continue to laugh and joke as the DJ restarts the party. The captain orders the crew to resume their duties while he escorts Ka'ren to her very large luxurious cabin. Witch is the size of some small yachts, it even has a private hospital room with everything needed to perform various types of emergency surgery, if needed. The medical staff are of course siblings of hers. So, their discretion of her condition is assured. What happens in their family, stays in their family! However, depending on the severity, it can make it to Eve!

"Well, my sister your ribs are definitely bruised."

Dr. Copper Tells her looking at her X-rays.

"What concerns me is that she did this damage with just her fingertips using snake fist kung fu and with such precision. It's a good thing you are physically Superior to her or you may have been hurt very badly my sister. How do you feel?"

"like I fought the most formidable opponent in my life!"

426

Dolores the assisting nurse walks over and asks.
"Did you hold back in the beginning of the fight as you always do?"
Ka'ren hesitates then answers.
"Yeah, But I'll never do that sh#t again with an Arch Nun. The next time I face one of them I'm gonna kill it, and bring its little nun hat home to MOTHER, I promise you!"
"That's nice, Ka'ren but for now let me give you something for your pain." The Doctor interrupts.
Ka'ren gives the doctor a cold look as she says to him.
"I find your condescending tone disturbing, doctor."
"No, Ka'ren my sister what's disturbing is the fighting skill and power of an Arch Nun!"
"Indeed" The nurse adds.
Ka'ren doesn't want her siblings to know how hard she was trying to hurt the Arch Nun, but could not she decides to lighten the mood. Besides the doctor and nurse are held high in Eve's favor as well.
"I'd better stop arguing with you. In my current condition I'm sure you can easily best me."
Ka'ren says putting her hand on his shoulder. Then they both turn to the nurse whom of course adds. "Best you indeed!"
Ka'ren stares at her for a moment and tells the doctor.
"Ya know, all doctors should have an obedient yes nurse like this one."
The nurse again replies. "indeed"
"God dam it, Dolores do you have ta repeat the same Fu#king word over and over again."
"Indeed, maybe if you stopped playing with your opponent so much. Just maybe you wouldn't have bruised ribs right now."
"You are Soooo Fu#king lucky I love or I would break every bone in your body."
Dolores knows repeating the same word during a conversation is another one of Ka'ren's many pet peeves. She

and Ka'ren are the type of sisters that argue over anything. But Dolores would never speak to her sister this way in front of anyone but family.

"INDEED!"

"Bit#h, STOP MAKING me laugh, it hurts when I laugh."

The doctor laughs and steps between them. Dolores continues attempting to jokingly fight and play with her sister. Ka'ren doesn't jest often but has successfully convinced her siblings that she wasn't trying hard to win the fight. The doctor gives Ka'ren a shot to ease her pain and wraps her sprained wrist.

"Listen to me Ka'ren." He says. "You have always been hailed a great fighter. But now your friends, guest and staff. Hold you in a higher regard than they ever have. Mother will be most pleased! I only wish the ship's cameras were able to capture it so the family can watch and hail you as the great warrior you are. Oh, and I'll use a condescending tone with you anytime I want young lady and don't you forget it."

He concludes with a friendly wink. She kisses him on the cheek and gives them both a hug before returning to the party.

On the main deck of the Sea Leggz. The partying and appreciation of her is in full swing. Ka'ren enters the main deck to a loud round of Applause and cheers. She is wearing dark sunglasses to conceal her black eye and long pants to hide the bruises on her pretty legs.

Those who love her, love her more. Those who hate her should never let her know and those who fear her should continue to do so.

She takes a seat on the upper deck overlooking the main Deck with her personal friends. The captain and first mate are among them. They are all still speaking of the fight as are the guests below. Ka'ren tells the captain to have someone bring Mr. Luciano to her.

Gloria Esteban a high-level drug dealer from Miami sits

down beside her and gives a toast in her honor.

"To Ka'ren, Ka'ren, Ka'ren you are the number one boss bit#h! if there ever was one."

Everyone raises a glass to her. A crew member approaches with Giovanni Luciano, he is still wearing the disguise she gave him. Leggz stands as they get closer. Mr. Luciano stops in front of her and rips off the beard. "I'm not wearing this stupid disguise anymore."

He says slamming the beard to the ground then turning to the rest of the guests.

"That was some catfight huh fellas? Looks like ya got ya ass handed to ya a little."

"WHAT" Leggz replies sharply.

"Yeah, I see ya wearing sunglasses ta cover that black eye that Arch Nun gave y...."

Before he can finish she punches him in the eye with such Force he flies backwards into three other seated guests, Knocking them to the floor. The guests immediately stand Mr. Luciano does not.

The captain immediately stands grabbing her around the waist and lifting her off her feet to contain her.

"A BLACK EYE LIKE THAT?" She screams.

Several of the guests stand as well helping to contain and calm her down.

"Calm down honey, calm down."

The captain says holding her tightly. She turns and clenches his chest trembling in pain.

That's when the captain realizes she's been hurt. He releases his tight hold as he puts her down. But continues to hold her gently close to him. She buries her head in his chest, breathing heavily.

"Ok honey, I got ya, I got ya!"

He whispers in her ear rocking her back and forth.

"This is the best day of your life, don't let him ruin it."

Her breathing studies and he feels her relax. she looks up at him and Whispers back.

"What would I do without you, Manly?"

"Probably kill everyone" He responds seriously.

Leggz apologizes to her friends and Whispers to the captain to check on the I.D.A.C and the status of Isabella if he can.

"Someone please get me a drink and Captain have the doctor look at him and let's get him ready for transport on the sub. I want him off my yacht, before I rip his Fu#king head off."

The captain calls the first mate over.

"Alright, Full Speed Ahead let's put some distance between us and that Arch Nun."

"No, HELL NO!" Ka'ren interrupts waving her finger.

"That bit#h didn't win no fight here, quarter speed and everybody party the fu#k on we're not running from them. Fu#k that Arch BIT#H!"

The Sea Leggz is equipped with its own private miniature submarine. This, like many of the Sea Leggz weapons and gadgets are not on any of its blueprints.

Onboard B.A.D-6 Sister Amira is being checked out by the medic, as they approach the disabled yacht.

"Who the fu#k was that woman, Boss? She had ta have been highly trained to give you a fight like that!"

The medic asks gently touching her ribs. She flinches a little but assures him she is fine.

"How's That feel Boss?"

"As I said, I'm fine I appreciate your concern but We have a job to do."

"Let me be the judge of that boss. You're tensing up before I touch you, that lets me know you're in a little more pain than you're letting on."

While she is talking to the medic, she is simultaneously communing with Mother Teresa.

'You've done well my dear, you will wear your pain and bruises for their natural duration. This will lead the presidents and your teammates to perceive you as vulnerable. After all we wouldn't want them to think you're a-- Well never mind! I love you my dear.'

Sister Amira becomes tickled in her communing with her grandmother.

'N-I-U grandma, but wait, wait, wait. We wouldn't want the presidents and everyone to think, we're what, grandma?'

'Oh dear lord Buffie please, REALLY?'

'Come on grandma, SAY IT!'

"NO'

'SAY IT PLEASE! I'll leave you alone after this promise.'

'SUPER HEROES! Ok Buffie, we wouldn't want the presidents and everyone to think you are a SUPER HERO. I can't believe you're 30 years old.'

While Mother Teresa is telepathically having this family moment with her granddaughter, she is simultaneously verbally reprimanding agent Valentina for buying her a $30 turkey sandwich for lunch.

The medic completes his evaluation of Sister Amira with some sound advice.

"Boss, try not ta let this woman get her hands on you again."

"Hey Boss, maybe she should join the team!"

Adds another agent laughing.

They are accustomed to making fun of each other when they're hurt. This goes on for a few minutes before Sister Amira stands abruptly and with full Arch Nun rhetoric tells them.

"I don't know how you conducted yourselves in serious situations in the jungles of the world. But need I remind you; we have a situation to assess!"

A.N.T 6 uses its advanced welding equipment to patch the hole and see to the family's well-being. They are a family of Chinese Americans, A little frightened but otherwise in good spirit

the man introduces himself and his family.

"Hello, I'm Billy Wong this is my wife Susie and my three daughters Donna she's 9, Miralda she's 7 and this is my oldest Susie she is 15. From the bottom of our hearts. Thank you, guys, so much."

The father says expressing his gratitude.

"I don't know what we would've done if you guys weren't in the area. The radio, satellite phone and our cell phones aren't working properly just texting. Again, thank you."

The man and his family are very grateful to the A.N.T. but couldn't keep their eyes off the B.A.D

and wondering if an Arch Nun is on board and if so, which one is it? The Sister Superior? one of the males? Their Curiosity has gotten the best of them and they couldn't help but to finally ask.

"That is one magnificent craft, sir." The mother says with her Three teenage daughters

standing behind her.

"We were just wondering, is there an Arch Nun in there?" The father asks nervously.

"Maybe, give me five bucks and I'll tell ya" The agent answers.

"Oh! I'll pay" The father responds quickly reaching in to the pocket of his shorts.

"No! Sir I was just kidding with you."

"Oh, I'm sorry I didn't think you guys joked around."

The teenage daughters shake their heads embarrassed at what their father just said. Realizing he may have insulted the female agent he immediately tries to redeem himself.

"I'm sorry, I'm usually calmer than this. I don't know what to say, I don't know how to act, I'm sorry!"

Agent Esmeralda finds him entertaining, his daughters, do not. "Dad, please stop talking, please!" His daughters bag.

"Sir, it's okay take it easy everything's fine."

The agent assures him.

"I tell ya what, I'll see if my boss will come out and say hello" He and his wife's eyes light up with joy. The daughters seem a bit nervous the agents notice this and decide to have a little fun with the teenagers.

"I will say this."

The agent says turning to the teenage girls.

"Anything you are attempting to hide from your parents, any forbidden activities you may be a part of will come to light in the presence of an Arch Nun!"
The teenage girls we're excited to meet the Arch Nun but Now they are petrified with fear. The agent turns to the parents and gives a playful wink.
Then turns and points to the teenagers.
"An Arch Nun knows what's in your heart!"
The girls want to protest to meeting the Arch Nun, but do not want to raise their parents' suspicion.
"We don't have to disturb the Arch Nun. I'm sure He or She is very busy, we can meet another time, maybe?"
Susie, the oldest says trying desperately to convince the agent.
"Don't be silly, Susie"
The father interrupts.
"This is a rare opportunity everything will be fine. you can tell all your friends."
Susie's younger sisters look at her and shake their heads.
The Sea Leggz has not departed from the area yet so the Comm system is still inoperative.
Agent Esmeralda sends a text message to Sister Amira telling her what's going on. She agrees to come out, meet the family and have fun with the teenagers. But first she's going to cover her Bruises with makeup.
Mr. And Mrs. Wong are enjoying the fun the agents are having with their daughters. Unknowing to the agents young Susie has been to the 'Scared Straight' program twice, didn't work. She like many teenage girls are rebellious and easily influenced by boys they have a crush on. In this case Susie has a crush on a twenty-three-year-old man, she is seventeen. He is in a gang and only interested in her because she is naive and her parents are rich.
"The Arch Nun will be here momentarily."
Agent Pal yen chow tells the Wong family. The teenage girls nervously stare at the ramp of the B.A.D. Susie has always

been the loud, tough angry teenager around police officers, Showing off in front of her friends or sisters. So, she builds her confidence to stand tall against the Arch Nun as she did in the Scared Straight program. She turns and Whispers to her sisters.

"Don't be scared Y'all it's just another law enforcement officer, right?"

Before they can answer the Arch Nun is walking down the ramp carrying her business tablet. Her makeup is flawless, the wind of the Open Sea gently blows her coat and Habit as she approaches the family. Mr. Wong stares at her with his mouth open Smitten by her beauty.

Mrs. Wong and her daughters are also impressed at how pretty the Arch Nun is. She gives her husband a gentle kick to get himself together.

Agent Esmeralda conducts the introduction.

"Wong family, I present to you the Arch Nun Sister Amira."

The agent moves back as Sister Amira steps forward Extending her hand.

"Mr. And Mrs. Wong, a pleasure to meet you."

Mr. Wong is a nervous Man by Nature and he is lost for words. Nor can he let go of the Arch Nun's hand.

"I,I don't know what to say sister."

"Perhaps, you can start with Hello."

Sister Amira responds continuing to shake his hand.

"May I have my hand back sir."

Everyone laughs then the Arch Nun switches from her traditional rhetoric to a more pleasant tone of voice. Mr. Wong introduces his family to her. The mood is light and joyful. The teenage girls stand with their parents staring at the Arch Nun. The more she and their parents Converse the calmer they become. Then Sister Amira begins to have fun with the girls. Playfully winking at their parents, she excuses herself from them and in full Arch Nun rhetoric asks young Susie to walk with her.

"What!" Susie surprisingly responds. "My sisters too, right?"

Sister Amira stops smiling and answers. "No! Little Susie, just you!"

They begin walking, in her mind young Susie thought of all the ways she was going to disrespect the Arch Nun and brag about it to her friends later. But now that she is truly walking with one, she is overtaken with fear.

Sister Amira waits until she is just far enough from everyone for privacy but Susie's parents can still see but not hear what's going on. Young Susie knows her parents didn't tell the Arch Nun anything regarding her behavior or activities. She and her sisters were standing there the whole time. She believes she's working herself up for nothing and begins to calm down.

"Well, Susie how are things in your life with your, friends?" Sister Amira asks with a serious emotionless look on her face. Susie is petrified.

Sister Amira continues to stare at her attempting to contain her laughter. But before the Arch Nun can laugh and tell her she's only joking with her. Susie grabs and hugs her sobbing. She holds the Arch Nun tightly, Sister Amira Returns the Embrace. Susie whom is a little shorter than Sister Amira, can't stop crying and apologizing.

"I'm sorry, I'm sorry, I'm sorry!"

"Why do you apologize child? you have done nothing to me."

Sister Amira asks looking down at Susie.

"I've been disrespectful to my parents, mean to my sisters, teachers, police officers. you name it, I just been a bit#h ta everybody. I think my boyfriend may have date raped me a few months ago and I'm afraid I might be pregnant. Oh God I hate myself I just want ta die!"

That was quite the unexpected earful Sister Amira says to herself, comforting the teenager. And in the words of her mother Hymiriam says to her.

"Gather yourself my Child, and know that the Lord loves you and will help you through this. I believe your family will be by your side every step of the way.

I hope and pray that this boyfriend of yours will do the same. But if he date raped you that my child that is a different situation. Does this boy go to your school?"

Susie is hesitant to answer but knows she must. Clearing her throat, she responds Softly

"No! He's outta school that's why my parents are so mad!"

"How old is he?"

"He told me he was 20, then my mom found out he was really twenty-three."

"So now your telling me a twenty-three-year-old man may have date raped you?"

Susie is silent.

"When your mother informed you of his true age what was your response?"

"It was bad and I stayed wit him anyway, behind my mom's back. He said he would wait till I was older before having sex wit me."

"And of course you believed him."

Susie hangs her head in shame and continues to cry her parents are very concerned. They want to run to her but they know she's in good hands.

Her sisters begin to cry as well in fear of whatever's going on over there, they will be next.

"But I've been really good this year, I said so in my letter to Santa!"

The youngest daughter says crying with her finger in her mouth.

"It's okay sweetie"

Agent Alfred tells the child kneeling in front of her.

"They're just talking, Arch Nuns are good people those are happy tears."

Mr. Wong picks up his daughter, wipes her tears as he rocks her back and forth. Agent Esmeralda turns to Mrs. Wong and Whispers.

"Not really happy tears, good tears, but happy not so much."

The agents begin laughing amongst themselves hoping it will calm the Children down. Young Susie goes on confessing to the Arch Nun, telling her the boy's name and the gang he's in. They call themselves the 'piped Pimpers' because they all have tricked out cars, but the name has a hidden meaning.

"Susie You Realize by giving me this information directly, this is something I cannot dismiss. Has he threatened you?"

"No! He offered ta protect me and my sisters."

"How"

"If anybody mess wit me or my sisters at school he got our back."

"Did that impress you?"

"A little he said he loved me."

"And you fell for that Susie?"

"No!"

"Why"

"I think he's trying ta get me and my sisters ta admire and depend on him."

"Well, how very interesting a spark of Common Sense. Now there's the Susie I know Mr. And Mrs. Wong raised."

The Arch Nun compliments her, then putting a hand on her shoulder she asks a very difficult question.

"Susie do you think he would put you on the street to make money for him?"

"I wish I could tell you no, but I'm not sure."

Sister Amira gives young Susie a few moments to think. Then something most wonderful happened right before the Arch Nun's eyes.

Susie wiped away her tears. Sister Amira reached into her bag to give her a tissue in which to wipe her nose. But Susie used the sleeve of her jacket instead, causing the Arch Nun to give her a weird look. Gone was the rebellious Headstrong teenager, gone was the hidden animosity she felt toward her parents for not treating her like a princess and gone was the immature little girl. Sister Amira can see the change upon her face. A Young woman now stands before her. And from this day forth, she shall be a woman for the rest of her Natural Life!

"I didn't mean ta be a snitch or anything like that."

Susie tells the Arch Nun looking into her face.

"I don't wanna get him in trouble, even if he was lying, he was good to me. But like so many stupid things I've done. I messed around and told an Arch Nun of ALL people, that I know some people in a gang."

Sister Amira takes hold of Susie's hand so she may know the severity of what she is about to say.

"Susie I will make a deal with you."

"Yes Sister, I'm listening."

"I hope so, young one. I have a previous engagement but I will ask one of my sisters to take a look at him and his criminal record immediately. If all he has is light gang activity the U.N.A will leave him alone. BUT if he is involved in pandering, human trafficking, crimes against children, or if he did truly date rape you. Then that what must be, will be! The U.N.A will do what must be done and you putting him in our path is the will of God! All my sister will do is have a talk with him. She will be discrete and respect him, there will be no U.N.A agents, just her and a few plain cloths police officers for her protection. Trust me Susie no one will Recognize her as an Arch Nun. I only hope this gang is as harmless as you believe they are."

"Thank you sister, thank you."

"You will do well to avoid him, see him NO MORE!"

"But what if I am pregnant with his baby?"

"Be still child, and know that you are NOT pregnant."

Susie knew in her mind, her heart and her very soul. The words of the Arch Nun were true!

"Your atonement with your family will be a blessing unto you, this is God's will!"

The Arch Nun concludes turning away from Susie.

Verbal Communications are still down. So, Sister Amira feels a message to Sister Navaeh, she is the closest to the city of Los Angeles.

Susie approaches her parents and hugs them both. Mrs. Wong is overjoyed it has been a very long time since her daughter gave her a warm hug.

"Susie you look different is everything all right?" Her mother asks.

"Mom, Dad we need ta talk. I love you so much and I wanna apologize for the way I've been acting these past few years." Mr. And Mrs. Wong look to the Arch Nun standing a few feet away. Sister Amira

Nods her head to them. Then begins to walk toward them and as she passes Mrs. Wong reaches out to her.

"Sister please, let us thank you."

Sister Amira stops briefly and smiles.

"There is no need to thank me for doing the Lord's work. It was a pleasure to meet you, good day. Hollowed be thy name."

The Wong's are speechless.

They watch as the Arch Nun walks away followed by her team. They cannot take their eyes off them as they approach the top of the B.A.D's ramp.

Sister Amira turns and gives a final wave to the Family. This is a day the Lord has made and this particular family are eternally grateful.

As for she who was once a rebellious teenage girl, she shall never forget the day an Arch Nun made a visit to 'The world of Susie Wong'.

On the ground at the unfinished Los Angeles A.N.T farm. B.A.D 2 is receiving a minor checkup from General Randolph's team. Sister Navaeh has received all information pertaining to Susie's now ex-boyfriend, Kevin Reed Known on the streets as 'Luv-Child' Susie thought this name was cool and that it meant he was a child of love. But it was given to him by older gang members because unknowing to Susie he has a lot of children with other Young girls. Some are currently selling themselves on the street and addicted to drugs.

For him there is a dark day coming, and it won't be long! For Arch Nun Sister Navaeh will be at his current address soon! In Washington 'The Cured' are still the topic of discussion in the news.

Hymiriam was instructed by Mother Teresa to stay close to Washington DC for the time being. President Ophelia is happy she can finally track 'Godspeed'.

"Madam president everything is working flawlessly." General Coleman tells her.

"Since Hymiriam left Langley she's only gone as far as New York, that's where they're landed right now. When she leaves there, we can track the craft anywhere in the world."

"That is excellent news General. I can stop stressing over her location and focus on running the country."

"Yes Madam president with knowing the location of the craft we can now start working on her exact physical location."

"Thank you General, I'll need that ASAP. She doesn't seem to carry that satellite phone much and when I order her to, she seems to conveniently lose it somewhere."

The president's personal cell phone rings. The general knows its Hymiriam because the president has a distinctive ringtone for her.

"Well, Speak of the Devil." The general comments sarcastically.

"No, No, No GENERAL!" The president reprimands. "She may be a lot of things,

DEVIL is most definitely NOT one of them. I'll thank you to NEVER refer to her as such EVER again sir!"

"My apologies Madam president, it was a figure of speech."

"Find ANOTHER figure of speech, GENERAL!"

If the general thought the president shared in his optimism and hidden animosity for Hymiriam.

He was mistaken, sadly mistaken!

Sister Navaeh didn't use her team for this endeavor because

this was considered a personal favor for Amira. She selects two California state Troopers from different precincts to accompany her. In light of what happened to her sister Donna, she wasn't taking any chances.

The two she selected Trooper Mark Henderson and sergeant Edward Friday are honored to serve her and are told to wear plain clothes. They arrive at the residence of Kevin Reed in an unmarked Ford F-250 Super Duty truck.

Parked along the sides of the street are several tricked out vehicles.

They park across the street from the house and sit for a few minutes.

The entire ride the troopers were courteous and respectful but deep down, they wanted to ask her a million questions, tell her how much they appreciate the U.N.A contribution to law enforcement. But most of all they really wanted to tell her how much they believe and love what her mother Hymiriam is doing for the world.

The house is mid-size with a swimming pool in the back Kevin is not the owner. On the pouch are several young women and a group of gang members.

A middle-aged African-American man is standing in front of the house yelling at them. He is crying and very upset.

"Give me back my daughter, I know Y'all got her in there."

The group on the pouch are making fun of him. The Troopers have had a crash course on how to conduct themselves when working with an Arch Nun. They want to jump out of the vehicle and tend to the situation. Sister Navaeh instructs Sergeant Friday to get out and talk to the man but never identify himself as law enforcement. He tells the trooper his fifteen-year-old daughter has been missing for a week and is in that house and they won't let her out.

"Sir, are you sure?"

Sergeant Friday asks.

"Yeah, when I walked up, they saw me and I saw her and they pulled her in the house."

"Have you told the police about this?"

"Yeah they ain't do sh#t!"

The group notices him telling what looks like an undercover officer. Because no matter what a State Trooper wears, they always look like law enforcement. This doesn't scare the gang because it's just one and may be another officer in the truck.

If they were here for an arrest there would be a lot more of them and they'd have a warrant. So, they continue to make fun of the man and the trooper as well. On multiple floors of the house curtains drawn back as more gang members look outside to see what's going on.

Sergeant Friday returns to the truck for further instructions.

"Well Sister, they know we're here now!"

The Arch Nun looks at the trooper and corrects him.

"No, Trooper they know you're here now."

She instructs both troopers to go to the porch and ask for Kevin. As they approach the group, four very large male gang members exit the house to stop them.

"You better be Po-Po coming up here like Dis, Cuz if you ain't. Y'all about ta get the a$s whippin of your life. On second thought I don't give a Fu#k, I'm Fu#king Y'all up anyway"

One of the large men says removing his shirt.

"Beat they a$s Y'all!" Shouts one of the young girls from the porch.

"He'll yeah fu#k them up!" Yells another girl as the men begin to surround the Troopers. The Troopers stand ready and show no fear. "Where ya badge at? Jus wat I thought Y'all ain't cops."

The Horn of the pickup truck is sounded. The gang stops thinking it is a signal to call more cops. They look around waiting for more officers. Sister Navaeh quickly communes with Mother Teresa. She tells her granddaughter it was wise to not use her team, to follow the guidance of the Lord, demonstrate the Power of God and be spectacular! So those

who have accompanied you will remember this day and
those who oppose you shall never forget it!
 Then the back door of the truck opens. Arch Nun Sister
Navaeh steps out, fixes her habit and reaches into the vehicle
to get her Nun bag. Everyone on the porch abruptly stops
what they are doing. As the Arch Nun starts to cross the
street several children run to her and hug her. Looking up at
her with a big smile one of the children says. "Them nig#ers
Dun now, rite?" Pointing to the Gang.
"Watch your language child!"
Sister Navaeh responds laughing and shaking her finger at
the child. The parents quickly rush over to get their children.
As does the man to tell the Arch Nun about his daughter.
Before he can speak, she stops him.
"I am aware of your situation."
She says holding her hand out to stop him.
'Take shelter and trust in the Lord'
She communes to his mind and soul. A sense of calmness
Falls over him as he turns it over to the Lord.
"Take your children and tell everyone on the street to go
inside and remain indoors."
She tells them in full rhetoric. But Everyone already noticed
the Arch Nun and immediately ran inside. For they knew
she was here for the gang down the street.
The gang now recognizes what approaches them.
"Get da fu#k outta here!" One of the gang members says to
everyone.
"Oooooooh, sh#t!" One of the larger gang members adds
putting his hands on his head.
"No, No, No PLEASE not one of them!" One of the young
girls screams opening the door and running into the house
followed by everyone on the porch. The Troopers smile at
each other, then turn to the large gang members whom have
surrounded them.
"Now, about that Royal a#s whipping?"
Trooper Henderson asks with an ear-to-ear grin. The large

men stand their ground not wanting to show fear or run like the others. These are hardened criminal ex-cons. The OG's of the Gang.

"I Ain't Going out like no punk."

One of them says softly to the group, they all agree.

"Imma get my hands on Dat bit#h and snap her neck, she can't take four of us. Then we get da other two!" All are in agreeance except one.

"Yo, I don't know about hittin that bit#h, man?" He questions.

"Nig#er you scared?"

"Nah, I ain't scared!"

"Better not be you just did ten years fa breakin ya baby Mama's back and killin the Nig#er she was cheatin on you wit. Now you wanna act like a Lil bit#t?"

This Twisted motivational speech helps encourage him.

"I'll sho you who the Fu#king bit#h is, Imma be the one ta break dis bit#he's neck! And imma get wit you later fa talkin that sh#t. That's reel, you can believe that"

The Troopers didn't hear this and are unaware of the gang's decision to kill them and the Arch Nun. They are a small-time gang, trying to impress larger gangs and criminal organizations. They consider this to be their big chance.

"It's on now" They say removing their shirts to show their incredibly large muscles in an attempt to intimidate the Troopers. Sister Navaeh approaches but remains behind the Troopers.

"Guys, why are you removing your clothing, I don't have any single dollar bills to give you. Please this is not that serious"

She says peeking between the troopers at the gang members. These men are to focused for jokes. The Arch Nun senses this and acts accordingly addressing them in full rhetoric.

"We will search the house for Kevin Reed he is wanted for questioning. You will stand aside,
Resistance to the U.N.A is futile!" Sister Navaeh warns.

The gang now realize they are here for Kevin and must protect him, not out of loyalty but in fear of what he may say if they take him and he is sarumed. This is something they cannot afford. But for bringing an Arch Nun to their door and what they feel they must do to her and what they perceive are two of her teammates. They are definitely going to kill Kevin next.

"You ain't searching this house, I ain't gonna say it no mo!" Responses a Gang member. The others agree with him Kevin is inside the house feeling and acting like a boss telling the other gang bangers what to do.

"Nig#er you ain't runnin sh#t. that's my big dog out there gettin ready ta wreck SH#T!" One of the girls tells him pointing in his face.

"And you can best believe win he dun wit them, MotherFu#ker you next" Everyone starts to laugh then out of nowhere Kevin punches her in the head so hard he knocks her unconscious. The laughter immediately stops.

"Bit#h! I don't know who the fu#k! you thought you were talking to. But you ain't talkin no mo are you, ARE YOU?" He yells kicking her limp body. "Anybody else wanna try me?" He asks drawing his gun from the back of his pants.

Kevin is a large African American man himself but not as muscular as the others. He's also very unattractive with a slightly larger than usual head and a lot of small facial scars. Sister Navaeh steps forward with the Troopers now behind her.

"I'll give you a moment to reevaluate your current decision." She says slowly assuming the prayer position and turning to address the Troopers.

"Gentlemen stand back. Do not interfere with the Lord's work, unless you are called by me to do so or if I fall in battle. No one will lay a hand on you. For they shall not pass me! Do you understand?"

The Troopers reluctantly agree but assure her they will comply. Unknowing to this gang they've made a critical error. They are about to do battle with The Arch Nun Sister Navaeh, also known as 'Heaven's weapon'.

She turns facing the gang her hands still in the prayer position. She turns her wrists and reaches into the sleeves of her coat. Slowly withdrawing a twelve inch titanium ruler in each hand, she raises her head and opening her eyes she tells them with the utmost serenity.

"Now witness the Power of God!"

With a smirk on his face one of the gang members tells the others to grab her quick and break her legs then finish her and move on to the others. They also find it funny that she chooses to fight them with just a pair of rulers.

Two of them start to rush the Arch Nun as the others go around to get to the troopers.

Time slows down. Sister Navaeh assesses the proximity of the two closest to her. She performs a spinning jump kick rotating left hitting the man on the arm breaking it instantly. The force was so great it knocks him sideways into the other two men knocking them to the ground. She continues the momentum Rolling over the back of the broken arm man, landing on one knee. Before he hits the ground, she holds the ruler under him impaling him. Despite his enormous size, with one hand she flips him off the ground and over like a pancake, quickly pulling the ruler from his neatly broken rib and slamming him to the ground breaking his back.

In those few milliseconds the fourth man has gotten closer to the Troopers whom are ready for battle.

Sister Navaeh reaches into her pocket and retrieves five pennies. She throws them at him and like bullets from a gun the pennies line up single-file. The first striking him to the side of his head lodging in his temple, the second and third striking that Penny driving it deeper into his skull. As his head turns from the impact. The fourth and fifth pennies

446

strike both eyes, bursting them like balloons. He falls before the Troopers and remains Motionless.

The last two men finally hit the ground rolling and immediately getting up. This is happening so fast they don't realize two of them have fallen. They continue to rush the Arch Nun trying to get their hands on her. One of them reaches for her throat. Just before he closes his hand.

She catches his wrist. With his arm fully extended she drives the flat tip of the ruler through his armpit, breaks his wrist and guide him to the ground. His adrenaline is so high he immediately attempts to get up causing the other man to trip over him. As he is falling, she places to flat tip of the ruler against the lower part of his spine. The second he hits the ground she drives the ruler into his vertebrae breaking his back. The Last Man Standing, rises bleeding profusely from his armpit. He swings his fist at her, she easily evades, maneuvering herself behind him, the last place anyone wants an Arch Nun during a fight. With lightning speed, she places the corner of the ruler against the back of his neck and moves it down his spine to his buttocks, splitting the skin down to the bone. Finally, she places the flat tip of the ruler against his lower vertebrae then taps it with the palm of her hand breaking his back, time resumes.

The Troopers stand staring in amazement. They've never seen anyone move so fast and so fluently. The gang watching from the windows were sure their biggest and strongest members together would defeat one little Arch Nun.

"Oooooooh sh#t, I think she jest killed dem motherfu#kers" One of them yells to everyone. They scramble around preparing themselves for what they know is about to happen next. The Arch Nun is coming into the house.

Kevin calls for some of the gang members to pick him up a few blocks away and to make sure they're driving one of their fastest cars. This gang hasn't kept up with the new laws and assumed they would be arrested under the new laws,

for being in the same house with Kevin and with that false
assumption, they are prepared to fight and die. Sister
Navaeh tells the Troopers to call for backup and medical
assistance, lots of medical assistance.
As she gives them further instructions. She touches the ends
of the rulers together electromagnetically they become one.
This amazes the Troopers.
"Pay attention! please gentlemen."
She tells them, pulling what looks like a bicycle handlebar
grip from her bag, and attaching it to the end of the joined
rulers.
 Pushing a button on the hand grip the flat end of the ruler
morphs into a sharp point becoming a very awkward
looking sword. The Troopers look at each other in confusion.
"What kind of weapons technology is this?" They inquire.
"Oh I'm afraid this is above your paygrade gentleman. But
know that you are blessed to have set eyes upon it!" The
Troopers stand silently with their mouths open. "Or should I
say, what weapon? I don't see anything!" Winking her eye at
them and laughing Softly.
She turns and walks toward the house adjusting her Nun
bag which has shifted positions during the fight.

President Ophelia is out enjoying lunch with her staff preparing for a meeting. Her approval rating continues to rise. She's enjoying herself and releasing a lot of stress. It's a great relief to her knowing she can now track Hymiriam's craft.

Her personal cell phone rings, it's Hymiriam.

"Salutations Madam president I just wanted to congratulate you on your recent approval rating. It most certainly looks like the sky is not the limit for you."

"Well thank you my dear and I do appreciate you remaining in the area for a few days."

While Hymiriam and the president are conversing. The engines of her craft can be heard through the president's phone revving up for interplanetary supersonic travel it's a distinctive sound the president is familiar with.

"Well Mary, I hear your engines powering up, Girl make sure you contact me soon. This steak is to die for." Referring to her lunch.

"Oh my! You guys are at Pesto's?" One of her and the president's favorite restaurants.

"I love their salad Soooo much!" Hymiriam says with Envy. Then suddenly an explosion is heard followed by a loud alarm.

"MARY!!!!" The president screams, the entire restaurant takes notice.

"Get me General Coleman now!" She says softly to her assistant.

"Yes Madam president"

The president apologizes to her lunch guests and excuses herself. Followed by her staff.

Her lunch guests are concerned and call their sources to find out what's going on. The President rushes outside and into her limo ordering everyone to remain outside so she may have some privacy. She tightly squeezes her eyes shut, rocking back and forth Softly praying to herself hoping

Hymiriam is all right.

"I have The General on the line Madam president."

Her assailant says tapping on the window and handing her the phone. She transfers the call to her private tablet for secure video-conferencing.

"General, please tell me you're tracking her."

"Yes Madam president. I'm talking to Peter now."

"Connect me, general"

"Right away ma'am"

"Peter, oh my God Peter what's going on up there?"

The president frantically asks.

"We accelerated to fifteen hundred miles an hour, charged supersonic engines. We were cruising along peacefully. We set course, but the moment we engaged the navigational computer. It and the primary engines blew out."

The president's heart drops. It wasn't her intention to cause harm to Hymiriam or damage her craft. "How's Mary Peter?"

"She's fine, Madam president you know her she was simply preparing for the end, her disciples were a little shaken up, but everyone on board is okay."

The president sighs in relief.

"Of course she was. I'm glad to hear everyone is alright. Let me speak to our girl, Pete"

"Right away Madam president."

Hymiriam is calm and jests as she speaks to the president.

"Madam president, I think Someone may have turned the microwave on at the wrong time."

She and Ophelia share a laugh. The president is very relieved she is in good spirits.

"Girl I can't believe you're taking this so lightly."

Hymiriam gives the president her warm smile.

"Well, you know tomorrow is not promised to any of us, Madam President that's one of the reasons I pray for strength when I wake and give thanks before I slumber."

The two women continue to talk for a few minutes while Peter and Angelica assess the situation.

Michael B. Randolph

450

"What's the status Pete?" The general asks.

"The engines are not too bad but the navigational computer is completely shot. I can replace the computer and have her up and running in a couple of days."

The general definitely doesn't want Peter or Angelica finding anything that doesn't belong on that damaged navigational computer system.

"That's a negative Pete." The general orders. "Do not! I repeat, do not! Repair. No one and I mean NO ONE is to enter the engine room. Seal it off until we can conduct a thorough investigation to rule out sabotage. This is a presidential order Pete."

Angelica looks at Peter then responds to the general.

"Sir, with all due respect. Presidential orders must come from, let me think, Oh yeah! The president!" She did not say nor mean this as a jest. The president immediately confirms the order.

"Where's the closest place you can land?-- Pete" The general asks directing his question to Peter.

"Nothing but water for miles, General."

"We have a destroyer in the area, Pete you can land there."

Before Peter can answer General Coleman can hear Hymiriam strongly protesting in the background.

"I am a woman of God and will not set foot on a Battle Destroyer, Military bases of operation are the only exceptions!"

The general grinds his teeth to keep from saying anything disrespectful.

The president orders the general to find an alternative location.

"OK Peter the closest body of land to your location is Chili, can you make it there?"

"Yes sir we were above the clouds when the engines blew, so we can coast most of the way reserving power until we get close to our destination."

"OK Peter land at our base in Chile. I'll have a team waiting for you."

"Copy that sir"

The president insists on everyone being checked thoroughly when they land. She wants to make sure Hymiriam is OK and wasn't injured in any way during the incident in the air. Godspeed makes its way to the military base in Chile near the City of Tongoy. General Coleman's team immediately escorts everyone off The Craft and to sick bay.

The president asks for an emergency meeting with General Coleman immediately! Once back at the White House she calls for the Secretary of Defense to join them.

"Thank you for coming gentlemen I'll be brief."

She says walking to her desk and taking a seat.

"I want you both on top of this. I need to know within the next 48 hours. That our device had nothing to do with damaging her craft. Please gentlemen! Get me an answer! I do not want us at fault for any possible harm that might have come to her."

"Yes Madam president, I have a chopper waiting to take me to Chile now."

"Thank you General" The general leaves the office but the Secretary of Defense stays behind.

"Madam president if our device did indeed damage the crafts navigational computer then it maybe sometime before we get a another chance to tag it!"

"Yes, Mr. secretary I'm well aware."

Mother Teresa's little scheme worked out exactly as planned. The president is remorseful of her attempt and her heart heavy. If anything happened to Hymiriam she would never forgive herself. Hopefully on this day she learned a valuable lesson.

That which the Lord does not wish you to see, thou shall not see!

But unfortunately, this is the U.S. government and there will be many more attempts in the future and Arch Guardian Angel Mother Teresa will be there to deter those as well!

Sister Navaeh approaches the stairs holding the sword behind her back. Step by step, inch by inch she slowly approaches the door. Behind the door is a gang member ready to shoot.

"I know this bit#h ain't bring a knife ta a gunfight!"

He says before squeezing the trigger. The bullet goes through the door and Sister Nevaeh's chest exiting from her back. The troopers were shocked and certain she was dead, but in a split-second Time slows down, but this time the Troopers are allowed to witness her movements slowly in time.

Sister Navaeh quickly turns extending the sword allowing the bullet to ride along its side. Guiding the bullet, she realigns it to its point of origin. Passing through the same hole from which it came striking the shooter directly in his chest. Another member of the gang is running down the stairs as the shooter stumbles back he falls at the base of the stairs tripping the other gang member. He stumbles forward striking his face hard against the wall breaking his teeth and nose. Sister Navaeh passes through the solid door stabbing the bloody faced man in the hip. His pain is so intense he loses consciousness. The second she stepped through the door, time resumes. A member of the gang appears to have been thrown from the third-floor window. With a loud thump he hits the lawn with glass falling around him. Both his legs break on impact. He was not thrown from the window. He was waiting for Sister Navaeh to come upstairs so he can shoot her. But found himself alone in the room with Sister Lin Whom transitioned into the room for a moment. So, the gang would tell the tale of seeing multiple Arch Nuns, as though they were high on drugs. But the Troopers would tell the tale of only one, Sister Navaeh. The gang member was so frightened of Sister Lin, he jumped on his own rather than face the Arch Nun known as the 'Alley Cat'!

453

Two female gang members unfamiliar with firearms, run at the Arch Nun attempting to shoot her, but did not cock the pistols before taking aim. They squeeze the triggers but nothing happens. They had every intention of shooting and killing the Arch Nun. For this they will lose the hand that held the gun. They cock the guns and are ready to fire. Time slows and the two women are allowed to witness the Arch Nun sever their right hands from their bodies.
Sister Navaeh releases the sword it separates becoming two blades, spinning so fast they become a blur, circling her body once before striking the women's wrists. Then becoming whole and returning to Sister Navaeh. As their hands fly upward still clutching the guns. Three men rapidly approach the Arch Nun, several shots are fired from the Guns of the severed hands, striking the men critically wounding them. The women are confused at how they are able to witness this but cannot move. Then Arch Nun Sister Anna appears before them and says to them with great conviction and full rhetoric.
"Hold thy heads in shame, and repent for that which you have done on this day. If not for your lack of firearm knowledge, you would have surely shot a servant of the Lord. You raised a hand to do harm. For this, your hand will never harm anyone again!"
Zip ties appear on their forearms to prevent them from bleeding to death.
Then Sister Anna disappears as time resumes. The bodies of the three Men and the severed hands hit the Floor simultaneously. The women fall to their knees holding their forearms in pain. They cannot believe what they have just seen and heard but they will remember it. TIL THE DAY THEY DIE! As they spend the rest of their lives in jail!
The two women begin to lose Consciousness from the excruciating pain. They are in agony and shock. As their vision blurs, they see the silhouette of Sister Navaeh walking away, time resumes. She walks down a hallway leading to

the kitchen. Two gang bangers emerge from the kitchen, pointing their guns and firing at the Arch Nun, a millisecond before the bullets strike her in the belly, she is gone! But the bullets stand still in time. She reappears behind them sitting at the kitchen table. Like the two women before them who we're of sound mind and body, meant harm to a true servant of the Lord. They are also allowed to witness what is about to happen to them. They cannot move but they are allowed to speak. Rather than ask for forgiveness and mercy from the Lord. They choose to call the Arch Nun names and threaten her.

"I don't know what you got me trippin on bit#h! But you better hope I don't get loose."

One of the gang bangers yells to Sister Navaeh. They both continue to shout threats to her. They can only see her through the corners of their eyes. But can see straight down the hall at the bullets held in time. The bullets reverse direction and slowly head toward the two men followed by another Arch Nun. They are no longer allowed to speak. For the voice of the Arch Nun Sister Dajairia takes precedence as she speaks to their minds, bodies and souls in full rhetoric and absolute conviction.

"Oh God most Powerful of ALL. Forgive them Lord for they know EXACTLY what they do!"

She prays aloud still walking behind the bullets. She stops a few feet from the men and watches as the bullets slowly pierce the skin of their bellies damaging their spines. Not that they will be free to do so, but they shall never walk again. The two men can feel the bullets slowly moving through their bodies. There are no words to describe the pain they are feeling. Sister Navaeh stands and walks between the men. They are in God's hands NOW as they are slowly and gently falling to the floor.

Time resumes, Sister Dajairia Fades away as Sister Navaeh walks down the hall toward the rear of the house. Seven of the gang's young High School females of different ethnic backgrounds are on the second floor, too frightened to join the fight. They were told by Kevin to go upstairs and get ready, should the Arch Nun make it into the house or upstairs. Sister Dajairia appears in the room with the females.

"Oooooooh Sh#t! How da fu#k she get in here?"

The girls shout hysterically Raising their hands high in the air, surrendering. They had no intentions of fighting or putting up resistance. They were hanging out with the gang to be popular at school and for Street Credibility. They recognized Sister Dajairia immediately and a few wet themselves in fear. Sister Dajairia takes a step toward them. The girls back away, still holding their hands in the air, until their backs touch the wall behind them.

Sister Dajairia knows the girls are frightened and had no intention of attacking her or her sister. But takes the opportunity to put the fear of God into them, so they may never seek gang affiliation again!

Looking the girls up and down, they lower their heads in shame.

"Did I tell you to bow your heads?"

Sister Dajairia shouts. Some attempt to answer verbally but are cut off.

"Nor did I grant you permission to speak!"

To hear the rhetoric of an Arch Nun for most is very intimidating. The girls instantly stop speaking. These are the girls of every High School, for every high school has them. Those who think they are grown, those who rebel against their parents, those who group together intimidating the other students and have no respect for adult Authority. They are always loud, obnoxious, self-centered and willing to physically fight anyone.

They didn't think they would ever be in the presence of an Arch Nun, especially under these circumstances. But now they stand before The Arch Nun Sister Dajairia and the Power of the Holy Spirit.

"You chose to stand with this gang. Now you will reap what you have sown."

Sister Dajairia says facing them with her hands behind her back.

"No! Sister please, I ain't do nuttin." One of them shouts.

"Neither did I, Sister I was just here cuz they said it was gonna be a party later and I wanted ta get hi--, I mean DANCE!" Shouts another.

"SILENCE!" Sister Dajairia commands. "How dare you attempt to deceive me!"

Then telepathically communicates to their minds addressing each of them by their full names. While simultaneously reciting the Lord's Prayer verbally.

'Your parents have repeatedly asked and begged you to NOT associate yourselves or be in the company of this gang. But time after time you chose to not heed their words. Now watch as your future ENDS!'

And at the same time completing the Lord's Prayer saying.

"Amen"

The girls state of fear has been heightened tenfold.

How can they hear her praying aloud, yet hear something else in their minds they wonder.

Although they all heard her speaking The Lord's Prayer. They couldn't help but focus on what they heard in their minds ending in 'WATCH AS YOUR FUTURE ENDS!'

Some of them silently weep but couldn't refrain from asking each other quick questions.

"I don't wanna sound krazy but I heard her talkin ta me in my head using my name."

One Whispers.

"I did too she used my name and told me I ain't got no future." Another says Softly.

"I hope we don't get arrested by da U.N.A nuttin can be worse than that!"

At that moment Sister Lin Passes through the ceiling landing on one knee then slowly stands before them with a cold piercing stare.

As if they weren't frightened enough. Now the 'Alley Cat' is in the room,

Perceived by the world to be the most vicious and FEARED fighter of all the Arch Nuns.

One of the girls begins to feel faint and soils herself. The girls catch her and lower her to the floor. As shocking as it was, they were in no position to comment.

'OMG! Lin please tell me she didn't just poop her pants right in front of us?' Dajairia feels to Lin.

'YES, she DID and YES, I'm LEAVING. LOL'

But before Sister Lin leaves, she not only has to speak to them, but must touch a couple of them so they may know she was truly in the room.

"let's make this quick, girls. Which one of you or how many of you are going to fight me?"

Sister Lin asks walking toward the frightened young girls. They collectively scream and begin crying, hugging each other and holding hands.

"BE SILENT" Sister Dajairia shouts. The girls attempt to stop sobering but it is difficult. They huddle closer together and are terrified. When one girl Whispers to another.

"Please don't wipe your nose on my shirt, I just got it."

"ENOUGH!" Sister Dajairia shouts. "CHOOSE YOUR CHAMPION!"

The girls know what that means they're heard it on YouTube. It is spoken before an Arch Nun is about to fight. They squeeze their eyes shut and tighten their holds on each other trembling. In school these girls are feared. They are known troublemakers and everyone is afraid of them, the Faculty included. On the street they flaunt their gang affiliation proudly. Now they sit sobbing, soiled and sorry. but this was their own doing, they have no one to blame but themselves.

They're sorry they didn't listen to their parents and family, who warned them of gang life and where it would lead them. All their visits to the Scared Straight programs where all the convicts can do is yell at them meant nothing. But in the presence of the Arch Nuns they were humbled before the Power of the God!

Sister Lin extends her hand to assist one of them in standing. The young girl is hesitant but she slowly holds out her hand. Sister Lin quickly grabs it and pulls her to her feet. The girl screams frantically in fear, assuming she's about to be hit or worse torn to shreds by the Alley Cat. The Arch Nuns let her scream until she was done. They wanted to assure this lesson was not in vain, these girls have been changed. After hearing the Lord's Prayer from what they know now, is truly a servant of the Lord. They will go forth and honor thy mother and father, heeding their words and life lessons. But most importantly they've opened their hearts and minds to the word of God! Like all teenagers they will not be perfect and they will work hard to maintain their popular cool girl status. But, with a little more Sunshine than Rain.

The girls step forward for a group hug with the Arch Nuns. But Sister Lin holds up her hand for them to stop immediately Sister Dajairia agrees.

"Due to circumstances beyond YOUR control (referring to she who pooped her pants) we're going to pass on that hug for now."

Sister Dajairia tells them with a very serious look on her face and judging by the look on Sister Lin's face the girls can tell she strongly agrees. The most popular girls in school can now add embarrassment to their long list of current feelings.

"We'll temporarily use the old 'Corona virus' social distancing rule for NOW!"

Sister Lin concludes turning away from them.

"Hold on a moment" Sister Dajairia says stopping Her sister. "I believe one or two of them still want to fight us."

"WAIT, WHAT? " One of them quickly responds.

"No, no, no, no, Nooooo! I think I speak for all of us, when I say we absolutely, positively do NOT! " All the girls immediately agree.

The Arch Nuns assume the prayer position and Sister Lin Stomps her foot hard to the floor. All the furniture in the room flies up and sticks to the ceiling. The girls look up at the furniture in amazement, then back to the Arch Nuns and with a serious gaze sister Lin simply says. "GOOD!"

Then the furniture comes crashing down around them and, in that moment, Sister Lin is gone.

"Go home and tell thy mother and father how much you love them. Remember this day AWAYS!"

Without hesitation the girls look through the room searching for garments to cover themselves with.

"We could just leave" One asks.

Sister Dajairia tells them they'll have safe Passage through the house and the officers outside will have instructions to take them home. They thank Sister Dajairia once more as they look upon her in wonder. She turns away from the girls and Stomps her foot hard to the floor then she too is gone!

Sister Navaeh enters the backyard of the house. Waiting for her are twelve adult gang members and Kevin Reed. They've all seen what she did to the smaller group of men and are taking no chances.

They draw their weapons and begin to fire. Sister Navaeh takes cover behind a bookshelf near the doorway. As mentioned before this is a small-time startup gang many of them are armed with guns but not all are fully loaded, some having as little as two bullets.

Out of fear the weapons are quickly emptied. But it's too late to turn back now.

Sister Navaeh peeks her head out and asks. "Is it okay to come out now gentlemen?"

"Yo Man, we gotta kill dis bit#h" Kevin tells them. Some of them drawn knives, others pick up sticks and large rocks. Kevin's gun is empty as well so he picks up a large heavy stick. He is more frightened than any of them, because he knows this whole mess is his fault. The owner of the house who is also the leader of the gang will most certainly be looking for him! The gang bangers Kevin called to pick him up are his cousins, so they will undoubtably help him.

Sister Navaeh reaches into her bag and pulls out an extendable titanium antenna and a 5-foot electrical ribbon. She extends the antenna and attaches the ribbon to the end of it. The ribbon is now charged and will have the same effect as a stun gun when it strikes someone.

She Twirls it with the Finesse of a Rhythmic Gymnast. The gang Bangers watch as she swirls it through the air and around her body then snaps it like a whip.

"What! You want us ta give you sum dallas?"

Kevin asks sarcastically, referring to her as a stripper performing for dollar bills.

Sister Navaeh is silent, but puts her hand on her hip with attitude and extends her Palm as a gesture for money.

"On second thought, it wouldn't be right to accept payment for what I am about to do! Rather than attend strip clubs gentleman, perhaps you should have spent your money on bullets!

Perhaps, Perhaps, Perhaps?" She answers tilting her head to the side and raising her eyebrows.

One of the gang bangers throws a large rock at her.

As the rock leaves his hand the two men closest to her seize the opportunity to attack. One of them extends his hands to grab her, time slows down.

She swirls the ribbon around both his hands barely touching them and with a quick snap, he makes a startling discovery For the Lord allows him to realize. The ribbon also has razor wire properties.

His eyes widen in Terror as he watches his fingers severed from his hands as he slowly continues to fall. The Arch Nun turns as the ribbon follows her body. The second man forgot to pull his sagging pants up, they hang under his buttocks displaying his underwear. She grabs his pants and yanks them to his ankles, causing him to trip, slowly falling to the ground. She turns to face the approaching Rock and whips the ribbon toward it splitting it in two.

The two halves fly passed her following the men to the ground striking them at the base of their skulls breaking their necks as they hit the ground, time resumes. Kevin receives a text from his cousins informing him they are two blocks away waiting for him. Like a true coward he throws his stick at Sister Navaeh and runs towards the backyard fence in hopes of climbing it while she's busy fighting the others. The Arch Nun evades the stick allowing it to pass her, striking one of the men in the forehead just as he is about to throw a fist-sized stone at her head. He stumbles backwards tripping on his untied shoelaces, tossing the stone in the air, continuing to fall backwards he strikes the back of his head on a large Stone protruding from the ground.

Sister Navaeh quickly Twirls the ribbon around the antenna, jumps sideways twirling her body and hits the rapidly falling stone increasing its downward velocity. It hits him in the nose, breaking it and causing further neurological damage.

She lands smoothly swirling the ribbon around her body forming a temporary defense perimeter. She pulls a titanium frisbee from her bag and places it on top of her habit it magnetically attaches, then touches the base of the antenna to the top of the frisbee. The two items are now locked in place with the ribbon flowing from the top of the antenna. Her habit now resembles (The Pungmul) A hat worn for the Korean head ribbon folk dance.

As stated earlier Kevin is a large man and having a difficult time attempting to climb the ten foot privacy fence.

Now pulling a pair of Nunchucks from her bag she prepares herself, before attacking the remaining gang bangers. Her movement is fast, fluent and hard to counter.

Her fighting Maneuvers are similar to the Korean head

ribbon folk dance, but she added Nunchucks. One of the men manages to grab her from behind. She lowers her head the ribbon follows then quickly whips her head back. The ribbon follows resting along his spine admitting an electrical charge splitting his shirt and spine! She pulls a second pair of Nunchucks from her bag. This is happening too fast for the gang bangers to realize how deadly the Ribbon is. The remaining men quickly run toward her, one attempts to catch the ribbon with his stick, it slices the stick with ease.
 The house only has outdoor security cameras to record their wild pool parties. Sister Navaeh doesn't destroy them so the world leaders May witness her magnificent fighting maneuvers.
There is a brief standoff, she twirls one of the Nunchucks around her right wrist catching it in her hand, with the chain facing her, she points it at one of the men. With the push of a button two spikes fly out puncturing his eyes then retracting. The men now realize there is no way these weapons can logically work. There must be a higher power involved! But it's too late, the Arch Nun is attacking. Swinging her head to maneuver the ribbon. Those who out maneuver the ribbon are rewarded with EXTREMELY hard strikes from the Nunchucks, causing massive head trauma or severe spinal damage.
For anyone who attacks with the intention of harming any of God's chosen Arch Nuns, the repercussions are quite severe. For it is not the skill of the Arch Nun they should worry about.
It is the 'WRATH OF GOD' channeled through the Arch Nun. The level of severity is the will of God. And they shall never physically be the same AGAIN!
Kevin has finally made it over the fence tearing a large gash in his forearm.
Desperate and frightened he runs through some of the neighbor's yards. They stay inside, closing their curtains as he runs by.

He has gotten a head start over the Arch Nun. He's out of breath but knows he must push on. One more block and he's home free. Sister Navaeh returns the weapons to her bag and runs toward the fence. With a single leap she Performs a gymnastic like Parkour maneuver using the wall of the house as a catapult clearing the fence and landing smoothly on one knee.

She's no longer in the view of the security cameras. Ordering the Troopers to supervise securing the house and tending to the wounded. She fixes her habit and tightens her bag around her waist.

The neighbors Peak from behind curtains with their families as the Arch Nun continues to give orders to the Troopers. Then she starts running at an inhuman speed, passing through solid fences as if they weren't there.

Kevin is jogging slowly, breathing heavily, with his cell phone to his ear, getting directions to his cousin's location for pickup. He keeps looking back to ensure no one is pursuing him. As he turns his head once more, he can clearly see no one is behind him. Then Time slows and he can't believe his own eyes as Sister Navaeh appears behind him. Time resumes and compensates for her arrival. She's now running forty feet behind him matching pace.

"WHAT THE FU#K, Yo this bit#h just came outta nowhere!" He says to his cousins quickening his pace. "Yo, where Y'all at" He yells into his cell phone. Then he sees them just ahead waiting in a bright lime green colored Ford Mustang 5.0 convertible with the top down. Normally this would be a fast-enough getaway car but, the custom work done to it hinders its performance. The car's lifted suspension and twenty-two-inch wheels with extremely low-profile tires being its biggest problem.

Kevin starting to smile with confidence, knowing he's far enough away from the Arch Nun to make it to the car, looks down checking the cut on his arm. In doing so like the classic horror movies of the 70s and 80s he trips, falling to the ground and dropping his cell phone.

The phone lies on the pavement and his cousins can be heard through the speaker laughing because he fell. Reaches out to retrieve it he is amazed at what he sees. The phone leaps from the ground and flies into the hand of Sister Navaeh. She slows her pace to a fast walk as she puts the phone into her bag.

Sitting on the ground watching, Kevin knows he must get up. He's so out of breath he can hardly stand. Gathering his strength to jog, he cannot help but look back at her. She's still walking twenty feet or so behind him offering him a final chance to surrender. He makes it to the car, breathing heavily and suffering from exhaustion. The passenger jumps in to the back seat. Kevin is too tired to open the door he just falls over it into the front seat.

"Who the fu#k is that chasin you, Nig#er?" The driver asks.

"Jes Go Mo-Fu#ker-GO!" Kevin responds still trying to catch his breath.

"Oooooooh SH#T!" The man in the backseat screams. "That's a Motherfu#king ARCH NUN ain't it?"

Kevin quickly tells his cousins a lie to deceive them hoping they'll start shooting at her.

"Nuh that ain't no Arch Nun it's another gang dressed up like em tryin ta Rob us.

We fightin them bac at the house."

Upon hearing this the man in the backseat draws his weapon and starts firing at her. like everyone else in this gang he only had a few rounds and his weapon empties quickly. The bullets stop in mid-air just before hitting her, she passes through them then they fall to the ground.   The look of Terror falls upon his face as he realizes without a shadow of doubt this is truly an Arch Nun! He tries to warn the driver whom did not witness this, but Kevin is screaming. "GO NIG#ER GO!"

He tries once more to warn him but Kevin gives him a hard elbow to the face.

The driver steps on the gas and the large rear tires spin violently causing a lot of smoke and the smell of burning rubber. The Mustang pulls into traffic. The sound of screeching tires can be heard as several vehicles are forced to make an emergency stop. Emerging from the alley and camouflaged by the smoke. Sister Navaeh extends her left hand, Time slows, the vehicles that were forced to stop are unable to restart their engines. If dashcams were in use they too were interrupted. All vehicles behind them come to a slow controlled stop preventing anyone from getting hurt. This is the work of God!

All pedestrians immediately run for Cover assuming this is gang activity. The passengers of the vehicles trapped in the smoke can barely make out the image of what they recognize to be the distinct image of an Arch Nun, but are uncertain and cannot remove their eyes from it. The smoke is lingering in the air for a usually long time. This is the POWER of an Arch Nun!

The Mustang has made it down the street and around the corner. Sister Navaeh pulls the titanium frisbee from her bag and with a hard fling tosses it through the smoke in the direction the Mustang was traveling. The Frisbee exits the smoke. Sister Navaeh then draws her gun from her bag and fires one time, waits a few seconds then fires again, waits a few more seconds and fires a third time. To the motorists in their vehicles this looks like flashes of lightning within a cloud, but there is no sound.

 The first bullet strikes the edge of the Frisbee increasing its rotation. The second bullet ricochets off a telephone pole striking the Frisbee to change its course. With the Frisbee now pursuing the Mustang and losing speed, the third bullet ricochets off the same telephone pole striking the edge of the frisbee increasing its speed a hundredfold. All three bullets upon striking it disappear and Time resumes.

It passes the Mustang, tapping and bouncing off the windshield of a car traveling in the opposite direction. This alerts the driver, a teenager texting on their cell phone who looks up just in time to slow down before hitting a child that has wandered in to the street. The Frisbee flies toward a Twenty-four-foot truck tapping and bouncing off its windshield, this time alerting the drowsy driver falling asleep at the wheel, drifting out of his Lane into oncoming traffic. The frisbee is now directly behind the Mustang, the car's engine wasn't in the best condition. With the harsh acceleration it has blown a head gasket and is now beginning to overheat and omit a small cloud of smoke. The frisbee strikes the driver in the back of his head, he hits his forehead on the steering wheel and loses control of the car. He slams on the brakes but because of the cars ridiculously large Wheels and thin tires it veers sideways. The rubber grinds down to the rim. There's a lot more smoke from the damaged engine filling the air.

There weren't many pedestrians on either side of the street but those few quickly took cover.

Several city blocks away. The faint image of the Arch Nun can still be seen in the dissipating smoke. Before she and the Smoke are completely gone.

Many of the pedestrians and motorists make the sign of the cross and look to the sky clasping their hands as they be held this beautiful sight.

The Mustang continues to slide sideways within the thick smoke. The twenty-two-inch custom wheels easily break.

Time slows as the car starts to roll over, no one was wearing a seatbelt, Kevin and his two cousins are slowly tossed from the vehicle. The frisbee dangles between the three men as they slowly fly through the air.

They watch as the disc slowly flips between them, as though it were laughing.

"Whaaaaat-------Daaaaaa----Fuuuuuuu#k?"

The three slowly say to each other. Kevin recognizes it as the disc the Arch Nun used against him in battle. They can feel themselves moving slowly like they were dreaming. Then a woman's hand reaches through the smoke grabbing the frisbee. Time completely stops, Sister Navaeh stands before them holding the frisbee. Kevin Smiles certain of this being a dream, the driver joins him in his optimism. The man in the backseat bursts into tears. Sister Navaeh allows them to speak one at a time starting with Kevin.

"I don't know how you drugged us Bit#h, but this some Gooooood SH#T!"

He says enjoying what he believes to be weightlessness.

"Like so many You fail to recognize the Power of the Lord. Dismissing it as narcotics affecting your mind. Now you find yourself currently in the process of truly knowing, the Power of the Lord!" The smiles fade from their faces as they realize in their hearts that, God is God! And Kevin is no longer allowed to speak.

"I only wanted to talk with you Kevin." She says. "I brought two unarmed plain-clothes officers whom would have brought you to the truck for a discreet conversation, regarding an acquaintance of yours. I deliberately did not show myself, until your gang chose to attack the officers. Something you manipulated them into, as you did these two. It rests upon your head, ALL the irreparable physical damage done to them on this day. And for this you shall drink bitter Waters!"

Kevin's eyes begin to tear as does the driver's who is only twenty years old and has not yet committed any violent crimes, only car theft. She turns her attention to the man in the back seat, his name is Arthur Clark and he is not so innocent.

"Sister imma keep it one hundred percent real wit you. Arthur says crying but still trying to sound tough.

"I ain't gonna try ta lie or nuttin like that. Straight up I did some fu#ked- up sh#t ta people. All my life I did that. I had plenty opportunities ta change, but deep down I just ain't Wanna. I know now there truly is a God and he can see my entire life. I ain't gonna blame it on my mother and I ain't gonna blame it on my father for not being there, it was me an imma man up ta that! I know I may be crying but them tears of joy, cuz I'm finally dun! I'll take my punishment Like a man an ask for God's forgiveness after that. Wit that said sister, I'm ready ta face God and move on!"

The Arch Nun stairs at him but says nothing. He has made his peace and so she silences him. The driver shall remain nameless for he represents every teenager that happened to be in the wrong place at the wrong time, doing something they will regret. He will remember every second of this encounter with an Arch Nun and hopefully he will grow to respect the mercy of the Lord!

He is eager to speak but she does not allow it. For the company he has kept and allowing their influence to take precedence in his life. His Natural Instinct under the circumstances would be to lie. She's doing him a favor by not allowing him to speak. He is Young and unknowing to him he will be spared permanent harm, This Time!

She turns their attention to an opening in the smoke so they may see their fate.

All three will impact on the back of a parked garbage truck. At the rate of speed their bodies are traveling it will be a most unforgettable experience.

Arthur will strike the back wall of the truck's garbage chute. For all the people he's killed in his gang life, His neck and back will be broken, he will be paralyzed from the neck down and spend the rest of his life in jail. For he who was simply the driver. He will land on Arthur's body and the soft garbage. he will be knocked unconscious suffering only minor cuts and bruises.

As for Kevin the man who turned what would have been a simple conversation into an assault. Manipulating his friends and family into attacking two police officers and an Arch Nun, With the intent to kill. He will strike the iron rear bumper of the truck, head first, breaking his neck and suffering severe brain damage.

He Shall Walk, See, Speak or Move NO MORE! But he will hear everything and spend the rest of his life in jail, regretting the decisions he has made and to make peace with the Lord.

She looks upon them one last time blessing them and praying to the Lord to have mercy on their souls on their day of final judgment as she disappears time resumes sending the three to their fate.

Pedestrians run to assistance the three men and as the smoke lifts, they are horrified by the mangled bodies, all they can do is call 911.

Sister Navaeh transitions back to the alley and heads to the house, there's a lot of commotion. Her troopers are doing an excellent job of handling the aftermath.

As she enters the backyard all the police officers and paramedics disregard what they are doing to acknowledge her.

Trooper Friday informed them that she was the only one to enter the house, they were ordered to remain outside and how she effortlessly defeated the gang bangers in the front yard single-handedly, making no mention of the distinct high-tech weapons she used.

Everyone is Beyond impressed by the combat skills of this Arch Nun.   They congratulate and shake her hand on a job well done. She tells the Troopers to secure   the video surveillance of the backyard, No one is to view it. The FBI is in route and should be there shortly. The house is riddled with bullets, there's blood everywhere and of course the two severed female hands on the floor, not to mention the completely destroyed bedroom upstairs, with female urine on the floor. It appears to be a House of Horrors. But it is no different than the villages found in biblical times when the kings at the time were cruel and merciless. It looks like a war took place within these walls, but it was just one of God's true chosen, The Arch Nun Sister Navaeh, 'Heaven's Weapon'.

The FBI arrive on the scene and quickly take charge, the Troopers turn everything over to them.

A few of the FBI agents are acquaintances of Sister Navaeh. They were with her at the 'Pole Position' during the Samuel Jenkins case.

"Oh my god sister, it's so nice to see you again" The special agent in charge says giving her a big hug.

"Agent Hernandez, always a pleasure." Sister Navaeh respond as they hug. "I wish the circumstances were different, this is most unfortunate agent."

"Well Sister, when they decided to make it a gun fight between you and your guys, they got what they deserved besides-!"

"Now, now agent" Sister Navaeh interrupts shaking her finger at her. "All life is precious and a gift from the Lord and should be cherished and embraced as such. Many of these poor souls simply did not know any better. They are the product of generations whom simply had no knowledge of how to raise children."

"Ok, Ok Sister please don't get all religious on me."
Agent Hernandez asks holding Sister Nevaeh's shoulders and laughing.

"Alright agent, I'll let you off the hook this time. Now please excuse me so I may pray for those who have fallen in battle on this day."

"Of course Sister"

The Arch Nun kneels and closes her eyes in the center of the yard amongst all the commotion. But before she can pray, she is interrupted by one of the First Responders.

"Excuse me, sister"

She opens her eyes to see a young woman standing over her. "I'm very sorry to bother you. But I know you're about to pray for all the people in this house you had to hurt in self-defense."

The Arch Nun looks up at her and stands to look her in the eye. Crossing her arms behind her back Sister Navaeh continues to listen. This is normal posture for an Arch Nun but it can also be misunderstood and quite intimidating. Considering she was Disturbed from prayer. She looks directly into the Arch Nun's eyes and says.

"I am a True Believer in the All Mighty father and I believe in your mother's work as well and I would like to join you in prayer for these people."

Sister Navaeh is shocked, normally police officers and paramedics are nervous or 'Starstruck' treating them as celebrities.

"What is your name" Sister Navaeh asks softly, extending her hand.

"Madilynn my name is Madilynn" The woman replies as the two shake hands.

"Well Madilynn I would be honored if you joined me in prayer."

The women kneel to pray but before Navaeh can speak, Madilynn begins to pray aloud.

"Oh, heavenly father, we kneel before you with the humblest of hearts, On this day. Oh, Heavenly Father many of our young fell prey to the Wicked Ways of this world, too early in life. Their little feet were put upon the path of treachery, deceit and violence. By those who are angry and lost. So, we ask of you Oh Merciful father forgive those who were to teach them, those who were to love them and those who have forsaken them, raising them with very little morals and no confidence to Prevail in life. And most of all Oh Heavenly Father, I ask for you to keep this Woman who kneels with me strong and Brave, in that request I represent the voice of many who always will truly believe in you. Thank you Oh Heavenly Father Amen!"

"Amen" Sister Navaeh repeats, the two women stand and immediately Madilynn starts to walk away.

"Thank you for your concern and prayer." Sister Navaeh says to her.

Madilynn stops, turns and politely responds.

"It doesn't matter who says the prayer. It can be a bum on
the street, the Pope, Mother Hymiriam or an Arch Nun. The
only thing that matters is that someone cares enough to say
the prayer and it was heard by the Lord! Good day to you
Sister."
"Good day to you as well, Madilynn."
This woman was not seeking Glory or praise from the Arch
Nun. Nor was she overwhelmed, Starstruck or intimidated.
She too has witnessed unspeakable Acts by despicable
people but stays strong, this is something she does with the
'Power of Prayer'!
Agent Hernandez has made it to the upstairs bedroom.
Officers are taking pictures and enduring the foul stench.
"No one thought to open a window. Come on now, don't let
me do all the thinking for you."
Agent Hernandez screams.
The officers laugh as they open the window.
"Why is all the furniture broken, yet there's no damage to the
windows or walls?"
She asks.
"Your guess is as good as mine Special Agent. The gang had
no video surveillance in the house."
One of the officers responds.
"Okay I gotta get out of here, it stinks too bad I'll see you
downstairs gentlemen."
She goes downstairs and returns to the backyard.
The two Troopers and Sister Navaeh are engaged in
conversation.
"We have the videos sister, buy their encrypted."
Sergeant Friday tells her. Agent Hernandez walks over and
asks to see the media card containing the footage.
"My team can decrypt this in the van" She tells the Arch
Nun. "I'll let you know in a few minutes." As she walks away
the Troopers follow.
"Hold on gentlemen where do you think you're going? This
is Federal Business!"

She tells them with a condescending tone. She doesn't know they were handpicked by Sister Navaeh.

"Agent Hernandez these two were personally selected by me. They are granted temporary A.N.T status for the duration of the day. Any courtesies you could extend to them would be greatly appreciated."

"Well my apologies gentlemen. That's an extraordinary career jump, temporarily!"

The Troopers almost fell over with excitement not just a U.N.A bump but an A.N.T bump, WOW! The only thing that can make this day complete is a ride in a B.A.D. Agent Hernandez allows the troopers to accompany her to the FBI Mobile command center.

The gang's weak encryption is quickly broken. As agent Hernandez and the Troopers watch the video. They are absolutely stunned by the fighting Maneuvers and weapons of the Arch Nun. Sister Navaeh turns everything over to the FBI, she and the troopers are leaving. On their way to the truck the people on the street applauded and cheer. The Troopers feel greatly appreciated.

None of the gang was killed during this altercation with an Arch Nun. But all of them will never forget the day they encountered 'Heavens Weapon'!

Once inside the truck she tells them they are allowed to speak of what they have witnessed by order of Mother Teresa. But to show discretion when mentioning the weapons used. The Troopers can no longer contain their enthusiasm.

"Sister I just wanna take a minute ta say what an honor it was ta serve with you today!"

Sergeant Friday tells her.

"Yes sister, we can't thank you enough!" Trooper Henderson adds.

The men continue to express their gratitude all the way back to their headquarters. Sister Navaeh accompanies them inside where they are met with strong admiration.

She asks for everyone's attention for a moment.

"Troopers, may I have your attention please" She says raising her hands for everyone to settle down. "I would like to thank all of you on behalf of U.N.A.

I personally would like to thank Troopers Eddie Friday and Mark Henderson

for assuring my safety. I would also like to bestow the blessings of the Arch Nunnery."

The Troopers cheer, whistle and applaud as the Arch Nun exits the room to speak with the captain before Sergeant Friday drives her back to the FBI building.

The submarine transporting Giovanni Luciano has arrived at its destination in Egypt. Ka'ren requested he remain sedated for the trip. He is transported to an underground bunker where he is revived and detained in a small holding cell. No one is allowed to speak to him. Several hours pass without food or water. The cell door opens and in walks three large men, they are wearing plain Black jumpsuits with no symbols or markings of any kind. Mr. Luciano is beginning to think this is the U.N.A.

"I don't know how, but I guess you Fu#king guys finally caught me! Well take me ta Mother Teresa." He says throwing his hands in the air. There is an awkward silence for a moment before one of the men politely ask if he would accompany them. He's taken to a dining area where there is a feast Fit for A King. Still believing he's in U.N.A custody, he trusts the food and immediately begins eating.

"I would ask you guys ta join me but' forget about it, more for me."

The three men remain silent until Mr. Luciano has finished eating then he is asked to accompany them once more. He's now taken to a luxury Suite, so he may shower and shave. On the bed he notices a garment bag containing a suit.

"Great, I see you guys bought my tux, now get the fu#k outta here so I take a shower."

"We will return for you shortly Mr. Luciano"
Giovanni's first instinct is to look around for something to
use as a weapon, but he finds nothing. Him being Giovanni
Luciano welcomes the luxurious accommodations. Relaxing
in the jacuzzi with his head back and a warm towel over his
eyes. He is startled by several hard knocks on the door
before the three men enter the room.
"Mr. Luciano your host will see you now. Get dressed and
come with us please."
Mr. Luciano dries himself and walks over to the bed.
Unzipping the garment bag, he's pleasantly surprised to find
a TaylorMade black pinstripe suit, white shirt and a yellow
silk tie. This suit looks familiar he thinks to himself as he
flips the collar on the suit to find his embroidered initials.
Realizing this is not just mere clothing provided for him, but
it's from his private personal apparel collection made
exclusively for him by his Taylor.
He knows everything he owned was seized and confiscated
by the U.N.A so this further confirms his belief of being in
their custody. But why are they allowing him this privilege
he wonders.
"So you guys bought me one of my suits, over here, what
gives?" He asks.
"You're going to meet the president" One of the men
responds.
"All right, top of the world ma, I made it!" He says
sarcastically. wondering what the president wants with him.
They take him to an elevator that goes directly to a private
office.

The elevator doors open to reveal a large luxurious office with the curtains drawn.

"Wow, now this is snazzy!" Mr. Luciano says exiting the elevator.

"The president will be with you in a moment."

Looking around the room he comments on the decor.

"It doesn't shock me that the president's into all this ethnic crap."

Mr. Luciano knows he's not at the White House or the Oval Office but all-in-all he thinks to himself this is still a nice office. Three more men in Black jumpsuits enter the office accompanied by a well-dressed middle-aged man.

He sits behind the desk, two of the men take positions at both sides of the desk.

"Please, have a seat." He asks Mr. Luciano.

"No thanks, I'd rather stand, who the fu#k are you?" Mr. Luciano shouts.

"I am the President!" He responds with a slight accent.

"The president of what, a corporation or organization?"

The man begins to grin, slowly leaning forward in his chair.

"I am 'Kalmin Seth' The president of Egypt!"

The guards draw back the curtains to reveal the city of Giza and a breathtaking view of the pyramids in the distance.

"WHAT THE FU#K AM I DOING IN EGYPT?"

Mr. Luciano screams hysterically standing quickly throwing his hands in the air. One of the guards calms him and asks him to sit back down.

"Calm down, my friend you are safe here, of that you can be certain!"

Kalmin assures him.

"Oh that little mully bit#h" Mr. Luciano Whispers to himself referring to Ka'ren.

Now he finds himself in Egypt with president Kalmin Seth whom is really one of many powerful men the world over whose true names are 'Cane' Blood of her Blood Sons of Eve! And they are held very high in her favor.

Mr. Luciano realizes if he's in Egypt with the president than he is protected by him. So Kalmin Seth will get the utmost respect from him. This is a relationship Mr. Luciano feels he can benefit from.

"My apologies sir, this just knocked me off my ass for a minute."

He says wiping his forehead.

"You're the man in charge of this country, that's the way it should be. The United States can learn a thing or two from this setup. Besides anything, and I mean ANYTHING is better than being around that crazy bit#h Leggz FU#KING Diamond!"

Kalmin and his guards laugh. He explains to Giovanni how he and the organization he belongs to are very interested in partnering with him to unite the most dangerous street gangs in Asia, similar to what he and Samuel Jenkins accomplished with the 'Thrones of Chicago' and if everything works in Asia perhaps rekindling his Supremacy in Chicago.

Giovanni doesn't want Kalmin to see how excited he is. After all he doesn't want to seem too eager. He knew how powerful Samuel Jenkins was, he had a few Mayors and governors on his payroll. But Sammy never had a president with full Military Support on his side.

"I like everything you're saying, and you can count me all the way in, over here."

The two continue taking a little while longer after a while there's a knock at the door. Kalmin tells his guards to answer it. Mr. Luciano whom was sitting, enjoying a cigar and the conversation, suddenly becomes silent as Leggz enters the office.

"Well look who it is!"

Mr. Luciano says standing with a devilish grin.

"The pretty little badass, who got her ass handed to her by an Arch Nun. Looks like your face is healing up a little bit."

Ka'ren stops dead in her tracks. Mr. Luciano is hoping she

has the gall to attack him now. Without her Goons or Entourage, he thinks he'll beat the crap out of her. She does not turn her head but cuts her eyes at him. Kalmin comes from behind the desk extending his hand. She takes his hand, slightly lowers her head and puts it to her forehead.

"Greetings Oh mighty Ruler of Egypt"

Mr. Luciano begins slowly clapping his hands, pointing at her and laughing.

"That's what I'm talkin about. You bow that pretty a#s down to a man. I knew a man held your leash!" Before she can respond Kalmin stops her turning to Mr. Luciano.

"Be silent my friend, show some respect."

"Yeah, I'll show some respect all right, not for this one!" He shouts pointing at Ka'ren. "I want this one working for me!" He concludes throwing his cigar at her.

With lightning fast reflexes Kalmin catches it. "Stop this NOW!" He says extinguishing it in the ashtray on his desk. Leggz Gives Mr. Luciano the most wicked of stares, if looks could kill!

"That's part of the deal Mr. President this one's gotta work under me, I gotta be her BOSS!"

"Do you not think it's a little too soon to be making demands my friend after all you have done nothing for us yet!"

"I understand Paisan, I understand I don't mind proving myself a little bit as long as I know that's going to be the prize."

With hatred in his eyes Mr. Luciano replies rubbing his hands together looking at Ka'ren.

Kalmin turns to Ka'ren and thanks her for delivering Mr. Luciano to Egypt safely, kisses her on the cheek and tells her he'll see her tonight at the banquet. As she is walking away Giovanni Shouts.

"Hey! aren't you gonna bow to man's superiority before you leave? Pretty little girl."

Ka'ren stops in her tracks once again only this time she turns
to him. Giovanni begins to take off his suit jacket and loosen
his tie.

"You haven't slipped me any drugs this time baby, I assure
you we fight now I'm going to put you through the floor and
the president can buy another two bid arms dealer, I'm sure
your kind come a dime a dozen!"

Ka'ren smiles but says nothing. This agitates Mr. Luciano.

"The only reason I'm not coming over there and wiping that
smile off that pretty face is because I don't wanna mess up
the president's office, capiche?"

"The reason you're not getting UP! off the floor right now is
because I'm Wearing a designer 'ZsaZsa La'more outfit right
now, and these are 'Burgundy Bottom shoes!"

(referring to her high heels)

Unwilling to participate in lowering herself to Mr. Luciano's
level, she leaves the office.   Patting Mr. Luciano on the
shoulder, Kalmin tells him.

"As I was informed you are very amusing my friend, I very
much look forward to working with you."

Giovanni gives him a very serious look as he responds.

"Mr. President with all due respect. I'm a lot of things,
amusing ain't one of them. So, I'm gonna respectfully ask
you not to refer to me as such, Alright!"

"Of course my friend of course."

Mr. Luciano was so consumed by his contempt for Ka'ren
that he barely noticed how fast and accurate Kalmin's
reflexes are for a man of his age, when he caught the cigar.
President Kalmin Seth disguises Mr. Luciano as one of his
aides. Adorned in Egyptian attire he is able to accompany
the president and his staff at a few small functions.
Everywhere they go president Kalmin Seth is hailed and
loved. With the deal the president has offered him, eluding
apprehension and finding sanctuary in Egypt. Mr. Luciano
will never tell anyone, but just this once. He will consider
himself to be very LUCKY!

The early evening approaches and the president is hosting a charity event in a few hours. But first he and his party must return to his office for a quick meeting.

Now that Mr. Luciano has seen the power and Prestige of Kalmin Seth.

He is more than impressed with him. As they enter the office the president sits at his desk. Everyone sits, relaxes and enjoys a drink.

Mister Luciano is beginning to feel comfortable and cannot help but compliment the president.

"Mr. president. I gotta tell ya I just can't wait ta get started. Been thinking about a working title what do you think of 'The Royalty of Asia' or something like that? "

Mr. Luciano suggestion sipping on his drink.

"So tell me Mr. President what's next?"

"Well my friend the TRUE! Boss of EVERYTHING! wants to meet with you before and if we are to proceed. Many world leaders are under the influence of this person but alas many like your president Ophelia Winfrey are not, For Now!"

"Oh my God are you telling me there's one man with that much Fu#king power, I KNEW IT, I Fu#king knew it. I used ta tell Sammy this all the time."

Mr. Luciano was almost in tears he is so happy.

"And now I'm here with the president of Egypt about ta meet the worlds powerful MAN!"

One single knock on the door is heard. Everyone in the room except Mr. Luciano becomes quiet.

"The ruler of ALL! is here." Kalmin says.

One of the guards opens the door and immediately stands back. Mr. Luciano fixes his hair and straightens his tie. His Palms begin to perspire, he has never been this nervous or excited in his entire life. But to his surprise the only person to walk through the door is a woman in her mid-50s or so accompanied by a younger female.

All the guards immediately fall to their knees and bow their heads.

Mr. Luciano doesn't know what to think.

The older woman is far too elegant to be a servant. Maybe they're the wife and daughter of someone important coming to the meeting, he thinks. They walk to the center of the office and stop. The younger woman stands to the side as Kalmin rushes to the elegantly dressed woman, falls to his knees and bowels to her. A horrified look be falls Mr. Luciano's face.

"Nooooo, please dear God no! Mr. president are you telling me this old-"

Before Mr. Luciano can finish saying 'OLD BROAD'.

Kalmin quickly jumps to his feet and lifts Mr. Luciano off his feet with one hand.

Mr. Luciano was so shocked and disappointed he didn't notice how unnaturally strong Kalmin is.

"My friend your tongue will be the end of you!"

Kalmin shouts shaking Giovanni like a rag doll.

"I can tolerate you insulting my sister, but to my mother you will show nothing but respect. Do this again and I will kill you where you stand!"

Mr. Luciano doesn't want to mess up his deal with the president, for at this moment, he has nothing and it may be time he shows a little respect if he wants to regain his status in the crime world. But in his mind, there is still a man more powerful than the woman now sitting at the president's desk, so he'll go along and play their game for now.

"Whoa I'm so Fu#king sorry Mr. President please forgive me I meant no disrespect! If I had known this was your mother, I would be on one knee shaking her hand, please forgive me my friend, please."

He says shaking his clasped hands in front of him in a begging motion.

Kalmin doesn't answer, this worries Mr. Luciano. He lowers Giovanni to the floor and guides him to the front of the desk.

Unknowing to Mr. Luciano he is in the presence of Absolute, Undisputed POWER! For he now stands before God's First Female Eve!.

With cold piercing eyes she stares at Mr. Luciano, like he is nothing!

For reasons not even he can explain Giovanni begins to feel inferior as he stands begging for forgiveness from this woman.

Normally he would be sarcastic, disrespectful and obnoxious. But he knows gazing deep into the eyes of this woman, it would surely be the end of him.

Still she says nothing, sitting behind the president's desk with her hands in her lap.

Everyone in the room with the exception of Kalmin Seth remains still with their heads bowed. Giovanni nervously looks around.

At this point he's almost frightened. All day he accompanied the president of Egypt, he witnessed with his own eyes his power and prestige. He observed interactions with world leaders to which some he is familiar. On this day he felt as though he were walking with a god! Until he met his MOTHER!

She has not yet uttered a word. But there is no doubt in Giovanni Luciano's mind. This woman is not just a big deal, she is the biggest deal!

She sits poised keeping the room silent and under her control for another 5 minutes or so, almost daring Giovanni to say something disrespectful, he does not. She puts her right hand on the desk and taps her index finger once before returning it to her lap. Everyone raises their heads but stands still in their place. Kalmin now stands behind Mr. Luciano.

Giovanni doesn't want anyone to see him sweat or show fear but he knows not to turn around. Then in a very Ancient Egyptian dialect with her wickedly sinister but sexy voice she speaks to her son 'Cane'.

"Your sister is right my son, his sharp tongue will be the end of him!"

"I agree mother, I have no doubt it will. But first he will serve us well."

"See that he does my son, see that he does!"

Giovanni is beginning to worry, the fact that he cannot understand a word they're saying is making him very uncomfortable.

Eve gives Giovanni a final look before turning to her son and saying in English.

"I will allow this, make sure I am not disappointed!"

The sound of three soft knocks are heard at the door.

Giovanni turns his head to see. The guards open it, in walks Ka'ren the one and only person who can make Mr. Luciano lose control. But alas not this time, he has too much to gain by remaining calm.

If she insists upon pushing his buttons, he must ignore her. Be cool he tells himself be cool!

She's dressed in a long black form-fitting gown and matching heels, complimenting her million-dollar legs. She is breathtaking, as always. But Mr. Luciano looks away in disgust. It doesn't matter who she knows or how connected she is to political power. He's still going to have his way with her and kill her very slowly.

She walks by him without so much as a glance walking around the desk and kneeling beside her mother. And in the same Ancient Egyptian dialect greets her.

"Greetings Mother, I hope you are pleased?"

Eve responds in English for Mr. Luciano to understand.

"I am content for now, my daughter."

She then turns to Kalmin still speaking in English. So, Mr. Luciano can have no question as to who is truly in charge.

"Make preparations for your guest, Kalmin! Now remove him from my sight, my son"

"I obey, oh great one!"

Kalmin responds in English, then escorts Giovanni from the

room. Ka'ren stands, Eve does the same. She gives her
mother a warm hug and a kiss on the cheek and with a smile
asks her.
"Was he not the obnoxious piece of sh#t! I spoke of?"
"Indeed he is, Ka'ren."
"Mother if I may ask, on the day he outlives his usefulness. I
respectfully request the right to kill him at my leisure and
your command."
"Yes, my daughter when the time comes, do with him as you
please."
"On that day my rejoicing will be great. Thank you Oh great
one, thank you!"
Eve Smiles at her daughter.
"Till that day, then!"
Ka'ren's face lights up with joy.
"Till that day, Mother."
  In the hallway Kalmin turns Giovanni over to his guards.
They will take him to a privately owned Island where he'll
be in charge of starting the new Asian street gang unification
project.
Giovanni apologizes once more to the president. After what
he just witnessed, he doesn't want to have any bad blood
between them.
Kalmin assures him everything is fine, but to be sure, he
doesn't disobey, dishonor or disappoint his mother and
never question decisions made by this organization, Ever!
Mr. Luciano desperately wants his old life back so he agrees.
But he has something he is compelled to ask Kalmin.
"No disrespect but I just wanna kinda clarify a few things. I
won't be working for Leggz Diamond, will I?"
"No you'll have interactions and business dealings but you
will not be working directly under her."
"Great that's great news and how come I didn't get an
introduction to your mother my friend."
"My Mother didn't deem you worthy of an introduction that
is something you'll have to earn, and it will not be an easy

Road!"
"I can imagine buddy. So Leggz is your adopted sister huh? I mean there's quite an age difference and no resemblance at all?"
"No!" Kalmin answers sharply.
"She is my blood sister, you need not concern yourself any further, but know this. She is held high in mother's favor. You will do well to remember that!"
Giovanni definitely notices a difference in the tone of Kalmin's voice and the way he speaks to him now. But considering how he almost insulted his mother, he understands. As long as he doesn't have to work with or under Leggz Diamond.
But as soon as he rises to power in this organization. He's going to carry out his plans to kill her.
"Mr. President I don't get a welcome to the family handshake or anything?"
"Of course, where are my manners?"
As they shake hands. Kalmin looks Giovanni directly in the eyes and says to him.
"Welcome to the next level, Lucky Luciano!"
Then walks away. As much as Giovanni hates to be called lucky, for this opportunity and to get his life back, he'll let this one slide. "Yeah! thanks." He replies watching president Kalmin Seth Walk Away.
    A helicopter approaches a small island off the coast of China. It lands at a military base. Mr. Luciano exits the helicopter and is greeted by Li wei the commanding officer of the base. He speaks with a heavy Asian accent and is a little hard to understand.
"Giovanni Luciano, we have been expecting you. Please sir, come this way."
He takes Giovanni on a tour of the base which is heavily-armed, introducing him to the other commanding officers. They leave the base and take him to a large twenty room mansion near a waterfall. There are three beautiful young

women sun bathing in lounge chairs flirting with him. A beautiful exotic woman exits the house carrying a tray with a drink and a cigar. Above the front door in gold lettering are the initials G.L. He's then giving a tour of the house and introduced to his staff.

"I HAVE ARRIVED!" Mr. Luciano says taking a sip of his drink.

"Well sir I'll let you unwind and relax; you have a big day tomorrow. Your representative and the rest of your team will be here at 8 a.m." Li wei says.

"OK that's great, you gentlemen enjoy the rest of your day." And Giovanni Luciano did unwind and relax. He made sure the women of the house knew he was in charge and to serve him well. He relished the status bestowed upon him by this most powerful unnamed organization. Mr. Luciano would drop dead if he knew there was no Powerful organization, just EVE!

The next day he is awakened by what he considers to be his servant girls, serving him breakfast in bed and massaging his feet.

"Life is Fu#king GOOD!" He shouts happily. Eight military Humvees pull up to the house and Park. The time is 8 a.m. and Mr. Luciano is just getting out of bed. He intends hosting the meeting in his bathrobe and slippers. After all it is HIS house, they are HIS team and HE is in charge.

He enters the meeting room everyone is talking amongst themselves and getting settled Giovanni takes a seat at the head of the table.

"Good morning everyone I apologize for my tardiness and attire but it's been one of those nights. For those of you who don't know me, I am Giovanni Luciano."

He is very happy to see his team consists of all men. The female members of his staff are serving them drinks. The men introduce themselves to him one at a time. They are an assortment of Asian politicians, police commissioners and high-level gang bosses from various organizations. Another military vehicle approaches the house. A woman exits the vehicle and is escorted to the meeting. Everyone is familiar with her accept Giovanni Luciano. She walks over greets him in Italian and hands him a tablet.

"Hey! Thanks baby, that's refreshing your Italian I like that. You must be my personal secretary?" She smiles and instructs him to turn on the tablet. It's a video message from President Kalmin Seth.

"Giovanni, I trust you have settled in comfortably. You have a lot to do in a short time in which to do it. So, I will be brief. The house is your home, the island is your domain. everyone employed there works under you, for the duration of your service to this organization. Everyone except the woman that stands before you. She is your boss; she is the organization's representative in the outside world. For this Endeavour you are the brains she is the beauty, we are the muscle! This is non-negotiable. She has instructions to call me directly within the next five minutes upon your refusal. At which time we will sever our relations with you and re-evaluate your existence."

  Mr. Luciano is so angry he can barely move but he doesn't want anyone to notice he gently puts the tablet on the table. As the tablet touches the table it self-destructs.

He knows this organization is great and they have him right where they want him.

He absolutely cannot afford to turn this down. It may take him a little while longer to move up the ranks but he is determined to return to his status in the crime world. Giovanni stands as not to look up at her, blows her a kiss and says.

"Well! it looks like it's you and I against the world, baby." Making a catching motion as if to catch his kiss, she rubs it on her buttock. Insinuating he has just kissed her butt. Giovanni doesn't find this amusing at all. He sits back down with an attitude and puts his feet up on the table.

"I didn't catch your name sweetheart."

He says clipping the tip of his cigar. One of his servant girls quickly runs over to light it for him but she's stopped by the woman.

"I didn't throw it." She replies in a condescending tone looking down at him.

"But since you must know it's Alfozaliyah Capone!"

In Chile the weather is not good at all, they are preparing for a tsunami. President Winfrey has ordered an immediate extraction of Hymiriam and her disciples but she refuses to leave. The president has arranged and insisted she and her disciples be moved to the Renaissance Hotel in the city of Santiago. Once the president receives conformation of their arrival, she calls Mary on the satellite phone.

"Mary, if it's your craft you're worried about I will take care of it. I just need to pull you out of there, don't make me pull seniority. Girl please, let me get you out of there!"

The president begs speaking to Hymiriam on the satellite phone. Hymiriam is staying at the hotel provided for her by the president, some of her disciples are out amongst the people preparing for the storm.

"Ophelia my dear, dear friend. That flying Tin Can is the least of my concerns.

I am guided here by the hand of the Lord and it be the will of God that I help them. If I am to die then I shall die helping as many as I can."

The president covers the microphone of her phone with her hand and orders General Coleman to dispatch a team immediately to extract her.

"Marry you and I had many conversations regarding your leisure activities and Mission and I promised I would never pull rank on you unless I absolutely felt I have to...But!"

The president is beginning to get a little emotional. She feels this is her fault for tampering with Hymiriam's craft and she wouldn't be in Chile if she had just waited a little while longer. She loves Hymiriam very much! And it is no secret Ophelia Winfrey loves everyone.

When her close friends and family talked her into running for the presidency, she was more than a little reluctant, because she was and still is one of the most beloved people in the world! But not even she was prepared for what's shaping up to look like the Second Coming of Christ.

It is only natural to be uncertain and to question yourself. Not just the United States stands behind president Winfrey a large percentage of the world does as well.

"But What, dear friend of mine. What weighs so heavy upon your heart?" Mary asks.

The president waves her hand repeatedly for everyone to clear the Oval Office. They can't leave fast enough as she continues waving her hand at them. Once she is alone, she continues talking to Hymiriam. "I'm sorry girl, I had to clear my office."

And clear it she did so she may have privacy for the content of this conversation.

"I was going to say, Mary you know your nunneries right-to-die hasn't felt right to me and frankly I doubt it ever will! I know you feel that you and your nunnery are closer to God than most. But Mary please, please don't stay there. Look I'm gonna tell you something girl, that's very important something the government of that country isn't letting everyone know the tsunami is said to be the worst on record!"

The president hesitates for a moment holding back her tears and sniffling.

"Just let me get you out of there. I'll take as many as we can, but let me get you guys out of there, please!" There is a brief silence.

"Remember Ophelia tomorrow is not promised to any of us. It's what you do and how you can help someone today that matters."

President Winfrey takes a deep breath knowing she can't convince her o leave and replies "Oooh kay Mary, you're absolutely right."

Wiping the tears from her eyes and changing to a more authoritative tone.

"I'll respect the fact that you feel you must do what you have to do, because I know you respect the things I must do. Be safe out there."

"Uh, thank you, I think" Hymiriam replies curiously. She knows the president is telling her what she wants to hear but is going to extract her anyway as soon as she gets off the phone. President Winfrey gave Secret orders to General Coleman to bring her and her disciples home unharmed at all costs and by any means necessary. Hymiriam doesn't want to frighten every one because weather reports are often exaggerated so, she tells the two remaining disciples by her side to accompany her outside.

"Outside whatever for Mary?" They ask.

"If I am to die! it will not be hidden away in a hotel room. It will be outside amongst the people with the wind upon my face helping anyone I can. I ask of you to accompany me and trust in the Lord."

The weather outside is rapidly getting worse. Several Hard knocks are heard at the door. When Hymiriam checked into the hotel it caused quite the Commotion, under the circumstances there was no time for discussion, everyone knows she's there. Her disciples open the door. The hallway is filled with True Believers and followers.

"It's the people, Mary" Her disciples tell her. "They wish to be with you and pray."

"Of course." She replies. "All may enter who love and believe in the Lord."

But Hymiriam spoke before truly seeing how many people are in the hallway. Her disciples let a few in and they quickly run to her.

"Everyone stop! please." The disciples asked of everyone, explaining there is simply not enough space for everyone to enter.

"Hold on everyone? please hold on, settle down please!" Hymiriam bags of them, they quickly comply. "My disciples and I were just on the way outside to help in any way we can. will you join me?" Everyone anxiously agrees.

"Lead the way, Hymiriam, Lead the way." A man in the crowd shouts.

Putting her hands on her hips and tilting her head to one side she replies Jestingly.

"Because you guys don't know how to get outside on your own!"

With laughter and song they exit the hotel room with hope and to bravely help as many of their neighbors as they can. Meanwhile the news media has not wasted any time in letting the world know she is here. Many are abandoning their homes, gathering their families and loved ones risking their lives, in hope of being near Hymiriam, if this should be their End.

The president wishes she could deploy Arch Nuns to retrieve their mother.

But this contradicts their mothers right to die. The president wants to demand this of Mother Teresa and face the repercussions later, if only it were that simple, she would order Mother Teresa to send her Grandsons Zachariah and Joshua to ready their A.N.Ts and prepare their B.A.D's for departure. But she'll settle for a covert mission and she's sure General Coleman will succeed.

 Outside the Wind is getting stronger and the rain is getting heavier. The city has lost most of its power and the hotel elevators are inoperative. In the lobby loud singing and laughter can be heard in the stairwells. The hotel staff is advising everyone to stay in the stairwells the winds have picked up and are uprooting trees and flinging Automobiles and debris through the air. A large crash is heard as the windows in the lobby are shattered, it's a good thing the staff were lured to the stairwells by the singing.

This was the work of the Lord. They were saved seconds before the inside of the lobby is completely destroyed. But heavy rain and wind continued for twenty minutes before calming down. It seemed as though the storm was over, but the worst was yet to come. The sound of the emergency weather Sirens begins. Everyone starts to panic in the stairwell.

"We must go back to our rooms and seek shelter!"
A woman screams hysterically holding her child.
"No! this is the safest place to be we're all safe here."
A member of the hotel staff screams over the loud talking and confusion.
"Everyone please listen to me, listen to me NOW!" A man screams.
"I work for the government I was sent here with a small group to provide secret security for Hymiriam. I'm going to share something with you that would otherwise get me fired or killed. The tsunami is said to be the Strongest ever recorded, more so than they are telling the public this is a MEGA TSUNAMI!"
He definitely has everyone's attention now Hymiriam's included.
"I say this because if I'm going to die with you, I don't want to lie to you or Hymiriam. This Mega tsunami could possibly destroy most of our country!"
The people begin to talk softly amongst themselves in fear. Hymiriam asks her disciples to help get everyone to the roof while the weather is somewhat calm. Maybe some of the helicopters can take the women and children. If only her craft where operational, she would call it in. They do as she asks quickly telling the people closest to them to go. Everyone notices them going up stairs and start to follow.
"Hymiriam is going to the roof!" Some yell so others can hear. The Secret Security trapped at the bottom of the stairs struggle and push their way through everyone attempting to reach her so they can prevent this. They believe someone would try to kill her and it would be a perfect time to do so. The door to the roof is locked, several large men force it open. The emergency Sirens can be heard throughout the entire city. The news media seize the opportunity to take video footage of the situation, reporting it to the world. Of course, many of the cameras are focused on the hotel Hymiriam is staying.

As the people rush onto the roof. Hymiriam asks them to try and remain calm. It's early evening and the sky is starting to darken. The cameras focus on the large group of people on the roof.

"There's a large group of people entering a rooftop." One of the helicopters reports. As they zoom in, they notice Hymiriam is among them. This is being broadcasted live and when the people of Chile saw Hymiriam on the roof, they too sought Higher Ground, seeking refuge on any rooftop they could find. Hymiriam's satellite phone has lost power and she can't call for help. The wind is getting stronger and the helicopters would crash.

President Winfrey realizes as she and her cabinet watch from the Oval Office this may be the end of Hymiriam! The short time she has been working with the governments of the world she has contributed so very much to humanity. World leaders from many countries are calling president Winfrey to offer their assistance in any way they can. They have put aside their grievances for the moment to focus on Hymiriam's rescue.

President Winfrey and president Andrei are relieved, they welcome the assistance from the world leaders. Because they know unlike the United States and Russia, they may NOT honor her right to die! Something president Winfrey is hoping on.

Hymiriam is unaware of president Winfrey allowing the coordinating of her rescue through other countries and making her a high-level priority. Something she would have definitely not approved of. But president Winfrey is of course a U.S. President and one way or another they find a way to pull rank. The world leaders are frantically attempting to coordinate their military forces, something that has never been done before. Mother Teresa enters the Oval Office. With the Arch Nuns having the right to die world leaders know they are never to be disturbed or interrupted during what maybe their final hours. It is the

Arch Nun's right, so they may commune with God and prepare themselves for the Everlasting.

Unfortunately, more than half of the world leaders participating in the rescue are only pretending to be concerned. Putting on a performance before the world to show a sign of good faith. But in reality, they could care less if she lives or dies, they'll finally be rid of her and what they believe to be her staged religious trickery!

These are the countries under the influence of Eve! Whom Watches from her Villa in Egypt enjoying a glass of white wine with a smug smile on her face. Keeping her promise not to harm Hymiriam, she finds it satisfying that she will die in a natural disaster. 'After all it serves her right trekking all over the globe helping this pestilence known as Humanity!

Hymiriam told her ten children at the beginning that her time on Earth may not be as long as theirs. This weighs heavily on the minds and hearts of her children. But wherever they are and whatever they are doing they know they must remain focused on their tasks at hand, For God's Great Purpose!

The people gather around Hymiriam in silence. Many of the women and children are crying, making their peace with God! Yet there are those among them who still do not believe. But they remain silent for they are few.

"I want to thank everyone for believing and loving me as you do the Lord."

Hymiriam shouts trying to speak over the sounds of the bad weather and sirens.

"We love you Hymiriam!" A man shouts to her.

"We'll follow you anywhere Hymiriam!"

A woman adds cradling her small child. When a man standing next to her leans over and Whispers.

"Speak for yourself, we're standing on a roof with her if she jumps, I'm not following."

"Shut up! poopy head." The child screams attempting to kick

him. The winds are getting stronger. Helicopters along the shoreline are recording a panoramic view of the devastation when suddenly the shoreline starts to recede, creating the largest tidal wave the world has seen in a while. Many are predicting the complete destruction of several cities. The approaching wave can be seen for miles. President Winfrey watches in horror struggling to hold back her tears. Many the world over want to turn off their televisions, but they cannot, all they can do is pray as hard as they can hoping she survives. Mother Teresa takes hold of Ophelia's hand. She looks into the Reverend mother's eyes. To spite the tough Persona, she portrays. President Winfrey sees the tears of a concerned mother trying to hold it together.

"Mother Teresa I wish there was a way we could have broken the Arch nunnery rules."

With tears running down her face the Reverend mother responds.

"My dear I am not unaware of your coordinating rescue efforts with the world leaders. But that will be our little secret." She says with a smile and a friendly wink.

"Deep down, I was praying for your success. She and everyone there are in the Lord's hands now." She concludes hugging the president, patting her on the back as the two women slowly rock back and forth. All rescue efforts are aborted, all anyone can do now is watch the destruction. Hymiriam is facing the people, the massive wave is behind her in the distance rapidly approaching. Those who do not believe can hold their silence no more.

"Hymiriam you were a fraud from the beginning sent by the government to deceive us."

A woman yells at her.

"Yeah! look around you these innocent children are gonna die and there's nothing you can do about it!" Screams another. A few more in the crowd are starting to join them. "Hymiriam Christ, my foot it's more like Hymiriam-don't look twice!"

A man yells laughing. Some join him in his laughter but it quickly quiets down as the Mega wave gets closer.

"Don't listen ta them Hymiriam!" A child yells, crying. Suddenly the ridicule and speculation turn to Fear. The Mega wave is but a few minutes away from the beach and has grown in size.

Hymiriam turns to face the wave. The Long-range news cameras on board the helicopters are having a hard time focusing due to the harsh weather. But they remain fixed on the Mega wave and Hymiriam.

Everyone around her with a cell phone is recording her. She falls to her knees. The people closest to her lay hands on her for emotional support. She bows her head, the clouds part and a small ray of light falls down upon her head, she looks up to the sky and begins to pray aloud.

"Oh Lord thy God, I pray to thee. Have mercy on those who do not believe. Grant them the serenity to behold thy love and to know there is no other, before you! Let them on this day know

YOU ARE, I AM, THIS IS-THE POWER OF GOD!"

And Hymiriam stood with her arms held high and wide. As a Mighty Wind swept through the city and the ground shook as an earthquake began and along the entire shoreline of the country the Earth opened consuming the large Mega Wave.   The people around her cannot believe their eyes. The people of the world are in Shock. President Winfrey's legs are so weak she falls backward into her chair, Mother Teresa attempts to hold her but she cannot as she stumbles forward, almost into the president's lap. For this is amazing even to her. President Andrei immediately calls the United States but cannot get through the phone lines are jammed, all cell phone towers are overwhelmed and beginning to overload. With all the governments communicating over their radios those signals are beginning to be affected as well. The world government quickly coordinate a systematic shutdown too slow all

Communications traffic. Fox, CNN, world news and every International news service. Urge everyone of an imminent shutdown of all non-essential communication Services if people do not refrain from calling their loved ones.

CNN is still on the scene filming everything! There is so much commotion between the rescue efforts and what the world is hailing as the GREATEST Miracle of Hymiriam Christ!

President Winfrey is still feeling a little faint, Mother Teresa is kneeling beside her tending to her. Everyone in the Oval Office rushes over to assist.

"It's okay everybody, I'm fine, I'm fine!" She tells them, standing and fixing her hair.

"Madam president, Russia's on the line. They say it's urgent."

"Thank you, I'm sure it is but right now nothing is more important than this! Tell him I'll get back to him I'm sure under the circumstances they'll understand!"

Continuing to fix her hair she pulls Mother Teresa to the side and Whispers in her ear.

"In my entire life, I've never been as confused and conflicted as I am now, please! Mother Teresa, I'm begging you. Tell me what's going on, what did I just see?"

The Reverend mother wipes a tear from the president's face and explains.

"My child you once told me you had a very dear friend named Maya and she told you before she passed away. That one day you would witness something so great that it could not be explained away or dismissed as an illusion. That you and the entire world would witness this. You told me she said to you, on that day follow your heart and what you truly believe and on that day you will truly know peace."

Mother Teresa pauses for a moment helping the president fix her hair.

"When you told me that I neglected to tell you based on the picture of her you've shown me. I believe I met her thirty years or so ago, on my many travels when Hymiriam was a little girl, Mary was fond of her poetry and Miss Angelo was quite kind to her. Remember Ophelia the Lord brings special people together, if only just for a moment. I cannot tell you or explain to you what you have seen, that is for you to determine, my child."

President Winfrey takes hold of Mother Teresa's hands gently holding them.

"Thank you Mother Teresa, thank you very much. Would you do me a great favor?"

"Of course Madam president, of course."

"I'm not asking you to this as the President of the United States I'm asking you this as Ophelia Winfrey."

The Reverend mother can sense the sincerity in her voice.

"On the day, the hour, the very minute I am no longer president. May we continue this conversation?"

"When you are no longer president within the hour we shall speak!"

"Thank you, thank you Mother Teresa."

The Reverend mother gives her a friendly smile and a piece of good advice.

"Now go forth my child and be conflicted no more, Hallowed be thy NAME!"

In Egypt Still watching in amazement. Eve Instructs some of the countries under her influence to assist Chile in every way and to contribute generously to the relief fund.

Eve has bared witness to many miracles of the Lord since the beginning of creation. She knows the Lord parted the Red Sea for Moses, Destroyed the walls of Jericho for Joshua and has now opened the Earth itself for Mary, mother of Jesus! Not that Eve has ever forgotten the power of the Lord! Hymiriam has come forth to rekindle her fear of it. But Eve feels she too has a special relationship with the Lord, this compels her to continue her endeavor and to increase her efforts a thousandfold!

On the ground in Chile the people are starting to leave their homes. Many have lost power; with no televisions or Internet they were unable to watch the miracle of the Lord. The sky is beginning to fill with helicopters from the military, news media and First Responders. There were a few casualties due to panic and crimes in the street. Every government involved in the rescue efforts are ordered to make Hymiriam a priority. She and those with her are still on the rooftop of the hotel.

Several helicopters representing numerous governments surround the Rooftop securing the area for the First Responders. Military forces lower themselves to the roof from the helicopters. The news media helicopters are not far away, they are told to hold their position. Now that the weather has calmed down, they are able to maintain camera focus on the rooftop. This is now broadcasting on every channel in the world not just the prime Networks. Word is quickly spreading through the streets of the city for those without electricity, cell phones or Internet.

They sing, they Rejoice they dance chanting. "HYMIRIAM IS CHRIST, HYMIRIAM IS CHRIST!"

In every corner of the world this is broadcasting, and the world is finally listening!

The toughest of the tough, the bravest of the brave shed tears of joy for they too rejoice and are not ashamed to do so.

 At Langley Air Force Base where the Cured still temporarily reside the cheers are ear-shattering.

General Coleman's team are the first to reach Hymiriam. She and the others are asked to remain on the roof while the joint military forces clear the building and assure there are no possible threats from the approaching crowds. Hymiriam refuses insisting upon going down to meet the approaching crowds. General Coleman orders them to comply and stay close to her.

The military cleared what debris in the lobby they could, then begin to exit the building first to meet the crowd but were stopped by Hymiriam.

"Gentlemen please, I doubt they have come to do me harm" She says to the commanding officer, gently putting her right hand on his shoulder. Looking into her eyes the soldier knows in his heart she will be safe.

Removing her hand from his shoulder he gently kisses it and holds it to his heart.

"Thank God for you, ma'am I thank God! you're here. I'll be by your side the whole time you're out there ma'am."

The commanding officer like most men are taller than her. Looking up at him she touches his face with her left hand, holding her hand to his face he bows his head and closes his eyes. Again, the people with her take pictures and video with their cell phones of everything they can.

These are the pictures the news media will not have access to and some hope to profit from them.

"Open your eyes, my child" Hymiriam tells him. "I have my disciples and the people at my side. I prefer not to be seen with anyone bearing arms."

Without hesitation the commanding officer immediately removes all of his weapons, helmet and body armor and gives them to his troops.

Hymiriam looks at him with her million-dollar smile asking. "May I know your name, sir?"

"Cody, ma'am my name is Cody and it is a great honor today to be by your side ma'am."

The people chuckle at how excited and anxious he is. His men Pat him on the back and join in the laughter.

"Well Cody, it is an honor to know you, you do realize this may get you in a bit of hot water with President Winfrey?"

"Ma'am I love my country, my flag and my president God knows I do. But today I want the Lord to know I love him more. And if that mob gets hostile ma'am, I'll fight them to the death with my bare hands to save his humble servant

'Hymiriam Christ' and proudly die a U.S Marine!"
"Hoorah" his men quickly and collectively yell there's even an applause from the people.
"As much as I love you Sarge you're gonna have ta face the heat from the president alone on this one, buddy!" One of his soldiers says patting him on the back.
Her disciples exit the building first, with her hair a mess and her clothes drenched. Hymiriam quickly follows. The crowd quickly rushes to her cheering and applauding. This makes Cody nervous as people reach over and around him to touch her. Her disciples ask that they step back to give her room so she may breathe and to be respectful. The crowd is massive but they slowly urge everyone to move back. With a reasonable amount of room around her and the news media filming from the air. Fox News and CNN are now on the ground standing with the crowd. The noise is so great it is impossible for the news reporter's commentary.
Hymiriam patiently waits for everyone to be quiet. Her disciples ask for their silence. It takes a few minutes for this request to circulate through the large crowd. They are expecting a long speech or prayer.
 The media want so badly to offer her a microphone but they know it is forbidden.
She bows her head briefly, says a quick silent prayer then gives her disciples instructions on what to do and to ask the news media to make this special request for her through their loudspeakers for all to hear. When the disciples deliver Hymiriam's request to the news reporters from Fox News and CNN There is a brief moment of arguing between them as to who will make the announcement, who will give the crowd this important request from Hymiriam Christ.
Cody suggests a coin toss the two parties agree, CNN wins the coin toss, but Fox news feels they were cheated somehow. Hymiriam notices this Petty bickering as does some of the crowd, recording them with their cell phones. Hymiriam walks over and politely asks each one for a

microphone, holding a CNN mic in one hand and a Fox
News mic in the other.

Both parties smile knowing both media companies will be
properly represented and they will look good in the eyes of
their bosses. She looks at the reporters, they all give her a
thumbs up, then she removes the logos from both
microphones, their smiles slowly fade.

"Is this thing on? testing 1 2 3 testing."

She says tapping the microphones one at a time.

She's going to speak into both. There's a piercing sound of
audio feedback confirming the microphones are on,
everyone holds their ears for a second.

"Oops my apologies everyone."

There's a brief moment of laughter.

"There will be no speech nor prayer at this time, for time is
of the essence.

There are still a lot of people out there that need help. I will
not stand here while others are in peril. I am going out there
and I am going to help as many as I physically can. I ask that
you help thy Neighbors. Do not do it for me or because there
are television cameras. Do it because it is the right thing to
do. I personally will reserve my rejoicing and go forth with
prayer and the strength of the Lord, God will guide you to
those in need, spread out and help anyone you can!"

   And with joy in their hearts the crowd did spread out
helping everyone they could. Hymiriam asked that the news
crews do not follow her, because it is not about her, but to
follow the people and to show the world how they have
come together.

And she who is now recognized as Christ! Dug through the
rubble with her bare hands assisting those in need.

   News reporters and cameramen joined in the efforts. The
military protected the streets from looters and those seeking
to do others harm, but they were few so the military assisted
in any way they could. If ever there was a day of Stillness,
this was that day!

One hour later all over the world in every major city, the people flocked to the streets. They danced, they cheered, they sung but most importantly they embraced each other, hugging and sharing tears. For this moment in New York City there were no ethnic barriers. Just people finally noticing each other. This has never been seen in modern times, and this was going on all over the world. President Winfrey has finally gotten herself together. Ordering the Secretary of Defense to make sure the rejoicing remains peaceful.

"I suggest we shut it down Madam president."

"That won't be necessary Mr. secretary, also any law enforcement agencies or military personnel displaying acts of aggression, I want you to bring their names to Mother Teresa and I personally!"

"I sure will Madam president, but between you and I, I have a good feeling about this!"

"So do I Mr. Secretary, so do I, carry on."

President Winfrey concludes winking her eye at Mother Teresa.

In Egypt the people also celebrate this miracle. Eve relaxes in her throne like lounge chair. Of all the things Mary has done in the world so far, she knows this cannot be dismissed as a simple hoax. Nor will she dare to call the power of the Lord 'Trickery'! On this day.

She puts her cocktail on the table beside her and picks up her tablet. These are her personal tablets they cannot be traced and self-destruct after use. She summons four of the world leaders under her influence. Two whom she calls Cain and two whom she calls Abel. Whenever she summons any of her sons that bare these names it is most certainly Paramount. She then summoned her daughter Aston vetta whom is visiting her at the Villa.

Aston enters the large balcony and kneels beside her mother. Speaking in their personal ancient Egyptian tongue Aston asks. "What is thy bidding? Oh, Great one!"

With the news of the miracle of the Lord still playing on the monitors around her. She gives her daughter these instructions.

"Increase the 'Forwaca' project Ten-fold worldwide, for now then accompany your brother and I shall see you on Mount Sinai."

Waving her hand to dismiss her daughter she stands, as Aston leaves the balcony. Eve with a smile, raises her glass to toast the Great miracle of the Lord!

Aston wonders why her mother decided to increase something she cut in half decades ago. But to summon Two 'Canes' and Two Abels changes everything. She calls for her personal assistants

Three male one female who are also Eve's children but under her command.

"With all this going on, Mother's anger must be GREAT?" One of the male assistants says.

"Surprisingly No!" Aston answers. "She is after all a firm believer in the Lord, being here since the beginning. Perhaps this Hymiriam thing reminds her of simpler times."

Aston gives them a few more minutes for their Pleasant conversation before continuing the business at hand.

"I do have a bit of good news from mother."

"What is it Aston, good news from mother, that's very rare these days what is it."

The female assistant anxiously asks.

"Well, she's increasing the funding and efforts to the 'Forwaca' project."

The assistants are very excited to hear that. The Forwaca project is Eve's fabricated word pronounced (for-way-ca) Recognized to the world as 4W.A.C.A meaning (For- Women- And- Children- Always.) A nonprofit organization funded by anonymous donations from wealthy corporations Worldwide, all of which are controlled by Eve.

The 4W.A.C.A organization shelters women and children who are victims of human trafficking and other unspeakable atrocities. This is one of the many things unknown to Hymiriam and Mother Teresa about Eve.

"Oh my god I'm so glad to hear this, Aston." One of the assistants' shouts. Approximately 80% of Eve's children love and support this project. It is one of the most recognized charity organizations in the world.

"This made my day; I'm so glad mother is in a happy mood." Adds another.

Ok, ok everyone!" Aston says raising her hand for them to settle down.

"I to share in your Enthusiasm. But I suggest you hurry with this assignment. You know how short-lived mother's happiness and good moods can be!"

They all agree. Aston gives them final instructions and dismisses them, then calls Ka'ren informing her of their mother's good spirit and to make arrangements with Benjamin in Singapore to prepare a very large shipment of women and children only. Also, to tell him the destination is London for the usual business. But their true destination will be the United States, there they will be fed, clothed, sheltered and educated. Holmes and citizenship will also be provided for a better life. A rare gift from God's First Female.

Ka'ren calls ZsaZsa asking for assistants she's still healing and doesn't want to tell her sister what happened during the fight against the Arch Nun.

"Hey girl, it's good mom amped up the Forwaca project." Ka'ren says.

"Yes, it is, that's Splendid news I've always been rather fond of the Forwaca project. That should keep you busy for a little while, little sister."

"Yeah sis that's why I'm calling, I have something to ask of you."

"Of course what is it."

"Can you supervise a shipment from Singapore for me before mother changes her mind, I gotta kind of take care of something."

ZsaZsa is happy to fill in for her sister. It gives her the opportunity to intimidate and Bully people. She enjoys doing this as International Fashion mogul ZsaZsa La'more but as Madame Butterfly she can do it violently!

Appreciative of her sisters help Ka'ren calls Benjamin giving him distinct instructions to exclude women with infants they are too unpredictable and cannot be kept quiet! This endeavor will require a high level of discretion.

"Will you be coming to Singapore to oversee this?" Benjamin asks.

"No not this time, baby"

"Dam! I was hoping ta see you."

"Well look at you Benny, Pushing up on me like That. Now that you're a big Boss. Be careful who you fall in love with BABY, you can't handle This!"

"Girl Ya know I fell for you the first time I saw you."

"I bet you say that Sh#t ta all the big booty bit#hes."

"Nah, it ain't like That."

"Okay baby, enough phone flirting. Get your hand out of your pants and pay attention. This little Mission comes from the top, make sure it goes smoothly. The butterfly will be there in my place."

Benjamin squeezes his eyes shut, shaking his head no and clenches his fist tightly in contempt,

just hearing the name Madame Butterfly.

He doesn't mind the way Leggz treats him because he has a crush on her but he absolutely loathes her sister Madame Butterfly and he's terrified of her.

Mother Teresa has authorized a few days off for her granddaughters. Next month Josh and Zac will have theirs. During this time, they are allowed to be themselves, using their alternative identities and the Grace of God to prevent being recognized.

It's been 48 hours since the miracle in Chile and the world is still celebrating.

Hymiriam has chosen to remain in the country for a little while longer helping the people. She is on the cover of every major magazine throughout the world. The news networks have pulled together and publicly offered her the sum of one billion dollars, if she would just do one television interview.
 They hoped by putting her on the spot publicly she would agree. But she turned the tables on them publicly stating if they have such Leisure Capital to donate it to children's charity organizations around the world. They gracefully, discreetly and quickly retracted their offer.

President's Winfrey and Andrei are again being praised in the spotlight. There's even talk
for the first time in history which would allow them to remain in their current positions for the next ten years, but that is just talk.

Both presidents are planning a large Gala and fundraiser for the country of Chile. This will be held in the United States and some of the most important people in the world will be in attendance. Some of which include the Pope himself and surprisingly ZsaZsa La'more to name a few. Eve Saint Adams will make a very rare appearance, not for the country of Chile but to honor the miracle of the Lord. She of course will be well hidden among ZsaZsa's Entourage of high-level fashion designers and very, very, very WELL protected!

She and the pope will be the only ones that know this was TRULY a miracle of God!

On the dock in Singapore Benjamin's crew oversee the loading of containers housing women and children. Benjamin inspects all the containers to assure they are properly ventilated and has provided battery operated fans. Yet he is still nervous. He doesn't want to end up like Giovanni Luciano and be number two on the U.N.A's most wanted list.

All of the women have small to mid-sized bags containing personal hygiene products, snacks, toys and clothing.

"Y'all stay sharp, check all these bit#hes out, make sure they got enough food and no kids under ten years old."

He tells his crew over the walkie-talkie. But two of his guys are busy on their cell phones not paying attention as one of the women carrying a large duffle bag with ventilation holes cut into the bottom smuggles a sleeping six-month-old infant into the container. The cargo ship is owned by one of Eve's children, all the fraudulent paperwork for the containers has been taken care of. However, creating so many false identities and Social Security numbers will take a bit more time and should be ready by the time they reach the United States.

Everyone on the dock is on Benjamin's payroll. Although the women and children are being taken to a better life. They must be transported illegally due to the extensive time-consuming paperwork and sometimes human trafficking requires operating within a certain window of time. Not to mention Eve's mood can change like the wind!

Benjamin stands with his bodyguards beside him, leaning on his Bentley, giving orders to his crew. He even has a couple of helicopters watching from the sky. A little added protection from his friend Leggz Diamond. Then a caravan consisting of two SUVs in the front one limousine in the center and two more SUVs at the rear enter the dock. Since the helicopters didn't blow them to smithereens. Benjamin gets a weird feeling in the pit of his stomach. He knows Madame Butterfly has arrived.

The chauffeur opens the door two women exit the Limo the first is the personal assistant, a tall gorgeous Italian supermodel carrying a briefcase she is the type of woman men dream of.

The second is Benjamin's nightmare as she exits the vehicle the wind catches her clothing, she's covered from head to toe similar to Arabic female attire and sporting a very

fashionable pair of sunglasses. Striking a Tee stand pose, she
waits a moment for her bodyguards to join her.
Benjamin reminds his boys again not to stare, giggle, make
eye contact or show any signs of disrespect, It can be fatal!
Fortunately for Benjamin he will not have to repeat himself
because these boys have seen her in action!
The personal assistant leads the way followed by Madame
Butterfly then four
Well-groomed male bodyguards. As they approach
Benjamin and his boys stand up straight. Her assistant steps
to one side and Madame Butterfly gives him a little hug.
Benny and his boys are shocked! What's going on he thinks
to himself, first Leggz is flirtatious on the phone with him,
now the meanest lady he's ever met hugs him. She's either
going to kill him in the next minute or this is a miracle from
God.
"This is a day of days; Benny upper management is most
pleased."
She says to him. Benny is so happy he forgets himself for a
minute with his response.
"He'll yeah 'B' I got this, Sorry, my bad, I mean Madame
Butterfly."
He quickly corrects himself holding up his hands.
"Were you referring to her as a bit#h?"
The assistant asks with a thick Italian accent stepping in
between them.
Benny remains cool on the outside but is more than a little
nervous on the inside.
Holding his ground respectfully he responds.
"No I didn't mean it like that I meant like Madame B or
something."
"I know you didn't mean it like that Benny."
Madame Butterfly says laughing.
"Sometimes my Personnel can be, shall we say
overprotective."
The assistant and Benny continue to stare each other down

for a few seconds more. Benny is letting the assistant know
he is no punk and she better remember that.

His bodyguards are very impressed at the way he handled
himself. Madame butterfly's assistant is No Child of Eve's.
like so many that work for her children they are just people
trying to impress their bosses. What a great day for
Benjamin, everything is running smoothly, he enjoyed
flirting with his dream girl Leggz Diamond and Madame
Butterfly is not belittling him.

The last of the containers is loaded, Benny inspects the
spacing and ventilation one last time to assure everything is
in order before he and his crew leave the dock. Madame
Butterfly and her Entourage will remain on the ship until it
reaches international waters then she will be picked up by
helicopter.

 The Arch Nuns are excited and preparing for their much-
needed mini vacations. Which they'll be taking on Earth in
various locations, trying some of their aliases for the first
time and using the Grace of God to hide their true identities.
Because their aliases are also protected by the U.N.A they
may have as many as they like. Each Arch Nun will have
two or five reserve A.N.T agents for security, Provided by
Mother Teresa. Their job will be to enjoy themselves with or
in the immediate vicinity of the assigned Arch Nun, keeping
a watchful eye and be on the ready. Part of their brother's
jobs is to take care of all arrangements and accommodations
under their aliases which will be treated as Undercover.
Only World leaders and High-level U.N.A agents will have
access to their locations and aliases. No other law
enforcement agency in the world will have this information.
This will allow them to make friends, allies and get in a little
mischief to gain Trust. Mother Teresa wants her
grandchildren to enjoy themselves but Needless to say she
was quite adamant regarding the level of mischief they
better not exceed!

They are however allowed to reveal themselves if they feel the need to do so. This will also be how the Arch Nuns are allowed to enjoy their Leisure Time and do some undercover type things while always doing the Lord's work. It may also be used to bring deep-cover operatives from various law enforcement agencies whom want to come in once and for all. Their countries and agencies may have forgotten them, but the Lord has not forsaken them.

Sister Elizabeth will be vacationing in Daytona Beach Florida, with her custom Street stunting motorcycle she custom built herself. She calls it 'Mi Lil Pone-E' she'll be under the alias 'Bi-ka, Ry-da-Di (biker, ride or die)' where she will definitely be with the Street Stunters and most likely get into a little mischief.

Sister Lin will be vacationing in Arizona. She too will be bringing her own personal vehicle. A 2028- 1,200 HP custom Chevy Camaro with a unique wide body kit. She's been working on it in her room at the Divine Ranch and can't wait to transition it to Earth. On the top of the windshield it reads, 'Vin-Diesel Powered' And on the back of the rear spoiler it reads, '2-Bad-U-Lose!'

She will most likely engage in some street racing under her alias 'Dominica Torretta' Mischief level let's just say she better keep it light!

Sister Donna will be vacationing in Silicon Valley California, under her alias 'Deleta' (De-le-ta). Her chances of Mischief are very low.

She better not hack into or delete anything showing off as she makes high-tech computer friends!

The Sister Superior Maria Will be vacationing in Paris France under her alias

'karisma De la Renta' she will undoubtedly be hanging out with the fashion Elite and attending all the Swank parties. Her Mischief level will be very low.

Sister Navaeh will be joining her Sister Superior in Paris, under her alias 'Ra'gina De Mornay' she and Maria share similar interests in fashion but will most likely make different friends. Her Mischief level will be very low as well, PERHAPS!

  Sister Amira will be vacationing in Las Vegas Nevada under the alias 'D.J Kinda Cool' then she's off to the city of Boom in Belgium in hopes of DJing at the Tomorrowland Music Festival. Possible Mischief level, ONLY GOD KNOWS! but Mother Teresa is sure she will be good, fingers crossed!

Sister Dajairia will be vacationing in London under her Alias 'Dance-a-rella' where she will attend many dance events including the World of Dance competition. Too bad she can't compete! Her Mischief level should be very low, SHOULD BE!

Sister Anna will be vacationing in Atlanta Georgia attending gardening and cooking seminars using her alias 'Victoria Goodie Tu'choos' she of course didn't give her alias as much thought as her sisters or maybe she did. Her Mischief level will be ABSOLUTELY Nun. Lol.

Zachariah and Joshua are still collaborating on cool Alias names for themselves and picking a destination spot. They're happy getting their sisters set up, making sure everything is ok.

Josh and Zac communicate some last-minute vacation instructions to their little sister Amira.

'Hey Buffie'

'Hey, what's up big brother?' 'I gotta tell ya two very important things while you're vacationing'

'Ok what is it josh?'

'Alright listen little sis, based on your chosen destinations, it's very important to remember these two things'

'Ok what' Amira is so excited about her vacation she doesn't notice her big brothers setting her up for their jokes.

'The first thing is, try to keep your PRETTY FACE off of people's Fists'

'That's so funny, I forgot ta laugh josh. Now I'm gonna be

stupid and ask, duh! what's the second thing?'
'Also Buff, if you see a group called 'Isis' don't join them it's
not a cool DJing School.' They all laugh enjoying the fun of
telepathic communicating.
The cargo transport is entering international waters. The
ship's crew constantly monitor the containers and walking in
between them. When the hidden sleeping infant awakens
hungry and crying. Immediately a redheaded woman in the
container runs to the woman and opens her duffle bag. She's
shocked to discover the infant. She can't believe the stupidity
of this woman. (Speaking in Mandarin Chinese.)
"What's wrong with you, are you crazy?"
The woman says violently shaking the mother of the infant.
"I couldn't leave my baby, I just couldn't!"
She responds bursting into tears. All the women in the
container are now very angry at her. They feel betrayed and
the Gang will surely take it out on all of them. Some begin to
pull her hair shouting at her. The red headed woman runs to
her personal belongings retrieves a doctor's bag and from it
a syringe. Assuring the mother everything will be alright,
this will only make the baby sleep. The mother is not sure if
she should trust the red headed woman, but the other
women are screaming and insisting. Benjamin wasn't
leaving any stone unturned inside each container among the
women he has a registered nurse in disguise. The red
headed woman identifies herself and tells the women she is
here to make sure they arrive at their destination safely this
sets the women at ease. Outside the container some of the
crew members heard the entire commotion and the crying
infant. They take a few minutes to discuss their options
before deciding on telling Madame Butterfly. One of the four
men is a deep under cover Interpol agent. He has been
under cover for a long time and is very good at his job. He is
said to be one of the best! He also has secret ways of
contacting numerous important law enforcement agencies
and world leaders when he needs to, this is one of those

times! His name is Lim Tan, head of engineering and he's been on this undercover assignment for the past twenty years. He's in his mid-fifties, scruffy-looking, reeks of engine oil with a partial uncombed head of gray hair. He loves to fish in his spare time and often gets that smell on his clothes as well. No one is aware that he does these things deliberately, so no one will want to be in the same room with him. Madame Butterfly likes and respects him but because of his foul stench she cannot stand to be around him. This always works to his advantage allowing him to be alone in the communications room, when radioing the Coast Guard after sabotaging parts of the ship. To avoid audio recording he never speaks of the emergency human trafficking situation,

he taps it out in Morse code with his pen while saying something completely different. In the twenty years he's been Undercover on this ship no one has ever caught on. Because he is considered to be a stressful man whom is always nervously tapping on something. As stated previously, he is one of the best!

But time is of the essence so he must act quickly. The three men are seriously considering telling Madame Butterfly. Whenever a person of importance is on board the security video recording systems are always off.

All of them have been heavily drinking, but Lim isn't as drunk as his three buddies, so he convinces them to hold off for a little while, at least until the alcohol wears off.

He quickly causes some temporary malfunctions and small problems with many of the ships systems which must be called in and reported immediately in case of engine failure, which would definitely bring the Coast Guard.

As expected, he and his small crew of repair men are called to service these malfunctions and Lim being head of Engineering is always the one to call in the problems and keep the Coast Guard away.

He enters the bridge and immediately everyone finds an

excuse to leave, some covering their noses. Most of the crew have known him for a long time and don't want to hurt his feelings. Madame Butterfly and her assistant wave hello covering their noses and leave as well.

"Did someone call break?"

He says sarcastically in broken English and waving his hand at them.

He looks around for a moment then passes gas heavily before taking a seat at the communication station. He never breaks his undercover characteristics and it is a good thing he doesn't because Madame Butterfly's personal assistant returned to the bridge, she forgot her walkie-talkie. Lim is the type of agent that always assumes he is being watched. This extreme paranoia has kept him alive all these years! While speaking to the Coast Guard and tapping his message. His three buddies enter the room, their intoxication has them relaxed but they can still fix the ship.

This is not new to Lim his buddies are normally like this, yet they always get the job done. Today he wishes they did not finish so quickly. Lim only had enough time to send the ship's position with a very brief message that says.

ATTENTION-2- U.N.A- EMERGENCY- EMERGENCY-HUMAN TRAFFICKING-INFANTS-ON-BOARD-IN-CONTAINER-EMERGENCY.

In case someone ever assumes or detects the use of Morse code, Lim over the years has constructed his own personal dialect for morse code. He has certain words to describe Human trafficking, Women, Infants and Children. Interpol secretly monitors all Coast Guard radio Transmissions and can decipher Lim's personal Morse code. This particular message has been forwarded to the U.N.A.

Madame Butterfly is quite the slide one herself. Yesterday she had one of her brothers 'Vincesco Cappadonia' a well-known millionaire in the fashion industry depart from the Miami Marina in one of his midsize Yachts with a middle-aged female whom is a ZsaZsa La'more look alike keeping her face partially covered. He makes sure they are noticed but the woman never speaks a word as he sneaks her on board. The captain and crew of The Yacht are also Eve's children. The yacht maintains a distance of eight Miles from the Cargo Carrier as it enters international waters but it is told to wait.

Walking down the hall at the United Nations building in New York. Mother Teresa and Sister Maria are discussing the president's big fundraiser party for Chile to which president Winfrey would like the Sister Superior to attend with her grandmother Teresa. The affair is set for this evening. Maria asks her grandmother if she could dress her up for the event.

"What's wrong with what I'm wearing right now, my child?" Mother Theresa asks in confusion looking down at her nun outfit.

"Come on, Abuela(Spanish for grandmother) I don't think anyone's seen you wear anything else since we started this thing. Please, please, Abuela." Maria pleads hugging her grandmother's arm.

"I will consider it my La nieta."(Spanish for granddaughter). Maria like her siblings waits exactly sixty seconds before pestering her grandmother to the point of annoyance. Then like all grandmothers she gives in.

"ALRIGHT! La nieta, ALRIGHT!" Mother Teresa screams. As people pass them giggling.

"But nothing like you have done for your brothers and sisters. I mean it and I'm wearing my habit."

"But I was counting on styling your hair-."

"I'M WEARING MY HABIT!" Mother Teresa says firmly cutting her off and shaking her finger at her.

"Hey, wait a minute Abuela. Do I have to wear my habit? I was counting on rockin a nice updo."

Her grandmother hesitates a moment then tells her. "No, my La nieta you do not."

Mother Teresa was hoping she would want to.

"Thank you Abuela."

To spite how cool the Sister Superior is, she like all grandchildren enjoys annoying her grandmother from time to time. Because of the transparency level of the U.N.A and Arch Nuns with the billions of YouTube views of their many fights. Which the world still views on a regular basis. It is a most welcome sight to see one casually strolling down the hallway arm in arm with her grandmother. It's such a shame that cell phone photography is not allowed by the staff within the walls of the United Nations building. Everyone Nods their head and smiles in passing and they notice the look of a proud grandmother on Mother Teresa's face as she walks with her loving granddaughter. But these rare moments are often interrupted by the business of the world. Mother Teresa receives a very urgent call on her personal tablet, it's the Governor of Georgia Harvey Stevens whom like President Winfrey was a very popular celebrity hosting a radio and game show. He informs her of gang activity in an abandon Factory. Involving forced teenage prostitution, Drugs, illegal firearms, explosives and the disposing of dead bodies for other gangs on the premises using the factories incinerator. These disturbing events have recently come to his attention and he would prefer Swift and Absolute Justice. This is what he feels makes it a U.N.A high priority because all of this gang's members are minors!   The oldest of them is sixteen some of the younger ones are seven years old. They have made so much money with their illegal activities that they can now afford to hire adult gang members from other gangs to protect them. These gangs accept their money assuming there is adult supervision controlling everything, but it is not just very smart teenagers.

Mother Teresa knows her granddaughters are preparing for their vacations and there will always be something to impede that. So, she feels to Anna whom isn't as excited as the others to go on vacation, Which Mother Teresa will most certainly be addressing with her shortly. But for now, she sends her to Atlanta to clean up this mess with the instructions to be Divine, Spectacular and Swift! Let these defiant teenagers witness the Power of thy Lord God!

"Go forth my child, for God's Great purpose!"

"SO SHALL IT BE WRITTEN, SO SHALL IT BE DONE!" Sister Anna responds.

Mother Teresa and Maria go back to her office. Soon as they close the door, Sister Dajairia transitions into the room. She's casually dressed and hugs them both.

"Hey Grandma the World of Dance Competition has been moved to next week you mind if I go on vacation next week instead of this week?"

"No my dear that would be fine. I just thought you all would prefer to have gone together."

"Oh, grandma every minute we get we'll be hanging out together transitioning to time."

"Why Yes, Abuela." Maria adds putting her hand on her grandmother's shoulder.

"I'm meeting Nevaeh in Paris later after the president's fundraiser, Dee are you coming?"

"Of course."

Mother Teresa is pleased to see her grandchildren reacquainting themselves with Earth. But with all the joyous sister chatter and excitement going on in her office. The coming of world business is inevitable. For she has received another call on her tablet.

"Ok, let me get outta here, I know your busy grandma. I'll see you later sis."

Dajairia says before transitioning back to the Divine Garden. This call is from Interpol it is the coded message from Lim Tan. When Mother Teresa and Maria hear this, they are astonished at how stupid some criminal organizations can be and assume this is the work of Giovanni Luciano.

"I'll go grandmother." Maria said sharply.

"No my dear, we have the fundraiser to attend tonight.

The Lord works in mysterious ways, my child. Perhaps that is why Dee is available and at leisure."

Dajairia is home at the Devine Garden dressed in a bathing suit and shorts, her preferred attire of choice. She's alone on the patio enjoying the Sun and Performing some dance moves while sipping a frozen margarita. When she receives a telepathic feeling from her

grandmother, informing her of the situation involving the infants.

Dajairia calls Mikolai whom is filling in as commander while she's vacationing, informing him of the situation and instructing him to go to the Cargo Carrier immediately she will meet the team there shortly. B.A.D seven acknowledges and sets a course to intercept the carrier. Lim's men eager to get on Madame butterfly's good side, decide to tell her what they've heard.

Madame Butterfly is on the bridge with the captain awaiting her extraction helicopter, when Lim's men enter the bridge asking to speak with her. They don't want her to think they withheld information, so Lim told them before entering the bridge to say they just heard it a few minutes ago. This works out exactly how Lim wanted it. Since his encoded distress massage was sent a little while earlier, he can never be considered a suspect.

Madame Butterfly is furious as she listens to Lim's men. After all her mother has done for these women, they dare sneak infants on board. She calls the captain and tells him to check it, take the cell phones from Benjamin's men and if it is true have them kill everyone inside the containers, dump them overboard and make sure the containers are cleaned thoroughly! Fuming with anger she decides to call Benjamin. Benjamin looks down at his temporary cell phone, which can only receive five calls from Leggz or Madame Butterfly. He just had good experiences with both of them, so he's eager to receive the call.

"What's good." He answers confidently.

"Benjamin, Benjamin, Benjamin." Madame Butterfly
responds wickedly. Benny is familiar with that tone of voice.
He hopes one of his boys didn't say something disrespectful
to her and mess up her mood.

"What's going on?" He cautiously asks.

"Captain, tell the men to hold on, I'm coming down I want to
see for myself."

She says over her walkie-talkie so Benny can hear yet still
making him hold on and he knows not to hang up for any
reason. The container's door is blocked with another
container to help hide it from the authorities. Madame
Butterfly joins the captain and several of Benny's men at the
containers believed to have the infants in side.

The women can hear the commotion outside and begin to
panic. The captain taps lightly on the container with a metal
crowbar.

"Is everything okay in there ladies?" He shouts so the
women inside can hear him. They are hesitant to answer but
know they must. Talking can be heard from within the
container as the women frantically decide what to do. Then
one of them nervously responds in broken English which
they are told to speak so Benjamin men can understand
them.

"Yeah, yes everything ok, everyone ok. A little hot but ok,
everything ok!"

"That's good ladies." The captain says in a calm and soothing
voice.

"You're going to hear a little noise out here, don't be scared
we're just making sure everything is okay." The captain has
lured them into a false sense of security, they believe they
are fine for now. Thirty seconds later the captain orders the
men to violently bang on the container as hard as they can
until he tells them to stop. The noise outside is Extremely
Loud but within the container it is unbearable, startling the
women and causing them to scream. This has the same effect
on the Infant as well. The captain orders them to stop. The

sound of crying women can be heard from within, along with the sound of a screaming INFANT. The medicine in the needle was too strong to be given to the baby, the nurse wasn't expecting it to be on board. Benjamin cannot believe what he's hearing, His men are equally shocked. He feels a sickening feeling in the pit of his stomach. "Madame Butterfly, Madame Butterfly!" He screams through the phone but she ignores him. When his men hear the panic in his voice, they too become nervous and begin blaming each other. Madame Butterfly holds her index finger up to them, for them to be quiet. Like children they immediately stop talking, she points to the container and says. "KILL THEM ALL!"

Benjamin is still on the phone and assumes she is referring to the captain's crew killing his boys. This frightens the gangster boss of Singapore. Then his worst fear is confirmed as she puts the phone to her ear and says. "SEE-YOU-SOON-BENJAMIN!" Then hangs up on him.

With his eyes wide as dinner plates, his heart is beating so fast it feels as though it's going to burst from his chest. He immediately calls Leggz whom is still in Singapore so he can have a chance to explain. She unlike Madame Butterfly will at least listen to him for a moment because of their friendship. She tells him to meet her at a popular restaurant in the city. There he explains to her how he took every precaution and had under cover registered nurses in every container to assure everyone's well-being. He asks his friend to speak to her sister on his behalf asking her not to kill everyone just yet and to set up a meeting with him, the nurses and his boys on board, so he can find out what happened and have the opportunity to take care of it. Ka'ren agrees to protect him for the moment advising him to go home and stay there until he hears from her. If what he tells her is true, he's safe for now, because her sister is still on the ship. Madame Butterfly and her assistant return to the bridge still angry she attempts to calm herself. Disrespecting a gift from her mother is one thing. But Madame Butterfly prefers not to kill children or infants. So, for putting her in the position of making such a cruel decision all the women in the containers will pay with their lives!

Madame Butterfly receives an urgent call from Kalmin Seth. She clears the bridge, her assistant must leave as well, when everyone is gone, she and her brother speak in their own dialect of Ancient Egyptian.

"I have important news my sister."

As do I and I am outraged at the audacity to say the least!"

"Steady yourself sister of mine. I do not have much time. I have no idea how but I think the U.N.A is aware of your cargo. A Battle Assault Drone has been deployed to your location. The Government has granted them a search warrant."

"Thank you Brother, I will take care of it!"

Madame Butterfly then calls her brother Vinny who's waiting seven miles away from the carrier's current position in his yacht with her look-alike. He's on the deck sunbathing with the look-alike when his cell phone rings.

"Hello." He says Softly sipping on a class of red wine.

Madame Butterfly gives him a coded phrase for him to carry out her plan. "No Time Like the Present" Then she hangs up the phone.

The look-alike is then taken below, strangled to death, dipped in liquid nitrogen, broken into small pieces and dumped overboard. Then the captain detonates a bomb strong enough to capsize and slowly sink the yacht. Vinny and the crew escape in a life raft, one of the crew is dressed as the look-alike. The Cargo Carrier rescues and brings them on board, keeping them in the medical Bay away from the main crew.

Both captains falsify the reports regarding the time of the explosion and Rescue. The rest will be taken care of by more of Eve's children. With the Battle Assault Drone on its way this had to be done. Because ZsaZsa's extraction helicopter can no longer enter the area and so her presence on board can be explained.

Madame Butterfly is still on the bridge making sure everything with the rescue is going according to her plan. When the assistant directs her attention to an unwelcomed but familiar sight. The signature streak of the Battle Assault Drone is seen in the distant sky rapidly approaching the Cargo Carrier. One of the mid-size drones detaches itself to check on the capsized yacht as B.A.D Seven stops in front of the Cargo Carrier.

Sounding the horn of Gabriel and ordering them to stop and prepare to be boarded.

The desperate Women within the container hear the horn and immediately begins screaming and banging on the container walls hoping to be saved by the A.N.T. Benjamin's men threaten to flood the container with gas if they aren't quiet. Although they have no way of truly doing this it's an empty threat but the women are so frightened they immediately become silent.

Madame Butterfly orders all of Benjamin's men to resist and engage the A.N.T at her command.

The accompanying crew are to hide so they may be found and considered hostages.

"Yo man, why she tell these motherfu#kers ta hide, they can fight too."

One of Benjamin's men says to another.

"You crazy, look at them! they skinny, dirty, old and drunk as fu#k! you can put your life in their hands, I'm not."

The other replies making sure his gun is locked and loaded. Benny's men know this is a gun fight they can't win, but they'll have a better chance against the A.N.T then against HER!

Madame Butterfly changes into her bullet-resistant outfit and redoes her makeup, putting on her War face but this time doesn't completely cover her face she wants the Arch Nun to see a little bit of ZsaZsa. Her assistant holds up a briefcase and opens it in front of her, Inside are two Custom-made Bulletproof Shaolin butterfly swords.

With magnesium properties within the blades which produce a blinding light when struck together. You don't want to have night vision goggles on when she uses these, for you will see no more!

Madame butterfly's assistant sends a text to benny's men informing them, the 'M.B' will be joining them in battle. This boosts their confidence, since many of them have seen her fight, but some hope she dies in this battle. But definitely not by their hand or bullets, they wouldn't want to explain that to Leggz Diamond.

"Everyone on Deck where we can see you, NOW! This is not a request your compliance is mandatory. By order of the United Nations Agency!"

Mikolai speaks authoritatively over the loudspeakers. This message circles through several languages known to be spoken by the ship's crew. Over a private radio signal Madame Butterfly orders the remaining crew members to the deck the captain included and make sure their hands are held high. She doesn't want them to be considered a threat or harmed. She tells the captain to inform them they have hostiles on board. Special protocol for ships at Sea when in danger of any kind is for the captain to make certain facial expressions. To alert the authorities when they arrive.

B.A.D Seven Has a camera fixed on the captain's face receiving his distress message.

"We also have wounded from the capsized yacht off the starboard bow that cannot be moved yet." He shouts.

Mikolai deploys a few of the mid-sized drones to watch everyone on deck. The captain tells everyone to keep their hands in the air. Benjamin's men remain in the hallways and lower decks waiting to ambush the A.N.T agents.

With the intimidating drones now watching everyone on deck. The A.N.T agents are free to start searching the ship. B.A.D Seven rotates 180 degrees and comes as close to the deck as possible. Body cams will be off for plausible deniability. World leaders are learning to exercise this regularly since the birth of the U.N.A.

Mikolai and five agents depart the Craft on high alert one is ordered to stay with the ship's crew while he and the others search the lower decks. Like all good bosses Benjamin has two military Commandos amongst those he sent to guard his Precious Cargo.

Mikolai tells three agents to search all top levels he and the other two will search the lower. They open the door and slowly descend down the stairs. They repeatedly identify themselves in the event there are still innocent bystanders roaming the Halls looking for help. Mikolai's Message can be heard looping through the crafts loudspeakers in all the spoken languages of the crew. They approach a locked door leading to a large corridor. Mikolai picks the lock and tells the two agents to continue searching the surrounding hallways and rooms.

For now, it is a game of cat-and-mouse as the agents move deeper into the ship. Madame Butterfly has not yet seen the Arch Nun leave the Craft. It is her intention to kill the Arch Nun and her entire team, leaving Benjamins men to take the blame or credit. Only her mother and siblings will know ZsaZsa La'more killed an Arch Nun and her team. For that she will take full credit within their family ranks!

Mikolai is beginning to feel a little uncomfortable so he commands his agents to hold position and tells the pilot to slowly Circle and x-ray the carrier.

But most of the walls and containers are lined with lead. The pilot reports to Mikolai whom tells him to continue circling the carrier then hold position above it. Madame Butterfly grows weary of waiting for the Arch Nun to show itself, so she orders Benjamin's men to attack. Gunfire is heard from the lower decks as the firefight ensues.

The crew becomes nervous and frightened not all of them are aware of what's going on.

Mikolai opens the door to the large corridor. Believing himself to be the hero and anxious to make an impression on Sister Dajairia, Mother Teresa and the World leaders. He enters the corridor alone, veering down the sight of his assault rifle, he can hardly wait to engage the enemy. Slowly walking down, the corridor he wishes the hostiles would attack. But like the old proverb says be careful what you wish for!

A door at the end of the corridor opens. Thank you, God Mikolai says to himself with a big smile. Then the look of disappointment comes over his face as the smile slowly Fades. He was hoping for Mercenaries, Commandos, inexperienced gang members with guns Maybe! But instead all he sees is a middle-aged woman wandering the Halls in what looks like a brightly colored Halloween costume. They must have been having some type of wild party here he thinks.

"Miss, are you okay? can you understand me? are you okay?"

Mikolai asks lowering his weapon. She doesn't answer but continues walking toward him. Mikolai isn't a fan of celebrities almost all are unfamiliar to him. He had no idea Ophelia Winfrey was an internationally known talk show host before she became president of the United States and he most certainly doesn't recognize The world's most renowned fashion Mongol ZsaZsa La'more wearing professional makeup to disguise herself and approaching him.

"Miss, I need you to stop, Please stop!"

Mikolai has been in many situations where children and the elderly were used as bombs or distractions and this is beginning to seem familiar to him. He quickly raises his assault rifle.

"STOP RIGHT NOW!" He demands. But it is too late she is now within range. Mikolai is no stranger to someone attempting to wrestle his weapon from him and sincerely hopes she doesn't try, he would hate it if he had to hurt the sweet older woman now standing six feet away from him, with unimaginable speed she leaps forward punching him in the chest, simultaneously grabbing his assault rifle yanking it from his hand and popping the strap which tethered it to his armor. The blow was so hard it knocks him back a few feet, He stumbles falling on his back and slides a few feet down the corridor. Mikolai quickly jumps to his feet and assumes an attack posture.

"I want to apologize, because now I have to hurt you, old woman!"

She stands in front of him holding his assault rifle. He's not worried because the gun will only fire for him.

"Oh no! please don't shoot me with my own gun old woman!" He says laughing.

Eager to get the name of her alter-ego in circulation again she offers to give his weapon back to him.

"I am called The MADAME BUTTERFLY!" She responds with her mother's Wicked tone, then bends the rifle over her knee and tosses it to him. He watches the weapon slide across the floor.

"That was a very expensive weapon, I'm afraid you're going to have to pay for that."

Madame Butterfly is wearing a wristband that controls the lights of each room and hallway. She deactivates the lights, Mikolai's helmet automatically switches to night vision. Madame Butterfly hasn't moved he can still see her standing in front of him. Again, with Incredible speed she draws her butterfly swords and strikes them together. The Magnesium flash blinds him the technology of His helmet didn't compensate for the Flash quick enough. It did however protect his eyes from being permanently damaged but he is temporarily blinded from the light. She luminates the corridor and Strikes him from all sides kicking and slapping him like a child to provoke his ego. With body cams dark Mother Teresa is unable to monitor this campaign and has no idea Madame Butterfly is there.

At the Devine Garden Sister Dajairia walks to the edge of the patio, assumes the prayer position, her casual attire morphs into her Arch Nun outfit, she dives into the water at the Divine Garden. One second later she emerges through the floors of the Cargo Carrier in the form of a spinning ball of water. Time slows down as the water comes to an abrupt stop, taking the form of sister Dajairia. Time resumes and the full form of the Arch Nun can be seen as the water splashes on the surrounding surfaces yet she is completely dry and now stands in the path of one of Benny's men, a large Ex-Navy Seal, dishonorably discharged for Unnecessary cruelty.

His name is Ta'maro and he cannot believe what he has just seen. He like many believe the Arch Nuns use magician's tricks to fool the mind. Because there's no way in the world he's going to believe she just came through the floor in the form of water then became solid.

"That's a good trick you, might wanna use it to get the fu#k out of my way!"

He says clenching his fists.

"You dare mock the Power of thy Lord God."

"It's not my God, it's yours since you believe in that sort of thing, Baby."

"Then know that on this day, at this moment, you chose to stand against the Power of God! And on this day at this moment you shall feel the wrath of thy Lord God!"

He waves his hand at the Arch Nun in disrespect then rushes at her attempting to grab her by the waist. With his head lowered he tries to tackle her. But he isn't fast enough. Time slows down, she leaps forward striking him in the face with her right knee, breaking his nose and knocking his body upright, with blinding speed she places her left foot on his chest using his body to flip herself backwards striking him under the chin with her right foot, breaking his teeth and both Jaws.

Time resumes as she lands and he stumbles back holding his face. With Extreme Rage he rushes toward her again, striking her in the chest, knocking her off her feet and through the air towards the wall behind her, before falling to one knee with his head down holding his Jaws. Time slows down, she absorbs the impact as she bounces off the wall performing a forward flip hitting him on top of the head with her left foot. Then performs a backflip Landing on her knees in the prayer position. Time resumes, the momentum from the flip and the power of her leg were too much for him to endure as his face slams to the floor. He lies on the floor motionless, his neck broken! He will be quadriplegic but will live to regret and repent for facing the wrath of God! The Arch Nun communes with his mind explaining this to him and asks the Lord to have mercy on him on his day of judgement. Sister Dajairia stands and says to him.

"No more harm shall come to you on this day. Someone will be here shortly to tend to you."

His hearing has been severely damaged in this very short fight and that is the last human voice he will ever hear! He watches as she walks down the hall, then his eyesight begins to blur and fade as he starts his descent into mental solitary. Never stand in the way of an Arch Nun when children are in PERIL!

Madame Butterfly continues to take advantage of Mikolai's temporary blindness. He swings and kicks but he hits nothing but air. He must be careful not to wear himself out. He can hear her Whispering taunts and insulting him. She toys with him, out maneuvering him to convince him his armor is slowing him down.

"You couldn't hit the broadside of a barn in that big heavy Knights of the Round Table armor you're wearing."

She says continuing to push him into walls and trip him to the floor. Mikolai can hear his helmet attempting to compensate for the lighting, but it cannot read the retinas of his eyes and Madame Butterfly has struck him several times hard to the Head causing further damage to the helmet. He assumes she's been striking him with a weapon of some sort. He knows there is no way this old woman can hit him that hard, but in reality, they were her hands and feet. Mikolai is forced to remove his malfunctioning helmet and some of his damaged body armor. This is exactly what Madame Butterfly was waiting for. With his helmet off he regains a little bit of his sight but doesn't let her know, he continues to stumble around and reach out. Overly confident she walks toward him from behind with her swords drawn. She intends to decapitate him and bring his head to her mother along with the Arch Nun's.

She slowly raises her sword, like so many she has beaten into submission before killing them, she doesn't use her superior speed or strength to finish the job. She swings the sword at his neck, he ducks, she misses and he unleashes a barrage of punches on her, knocking the swords from her hands and throwing her to the ground. This throws her completely off guard. Not many can take her to the mat, but she is pleased to have a worthy adversary. But will absolutely not allow him to damage her face or mess up her makeup. She throws an upward punch; he catches it and puts her in an arm lock.

"Mikolai what's your position?"

Sister Dajairia asks over the comlink. Aside from his primary Communications within his helmet he also has a small voice activated wrist watch communicator. Struggling to maintain his arm lock between the grunting and groaning he responds.

"Heeeey bossss, welcome to the parrrrty."

"Mikolai, what are you doing? OH MY GOSH! are you using the bathroom?"

"What, Nooooo!"

Hearing Sister Dajairia's voice Delights Madame Butterfly, finally the Arch Nun has arrived.

As Mikolai struggles to maintain his hold, Madame Butterfly begins to stand lifting him off the floor with ease. Mikolai is a very tactical fighter, as he feels his body leave the floor he releases his hold on her arm and grabs her by the legs throwing her to the floor once more.

"GOD-DAM-IT, YOU LITTLE SOVIET SH#T!" Madame Butterfly screams in anger.

"I think you broke my fingernail."

Mikolai laughs a little as he repeatedly tries to punch her in the face but she blocks his attempts.

"Come on, move your hands give that face to Mikolai."

Sister Dajairia is walking down the hallway wondering why her chest is still in pain from the previous fight.

"Mikolai what's taking you so long with that female Soldier?"

"She's a tough old coot boss, I think she's on some kind of drugs and she's wearing bullet resistant material."

His description of her sends chills down Sister Dajairia's spine.

"OLD COOT!" Madame Butterfly interrupts forgetting herself and speaking in her natural voice.

"I WILL NOT TOLERATE THIS INSOLENCE, ESPECIALLY FROM A VODKA DRINKING HOOLIGAN LIKE YOU!"

She concludes kicking him off her and into the wall behind him leaving an imprint from the impact. Mikolai left his comlink open so Sister Dajairia could hear. What she heard confirmed her worst fear. An older woman, bullet resistant clothing, her second-in-command unable to defeat her and not to mention that overbearing, condescending British tone of voice. Oh Lord thy God, it's ZsaZsa La'more the MADAME BUTTERFLY!

She immediately feels this information to her grandmother. Mother Teresa immediately telepathically responds. 'Find her Dajairia before she kills your ENTIRE TEAM!'

Madame Butterfly slowly stands to face Mikolai, he's still attempting to stand after hitting the wall. Mikolai being tough as Nails, not only stands but shakes it off.

As the two slowly circle each other Madame Butterfly describes to him exactly what she's going to do.

"I was going to cut your head off clean and quick, but now you little Soviet prick, I'm going to rip it off slowly, very slowly!"

Mikolai makes a painful face covering his crotch. "Not that HEAD, you idiot!" Madam Butterfly says. If he only knew how close to death he is, he would not be making jokes. with his vision still blurred, he puts his hands up ready to fight. But Madame Butterfly is done playing!

She holds her finger up for him to wait a minute. She unzips her jacket; extra material drops just below her knees extending its length. Mikolai gives her a round of applause and asks if she's ready to fight now.

Before she can answer there are several hard pounds on the door. It's the Arch Nun attempting to enter the corridor but the door is locked.

"Well, it appears we have a guest." Madame Butterfly says grinning at Mikolai who is standing in a doorway to one of the offices. The office has a large window with two-inch-thick tempered glass looking out into the corridor. Sister Dajairia kicks the door open and cautiously enters the corridor. Madame Butterfly uses her Superior speed and strength to grab Mikolai, throw him into the office and break the inside door handle so he cannot escape then pulls the door shut, locking him inside.

Madame butterfly was eager to fight an Arch Nun, Now she stands before one.

"How nice of you to finally join us my dear." Madame Butterfly says politely, but still with her mother's rhetoric. Sister Dajairia is glad to see Mikolai is still alive as he bangs on the glass screaming to be released. Then she notices his helmet and some of his body armor lying on the floor.

"Don't be shocked darling, this isn't the first time I've talked a man out of his clothes."

Madame Butterfly says with a seductive wink.

"Dajairia, Dajairia can you hear me?"

Mikolai screams rapidly tapping on the glass. Dajairia notices he is not looking directly at her and keeps squeezing his eyes shut. I hope this chick didn't damage his brain' she thinks to herself looking down at the damaged helmet.

"I'll give you a moment to say goodbye to your boyfriend darling, before I kill the two of you!"

Madame Butterfly tells her backing away with open arms allowing the Arch Nun to speak to him. She comes close to the window but Mikolai doesn't turn to face her. She takes another step closer and he quickly turns to face her.

"Dajairia, Dajairia I'm okay my vision is blurry like sh#t. She Blinded me with something somehow. Do me the favor for me, beat sh#t outta her for Mikolai, Da?(Da is a Russian word meaning yes). With his vision blurry he cannot Witness the superior fighting Maneuvers the two women are about to display. Mikolai heard the Madame refer to him as her boyfriend, he also noticed Sister Dajairia didn't correct her. With his face close to the glass he can barely see what's directly in front of him.

Sister Dajairia gently places the palm of her hand on the glass, Mikolai does the same wishing he could see her face clearly. Looking into the eyes of her Fallen second-in-command Sister Dajairia blows him a Playful Kiss and responds with a little street slang.

"Yeah BABY, Mama's got THIS!"

Mother Teresa feels to Dajairia telling her not to defeat Madame Butterfly.

'Dajairia listen to me, she must believe she is superior to an Arch Nun. Allow her to dominate the fight, believing she is hurting you. Remember child, it is imperative that Eve's children have that delusion of grandeur for now and when she's ready to escape allow her to do so, do not pursue. To assist you in this. Use only 2% of your speed and strength, this will allow us to gauge the power of Eve's top Children.'

The Arch Nun turns facing Madame Butterfly, says a quick prayer to herself then opens her eyes and says. "NOW WITNESS THE POWER OF GOD!"

Madame Butterfly immediately responds.

"What a coincidence darling, I was just about to tell you the same thing!"

Unlike her sister Ka'ren whom plays with her opponents/pray giving them the opportunity to get the best of her. The Madame intends to kill the Arch Nun quickly and with fabulous Style.

The Arch Nun attacks her with a series of kicks which are easily blocked by The Madame. Mikolai presses his forehead to the window trying to get a clear view of what's going on. Sister Dajairia jumps high in the air performing a spinning axe kick. Time slows down, The Madame jumps as well executing a similar kick with superb form but faster and more powerful, striking Sister Dajairia to the side of the head breaking her neck. Dajairia feels her neck snap for a millisecond before repairing itself as her body Twirls through the air striking the wall. Falling to the floor She instinctively grabs her neck and struggles to stand.

"Well, I see that didn't work!" The Madame says throwing her hands in the air in disappointment.

"That's a pretty strong alloy in your body armor darling, I can see how it hinders your movement and speed. Perhaps you care to remove some of it?"

Mother Teresa is with her granddaughter spiritually communicating during this most important battle.

'Excellent my child she believes the body armor is protecting you, proceed.'

Sister Dajairia slowly stands, still holding her neck and responds to the Madame.

"Chick! I was born at night, but it wasn't last night. I'll keep my armor on, thank you and if you know what's good for you. I suggest you do the same!"

"Indeed darling indeed! But I'm afraid you'll find me far

more formidable than those inferior Street punks you've been fighting. Now, ready or not here I come!"

Then the Madame viciously attacks striking the Arch Nun with beautifully executed maneuvers. Her long clothing flows with her body movement magnificently as she uses it to misguide and distract the Arch Nun.

With her great speed she kicks Dajairia in the stomach, both shoulders than eight times to the forehead knocking her to the wall behind her. Time slows down. She then performs a spin kick pinning the Arch Nun's head against the wall, holding her there for a few seconds attempting to crush her skull with her foot. Time resumes, Dajairia being the extreme contortionist, kicks her leg over the Madam's breaking her hold. Then demonstrates a little speed of her own. Using only her right leg, she kicks the Madame in both her knees and lower abdomen as her body leans forward from the blow. Sister Dajairia gently places her foot under the Madam's neck preventing her from leaning over. Then she kicks The Madame three times in the chest with the heel of her foot. Returning the favor and knocking her to the wall. The madame's back hits the wall hard, so hard it leaves an imprint right next to Mikolai's. She immediately steps away from the wall but is met by Sister Dajairia's roundhouse kick, then a spinning back kick, then another, then another. The Madam Falls to her hands and knees, time slows down, with the momentum of the spins Sister Dajairia holds her right leg straight in the air with both hands spinning on the tip of her left foot three times, before bringing her right foot down hard on the madame's back. Being extra careful as not to break it time resumes.

Madame Butterfly falls flat to the floor, rolls over and quickly jumps to her feet.

'Sorry Grandma, I couldn't help myself.' She feels to Mother Teresa.

Sister Dajairia continues to attack the Madame but can no longer hit her. Madame Butterfly is now using all of her speed and strength.

She strikes Sister Dajairia hard, fast and mercilessly easily breaking her bones.

Turning, jumping and flipping through the air, she is not only impervious to the Arch Nuns attacks. She is also Unstoppable! Sister Dajairia now understands why she is called Madame Butterfly. She bests the Arch Nun in every maneuver with such Style and Grace. It's hard to believe she too was not chosen by God!

Sister Dajairia is feeling all of this to her grandmother who has come to the conclusion.

If the Arch Nuns did not have 10% Grace of God and the Holy Spirit, there would be no way they could possibly defeat such Superior specimens of humanity.

'Grandma this REALLY, REALLY, REALLY hurts, can I stop now? I lost track of how many times my bones have been broken!'

Gunfire can still be heard in the distance as the firefight continues.

'just a few moments more my child. Your team is wrapping everything up and the hallways need to be clear so she may choose to escape.'

To take her mind off the pain she calls to some of her brothers and sisters so they may commune with her.

'O.M.G Dee your fighting The Madame Butterfly.'

Navaeh says trying to contain her laughter.

"Hey, I thought grandma said when it comes to celebrities whichever one of us is a fan of that Celebrity, must deal with that celebrity. Where the heck is Maria? She's a ZsaZsa La'more fan!'

Zac asks.

'Shut up Zac, the Lord works in mysterious ways and besides grandma and I have a very important party to attend this evening and I have to do our hair.' Maria replies.

'Hey Dee does it hurt bad?' Anna asks with concern.
'No! Anna, I enjoy having every bone in my body repeatedly broken, WHAT DO YOU THINK?'
'it's a shame grandmother and I have a previous engagement this evening or I would have gladly taken your place.'
'Oh, REALLY sis?'
'Nooooo, absolutely NOT really!' Maria says laughing.
'Keep your chin up Dee.' Amira says.
'Thanks Buff'
'On second thought don't she'll only kick you in it!'
Sister Dajairia is enjoying having her siblings telepathically communicating with her during this, even though they're roasting her good.
But Dajairia has a little joke of her own up her sleeve. She didn't inform them she was communing with Grandmother when she asked them to comfort her.
'Wow! This chick hits harder than Mike Tyson!'
Dajairia feels to all of them. Zac can hardly contain his enthusiasm as he shouts.
'O.M.G, I KNOW HIM, I KNOW HIM!'
Imitating Will Ferrell from the movie Elf.
'Hey Buff this feels like when Leggz stomped on you.'
'I know I can't believe that bitty stomped on my boobies like that.'
And right on cue all the female Arch Nuns begin joking and talking about boobies. Even the Sister Superior who is sitting in the same room with Mother Teresa but unaware her grandmother was multitasking and communing with Dajairia.
The Reverend mother allow this to go on a few seconds before they all heard the most disturbing of communes.
'WHAT IN THE BLUE BLAZERS IS GOING ON HERE?'
Instantly all communes stop!
Dajairia and her grandmother are laughing still connected by their commune. As mother Teresa seriously stairs at the Sister Superior.

"Excuse me Abuela I'm going to go do my hair now." Maria says quickly leaving the office.

The Madame Butterfly continues to beat Sister Dajairia, hammering away believing she is weakening what she believes to be her body armor. The gunfire has stopped, Mikolai has been trying to punch through the tempered glass window to help Sister Dajairia.

With his hands bleeding he continues to punch the glass, screaming her name.

The Madame had hoped to have killed the Arch Nun by now but time is a luxury she no longer has so she must now go. "My compliments to the inventor of your body armor my dear, I can assure you the next time we meet darling, I'll cut through it as though you are wearing nothing!"

She picks up her butterfly swords looks at Mikolai. "And your little dog Too!" She concludes reciting the famous line from 'The Wizard of Oz' punching the tampered glass window almost shattering it as she walks away. The Madam quickly makes her way to the medical section of the ship, the crew member dressed as the look-alike gives her the outfit. Removing her makeup and messing up her hair she takes her place among them. They shut the door lock it and pull a desk in front of it, pretending to be shook up and frightened. One of the agents finally makes it to the medical section, banging on the door he asks is everyone all right?

Miss La'more is upset and crying standing behind the men. They cautiously open the door and let the agent in backing up with their Hands in the air, with his assault rifle at the ready he enters asking again is everyone all right. He quickly and thoroughly checks the room before announcing over the comlink.

"Med section clear"

Sister Dajairia lets Mikolai out of the office. With his vision still blurry and his hands broken. She helps him out and sits him on the floor.

"What happened? it sounded like you were getting sh#t

kicked out of you?" He asks.

"Sounds can be deceiving Mikolai, now let's talk about this body armor on the floor."

"What body armor? I don't see any."

She reaches over him picks up his helmet and holding it in front of his face."

"How about now?"

"I can't see a thing boss."

She stands up with her back to him. "That was a pretty hard fight that chick sure could hit."

She says stretching and bending over to pick up the rest of his body armor.

"OH MY GOOOOOOD" He grunts.

With her legs straight and still bending she looks back at him and says.

"I see you looking at my Butt, Mikolai."

"I can see nothing boss, nothing!"

At that moment more agents enter the corridor and are shocked at what they see.

"WHAT KIND OF NUNS ARE THESE?" One of them shouts.

The Coast Guard Searches the Cargo Carrier finding the containers with the women and infant inside. Miss La'more and her group are kept in the medical section. Her female assistant is dressed as a member of the Cargo Carrier's crew assisting the captain and staying far away from ZsaZsa. All but a few of Benny's men were killed by the A.N.T. Those who survived are badly wounded and taken to the Coast Guard Medical ship. The A.N.T medic is tending to ZsaZsa she's crying, terribly frightened and hysterical. The Coast Guard's medical staff relieve him so he may tend to his team. They give ZsaZsa a mild sedative to ease her nerves.

"Thank you, thank you so much darling"

ZsaZsa says literally patting the female nurse on the top of her head like a pet, as she kneels beside her administering the shot.

The nurse doesn't mind at all. She's Starstruck and a fan of high fashion and knows exactly who Lady ZsaZsa La'more is. She asks the ship's chief medical officer if she may be separated from her group, after all they're just the staff of the yacht, with the exception of Vinny who she wants to distance herself from. The nurse is so smitten with her she offers to take her to a private room and tend to her personally. The chief medical officer agrees but sends two more nurses to assist her, one of which is male. ZsaZsa doesn't mind she adores the attention. Still very emotional and traumatized the nurses assist her to a private section of the medical Bay. Which is just a curtained-off section of the larger room.

"Is this the best you can do, darling?" She asks.

"I'm afraid so ma'am, this is a nasty, stinking Cargo Carrier not the luxury Hotel suite you most certainly deserve Miss La'more, sorry."

The male nurse nervously responds. He's LGBTQ, a fan of high fashion and very familiar with ZsaZsa La'more and feels he is in the presence of his fashion Queen. No cell phones are allowed by the Coast Guard during a rescue. But if they were, he would definitely be asking for a selfie with her.

   In the corridor the A.N.T tend to Mikolai helping him with his armor and fixing him up enough so he can walk back to the Battle Assault Drone. Sister Dajairia is wondering why the pain in her chest from the previous fight has returned. It was gone during her fight with Madame Butterfly now it's back! Inside the medical section there is a lot of commotion. The women and infant from the containers are being brought in. The infant is screaming and crying.

ZsaZsa asks her nurses what's going on. They explain to her the ship was being used for human trafficking. Miss La'more becomes concerned, snatching the curtain back to see for herself.

"You don't say, darling!"

She struggles to stand the nurses rush to assist her. She tells them to take her into the main medical section so she may see the women and infant.
"Good gracious, there's so many of them."
ZsaZsa shouts in amazement. With human trafficking confirmed and all the victims safe and secure the Coast Guard now takes charge of the situation. The case is still under U.N.A jurisdiction so one of the team members will remain behind when the A.N.T depart shortly.
"Where's the captain? I demand to see the captain immediately!"
ZsaZsa demands.
"Someone please get me the captain, please!"
The ship's Chief medical officer asks her to calm down. Explaining that the captain is busy and if she continues to act this way she will be sedated. She immediately stops talking and gives him such I look.
"No, he didn't." Her male nurse whispers to the others. The medical officer is putting on quite the show, it isn't every day he gets to tell ZsaZsa La'more to shut up.
Her male nurse decides to take matters into his own hands and confront the Chief medical officer because he is not a member of his crew, he's with the Coast Guard.
"Hold on, you need to watch who you talkin to, she's a victim!"
He tells the officer pointing in his face.
"Get your hand out of my face, NOW! What's your name and who's your supervisor?"
"My dear, the names 'Gorden Jesabee' But they call me 'Gor-Jes' and I AM
the supervising R.N on duty, TA NIGHT!"
He responds snapping his finger in the Chief medical officer's face. With all the commotion going on in the medical section not many noticed the conversation. Then the captain of Vinny's yacht uses his influence to call the captain for her. He comes to the medical section accompanied by

more members of the Coast Guard. ZsaZsa asks to speak to both captains privately but allows her nurses to accompany her because she wants them to witness the meeting.

"Captains thank you for meeting with me I know you're very busy and there's a lot going on so I'll be very, very brief, Darling."

This appears to the nurses as a meeting and a celebrity making a request, but in reality its ZsaZsa laying out a new plan and giving them Orders. Since there's no longer a threat of violence the media helicopters are allowed closer but cannot land on the carrier yet. ZsaZsa asks the Captains to inform the media of her situation and how she came to be on board this carrier. listening to this the nurses understand she doesn't want the world to think she was involved. She also tells them she would like to express her gratitude by using every resource at her disposal to assure these women and infant are completely taken care of and she will finance everything!

"What about the Singapore government they're going to want these people back."

The captain of the Cargo Carrier asks.

"Well I'll see if I have any friends who can assist with me with them, if not I'll go through however many channels I need, to make this happen, Darling! Please assist me in starting this gentleman and I want to thank you in advance for your anticipated cooperation, Darling."

The two captains listen to her request but in front of the nurses make no promises to her. But know they had better get it done immediately.

As the mock meeting concludes the nurses give High Praise to ZsaZsa, assuring her they will spread this news on their social media pages and encourage their friends to do the same. ZsaZsa is escorted by the nurses throughout the medical section introducing herself to the women. The nurses translate for her but many of them have no idea who she is.

Now that some of the media helicopters are allowed to land the captains begin carrying out ZsaZsa's plan. The media covers some sort of human trafficking news almost weekly but this is a very special case. The captains made absolutely sure the media understood and knew how Miss La'more came to be on the Cargo Carrier the slow sinking yacht is still in the distance confirming everything.

The news crews quickly report everyone's safety to the world, so they can begin interviewing Lady ZsaZsa La'more. Normally she would never allow herself to be seen, photographed or filmed with no makeup and her hair a mess. But she needs the world to believe she was pulled from a sinking yacht and was in terrible Danger also very frightened. She did however ask nurse Gor-Jes to at least do something with her hair.

With the three nurses by her side CNN, Fox News and many others start the interview in a curtained-off part of the medical section. ZsaZsa is extremely convincing, her interviewers are very sympathetic. She explains how traumatized she is on top of being rescued by a human trafficking boat. But how grateful she is they were in the vicinity. With most of the attention now focused on her. She goes on to express her views on human trafficking and how appalled she is by it. The interviewers must stop from time to time due to her crying. She also takes the opportunity to plug some of the charity organizations she supports that help women and children in trouble. She Praises Hymiriam's work and says she's inspired by her, taking a moment to get herself together then telling her interviewers she was on the guest list for president Winfrey's fundraiser for chili tonight but of course will not be attending and makes a fifty-million-dollar pledge. The interviewers are amazed.

She has thrown down the gauntlet making such a large donation. President Winfrey is not watching the interview but her public relations department is and they make an emergency call to the interviewers while it is being televised to publicly express the president's gratitude.

ZsaZsa has everyone eating out of the palm of her hand like only she can, even expressing her appreciation to the Arch Nun and her team for rescuing her from those wretched thugs.

By the end of the interview Lady ZsaZsa La'more is hailed the hero. The only thing that would have gotten more attention would have been an interview with The Arch Nun or any of her team.

But that will NEVER happen!

On board B.A.D Seven Sister Dajairia tells Mikolai to speak to No one regarding what happened in the corridor until he Debriefs Mother Teresa.

The team can't wait to hear what happened to him.

Something they'll all talk about over a great many Beers! On the deck of the carrier the news media have cameras fixed on the Battle Assault Drone hoping to get a glimpse at the Arch Nun.

"Ok okay agent Alex you have command of the site. We'll be departing in a few minutes, see you back at the base."

Sister Dajairia says over the comlink to the agent left on the Cargo Carrier.

"Okay boss tell Mikolai not to touch my stuff."

The agents laugh knowing his hands are broken. Like always it is Mother Teresa's instructions for all B.A.D Pilots to demonstrate the crafts extreme maneuverability during departures. B.A.D Seven slowly Rises, flips backwards, rolls over and quickly speeds off. Something no other aircraft in the world that can do. With the exception of 'Godspeed' of course.

"I love to see those things fly!"

One of the Fox news reporter says to his camera crew.

Mother Teresa tells agent Alex on board the Cargo Carrier if there are any discrepancies say nothing, they are to be reported directly to her.

   In Atlanta Sister Anna meets with Governor Stevens.
The two are sitting in his office. He met with Mother Teresa
a few times for a group lunch and finds her to be very
Pleasant and easy to talk to. But being around one of her
grandchildren is a little unsettling at first. The Arch Nun
rhetoric doesn't help much either.
"Thank you, sister, for coming on such short notice I really
appreciate this. I'm a big fan, believer and supporter of your
mother's work."
"Salutations governor, my mother would be pleased to know
that."
"Please sister please let her know when you see her for me."
Governor Stevens is quickly becoming comfortable with the
Arch Nun, rambling on and praising her mother. Then Sister
Anna sharply brings him back to his senses.
"Let's stay focused and tend to the business at hand, sir!"
She interrupts in full Arch Nun rhetoric. The governor
realizes he was getting a bit carried away and apologizes.
Sister Anna responds with a single nod of her head. He
provides her with all necessary information. But the
governor has one final concern and request.
"Sister a portion of this gang consists of small children. Like I
was telling Mother Teresa some of them are only seven years
old, born into the life. I know you're not going in there ta do
them any harm. I feel only an Arch Nun can do this, that's
why I reached out ta Mother Teresa. And if you would
honor me Sister Anna I would like to pray for their safety
and yours. Will you join me, sister?"
"It would be my pleasure to pray with you governor."
The two join hands and the governor starts the prayer.
"Oh Heavenly Father if it wasn't for you, I wouldn't be
standing here today. You've seen me through some of the
toughest times of my life, Lord. But it's not about me Lord I
just wanted ta take a moment to thank you, before I ask you
ta watch over these poor misguided children who are about
to stand against a power this world has never seen! A power

I KNOW resides in this Arch Nun praying with me today. I would ask you ta watch over her, but I know she walks with YOU like no other. I went outside my jurisdiction Lord because I couldn't wait for the slow-moving justice system. So, I had ta ask a group I know is sent here by you. Please God I am begging you, see these children through this, safely! And now that I've prayed about it Lord, you know I'm not gonna worry about it! Thank you Oh Heavenly Father Amen!"

Before Sister Anna says Amen, she adds a little prayer of her own.

"Oh Lord, thy God I shall not procrastinate in doing thy bidding. I will be Swift in administering the spiritual chastising their parents should have given them and put them on the path to a better life. Amen"

"Wow, sister that was short and sweet"

"Short yes, sweet remains to be seen!"

"Well sister I said and did all I can do. It's in God's hands now!"

"Indeed it is Governor, Hallowed be thy name!" Then the Arch Nun is on her way to do the Lord's work.

"Lord please don't let those children do anything stupid!" Governor Harvey says looking up at the ceiling and wiping the sweat from his forehead.

On the streets of Atlanta not too far from the warehouse they occupy the teenage Street gang solicits prostitution of minors. They have a fixed clientele and are very careful who they approach. If they do encounter an undercover police officer. They simply say they were just playing or someone dared then to say that. They're familiar with most of the vehicles in the vicinity and have numerous Lookouts. Sister Anna and her team are sitting in an unmarked vehicle a few blocks away using the traffic cams to monitor them. As Twilight approaches some of the gang members had back to the warehouse to get the girls ready for their customers. The A.N.T follow telling the undercover officers to continue monitoring those still on the street. With lookouts on the roof and throughout the property, Sister Anna comes to the conclusion there are definitely adults in charge but may not be on the property. The Arch Nun is only half right some of the older gang members are twenty-three, they look, dress and act like teenagers. They never applied for Social Security numbers or had any real jobs and the young seven-year-old children born into the life, we're born in abandoned buildings and it is their twenty-three-year-old parents they work for.

As for the parents of the twenty-three-year olds. They are either incarcerated or dead leaving their offspring to be raised by the streets.

Sister Anna tells her team to take her down the street, drop her off and standby. She alone will find a way to infiltrate the building. They pull into an Alleyway as not to be seen. "Gentleman I will tend to the minors and children; I'll have them all contained in a single room. I'll electronically mark it, so you guys don't blow holes through it. On second thought I'll just wait in the room with the children I'm sure they'll be frightened."

"The sh#t kids do these days boss is un-Fu#king - believable!"

549

Sister Anna grabs her bag and exits the vehicle, The Gangs look outs immediately spot her, from the rooftops of neighboring buildings. The vehicle exits the alley to return to the warehouse.

"Yo, Y'all stay Sharp. I jus saw one of them Arch Nuns get out a blue truck, the truck heading back your way." Philip, one of the Lookouts says over the walkie-talkie warning the others.

"Oooh Sh#t you got eyes on that Bit#h?" Hector, a sixteen-year-old boy responds. He's a handsome young man with a slight developing mustache and one of the leaders of this Motley Crew of teenagers and children.

"He'll yeah, I'm looking at her right now." Philip tells him, and as he looks at her through his binoculars, The Arch Nun disappears right before his eyes. "Oh sh#t that bit#h GONE!" A millisecond later in a spectacular display of light Sister Anna appears in the warehouse, in front of Hector, several armed adult guards and all of the small children.

"What-Da-Fu#k!" Hector says to himself.

"Oh HELLLLLL NO!" One of the adult guards' shouts pointing his gun at her, then all the guards point their guns at her. The small children jump up and down clapping their hands yelling. "DO IT AGAIN, DO IT AGAIN, DO IT AGAIN!"

"SHUT THE FU#K UP!" Hector yells. "Y'all kids come wit me now! ALL You other motherfu#kers, KILL THAT BIT#H! or we all going ta jail!"

Hector picks up a seven year old girl and tells the other children to follow him.

"MAKE SURE THAT BIT#H DEAD AND I'LL TRIPLE ALL Y'ALL PAY, TELL EVERYBODY!"

The children are now out of Harm's Way but the guards are still a little hesitant.

"Yo, don't be scared of this bit#h tricks." One of the guards named Jamil says to the others.

"That's all they are, is tricks! This ain't no magic show, treat

her like we do everybody else and let's get this MONEY!"
Suddenly the lights go out and the room is completely dark.
Before the guards can Panic Peecan, another loudmouth
adult gang member yells to everyone.
"HOLD UP, HOLD UP Y'ALL DON'T SHOOT, DON'T
SHOOT. WE MIGHT HIT EACH OTHER! I heard that's how
they like ta fool you into shooting each other. All they sh#t is
fake and can be explained! Like any other magic trick."
Then from all directions they hear the voice of The Arch
Nun echoing in the Darkness.
"Then allow me gentleman to do that which cannot be
explained. Now BE HOLD THE POWER OF THY LORD
GOD!"
Then the room is mysteriously lit by an unknown source
coming from the center of the room. It becomes a ball of light
hovering in place.
One of the guards is only sixteen but looks older. His name
is Thomas Adamos
His father is from Greece, his mother Italian-American. He's
known on the streets as 'Tommy the Greek'. He has watched
the YouTube videos countless times of the Arch Nuns
fighting and like many gang members secretly hope they
NEVER have to face one. Tommy has been a thief all his life
working with the smaller children breaking into people's
homes. He was caught once by a homeowner who didn't call
the police but rather gave him a vicious beating before
letting him go. Tommy took his lumps like a man on that
day and chose not to report the beating to his gang, because
he knew they would kill the person who beat him. Instead
he told them it was a one-on-one fight with someone his age
over a girl and everything was okay. But today he seriously
doubts everything is going to be alright. He stands with the
armed men but has not yet pointed his weapon at the Arch
Nun. Upon hearing her words, he has a strong,
overwhelming feeling he shouldn't do this. He may be a
thief but a murderer he is not. As the gang members Point

their weapons at Sister Anna. Thomas looks around at the
adult gang members and knows he is gazing into the eyes of
truly ruthless murderers.

"No, I can't do this sh#t, I just can't!" He says throwing his
gun to the floor.

"You punk as$ bit#h!" Shouts one of the gang bangers.

"Shoot Dat motherfu#ker!" Another adds.

All the gang bangers open fire on Tommy and the Arch
Nun, a second before the bullets strike Tommy's head and
body, time stops and none of them are allowed to shut their
eyes.

For as the Arch Nun said unto them. Behold the Power of
thy Lord God!

And Sister Anna walked through their bullets as they were
suspended in time. The gang members watch but cannot
deny what their eyes are saying. She approaches Thomas
and gently places her hand on his left shoulder, attempting
to comfort him.

But with bullets a few inches from his face and body, he
can't help but to panic.

"Everything will be alright for you my child, have faith in
the lord!"

Sister Anna says softly to him but loud enough for everyone
to hear. But alas poor Thomas cannot, he doubts the bullets
will pass through him as they did the Arch Nun.

The ball of light slowly approaches Thomas. He's so scared
the only thing he can do is attempt to weep but he cannot.
Sister Anna removes her hand and stands to the right side of
him assuming the prayer position. The ball of light stops
behind Thomas and forms the silhouette of a woman. The
image of Hymiriam can almost be seen within the light.

Then he feels a hand upon his right shoulder, time resumes
very slowly.

The first bullet passes through him, he is unharmed then another then another, and so on until the last bullet approaches his right shoulder. Still unable to move and a little doubtful of his survival. All he wants to do is Scream! With her hand still upon his shoulder, Hymiriam walks around to face him. Looking deep into his eyes she asks him. "Why do you deny that which is in your heart? Stop Doubting Thomas and believe!"

But he is still a little uncertain as the last bullet grazes his shoulder breaking the skin and drawing blood. And in that instant Hymiriam is gone but the room is still mysteriously lit. The Lord illuminates the path for the Arch Nun in hopes that all who mean her harm will see the light! Because of Hymiriam's appearance and her designation of Christ. The Arch Nun cannot harm them unless she is attacked again, even though they had every intention of killing her, this gives them one chance to repent. With time still moving slowly Sister Anna says to them.

"You have all witnessed a miracle of the Lord first hand. Realize the error of your ways and you shall be spared the Lord's punishment on this day."

If all the rumors they've heard are true. They know the Lord's punishment for attacking an Arch Nun is quite severe and ALWAYS ending with permanent damage!

They are allowed to speak freely Thomas included.

"I'll never doubt God again! I wanna atone for my sins sister, please help me?" Thomas says with great remorse.

The adult gang members agree, all but one, his name is Fabian he is a twenty-eight-year-old murderer and rapist of women and has no intention of changing his ways.

"I ain't changing sh#t, you think that little magic show mean something ta me?

IT DON'T! LET ME GO BIT#H SO I CAN SHOW YOU JUST HOW FAKE YOU ARE!"

Why is there always one? Sister Anna thinks to herself as she shakes her head in disbelief.

She allows Fabian to move freely while still holding the others in time. The moment he's free, he does nothing! Fabian is all talk without his friends behind him, he is just a coward. Staring at the Arch Nun he throws his gun to the floor and turns to run but his loose-fitting pants fall to his knees tripping him, yet he does not fall. Once again, he is suspended in time, she asks the others if they feel the same as he. She allows them to move they quickly throw their hands in the air disagreeing with him and surrendering.
"Put your hands on your heads gentleman and keep them there!" She commands. "And for Heaven's sake pull up your pants and fix your clothing!"
They immediately obey without hesitation.
"What's gonna happen ta Fabian sister?"
The Arch Nun looks at them but does not respond to the question, instead tells them to take hold of him and carry him out, she releases him from time and he drops to the hard concrete floor unconscious. She stands over Fabian and reminds them exactly how blessed they are.
If not for the special appearance of 'Hymiriam Christ' Sister Anna would have been at full Liberty to administer the Lord's punishment!
 She points to the door ordering them to leave and surrender to her team outside without resistance, something they are more than glad to do.
Thomas's shoulder is bleeding and a little sore so Sister Anna tells him to walk ahead of the others. She watches as they leave the warehouse carrying Fabian and lead by Thomas.
Watching the gang members exit the warehouse, her team can't help but wonder why their coming out so soon?
"What the fu#k! Boss you've only been in there less than a minute, everything okay?"
Bernardo asks in confusion.
"Yes everything's fine Take all of them into custody. The one their carrying is unconscious.

I don't believe there's going to be much of a fight in here! Stand by."

"Hey boss you secure those kids yet?" Arsenio Jokingly asks knowing she's only been in there sixty-seconds.

"For Heaven's Sake guys I just got here, and I had to use the restroom."

Her team laughs as they playfully urge her to hurry.

Only those gang members present in the room at the time of Hymiriam's appearance are exempt from the Lord's punishment. For those in waiting to Ambush the Arch Nun, they would do well to yield to the Power of God!

Sister Anna ventures further into the warehouse entering another large room with the light of the Lord coming from her body. All is silent but she is in the sight of a female sniper's 50 caliber rifle. The sniper looks through the scope and decides to shoot her between the eyes.

Sister Anna is well aware of the sniper and where she plans to shoot her.

She assumes the prayer position looking up directly at the sniper then closes her eyes giving the sniper an opportunity to cease.

 The sniper takes the shot, the Arch Nun does not move just before the bullet hits the Arch Nun between the eyes, time slows down, she opens her eyes. The sniper is still watching through the scope as all snipers do assuring, they hit their mark. Sister Anna opens her eyes with an intense stare. The sniper can see the Arch Nun's lips moving as though she is saying something. Then the sniper can hear clearly in her mind the words the Arch Nun Speaks.

"NOW WITNESS THE POWER OF GOD!"

Still staring at the sniper the bullet strikes the Arch Nun right between the eyes, flattening on impact and dropping at her feet, time resumes.

"What the Fu#k!" The sniper says to herself taking her eye from the scope for a moment to chamber another round. Looking through the scope again she notices the Arch Nun is

holding what appears to be a small compound bow, no
bigger than a coat hanger. Unknowing to her this is no
ordinary weapon. For this is the Arch Nun's exclusive
weapon The Arc Bow!

"What'cha gonna do with that, Pocahontas?"
The sniper says to herself. Referring to Sister Anna as the
animated Disney Native American female character. The
sniper pulls the trigger once more as the bullet exits the
barrel, time slows down. Sister Anna reaches in her bag and
retrieves one Arc-Bow-Arrow. The feathers auto adjust for
custom flight, she loads the bow, aims at the sniper and
draws the string back. The Wheels on the Arc Bow make a
winding sound adjusting in size to compensate for pressure
as the arms of the bow mechanically tighten making a very
distinctive clicking sound. A loud single Harp-like plucking
sound is heard as the string is released. The arrow separates
into four arrows. The first Arrow strikes the 50 cal. bullet
altering its course as it continues toward the sniper. It
penetrates the sniper's scope traveling through it and
puncturing her eye. Followed by the second Arrow which
punctures her other eye. The third and fourth arrows
simultaneously curve upward and back toward the Arch
Nun traveling past her and striking two rapidly approaching
assailants through the mouth attempting to ambush her
from behind.

   The arrows penetrate the backs of the necks causing severe
neuro damage to their spines. With time still moving slowly
they begin to fall. To prevent any further damage to them
brothers Zacharia and Joshua appear and gently guide each
one to the floor laying them to rest comfortably until help
arrives. The 50 caliber bullet ricochets around the room
becoming weaker before hitting the sniper in the back
paralyzing her. Her name is Carol a twenty-six-year-old ex-
military sniper dishonorably discharged for allegedly
sleeping with underage boys. Now She's a gun-for-hire and
would have shown No Remorse had her bullet penetrated

the Arch Nun's skull. For that she shall see and move, NO MORE! Now she will spend the rest of her life in jail unable to move in total darkness, until her day of judgement.

Time resumes, Carol's painfully horrible screams can be heard throughout the warehouse.

The gang recognize her voice and become a little uneasy hearing her agony. She screams a few minutes more before passing out from the extreme pain. At that moment the light of the Lord leaves the Arch Nun.

Sister Anna enters another section of the warehouse there are more gang members waiting to attack her but are very hesitant after what they've just heard. The room is dimly lit from a dropped flashlight. Eight-armed gang members are waiting to attack her. Two are hiding behind old factory equipment, three are hiding on elevated scaffolding just above the entrance. The last three are also on elevated scaffolding on the other side of the room. Sister Anna slowly enters the room. The gang can barely make out her silhouette in the Darkness.

"Surrender and no harm shall befall you. Resist and thou shall know the Wrath of God!"

She warns but unfortunately it fell upon deaf ears. The gang members empty their guns at the Arch Nun, hoping she is dead! They quickly reload and wait.

"Go see if that Bit#h is dead." One of them Whispers.

"FU#K THAT! you go see if she dead." He answers.

"She gotta be dead, where I'm standing, I saw all those bullets hit her."

They turn on their flashlights and see the Arch Nun lying in a pool of blood. They start cheering when their flashlights mysteriously turn off. They immediately turn them back on and to their horror, they see Sister Anna standing with her hands on her hips tapping her foot. The bullets did not harm her, for no bullet can harm an Arch Nun unless it be God's will. She merely wanted them to believe they killed her, to see their response and a very disappointing one it was.

"Oooooooh FUDGE!" One of them says slowly.

Sister Anna stops tapping her foot and the room goes dark again, they try their flashlights but they don't work. The only light in the room is from the flashlight dropped earlier. Too petrified to move or whisper to each other they remain perfectly still, hoping she can't see them. Then they hear the most terrifying sounds in the Darkness. The sound of the Arc bow's wheels turning and the clicking of its arms locking. Anxiously waiting for their eyes to adjust to the dim light, they wonder in fear who she is targeting. Then they hear the single harp-like plucking sound as the string is released.

"Ahhhhhh!" One of the men hiding behind the old equipment screams. The arrow has gone between his rib cage and lodged in his spine. The pain is so excruciating he only had a moment to scream before passing out. Once again, the room is completely silent. The men are very tense. Sister Anna keeps them in suspense a few minutes before drawing the bowstring again. The sound in the darkness is intimidating, very INTIMIDATING!

They want to shoot her but know the bullets won't penetrate her armor. Then they hear the releasing of the bowstring. Their eyes adjust to the light, just in time to see the arrow curve around the room hitting the metal scaffolding over the entrance behind the Arch Nun. The scaffolding holding the three men comes crashing down, on top of the gang member hiding behind the other piece of Factory equipment. Breaking their necks, all four men lie motionless but are allowed to continue witnessing the Arch Nun performing The Lord's work. With Sister Anna appearing to be trapped within the rubble. One of the last three men on the other side of the room, jumps from the scaffolding and runs towards the Arch Nun hoping to get his hands on her so he can shoot in the face at point-blank range. He can see her silhouette standing in the center of the rubble. Without thinking he hastens his pace. He can clearly see her in the dimly lit room now, he reaches out with his left hand to grab her by the throat. The thought of getting his hands on her excites him. Holding his pistol in his right hand. All he can think about is grabbing her by the throat, putting his gun in her mouth and blowing the top of her head off!

The other two men are too scared to move. They remain on the scaffolding watching their friend run toward the Arch Nun. As he reaches out to grab Sister Anna, he impales himself on a piece of the sharp scaffolding.

"Ohhhhhhhh SH#T!" The two men say collectively in disbelief grabbing their hair.

As for he who intended to kill an Arch Nun on this day. He will spend the rest of his life regretting it. Looking into Sister Anna's eyes he is in shock with his hand still extended. She takes his hand into hers bows her head and prays for his soul. The last two men assume she is trapped. They jump down and start to run from the room. They stop for a moment turning to look back at the Arch Nun to ensure she is still standing there, to their brief delight she is. She releases his hand, assumes the prayer position and walks, passing through the rubble as though it were not there. They stand watching in amazement not knowing what to do. She lowers her hands and the Arc Bow slowly appears in her left hand, an arrow in her right, they do the only thing they can, RUN! The two keep looking back firing their guns hoping to hit her in a vulnerable spot. But when administering the Lord's punishment an Arch Nun has no vulnerabilities!

This long corridor has Sky lighting and is not as dark as some of the rooms. Sister Anna allows them to get ninety feet or so away from her. She loads the bow and draws the string.

At ninety feet away the men can still hear the chilling sound of the Arc Bow! She releases the string the arrow leaves the bow as it flies through the air it becomes two. The first Arrow curves upward hitting a rusty light fixture, knocking it loose. It falls striking one of them on top of his head, he falls breaking his neck. The second Arrow flies straight striking the last man in the center of his back paralyzing him. He falls face-first onto the hard-concrete floor sliding, grinding the skin from his face. He comes to a stop at the feet of his girlfriend who was running toward him.

Her name is Gretchen Estes, she appears to be a seventeen-year-old girl but she's really a twenty-three-year-old woman and an abuser of children. When the children disobey or simply don't want to commit crimes, she severely beats them. She has broken their limbs and caused one to lose an eye. She's Despicable and heartless. Now she faces an Arch Nun. Looking down at her boyfriend's limp body, she is saddened and becomes angry. She slowly raises her head looking at Sister Anna whom is standing in the doorway almost a hundred feet away holding the Arc Bow. Gretchen is an excellent shot and very good with a pistol, she also comes to work very prepared. She unzips and removes her jacket revealing twin 45 caliber handguns in shoulder holsters under each arm. She is determined to kill Sister Anna and she knows this Warehouse like the back of her hand. She draws her weapons and repeatedly Fires at the Arch Nun. The bullets pass through her. Gretchen takes cover and reloads her weapons. Hiding behind a support column, she waits for Sister Anna to come closer. She can see the Arch Nun hasn't moved yet.

She peeks out to assure the Arch Nun is still standing in the doorway.

The sound of the Arc bow is heard as Sister Anna draws the string. What the hell is that Gretchen wonders taking a few deep breaths. The plucking sound of the Arc Bow is heard as Sister Anna releases the string.

The arrow separates in two, the two arrows swirl around each other as they dance through the air. As the arrows get closer to the column, time slows down. Gretchen leans outside the column, she points her guns and squeezes the triggers but before the bullets exit the barrels the arrows go down them causing the guns to explode in her hands, blowing all the fingers off her left hand and lightly damaging her right. Ducking behind the column and Biting her shoulder to keep from screaming she slides to the floor; her fingers lie spread out around her. The pain is almost unbearable. Trembling and heavily perspiring she pulls a small 9 mm handgun from her ankle holster. With nothing to wrap her left hand, she begins to tear small pieces of her shirt. She sees her jacket lying on the floor where she dropped it before shooting at the Arch Nun. But if she reaches for it, she'll be out in the open. She can hear the heels of the Arch Nun's boots as she slowly walks down the corridor toward her.

"Gretchen Jennifer Estes. The Lord took your left hand for standing against the Power of God! And spared your right hand so you may know the mercy of the Lord! Surrender and be harmed no more." Sister Anna tells her but Gretchen is too angry to heed the Arch Nun's warning.

"Yeah, yeah! let me get my jacket, then I'll give up."

Sister Anna stops walking. Gretchen has no intention of surrendering but she can really use that jacket to cover her hand and stop the bleeding. Holding the gun in her right hand, she hides it under her left arm.

"Stay there Gretchen I'll get your jacket for you."

This works out perfectly Gretchen thinks to herself. When the Arch Nun gets close enough, she can shoot her in the head.

"Okay" Gretchen says tossing both 45's out into the open so the Arch Nun can see them, attempting to lure her into a false sense of security.

Then before her very eyes the jacket rises from the floor as if by Magic. She watches as it slowly floats toward her and lands in her lap, but she is not impressed. She believes it to be a magician's trick done with wires. Gretchen is too angry and in too much pain to recognize the power of the Lord.

She wraps the jacket around her bloody left hand further concealing the gun under her arm and squeezing her eyes shut to deal with the pain.

"Your pain must be great Gretchen? The lord giveth pain and the lord taketh it away. Now feel the Mercy of thy lord and know that God is God!"

The lord relieves Gretchen of her pain and stops the bleeding. With her body now calm and her right hand steady. She wipes the sweat from her brow and slowly walks from behind the column from which she hid. Now standing seventy feet from the Arch Nun still holding the gun under her arm. She stares at Sister Anna with anger and hatred in her heart. Turning 180 degrees away from the Arch Nun with the gun hidden under her arm, partially covered by the jacket and now secretly pointing at Sister Anna.

She squeezes the trigger, Time slows down. Sister Anna draws the string of the Arc Bow and releases. The arrow passes by the bullet and splits in two. The bullet hits the Arch Nun in the chest leaving a mark on her body armor but doesn't penetrate. As the bullet falls at sister Anna's feet, Gretchen turns to watch the Arch Nun die. Upon turning she is met by the two arrows.

She watches has they pierce her eyes, that is the last thing she'll ever see!

Time resumes. Gretchen screams in agony, not only has she lost the gift of sight but all the pain she has received thus far returns tenfold.

She stumbles backwards, tripping over debris and falls, striking the back of her head on the hard-concrete floor. Sister Anna goes to her and kneels beside her. Gretchen's eyes are destroyed but she can see the Arch Nun clearly. Still conscious and coherent her physical, mental and emotional pain is great. Because of this sister Anna will speak directly to her.

"Gretchen my child someone will be here soon to take you to the hospital."

Sister Anna says Softly placing a hand on her face.
"Don't call me your Fu#king child. If there is a God, he don't
love me! The only person that loves me is me!" She angrily
responds slapping Anna's hand from her face.
"God does love you, as do I. You cannot blame the choices
you've made on the Lord. Even now Gretchen you deny
God's existence."
Gretchen says nothing, she lies on her back breathing
heavily, knowing she'll never be the same again. She reaches
up for Sister Anna to take her hand.
"Open your heart to God Gretchen, take but one step toward
the lord and the Lord will never stop talking steps toward
you."
Sister Anna says bowing her head, tightly holding her hand
and bringing it close to her heart.
The image of Sister Anna fades from Gretchen's mind as she
finally passes out from the unbearable pain. For all the pain
she has inflicted upon children, for bringing her own child
into the life of prostitution, for all the families she has
destroyed accusing men of raping her during consensual
sex, for all the teenage girls who faces she scarred for life in
jealous fits. This WAS a young woman whom was very lost!
But Gretchen was given the opportunity to experience God's
mercy first hand. She chose to deny what her eyes were
allowed to see and her body has felt. Now the Lord will
allow her to live till the age of ninety-three incarcerated, in
darkness and in solitude. On that day the Lord will take her.
Hopefully in that time span she will truly know that, God is
God!
The Arch Nun makes the sign of the cross, then Rises to her
feet. Before she can take a single step. Two handguns slide
across the floor stopping where Gretchen lies unconscious.
Three adult gang members walk toward her, they saw and
heard everything. Rapidly approaching her they
immediately stop when the Arc Bow materializes in her
hand.

They QUICKLY fall to their knees begging her not to shoot.
"STAND" She commands.
"Sister we saw the whole thing." One of them shouts.
"Of course you did it was God's will." The Arch Nun tells them.
"Yeah, whatever all we know is we don't want none of this."
Sister Anna steps closer.
"Really, did you just refer to the Power of God as WHATEVER?"
"Nah, nah, I ain't mean it like that, I ain't mean it like that now." He quickly explains holding his hands in front of him. "I meant we surrendering ta you."
Sister Anna steps a little closer, squinting her eyes at them.
"WHATEVER, doesn't sound like I Surrender."
"My bad, my bad sister I'm sorry, I'm sorry!"
"What are your names?" She asks they are hesitant to answer but figure she already knows. Before they can answer she holds up her hand and urges them to give her their government names not the ridiculous street names they tend to give themselves.
"My name fuquan." (a very common name. lol)
Sister Anna couldn't help herself she had to correct his grammar.
"Is, my name IS FUQUAN! Now try it again."
"I'm sorry, I'm sorry." Fuquan says nervously still shaking his hands in front of him.
"For Heaven's Sake, man pull yourself together and by ALL that is Holy, stop repeating yourself."
Sister Anna shouts stopping her foot to the floor. Brothers Zacharia and Joshua are in commune with her and can't stop laughing. Fuquan's eyes begin to water, not so Much from the reprimand but the fact that this is all happening in front of his boys.

He never respected his mother enough to ever pay attention to anything she told him. But to spite the embarrassment of it all he sort of welcomes it from the Arch Nun.

Sister Anna immediately turns her attention to the other two.

"And what may I ask is your name?" He takes a deep breath before answering. "Wayne, my name is Wayne ma'am."

"Well, that's more like it!"

The third gang member attempts to give his name but Sister Anna abruptly stops him, squeezing his lips shut.

"That's rude, to interrupt someone when they are speaking. Now kindly wait until this conversation has ended and you are addressed!"

"Yes ma'am I apologize." He says biting his lip.

"NO! You ARE sorry, but I will accept your apology."

Sister Anna takes a moment to look at him before asking.

"What is your name sir?"

"Herbert" He nervously answers. Sister Anna takes a few steps back and looks at them.

"let's get on with the surrendering, shall we gentlemen?"

They all agreed anything would be better than being treated like children by a Nun!

"Gentleman make no mistake everything I say to you is not a request, you are to follow my instructions to the letter. Do I make myself clear?"

They all agree. Brothers Zachariah and Joshua are still laughing hysterically in Anna's head.

"Gentlemen put your feet together, hands on your head and interlock your fingers."

Like soldiers they follow her orders.

"Now that we have an understanding. Know this, you are my prisoners any attempt to harm me or escape may be met with deadly force. I will allow you to speak but be wary of what you say in my presence, understood?"

The three rapidly shake their heads in agreeance choosing not to speak.

"If you have any doubts regarding the Power of thy Lord God. Let me assure you when this is over you will NOT! Believing will be your choice."

At this point the three gang members are becoming frightened. They are tough as Nails on the streets of Atlanta but standing before an Arch Nun. They are like putty in her hands.

"Gentlemen try to move your hands from your heads and walk toward me."

To their surprise they can do neither. Struggling to break free one of them passes gas. They Immediately stop moving but are breathing heavily from their efforts.

Although the Arch Nun allows them to speak, they are now terrified so they remain silent. A wise choice considering they would have undoubtedly used profanity.

"Now that you feel the Power of God! Gentlemen follow me."

She turns and begins to walk away. The three men nervously shout out to her.

"Sister we can't move!"

The Arch Nun Stomps her foot to the floor and the three men rise four feet in the air, levitating behind her as she walks. With their eyes wide in amazement they still remain silent. To take their minds off of what is happening to them, they do the only thing they know. They watch her BUTT as she walks.   Before they leave the room their approached by a twelve-year-old boy. His name is James the younger brother of Fuquan. He's nervously pointing a gun at the Arch Nun.

"Let my Motherfu#king brother go, let my Motherfu#king brother go!" He demands trying to hold back his tears. The three men immediately break their silence yelling at him to put the gun down. James is anxious to show his brother how much of a man he is. He doesn't want to shoot the Arch Nun, for he has never shot anyone in his short life. But he so desperately wants to prove to his brother he's worthy of being in the Gang. Shaking like a leaf, he can no longer hold back his tears. The men are still shouting at him, hoping his brother didn't see him cry James struggles to hold himself together. Then to the three men's horror they notice the Arc Bow slowly appearing in the left hand of the Arch Nun. The men continued to scream as loud as they can ordering James to drop the gun.

"Drop the gun, BOY drop the FUC#KING GUN NOW!" Fuquan frantically yells to his younger brother. Then they hear a sound, a sound they hoped they would never hear again! The sound of the Arc Bow's wheels turning and the clicking of its arms locking. Fuquan begins to cry pleading and yelling at his younger brother to put the gun down. He knows he's going to jail for a long time but he cannot watch his baby brother die today.

Sister Anna has no intention of shooting the young boy but he will witness the Power of God on this day. With his finger on the trigger he's still ordering the Arch Nun to let them go. Sister Anna Stomps her foot to the floor, the Arc Bow disappears and the three men form a circle, levitating around her creating a barrier between her and the young boy. James didn't notice that the men were levitating before due to the excitement and his adrenaline. But now he can clearly see they are four feet off the ground and circling the Arch Nun.

All James has ever known is the gang's way of life and with everything going on in front of him, he still wants to impress his brother. Sister Anna realizes the young boy is too brainwashed to realize the seriousness of his situation and with that she saves James from himself. Holding out her hand the gun flies from his and into hers. James is then telepathically lifted into the air and placed in the same surrendering position as the others, but he unlike the others will not be allowed to speak.

"Sister, Sister." Fuquan calls out.

"SILENCE fuquan, I would not have harmed your younger

567

brother. Judging from my observation you have done more harm to him than anyone, something you'll undoubtedly answer to the Lord for, on your day of final judgement!" Fuquan hangs his head in shame and asks.
"Sister how'd you know he was my little brother."
"like you fuquan he says everything twice! Gentlemen let's move on."
Now James joins the men levitating behind the Arch Nun. They pass through a few small rooms before coming to a staircase. There's a door at the top of the stairs, this is where Hector is hiding with the children. Sister Anna turns to her four prisoners.
"Wait here gentlemen I will return momentarily."
Still levitating the four form a tight square formation slowly rotating. Fuquan can see the struggle in his little brother's face as he tries to break free from the Arch Nun's hold, but it is not the Power of the Arch Nun that Holds him. It is the Power of the God and if it not be the will of the Lord, nothing can free him.
   Sister Anna climbs the stairs and politely knocks on the door. Hector told the children this was a game of hide and seek so they would be quiet. He read how the Thrones of Chicago held children hostage and the high price they paid. Unknown to the outside gang members Hector's group paid to help protect him. He has a secret very few know.
Like Gretchen he's a legal adult, twenty-two years of age. The Arch Nun knocks again.
"Hector, let me in!" Sister Anna says calmly. "You cannot avoid that which is inevitable. I pray the Lord grant you the wisdom to acknowledge defeat. Resistance to the power of God is futile!"
She can hear the children giggling behind the door. Hector is torn between making a Last Stand or surrendering. Then he has a thought, the Arch Nun thinks he's sixteen. If he can maintain that he won't go to jail they'll still treat him like a juvenile. He places his gun on the floor where she can see it

as she enters the room, then calls to the Arch Nun.

"Ok , I give up!" He shouts to her laughing.

Before everyone's eyes Sister Anna passes through the solid door as though it were not there.

The gun leaves the floor and flies into her hand. She places it in her bag continuing to walk toward them. How is she doing all these tricks he wonders.

Hector and the children have already witnessed the Power of an Arch Nun and he is becoming afraid. The children on the other hand are finding all of this very entertaining and exciting. Laughing and running to the Arch Nun hugging her legs. "It's the magic lady." They shout.

"Do we get to hide again?" Some of the children ask.

"No, my children there will be no more hiding." Sister Anna answers, smiling.

"You see sister everybody's alright." Hector adds laughing with the children. "I wouldn't let no harm come ta them, Imma kid caught up in this sh#t myself!" Hector continues attempting to fool the Arch Nun.

"Caught up indeed!" Sister Anna responds cutting her eyes at him. "But you didn't seem too caught up, when you gave the order for the others to kill me!"

"Oh, I was just talkin big trying ta sound tough in front of the others, that all."

"REALLY, is that what happened." She asks.

"Actually what had happened was. They told me to act like I was in charge so you wouldn't think it was them, so they could get close enough so they could get you."

Sister Anna is astonished at how quickly he's fabricating his story.

"Well the Courts seem to go easy on juveniles committing crimes under the influence of adults."

Sister Anna states. Confident he is completely convincing the Arch Nun he is a minor, he continues. "Yeah Sister they had me doing all kinds of sh#t cuz I was scared."

"I'm sure it must have been horrible for you, Hector?"

The children are still clinging around the Arch Nun.

"Are you gonna do more Magic?" One of them asks.

"If your good." Sister Anna answers picking the child up.

"What is your name sweetheart?"

"Speechie."

"Well, speechie it's impolite to--"

Sister Anna pauses for a second to look at Hector before continuing.

"Interrupt ADULTS when they're talking!"

Hector's eyes widen but he doesn't want to give the impression he's lying case the Arch Nun is just trying to trick him into telling the truth.

"Yeah sister. I made them think I was older, so I can hang with them. You know so I could drink and get high."

"Of course Hector! Because being a MINOR like YOUR SELF, you were unable to acquire marijuana and alcoholic beverages, on your own. Because you're ONLY sixteen."

"Yeah, yeah, yeah Sister you get it, see you was a good girl when you were younger, so you don't know nothing bout that!"

"Hector, I may have been a good girl when I was younger, but I know a tall tale when I hear one and you sir are telling the tallest of tales!"

"What you saying Sister?"

"You proceed in your Endeavor to deceive me from a false assumption sir, that assumption being that you can manipulate me." Hector gets a bad feeling in the pit of his stomach. He knows the Arch Nun isn't buying it. Now desperate knowing he's going to be convicted as an adult immediately under the new law. He reaches into the back of his pants and draws a pistol, points the gun at the Arch Nun holding the child and squeezes the trigger, time slows down, Sister Anna suspends the children in time to protect them yet still controlling time Allowing Hector to move slowly. The bullet is heading straight toward little speechie's back, before the bullet can strike the child, all the children disappear and reappear downstairs with her four prisoners. They are still suspended in time, levitating a few feet off the ground with speechie in the center.

The four men, again cannot believe what they are seeing, with the Arch Nun out of their sight they break their silence. "Yo, MAN WHAT THE FU#K, Y'ALL SEEING THIS SH#T?" Fuquan yells.

"I don't think this sh#t is a trick anymore!" Wayne adds. With the children Frozen before them. it is uncomfortable and a very eerie sight. The men take the opportunity to discuss what's going on.

Now alone in the room with the Arch Nun, Hector will see his fate. A millisecond before the bullet touches the Arch Nun, she and Hector trade places, time resumes for Hector. The bullet pierces his abdomen and lodges in his spine. The force of the bullet is controlled by the Lord, blowing his body into the door, the door is forced from its hinges, soaring through the air with Hector's body lying flat on top, it slides perfectly down the stairs with his body held in place by the hand of God.

It slides a few more feet before stopping in front of her prisoners. They are allowed to move their heads for a moment. Looking first at each other Then up at the doorway. They see Sister Anna slowly walking through it in the prayer position.

"When I get outta jail, I ain't EVER doing anything wrong AGAIN!" Fuquan says to the others.

"I ain't ever gonna THINK about anything wrong again!" Herbert says in agreeance.

"When I get outta jail, imma be a PREACHER!" Wayne adds. As the men stare up at the Arch Nun. She disappears instantly appearing beside Hector and unfreezing the children. Clapping their hands and laughing again they run to the Arch Nun. These children unfortunately know death, for they have seen Fallen gang members.

They stop laughing and stand quietly beside her. She kneels beside him and communes with him.

'This ain't fair, this ain't Fu#king fair!' Hector says crying.

'Why do you say that. Hector?'

'I was born with nothing, grew up with nothing and when I do what I gotta do, this sh#t happens!'

'Hector, again my child you are under the assumption the world owed you something and if it didn't give it to you, you'd take it by any means necessary!'

'Nah, you got it wrong."

'Hector stop, calm thyself, even now after what thy eyes have beheld, you still doubt the Power of the Lord! And Accuse thy God of being wrong. Listen to your heart and humble thyself Hector before it is too late!'

'You said you already convicted me, so how you gonna say God forgives?'

'You have been convicted for the many EARTHLY laws you've broken. Those cannot go unpunished. I came for you on this day to answer for these crimes. But when you chose to attack me and challenge the Power of God, you felt the Wrath of God!'

'With my conviction how many years you giving me, sister?'

'I gave you forty years Hector.'

'I'll be forty-two when I get out, it'll give me time ta heal and I'll be big and strong when I get out.'

'No Hector you'll be sixty-two when you get out. You will not be strong and you will never walk again!'

'This is how God Saves, he sent you to do this sh#t, sister?

'Yes Hector, this is how the Lord saves. God sent me to save those children from you!'

He begins to scream obscenities at her and asking God to kill him, so she prevents him from communicating with her, now all you can do is hear her in his mind.

'you will live a long life, Hector. I will pray for you often. In that time, I hope you find it in your heart to let the Lord in. I beg of you, repent! And know the Love of the Lord.'

Hector lies sprawled on his back atop the door. His blood loss will be minimum until help arrives for now, he is held by the Lord. While sister Anna was praying the children closed their eyes and pretended to pray as well. They pretend for no one has ever taught them how, but in their little hearts they know it is right.

"Is Hector gonna be ok?" One of the children asks.

"I certainly hope so children." Sister Anna answers starting to stand. The children assist her as though she needed help.

"Can we say goodbye ta Hector?" Speechie asks the Arch Nun. Sister Anna looks down at the children and responds smiling.

"Why of course you may children, by all means."

Sister Anna allows Hector to hear their words. All the children say and wave goodbye with their sweet little Innocent Voices. These are the last words Hector will ever hear and they will undoubtedly haunt him for a very long time.

The Arch Nun looks at her prisoners and tells them. "These are the lives you intended to ruin gentleman. Know that these children will have every opportunity to be a thousand times better than you. I hope and pray you did not scar them too deeply!"

The men are silent hanging their heads in shame.

"Can I say something sister?" Wayne asks.

"You may, but be mindful of the children and be quick."

Wayne looks at fuquan and his eyes begin to tear as he unexpectedly extends his gratitude.

"Thank you, Fuquan."

"For what, you trying ta be funny?" He asks assuming Wayne is being sarcastic for their situation.

"Nah man, nothing like that. I just wanna thank ya for convincing me ta surrender and not go through with what we had planned. Thank you man, I know we all going ta jail but we going in one piece and however many years I get I'm gonna take that time ta try ta find the Lord cuz that's something I ain't never know til taday, so nah man I ain't being funny, I'm being real."

Herbert agrees with him 100%. All three men are fighting to hold back tears. Fuquan pulls himself together enough to respond.

" I only remember one thing my mama ever said to me when I was young before, she ran out on me and my little brother. She said if I ever see the Power of God be smart enough to be humbled by it. I'm glad I was able to share that with Y'all. Thank you, sister, thank you for not harming my little brother today. I know you not letting him talk and that's probably a good thing. I know he's probably thinking I'm acting like a little bit#h right about now. But hopefully he'll be all right. I don't have nothing to say ta these little kids cuz I ain't never seen them before until today. But real quick ta my little brother, I'm sorry for trying ta turn you inta a little monster. And I don't deserve to ever see you again so I'm not, I'm ready ta go Arch Nun!"

Sister Anna silences them. with her body cam off their statements will be in her final report. The Arch Nun tells the children to form two lines, join hands and start walking ahead of her.

She controls the levitating prisoners as they follow behind. Before they can leave the room speechie whom is closest to the Arch Nun shouts.

"You said if we were good you do more Magic!"

"I did say that children, didn't I?"

It is written in the book of The Arch Nunhood. Thou shall not perform exhibitions. Without express permission from the Mother or Grandmother Superior!

Sister Anna questions herself on what she should do. She's not performing a martial art exhibition or showing off in any way. She feels to her grandmother for advice, then she receives a commune from her grandmother.

'For all the things these children have endured. Let them feel the love and Power of thy Lord God. And hopefully as they grow, they will always remember and know that God is God'

And with that Mother Teresa allows Sister Anna to levitate the children ten feet off the ground and dance on air.

These children have never been to Disneyland or an amusement park of any kind. So, for ten minutes the Lord allowed them to fly around the room and it was truly the best time of their life.

"Boss it's been a few minutes is everything okay, it's pretty quiet in there."

Johnny asks over the comlink.

"Yes indeed it is, Johnny we're coming out. I have all of the children, prepare to sweep the building."

This is music to her agent's ears they're always ready for a firefight. Sister Anna, her prisoners and the children exit the building. As her team immediately rushes in.

Unlike higher-level gangs, this unnamed gang of young adults and children didn't have the resources to acquire adequate Firepower to engage a S.W.A.T team let alone the A.N.T.

There are still twenty or so gang members still hiding in the building. Sister Anna's team make Swift work of the inexperienced gang. S.W.A.T teams and local law enforcement apprehended all those who attempted to escape. Governor Stevens is containing the media for now he won't allow the story to break until tomorrow. The children will be taken to Langley Air Force Base and will remain under U.N.A jurisdiction until they are placed into proper homes and redistributed into society. Mother Teresa intends to dissolve the traditional orphanage within the next few years replacing them with a more home-like atmosphere for children and far better assistance if they should age out. This should not be a problem since it is something Nuns have always controlled anyway.

Meanwhile Sister Anna has a most serious meeting with her grandmother regarding her lack of enthusiasm or interest in vacationing.

She is told to transition to the Divine Elysium so they may speak.

"Why do you not wish to go have fun like your brothers and sisters? My child."

"It's not that I don't want to go Oma (German for grandmother). It's just that, well there's probably too much to do and-"

"Enough, my child." Mother Teresa interrupts holding up her hand.

"Ever since you were a little girl, you never thought you were deserving of anything. Your mother and I have always known you wonder why you were chosen to do God's work when your brothers and sisters have dismissed those thoughts a long time ago and embraced it, enjoying God's gift to the fullest. That is what the Lord intended, that is why you were chosen."

"BUT-"

"No, my child do you think the Lord makes MISTAKES?"

"No! Oma not at all."

"Then believe me, she who was Victoria Marsha Brady and she who IS

ARCH NUN SISTER ANNA!

Enjoy these vacations you will receive, my child. Because if you don't and your brothers and sisters find out, their love for you is so great they will be unable to enjoy theirs."

"Perhaps"

"There is no PERHAPS my child, we are your family and God wants you to enjoy your life so my child will you embrace the gift that the Lord has given unto you or will you question and deny it?"

"I never looked at it like that Oma. Why haven't you spoken to me about this earlier in my life?"

"Because my child it is something you have to work out on

your own. All parents can do is sit back and watch hoping you'll make the right decisions and I have the utmost confidence you will." She concludes hugging her granddaughter tightly. A few tears fall from Sister Anna's eyes as she embraces her grandmother and promises to heed her advice.

"Now, go have fun my child and please rethink the name of Victoria Goodie Tu'choos."

Sister Anna Smiles wiping the tears from her eyes.

"Thank you Oma, I love you so much!"

"N.I.U my child, now go and see Maria later after the fundraiser."

Mother Teresa transitions back to her room at the U.N building in New York where Sister Maria is waiting for her. She is delightfully surprised to find Maria in one of her high fashion Black and Red Spanish flamingo outfits, topped off with a matching habit. She had every intention of wearing her habit for it represents all Nuns! Besides she didn't want to disappoint her grandmother.

"You look like me when I was younger, my child."

Mother Teresa says laughing and hugging her.

"Don't be silly my Abuela you couldn't look this good if you tried."

"Maria that sounds like something your sister Buffie would say."

Mother Teresa replies playfully slapping her on the butt.

"While we're on the subject of attire my child you did look after your brothers I trust?"

"Of course you know what Zach would wear, if I didn't pick his outfits for him and Josh would dress Like a Rockstar! Fear not Abuela they won't be embarrassing us dressing like circus clowns tonight. Surprisingly they've been asking me for fashion advice a lot lately."

She concludes looking in the mirror checking her makeup and shrugging her shoulders in wonder.

Mother Teresa laughs for she truly knows why her grandsons are so suddenly interested in fashion tips. Outside the newly renovated Top Town Loft & Terrace the largest event venue in Manhattan, it is a parade of limousines and fancy automobiles as the world's Elite and Mega Rich gather for president Winfrey's fundraiser. The media is in full swing. Cameras and news crews are everywhere, Since the rumor was leaked that one of the female Arch Nun other than Mother Teresa will be in attendance it has been a madhouse. Due to the level of prestigious guests the General public is not allowed near the building. The public crowd is not very large right now, no more than three or four hundred appear to be in the immediate area, hoping to see their favorite celebrities who were invited. But the night is young and more of the General public are more likely to show up. The Arch Nun is not the focus of their attention. After all they're more likely to see an Arch Nun then most of President Ophelia's guests.

The News helicopters share the air with Apache helicopters maintaining a safe distance. President Winfrey has ordered not one, not two, but three Battle Assault Drones for absolute security and Due to the possibility of an attack and how serious it would be. President Winfrey invited every leader in the world and from the look of things most of them showed up, hoping the attending Arch Nun is Hymiriam.

President Winfrey and Mother Teresa have been bending some of their protocols so they may have a peaceful business relationship. If it were up to Mother Teresa Sister Maria would not be attending this affair but nothing could prepare the Reverend mother for the entrance president Winfrey has in mind. Inside the limo are the president's personal chauffeur and an A.N.T agent in the passenger seat. In the rear are Mother Teresa, Sister Maria, Brother Zachariah, Brother Joshua, president Ophelia and her husband Edmond.

The president calls ahead and tells her private security team to get everyone and everything ready for their arrival. The chauffeur slows down allowing the police escort motorcycles and vehicles in front to go first.

A twenty-five foot temporary tunnel was built to conceal the vehicles and some of the occupants before they approach the entrance for security purposes.

"Girl don't be mad but we have to make a Big statement to deter any would-be terrorists and besides the Apache helicopter just isn't as intimidating as it used to be since the birth of the Battle Assault Drone!"

The President tells Mother Teresa taking her hand and patting it to comfort her.

The Reverend mother is not a fan of showing off or displaying Unnecessary military power. But the president is of course in charge and it is her big night.

"Why are we stopping, what's going on now" The Reverend mother asks.

Everyone is laughing at Mother Teresa's meltdown.

"Maybe this will calm you nerves Mother Teresa."

Edmond says pouring her a glass of wine.

"Not too much, not too much."

She shouts waving her hand. Then a mid-sized B.A.D passes over the limo and hovers in front waiting to escort them.

"A mid-sized B.A.D for an Escort?" Mother Teresa shouts. "Pour me some more wine."

President Winfrey takes a moment to just look at her family and friends she considers herself so blessed to have them in her life and thanks the Lord for sending them to her.

"You okay baby?" Edmond asks. Putting his arm around his wife. She leans over and softly whispers in his ear.

"I-AM-FINE Baby. Just thanking the Lord for everything in my life. You know I can't say that too loud as president of the United States."

Edmond looks her in the eyes and Whispers back.

"Honey, I think you can shout that to high heaven in front of everybody in this vehicle!"

She smiles and gives him a big hug then a kiss.

"Okay Madam president we're clear to go."

The chauffeur says. The mid-sized B.A.D disperses four smaller Drones taking a position behind the limo before slowly moving forward followed by the President's limousine.

Not since the days when Ophelia Winfrey dominated Hollywood has there been in entrance as great as this.

The mid-sized B.A.D emerges from the tunnel. As it approaches the entrance it slowly rises as the president's limousine slowly drives under it and comes to a stop, With the mid-sized B.A.D hovering ten feet above its roof, scanning the immediate crowd with its thick fat beam lasers. The smaller Drones hover above the entrance of the building. A member of the president's staff opens the door. Edmond is the first to exit the limo, he extends his hand to assist his wife.

The people applaud the first family. Brother Joshua exits next; he assists his Grandmother from the vehicle. The people are still applauding and cheering.

Next brother Zachariah exits the limo; he extends his hand Sister Maria takes his hand and elegantly exits the limo. The crowd gasps at how stunning she looks, her outfit, her Style and the way She carries herself.

ZsaZsa watches from her private luxury hospital room with the naval medical staff she insisted upon keeping for a little while. With her power and influence it wasn't very hard and they didn't mind staying with her.

"Oooh Sh#t That SISTER is fierce in that outfit, WORK it Girl, WORK it!" Gor'jes shouts at the television screen. All the nurses agree.

"I wish there was a way I can get her to do some modeling for me or at least wear some of my designers." ZsaZsa adds.

"Talk ta God he'll make her sign with you!" Gor'jes tells her. They all laugh continuing to watch the fundraiser.

The crowds cheering and applauding become louder.
"The Arch Nun in attendance is Sister Maria. I repeat the
Arch Nun Sister Superior Maria is accompanying the
president."
Is reported to the World by the news media.
Some of the young fans of the Arch Nuns sing a verse from
the song 'Maria' from Steven Spielberg's remake of 'West
Side Story'.
" ♫Ma-ri-a, I just met a girl♪ named Ma-ri-a ♫." A lot of the
crowd are amused and join in.
The Sister Superior Makes the sign of the heart and bows her
head in appreciation. The media and world have seen the
President ,Mother Teresa and the male Arch Nuns more
than a few times casually out and about. Not that they're old
news by any means it's just people are more accustom to
seeing them, but to see one of the females, not on official
Duty and out in public enjoying herself is rare!
The two doormen open the doors to the building, the small
drones fly in followed by the Arch Nuns then everyone else.
They wait inside for the president and Homeland Security to
lead them down the hall, into the elevator and finally into
the main room.
   There's a standing ovation as the president and her party
enter the main Ballroom. The small drones fly in and take
their positions on the ceiling.
Oh how the rich and powerful wish they were sitting at the
president's table tonight with the Arch Nuns. No doubt
many will attempt to get close enough to have conversations
with them.
One in particular is Salman Bin Talal, The Prince of Saudi
Arabia. He like many men in the room were taken with the
Sister Superior's Beauty, style and elegance the moment she
entered the room. It's one thing to see a female Arch Nun
fighting on YouTube or briefly walking by a camera on the
news. But to be in the presence of one under pleasant
circumstances especially the Sister Superior is breathtaking.

If they could have met and spoke to the Mother Superior 'Hymiriam Christ' what an evening this would have been. President Andrei and his staff join president Winfrey's party as they begin personally introducing Maria to some of the guests but there are far too many. So, they are taking to their table. The television cameras are rolling, capturing and documenting every second of this most joyous event.
Sister Dajairia is home at the Divine Elysium communing with her sisters Nevaeh and Amira who are in Paris at the Hotel de Crillon waiting for Anna who is running a little late. The three are making fun of each other's Alter Ego names but they are really making fun of Anna's.
'Instead of calling herself Victoria Goodie Tu'choos. She should have called herself Princess Diana Du'rite.'
Buffie says laughing while at the pool drinking Mai Tais with Navaeh. The two are wearing bikinis and getting quite a lot of attention, maybe a little too much attention. It's a good thing they're using the Grace of God to be unrecognizable or Mother Teresa would be Furious.
Back at the fundraiser everything is going smoothly the donations are pouring in from around the world and it looks like the country of Chile will make a speedy recovery. Everyone is socializing and enjoying themselves. Many of the attendees are children of Eve whom decided not to attend. Her children know when it comes to public affairs their mother will change her mind on a whim. She urges them to enjoy themselves unless she instructs otherwise. Edmond and the Arch Nuns takes a moment to return to their table for a drink of water.
Prince Salman who has been waiting all evening to ask the Sister Superior for a dance, finally sees his opportunity. He is very respectful with his approach, speaking in Arabic asking the Reverend mother if he may ask her granddaughter for a dance. The two Converse for a few minutes. She tells him her granddaughter is quite the accomplished Ballroom dancer and it is a great passion of

hers. The Prince is overwhelmed with joy.
"What a coincidence" he says."
"How so?" Mother Theresa asks.
"I also have a passion for Ballroom dancing."
The Reverend mother is delighted she takes his hand and directs him to her granddaughter.
The prince has met the Reverend mother and her grandsons a few months ago, but never any of the females and up until recently he thought he had a crush on Sister Amira. But when he laid His Eyes Upon Maria his heart beat quickened! Mother Teresa communes with Maria briefly to ask if she has taking a moment to meet with Anna at home. Maria confirms that she has then her Grandmother speaks to her.
"Maria My child, I'd like you to meet someone. This is the Prince Salman Bin Talal of Saudi Arabia."
She extends her and speaks to him in his native tongue of Arabic. The prince takes hold of it and gently rubs it between his hands. Before she can stand, he quickly kneels as not to stand over her or look down at her and so he can speak directly to her. To the other guests casually watching it appeared as though he were proposing, but he was complimenting her appearance and asking for a dance.

The Sister Superior agrees to dance with him. She turns to her brother Joshua and ask him to ask the band to play something appropriate. They continue their conversation while Joshua takes care of the band. He returns a few minutes later telling them the next tune is theirs.

'Josh what did you tell them to play?' She feels to her brother.

'Don't worry sis I gave them some music, relax!'

'Josh I will throw you off the roof of this building if they play something stupid.'

'I said relax sis, I got it you'll be happy.'

The band concludes the current tune. The guest applauds from the crowded dance floor. There is no special announcement or warning. The band begins playing everyone on the Dance Floor starts dancing.

The prince takes Sister Maria by the hand and escorts her to the dance floor. All the guests stand at their tables hoping to get a good view. President Winfrey rushes back to her table which is on an elevated platform, to sit with her husband and watch the dance. She sits between Mother Teresa and her husband.

President Andrei and his wife chose to stay at floor level so Maria can see them. It may not have been Maria's intention but the guest clear the Dance Floor, forming a large circle for The Prince and The Sister Superior.

The Music Stops so the crowd may applaud and cheer. Her outfit like much of her apparel is combat-ready. They stand at the edge of the Dance Floor, the prince walks to the center, looks back and extends his hand to her.

She pulls a Spanish flamingo fan from her sleeve, it coordinates with her outfit perfectly. She snaps it open and fans her face, and with her super sexy supermodel Catwalk strut she approaches him and takes his hand. Her walk was so sexy it captivated the entire room. She takes hold of his hand and Spins into his arms.

The moment he Embraces her the second piece of music Josh has given the band begins to play. it's a piece he composed and Amira remixed for just such an occasion.

The crowd applaud as they begin dancing.

"No wonder you fight so gracefully, you move as if you are walking on air." The prince says.

"And may I say you dance divinely as well sir."

They dance the Mambo with a little Rumba and just a touch of Bachata. Many of the attendees have seen the prince dance, but never with such an elegant partner. If This Were an episode of 'Dancing with the Stars' they would surely be the victors. As they dance the prince tries to impress Maria by telling her how rich and powerful, he is and all the things he owns. He tells her how bored he is with the common woman and how he seeks someone truly worthy of his stature. The more he brags, the more she is amused. But then she realizes why she's been here for two hours and no man has asked her to dance. Surely the prince has asked them not to as a favor to him or something and they simply indulged him for whatever reason. Or perhaps they were simply more intimidated of her grandmother.

Nevertheless, she is flattered and she can rub it in Buffie's face later.

"You speak my language so effortlessly, Sister."

"I am fluent in many languages, sir."

"Sir! For one such as yourself you may call me Salman."

"How flattering, I bet you say that to all the girls."

The prince maneuvers Maria into a dip and responds. "No, they address me as your Highness!"

She bats her eyes at him flirtatiously and smiles.

The dance concludes and they to take a bow. All the attendees applaud and raise their glasses toasting the two.

The Applause continues as the prince escorts the Sister Superior back to her table.

"Thank you for this opportunity Mother Teresa."

Before the Reverend mother can respond Maria interrupts.

"What are you thanking my grandmother for? it was not she who danced with you!"

Mother Teresa and president Winfrey throw their hands in the air in agreeance. President Winfrey has known prince Salman for some time and knows him to be quite arrogant, especially to women. But the Sister Superior is no ordinary woman. She also finds it highly amusing to see him humbled before such Greatness. He is a good man at heart but perhaps this time he bit off more than he can chew.

"My apologies, I did not mean to offend!" Prince Salman says. "Please allow me to make it up to--" Maria holds her hand up and tells him she was only kidding. Everyone at the table enjoys a laugh the prince is a little red-faced but amused. Putting his hand over his heart and kneeling beside Maria he tells her. "I would rather die a thousand deaths than offend you, most elegant of ones."

Mother Teresa leans over and taps the prince on the shoulder.

"Thank you for dancing with my granddaughter Prince Salman. Now if you don't mind, I will have a word with her now."

"But of course Mother Teresa, but of course"

He turns to Maria and once again takes her hand. "I hope to see you again, very soon Sister Superior, please excuse me." He bids everyone at the table of fond farewell before walking away, he turns to see if Maria is watching him, alas she is not! He returns to his table where his friends and staff all male of course raise their glasses to him as he arrives. He is handed a glass of champagne. Before he sips, he raises his glass and tells them. "Gentleman, heed my words. She will be my wife!"

"What is it you plan on honoring and embracing, sweetie?"
"My death!"
Hymiriam stops hugging her and holds both her hands.
"Why do you believe you're going to die, my child?"
She asks with great concern. Dee begins to weep as they start
to sit, a bench materializes so they may sit.
"Well mom during this last campaign. This big guy hit me in
the chest. I absorbed the impact and countered; my body
instantly repaired itself as always but when I was finished
administering God's law. I was still in pain, not really bad at
first but as I went on the pain fluctuated then became very
irritating."
Dee begins rubbing her chest as the pain begins to flare once
more.
"Is it hurting you now?"
"Yeah, it is but that's not the worst of it."
Hymiriam wipes her daughter's tears and kneels in front of
her. Looking up into her daughter's eyes she can see she is
very upset and also very brave.
"This hit hurt you that bad my daughter?"
"It sorta did Mom, I know I got little boobs, but WHAT THE
HECK? I'm pretty sure Donna and Buffie could have taken
that hit and not felt a thing with all that bosom they've got!"
Hymiriam stands, puts a hand on her daughter's face then
sits beside her.
"My child you are not going to die. All of you are going to
have a little pain with your injuries from time to time. You
see my child if you didn't, when these things happen to you
and your teammates and Friends notice. You would have no
choice but to lie to them and we my child most certainly do
not bear false witness, now I know in your line of work there
may be times when you may have to twist or bend the truth,
but that I leave up to Mother Teresa through her, you'll be
protected by the Guardian Angel Act because they are
allowed to bend the truth for the greater good but that's
okay.

The Lord knows all of you better than you know yourselves and the Lord will see you through this. With these great gifts from the Lord it is only natural for anyone to feel like a- let's see how would your little sister Buffie put it, oh now I remember a SUPER HERO! So, don't worry, you've only just begun. I trust you will all get those feelings and get them under control quite quickly. So, you see my child when you are asked, does that hurt? you can honestly say YES IT DOES! But you'll be fine, you will all be fine. After all we raised you all to endure and persevere. But that does not tomorrow is promised to any of you."

"O.M.G I feel so much better. Thank you, Mom, thank you." Dee shouts wrapping her arms around her mother and hugging, squeezing and kissing her. Hymiriam loves every minute of it. But she must now get back to humanity whose problems will not be so easily solved. She stands and holds out her hand.

"Come my daughter walk with me for a bit."

Dee takes her mother's hand and the two begin to walk and Converse.

"Wait a minute Mom, I just had a thought."

"What is it sweetheart?"

"That's probably why Buffie couldn't sense or react quick enough when Joey Get Down punched her in the face. We were all wondering with us being so fast how that happened.

Okay I get it; I truly get it Mom. The Lord does indeed teach lessons in the most mysterious of ways!"

"That is correct my child."

"Cause we was all wondering why Buffie couldn't slow down time and prevent herself from being hit."

"I'll bet Buffie was REALLY wondering why she couldn't slow down time."

"Can I share this with them mother?"

"Of course Dee, my lessons are not just for one, they are for all of you."

"Mom I was just wondering since I'm going on vacation and everything if you could just--"

"NO! Dee you are going to wear that pain the lord gave you."

"That's not what I was going to say Ma." Dee says laughing.

"Then what was you going to ask my child?"

"I was going to see if you had Ten dollars I can have for vacation?"

They both laugh and hug each other one final time before departing. Dee learned in a short time the pain will soon subside. She leaves happier and much wiser. Now she's ready to join her sisters on vacation in Paris, transitioning to their hotel room she communes with them letting them know she has arrived. A few seconds later Anna transitions to the hotel room.

"Anna, well look at you." Dee says with amazement.

"I thought you were going to a gardening seminar."

"I still may, but first I'm going to have a few drinks with my sisters, after all we deserve it."

At the pool Amira and Navaeh can't believe their eyes as they watch their sisters walking toward them. Dee is wearing a revealing one-piece bathing suit; mom would definitely NOT approve of! Showing off her gorgeous figure and beautiful black Nubian skin. But who can this possibly be walking beside her wearing a revealing bathing suit as well?

It looks like Anna, Walks Like Anna. The two sit in their lounge chairs with their mouths open, staring.

"Is that Victoria Goodie Tu'choos?" Navaeh asks.

"Dee did you do this? Who is this person? We lost Anna grandma's gonna kill us!" Amira shouts.

"Hold on you two. First off, no I didn't do THIS!" Dee responds pointing at Anna. "And second this is most definitely NOT Victoria Goodie Tu'choos. Ladies I'll let her introduce herself"

Anna waits a few seconds then tells them. "The names 'Martina, Martina Alo Rell."

Her sisters stand applauding, blowing her kisses and jumping up and down. They definitely approve of their sister's new look and Anna couldn't be more happier.

Navaeh communes to Elizabeth and lin telling them to come to Paris for a moment there's something they absolutely, positively have to see.

Sister Lin or shall we say Dominica Torretta is driving onto the street racing scene in Las Vegas with five undercover agents, all in tricked out street racing cars.

They slowly cruise the circuit making themselves known. There's definitely going to be some action in the illegal street racing world tonight. But first sister Lin is going to find a restroom so she can transition to Paris and see what her sisters are talking about.

Sister Elizabeth A.K.A Ry-da-Di seems to be already getting in a little trouble of her own. She's riding on I-95 with a bunch of bikers performing wheelies and dangerous stunts. President Winfrey's fundraiser wrapped up with great success. The country of Chile will make a full recovery thanks to ZsaZsa La'more throwing down the gauntlet with such a high donation and is praised as one of the biggest contributors and heroes of the evening. This will put the country of Chile under Eve's influence. ZsaZsa has made her mother proud. She is so happy she decides to forgive Benny. He accidentally made her the hero so she tells Ka'ren to meet with Benjamin and make sure she lets him know how lucky he is! In fact, he is luckier than Mr. Luciano will ever be. For he has done something not many can do, he has returned to the good graces of Madame Butterfly. This makes him the happiest man in the world!

In Savannah Georgia in a small Park at the end of the famous River Street. Reverend Lolita Brown has been working on a fundraiser she gives every year to feed the children of Savannah. With all that has happened and gone on this year she has expanded it to feeding the children of Georgia. She always has a good turnout but is not expecting as much this year due to everyone wanting to give to Chile. She and her congregation have also donated large sums of money to Chile. She receives assistance from many charitable organizations throughout the South.

'Our Lady of the Sacred Veil'. One of the oldest charitable organizations in Savannah is attending the event. They are a group of elderly women whom have served in various nunneries throughout the South and are involved in many other organizations helping children. They have assisted The One and Only Jerry Lewis with his telethons for children with muscular dystrophy and Kidd Chronic's organization 'Kidd's Kids' and countless others. They have known Reverend Brown for twenty years and are always glad to help her in any way they can. Also, in attendance will be The McIntosh County shouters from Brunswick Georgia. They are one of the many groups performing. The Songbird 'Chapellet' the oldest female gospel singer in the south will also be performing. Being a small annual local event, it is only covered by the SAV news. But it generates enough Buzz to keep Savannah interested. Before the event comes to a close Lady Shalonca a member of Our Lady of the Sacred Veil asks Reverend Brown if she may speak to the crowd briefly.

"Of Course, Y'all speak every year I was wondering why you were so quiet. is everything all right?" Reverend Brown asks with concern.

"Yes Reverend everything is fine, my apologies, it's not me who wishes to speak. It is someone with us in need. If you would be so kind." The Reverend gives her a hug and tells her. "If someone in need wants to address the crowd or give

At the Divine Elysium Sister Dajairia is still very concerned about the pain in her chest. She doesn't want to disturb her Grandmother who she feels is having a much-needed good time at the fundraiser, so she reaches out to her Mother Superior Hymiriam.
"Dee, sweetheart I thought you'd be on vacation by now. Is everything okay my child."
Her mother asks.
"Well yeah, but there's something I'd like to talk to you about. I know you're probably busy standing in mud up to your waist helping people in a small village with very little or no technology. but I really need to talk to you. Is there a porta potty or something nearby you can excuse yourself to?"
"Give me a few minutes to find some privacy my child then I'll meet you at your home."
"Can we meet at your church?"
"Of course, my child I'll see you there."
The Church of Hymiriam is the equivalent of a mother's bedroom since she is only half celestial she cannot transition to heaven. So, God gave her this sanctuary where she may be at peace when she is not serving Humanity, here she can communicate with angels.
The Arch Nuns refer to it as mom's Church or Bedroom. Mother Teresa being full celestial has no need for such a place being a Guardian Angel, warrior class she can transition to heaven at will. Hymiriam finds a porta potty and converts her time from seconds on earth to hours at her home so she may spend some time with her daughter. Dee runs to her mother giving her a long hug squeezing her tight.
A mother can always tell when something is troubling her child.
"Dee sweetie what's wrong?"
"If what I think is true, I will not be afraid. I will honor you and embrace it."

587

thanks, by all means yes lord they can, bring em on."

Lady Shalonca escorts a woman to the stage, she's wearing a hood with a full Veil covering her face. The crowd is talking among themselves, watching but not paying much attention. She remains silent Reverend Brown becomes concerned.

"Two of Y'all go up there and stand by her please, She don't look to well."

Reverend Brown says to some of the male members of her congregation.

"Jesus, please don't let her fall out on that stage."

The Reverend says urging the men to stay close.

"We got her Rev, she ain't gonna fall." One of them answers.

She takes hold of one of their arms and says. "I am honored to have you stand beside me if I should need you. Will you show the same concern for a stranger?"

Without giving it much thought one says. "I guess so."

The other answers with confidence. "You are a stranger and I am here."

She removes her Hood and the crowd begins to quiet down a little. Then she removes the Veil.

With the river running calmly behind her the crowd stares in amazement too shocked to

do or say anything. WSAV news was not paying attention they were busy filming the festivities of River Street. Then instantly there is applause and very, very loud cheering.

Everyone now recognizes who is on the stage and quickly rush to get as close as they can. More people flood the area to see what's going on.

Reverend Brown's back was turned; she was briefly speaking to someone. But when she turned around, she almost fell over.

"Oh Lord Jesus' Oh Lord Jesus." Reverend Brown shouts almost straining her throat.

"TELL ME THATS NOT THE MOTHER SUPERIOR HYMIRIAM CHRIST ON MY STAGE RIGHT NOW, LORD JESUS! OH MY GOD, JESUS!"

She's so excited she exhausts herself to the point of almost fainting.

By now WSAV news realizes what's going on and who is here. They try to push their way through the crowd but no one is moving. Not wanting to waste any more time they decide to stay where they are and use the zoom lens. The police are frantic they weren't expecting anything like this. Hymiriam raises her hands for everyone to settle down.

"Please everyone I only have a few moments; I did not mean to cause a Ruckus please settle down."

There are a few gang members in the crowd. They're not here for the fundraiser they're here to sell drugs. Some of them are fugitives leftover from the 'Thrones of Chicago' who have migrated to Savannah.

"Ah man look it's the leader of them Arch Bit#hes." One of them says.

"I bet if we kill her, those Arch bit#hes will be lost as sh#t and we can get our city back."

Another adds. The gang try to move closer but the crowd is too thick and refusing to move. They don't want to push anyone or cause a scene so they find a slightly elevated position and get ready to shoot. The crowd quickly settles down eager to hear what Hymiriam has to say.

"Thank you as I stated before I must be brief, but I will say this. The children are our future we must Embrace and nurture them. We must do better and be better if not for ourselves then for them. I ask that you never, never let the children forget that God loves them. Raise and help them to Love Thy Neighbor. Teach them to endure hardship and emerge triumphant. But most importantly if they should ask is there a God? Don't deter or discourage them.

If they are guided to the Lord, then by all that is Holy LET THEM KNOW GOD! HALLOWED BE THY NAME!"

She raises her hands to the sky then lowers them into the prayer position and bows her head.

A Mighty Applause is heard throughout River Street.

The gang members decide this is the perfect time, with so much noise it would take a few minutes before anyone realized what happened. They slowly put their hands on their guns. The noise from the applauding is unbearable. Then something large begins to emerge from the river, her craft Godspeed slowly rises from the water behind her. The Crowd Goes Wild, the gang members abort their endeavor and the police are able to get the rapidly approaching crowds from the surrounding area under control. The gang watch as Hymiriam stands on the stage waving at everyone with her craft hovering strongly behind her.

They'll be another day. They think to themselves, BUT NOT TODAY!

Hymiriam asks a few members from visiting churches to assist Reverend Brown with getting the situation under control. Shirley Ann and her daughter Tabitha are happy to do so. Almost everyone is praising her and attempting to get pictures with their cell phones.

WSAV news is proud to announce Hymiriam Christ on River Street in Savannah Georgia.

Godspeed rotates 180 degrees and lowers its rear ramp, so she may enter the craft, her disciples are standing proudly, waiting to assist her onboard. She turns to face the crowd once more opening her arms wide to let everyone know, ALL ARE WELCOME IN THE ARMS OF THE LORD!

The people continue to shout praise, cheer and rejoice, as the door closes and it slowly departs. They continue to watch as it disappears in the distant clouds.

On a commercial airliner the passengers can see Godspeed pulling alongside them and matching their speed, watching as it gracefully flies among the clouds. What a beautiful sight to behold. The captain takes a chance and calls them on the radio hoping they'll answer, to his surprise they do. Peter and Angelica extend a salutation and wish everyone well. Then Hymiriam does the same. Everyone on the plane makes so much noise the captain is forced to ask them to quiet down. Godspeed slowly moves ahead of the airliner, chargers it's engines and accelerates through the clouds creating a swirl effect behind it. Now it is the cockpit crew cheering too loud....

Thousands of years ago Moses freed the Hebrew slaves because of the terrible Injustice that was done un to them by the Pharaohs of Egypt. Now Hymiriam and The Arch Nuns will continue their endeavor to free all of humanity for God's Great Purpose! And to make this world truly 'GOD'S HOLY MOUNTAIN'.................

(if this were a movie the credits would roll here, THEN---)
At a private location on Mount Sinai Eve is on her knees silently praying over a large Rock. She is naked and accompanied by Twenty of her high held children, among them are ZsaZsa La'more, Ka'ren Elaganza, Aston vetta and Kalmin Seth. Everyone is naked, silently standing behind her. She completes her prayer then stands. As she turns to face them, they all kneel and slowly bow their heads.
"Raise thy heads and look upon me, my children."
She says softly with her Eerie, Sinister, Sexy voice.
They collectively raise their heads and gaze upon their mother and before their very eyes they bear witness as she changes from a middle-aged Caucasian woman to a young twenty year old Chinese woman.
Because of the progress and acceptance of the Arch Nuns by most of the world. She decided to reset herself and make this DNA change to assist her children in destroying 'The Arch Nunhood of Mother Hymiriam'!........

The End, Perhaps?

The Saved
of
Hymiriam

ABOUT THE AUTHOR

I am a first-time writer; I made all the illustrations and cover art myself. It was also my first time editing and formatting. Unfortunately for the paperback/Hardcover to cut down on printing cost most of the illustrations had to be removed but are still available in the eBook. I will have a website soon with a lot of illustrations and hopefully music. For it would be my pleasure to show you my visualization of:
The Saved of Hymiriam.
May God Be With Us All!
THANK YOU.

www.ingramcontent.com/pod-product-compliance
Lightning Source LLC
Chambersburg PA
CBHW030840030726
47495CB00005B/1301